EASTWARD BEYOND THE SKY
THE GLORIOUS VICTORIES OF ELEANOR MACLEOD
VOLUME FOUR
by Ashley Mayers

First Printing: 2019
ISBN 978-1-943918-22-5
International Print Edition

Grass Roof Publishing
P.O. Box 14908
San Francisco, California, 94114
www.GloriousVictories.com

Also by Ashley Mayers:
THE SITA CHRONICLES:
Red Sapphire
Violet Sapphire
White Sapphire
Golden Sapphire
Cerulean Sapphire
Green Sapphire
Black Sapphire

THE GLORIOUS VICTORIES OF ELEANOR MACLEOD:
The Cursed Baron
Angels in Disguise
Damsels and Demons
Eastward Beyond the Sky
Before Midnight Ends

Notes from the Publisher:

The Glorious Victories of Eleanor MacLeod is a new five-book epic that adds another layer to the rich fantasy world created by Ashley Mayers and first published in 2015-16 in her seven-book modern multicultural epic, *The Sita Chronicles.*

Eastward Beyond the Sky, the fourth book of Eleanor MacLeod's story, continues the modern story from *The Sita Chronicles*, in juxtaposition to Eleanor's prequel epic unfolding in the 1920s. As an homage to the genres that Ashley Mayers found most fascinating as a young reader herself, each book in Eleanor's epic plays with elements of a classic genre. *Eastward Beyond the Sky* incorporates elements of an American western, taking place in Western Australia with a unique Ashley Mayers twist.

Throughout this series, it is the author's intention to give enough background for an uninitiated reader to develop a relationship with the world of *The Sita Chronicles,* while introducing them to several new heroines whose stories haven't yet been told. Both series fit together as puzzle pieces, creating unique insights into characters who are lovingly developed over the combined set of twelve books. All five books of Eleanor's story are intended to be read in order.

This series, like *The Sita Chronicles*, is a completely original, multicultural saga with roots in Hindu mythology. It exists in a world not dissimilar to ours, where Avatars (deities on Earth), Rakshasas (shapeshifting demons originating on Venus), and Yakshas (shapeshifting nature spirits) are real. While knowledge of Hinduism is not required to enjoy this series, a short glossary is provided in the back of the book to offer readers more context on Hindu cultural references.

This is a work of fiction.

Names, characters, businesses, places, events, and incidents are either products of the author's imagination or used in a fictitious manner. While many of the referenced historical events, figures, and places are inspired by fact, their treatment in this work are fictitious and should not be construed as real.

This book is written in American English using the grammatical, punctuation, and spelling conventions therein. The author has taken great care to apply a professional level of editing and proofreading to her works, while intentionally reflecting various accents, idioms, and dialects appropriate to each character's background, including Scots English, Australian Strine, and Indian English. Readers are kindly requested to approach the linguistic diversity of the series with curiosity and appreciation, rather than nitpicking. Anyone who judges Agatha Christie's English by Poirot's grammar needn't read any further.

TABLE OF CONTENTS

PROLOGUE

Early December, 2016 – A Divine Sri Lankan Palace

"My lord? My lord, you must wake up!"

Edmund stirred and then nestled back into the spiked, naked arms of his loving Rakshasa wife.

"Master Edmund? Lady Supriya? WAKE UP!"

Supriya groggily opened her eyes, and then she blocked the bright light of Kuveni's shimmering Yakshini form with her arm.

"Kuveni? What are you doing here? Didn't we order you not to spy on our marital activities?"

"Oh for god's sake, you must get up!" Kuveni exclaimed.

"What time is it? It's still the middle of the night," Supriya protested.

Kuveni snapped her fingers, and the water of their Rakshasa bed evaporated. A row of flickering fire torches lit up all around the marble walls of their cavernous bedroom in Vibhishana's ancient palace hidden away in the mountains of Sri Lanka. The cicadas hummed their nightly song louder as Kuveni's ruckus echoed out of the open veranda, into the jungle gorge below.

"My lord, there's been an accident! Charlie…"

In a blur, Edmund subverted his demon, wiggled on a perfectly fitted suit, and was standing in front of Kuveni, fully alert.

"What happened to Charlie?" he exclaimed. "Where is he? We must go now!"

Supriya absorbed her spikes and wiggled on a fashionable outfit with tight jeans, boots, and a cashmere sweater, gathering her hair up into a long, silky ponytail.

"Is he in Cambridge?" she asked. "What time is it there? Kuveni, please take us at once!"

"Charlie isn't injured," Kuveni reported, now that she had their attention. Edmund's eyes turned black with rage, and Kuveni rushed to explain herself. "Charlie was with Grace, doing their Christmas shopping in London. There was a car… they were crossing the street… Grace was hit!"

"Good lord," Edmund murmured. "Is she alright?"

"She isn't!" Kuveni exclaimed. "She's in the ambulance now! She's not doing well at all, and Charlie is with her!"

"Why didn't Charlie summon me?" he demanded.

"I don't bloody know! Does it matter?" Kuveni shot back.

"Take us." Edmund took in a deep, calming breath, preparing himself. "Please, Kuveni. Take us to them now."

"It's very difficult to transport corporeal beings into a moving vehicle!" Kuveni exclaimed. "It's going very fast!"

"Can you do it or not?" Supriya pushed. "If you can't do it, we need another plan. Can you stop the ambulance?"

"That would be very dangerous indeed… Charlie would be in grave danger if something went wrong."

"Take us into the ambulance," Edmund reiterated. He grabbed her hand and stared straight into her eyes. "You can do it, Kuveni. You are the most skilled Yakshini in the world, and we have *always* been able to count on you."

"Oh, Master Edmund, how I love you," Kuveni sighed. She gathered him and Supriya into her arms. "Hold on tight."

With a moment of lightheadedness, all three of them dissolved.

"She needs oxygen, stat!"

"She's going into shock."

"Call the hospital! Tell them to page a trauma surgeon!"

Charlie whimpered. He watched from a metal bench along the inner wall of the ambulance as three EMTs hovered over his mother's struggling body.

"Daddy, please, please, please," he whispered. "Please come. Please help. Please come."

In a flash of light, Edmund and Supriya materialized inside the moving ambulance. They were both thrown against the wall as the vehicle made a screeching turn.

All of the EMTs looked over at their commotion. "God almighty, it's them," one whispered. "It's the Rakshasas of Venus."

"Daddy!" Charlie cried. "Daddy, I was so afraid you wouldn't come!!!"

Edmund sat down on the bench and pulled Charlie into his arms. "I'm here, Charlie. I'm right here."

Two of the EMTs stopped what they were doing to watch.

"Back to work!" Supriya stood up and pushed her way into their group. "Report!"

The EMTs looked at each other, unsure of what to do.

"REPORT!" Supriya boomed. "I have five MDs and thousands of years of experience. Now tell me what's going on here so I can help you!"

"The victim has suffered acute trauma to the head and chest region," one of them replied nervously. "She has lost a lot of blood, and she appears to be suffering from internal bleeding as well. Her lungs are filling with fluids, and her pulse has been steadily declining for the last nine minutes, since we arrived at the scene."

Supriya placed her hands on Grace's forehead and chest, avoiding several ugly, gaping wounds. She could feel the life-force fading, and then she smelled the wretched tell-tale scent of death.

Edmund stood up and pushed his way in beside her. "She's dying," he whispered. Charlie whimpered again.

"Stand back!" Supriya ordered as she rubbed her hands together until the glowing silver light of her healing power emerged.

Edmund took her hands into his. "I will do it, my love. There is no need for you to take on this pain on her behalf. She is my responsibility. Please comfort Charlie until I recover."

Supriya nodded her agreement and took a seat on the bench beside Charlie. She took his hand, but he leaned forward to watch intently as his father rubbed his hands together, bringing forth the same divine healing light of the Preserver of the Universe.

Edmund slammed his hands onto Grace's forehead and her chest, and as he engaged her in a dance of frenetic shaking, the EMTs stepped back and watched with some combination of awe and dread.

After almost a minute of increasingly violent movements, Edmund let go and collapsed unconscious onto the floor. His illusory Rakshasa shirt and jacket dissolved as the ugly wounds from Grace's chest and head opened up in his flesh. Supriya fought off a bout of nausea as their shared life-force temporarily depleted.

The EMTs gasped as his violet metallic plasma worked its way to the surface to start healing his wounds. Supriya leaned forward and looked around for any reasonable place for Edmund to rest, but there was none, and so she left him on the floor.

"Check on the victim," she said as the EMTs stared at Edmund's spectacle.

They broke themselves out of their curiosity and returned their attention to Grace.

"She's... she's perfectly fine! There's no evidence of an injury at all!" one of them exclaimed.

"So it's real? The Rakshasas really can heal people?!"

"Why don't they do it all the bloody time?! What about all those people with cancer?!"

"Or malaria?!"

"Or third degree burns?!"

"They should at least heal the children!"

They all stared accusingly at Supriya.

"Healing is not a Rakshasa ability. It is a talent unique to the Preservers of the Universe, to me and my husband," Supriya corrected them.

Edmund moaned with pain as his plasma flooded into his largest gaping chest wound.

"You can see the toll it takes on us," Supriya added. "We can't heal everyone for many reasons, including that one. Two people, even two gods, do not provide the scale necessary to save everyone who deserves to be saved. Humanity must continue moving forward and healing itself. That is why we have spent so much time in recent months building hospitals and teaching medicine. Those efforts have already saved more lives than our glowing hands ever can."

They calmed down as they begrudgingly accepted her argument.

"Will he be alright?" the closest EMT asked. "Do we need to do anything to stabilize him?"

"He is immortal," Supriya replied. "He will be fine in a few minutes... but thank you for asking."

"Right...yeah, I read something about that... didn't think it could really be true, though..."

"Well, you'll see the evidence yourself in a few minutes. Why don't you make sure that the victim is continuing to recover in the meantime."

As the EMTs dutifully followed Supriya's suggestion, Charlie took one final look at his peacefully sleeping mother, then down at his father's sacrificial injuries, and he burst into wailing sobs.

Supriya gathered him into her arms and let him cry into her shoulder.

"Hey," she whispered. "Everything's alright. They're both going to be perfectly fine in no time."

"I... I... I wasn't sure... I wasn't sure he'd heal her!" Charlie sobbed. "I left my talisman at home so no one would steal it in London, and then I couldn't call Dad for help!"

Supriya rubbed his back soothingly. "Kuveni will always be around to help. See how fast she got us here from Sri Lanka? In the blink of an eye!"

"That isn't all of it!" Charlie wailed. "I was afraid... I was afraid he *wouldn't* do it! Mum's been so mean to him, and you've refused to heal so many people who were dying. Good people! People who were nice! Why does Mum get special treatment? It's not bloody fair! But then... God, I wanted so badly for him to heal her anyway..."

Supriya threw a ferocious look at the EMTs who glanced over at them, eavesdropping on their painfully complicated conversation.

"Sshhh... Charlie. Let us bear our divine burden alone, okay? It's bad enough that we have to worry about it. You shouldn't try to make heads or tails of it. We have thousands of years of experience and so many ancient voices in our heads to help us make these decisions, and they are still excruciating every single time. Edmund chose to heal your mum, and that is what you should focus on."

Edmund stirred and took in his awakening Rakshasa breath.

"Charlie?"

Charlie kneeled down onto the floor beside him, and Supriya helped him sit up. He grunted as Charlie pummeled him into a hug, and then he squeezed him lovingly.

"Everything is going to be fine, Charlie. I'm already feeling better, and so is your mother."

"Thank you, thank you, thank you, Daddy," Charlie whispered.

Edmund looked searchingly to Supriya.

He wasn't sure you'd do it, she explained through their glowing green sapphire Rakshasa wedding rings that served as their constant telepathic connection. *He thought you might refuse.*

Refuse? How could he possibly think that?

He knows that we often refuse, my love. And he was afraid that Grace had been too mean to you, that she didn't deserve to be healed.

Blimey.

He's not wrong. If she weren't Charlie's mother, you wouldn't have done it, and neither would I.

Blimey.

These medics have also noticed the hypocrisy; we must be careful what we say in front of them.

No child of mine will grow up without a mother ever again. I finally had the power to stop it, and I did.

I know, my love. I know.

Supriya helped Edmund woozily stand up, and she sat him back down beside Charlie on the bench. He blushed as he noticed the EMTs eying his freshly healed bare chest, although he was grateful that he'd managed to develop enough control over his Rakshasa clothing to keep his trousers intact, even while unconscious.

Charlie leaned into the nook of his arm and squeezed him, letting gentler tears come as he watched his healed mother sleeping soundly in her blood-stained clothes. Edmund kissed the top of his head.

"Everything is going to be alright, Charlie. I'm here," he whispered. "Daddy's here."

As he noticed the EMTs attention, he sighed. "If you could heal the ones you love, wouldn't you? Wouldn't you do anything you could to spare your children the pain of losing their mother? We are, in the end, very human, despite everything else that we are.

I made a very human decision just now. I hope you can forgive me."

As the ambulance began to slow down, Kuveni's disembodied voice echoed eerily. "Hold on tight. There is a mob of paparazzi waiting at the ER door. We will transport all of you to Shambhala before they can tear you apart."

With a pleasant breeze, Supriya, Charlie, Edmund, and Grace were gone, and the three EMTs were standing alone, left to contemplate the complicated implications of their divine encounter to the flashes of some very disappointed photographers.

PART ONE
DEVI

CHAPTER 1 – WHILE HE'S AWAY

September, 1924 – The mountains beyond Munnar, India

"Dearest, wake up."

Eleanor stirred and then stretched languidly. She smiled as Edmund looked down at her. He was already dressed.

"Good morning, darling."

She sighed as he ran his cool finger along her naked breast and then enticed her into a gentle kiss.

"What time is it? Is Mr. Valov already stewing about your tardiness?" she yawned as she glanced over at the billowing white curtains.

The sun was shining outside, and she sighed once again with satisfaction. It had been weeks since the sun had broken through the misty mountainous fog of the humble hilltown in the Western Ghats where they'd been living in blissful domesticity for over a year.

"It is a quarter past eleven. We really should be going, or we'll miss the train, and there is only one connection we can make in

Kochi this afternoon. Otherwise, we'll be a day late to the conference."

"What a shame," Eleanor winked.

"Don't tempt me, dearest. You know I don't want to go at all. I almost retired right there on the spot when they said that all of the colonial magistrates would have to be cooped up in the royal magistrate's hall for two *weeks* of policy meetings. At the end of it, they're just going to bloody do what they want anyway!"

"Oh darling, you know as well as I do that you care more about bringing fair and unbiased justice to our little hamlet than you care about these trivial inconveniences. Otherwise, you'd still be a retired colonel, painting away your afternoons."

"Being away from you for two whole weeks is hardly a triviality, Eleanor. We haven't been apart this long since before we were married."

"Darling, it will be perfectly lovely. You will spend lots of time with Ravi and Shruti, Mr. Valov will enjoy his time with the other miserable foreign butlers, and I will be reminded of how lonely I was before I met you as I pine away longingly from my empty bed."

Edmund laughed. "Hardly, dearest. I know you've been looking forward to your time alone for weeks."

Eleanor was taken aback, and she sat right up to address him more seriously. "Darling, why do you think that? I love all of our time together, and I always have!"

"Eleanor, you were so quick to console me in my plight when I told you about the conference that I didn't even have time to invite you to join me, and then you announced your time off from the medical clinic by that afternoon." He leaned forward and kissed her again. "You are allowed to enjoy your time alone, dearest. You've hardly had any of it since I seduced you."

Eleanor lured him into a deeper kiss. "I love you, Edmund."

He shifted uncomfortably. "I did, however, mention to Ravi that you would be here alone without Mr. Valov, and he… er… sent a reinforcement to guard you."

12

"A reinforcement?!" Eleanor worked to hide her annoyance.

Edmund had not been wrong in his astute observation. She had been desperately counting down the days until he'd be away, not because she didn't love him, but because it had been far too long since she'd been able to meander about completely on her own without thinking about another person.

Over the past year and a half, ever since an ancient goddess had taken up residence inside of her, she'd developed too many foreign habits in the moments when her husband wasn't looking that were just itching to burst out of her. She'd been anticipating the freedom to indulge them for weeks, and the news of a visitor took the wind right out of her sails.

Edmund shrugged apologetically. "Jaap Sahib is waiting out front."

Eleanor breathed in a deep sigh of relief. "Of all the reinforcements to send, I suppose Jaap Sahib is the best I could have hoped for."

She was intensely grateful that Ravi had sent the one guard who knew all of her secrets, who knew more about who she really was than her own husband did.

"He is very accommodating," Edmund agreed. "I'm sure he will do whatever you'd like him to do, Eleanor. But I must admit, I will feel better knowing that he's here."

"I know you will, darling," Eleanor conceded. "If only we'd trained Ovid and Pliny to be more vicious, you could have counted on them to guard me."

At the sound of their names, two fluffy golden retrievers barreled into the bedroom and hopped onto the bed, surrounding Eleanor and licking her face. She laughed and scratched their ears.

Edmund closed his eyes as Pliny lunged forward to lick his face. "They are rather terrifying," he laughed.

After several minutes of letting the dogs distract them, Mr. Valov began pacing in the front hallway, and Eleanor smelled the tell-tale smoke of his nervous cigarette. As he began coughing and walked out onto the porch to continue his impatient pacing in the fresh air, she ripped herself out of bed and gathered up a silk robe from the floor. The dogs jumped down, readier than ever to follow them into action, and Edmund enticed her into one more naughty embrace, squeezed her bum, and licked her tongue with the rich taste of fresh rosemary that she'd become so addicted to over the year and a half of their mostly blissful marriage.

"You know, darling, being away from each other for so long will mean a very passionate reunion." He perked up with excitement. "Take that idea with you." She winked.

Edmund took several calming breaths until his excitement dispersed. "Please be safe, Eleanor."

"That goes for you too, Colonel." She slapped him playfully on the bum. "Tell Jaap Sahib that I will be out in a minute to give him his orders."

She kissed him one last time and waved him away. "I'll miss you, darling!"

"I love you, Eleanor."

Edmund smiled and waved, and then she listened as the dogs followed him through the airy hallway of their old plantation house towards the front door. He said a few words to Jaap Sahib, who responded with pious agreement, and then he engaged Mr. Valov in amicable conversation as they walked down the creaky wooden stairs of their wrap-around deck, across the stones of the walking path, and to the muddy drive. The dogs whined their displeasure as the doors to the car slammed shut. As it sput-sputted away, Eleanor finally gave into her excitement.

She ripped open the wardrobe and stared at her options, landing on a bright yellow traditional Keralan silk sari that she wore often. She slipped on the blouse and the petticoat, and with only a few expert folds, she wrapped herself up and rushed out to greet her loyal ally.

"Jaap Sahib!" she exclaimed. "Welcome to our home!"

Ovid and Pliny wagged their tails vigorously as they flanked him.

He bowed. "It is an honor to serve you, my lady."

"I'm so glad you are the one Ravi sent. I trust that Jyoti and Amit are well?"

"Yes, my lady. Thank you, my lady. Sri Bidkar dotes on them as if they were his own flesh and blood. Amit is almost a year old now, and he is very healthy and strong. He laughs at everything."

Eleanor smiled. "I'm glad to hear it. Was it difficult for you to leave them to come down here for your little assignment?"

Jaap Sahib looked torn. "It was an honor to be asked to serve you, my lady." Eleanor stared him down until he offered her a truthful answer. "It was the most difficult thing I've ever done in my life. It was harder than resigning my commission from the maharaja."

"I'm glad that your life is so beautiful that leaving it for a couple weeks feels like torment."

"It is a blessing that I never imagined, to live the life we have now, my lady. There aren't words to thank you enough for everything you've given us."

She took his hands into hers and let Uma say her piece. *May you revel in Shakti's blessings, my child. You have earned them.*

"Thank you, my lady," he whispered.

Eleanor smiled as she felt Sheranee break free from her divine perch. She looked past Jaap Sahib to spy her loyal mount emerging from the jungle just past the garden. Ovid and Pliny barked and growled with excitement as Sheranee barreled towards them, and Jaap Sahib jumped out of the way as she pounced playfully on top of Eleanor.

"My lady, are you alright?" He placed his hand on the handle of his sword, ready to attack the enormous tigress at Eleanor's command.

"Perfectly fine!" she laughed as she rolled around on the mossy grass with Sheranee, scratching her tummy and then her ears as Sheranee licked her face. "You never need to worry about Sheranee, Jaap Sahib. She is my loyal mount, and she understands the delicate nature of a human body."

The dogs watched jealously from the sidelines, and then Ovid jumped on Jaap Sahib, hoping for a new source of attention.

"Yes, my lady." Jaap Sahib worked dutifully to hide his bewilderment as he patted Ovid and Pliny.

Eleanor finally broke out of her game and sat up beside Sheranee to address Jaap Sahib, who kneeled down before her, ready to receive his orders.

"My lady, how may I serve you?"

"Would you like to pet her?" she asked. "She is really very gentle to our allies. She plays with the dogs as if they're her cubs."

Jaap Sahib nervously reached his hand forward, but he flinched and pulled away as Sheranee sniffed it.

"Well, you don't have to be best friends just yet. It does take time to get used to unexpected truths sometimes, and tigers have earned their reputations as formidable predators."

"Yes, my lady." He fought back his fear and patted Sheranee's head. She purred encouragingly.

"Very good, Jaap Sahib. Now, first things first. I have already dismissed the rest of the staff. Everyone has gone home with paid leave. There is an extra room in the servants' quarters that you can use, just at the top of the stairs, and there might be some food left, although you should feel free to pop into town to get whatever you need."

"Thank you, my lady. But, may I ask what you will be eating?"

"I have some very special friends with whom I will be dining, Jaap Sahib. They will feed me well."

"Yes... yes, of course..." He did not know what she meant––that her loving Yakshini allies would be dining with her at her whim—but he knew it wasn't his place to ask, and she was grateful for it.

"I would like to revel in my privacy this week, Jaap Sahib, and so I must enlist you to help me. No one is to come onto the property. No one should be let inside the gates, nor into the gardens, the tea fields, or the jungle beyond. Sheranee and I need some time to relax, and it is important for all of the wild tigers in the region that no one sees her so close to civilization. We don't want anyone getting the wrong idea."

"Yes, my lady."

"Good! Now, the other thing is… I'd like to dress as I please, and it will be very awkward for both of us if you and I have an unexpected encounter, so I must ask you to avoid our main house and wandering around the grounds. If you need to reach me, please telephone first from the staff house to the main house. I know it's an odd request."

"No, my lady. I am at your command."

Eleanor smiled. "I knew I could count on you. Oh, and perhaps you can see to the dogs. They should be fed twice a day, morning and evening, and otherwise they are free to roam around the grounds as they please. We have a fence that keeps them out of the jungle, but please do take care to close the front gate. We want to keep them off the road."

"Yes, my lady. Will I need to tend to the dogs' sleeping arrangements?"

Eleanor grinned. "The zoo will be sleeping with me. I'm not sure we'd all fit on the bed if we hadn't ordered an extra-large one to accommodate Edmund's height. But as it is, we all fit nicely together. It is wonderfully warm to sleep with a zoo, you know."

"If you say so, my lady."

Eleanor stood up, and Jaap Sahib rushed to join her, but as he buckled woozily, she steadied him.

"Are you alright?"

"I'm not as young as I used to be," he admitted. "The blood rushed into my head after kneeling."

"Well, hopefully you will get some rest while you're here. I suspect you haven't been sleeping so well these last several months with Amit keeping you up."

"No, my lady. I haven't," he agreed.

Eleanor squeezed his hand encouragingly. "Try to relax a bit, Jaap Sahib. Edmund knew to lock the gate to the road when they left, and Sheranee will be a fine guardian. Together, she and I are more than capable of looking after ourselves."

"Thank you, my lady."

Sheranee stood up and stretched, and Eleanor grinned and hopped right onto her back.

"We have some exploring to do, don't we, Sheranee?"

Sheranee roared her approval, and as Jaap Sahib stepped back and the dogs barked with excitement, Eleanor leaned in, let her wild tendrils whip in the wind, and rode Sheranee across the garden, over the dogs' fence, and straight into the jungle beyond.

CHAPTER 2 – THE LOCAL DEITY

Around noon the next day, Eleanor awoke as the heat of another sunny morning invigorated her senses. She snuggled into Sheranee, who had taken Edmund's spot on the bed beside her, and yawned. The dogs turned over at the foot of the bed and snored. She hadn't felt so relaxed in months. It reminded her of the lazy weekends she'd enjoyed as a spinster back in Edinburgh, when eating and sleeping and meandering about were all that she ever had to do, except that now, of course, her meandering involved a divine pet tiger. She had to admit, it was a nice development.

After she'd left Jaap Sahib to guard the house, she'd ridden around with the wind in her hair all day, laughing and squealing as Sheranee leapt across trickling jungle streams and crouched underneath low-hanging vines, until they'd reached a remote watering hole with a lovely artesian waterfall. She made a note to pay attention to the exact location so that she and Edmund might return another time for some wet romantic fun, and then she stripped off her sari and floated for hours in the fresh, clear water while Sheranee lazed about on the edge, keeping her ears perked for any intruders.

When she was tired, and the shadows were long, Sheranee brought her back to the garden, to the comfortable wicker dining set on the mossy lawn where she and Edmund enjoyed eating their relaxed weekend lunches, and Kuveni joined her for a delightful Yakshini feast.

Now, she only had one decision to make: to roll over and sleep the day away, or to get up and meander about. She loved her options.

She lay around for another many minutes, until the cawing of a bird outside distracted her, and she finally decided to get moving. Sheranee stretched and yawned and rolled back over, not particularly supportive of her plan. As Pliny snuck up to cuddle in Sheranee's nook, and then Ovid joined her, Eleanor wished desperately that Edmund could enjoy the absurdly adorable scene with her. It was a sight that destiny had decreed he would never, ever see. She sighed with disappointment.

She wandered over to the WC, and when she was finished, standing at her wardrobe, contemplating her day's activities and feeling rather uninspired to put clothes on at all (an option she'd specifically planned for when she gave Jaap Sahib his orders), a steaming hot carpenter's pie appeared on the vanity beside her along with a fork and an aromatic pot of coffee.

"Thanks, Kuveni!" she whispered. She poured herself a cup and drank the entire thing down, pouring herself a second as she stared at her options again.

Let us tend to our sacred duties, Eleanor. Tonight is the full moon, and it is Dasara—the end of our people's nine nights of fasting in our honor. This is a very auspicious time, the most auspicious.

I did think they'd been looking a bit unhealthy this week. Why didn't you tell me they were fasting?

I thought you knew, my child.

20

I would have told them to eat something if I'd known!

My child, they achieve spiritual awakening through the trials of their abstinence. It helps them feel more connected to God.

Maybe I should try it. I still feel like I have too much to learn. Every time I learn more about your divinity, I feel less worthy of bearing it.

I have abstained enough for both of us, Eleanor. There are many ways one can become closer to God. You have chosen a different path, and together, we make a perfectly balanced pair.

Perhaps I shouldn't have sent Edmund away. We could have celebrated together... naked.

It is better this way. We can be our true selves for our holiest festival without explaining it to him. There will be many worshippers to bless.

I thought we were on holiday, Eleanor humphed.

Sacred duties never cease, my child. Someday you will find them fulfilling.

Eleanor sighed with ambivalence. *I don't see how our blessings help them, when we don't actually have any power to influence their lives.*

What makes you think that Shakti's blessings don't influence their lives, my child? Knowing that we support them, and that they have touched God, is often enough to inspire action.

It doesn't give them what they're praying for. It doesn't save their children or cure their infertility. It misleads them into believing that prayer is the answer, when really they should be taking more action—human action—to solve their own problems.

Why are you so certain that our blessings do not answer their prayers?

Eleanor paused to think about the question. She had always subtly assumed that as Uma had reached out her hands to offer her unspoken blessings, the sentiment was all that was being transferred. She had never seen any immediate impact from the interaction, never any godly light that glowed as she touched them or anything of the sort. The implications of her actually being able to answer their prayers was overwhelming.

Do they?

What do you think, my child?

I don't bloody know! Do they? This is no time for rhetorical questions! Can we answer people's prayers? Can we save their children and cure their infertility?!

Why does it matter, my child? Would you not bestow our blessings if you believed they were more literal?

If we can actually answer their prayers, we must be more careful! We must learn more about them to decide whether their prayers should be answered! We shouldn't heal rapists or bestow riches upon selfish fools!

Making the decision for each and every person you touch is very difficult, Eleanor. Lord Vibhishana has been practicing for five thousand years, and he still finds the process utterly unbearable. It is even worse for Lord Rama, who has the ability to heal with his hands. Every time he is faced with an injured human, he must decide whether or not to heal them. But he cannot heal everyone, and so how is he to decide when the desperate, inconsolable mother brings him her child? The child who may grow into a saint or a monster or a dullard? And then the next mother comes, and then the next… How can he possibly choose? You do not want that burden, and neither do I.

So we can't heal people? We can't answer that prayer?

We cannot heal injuries or diseases. Only the Preservers of the Universe can do that.

Edmund… poor Edmund will be able to do that…

Yes, my child. He will. But he is not ready yet.

Neither am I. I shouldn't be answering anyone's prayers.

My child, I will help you. Together, we have six hundred years of wisdom.

So… what exactly can we do?

We can catalyze change, Eleanor. In all sorts of unusual ways. Ways that humans do not usually perceive, but that affect them mightily. We can make them who they are meant to be.

That sounds rather vague.

They do not always know what they need, Eleanor. When they pray, they pray for what they want, but it is not always what will make them better. We give them what they truly need, not what they think they want.

How do we know what that is?

We do not have to be so prescriptive. We bless them, and Shakti makes the decision.

That doesn't seem particularly divine.

It is a great gift that we do not have to shoulder the same burden as the other avatars, my child, and that is why it is not such a risk to bestow our blessings upon everyone we meet. Slowly but surely, we are improving the world around us with each subtle change.

I guess that's something…

It is everything, my child.

Eleanor sighed her concession and dug into her wardrobe, sniffling as the abrasive scent of cedar assaulted her nose.

Any suggestions?

Tonight, we will be a goddess, Eleanor. And there will be a wild, raging party with us as the guest of honor. We should dress the part.

I'm always up for a wild, raging party, but you realize that everyone is going to stare at us if we wear something too obvious? With my pale skin and red hair? All the villagers already know who I am! I'm the firang nurse from the medical clinic. We will give away our identity. Leo would not be pleased at all.

It is a good thing he isn't here then, isn't it?

Eleanor smiled. Suddenly, the idea of thwarting Mr. Valov's spying rules made the entire proposition more interesting, but then she couldn't ignore the sensible voice in her head.

If Edmund returns next week and everyone tells him that I am an avatar, certainly he will begin to suspect something. You always remind me that Lord Kalki must remain in the dark about us.

You are right, my child. But we will not relegate ourselves to the village temple tonight. Let us hear the prayers of our neighbors this afternoon, and in the evening, we will ask Kuveni and Lady Mélusine to accompany us to our festivals. It has been centuries since I have let myself enjoy this most auspicious of occasions.

Festivals? There is more than one?

Tonight, we will bless all of India!

Eleanor felt Uma's excitement brewing, and she let herself relax and be swept up by the rare feeling.

She dug through her wardrobe more enthusiastically, until she reached the box with Kuveni's first offerings, the offerings she'd made while Eleanor was still on her honeymoon, crying about Shakti's abrupt change to her bust. The memory was so distant that it hardly seemed real. In fact, her entire life before Uma and Edmund seemed like someone else's life completely. She didn't mourn it.

She gathered up an emerald green sari made of delicate Mysore silk that matched Mélusine's talisman and her eyes, and draped it over the blouse and petticoat in the Southern style that she had become so used to using ever since she'd realized that wearing a sari to the medical clinic helped her prove to the locals that she was, indeed, a trustworthy friend in whom they could confide their most frightening medical concerns. Her perfect grasp of the local Malayalam dialect helped too...

As soon as she was finished, she smoothed out her hair into calm ringlets and pulled them into a loose ponytail, and as she dug into Kuveni's carpenter's pie and drank down her second and then her third cup of coffee, she smiled as a strand of fresh jasmine appeared on the vanity beside her.

"Thanks, Kuveni!" She clipped the jasmine into her hair, just as the local women did, positioned Mélusine's green sapphire talisman around her neck, and then finished off her look with some dangling gold earrings and ordinary gold and green bangles that matched the gold threading of her sari.

As Sheranee noticed her movement, she climbed off the bed, stretched, and then humphed her disapproval. The dogs followed her lead, circling Eleanor as she attempted to leave her zoo behind.

"You can't come, my love." Eleanor scratched Sheranee's ears. "We must protect the other tigers of the province by keeping you a secret. You may stay here and stalk the grounds if you promise to be nice to Jaap Sahib. Ovid and Pliny, you will do as Sheranee and Jaap Sahib say."

Sheranee licked her hands, and Eleanor kissed her forehead. Then, three bowls of mysterious meat appeared beside the wardrobe, and all three members of Eleanor's zoo barreled over to their breakfast.

"Thanks, Kuveni!" She finished off the last coffee from the pot and skipped out the door while the zoo was still occupied, slipping on her ordinary flat golden sandals as she went.

She walked across the mossy lawn, down the long, muddy drive through the manicured tea fields, just as she did most days of the week when she was walking her scenic twenty-minute commute to the local medical clinic in the heart of town. She took an extra moment to breathe in the rich scent of the sun beating down on the damp earth, evaporating the moisture and creating a delicious coat of humidity that Uma loved.

She felt a passing sense of guilt that she felt so much freedom in Edmund's absence, but then she relegated it as she often did, with the reminder that her heavy yoke was borne out of love. His absence was freeing because she was free from her web of lies. She sighed. No one knew better than she did that life wasn't fair, and the benefits of her unorthodox marriage had indeed far outweighed the drawbacks. She was grateful.

She let her mind wander, wondering what the night's festivities might be like, and whether or not the villagers would notice anything unusual about her on this most auspicious day. She wasn't sure whether or not she was hoping that they would.

A year earlier, at Uma's behest, when she and Edmund had finally settled into their adorable white-washed plantation house, and she'd rallied the British authorities to allow her to create a rural medical clinic so that the locals would no longer have to travel the muddy hour's drive to Munnar for treatment, she'd secretly assessed each temple's suitability for them to conduct their sacred duties. The first temple wouldn't allow a woman of menstruating age inside at all, while the next three temples would not allow a foreign woman inside, even when she was dressed in a modest, traditional sari. The next two had no altar to the Goddess. And then she'd reached a small, crumbling old temple at the edge of town with a cute little courtyard built around a natural spring. The whole thing backed straight onto the dark jungle beyond, and Eleanor found its mixture of artistry and nature to be strangely captivating. She knew she'd found the special place for Uma's plan when she spied an altar to the Tridevi—Shakti's three primary forms as Creator, Preserver, and Transformer. She was even more convinced when she stumbled upon a dark corner devoted solely to Parvati, a benevolent, wifely form of the Goddess that she and Uma particularly identified with now that they were living in domestic bliss with Edmund. Uma agreed.

Ever since, on her way to and from work, Uma had enticed her into sitting silently in Parvati's corner for a few minutes, offering blessings to anyone who dared to indulge their curiosity by asking her a question. It had taken the priest nearly three weeks to ask her what exactly she was doing there. Uma had responded with a blessing (alongside a request for discretion), and ever since, a steady stream of worshippers had started coming by to commune with the *firang* goddess.

As the months passed by, Eleanor had been finding their position increasingly precarious, but Uma had remained undeterred. *It is our sacred duty. Shakti will make it work.* She often reassured Eleanor as they caught the enamored eye of their worshippers at the Saturday morning farmer's market.

On this particularly auspicious day, as Eleanor reached the edge of town, the streets were unusually quiet for a Saturday morning. Many of the typical fruit vendors were nowhere to be seen, and only a few rickshaws were out and about. None of them were hauling any customers.

She fought back a sense of foreboding as she walked down the empty street, through the center of town, until a young girl, a worshipper whom she'd known for many months, ran out from the small mercantile and bowed before her, holding up a jasmine garland.

"Victory to the Mother," she whispered.

Eleanor kneeled down and let the girl put the garland around her neck.

"Thank you, Tanvi." Eleanor looked around again. "Is there something going on today? It seems unusually quiet."

Tanvi was surprised by the question. "It is Vijayadashami! Dasara! The final day of your festival, my lady! We are celebrating your triumph of light over darkness!"

"I see. So is there a party going on somewhere that I haven't been invited to?"

"May I lead you, Holy Mother?"

Eleanor had always liked the girl's boldness. She had, in fact, been one of the first villagers to ask her a question in the temple.

"Please do!" Eleanor agreed.

Eleanor followed her past several closed shops, past her medical clinic, the one room school, and the cute little library that Edmund had erected early on in their stay as an investment in the intellectual curiosity of the villagers, until they reached her temple. Out front, filling the muddy streets, all of the villagers milled about, awaiting her arrival.

They whispered and parted to make way for her as she approached.

The priest rushed out of the temple's courtyard and kneeled before her.

"Victory to the Mother."

Two child brahmins approached from behind him, each carrying garlands. Eleanor looked around at her large audience, who was watching her with a combination of curiosity, reverence, and skepticism. She kneeled down and let the children put the garlands around her neck.

"Please come, Holy Mother. We have made you a proper altar. We have been so embarrassed that our humble temple does not have an altar worthy of the Avatar of Shakti, but now… we pray that it will be to your liking."

Eleanor followed him inside, channeling Uma's optimism to push back her own anxiety at the development.

In the center of the courtyard, in front of the fountain fed by the natural spring, was an enormous, intricately carved wooden throne atop a series of matching wooden steps, all of which were adorned with thousands of clusters of jasmine and marigolds. They were already wilting in the midday sun.

"This is for me?" she asked him.

He bowed his head. "Yes, Holy Mother. If it pleases you?"

"Panditji, how long have you been working on this?"

"Several months, Holy Mother. We were worried we wouldn't have it finished in time for Dasara, but with your inspiration, we were able to do it. We enlisted the help of artisans from as far away as Kottayam to help us."

Eleanor looked up again at the conspicuous throne and sighed. "So, you would like me to sit there, on the throne?"

"The people have brought you offerings, Holy Mother. As thanks for your blessings on this most auspicious day. We wish dearly to bow to you, Holy Mother, if you will let us."

We should reward them, Eleanor. They have achieved a great feat in our honor.

This is folly. Lord Vibhishana learned only too well that indulging their desires for elaborate ritual only leads them astray. It focuses them on something other than helping each other. Next there will be a gilded golden cathedral in the center of town, and the people will be starving.

My child, you are too pessimistic sometimes. The entire community came together to do this. We are a uniting force amongst them. Look at your audience. The brahmins from the temples that sent you away are in the back. Even they have come to see if the rumors that we are the Goddess are true.

So we will confirm the rumors? And when Edmund returns from Bombay, our entire village will be worshipping his wife? That won't make him suspicious at all…

Destiny will find a way, my child. It is not a coincidence that his conference is now, during the most auspicious Dasara in centuries. Sometimes we must have faith in Shakti's greater plan.

In for a penny, then?

In for a pound, my child.

Eleanor closed her eyes and called forth her green, glowing trident, commanding it to come slowly so the audience could watch. As she felt it materialize in her hand, she also felt an unusual weight on her head. As the audience gasped and kneeled at the sight, she reached up and felt an elaborate golden crown.

Come join me, Sheranee. It is your lucky day.

A roar of excitement echoed in the distance, and the crowd parted with shrieks of fear and awe, making way for her as she bounded from the main road right through the temple to Eleanor's side. She took a regal seat in front of Eleanor and stared down the crowd. The skeptical priests in the back whispered to each other with disbelief, and then kneeled, trembling and muttering with self-castigation.

"Victory to the Mother," an elderly man in the front row whispered.

"Victory to the Mother!" the crowd cheered.

Eleanor climbed up the staircase and took her seat in the throne, gathering her feet up underneath her in a lotus position that Uma had been insisting upon for months. She placed her trident next to her and the green glow dissolved, leaving the trident to its golden hue that she had first seen in the dark caves of Elephanta. In the bright sunlight, it shimmered with an otherworldly glow that she had never noticed before.

Sheranee kept her position at the bottom of the stairs, aggressively eyeing the crowd.

I don't need a guard, my love. I want them to get as close as they usually do, so I can touch them with our blessings.

Sheranee obediently slinked up the stairs to take a seat beside her, knocking a pile of flowers onto the ground to make room.

Eleanor gestured for the first man in the front to climb up the stairs. He hesitated.

"Come," Uma coaxed in Malayalam. "There is no need to fear us. We are only here to bestow our blessings upon you, our beloved children."

When he arrived at her feet, kneeling and trembling with emotion, Eleanor took his hand gently.

Take with you peace and joy, my child. Revel in Shakti's blessings and share your good fortune with others through your own kind deeds.

"Thank you, Holy Mother," he whispered.

Eleanor squeezed his hand, and he let go and stumbled down the stairs. His daughter placed a coconut and a strand of jasmine at the edge of the staircase, but as she turned around to scamper away, Eleanor called to her.

"Come, my child. You too shall have Shakti's blessings."

The girl looked nervously at her father, and then obeyed Eleanor's command. When she reached her, Eleanor took her hand.

There is no need for timidity, my child. Share your good tidings with the world, and take with you Shakti's blessings.

The girl reached forward and pet Sheranee, who licked her. The girl squealed with excitement, and then scampered down the stairs.

"Who's next?" Eleanor called as a haphazard line formed, and she buckled down, preparing herself for a very long afternoon. She gestured for the next devotee to greet her.

She sat for hours soaking in the unusually warm sun while the line of worshippers seemed to grow rather than shrink. After only a few hours, when her legs were solidly asleep, she realized that she no longer recognized anyone in the temple except for the priest who continued to dutifully chant, leading the worshippers with the same peaceful Sanskrit mantras she'd come to love over the months—*ya devi sarva bhuteshu, Shakti rupena sangsthita*—while they each waited for their turn to touch divinity.

Finally, as a bank of fog overtook the late afternoon sun, Eleanor gratefully spotted the end of the line.

You have been wonderfully patient, my child. I hope that you will eventually find our efforts to be worth your discomfort.

Can you feel the shooting pain in my legs?

I can, my child. I can feel everything that you feel.

I will try not to think about that the next time I'm enjoying my time with Edmund.

It is best for both of us not to think of it, Eleanor.

As Eleanor was finishing up with the last of the worshippers, she suddenly felt faint, and leaned over to brace herself on Sheranee. A moment of confusion morphed into recognition, and then into panic.

"Blimey. Edmund? How are we going to explain this?! What is he doing back so soon?!"

She looked around for the source of the familiar pulsating power, but this power was far more acute than anything she'd ever felt from her husband, not even in his most divine moments.

She stood up, leaning on Sheranee for support as her legs exploded into painful tingling, but as a very regal young Indian man with dark skin, red eyes, and angular features that made him look strangely ancient (and rather interesting) approached with a similarly ancient-looking dwarfish brahmin, both clad in the holy orange robes of sadhus, Uma practically squealed with excitement.

It's about time! she exclaimed.

CHAPTER 3 – OLD WOUNDS

What do we do, Uma? How are we going to explain this?!!

It is not Lord Kalki. It is two very old friends. Oh, please do indulge me, Eleanor. I must say hello for myself.

Don't do anything that Lord Kalki wouldn't approve of.

Never fear, my child. I can control myself as long as Lord Vibhishana is nowhere in sight.

Eleanor gave in and relaxed, allowing Uma to take control of her movements. With the transition, the acute pain in her legs subsided.

Shiva's wrath, Eleanor, your legs were hurting, weren't they?

So you can't feel exactly what I feel? Somehow that makes me feel better, although I suppose it is quite sad for you.

I feel more in you than I felt in my own body for centuries, my child. You are a very generous vessel.

"My lord, I told you this was just a hoax. Look at this imposter! She is a *firang*! Can you believe the British would stoop so low?!" the dwarfish brahmin whispered in a strange ancient tongue as they approached the center of the courtyard, which was now entirely covered in layers and layers of jasmine offerings, coconuts, and a wide variety of fresh vegetables, which Eleanor felt somewhat guilty about. Would they just rot now? She made a mental note to suggest to the priest that it was the Goddess's will for the village to end their fast with a feast of the offerings.

Uma grabbed her trident and rushed down the stairs.

"My lords!" she exclaimed. "What a gift it is to see you on this most auspicious day!"

They looked skeptically to each other as they eyed her red hair and pale skin, but as Sheranee rushed past her and pounced onto the dwarfish brahmin playfully, the regal young man was taken aback.

He took another long look at her, staring at her crown and trident, and then he bowed rigidly.

"My lady, I am Lord Rama, Seventh Avatar of Vishnu."

"I know, old friend." Uma dissolved her trident and took both of his hands into hers to communicate the rest of her message silently in the ancient language of his childhood that she knew he loved so much. *I am Uma, old friend. Eleanor is the beautiful woman you see before you, and she is my anointed vessel now. Together, we are continuing my sacred duties on Earth until my next incarnation is born.*

"Uma…" Rama murmured.

"Uma?!" the brahmin exclaimed as he escaped Sheranee's playful grip and hopped up nimbly. "It can't be!"

She took his hands into hers. *And yet it is, old friend. Destiny often deals us unexpected cards, doesn't she?*

He looked around the courtyard and spied their pious hosting priest, who was sweeping up the dust and mud left by the horde of worshippers.

"He is a virtuous soul, worthy of keeping our secrets," she reassured him.

The brahmin nodded his agreement, closed his eyes, scrunched his nose, and looked as if he was squeezing as hard as he possibly could until, with a move far clumsier than Vibhishana's subtle Rakshasa wiggle, he morphed into a monkey the size of a very large human.

"Aren't you a sight for sore eyes!" Uma pulled him into a tight hug. "I've missed you, Hanuman. It has been too long."

"You were much more pleasant to hug before. Now you just feel human." He couched his insult as a friendly jab, even though Eleanor and Uma both knew that he meant it.

"We were a dying breed, weren't we, old friend? Is Sugriva still around?"

"I haven't seen him in two hundred years. He went to Mount Kailash to die. I thought for quite some time that I was the only Vanara left."

Uma felt a wave of overwhelming sadness. "You are, old friend. I'm dead. You and I are only talking directly because Eleanor is a very obliging vessel. She is letting me be in control right now so that we can have our proper greeting."

Hanuman grimaced. "We could have saved our species, you know."

Eleanor felt a burst of someone's fiery temper working its way to the surface (she wasn't sure if it was hers or Uma's), mixing dangerously with the melancholy.

"Do not start with that again, old friend. There is a reason we have not crossed paths in many centuries. I am Lord Shiva's wife. I could not marry anyone else, even a lord as powerful and ancient as you are."

"But how do you know I'm not the Avatar of Lord Shiva? Some of the scriptures say that I am!" Hanuman exclaimed.

The priest glanced over and began whispering mantras as he continued on his sweeping, listening in on every word.

"I just know, Hanu. I can always tell. Avatars can feel when we are connected with our other halves. It feels singularly unique. Rama knows exactly what I'm talking about." She glanced over at him, and he offered her a nod of agreement. "It is why he ignores his sacred duties whenever he's on the trail of Sita's next incarnation."

"I wouldn't use the word *ignore*," Rama countered half-heartedly.

"Did you come because you thought I might tell you where she is?" Uma asked.

"There were rumors in Kottayam that an avatar of the Goddess was living in a village near Munnar. We had to come and see for ourselves," Rama replied. "There aren't so many avatars… it's good to keep a good eye on who's around."

"You hoped a different avatar would give you a more satisfying answer than I did, didn't you, old friend?" Uma stared him down.

"The avatars are not all the same. I thought it was possible I could find a more obliging ally," he admitted.

Uma sighed. "Rama, I don't refuse to help you because I'm cold-hearted. I refuse to help you because I don't think you should be so actively seeking Sita. For five thousand years, she has died painful deaths, and you have mourned her. You have both suffered mightily. You have it within yourself to break out of that cycle, and yet you choose not to. Why?"

"I must find her!" Rama exclaimed, giving away his desperation. "I must save her! I must fix all of the wrongs that have caused her great suffering! One of these times I will save her, and everything will be okay again. I will finally make up for her suffering! I can't just walk away! I need her! It is her strength that will help me defeat Ravana, the prophecies said so!"

Uma squeezed his hands. *My friend, you are tormenting yourself. You are enforcing your own karmic punishment, and Sita's. Why not focus on your sacred duties for a lifetime or two, avoid Sita altogether, and see where it takes you? Destiny has an uncanny way of leading the avatars together who are meant to connect. Have you ever asked yourself whether or not you are meant to still be with Sita after so long?*

"She is my wife!" Rama exclaimed. "How could I not be meant to be with her?! We are joined in eternal matrimony! Surely you must support that, my lady. You are the Avatar of Parvati! You let your entire species become extinct out of loyalty to Lord Shiva!"

I understand now what Padma meant, Eleanor murmured. *What a mess.*

It made Eleanor somewhat relieved that the relationships of the avatars were all just as complicated as her web of lies was with Edmund. In fact, it seemed like her relationship with Edmund was relatively healthy in comparison.

"Careful now, Rama. You're letting your passion get the best of you again. We do not need to awaken the wrath of Durga during our auspicious reunion," Uma warned.

He straightened his posture. "I'm sorry, my lady. You're right. It has just been too long... decades since I lost her. Now I'm of marrying age, and I haven't found a single clue."

"You must trust Shakti's plan, old friend."

"I trust Lord Vishnu's plan," he countered.

"Do you know what it is?" Uma asked. "Have his holy voices emerged in your consciousness to guide you?"

"No," Rama begrudgingly admitted.

"Then perhaps you'd best be careful to separate your own human desires from the deeper divine presence within you. I know more than anyone how difficult the dichotomy can be, but perhaps you should meditate more, refocus yourself. Eleanor and I have been working steadily to obtain a balance, and I'd say we've made some excellent progress."

Rama sighed with disappointment.

"You did not come here for a familiar lecture from an old friend?" Uma took Rama's hand and Hanuman's hand. "Come, my lords. Let us eat something together before you leave. I don't want to part on bad terms after so long, especially on the day of my most holy of celebrations. Will you do me the honor?"

"Yes. Yes, of course, my lady," Rama agreed.

"Panditji, please gather up these offerings and organize the people of the village to make a community feast for this evening."

"Yes, Holy Mother!" he agreed.

"Come, my lords, let's go to Eleanor's home. We can eat there in privacy."

Hanuman and Rama followed Uma, but they stopped as they reached the front of the temple. The streets were now bustling with an unusual energy as the villagers and the many visitors set about following Shakti's orders to share their joy with acts of kindness. One group at a neighboring temple was acting out an elaborate puppet show of Durga defeating Mahishasura, while a parade of housewives was offering homemade snacks to everyone they met. A whole group of teenagers were escorting an elderly man across the muddy street.

"*Jai mata di*," Rama murmured. "It is like the age of peace in Lanka after I defeated Ravana the very first time."

"You have been honest with them about who you are?" Hanuman asked. "We have avoided being honest for centuries now. It has always caused such problems. The modern world cannot handle our divinity in the way the ancients could. They have become so quick to covet our power for their own selfish ends."

"You have more to worry about than I do," Uma reminded them. "I cannot heal them. It makes being honest much simpler. Shall we?"

Hanuman looked down at his furry form, took a deep breath, and nodded his agreement. In his true Vanara form, he walked beside Sheranee, Rama, and the Goddess, right into the public square. It was the first time he'd used his natural form in public in almost three hundred years.

The entire village stopped to stare.

"Victory to the Mother," he declared.

"Victory to the Mother!" the crowd cheered.

They kept a curious eye on him as they returned to their activities, while Uma guided the gods through the streets of her holy village. Several children approached, offering more garlands of jasmine and marigolds, until all of their necks were completely obscured with the aromatic flowers.

They walked up the muddy road, past the tea fields and patches of bush, across little wooden bridges over roaring streams, to the whitewashed iron gate of her estate. Eleanor wondered if Edmund would be able to sense that another Avatar of Vishnu had been inside. She was certain that if he did, any explanation he'd concoct would be very far from the truth.

When she opened the gate, Ovid and Pliny barreled through the tea fields to greet her, jumping up on Rama and Hanuman with their muddy paws.

"Dogs? You have *dogs*?" Hanuman exclaimed disapprovingly as he wiped the mud off of his legs and hissed at them in a decidedly primate style. "Since when did you like dogs?!"

"Down!" Uma ordered. "You know better than that, my children!"

Ovid and Pliny obeyed, running in wide circles around them as they escorted the group up the driveway.

"People change, Hanu. I am not a miserly Vanara recluse anymore. Eleanor has rescued me from my misery."

Hanuman humphed.

"They are very nice dogs," Rama said diplomatically. "If a bit… overly enthusiastic."

Hanuman stopped as they reached the white wooden colonial house surrounded by mossy lawns and manicured gardens. "This is not the home I would have expected you to choose. It's so… British."

"It is Eleanor's. She lives here with her husband. They bought it to preserve the jungles beyond. There was a plan to raze them to the ground for more tea plantations, and so they bought it and kept the jungles intact. It was exactly the plan I would have expected from them. They have since bought two more estates in the mountains with exactly the same plan. *That*, my lords, is one way to preserve things in this modern world." Eleanor loved that Uma indulged in such a clever, subtle jab.

"Her husband?!" Hanuman exclaimed.

"Destiny's cards," Uma reminded him. "He is not here now. He is away in Bombay for a conference of colonial magistrates."

"Colonial magistrates?!! He's *British*?!"

"Eleanor is a *firang*," Uma shrugged. "It should not be surprising that she is married to one."

"But why didn't you choose a more suitable vessel? A nun, or at least an unmarried brahmin girl!" Uma could see the jealousy and hurt in Hanuman's expression at the idea of her living a domestic life with someone else after centuries of refusing to marry him.

"My friend, there is no worthier vessel on Earth than Eleanor. Destiny brought her right to my door. It is a great blessing that I was sent a vessel who lives such a beautiful life. Her husband is very loving, and she finds great value in her work."

"Her *work*?!"

"She is a nurse. She runs the local medical clinic."

"That is not suitable at all for the Avatar of Shakti..." Hanuman muttered.

"My friend, you have always had such specific ideas of how we should be. Someday, you will have to let go of them. If you cannot do it yourself, Lord Vishnu will find a way to make you."

Yes, he will, Eleanor murmured. *Wait until he sees Lord Vishnu in the body of Ravana's son.*

You are right that Lord Vishnu's plan was very strategic, Eleanor. Hanuman is not the only one who will have to face a new world, but that time is not here yet. There is no point in trying to change ideas that have been ingrained for five thousand years.

"Now, come. Let us take an early dinner together. Eleanor and I will have to get ready early so that we can join our worshippers for their festivals tonight. We will start in Bengal."

"Bengal?!" Hanuman exclaimed. "How do you plan on getting to Bengal in one night?"

"Oh, I will have the help of some old friends."

"We are not going to Bengal," Hanuman countered.

"My dear man, what makes you think I'd even invite you?" Uma laughed. "Kuveni and Mélusine will be joining me."

"I've never liked that Mélusine," Hanuman muttered. "She's always been too unpredictable, too surly… and she's half Rakshasa! Any minute she might run right back to Ravana."

"My friend, for the sake of our friendship, I will ignore all of your ignorance on the topic. You'd best keep your opinions to yourself around Vibhi, as well."

"Vibhi isn't a real Rakshasa," Hanuman argued. "He's practically human."

Ha! What an expert Vibhi must be at hiding his secrets!

He is. They do not even know that the Patels are Rakshasas. Protecting them is one of Vibhishana's most established farces.

Uma guided them to the outdoor wicker table in the middle of the garden.

"Is Kuveni going to feed us?" Hanuman asked bluntly.

"I suppose I could ask her to drop what she's doing to feed the gods. She is certainly used to such requests," Uma replied. "But, I was thinking that perhaps a different Yaksha might enjoy the task more."

She closed her eyes and whispered a quiet mantra. Mr. Montero materialized beside them.

"Oberon, would you like to join the gods for dinner?" she asked.

Mr. Montero observed Rama and Hanuman and then dropped into a pious bow. "It would be my honor, my lady."

"Thank you, Oberon. Perhaps some Vanara korma, and some of those spiced plantain things that Sita always made for Rama?" she suggested.

"Thank you, Monty," Rama said sadly. "It has been a long time since Sita cooked for me. I've almost forgotten how it tasted."

"My cooking will not be as good as hers was," Monty reminded him.

"It will be something," Rama sighed.

Mr. Montero snapped his fingers, and a feast materialized on the table, complete with silver platters, a steaming pot of chai, four place-settings, and a green silk tablecloth. He even included a large bone for Sheranee and two smaller ones for the dogs. While Sheranee roared thankfully and whisked hers onto the lawn to start working, the dogs only licked Mr. Montero's hands in thanks, to his unspoken displeasure.

Uma took a seat and then gestured for the men to join her.

"*Jai mata di*," Rama said as he raised a tea cup.

"*Jai mata di*," Monty and Hanuman toasted.

And so, as the sun dropped slowly out of the sky, Uma and Eleanor passed the time in the company of old friends, avoiding the melancholy of old woes, and awaiting with growing anticipation the auspicious festivities to come.

CHAPTER 4 – THE GODDESS PREPARES

As the cicadas hummed and the dark jungle rustled with another blustery gust of evening wind, Hanuman shivered. "You've chosen the coldest place in India to live, you know."

"That is most certainly not true, old friend. Have you been away from Mount Kailash for so long that you've forgotten what real mountains feel like?"

Hanuman humphed again.

"This temperature is better for Eleanor's *firang* family. She and I both soak in as much sun as we can get, and it is usually sufficient."

"You have a very strange relationship with this vessel. This conscious human woman has just let you control her for hours upon hours?" Rama asked.

"Eleanor is too obliging," Uma replied. "She is the most unique human I have ever encountered. It would have been a privilege for you to meet her, but I simply couldn't help myself. I have missed you both so much."

"Have you?" Hanuman asked as his demeanor softened. "Have you really missed us?"

"Of course I have!" Uma exclaimed.

"Even with our... er... disagreements?"

"My lord, it takes great intimacy to banter as we do, don't you think?" Uma reached forward and squeezed his warm hand. "Do you know anyone you can disagree with so freely as we disagree with each other?"

"I've never thought about it like that," Hanuman admitted. "I thought... I thought that perhaps we'd fallen out of your favor."

"You do annoy me, old friend. Make no mistake of it." Hanuman snorted at her insult. "But does anyone else have the freedom to tell you so?" She glanced over at Mr. Montero, who had spent most of their leisurely dinner dining in silence. "It is good for you, Hanu. And for you, Rama. You should surround yourselves with equals who can be honest with you. It is the only way for you to be honest with yourselves."

"We are honest with ourselves!" Hanuman exclaimed indignantly.

Uma raised her eyebrows. "Are you?"

"This vessel can hear you? She can hear your voice in her head, and you have conversations with each other?" Rama interrupted distractedly.

"We are very good friends, in fact," Uma replied.

Rama looked troubled.

"Does that bother you, my lord? Because it is such an unusual arrangement?" Rama didn't answer. "I agree that it has a degree of symbiosis that I never expected, but I rather like it, to be honest, and I believe Eleanor does too. We benefit from each other's many unique qualities. She helps me relax and enjoy life, finding meaning in human interactions that I never cared too much about before, and I help her understand our divinity with the centuries of painful experience I've had understanding it for myself. Not having to

44

learn everything from the beginning is a great gift to her, and together we are a greater goddess than I ever was on my own."

"I suppose I didn't think that any of the avatars could hear God's voice so explicitly. It makes me wonder…" Rama trailed off with a grimace.

"What, old friend?" Uma coaxed.

"It makes me wonder if the instinctual feelings I've always attributed to Lord Vishnu are just my own. Perhaps his voices haven't surfaced in me at all. Perhaps I haven't even fully ascended yet, and *that* is why I cannot defeat Ravana, no matter how hard I try. You should have seen him last time, my lady. I stabbed him straight through the belly! He splattered into a lifeless puddle, and I was certain I'd triumphed! And then four years later, Vibhi showed up at my door to inform me that Ravana was back again, stirring up the same old hateful chaos as always."

"His excessive immortality is curious," Uma admitted. "But I do not have your answers, my lord."

"I find that hard to believe. Certainly, you could…" He trailed off again, as he eyed her reaction.

"Yes, old friend?" Eleanor felt Uma cringe in anticipation. She knew exactly what he was going to ask, because he had asked the same question so many times before.

"Could you not consult the Oracle, my lady? Surely it is in both of our best interests to learn what we can about defeating Ravana? We are both still Avatars of Light, allied in the fight against darkness, aren't we?"

Uma sighed disappointedly. "My lord, I have told you so many times over the centuries, just as Lord Vibhishana has told you: The Oracle is a dangerous, meddling fiend. The prophecies are perplexing. It is enough of a curse that I must manage its mischief. It is a great gift that I am giving you by keeping its misery away from you."

"Yes… yes, you have told me that," Rama shrugged.

As the last hint of light dissolved from the sky, Mr. Montero snapped his fingers, and flickering fire torches appeared all around them on the lawn.

"My lords, I'd best be getting ready. I have quite an evening ahead of me." Uma stood up.

As Hanuman stood up, Uma gathered him into a friendly hug. "Until next time, old friend."

He reached into his pocket and handed her a small Hanuman figurine. "Call me if you need anything. I will be at your service, as I have always been, my lady."

"Thank you, old friend," Uma said as she squeezed his hands affectionately. "I hope that I will not need to bother you, but it is comforting to know that I have the option."

He coaxed her into another hug, and Uma felt his heart racing with emotion. "You are never a bother, Uma. I have cherished every moment we've ever spent together."

She gave into the warmth of his fluffy embrace for a bit longer than she'd intended, and then she pulled away with a resigned sigh.

"Take with you Shakti's blessings," she said as she squeezed Rama's hands.

"Thank you, my lady," he replied with a hint of dejectedness in his voice. "*Jai mata di.*"

"Until next time, old friends, take care of yourselves." Eleanor could feel Uma's impatience growing as she waved them away with a cheerful smile.

Hanuman rolled his shoulders and gathered Rama into his arms, and with a burst of white light, he shot them into the evening sky.

How does he manage to fly without any wings? Eleanor wondered.

I could never figure out why it worked myself, but there was nothing quite like feeling the wind in my face as I climbed higher and higher into the sky… Uma sighed nostalgically.

You must feel very constrained now in my human body.

I do miss flying, but I am freer now than I ever was before, Eleanor. It is an irony so great, I cannot contemplate it too much, or I find it dreadfully distracting from our sacred duties.

Uma turned her attention onto Mr. Montero. "Thank you, Oberon. You were wonderfully obliging."

"It was my pleasure to serve you, my lady," he said with a pious nod.

"Tell me, my friend, how is the Lady Padma faring after our encounter in the garden?"

He shifted uncomfortably and looked around into the dark sky. "She is very private with her sorrow, my lady. It is not my place to discuss her woes, even with you."

Uma smiled. "I knew that you were the right one for the task, Oberon." She took his hands into hers. "Take with you Shakti's blessings."

"*Jai mata di,*" he replied with another pious nod.

Kuveni materialized beside her.

"Oh, Oberon, it was such a treat to have the afternoon off!" she exclaimed as she pulled him into an awkward hug.

"You're welcome. Now, I'd best get back to Baroda. The Patels are headed to the maharaja's palace for a dandiya celebration, and I am sure they will need my assistance."

"What fun!" Kuveni exclaimed. "Perhaps we'll join you later!"

Mr. Montero eyed Uma. "Lord Vibhishana will be there. If you wish to maintain your anonymity with him, you'd best avoid the party. It has a tendency to get out of hand every year, and this year is sure to be no exception."

"Thank you for the warning," Uma replied.

Don't get any ideas, Eleanor warned her. *And if I'm not mistaken, I've been very obliging.*

You have, my child. You have been exceptionally obliging.

Eleanor took in a deep breath as Uma relegated herself back to the core of Eleanor's being, and Eleanor regained control of her faculties. She wiggled her fingers and her toes, relishing the depth of her sensory perception.

"Thank you, Monty. You may go." Eleanor released him with a wave of her hand, but then she found the gesture oddly aristocratic. *Uma, that's enough!* She pushed the remnants of Uma's control as far down into the core of her being as she could manage.

He bowed and dissolved.

"My darling girl, was Uma in control all afternoon?!" Kuveni exclaimed. "You are too accommodating!"

"I know," Eleanor shrugged.

"Well then, now we will revel in *your* divinity for the rest of the evening, Eleanor."

"I don't have any divinity of my own, other than being divinely patient about sharing my body with an uninvited avatar."

"Hogwash! You are more divine than most of the avatars I know, my dear girl! I knew there was something special about you the moment I laid eyes on you, and you have only proven to be more and more divine at every juncture."

"If you say so."

"I do," Kuveni countered matter-of-factly. "Now come, I have something for you, for your first public parade as the Goddess. I've been conjuring it all afternoon."

"That's what you were doing with your afternoon off?" Eleanor laughed.

"It was easier than what you were doing with your afternoon off," Kuveni winked. "Sacred duties never cease, Eleanor."

Eleanor suddenly had an uncomfortable thought. "You aren't serving me as a sacred duty, are you, Kuveni? I thought... I thought you were helping me because you enjoyed it, and because it brought you closer to Edmund."

Kuveni pulled her into a motherly hug. "My dearest girl, I have known no better joy than to serve such a divine mistress as you. It has been one of the greatest privileges of my six thousand years on Earth."

Eleanor pulled away from her grip. "But, Kuveni, surely you don't need to serve any mistress."

"My dear girl, it is our nature! Yakshinis and Yakshas are born to serve! We feel no greater pleasure than when we are serving a worthy cause. It gives us a sense of intense fulfillment that cannot be achieved any other way."

Eleanor could not hide her distaste for the development, but she couldn't decide on the appropriate response.

"The concept is not as foreign as you think it is, Eleanor. Consider it similar to your personal requirement for the fulfillment of work. Would you be happy sitting around like the lazy lout Edmund is always afraid of becoming?"

"I suppose not," Eleanor conceded. "But, still, Kuveni. *I* am not a worthy cause. Wouldn't you be happier using your Yakshini talents to save flooded villages or the like?"

"Big picture, my dear girl! You must think bigger picture! Helping a worthy deity ascend to lead the world into peace is far more important than stopping any one regional disaster. Besides, destiny gets very testy when we try to meddle in Earth's affairs in certain ways. There is a balance that must be maintained."

"But what is the point of helping me ascend? I will die soon enough, and then you will all have to wait around for Edmund and Padma to figure out their fairy tale demon romance before you will have your messiahs."

Kuveni was taken aback, and then she pulled Eleanor into an even tighter hug. "My poor, poor girl, you mustn't borrow trouble. Uma has told you too many things. Things that must be very troubling for you. But the prophecies and the scriptures are not set in stone, Eleanor. No one, not even Lord Vibhishana, had any inkling that *you* would be the Avatar of Shakti. It is only one of countless examples of the prophecies leading too many gods astray. For all anyone knows, even Uma and Lady Mélusine and Lord Vibhishana, *you* will be the greatest goddess the world has ever known. Now, you must release this burden from your mind, or it will only lead to unnecessary suffering."

"That's easier said than done," Eleanor humphed.

"And yet I know you will try all the same, darling girl." Kuveni took her hand and led her into the house. "Let's revel in your power tonight, Eleanor. When the crowds are cheering with adoration and chanting your mantras, you will feel more powerful than you ever have. You will learn what it truly means to be Shakti's anointed vessel."

Laid out on the bed were layers upon layers of heavy crimson silk, accented by sparkling gold embroidery and clusters of jewels encrusted into the fabric. A heavy golden belt and a stack of other glistening, chunky jewelry were laid out right beside it.

"Now, Eleanor dearest, let's get you all squared away. You already have the lovely crown, and I've made you an outfit worthy of the Holy Mother. It is of the finest silk in the world, of a very ancient style that her avatars have worn for millennia. I will help you put it on."

Eleanor pulled off her sari, leaving it in a crumpled pile on the floor, and stood still as Kuveni buttoned her blouse and then wrapped the fabric around her, folding and tightening it around her hourglass curves until she realized that Kuveni was just doing an unusual draping of the sari, covering her legs like baggy pants, allowing her complete freedom of movement for riding Sheranee without worrying about stray eyes catching a glimpse of anything they shouldn't. She secured the sari with the belt, and then noticed that the stack of jewelry was entirely made up of layers and layers of necklaces, some long, some short, and all sparkling gold with red and green gemstones that glowed eerily in the muted light.

"Are these green and red sapphires?" Eleanor asked.

"They are. They are only for you to wear tonight, my dear, and I will take them back in the morning. They are more valuable than anything else on Earth, and are best guarded by quite a bit of Yakshini magic."

"Really, Kuveni, I'm sure paste will do just fine," Eleanor protested.

"The Goddess will be real on Dasara," Kuveni countered. "Oh, and I almost forgot!"

Kuveni took Eleanor's wrists into her hands and closed her eyes with deep concentration. Eleanor shivered as a wave of pleasant Yakshini warmth worked its way up her arms and down into her feet, bringing along with it an intricate geometric mehendi design filled with peacocks, lotuses, and even a scene of Durga's defeat of Mahishasura stained across her arms and her legs that rivaled the one Shruti had done for her on her honeymoon.

Eleanor held up her hands to inspect Kuveni's complex artistry. "It's beautiful. Thank you."

"It is my pleasure, darling girl."

As Eleanor looked at herself in the mirror, contemplating how strange her red hair looked with the rest of the outfit, a half-moon appeared on her forehead above a red bindi that sparkled with the same otherworldly glow as the other red sapphires.

Eleanor laughed. "Did you do that too, Kuveni?"

I did it. It represents our third eye, my child.

At least I didn't grow a real third eye, I suppose. Vibhi's does look rather alien.

Uma sighed longingly at the thought, and Eleanor sighed with annoyance as she relegated the swoon that wasn't hers. She pulled her hair back and folded her ringlets up under the crown.

"Do not hide your lovely hair, Eleanor. The Goddess always lets her hair flow free," Kuveni admonished gently as she unraveled Eleanor's work.

Eleanor sighed with resignation and took a step back to look at the reflection of the strange woman who had taken her place. She hardly recognized herself, but standing in her stead was not the goddess from the pictures hanging for sale by the temples in town. She looked like something else entirely. Some odd blend of a highland lass and a warrior queen.

"Won't they be disappointed that I don't look how they think I should?"

"What makes you think that you won't?" Kuveni asked.

Eleanor rolled her eyes. "I'm as foreign as they come, Kuveni. I don't look anything like the idols of the Goddess."

"On Dasara, your people will see their goddess as they want to see her, Eleanor. Your human physicality is irrelevant. They will see through your exterior to the divinity within you. *That* is what makes the night so auspicious."

"Are you saying that I'll look different to them? They'll see the Maa Durga that they know from the temples as I ride Sheranee through the streets?"

How do you think a Vanara avatar got away with leading them for so many centuries, my child?

Kuveni grinned. "We have created the canvas, and Shakti will take care of the rest, my dear girl. Now, you are looking perfectly ravishing tonight, and it will only be fitting for your entourage to do the same."

Kuveni closed her eyes and dissolved herself momentarily, reappearing in a form Eleanor had never seen before. She was Indic, perhaps Lankan, not dissimilar to Vibhishana's Lankan form in some ways, although much, much shorter (even shorter than Eleanor), and she looked like she was in her late twenties (quite a bit younger than she usually chose to look). She wore shimmering golden jewelry in her braided silky black hair that connected to a dangling pair of earrings encrusted with red and green sapphires. A golden chain dotted with more jewels connected the earrings to a nose ring, producing the distinct effect of a Hindu bride. The heavily beaded silk of a bright red sari added to the effect, but the garment was draped in a style that looked quite different than any style Eleanor had seen in India, with quite a bit of extra material bunched up around her waist, held together with a sparkling golden sari belt that was accented by an enormous bejeweled sheath housing a long, curved dagger with a similarly decorated handle. Kuveni looked down at her hands and watched with satisfaction as ornate mehendi worked its way up from her fingertips, all the way to the heavy sleeves of her blouse.

"You look beautiful, Kuveni," Eleanor said as she reached out to feel the silk of the sari.

"This is my most natural human form," Kuveni revealed. "I almost never use it."

"Why not?" Eleanor touched the handle of the dagger and shivered as the red sapphires sent a pang of power up into her fingertips.

Kuveni felt the heavy earrings connected to her nose and smiled wistfully. "This is the ancient Lankan style... the style reserved for the queen. I suffered mightily in this form, my dear girl. I avoid it to avoid the memories, but perhaps together we can create some newer, happier ones."

Eleanor pulled Kuveni into a hug. "It is a privilege for me to see it."

"It is a privilege for me to share it with you, Mistress Eleanor."

When they pulled away from each other, Kuveni closed her eyes and whispered a quiet mantra, and Mélusine appeared by her side.

"Kuveni?!" Mélusine exclaimed. "*Mon dieu*, it is a rare occasion, isn't it?!"

"Perhaps you too would like to give into your most natural human form for the occasion," Kuveni suggested.

Mélusine threw her an annoyed look, and then eyed Eleanor, debating the prospect.

"You should use whichever form you want," Eleanor suggested. "The most important point is to enjoy ourselves, isn't it? At least, that's what I say it is, and I am the Goddess, after all. It's my night."

Mélusine paced back and forth, muttering to herself and glancing between Eleanor and Kuveni, until finally she shrugged, took a deep breath, and morphed into a handsome, muscular blond man, who did not look particularly dissimilar to her usual female form, nor that of Lord Blakeney, although there were several subtle differences that made her look like the younger brother of her other two forms.

"Are you happy now?" she asked Kuveni testily.

She is Lord Brahma… I understand now…

Yes, my child. But the dear girl took centuries to escape from the torment she endured in this form. It is not time yet for her to embrace it again. It must be her choice entirely.

Mélusine looked down self-consciously as Eleanor approached her. "You are quite handsome, but don't you think it would be more fitting for the Goddess to be accompanied by two of her most loyal Yakshini allies?"

She took Mélusine's hand. *Be yourself, Melysium. You get to decide who that is.*

Mélusine wiggled subtly, returning to her normal feminine form, wearing a rich emerald green and gold sari in a modern style, and weaving fragrant jasmine into her long locks of blonde fairy hair. She sighed with relief.

"The Goddess has spoken," Mélusine declared. "*On y va.* The celebrations have already begun."

"Come, Sheranee!" Eleanor called. "It's time to go!"

Sheranee roared with excitement as she barreled into the open front door of the house, down the hallway, and into Eleanor's room, barely bringing herself to a halt before pummeling her.

Ovid and Pliny barked as they chased her, but before they could tag along for the evening's festivities, Eleanor climbed right onto Sheranee's back, and Kuveni and Mélusine surrounded her.

"Tonight, the Goddess lives!" Kuveni declared.

And with a moment of lightheadedness, Eleanor and her entourage dissolved, leaving two very disappointed dogs behind.

CHAPTER 5 – PUJA HOPPING

The air was filled with the rich smoke of gunpowder explosions as fireworks lit up the sky in a rainbow of colors, drowning out the shouts and cheers of revelers who filled every inch of space in the bustling streets of Calcutta.

Eleanor took a moment to get her bearings as she materialized on Sheranee's back right in the middle of the crowded streets with Kuveni and Mélusine by her side.

"Very subtle!" she whispered. "All of India will know who we are by morning!"

"Tonight is not about subtlety, it is about victory!" Kuveni declared.

As the smoke of another round of fireworks cleared, the revelers stopped, bumping into each other to look as they noticed the conspicuous presence of Eleanor and her entourage. They began pointing and shouting.

Uma, I hope you know what you're doing, making a spectacle like this.

Relax, Eleanor. Listen to their words. Let their prayers and their awe wash over you and infuse you with the power of their love and devotion.

Eleanor rolled her shoulders and attempted to take Uma's advice. When she had achieved some minor progress (as much progress as anyone could reasonably expect her to make as thousands of people watched her ride her divine tiger through the smoky streets), she held out her hand and summoned her green glowing trident to come to her slowly so that her increasingly enamored audience could watch.

As the revelers burst into emotion—cheering, crying, shouting, praying—she felt a wave of Shakti's power burst forth from the center of her being and infuse her with a form of giddy intoxication that she had only ever felt once in her life, during her first beautiful moments of making love to Edmund, when the full force of his divine passion had filled her with a unique brand of heavenly euphoria. This time, though, the feeling was accompanied by a wave of utter satisfaction, as if she had always meant to be the mistress of the chaos all around her.

"Victory to the Mother!" Kuveni declared as she snapped her fingers and another round of fireworks, much more elaborate and artistic than the earlier ones, exploded in the skies above them.

Sheranee roared her approval as she bucked. Eleanor held on with one hand while her trident erupted into green flames in the other. She pulled back until she realized that the flames were not made of earthly fire. They weren't even hot.

As they burned all around her, she realized that they were also burning within her, infusing her with more of the intoxicating power that had begun emanating in increasingly potent waves from somewhere deep inside of her.

Eleanor flinched as the shadow of a dark arm loomed above her, but as her adrenaline exploded, she realized that the arm was hers. It was not the only one. She looked up and watched as the eight arms of Durga extended all around her, each wielding a divine weapon that flickered in the eerie green flames.

There was a bow, an arrow, a sword, a javelin, a discus... there were more, but she had to pause as she almost passed out with a wave of hot nausea... Her eyes couldn't focus.

The arms were somehow anchored to her, but not physically. They weren't some Rakshasa extension of her human form, or even a Yakshini illusion. They were real, and yet they weren't. It was as if they'd burst forth from her soul itself, taking on just enough matter from the smoky air around her to be visible. She glanced over at her reflection in the window of a small shop. There, amongst the green flames, Maa Durga, the most powerful warrior form of the Holy Mother in her full divine glory, looked back at her and smiled. She collapsed forward onto Sheranee, but Uma pulled her body back up into a regal riding position.

"Victory to the Mother!" the revelers cheered.

The crowds parted, shouting their prayers and praise as Uma rode Sheranee through the streets with Kuveni and Mélusine by her side, adorning her loving followers with handfuls of fresh jasmine and marigolds that they pulled from an endless supply in their hidden Yakshini pockets.

Eleanor's head felt like it might implode as the sensory overload of smoke and screams, of flowers and fireworks, and the millions of other intense sights and sounds unfolding all around her beat against her human body, but she fought with all her might to stay awake.

After a long parade surrounded by increasingly fervent followers, they reached a huge golden pandal that shimmered in the dramatic light of thousands of fire torches. At the very top, an effigy of an animalistic demon with red spikes jutting from its fanged face and the curved horns of a water buffalo protruding from its bulbous forehead awaited her. Eleanor did not like its resemblance to Vibhi's and Edmund's demonic forms.

It is not an effigy of our virtuous Rakshasa beloveds, Eleanor. It is Mahishasura. Let us ignite him and celebrate with the crowd.

Should we really celebrate killing demons? After everything we know about them?

Mahishasura was one evil bastard, Eleanor. We should celebrate the triumph of light over darkness. Just as not all demons are evil, not all demons are worthy of our mercy. He was not.

Eleanor gave in, as she was finding it increasingly difficult to keep her mind focused on the complicated issue, and so she let Uma lean forward and whisper into Sheranee's ear.

"Let us go into battle, my love."

Sheranee roared and pounced up the stairs. Uma didn't look back at the crowd as she thrust her flaming green trident into the belly of the effigy. It ignited into a bonfire of green flames, and she almost collapsed with another burst of overwhelming intoxication.

Eleanor barely held onto her consciousness as Uma looked back at the crowd with glee. Thousands of people danced and cheered as she stood before the flames of her own divine power, and the effigy of one evil bastard lit up the night sky.

"Come, Eleanor. Let us skip to the next celebration," Kuveni's disembodied voice whispered into her ear. "We have a long night ahead of us."

Eleanor couldn't respond as the growing power of the Holy Mother pumped through her human veins.

"To Mysore!" Uma declared on her behalf.

Eleanor felt the delightful warm breeze of her Yakshini allies encompassing her, and as her mind went blank, she dissolved, leaving the crowds of Calcutta behind to continue on their Durga Puja with Shakti's blessings.

They materialized in front of an enormous palace illuminated by millions of twinkling electric lights. The bulbous towers and spiked turrets were somewhat reminiscent of Hyderabad, but a series of imposing archways highlighted by the lights reminded her of Harrods at Christmastime. The idea that a maharaja's palace and a London department store could look so similar felt fanciful, but the more she stared at it in her woozy state, the more she expected to see a red double-decker bus driving past.

She caught her mind wandering and focused with all her might on staying in the present. There was already an audience of thousands assembled, and she was grateful that Kuveni had had the sense to materialize them at the back of the crowd this time. She kept her flaming trident at bay (back wherever its divine perch was—she still wasn't sure), hoping to reduce the intoxicating effects so that she could fully retake control of her faculties.

"How did they even procure this much electricity?" Eleanor murmured as she took a deep breath and reveled in a moment of humanity.

Twelve elephants trumpeted from an elevated platform just inside the palace's largest, most central arch. They were each painted in a unique design made up of the bright colors and patterns so common to the sacred elephants across India, and each carried an empty golden sedan, except for the front-most elephant, whose sedan already contained a large glistening idol of the Goddess, illuminated by flickering fire torches. The maharaja and his court stood beside them as several brahmins finished off some devotional rituals involving holy water, garlands, incense, and coconuts, but as the elephants noticed Eleanor's abrupt entrance, so did the court, and the vast audience turned to see what had garnered their attention.

In for a penny, Eleanor sighed.

In for a pound, Uma agreed.

The crowds gasped and scampered out of the way as she rode Sheranee right through the center of their gathering, straight up the stairs, and onto the platform.

While the royal children whispered and pointed at her with excited ogling, the maharani and the priests gasped with some combination of awe and fear, while the maharaja watched her with puzzlement.

Uma reached forward and grabbed the closest brahmin's hand, forcing him to stand. *Take with you our blessings on this most auspicious eve, my child. Never forget what it is you are here to celebrate.*

As Uma let go and the brahmin stumbled backwards, whispering to the other priests, who bowed their heads and began chanting heated mantras, Sheranee growled a low warning of displeasure at the unwelcoming expression on the maharaja's face, and the maharani subtly nudged her children behind her husband. She hissed at the guards to step in, but they only stared at the Goddess and her mount standing before them, stunned with disbelief.

"There is no need to fear us, my children. I am the vessel of Uma, Avatar of Shakti, and I have come to celebrate the Holy Mother's triumphs with you on this most auspicious night."

Uma summoned her flaming trident, and Eleanor felt the burden of Durga's full divine form engulf her.

"Good lord," the maharaja murmured. "How is this possible? How can you be the Holy Mother here, in the flesh?"

Uma laughed. "Surely, you've heard of avatars, Your Highness."

"Yes, of course! But they were alive in the past! In the days of Lord Rama himself! I've never heard of such a thing in the modern world!"

"We keep a low profile these days, my friend. But, just as I helped your grandmother's grandmother celebrate Dasara, I have come to offer you my blessings tonight. Your celebrations have always been some of my favorites."

He kneeled and bowed his head. "It is an utmost honor to serve you, Holy Mother."

"Then you can serve me by getting started! Your people are waiting!"

"We were just about to begin the procession to the sacred banni tree, my lady," the maharaja replied as he glanced passed

Eleanor to spot Kuveni and Mélusine waiting impatiently for their pleasantries to be done with.

"Then by all means, let us proceed together!" Uma declared.

"As you wish, Holy Mother," the maharaja whispered.

He gestured to the guards, and Eleanor cringed for a split second, hoping that he hadn't just done something incredibly foolish, but the guards rushed forward and guided the maharani and the children onto the steps that were already set up to help them mount two of the beautifully painted sacred elephants.

The maharaja followed their lead, stepping up onto the third sacred elephant, and Uma reached forward and laid her hand on Sheranee's soft head.

Let's give them the parade of the century, my love.

Sheranee growled her agreement and leapt down off the stage, mischievously scattering the front rows of the crowd before she returned to her duty and took her position at the front of the procession. The elephant carrying the idol followed, then the maharaja and his family, and then the rest of the court. Men, women and children in glittering ceremonial silks walked in rows between groups of dancers who moved to the frenetic beat of traditional drums. The sound reverberated through her, compounding her giddy intoxication until she made a brash move, ripping Uma out of her primary position and retaking control of her body.

As you wish, my child. Please take your turn.

Eleanor wiggled her fingers and toes, reveling in her human sensory perception with an extra dose of determination not to let it overwhelm her again. She ignored the unsettling feeling of Durga's divine form all around her, and instead focused on the humanity of the present. She reached her free human hands out as worshippers bowed and whispered quiet prayers and offered Shakti's blessings to anyone who had the courage to reach out to her.

As they continued out of the palace grounds, into the streets of Mysore, news of Uma's presence spread, and the thousands of revelers gathered along the processional route became more somber than their counterparts in Calcutta had been. They prayed and cried, reaching their hands up into the air and calling out, "Victory to the Mother!" as if it were a call to prayer rather than a victory chant. Eleanor found the difference in their reaction fascinating.

We are their divine patroness, Eleanor. Their city is named after our victory. Our story inspires them to fight evil in their own daily lives.

Many people would assume Edmund and Vibhi are evil. Would these worshippers not chase down the demons with pitchforks, ready to slay them? We must be careful what we inspire them to do.

Let us bless them, Eleanor. We will bless them to see the difference between good and evil, no matter what forms they take.

Eleanor doubled-down her efforts to reach out to the crowd, blessing every devotee she could reach. She continued as her arms became more and more fatigued, and the waves of intoxicating power became increasingly tiresome, until she noticed two familiar faces watching from the balcony of a building.

"My lords!" she called to them. "Don't just watch from the sidelines! Come join me!"

Rama scrunched his nose and squinted as he stared at her, while Hanuman scratched his head with puzzlement.

"Come along for some fun! The Goddess commands it!" Eleanor called cheekily. She could feel the intoxication taking hold of her better judgment.

They debated heatedly for a minute, and then the small ancient brahmin shrugged his begrudging obedience, rolled his shoulders, and burst into his fluffy Vanara form. The crowds were too focused on Eleanor to notice his transition.

Hanuman gathered Rama into his arms and leapt from the balcony straight into the center of the processional route. The crowds went wild as soon as they saw him, and he and Rama both looked around nervously. Eleanor held out her flaming trident, and the bustling worshippers stepped back.

"I told you this was great folly, my lord," Hanuman muttered.

"If the Holy Mother can do it, certainly we can too," Rama argued. He bowed his head. "But, if my lady will indulge a foolish question, how, may I ask, are you achieving this feat?"

"And which feat is that?" Eleanor asked.

Rama squinted at her again. "You are… you are two people at once. I see Maa Durga in all her glory, but I also see your human vessel."

"I suppose I shouldn't be surprised that the gods can see more truth than humans can. Do you see my human vessel too?" she asked Hanuman curiously.

"I only see the Holy Mother, my lady."

"Don't sound so disappointed!" Eleanor was starting to regain her energy. "We can't change what we are, my friend. Just because you aren't an avatar, it doesn't mean you aren't a god in your own right."

He looked even more upset by her attempt to cheer him up.

"Have I offended you?"

"Yes, I mean no… I mean, I'm sorry, my lady… I just wish… I was just hoping… If Rama can see your human vessel, I was wishing I could see Uma. I'm sorry. It was a selfish thought."

Eleanor smiled. "I forgive you, my child."

"Thank you, Holy Mother."

Rama reached forward to poke one of Maa Durga's arms, but his hand went right through it. He shivered.

"Are the Yakshinis doing this for you? It's a rather clever idea for them to help you disguise yourself like this. I wish I'd thought of it centuries ago."

"Nope. No Yakshinis were involved in the making of this divine form. It is Shakti's will entirely for the people to see a deeper divine truth tonight."

"Then which truth am I seeing?" he asked dejectedly. "These villagers are seeing a deeper truth than I am."

"Their minds don't accept plurality like yours can, my lord. You've spent thousands of years learning to see past the changing forms of the people around you. It is a useful skill."

"I suppose." He didn't seem convinced.

"Surely you must agree that many truths can exist at once? I'm Maa Durga, Shakti, Parvati, Uma, and Eleanor. You're lucky you aren't seeing five of me!"

Rama looked to Hanuman who shared his expression of discomfort.

"Have I offended you now? Just give me some time, I'm sure I'll find a way," Eleanor winked.

"My lady, it's just... you're so different from Uma. You're so... er... lively and irreverent but somehow familiar all the same, and your accent... it's very... er... foreign."

Eleanor laughed. She appreciated their honesty. She realized that Uma had spoken with her own perfect lilting Anglo-Indian intonation throughout their entire interaction earlier in the day, and if she'd been in their shoes, just as she had when Leo had revealed his true accent, she would be feeling strange about the transition too.

"Don't fret, my lords. Half the English-speaking world can't understand my brogue."

She hopped off of Sheranee to walk beside them, and looked back to spy the maharaja and his entourage watching their exchange with some combination of awe and bewilderment. Kuveni and Mélusine were conspicuously absent.

"I don't believe we've had the pleasure, my lord, at least not formally. I am Eleanor MacLeod Marriner, vessel of Uma, Avatar of Shakti." She offered him her human hand to shake.

He looked at it for an awkwardly long moment, and then reluctantly shook it.

"Was that too foreign of me, to offer you my hand?" Eleanor asked. "I thought that since you hugged me several times already today, a handshake would be perfectly apropos."

"You were conscious? For everything we said and did earlier?" Hanuman asked with a hint of discomfort.

"Just as Uma is conscious now. That is how our partnership works. I'm certain she explained it earlier."

"Yes... yes, she did explain it. I suppose we just... we didn't fully comprehend that you would be so different from her... so separate," Rama admitted. "You are... you are a stranger, but she was an old friend."

Eleanor smiled encouragingly at his honest admission. There was something strangely familiar about him, something that reminded her of Edmund.

"There is no need to apologize. I am a stranger, but perhaps we will become friends in our own right. I have it on good authority that I get along swimmingly with Lord Vishnu's avatars."

Uma stirred disapprovingly at Eleanor's risky quip.

"Lord Vishnu's avatars? Have you met Parashurama then?" Rama asked. "Yes... Yes, I suppose you must have spent some time on Mount Kailash... You should know that he and I are very different. I like to think of myself as more... er... evolved than he is. I don't enjoy killing my enemies like he does."

Eleanor suddenly realized the mess she'd just made, but as the consummate liar that she was, she simply fell back on one of her classic avoidant responses. "We have a lot to learn about each other, my lord. In the meantime, shall we bless our followers together?"

Eleanor reached out into the crowd and returned to offering her blessings, while Rama watched. She looked back at him, and he shifted uncomfortably as he prepared to contradict her. "I should not make it clear who I am, or we will have a riot on our hands. It has happened too many times to count, and I do not wish to repeat it again tonight."

"Do they not recognize you?" Eleanor asked curiously. "I would have thought that your unique features would give you away." He looked like he wasn't entirely sure what she was referring to. "Your red eyes are quite striking." She glanced at Hanuman and decided not to point out that he was the only walking, talking, flying monkey left on Earth.

"They think I should be blue," Rama shrugged. "The art has been too stylized for millennia."

"Blue? The color blue?" Eleanor asked.

"Very, very blue," Hanuman reiterated.

"But aren't you human? Isn't it an important detail in the epic that you're human? Why would they paint you as a color that isn't natural to a human?"

"You have read our epics?" Rama asked.

"Not really." Eleanor veered out of dangerous territory before she gave away anything about Edmund or Vibhi. "I saw a dance performance depicting *The Ramayana* several years back, and I've seen various artistic murals in temples from time to time. Now that you mention it, though, you were quite blue in those murals."

"The blue represents my divine virtue. They want us to be human when they are trying to understand us, and divine when they need our help," he explained. "Surely you have already come to notice the contradiction? We must straddle two intensely different worlds while they are watching our every move, venerating our human follies with just as much enthusiasm as they have for our divine victories."

"I suppose they don't know me well enough to venerate much of anything other than my divinity." She reached forward and continued on offering her blessings. "That is certainly how it should be. I will disappear into oblivion in a human lifetime, and Shakti will continue on her work in another form."

Rama took a long look at her, reassessing something in his mind. "You are a very curious woman. You do not wish to fight your mortality?"

"Not any more than I wish to move a mountain," Eleanor laughed. "They are both futile endeavors marked by unnecessary pain. Change and death and transformation are necessary. They are fundamental aspects of the nature of the universe. I cannot escape them anymore than you can, my lord."

"I am still here five thousand years after my first death," Rama countered.

"I suppose Lord Vishnu works in mysterious ways," Eleanor conceded amicably with a wink, moving the conversation swiftly along.

Rama and Hanuman walked alongside her and Sheranee as she reached into the crowd for street after street after street of the parade, until Eleanor felt her second wind of energy and her enthusiasm waning. She'd finally gotten used to the waves of intoxication, and now, as was often true by the end of a night of tippling, she was ready to return to her normal, clear-headed state of being. She wondered if she'd have a hangover in the morning...

Kuveni must have sensed her struggle, and with a warm breeze, she and Mélusine materialized beside her.

"Where have you been?" Eleanor asked curiously.

"Oh, we were just enjoying ourselves out and about," Kuveni replied. "We thought you might enjoy your time alone together."

Eleanor looked around at the hundreds of people actively watching them. "We were hardly alone."

"Ma chérie, are you going to refuse a moment of privacy offered by your Yakshini handmaidens? If you aren't grateful, Kuveni will never offer you another!"

"Yakshini, huh?" Hanuman muttered as he eyed her suspiciously.

Mélusine's cheer morphed into annoyance. "Should I have said Rakshini and Yakshini handmaidens? It is important that we clearly specify the exact composition of everyone involved when we put together a sentence, isn't it? And what exactly should we say about you and Rama? A human avatar and his sidekick? We mustn't refer to you as gods in the plural, if we're going to be precise about it, as I only see one very human god in our midst, regardless of how many millions of lemmings have decided to worship a monkey."

As Hanuman stuttered angrily, Rama stepped in diplomatically. "Thank you, Kuveni. It is an unusual privilege indeed to be left alone in the presence of any mistress of yours."

"Indeed," Kuveni replied curtly to his subtle jab. "Now, Eleanor, the procession is just about to reach the banni tree. We have many more parties we can attend tonight. Would you like to stay for the ceremony, or shall we make our exit?"

"I think we've done enough for Mysore for one night," Eleanor decided as she glanced back up at the maharaja's elephants, which were now waiting for her entourage to clear the path to the sacred tree. She took Rama's hands into hers. "It was a pleasure meeting you, my lord. I hope we can continue our friendship on more auspicious occasions." She glanced over to Hanuman. "Perhaps you should avoid insulting my Yakshini handmaidens in the future, my lord. You may find that they are much nicer when properly addressed as the friends and allies that they are."

"I... I..." Hanuman looked so dejected that Uma couldn't let him squirm any longer. She took his hands into hers. "Remember, old friend, what a privilege it is to have friends and allies who can be honest with you."

"It is a privilege," he agreed begrudgingly.

She smiled, and then let him go. Eleanor relegated Uma back to the core of her being and mounted Sheranee. "Onward, Kuveni!"

With a moment of lightheadedness and a chorus of gasps from the crowd, they dissolved.

CHAPTER 6 – DANDIYA

They skipped around India for several more hours, setting more demonic effigies on fire, and parading through the crowded streets offering Shakti's blessings, until Eleanor's weak human body could no longer ignore the shooting pain in her back and her legs from her long day of unusually rigorous movement. Even Uma had reached her limit.

"How much longer are these parties going to last?" Eleanor asked as she ascended another sparkling golden pandal before a roaring crowd in a city she didn't even recognize.

"All night!" Kuveni exclaimed. "You have given them enough joy to last a lifetime, Eleanor. Dancing all night in your honor is hardly a feat."

"Maybe for them it isn't..." she muttered. "Surely we should go home soon. I'm sure the dogs are lonely."

"But it is your most auspicious night!" Kuveni argued.

"I'm not as young as I used to be," Eleanor countered.

"My dear girl, you are so young, you would be considered an infant if you were a Yakshini," Kuveni shot back.

"In case you've forgotten, I'm still a mere mortal."

"I had forgotten," Kuveni sighed sadly. "What wonderful bliss it was while it lasted. I suppose we should take you home. We must keep you healthy and hearty for the rest of your human lifetime."

"Ma chérie, you should at least go to one dandiya party. The sacred dances are one of the most entrancing celebrations of the Goddess anywhere."

"We are *not* going to Baroda," Eleanor declared steadfastly.

With her fatigue, and the intoxication of Shakti's power that was still pumping through her veins, there was no telling what she might do in the presence of her other half.

"I know, ma chérie. You are very wise to stay away from the nest of Rakshasas. They mustn't learn who you are. But Baroda is not the only palace hosting a dandiya celebration. *Viens.* I have an idea that I'm sure you will like."

Mélusine whispered something to Kuveni, who smiled approvingly, and then they flanked Eleanor and Sheranee, and dissolved them once more.

They materialized beside the grandest swimming pool Eleanor had ever seen, so big that there was a row boat tied up along the edge. The water vibrated with the movement of frenzied folk-drumming echoing from somewhere beyond. Twenty-foot-tall marble columns held up domed ceilings covered in whimsical murals, and beautiful chaises with carved wooden edges and artistic brocade silks lined the veranda, looking out upon the pool and the gardens beyond. The furniture looked slightly familiar, but Eleanor did not recognize anything else about their setting.

Sheranee stretched and yawned, and Eleanor felt a sudden urge to cuddle up with her on one of the divans for a nice long nap.

"Where are we?" she asked as she watched several servants run across the lawn just beyond the edge of the pool, carrying silver trays of dirty glasses. They paid no attention to her at all.

Mélusine grinned. "We are in Gwalior. Now come, ma chérie. They're almost finished. The Maharaja of Baroda sent over some dandiya dancers as a peace-offering, and the royal family has been enjoying their most festive Dasara in decades. I'm sure that they will be thrilled to welcome you."

Eleanor suddenly felt self-conscious. She hadn't seen the Maharaja of Gwalior or his family in almost two years, since she and Edmund used their unique talents to save the maharaja's children from a violent troop of thieving bastards. The Maharaja of Gwalior, and his daughter Anya, had in fact been there the moment that Eleanor learned that she was an avatar. The idea of them seeing her displaying Maa Durga in her full glory suddenly felt like too much. She was ready to have a human experience.

"Come," Kuveni urged her. "There is no need to be shy, my dear girl."

"Do you think I can just come as myself? Will Shakti let me?"

"Why don't you ask her?" Kuveni suggested.

Eleanor closed her eyes. *Uma? Shakti? Maa Durga? May I please be myself again?*

She felt her heavy crown dissolve. "Thank god!"

"Thank the goddess," Kuveni corrected her.

Eleanor looked down at her sari and her mehendi, and then at Sheranee. Suddenly she had second thoughts... She wanted to be back home in bed.

"I'm going to be a spectacle, aren't I? Eleanor MacLeod, the silly *firang* imposter."

"You aren't an imposter, ma chérie. I don't know how you could come out of this night thinking anything of the sort," Mélusine said sternly.

"Besides, they love you," Kuveni added more diplomatically. "At the worst, the uninitiated members of the audience will think that you've come as an impersonator... a living idol to help them celebrate."

"They'll think I'm like one of those department store Santa Clauses, hopping about the streets of Edinburgh giving out sweets before Christmas?"

"*Exactement!*" Mélusine agreed.

"With a pet tiger?" Eleanor asked skeptically.

"They will not question it, ma chérie. Trained animals are a dime a dozen in India. Now *viens!*"

Kuveni skipped ahead, while Mélusine stayed by Eleanor's side, escorting her and Sheranee through the marble hallways, towards the music. As she reached the edge of the massive, glittery marble ballroom illuminated by millions of crystals in its huge chandeliers, the music came to a grinding halt, and a large circle of frenzied dancers in colorful costumes embroidered with thousands of tiny mirrors that sparkled in the lights of the chandeliers stopped confusedly to see what was wrong.

"Good lord, Madho Rao. How did she possibly know to come…" the maharani murmured from her position beside her husband and her children on a gilded platform overlooking the festivities.

"Good lord," he seconded. "We should have prepared!"

"Eleanor!!!" Anya exclaimed. "I knew you'd come!"

The entire room watched as Anya rushed down the stairs of the platform, across the room, through the circle of dancers, and straight into Eleanor's arms.

Eleanor hugged her happily. "You are such a beautiful young woman now! I can't believe you've grown so much!"

"We're not supposed to comment on how people look," Anya winked.

"The Goddess has given us both permission tonight."

"You're the prettiest avatar in the world," Anya said as she hugged Eleanor again. "I'm so glad you got my invitation. I told them you'd get it!"

"Invitation?" Eleanor asked.

"To the Dasara party! We've had the dancers practicing for all nine nights of Navratri just so it would be perfect tonight. I told them it needed to be perfect for when you came!"

As Eleanor glanced back at the royal family, she saw Rane look down nervously and whisper something to her husband, who threw her a look of intense disapproval, and then glanced apologetically to Eleanor.

Eleanor made a mental note to check in later on Rane's foolish role in keeping the invitation from being sent. "Well, darling, I'm here now. Don't let me spoil your festivities." Eleanor watched as Anya eyed Sheranee with a combination of wonder and nerves. "Would you like to say hello to my mount? She's very gentle."

Eleanor pet Sheranee on the head and scratched her ears, and then Anya reached forward and copied her movements. Sheranee purred, and the entire room watched the exchange with disbelief.

"*Jai mata di,*" Anya murmured. "Would you like to watch the dandiya with us, Eleanor? You can have my chair at the royal table."

"Watch?" Kuveni chimed in. "My dearest child, we should not watch, we should dance! What better way to celebrate the Goddess's triumph?"

"We don't know how to do it!" Anya protested.

"You don't know how to do it *yet!*" Kuveni corrected her.

"But it's Gujarati! Gujarat is miles and miles away from here!"

"Well, my dearest child, I am Lankan, and I know how to do it, so you really have no excuse now, do you?"

Kuveni grabbed Eleanor's and Anya's hands and guided them straight into the circle of dancers.

Several servants stood behind Sheranee at the door, trapped in the hallway with their trays of fresh drinks, refusing to come any closer.

"Come, ma chérie." Mélusine coaxed Sheranee out of the way, and several guests scurried away from them. "She won't hurt you, unless you do something very foolish," Mélusine explained in a failed attempt to calm their nerves. She shrugged and leaned casually against the wall, petting Sheranee's head as the tigress took a regal seat beside her.

Kuveni materialized two sets of wooden sticks that matched the ones in the dancers' hands and handed them to Eleanor and Anya.

"Now, my dear girls, you will be partners in our dance, and I will show you what you need to do, with the help of our obliging friends..." She looked around at the circle of dancers, who were still staring at Kuveni's hands where she'd conjured the sticks out of thin air. Kuveni did not acknowledge their intrigue. "Hrm. I need a partner. This won't work at all with an uneven number. Rane, perhaps you'd like to join us?"

The maharani was startled by the attention. She glanced at Eleanor, who nodded her support, and then the maharani stood up, straightened her posture, and ignored the many eyes watching her as she joined them in the center of the ballroom.

Kuveni materialized two more sets of sticks, to the subtle gasps of the dancers who were now paying very close attention. She handed one to Rane and kept one for herself.

"Now, my dearest girls, do exactly what I do. We will dance in a circle with some basic movements like this... and this... and this... And it is important that we strike the sticks against one another at just the right time or else it may get very messy. Remember, this dance is commemorating Maa Durga's battle and victory over Mahishasura, the scoundrel. The movements should feel a bit like swordplay, without the injuries, of course."

They followed Kuveni's demonstration of various strokes, until she was satisfied with their understanding of the basics. She coaxed her way into the circle of expert dancers, who were continuing to watch her with some combination of confusion and intrigue. They did not, Eleanor was quite sure from their casual posture, realize that an avatar of the Goddess was amongst them. She was grateful for the reprieve.

"*Jai mata di!*" Kuveni declared. "Let the music begin!"

"*Jai mata di!*" Rane seconded.

With the maharani's declaration, the music began.

"Please forgive me, my lady," Rane whispered as she took her position beside Eleanor. "Anya begged us to send you an invitation, but we did not want you to feel obligated on this most auspicious of days. I was sure you had more important things to do than to attend our dinner party."

Eleanor smiled forgivingly. "Next time, let me decide for myself?"

"Yes, my lady. Of course, my lady."

Eleanor held both of her sticks in one hand to grab Rane's arm. *Take with you Shakti's blessings, my child.*

"Thank you, Holy Mother," she whispered with a pious bow.

Eleanor looked up self-consciously to the whole circle of dancers watching them, waiting for their cue to begin.

"*Jai mata di!*" Kuveni repeated again. She slammed her sticks against Eleanor's and began the movement of the circle clockwise with several of the strokes she'd demonstrated, clicking her sticks against the other dancers' and twirling around, helping Anya and Rane keep up and begin anticipating the changes until the group was moving in a smooth, swooping, graceful pattern around a sacred lantern with a flickering flame right in the center of their circle.

Eleanor relaxed and let Uma's comfort with the movements work its way into her muscles. She clicked her sticks against Anya's, following the dancers and Kuveni's lead as they improvised and expanded their strokes into increasingly frenzied action. She wove in and out of the circle, smacking her sticks against theirs with growing force until some of the dancers started bowing out, leaving only the heartiest to combat her.

Eleanor's head swam as fresh waves of Shakti's power wafted up from the center of her being. As she fought against more bursts of intoxication, she noticed that the lantern's flames were the same green as her trident and her eyes. The other dancers noticed the strange flames too, and as the lantern exploded into a bonfire, the circle widened, and the dancers' determination to maintain the rhythm morphed into panic.

Eleanor could not rip herself out of the circle. Her head was spinning. A wave of heat engulfed her, and she closed her eyes to make it stop. Her body kept moving.

"Eleanor?" she heard Anya's voice calling. It sounded as if she was far away, at the end of a very long tunnel.

"Holy Mother, what's happening?" Rane yelled.

"Eleanor?" Kuveni called, her voice even more distant. "Eleanor, dear girl, snap out of it!"

As a final burst of power almost knocked her off her feet, she caught herself and forced her eyes back open. She looked around. The dancers were back. The dandiya circle was weaving around her. Gasps and murmurs and shouts rang out, but Eleanor was too dizzy to see past the movement of the dancers encircling her.

Suddenly, she felt an anchor. She focused all of her energy on grasping onto the familiar surge of power that had just infused her. She slammed her sticks against a passing dancer's, and as he held on for an extra beat, twirling with her and contemplating her presence with confusion and then acute desire, she pulled him out of the circle and engaged him in a one-on-one battle in the center of the dancefloor.

In a daze, they both slammed their sticks against each other's, circling the center of the ballroom as the crowds parted to watch their feverish match. While Eleanor struggled to maintain her consciousness in the wake of overwhelming intoxication, Uma emerged, taking over her faculties completely and engaging their other half in a dance so furious that each movement lost its identity, morphing instead into one greater entity.

The sticks burst into flames.

The momentum could not be broken.

Eleanor's waning consciousness realized that her body was imprisoned in the exchange. She did not have the strength to fight back.

Uma kept their partner transfixed, yanking his energy into her being until an explosion of euphoric pleasure unlike anything Eleanor had ever felt in her life infused every last cell of her being. Nothing corporeal could possibly compare with the ecstasy of their energy becoming one.

The dance pushed on.

Eleanor lost track of the crowd, then of her own mind.

She couldn't feel her limbs as the frenzy accelerated, until an explosion of acute, ravaging pain in her hands traveled up her arms and into every inch of her nervous system.

Stop! She begged Uma.

"Stop!" she finally squeaked out the word.

In the distance, as if through rippling water, she felt the music stop. She dropped the flaming sticks and collapsed onto the cool marble floor. She glanced down at the oozing, blistering burns on her hands and her arms, and then she looked into the terrified face of her other half.

"Vibhi?" she murmured.

"Shiva's wrath," he whispered. "What have I done?"

CHAPTER 7 – D.H.'S FOLLY

Vibhishana looked around at the enamored, gasping crowd and then down at her dismal state. He dropped his flaming sticks onto the floor. An expression of terrified desperation darkened his gentle Lankan features. The pleasure of his power still intertwining with hers was almost enough to overwhelm the agony of the burns… almost. Eleanor whimpered as a burst of pain shot up her arms.

"Eleanor?" a familiar female voice called. "Eleanor, are you alright? What was that? Mr. Vishravan? Are you alright?"

"Get a doctor. Find Doctor Desai now! He was smoking in the garden an hour ago." Another familiar voice, this one male. How did she know it?

Eleanor did not have the energy to see who it was. It wasn't Kuveni. It wasn't Mélusine. It wasn't Anya or Rane or Madho Rao.

Where am I? How in the hell did I get here?

Uma remained unsettlingly silent.

Vibhishana whisked her up into his delightfully frigid arms. "Hold on tight, Eleanor," he whispered into her ear. "We must get out of here now, before they see anything even more incriminating."

At an admirable approximation of human speed, Vibhishana ran with Eleanor in his arms out of the ballroom, through several hallways, and finally into a vast marble bathroom. He slammed the door closed behind him with his foot, and as he lay her down on the cold floor, she opened her eyes to observe his divine Shiva form. He looked down with his three eyes at his ashen skin, skull necklace, and the white and yellow snake of life that slithered across his bare shoulders, and he sighed with stress.

"You're looking mighty handsome in that loin cloth, Lord Shiva," she murmured. The intoxication had apparently not worn off yet.

"Eleanor, I'm so sorry!" he wailed. "What wicked, wretched, worthless folly!" He buried his head in his hands and sat back against the wall several feet away from her. "I should have realized this could happen! I should have been more careful! It's just... I didn't think you'd be so active in fulfilling your sacred duties." Suddenly another wave of panic blanketed his face. "Where is Edmund?!"

"He's in Bombay at a conference of colonial magistrates. He's staying with the Bidkars and our loyal spying butler," Eleanor replied calmly.

"Well, that is one small respite for my undeserving mind..." He took in a deep breath of relief, and then he paused with another troubling thought. "He isn't waiting for you, is he?"

"He is away for two weeks. I stayed back at home, and Uma convinced me to bless all of India tonight with the help of my Yakshini handmaidens. It seems there was wicked folly all around... speaking of which... I am going to *kill* those Yakshinis for this."

"It wasn't them," Vibhi said as he crawled over and kneeled by her side. "It was me, Eleanor. It was entirely my fault."

"May I ask *how*?" Eleanor didn't like his guilty tone.

"I'm not entirely certain how it works, but it has happened a few times before… each time on Dasara, while Uma was engaged in her sacred duties. Her power… your power… I can feel it brewing from afar, and it intoxicates me. It entices me to summon you, and when the conditions are right, I can make you come to me."

Eleanor raised her eyebrows at the unlikeliness of the story. "I'm human. I have a human body. How can I be summoned like a genie?"

"I don't know! I didn't think it could happen!" he exclaimed before he got his emotions back under control. "But you still somehow traveled through the divine flames of the yajna, until our energy connected into the whole being that we are meant to be. It was an utterly bewitching feeling." Vibhishana looked down sheepishly. "I swear to you, Eleanor, I didn't mean to do it. I have been working harder than I ever have to keep my distance. I have missed you both so dearly since Edmund's birthday breakfast at the Bidkars, and I suppose I was thinking about what you both might be up to… and wishing that you could be in Baroda for the cheerful festivities. What wretched folly…"

Eleanor hissed as another burst of pain traveled up her arms, and Vibhishana shivered, glancing down at his own arms with a grimace. He coaxed the snake of life off of his shoulders and onto hers. It coiled gently around her arms, and the pain transitioned from acute to throbbing. Eleanor sighed with relief.

Vibhishana rubbed his hands together, and Eleanor caught a subtle expression of pain on his face.

"Are you alright?"

"I'm perfectly fine," he lied.

"Are your hands hurting because mine are?"

"I would endure a million times the pain if I could undo what I just did to you, Eleanor."

"You didn't answer my question."

"We are linked, Eleanor, as two halves of a more perfect whole. When you feel extreme... er... sensations... they resonate within my being."

"Blimey..." she murmured. "Does that include pleasurable sensations?"

His cheeks flushed as he stared at the floor.

"Blimey... but does it work the other way around? How come I've never felt an unexplained burst of your pleasure?"

"Because in this ascetic stage of my life, I don't have any feelings that are strong enough to resonate... at least when you aren't around." He refused to look at her. "Now, tell me what else I can do for you, Eleanor. Uma was never impacted like this when we did the fiery Nataraja together."

"Was our dance really so fiery? Even for you? I suppose she did say that she's felt more in my body than she ever felt on her own."

"It was unusually... er... hot... for me as well. I haven't felt anything like it in five thousand years." Vibhishana shifted uncomfortably. "But what I meant was that Vanaras cannot burn. It is a unique heartiness shared by all members of their race. I should have realized that you wouldn't share it... I should have stopped... but I couldn't! I was completely enraptured! It was like my body wasn't mine."

"I know the feeling," Eleanor reassured him.

"Yes, I'm sure you do," he murmured.

Eleanor fought back a wave of nausea and realized that she was shivering.

"I am going to need help, Vibhi. These burns are dangerous. I can feel my body going into shock."

"I don't know what to do. I can't change out of this form."

"Surely the damage is done?"

"It isn't. By Lord Shiva's grace, I had the discipline to ward off the transition until we were out of the crowd's sight."

"Don't you mean by your own grace, Lord Shiva?"

He looked down at his ashen hands. "I am Lord Shiva, but he is much vaster than me. His divine will always supersedes mine if there is a difference of opinion."

"I know the feeling," Eleanor said as she glanced down at the hourglass figure Shakti had endowed her with against her will. "I wanted to be in bed hours ago, snuggling with Sheranee and the dogs. Instead... here I am."

"Uma has spent many ascetic centuries looking within herself, as have I, and I must admit that neither of us have been able to transcend the limitations of our corporeal desires. I can only conclude that our limitations are part of the plan, but it is an unhelpful conclusion when dastardly difficult circumstances like this one arise..." He looked around the windowless room, furrowing his brow as footsteps resonated in the hallway. He sighed with stress as he eyed the only exit, right into the public hallway. "The last time this happened, I was trapped in this form for three days before I could calm down enough to switch out of it. I *cannot* be revealed to the world like this, Eleanor. The prophecies were very clear about that."

"I will summon..."

"Don't say her name," Vibhishana interrupted before Eleanor could finish her sentence. "None of them can know who I really am. It is absolutely imperative. The future of the world depends on it."

"Well, my lord, do you have any other suggestions?" Eleanor asked with minor annoyance at his refusal to join her in problem solving.

Their exchange was interrupted by a subtle knock on the door.

"Vibhi?" the familiar male voice called. "Vibhi, is everything alright?"

"Perfectly fine, Rohit," Vibhishana called back. He looked to Eleanor in a panic. "I don't know what to do, Eleanor. Clearly my judgment has been wretched all night. Tell me what you need."

"You trust him, don't you? You described him as one of the most virtuous humans you'd ever encountered?"

"I did…"

"Then let him in, for god's sake. We need an ally!"

Vibhishana glanced nervously at the door.

"We have to do something, Vibhi. If you won't let him in, I will."

He stood up and walked to the door, taking in several nervous breaths in a row.

"Why do you do that?" Eleanor asked distractedly. "You don't need to breathe, I assume, if you enjoy sleeping as a puddle of liquid in the bath?"

"It is still calming to feel the air on my internal plasma," Vibhishana explained. "It grounds me."

"Huh…"

He glanced back at her, rolled his shoulders, ripped open the door, pulled Rohit inside, and slammed it behind him.

Rohit Patel glanced down at Eleanor. "Shiva's wrath! Eleanor? What are you doing in Baroda? It was like you just appeared in the sacred fire!" Eleanor hissed again as a fresh burst of pain traveled up her arms. "We need to get Doctor Desai in here! Miss Smith is looking for him now. What in god's name…" He trailed off as his eyes landed on the snake of life coiling around her arms and slithering across her chest.

Vibhishana was leaning up against the door behind him, whispering a set of mantras. Rohit's eyes widened as he took in his foreign form.

"Vibhi?" he whispered.

Vibhishana looked down at his unchanged body and sighed with resignation. He turned around to face his old friend.

84

"You cannot tell anyone anything about this," Vibhishana warned. "Not Maya, not Monty, or Rama or Hanuman or anyone else. Do you understand?"

"What would I tell them, my lord? What is it that I'm seeing?"

He waved his hand in front of Vibhi's three eyes, and they watched him eerily.

Vibhi lowered his voice into a barely audible whisper. "Rohit, I am, and I have always been, the Immortal Avatar of Shiva."

"My god," he murmured.

"And Eleanor is the Avatar of Parvati."

"My god," Rohit repeated, as he eyed the snake of life again.

"But Eleanor is Edmund's devoted wife on the earthly plane, and that is how it is going to stay. Now, we need your help. Our Nataraja has left Eleanor with wicked burns."

"I'm going into shock," Eleanor whispered as her teeth began chattering. "I need you to bring me some blankets, some lukewarm tea, some room temperature water, and some aspirin. When you find the doctor, you must bring him here. Tell him to bring bandages and gauze and whatever else he has to clean the wounds."

"You must keep everyone away from here, including your family," Vibhishana added. "I cannot change back into my human form right now. The divine energy of our dance is too overwhelming."

"My lord..." Rohit was working hard not to give away his reaction to the shocking revelations. "My lord, would it not be prudent... with all the people who saw you in the ballroom... who saw your unique Rakshasa speed on the dancefloor... for you to escape from here until you are in a state in which you can explain yourself? I can stay with Eleanor, or perhaps Maya can stay with her while I find Doctor Desai. I can wait in the hallway and tell you when the coast is clear."

"I will not leave my divine wife in a wounded pile on the floor," Vibhi countered. "I did this to her, and I will stay with her until she is healed."

It was the first time Eleanor had heard him refer to her in that way. She didn't like it... but some part of her did. She pushed it down. She did not have the energy to deal with the complications of the other souls creating feelings inside if her that weren't her own.

"Yes, my lord," Rohit said quietly. "I will go find Doctor Desai and give him your orders, my lady."

Vibhishana grabbed Rohit's hand. "Thank you, my friend. I am trusting you with a secret dangerous enough to destroy the world... perhaps even two or three worlds..."

"It is a privilege to serve you, my lord," Rohit replied with a pious nod. "Now more than ever."

Vibhishana hid behind the door as Rohit slipped out, and then he locked it and returned to his position kneeling by Eleanor's side.

"I'm so sorry, Eleanor," he reiterated. "What a wicked disaster I've wrought."

"We have a bigger problem, my divine husband."

Vibhishana raised his eyebrows.

"Perhaps I will call you D.H. from now on. That seems sufficiently unromantic, don't you think? It is like an acronym for a disease."

"You may call me whatever you want, Eleanor. I am at your mercy."

"As you wish, D.H. My point was: even if my immediate health improves, these burns are sure to leave ugly scars. How am I going to explain this to Edmund? He will never leave me alone again if I tell him I had some kitchen accident without him. I need him to have faith in my ability to take care of myself. It is pivotal to my future happiness and our marriage."

"There is another solution..." Vibhishana trailed off in deep thought. "But what a great risk that would be..."

"Yes? What is it?" Eleanor pushed.

Another knock at the door distracted them.

"Eleanor? It's Mae. Mabel Smith? You remember me, don't you?" Mae's voice called. "Eleanor, are you in there? Mr. Vishravan? I have Doctor Desai here."

"Where is Rohit?" Eleanor called back.

"The maharaja pulled him into his library," Mae called.

"Shiva's wrath, explaining our show will keep him occupied all night," Vibhi muttered. "I promised the maharaja not to give away our Rakshasa nature to the masses, and I made him promise to keep our secrets, but *this* secret... He can't know this secret... But Rohit doesn't have five thousand years of experience with lies!"

"Neither do I, D.H., and look at the cunning little vixen I've become." Eleanor smiled reassuringly, even though the truth of the statement hurt.

"What wretched folly..." he whispered.

"I need help, Vibhi. You must let them in," Eleanor reiterated.

Vibhishana looked down at his divine form again.

"You chose not to leave when Rohit gave you the chance, and now you're stuck with the consequences," Eleanor whispered. "Now let them in, and we'll figure everything else out later!"

Vibhishana coaxed the snake of life off of Eleanor's wounds and back across his shoulders, and she gasped as a burst of agony erupted from her burns.

She shooed him away as he grimaced with some combination of pain and guilt. "I need help, D.H."

He relegated his emotions, hopped up, and hid behind the door as he pulled it open. As soon as Mae and Doctor Desai were inside, he shut and locked the door behind them.

"Eleanor?!" Mae exclaimed as she kneeled down beside her. "You're terribly burned! You were moving so fast we could hardly make heads or tails of what was happening! How did this happen?"

"No need to get hysterical, Miss Smith." Doctor Desai kneeled down across from Mae. He didn't have any of the supplies that Eleanor had asked for, and the scent of fresh tobacco wafted off of his ill-fitting kurta.

"Hysterical?!" Mae exclaimed. "You weren't even in the ballroom! You didn't see what happened!"

"Let me see, little lady. I'm sure it's nothing." He grabbed Eleanor's burned hand, and she screamed with pain.

"It's *nothing*?! Does this look like nothing to you?" Eleanor exclaimed indignantly as soon as she got control of her nerves.

Doctor Desai fished into his pocket, but instead of pulling out a stethoscope, a bandage, or any similarly useful item, he pulled out a box of cigarettes.

"Are you bloody joking?!" Eleanor exclaimed. "I've been *burned*, and all you can do is light up a bloody cigarette?!"

Vibhishana lost his patience. In a blur, he reached forward, grabbed Doctor Desai, ripped open the door, and threw him into the hallway. He slammed it closed again and locked it.

"Thank you, D.H. I would have done the same thing myself if my hands weren't out of commission," Eleanor said casually.

Mae stared at Vibhishana with disbelief as he leaned up against the door again, refusing to face her. "Mr. Vishravan?" she murmured as she watched the snake slithering across his ashen shoulders.

Eleanor's teeth began chattering more violently. "We appear to be out of options, D.H. I'm certain that Kuveni already knows who you are. We must enlist her help, or we will be trapped in this bathroom until all of Baroda knows our secrets."

"Kuveni already knows?"

Mae let out a quiet gasp as he turned around to face Eleanor.

"I'm quite sure that she does," Eleanor reiterated. "I didn't tell her, so I assume she must have already known for quite some time. She can be discreet, you know, when it truly matters. She managed to keep my secrets from you, and she has done an admirable job of keeping Lord Brahma and Lord Kalki in the dark about themselves."

"She knows…" he murmured.

"Kuveni!" Eleanor called. "Kuveni, please help us!"

With a pleasant breeze, Kuveni was standing beside her, still donning her ancient Lankan form. Vibhishana was intrigued by the development, but he quickly relegated his reaction into a stoic expression.

"Mistress Eleanor?!" she exclaimed. "We've been going mad trying to find you! We thought you might have been ripped right into the heavens! What happened?!" She kneeled down beside Eleanor and inspected her wounds. Then she looked over at Mae, and then up at Vibhishana. "Shiva's wrath," she murmured as he cringed self-consciously at her reaction. "I will tell Lady Mélusine to remain in Gwalior to manage the crowds there. They were quite concerned about your abrupt disappearance, my dear." She closed her eyes and whispered a quiet mantra.

"Kuveni…" Vibhishana hedged.

"I will keep your secrets safe, my lord, just as I have for five thousand years. We needn't discuss your lack of faith in my discretion when our dearest girl is in such dire straits."

"You've known for that long?" he asked. "And you've never said one word about it?"

"I am a citadel of secrets, my lord, as long as they are worthy of being kept. One of these days you will realize that you and I are not as different as you'd like to think."

"Kuveni, you must get us out of here," Eleanor whispered as her shivering escalated. "Please take me home; then you and Mae can follow my instructions to help me treat the burns. Mae, please come. I promise I will explain everything."

Eleanor wasn't quite sure what her plan was for Mae, but she was certain that she shouldn't just leave her behind to her own imaginative explanations for their wild display of divine shenanigans.

"I need to be at the school on Monday morning…" Mae hedged.

"My dear girl, we will have you back with plenty of time," Kuveni reassured her.

"But you don't live in Baroda, do you? Surely we would have crossed paths," Mae asked skeptically.

"Have we not already demonstrated that we are not limited by human constraints, dear girl?" Mae suddenly looked pensive, and Kuveni took her silence as agreement. "Shall I take all of you, my lord?"

"I will stay with my divine wife," Vibhishana replied.

"Oh dear, this is dreadfully complicated, isn't it?" Kuveni sighed. "First Uma was a Vanara, and now Eleanor is married to Edmund. Destiny can be so cruel."

"Perhaps we can discuss my romantic woes later... privately," he said as he eyed Mae.

"Yes, my lord," Kuveni agreed. "I will take you in batches to keep the other Yakshas out of it."

Kuveni dissolved, and with a moment of lightheadedness, Eleanor rematerialized on her messy bed. With only a few more seconds of delay, Mae was standing beside her, and then Vibhishana. As the electric lights clicked on, Kuveni reappeared in her chubby middle-aged form, clad in an empire-waisted, old-fashioned nurse's outfit.

"Now, Mistress Eleanor, tell us what exactly you need us to do."

CHAPTER 8 – THE OTHER SOLUTION

"Kuveni, I need more blankets and cool, clean water to drink and to clean the wounds, and some lukewarm tea, and some fresh bandages... perhaps with Mélusine's Roman remedy."

Kuveni snapped her fingers and materialized a nursing cart with all of Eleanor's requested items.

"Good lord," Mae murmured.

Vibhishana began pacing back and forth.

"Cover me up, Kuveni... Mind the burns, we mustn't touch them yet," Eleanor whispered. "And help me drink some tea."

Kuveni bundled Eleanor into the bed, covering her up with several additional blankets, which were the softest cashmere she'd ever felt, and then like a doting mother, Kuveni held up a cup of tea and fed it to Eleanor.

"Is it warm enough?" Kuveni asked.

"It's perfect," Eleanor sighed. When she was finished with her first two cups, she gestured towards the water, and Kuveni dutifully held up a glass while Eleanor drank the entire serving in one go. "I shouldn't have let myself become so dreadfully dehydrated. I didn't have anything to drink at all after Rama and Hanuman left."

Vibhishana stopped in position. "Rama? Lord Rama and Hanuman?"

Eleanor wasn't about to initiate any more lies, even though she felt a stirring of Uma's desire to be less than honest about their divine encounter. "They came earlier to the village temple where I was offering my blessings. They'd heard lore of an avatar of the Goddess and came to assess my claims."

"And?" he asked nervously.

"And they found them to be true." Eleanor shrugged, and then hissed with the pain of the minor movement. "I let Uma entertain them all afternoon before we went out to the festivals. Monty even came by to help us with an early dinner."

"Monty was *here* all afternoon?"

"You are not the only one who keeps secrets, my lord," Kuveni pointed out.

"How many of the Yakshas do you know, Eleanor? How many are actively serving you?"

"Enough?" Eleanor glanced at Kuveni. She wasn't sure what the right answer was, or what the answer that would not get Kuveni and Mélusine in trouble for meddling would be.

"Shakti is our mistress, my lord," Kuveni stepped in. "You know as well as anyone that we serve the gods above all else. Perhaps if you'd like more loyal service, you should make it clear who you really are. I'm sure you'd have a line out the door of qualified Yakshas ready to join the cause."

"That will not be necessary," Vibhishana replied testily.

"Then do not fault us when we follow Eleanor's orders above yours," Kuveni replied. "Now, Mistress Eleanor, what else do you need?"

"We must clean the wounds."

Kuveni moved a bowl of cool water to the bed beside Eleanor and began dabbing the wounds with a clean cloth.

"You've done this before," Eleanor observed.

"Too many times," Kuveni agreed.

They all watched in silence as Kuveni conscientiously cleaned every inch of Eleanor's blistering skin.

"Now what, my lady?" she asked when she was finished.

"The Roman remedy," Eleanor whispered. "And the bandages. You will need Mae's help with this step, I think. Mae…"

Eleanor suddenly became self-conscious as she forced herself to deal with her uncomfortable revelation.

Mae startled at the attention and then stepped forward to help, focusing dutifully on Eleanor's wounds without a word about the wild circumstances.

"We must be very strange to you, Mae?" Eleanor asked as Kuveni showed her how to gently dab the Roman cream onto Eleanor's wounds.

"Yes, strange is one word to describe it," Mae replied. "I'm sure I will forget everything as soon as I wake up."

Eleanor smiled. "I thought I was dreaming the first time I got sucked into this madness too. I suppose I might still be asleep…"

Eleanor realized as she made the quip that she didn't like the idea one bit. Despite every tribulation, she was exceedingly happy that her wild life with Edmund was real. Going back to changing bedpans and reading vapid magazines alone in bed on Sundays with a box of shortbread in her lap suddenly seemed utterly unbearable.

"You cannot tell anyone about this," Vibhishana interjected. "Only Rohit knows, and it must stay that way."

Mae eyed the snake of life and then his third eye. "I wouldn't even know what to say… Mr. Vishravan?"

"That is one of my names," Vibhi replied.

"Then Lord Shiva, is it?" she asked casually. "With the snake and the skulls and the third eye? Does the river Ganges flow through your hair?" Eleanor was quite sure that Mae had resigned herself to playing along with the dream.

"That is another of my names."

"Yes… yes, of course, just like the statue across from the school… We've been studying Hindu iconography all semester, but the girls are still so obsessed with that one… I wonder what it means… Perhaps I should ask Mr. Vishravan for some patronage for next year… or perhaps the Patels… I could use a few new teachers…"

"You are not asleep," Eleanor reiterated.

"My companions often say that in my dreams," Mae winked. "But, anyway, there's really no point in fighting it. I must let it play out and learn what I can from the symbolism…" She eyed Vibhishana again. "I must admit, I didn't think any of this Hindu stuff was real. It seemed far too colorful to even have a hint of truth to it. I suppose I'll have to rethink some philosophy. Perhaps I've been too close-minded with the girls' religious assertions at school…"

Vibhishana paused as he considered his response. "Most religions have some truth to them, Mae, whether they are about the senseless crucifixion of a kind-hearted carpenter or a virtuous demon defecting to the cause of righteousness. What is important is that you hold onto the universal message of peace and acceptance."

"Does that mean that you are also Lord Vibhishana?" Mae asked curiously. "*The* Lord Vibhishana? You are not just named after him?"

"You are familiar with Lord Vibhishana's story?" he asked. Eleanor could not tell if he was more or less pleased with her astute observation about his name.

"The Chiranjivi from the ancient epics? He is the virtuous demon who became immortal after he defected to the cause of righteousness, isn't he?" Mae asked.

Vibhi looked down at his divine form and gave in. "I didn't realize news of my identity had traveled all the way into the British community."

94

Eleanor wondered if he was using Mae's belief that she was asleep to cleverly fish for intel.

"The girls at the school go on and on about you," Mae admitted. "When we read *The Ramayana* back in June, they insisted that we had our very own family of Rakshasas right here in Baroda, and that Lord Vibhishana himself was living with them."

"Family of Rakshasas?" Vibhi asked, only somewhat masking his panic at the development. "And which family of Rakshasas might that be?"

"The Patels, of course. The children make up all sorts of tall tales about them."

"Such as?"

"Well, let me think about it... some of them have been very amusing... They can turn into anything they want... Their butler is a wizard... They have purple blood... They eat misbehaving children... Oh, and of course they can fly... with bird wings (or bat wings, they argue about it often). I mean really, wings would need to be absolutely enormous to carry anything bigger than a bird..."

"This is very, very bad..." Vibhishana muttered.

"Are the tales true, then? I have quite a list of misbehaving children to send along!" Mae burst into laughter at her facetious joke, but when she remained the only one laughing, she calmed herself awkwardly. "I'm sure it's nothing to worry about. The architecture of the Patel Estate is enough to inspire anyone's imagination. Like my sleeping mind's right now..."

Vibhishana pulled up a chair from the corner and took a seat beside them. Eleanor found the casual gesture to look especially odd in his unusual form. "Do the children tell these stories to Rahul Patel?"

"I'm not sure. The boys are in the maharaja's English medium school across the road. But it is not uncommon for children to make up stories like this. British schoolchildren make up ghost stories all the time about the castles in their villages. I think it is their way of connecting the past to the present, and the Patel estate really is one of the oldest in Baroda. It's all perfectly healthy, as long as it doesn't cause problems for the Patels… or for you, I suppose. But surely as an ancient god, you shouldn't be worried about what schoolchildren are saying about you? Perhaps it means that I am too concerned about what they are saying about me… I do seem ancient to them, and rather powerful…"

"They are repeating what they hear from their parents. It would be less problematic if it weren't mostly true."

Eleanor watched curiously as he reached out his hand and dissolved it momentarily into his violet metallic plasma, grimacing as he forced it into his clawed, spiked demonic hand. It reverted stubbornly back into his ashen divine hand, and he sighed with subtle annoyance. "I still cannot escape from Lord Shiva's form."

"Good lord," Mae murmured. "This really is the strangest dream." She reached out and poked his open palm. "But it doesn't feel like a dream…"

"You are not asleep," Eleanor reiterated.

Kuveni reached over and pinched Mae's arm.

"Ow!" Mae exclaimed.

"My dear girl, what must we do to convince you that you are awake?"

Kuveni materialized a glass of water in her hand. She splashed it right into Mae's face, and Mae squealed with surprise. As Mae wiped the water off of her eyes, she glanced at Eleanor, and then landed her gaze on Vibhishana.

"So, you are telling me that an ancient god, the Avatar of Shiva, whose statue looms over our humble city *and* a primary character from one of the most famous Hindu epics, is living in the center of Baroda with a family of flying demons?"

"I am also a demon," he corrected her. "But we don't eat children, or humans of any age, for that matter. I'm sure that detail was added by the children's parents to scare them into behaving. The Rakshasas of Baroda have always been unquestionably virtuous. We have protected the city against more plagues than anyone would care to know about."

"And you have a wizard as your butler?" Mae asked with disbelief.

Kuveni smiled and snapped her fingers. Suddenly the room was filled with heaps of freshly cut jasmine and marigolds.

"We look like wizards to children who don't know any better, but we are far more interesting than that. We are Yakshinis, my dear girl."

"Yakshinis? From the local folklore? The fairies in the woods that lead travelers astray?" Mae reached forward and collected a handful of flowers. She sniffed them, and then crumbled the petals, dropping them onto the floor. "How fantastical."

"We are *not* fairies. We are nature spirits and the sacred guardians of Earth," Kuveni explained.

Vibhishana leaned in. "It is imperative that Rahul does not know anything about this. Not about the Yakshinis, and not the rumors about his family. Perhaps I will talk to Maya and Rohit about being more honest with him before he learns too much in the schoolyard... but we wouldn't want to be too premature..."

"I can ask the male teachers if they've heard any rumors and report back, if you'd like?" Mae offered.

Vibhishana's posture relaxed. "You would be a valuable ally, Miss Smith, in many capacities."

"I don't know what I could really do. Whatever is going on here is totally beyond me," Mae demurred.

"Humans are often our most valuable allies," Vibhishana reassured her. "And I have observed your earnest virtue for years as you've built up the school. Let me think about your suggestion... Rahul hasn't mentioned anything at home about any of it... Sometimes it is best to leave well enough alone..."

A burst of shooting, freezing pain distracted Eleanor as Kuveni began rubbing Mélusine's remedy onto a particularly crispy patch of skin. "This isn't the same as Mélusine's usual recipe."

"I'm sorry, my dear girl. It has eucalyptus… and a few other ingredients to dull the pain and help the burns heal. Burns need unique treatment, you know. The Romans had many centuries to refine their techniques with so many temple fires running amuck."

Vibhishana coaxed the snake of life off of his shoulders and around Eleanor's wounds, and Eleanor sighed with relief. While Kuveni didn't pay it any mind and continued on with her task, Mae stepped away, backing up against the window.

"It isn't dangerous," Eleanor reassured her. "It isn't even really a snake. Isn't that right, Vibhi?"

"It is the snake of life," Vibhishana replied. "It is a manifestation of our power—Eleanor's and mine—when we are together as one, managing the underlying transformation of the universe."

"That was my next guess," Mae quipped. Then she glanced around at the fresh flowers Kuveni had produced, and reminded herself that there was a chance she was awake. She became somber. "This is all utterly mad. Gods and demons and magical spirits all in the center of an unimportant principality in Gujarat? How can it not be a dream? Eleanor, aren't you married to that handsome tall colonel? You burned a chicken together on your honeymoon in Baroda the day we all met."

"I am married to my tall, handsome, kind, gentle colonel. Through the cruelest joke the universe could have possibly concocted, the goddess inside of me is married to Vibhi."

"Blimey, that is complicated," Mae murmured.

Eleanor hissed again as a burst of pain shot through her arms, and Vibhishana was distracted by a momentary internal debate. He glanced at Kuveni guiltily, took a deep breath, gathered up some of the cream, and began gently massaging it into Eleanor's skin underneath the snake with his delightfully cold hands, pushing the snake out of the way to make sure that he was covering every inch of her wounds. Eleanor fought back Uma's pleasure at his touch, and watched curiously as none of the substance wiped off on the snake's smooth white scales, as if the snake weren't there at all. She took a moment to consider the possibility that it was entirely an illusion, but she felt its weight and its energy infusing her with a calming sense of well-being.

"Thank you," she whispered when he and Kuveni were finished. "It is feeling much better, but I don't know what we're going to do about the scars."

Vibhishana glanced at Kuveni and then leaned in. "Rama will heal you if you ask him. He owes Uma and me a great number of favors."

Eleanor chuckled. "We'll have to call in one of Uma's, D.H. Unless you'd like to explain to him what exactly Lord Shiva is doing here. Hanuman might never forgive you for keeping Uma from marrying him."

"That was Uma's decision entirely. It took all of my self-discipline to stay out of it." Eleanor was intrigued by the hint of defensiveness in his tone.

"Still, Vibhi, do you think he'd believe that if he knew that Lord Shiva's avatar was hopping about in secret this entire time? That *you*, his old Rakshasa friend, have been Lord Shiva as long as you have known him, and you never told him or Rama anything about it?"

"You're right, Eleanor. It is not time for them to know. They will not learn of this secret until the greatest transformation the worlds have ever known is upon us. If I do anything to change that course, the consequences will be catastrophic."

"Worlds?" Eleanor asked astutely. "As in, more than one?"

Vibhishana glanced at Kuveni.

"Don't look at me, my lord. It was your plural."

He sighed. "I don't know what it means, to be honest. The prophecies always use the plural, no matter what language the Oracle is speaking. I don't have any clue about what other world might be involved." He glanced nervously at Mae. "We'd best not say anything else about it."

Be careful, Eleanor. Mae has not yet been chosen by the Oracle to receive its prophecies.

"Uma agrees with you."

"She has always been very wise…" He trailed off and then caught himself and cleared his throat. "Do you have Hanuman's talisman, or shall we use mine?"

"He gave me a new one just today." Vibhishana raised his eyebrows disapprovingly, but said nothing. "I left it on the vanity, just there." She pointed.

"You shouldn't leave something so valuable just lying around." He gathered it up and brought it over to her. "Anyone who gets ahold of it can summon him at will. He will get very testy if another desperate human summons him on a selfish whim."

"How does it work?" Eleanor asked.

"You must hold it in your hand and think the message you want him to hear, just as you do for Mélusine's…" He trailed off and gave into a grimace of intense internal debate. After another guilty glance towards Kuveni, he reached into a hidden pocket in his form and pulled out a bangle covered in eerily glowing green stones that perfectly matched the pendant in Mélusine's talisman. "And for mine. You should summon whichever one of us you need from now on, Eleanor. There are certain things that I can do… that you and I can do together… that exceed the Yakshinis' capabilities."

"Like what?" Eleanor felt Uma cringe as she asked.

Vibhishana glanced at Mae and then Kuveni. "We can discuss it later."

"As you wish, D.H. But how are we going to summon Hanuman now? I am not in a position to squeeze a talisman in either of my hands, and he mustn't know you're here."

"I will do it," Kuveni volunteered. "He knows we're enjoying your festival together, and he will know to treat the summons seriously if it comes from me."

Kuveni took it into her hand, closed her eyes, and whispered her message.

"You'd best find a place to make yourself scarce, my lord. They are on their way from Mysore. You have ten minutes at most."

"Mysore?" Vibhi asked distractedly. "*They* were celebrating Dasara in public?"

"We ran into them earlier, actually. I convinced them to enjoy the night with their people," Eleanor replied.

"I didn't expect them to become active so soon..." Vibhi murmured. "Maybe that's what the prophecy meant, after all..."

"My lord, you must hide yourself away promptly if you wish to remain anonymous. Shall I escort you somewhere?" Kuveni offered. "Eleanor will recover quickly with Lord Rama's intervention."

"I will not leave until I see it is done," Vibhishana declined.

"There is a natural spring in the jungle beyond the property," Eleanor suggested. "You could rest there and try to retake control of your form."

"That is a better idea." He leaned towards her and then caught himself. He stood up and backed away. "Can you tell me roughly where it is?"

"I can do better than that." Eleanor closed her eyes.

Sheranee, come now. Your mistress needs your help.

With a resonating roar, Sheranee burst through the front door of the house and barreled into the bedroom. Mae screamed and stepped back into the corner, while Kuveni stepped away from Eleanor to make room for their touching reunion.

Eleanor laughed as Sheranee licked her face.

"I know you were worried, my love. But I will be perfectly alright. Now, go show my divine husband that lovely natural spring that we found a few days ago." Sheranee humphed her disapproval as she nuzzled into Eleanor's blankets. "Go, my love, your mistress commands it. I will summon you when we are ready for his return."

With a final lick of Eleanor's face, Sheranee begrudgingly obeyed. Vibhishana offered Eleanor a determined nod, glanced at Kuveni and Mae with an awkward goodbye, and followed his divine wife's loyal mount down the dark hallway and out the wide-open front door.

Mae took his vacated seat next to Eleanor.

"Mae..." Eleanor hedged. "Mae, you must promise me truly that you will not tell anyone anything about this... including Edmund."

"I don't know when I'd even have the opportunity, but I promise you, Eleanor. You will not need to add me to your list of worries."

Eleanor smiled. "I wish we could have stayed in Baroda. I think you and I would have been great friends."

Mae glanced out the window to the edge of the jungle. "I understand why you left us in such a hurry now. It was to avoid him, wasn't it?"

"That was a big piece of it, yes. Baroda has a number of people living there that Edmund and I really should stay far away from..." Eleanor thought momentarily about how much she was willing to share, and suddenly the idea of an unbiased human friend overwhelmed all of her reticence. She lowered her voice. "It is so complicated, Mae. So much more bloody complicated than you can imagine. Edmund believes that Vibhi is his father."

"Good lord... is he?"

"Vibhi is his really his uncle, but he has taken it upon himself to look after Edmund. He's even the one who officiated our wedding ceremony."

"Good lord... Does that mean then that Edmund is also a demon? You are married to two different, related demons at once?" Eleanor nodded her agreement. "Blimey, I thought my love life was complicated..."

"But it gets worse!" Eleanor exclaimed, ignited by the novelty of voicing her woes to someone other than Kuveni. "Edmund is also an avatar, an avatar of a god who is *not* married to the goddess inside of me. And the avatar of his divine wife is *also* in Baroda. When he is anywhere near her, he is utterly bewitched, and he doesn't even bloody know why. Only I know, because the goddess inside of me knows far too much about most things. And *that* is why we ran away from Baroda. It's the center of one of the cruelest romantic jokes in history."

Kuveni suddenly dissolved.

"Does she do that often?" Mae asked curiously.

"Yes, quite often. She prefers her non-corporeal form." Eleanor relished the novelty of her honesty.

Kuveni reappeared. "They are here, my dear girl. They just landed in the garden. I will go outside and gather them up. Prepare yourself. Hanuman will be unhappy with this development, and he has never been particularly good at controlling his emotions."

"Are you ready to meet some more gods, Mae?" Eleanor asked as she took a deep breath, readying herself for her third encounter in one night. It was sure to be the least pleasant.

"You will have your own epic soon enough," Mae winked.

"I feel like I already do."

They all held their breath as they listened to the heavy, creaking footsteps approaching at a panicked speed.

"Uma?!!" Hanuman barreled into the bedroom.

"Good lord, he really is Lord Hanuman." Mae eyed his fluffy primate form.

He ignored her. "Uma, what happened?" He took one look at Eleanor's charred, glistening arms. "I knew you shouldn't have gone out alone with those irresponsible escorts! This was Mélusine's doing, wasn't it?! Ravana put her up to it!"

"We were *not* irresponsible!" Kuveni rebuked.

"Please do not overreact," Eleanor implored. "Mélusine had nothing to do with this."

"Don't overreact?!" Hanuman exclaimed. "Look at you! You could have died, and then where would Uma be? She'd be dead! Truly dead!"

"I am already dead, my dearest old friend," Uma replied.

"You are talking to me right now," he countered. "It is a privilege I do not take lightly."

Uma and Eleanor did not have a proper rebuttal.

Rama kneeled down beside her more calmly. "My lady, you really do look affright. Did the fireworks get out of hand?"

"Yes, you could describe it that way," Eleanor agreed.

Rama glanced at Mae.

"She is a discreet and devoted ally, my lord," Eleanor reassured him. "You needn't withhold anything for her sake, but you may ask her to leave if you do not want her to watch."

"I trust your judgment, my lady."

Hanuman humphed his disapproval, but said nothing as Rama rubbed his hands together until the divine silver light of his healing power emerged.

"Good lord..." Eleanor barely caught herself before the words fell out of her mouth. *Edmund will be able to do that.*

As Rama ran his hands gently over Eleanor's wounds, Hanuman paced back and forth humphing and hawing with unfocused disapproval and throwing accusatory looks towards Kuveni.

Eleanor shivered as the warmth of Rama's touch dissolved into the utterly novel feeling of immediate relief from agonizing pain. The contrast created a sense of euphoria that was not entirely different from what Mélusine often produced, although it was much more localized.

When he was done, Rama crossed his arms on the bed beside her and put his head down, shading his eyes from the electric lights.

"Are you alright?" Eleanor asked concernedly. She flexed her fingers, focusing on the odd sensation of their complete recovery.

"He is weak," Hanuman replied on Rama's behalf. "Lord Vishnu's healing power drains his human life-force. It leaves him in a highly vulnerable state."

He eyed Mae and then positioned himself between her and Rama.

"My lord, do you think I intend to hurt Lord Rama?" Mae asked with puzzlement. "That wouldn't be very Christian of me, you know."

"With Rakshasas hopping about on the loose, we can never be too careful," Hanuman replied.

"Rakshasas? Are they not your allies?" Mae asked.

Hanuman snorted. "Rakshasas? They're bloodthirsty fiends, the lot of them! Perhaps you should educate yourself on the ancient epics."

"But isn't Lord Vibhishana a Rakshasa?" Mae caught herself and then trailed off. "Never mind."

"Lord Vibhishana is practically human, and he has been for many thousands of years now," Hanuman informed her confidently.

"Right then, I suppose I should read up on it..." Mae agreed disingenuously with a subtle glance at Eleanor.

"Thank you for your help, Rama. You have done me a great service, and I owe you a debt of gratitude," Eleanor whispered.

Rama only humphed.

Eleanor debated her next move, and then she let Uma guide her. She ran her hand through Rama's hair, massaging his scalp as she often did to calm Edmund. She noticed with passing intrigue that the green glowing divine power of Shakti was emanating from her palms.

Hanuman watched with an expression of distinct melancholy for almost a minute as Eleanor tended to her struggling ally, until he shivered and then looked up at her and smiled wistfully.

He leaned heavily on the bed, and Hanuman rushed to help him stand up. Rama leaned on him woozily.

"Thank you, my lady. I have not felt Shakti's energy in decades. Your touch has reinvigorated me, even if your energy is a bit... morbid."

"Is it?" Eleanor asked curiously. She wondered if Edmund felt the same sensation and simply didn't recognize it.

"Sita's energy feels alive. It feels warm and loving, as if I'm home..." He trailed off into a sad sigh.

"I suppose it is not strange for my energy to feel dark to you. It is the energy of the destroyer. But destruction is necessary for rebirth, Rama. It is a natural and necessary aspect of life on Earth, and it is not innately bad. If everything always stayed the same, there wouldn't be room for anything new." Eleanor wasn't sure if it was her or Uma speaking.

"I have never really felt connected with Lord Shiva," he admitted. "You are the closest I've come. I suppose if he had an avatar, I might understand him better."

"I'm certain that you know him better than you think," Eleanor replied.

Rama straightened his posture. "You're certain? Because the Oracle told you so?"

Eleanor felt Uma cringe as a hint of dangerous desperation darkened his expression.

"I know a great many things," Eleanor evaded.

Rama got down on his knees and bowed his head. "My lady, I implore you from one avatar to another, please let me commune with the Oracle. There are so many things I must know! They have been tormenting me for centuries!"

"My lord, how many times must I save you from yourself?" Uma replied on their behalf. "The Oracle is evil. Its meddling causes the greatest misery in the world. Someday Shakti will fully control it, but that day is not here yet. You must fight these human urges and connect to your divinity, or your desperation will lead you into darkness."

Hanuman put his hand on Rama's shoulder and threw Uma a supportive glance.

"My lord, let's go. You are still weak. You will be safer back home in your compound."

Eleanor wiggled up out of the bed and stood up. She let Uma take his hands and lead him back into a standing position.

"Take with you Shakti's blessings, Rama. May they lead you past the darkness, onto the most righteous path."

Rama's eyes teared up, and without another word, before he gave into his emotions, he ran right of the bedroom, down the hall, and out into the back garden. Eleanor caught a glimpse of him pacing back and forth, muttering to himself and growling with unrequited anger.

"Please take better care of yourself," Hanuman whispered as he pulled her into a warm, fluffy hug. As Rama let out a wail of frustration, Hanuman pulled away. "I'd best get him to safety."

Without a glance at Kuveni or Mae, Hanuman lumbered outside and gathered Rama into his arms. In a flash of light, they burst into the dark, hazy sky.

"Good lord, I'm tired," Eleanor murmured.

Mae and Kuveni both came to her side to inspect her wounds.

"Remarkable," Mae whispered. "How utterly divine."

Eleanor yawned and sat back down on the bed. "I suppose I'm not fully recovered yet."

"You have had quite a tiring day, my dear girl. Why don't you sleep? I will escort Mae to one of your guest rooms, and in the morning, I will make you both a delightful Yakshini breakfast before I escort Mae back to Baroda. If that pleases you, Mae?"

"If it's not an imposition?" Mae agreed.

"Not at all!" Kuveni guided her to the door. "Sleep, Mistress Eleanor. All will be right in the morning."

As Kuveni took Mae's hand, Mae paused and squeezed her curiously. "You really are very solid for a spirit."

"I am solid, my dear girl... when I want to be." Kuveni winked and escorted her into the hallway. "Nighty night, Eleanor dearest!"

Eleanor leaned back onto the bed, and as the remnants of the familiar energy of the Preserver of the Universe's life-force coursed through her, she closed her eyes and slept.

CHAPTER 9 – A GLIMPSE

Eleanor awoke with a start as the midday sun warmed her face through the open window. She took a moment to process her surroundings. Sheranee and the dogs were nowhere in sight, and she was still wearing the thick layers of royal silk and jewelry from her long night of festivities.

She held up her hands and wiggled her fingers, observing with wonder and a hint of unfocused guilt that the injuries were completely healed. She smiled bemusedly that Kuveni's mehendi was also still perfectly intact.

As she threw her feet over the side of the bed, a pleasant breeze tickled her face, and Kuveni appeared.

"Oh, Mistress Eleanor, I'm so glad you're awake! I was beginning to worry!"

"Really? Why? How long did I sleep?"

"Twelve hours!"

Eleanor laughed. "You didn't know me before I met Edmund. On my weekends off from nursing, sometimes I'd sleep for fifteen hours at a time." She stood up and began gathering her wits. "Is Mae still here, or did we scare her away?"

"Oh, never you worry, Mistress Eleanor. Mae is a worthy human ally. She's been patiently taking in the serenity of the garden with Sheranee for a few hours already."

"With Sheranee!" Eleanor laughed. "She's really settled into our world quickly then, hasn't she? Sheranee doesn't usually like humans."

"Sheranee knows when humans are worthy of her affection, just as I do, Eleanor. I knew you were worthy of our affection the moment I met you, and you were right that Mae is too."

"I don't suppose we can convince her to move down here? I could use a friend. I didn't realize until last night how lonely I was for friendship. It has been years since I've had a normal human woman to confide in."

"You could always suggest it."

Eleanor thought about the fanciful idea, and then she shrugged with resignation. "Nah. She's too invested in the school in Baroda. I won't steal her away from them. She will have a bigger impact there anyway. Our village is too small for a woman of her talents."

"Well, perhaps I can help you see each other more often, when Master Edmund is otherwise occupied, of course."

"Yes, I suppose…" Eleanor pushed back a wave of melancholy. "I shouldn't keep her waiting."

"As you wish, Mistress Eleanor. I've been satiating her with coffee and canelés, but I do believe she may still have room for a bit of a late Yakshini lunch."

As Kuveni noticed Eleanor's bewilderment at removing the complicated sari and jewelry, she rushed to her side and began untangling her, dissolving each necklace, bangle, and belt as she removed them.

"Where do things go when you do that? They don't disappear from existence, do they?"

Kuveni laughed. "Only if we desire it. Mostly they go back into storage. We have quite a few little treasure troves cached away across the earth. Lady Mélusine's divine power keeps them safe."

As Kuveni removed the last of the silk, Eleanor darted naked past the open window to her wardrobe and pulled out a thin yellow cotton sundress that she hadn't worn in many months. She slipped it on and noted in passing that it looked slightly scandalous without one of the modern bras Kuveni had made for her, but then she ignored her concern in favor of the comfort of a leisurely unrestrained lunch in the company of female friends.

She ran her fingers through her wild hair, calming her frizzy tendrils and gathering them into a loose ponytail tied back with a white ribbon, and then she scampered outside barefoot, relishing the feeling of the warm moss between her toes as she waved happily at Mae.

Sheranee jumped up out of her sunbathing position beside Mae and bounded across the lawn to greet her with loving licks.

"Good morning, sleepy head!" Mae called as she stood up from the table and walked towards her.

Eleanor kissed Sheranee's forehead, and then escorted her towards Mae. "I'm sorry to keep you waiting. Yesterday was more tiring than I realized."

"Please, do not apologize. I'm sure a goddess's life is busier than I can imagine." Mae hugged her, but then pulled away. "I'm sorry. Should I not hug you? It is a rather informal gesture. Should I bow or kneel instead? I don't know what the proper protocol is to greet a goddess."

Eleanor pulled her into a tighter hug. "Please, Mae, treat me like a casual friend. It has been ages since I've had a break from my divine throne, and it has been thoroughly refreshing."

Eleanor walked her back to the wicker table in the middle of the mossy lawn, and Sheranee followed.

"I was afraid we might have scared you off," Eleanor admitted as she took a seat at the table and poured herself a cup of coffee.

"I must confess that when I went to bed last night, I was absolutely certain I'd wake up in my bed in Baroda with all of the evening's drama having been an intoxicated dream. I did have quite a bit of champagne last night... But I have spent the morning hours contemplating what it means that it is all real. I think I will have to reconsider my faith."

"There are so many layers, you should probably withhold judgment until you know us better."

"I suppose..." Mae trailed off as Sheranee put her head in Eleanor's lap, and Eleanor began gently stroking her ears.

Kuveni materialized beside them, snapped her fingers, and produced three steaming carpenter's pies.

Eleanor smiled. "Thank you, Kuveni. I think this is a fitting meal to properly introduce Mae to our world."

"What's it called? It smells wonderful," Mae said as she looked around the table for a fork.

"It is a carpenter's pie, dear girl. It has been one of our specialties for exactly two thousand years."

"May we have some forks?" Eleanor asked politely, even though she knew full well that Kuveni had purposely omitted them.

Kuveni shrugged with melodramatic disagreement. "If you insist on eating like Scottish barbarians, then be my guest."

She snapped her fingers and produced two forks.

"Thank you for indulging us," Eleanor winked.

As Eleanor dug in, she watched curiously as Kuveni gracefully set about eating her pie with her right hand. The style was different than Edmund's, although it seemed similarly foreign.

"Is that really how the Romans ate?" Eleanor asked.

"It is, dear girl. They knew how to be elegant in their simplicity... until they lost their senses in the second century."

"How remarkable," Mae whispered. "What a privilege it is to hear firsthand stories of times long past. Do tell us more!"

"What would you like to know?" Kuveni asked casually.

"Anything! Everything! Did you ever see the great library of Alexandria?"

"But of course! Who do you think built it?" Kuveni asked.

"You didn't!" Eleanor exclaimed.

"Ha! Not me personally, no. An ancient Yaksha who has long since left this world. He was the Yaksha who trained Mélusine a few centuries later in the techniques she used to expand Lord Vibhishana's Anglo-Roman estate in Bath."

"In Bath? In England?" Mae asked with surprise.

"We have had quite a global footprint," Kuveni replied.

"How extraordinary. So, you've been hopping about as deities all across the earth for thousands of years? How is it that you do not have a global religion?"

"What makes you think that we don't?"

"Well, there isn't really a global religion, is there? The only real contender is Christianity, and that is only because the conquistadores force-converted the American natives, just like the Portuguese force-converted so many people here in the southwest."

Kuveni rolled her eyes. "Do not get me started on the violence and fear-mongering that have been perpetuated in the name of a kind-hearted carpenter. It is a sore subject for all of us. But you are a unique human, Mae. Often humans believe that violence in the name of their own religion is acceptable."

"I'm not a proponent of violence in any circumstance. I think a lot of people would agree with me, Christians and Buddhists and Hindus alike."

"Yes, but there are still violent followers of those religions," Eleanor interjected. "I suppose in the end, human nature is rather violent. It plays out in religion just like everything else."

"Can you and your... er... fellow deities not lead humans away from it? Into a more enlightened state?"

"We can lead, yes, but as my mother always said, you can lead a horse to water, but you can't make it drink." Eleanor paused to contemplate the utterly bizarre truth that she was speaking on behalf of the gods… and that she'd just quoted her mother.

"Our meddling has produced a wide range of unintended consequences that have unduly impacted the course of human history," Kuveni added.

"Unduly? But if your pantheon was the source of the impact, would that not be… God's will?"

Kuveni stopped to consider the astute point. "Perhaps we should speak of more frivolous things for now."

"What was the most extraordinary city you've ever seen?" Mae politely changed the subject.

"Certainly it was Rome," Kuveni said without a moment's hesitation. "At its height, it dwarfed any other city that ever existed before or since. It was a great tragedy to watch it fall as it did. Slowly, as each selfish decision led to the next, until they could not extricate themselves from their own doom…" As Kuveni noticed Mae's enthusiasm deflate at the dark thought, she smiled reassuringly and led them back to a happier topic. "Mohenjo Daro was also quite unique. It was a wonder you humans achieved such a feat so early on in your civilization. It was a place of great learning and culture, with a street plan that was fanciful in its originality. They didn't even have streets, just hatches in their flat roofs that they could use to pop up and wander about across the rooftops of the city, while all of their homes and businesses were entirely contiguous below. From above, it looked very much like an ant hill."

"How extraordinary!" Mae exclaimed. "Oh, how I wish you could speak to my girls at the school. What an experience that would be for them!"

"Lord Vibhishana would not be supportive of that plan," Kuveni demurred. "Speak of the devil…"

Eleanor's heart skipped a beat as Vibhishana emerged from the edge of the jungle, fully returned to his natural Lankan form and clad in a relaxed Indian suit of a subtly embroidered navy blue kurta and ivory pyjamas. She looked down at the curves of her breasts showing through the scandalous dress and berated herself for forgetting that he was lurking about. A pang of desire stirred inside of Uma, and Eleanor pushed it away.

Vibhishana walked casually across the lawn to their table and offered them a polite *namaste*.

"I see we've beaten your three-day record, D.H." Eleanor hoped that his highly attuned senses would not pick up on her burbling cauldron of confusing emotions.

"I'm grateful for the reprieve. I find it very disconcerting to be out of control of my form." He eyed her hands. "You are fully recovered?"

"I am."

"I'm glad. Did Rama give you any trouble?"

"A bit, but nothing Uma and I couldn't handle... with Hanuman's help."

"His help?" He raised his eyebrows in a gesture that looked distinctly like Edmund. She found the family resemblance puzzling.

"Yes, I was surprised by it too. I suppose he must have enough life experience to recognize that meddling with the Oracle is bad."

"Rama wanted you to access the Oracle?"

"He did."

"You didn't, did you?"

Eleanor relegated a pang of annoyance at the question. "I did not."

Vibhi sighed with relief. "Thank you, Eleanor. Keeping him away from it has been a wickedly difficult task. I am grateful to have you as an ally."

"It wasn't that difficult. I just refused, and Hanuman took him home."

"I'm glad that you have not witnessed the full extent of his desperation yet."

"I suppose I am too."

Kuveni snapped her fingers, and another steaming carpenter's pie alongside two carafes of hot honeyed milk appeared on the table.

"Come. Sit with us, my lord. Enjoy a Yakshini meal before you go."

"You like carpenter's pie?" he asked Eleanor.

"It has been one of my favorites for years now."

Kuveni cringed as Vibhi threw her a sideways glance. "Years, you say?"

"Come, my lord. Sit with us and enjoy this lovely afternoon," Kuveni reiterated. "I made the pie using Miriam's exact recipe."

A grimace of sadness darkened his expression momentarily, until he relegated it and took a seat at the table.

"Thank you, Kuveni. It has been too long."

"Miriam?" Eleanor asked. The name was familiar, but she couldn't remember from where.

He took a bite using the exact Roman technique that Kuveni had used, and concentrated for a long moment before swallowing it. He smiled wistfully.

"She was my last human wife. She never understood the full extent of my foreign nature… or that I didn't actually need to eat any human food. She worked for years to find something I would like, and eventually she concocted this. It is the only solid food I have ever eaten that is worth the trouble of producing a digestive system."

"How extraordinary," Mae murmured.

"I really am quite foreign to human sensibilities." He drank down one of the carafes of hot honeyed milk in one long Rakshasa gulp. "But you seem to be adjusting well to your new knowledge of our world?"

"It is extraordinary," Mae reiterated. "I have spent the morning rethinking what it means for my faith. There is such a diversity of divinity that I never remotely considered before."

116

Vibhishana took another bite, relishing the flavor before swallowing with great concentration.

He glanced at Mae, and then at Kuveni, landing his gaze on Eleanor as he wrestled with an unspoken debate. As Eleanor attempted to distract herself from Uma's excessive interest in what was going on in his head, he wiggled ever so subtly and presented a form Eleanor had only ever seen once before. Thomas had placed an icon of it in the church in Sofia on her honeymoon.

He wore a simple white Roman tunic, and his skin was a beautiful olive color of brown. His deep brown, soulful eyes looked the same as they did in his gentle Lankan form, but his long frizzy hair was brown rather than black, and something about his facial structure made him look distinctly middle eastern. Despite a thick beard masking his chin and jawline, there was a softness to his features that even his gentle Lankan form somehow lacked, as if the form was actively hiding the ferocity of the destructive power that brewed deep within him.

"Good lord," Mae murmured. "That is what the children meant. You really can be anything, can't you?"

"I can," he agreed. He turned his attention to Eleanor. "This is the form that Miriam knew. I haven't used it in almost two thousand years."

"So this is what you looked like during your... er... stint in the Holy Land?"

"It is." He glanced at Mae. "It is one of my best kept secrets."

"Your stint in the Holy Land?" Mae asked. "Does that mean that you were there when Jesus was preaching?"

He threw a nervous look to Eleanor. She could tell that he had hoped that Mae had already understood what he was trying to reveal without so many words. "It does."

"What a thrill to meet someone who was actually there! Did you witness the Sermon on the Mount?"

Vibhishana now looked pained with the burden of his unplanned revelation. "Yes, I was there."

"Well, what was He like?!" she asked excitedly.

"He was like this," he said as he held out his arms with his palms up. "*Exactly* like this."

Mae's enthusiasm dissolved into momentary confusion and then bewilderment as the true meaning of his words finally dawned on her.

"Exactly?" she asked as her eyes widened.

"Exactly," he reiterated.

"Good lord," she murmured.

"Exactly."

Mae became silent, and Vibhishana threw Eleanor another nervous look.

"We were just talking earlier about the global impact of your efforts on the course of human history," Eleanor said casually in an attempt to lighten the mood. She should, perhaps, have picked a different topic.

"My actions often have far-reaching consequences. No matter how many ways I try to lead humans to peace, they find reasons within themselves to twist my simple messages to their own selfish ends. I spend much of my life mitigating the pain that humans inflict on each other in my names."

Mae grimaced as she battled with a flood of unspoken thoughts.

"Have I upset you?" Vibhishana asked. "I almost never share this truth with humans because it is so different than how the scripture told the story. Most humans do not want to know the truth."

"It's not that," Mae whispered.

Vibhi reached across the table and took her hand. She shivered, despite the warmth that was coursing through him from the hot honeyed milk.

He looked at her straight in the eye, and Uma gasped with pleasure as a wave of divine power wafted off of him. "You may be honest with me, my child. Tell me what is troubling you."

118

"I don't know what to say… If I'd known, I would have done everything differently! Surely I've embarrassed myself in front of you too many times, acting like a cheeky schoolgirl! I was teasing you just last week about that wild suit you were wearing to dinner at the maharaja's!" Her cheeks turned bright red. "I should not have done that."

Vibhishana smiled. "You needn't worry about hurting my feelings, Mae. I far prefer that people act like themselves when they are around me. It is one of many reasons that I have kept the full extent of my divine nature such a secret."

"Still… what a fool I was…"

"The suit was a bit over the top." He relaxed, let go of her hand, and returned to his carpenter's pie. "I myself found it hard to believe that it was in style, but there it was right there in *Vogue*."

"You read *Vogue*?" Eleanor laughed. He didn't appear to understand the source of her humor. "You have to admit that the idea of a god of your stature reading a fashion magazine is a bit absurd."

"When one makes his own clothing, it is important to keep up to date on current fashions. Otherwise, I'd still be wearing this." He glanced down at his tunic.

"I think it's rather charming," Eleanor winked.

"Miriam liked it as well. I switched from the Hebrew to the Roman style after we moved to my Anglo-Roman estate for our retirement."

"Retirement is not the word I would have expected you to use," Mae murmured.

"Yes, well, a handful of misguided human lemmings brought my preaching to an earlier end than I'd intended. My original plan when I set out on the endeavor was to lead humans in that way for a full human lifetime, to live entirely amongst them and age myself physically so that I could connect with them in a way I never had before. I succeeded in some ways and failed in others, but in the end, the entire experiment had a much greater impact than I expected."

"I'd say," Mae said distractedly. "And you were married at the time?"

"I was."

Mae paused, and he nodded for her to continue. "Was Miriam... was she Mary Magdalen?"

He sighed with resignation. "She was never a prostitute. My evil brother added that detail to the story to spite me several centuries later. I let it stand because it provided such an excellent model of acceptance for humans to follow; although, I must admit, the thought of her memory being twisted in that way still stings."

"How extraordinary."

He leaned in, and another tantalizing wave of divine power wafted off of him. "I trust that you are worthy of keeping this secret, Mae. You are the only ordinary human alive who knows it. I haven't seen fit to tell anyone since Miriam died. It is really only the giddiness that my divine wife is stirring within me that has led me to give into the foolish idea today. I hope that my trust was not misplaced?"

She snapped herself out of her thoughts. "I will do whatever you ask of me, my lord. I will be discretion itself."

He smiled. "I expected nothing less."

They each continued eating in silence as the fog began working its way over the hill, masking the sun and whipping up the breeze, which blew through Eleanor's and Vibhishana's flowing hair with similar assertiveness. But, as Eleanor finished up the last bite of her carpenter's pie, and she caught a glimpse of guilt in Vibhishana's expression, an odd queasiness overtook her, and she almost passed out.

"Shiva's wrath," Kuveni hissed. "Not this again! Leave her alone! Leave all of us alone, you fiend!"

As Eleanor struggled to hold onto her consciousness, the world turned green, as if she were looking through tinted glasses.

120

She felt like she was going to crawl out of her skin, and as her body convulsed, Vibhishana knocked over his chair and blurred to her side, gathering her into his arms.

"Do not fight it, Eleanor," he whispered into her ear. "You must be its ally, not its foe, or it will consume all that you are. Now relax, and let the Oracle deliver its prophecy."

A dark, booming voice that was not hers or Uma's scratched its way to the surface.

Upon the return of the blind changeling child to the land of her destiny, the gods will weep, the world will bathe in blood, and the darkness of men shall know no bounds.

The Oracle ripped Eleanor's hands out of Vibhishana's, and forced her to grab Mae by the shoulders.

You will summon the child to her destiny.

"Me? But I don't want to!"

"Do not argue with it, Mae," Vibhishana whispered.

Upon her return to the land of her destiny, the two perfect halves of the Destroyer of the Universe shall unite, and the ultimate apocalypse shall be inevitable.

Eleanor collapsed into Vibhi's arms, and then awoke with a start and ignored Uma's raging desire to stay held in a swoon, instead scrambling out of his arms and into the open neighboring chair. A look of horror blanketed Mae's completely white face.

"*I'm* going to destroy the world?" she squeaked.

"The Oracle speaks in riddles. You mustn't panic." Vibhishana didn't look like he entirely believed his own assertion.

"But it said that I would unite the Destroyers of the Universe!"

"Mae, *I* am the Destroyer of the Universe, and so is Eleanor." She tried to hide her fear, but as Vibhi's eyes lit up momentarily before he smoothed out his expression, Eleanor could tell that he tasted it. "Lord Shiva and Parvati manage the natural destructive cycles that govern Earth's evolution. Destruction is required for transformation and rebirth. It is not innately evil."

She did not look convinced.

He calmly set about demonstrating his point. "When you decided to move to Baroda, what did you leave behind?"

"My family, my friends, my childhood sweetheart… my teaching position in Cambridge."

"You destroyed the status quo for each of those things, did you not? You destroyed the close proximity of your relationship to your family in favor of a new relationship, a different one? Did you destroy your relationship with your childhood sweetheart?"

Mae sighed regretfully. "I certainly did. The poor bloke was devastated, but I simply didn't love him."

"Is he married now?"

She smiled wistfully. "With two children, which is what he always wanted anyway. He and I didn't share that desire."

"So when you destroyed something that had reached its natural end, you made room for something new," Vibhishana explained. "Nothing about that natural process was evil."

Mae paused to contemplate the idea. "But it said that the ultimate apocalypse will be inevitable. Surely that must be stopped? That can't be natural? Think of the suffering!"

He sighed with resignation. "It is already inevitable. Nothing that any of us do will change that. What is most important is that you do not change your behavior to avoid the prophecy. It will be true one way or another, and attempting to combat it will only bring greater misery to you, and to others."

"This child… this child will be my divine heir," Eleanor whispered. "She will be Uma's next incarnation. A blind changeling, though? That doesn't sound very divine."

"Prophecies are rarely literal. We must be very careful not to jump to conclusions. The Oracle is wickedly good at misleading the cleverest of gods and men."

"Then it's a good thing there are some goddesses and women around," Eleanor winked.

He smiled with relief as she regained her energy. "We are very lucky to have you around, Eleanor. And you, as well, Mae. It has been thousands of years since we've had such worthy additions to the Celestial Court."

"I do not feel very worthy," Mae admitted. "This is all intensely overwhelming, if I'm going to be honest about it... my lord."

Vibhi smiled and squeezed her hand reassuringly. "It is perfectly natural for you to be overwhelmed. I would be concerned if you weren't. But I will help you navigate, and you, apparently, will eventually help me connect with my other half..." He glanced at Eleanor. "The other half I am destined to be with, that is. It is strange, though..."

"What is?" Eleanor asked, unsure of whether she really wanted to know the answer.

"When I set out last night with the Patels for the party, I did not expect an encounter with destiny. Even after five thousand years, the Oracle still has a knack for surprising me. I suppose there's something comforting in that. It means I am not too old to be surprised."

He stood up, rolled his shoulders, and sighed. "Speaking of the Patels, I have already procrastinated enough. Lord Shiva must have a discussion with Rohit, and I must make my excuses to the maharaja for our little show last night. If you would like to return to Baroda with me, Mae, I will take you."

"May I ask how, my lord?" Mae asked with nervous excitement.

Eleanor grinned in anticipation of his most entertaining revelation, and he smiled with his own thrill at the revelation as he burst forth his sparkling golden falcon wings.

"Good lord," Mae murmured.

"My mother would go utterly mad if she saw this and knew what it meant," Eleanor whispered.

Kuveni cheered. "You are a sight for sore eyes if ever I've seen one, my lord!"

As Vibhishana realized that he was still using his Christian form, he wiggled subtly and returned to his gentle Lankan form, transforming his Roman tunic back into his relaxed Indian suit.

They all stood up to say their goodbyes. Eleanor squeezed Mae into a tight hug. "Don't be a stranger," she whispered. "And take with you Shakti's blessings."

"Thank you, Eleanor," Mae said as she fought back her emotions. "My life has changed today."

"May it be for the better." Eleanor smiled reassuringly as she squeezed Mae's hands.

"My dear girl, I will see you soon. If you ever need anything, anything at all, just whisper my name, and I'll be there in the blink of an eye," Kuveni said as she hugged Mae. "And, my lord, feel free to summon me the next time you need discreet Yakshini help."

He nodded. "You have given me a lot to think about, Kuveni. I should have trusted you long ago. It would have made many things easier."

"May that be a lesson to you, my lord," she winked.

"It will be."

He eyed Eleanor, debating his final move, and then she gave in and let Uma spend one last moment in his arms.

He kissed her forehead, and then she kissed his, and as they felt the magnetic pull of their energy connecting, Eleanor ripped herself away and stumbled backwards, calming herself with several frenzied breaths.

"Go, D.H. Before we both do something we'll regret."

She refused to let Uma swoon.

He gathered Mae into his arms, and she squealed with the thrill as he glided gracefully up into the air. In a blur, they were gone.

Eleanor collapsed onto the closest chair.

"For god's sake," she whispered angrily. "Uma, I swear you will be the death of me!"

"You demonstrated exceptional self-control, Eleanor. Truly exceptional." Kuveni took the seat beside her. "Would you like another canelé?"

Eleanor laughed. "Yes, I suppose I'd like ten. I must give into my urges on something, or I'll go mad."

Kuveni smiled, snapped her fingers, and produced a heaping pile of canelés. Eleanor ate the first, and then tossed one to Sheranee.

"I'm not sure I'm actually going to be able to eat these…" She trailed off as she suddenly noticed a conspicuous absence that hadn't crossed her mind with all of the other drama.

"Kuveni, do you know where the dogs are? I haven't seen them since yesterday morning."

"I haven't seen them. Perhaps they are with Jaap Sahib in the servants' quarters?"

"I did tell him to leave me alone…" Eleanor worked hard to push down her anxiety. "Still, they are usually very present, following us around all day and night…"

Kuveni dissolved herself, and Eleanor ate another canelé while she waited for her report. But instead of a quick return, Kuveni's disembodied voice only resonated eerily in the air around her.

"Oh dear, Mistress Eleanor. This is bad. Very, very bad."

CHAPTER 10 – IN THE ABSENCE OF DIVINITY

At the dire warning, Eleanor jumped out of her seat, summoning her trident, and Sheranee growled.

"What is it? Are we under attack? Is Surpanakha here?"

"No, dear girl. You are not in danger. But you must come now to the servants' quarters. Jaap Sahib is in a horrible state."

"Is he alive?"

"Yes. But not for much longer."

Eleanor felt Kuveni's warm essence encompass her, and she braced herself for the typical moment of disorientation before she rematerialized in the foyer of the servants' quarters. She barely held in a vomit reflex at the horrific scent that assaulted her.

Ovid and Pliny whimpered and barked as they rushed towards her, pummeling her into a desperate embrace. She dissolved her trident and kneeled down, letting them lick her face.

"My loves, were you trapped inside this house since yesterday? I'm so sorry!" She scratched their ears and swung open the front door to let air move through the house, but even after their time trapped indoors, the dogs refused to leave her side. Sheranee leapt up the porch stairs from the garden to Eleanor's side, and swiftly began licking Ovid and Pliny clean.

"Kuveni, can you give them some food and water?"

Two bowls of mysterious meat and water appeared by the front door, but the dogs would not be distracted.

Kuveni materialized beside Eleanor, clad in her empire-waisted nursing outfit and holding Eleanor's medical bag.

"Come, Eleanor. You must see if there is something you can do for him. He is beyond anything a Yakshini can cure."

"Sheranee, please keep Ovid and Pliny occupied down here," Eleanor commanded gently.

Eleanor followed Kuveni up the stairs, and a low growl indicated that Sheranee had begun her dog herding duties. Eleanor relaxed at the minor victory, and walked past the room she'd offered Jaap Sahib to the bathroom, but her heart returned to its sprinting pace as she approached. She didn't need Edmund's Rakshasa senses to recognize the smell of diseased death wafting through the cracked-open door.

Kuveni handed Eleanor a scented handkerchief, and she covered her mouth and nose as she pushed open the door. Next to the toilet, Jaap Sahib was collapsed naked, unconscious amongst his own mess. Sweat still oozed from every inch of his body, and he mumbled feverishly.

"Blimey," Eleanor whispered.

She leaned down and felt his parched back. "He doesn't have a fever, but he is dangerously dehydrated. Help me turn him over."

"Is that wise? In this mess? Shall I clean it up first?"

"Don't!" Eleanor exclaimed. "Not yet," she calmed herself. "I must get a better understanding of the exact symptoms." She glanced around the room again and sighed with resignation as she noticed the white, milky tint to the mess. "He has cholera. This is very, very bad…"

128

"What can we do, my lady?"

"We must hydrate him, but I honestly don't know if we have time. He is in an altered state. I don't know if we can make him drink without choking. I can feel his life-force fading."

"Would it not be prudent to attempt this in his bedroom?"

"Fine," Eleanor gave in. "Yes, Kuveni, you're right. Can you help me cleanse him too?"

"I am at your service, Eleanor."

Kuveni dissolved herself, and with a few seconds' delay, Jaap Sahib disappeared. Eleanor sighed with resignation, and then walked down the hallway to his room.

She sat down on the bed beside him and placed her hand gently on his forehead. The green glow of Shakti's power emerged, and his feverish murmurs dissolved into silence. Eleanor felt his life-force dissolving.

"Wait!" She pulled her hand away in a panic. "What just happened?!"

"I transported him," Kuveni replied. "I cleansed him in transit."

"No, I mean, what did I just do?!" Eleanor exclaimed. "Uma! What power is this!"

It is the power to ease his suffering, my child. It is all we can do for him now.

What?! No! We must try to save him! Jyoti and Amit are waiting for him to come home! He has been a loyal and virtuous servant!

We do not have the power to heal him, my child. We must not fight our nature. It is Shakti's will for him to transition into the next life.

No! It is Shakti's will for him to live!

Careful, my child. You must separate your human urges from your divinity, just as Lord Rama must, or you will bring great misery on us all.

Without another word, Eleanor left Kuveni and Jaap Sahib and ran down the stairs, past her zoo, across the lawn, into the house, and finally into her messy bedroom. She spied Hanuman's talisman on her vanity, and fought Uma's attempts to take over control of her body with all her might as she squeezed it into her hand and initiated her summons.

Come, my friend. The Goddess requires your help.

This is folly, Eleanor, and we both know it.

I will not let him die! For all we know, it was our fault! What if he contracted the cholera on the journey down here?!

Then he will die tragically like millions of other humans do every day, Eleanor. We cannot save all of them, and neither can Lord Rama. We must embrace the natural cycles of Shakti's ever-changing universe.

Hogwash. We are talking about saving one man out of billions. How many devoted human allies do we have, Uma? I can count them on one hand. Surely they deserve divine intervention after their loyal service?

It is not your divine intervention that you are offering, my child. It is Lord Rama's. We have the power to end his suffering, and we should use it.

No!

Eleanor rushed down the stairs, back across the lawn, past her increasingly concerned zoo, up the stairs, and into Jaap Sahib's bedroom. Kuveni was dabbing his sweaty forehead with cool water from a wash basin.

She glanced at the talisman in Eleanor's hand, and froze in position.

"My dear girl, you did not just summon them, did you?"

"Jaap Sahib is a loyal servant. He has a baby, Kuveni. He has been living a beautiful life that I gave him, and I will not let fate take it away like this."

"This is folly, Eleanor."

"Isn't everything?!" Eleanor exclaimed. "Every bloody thing is folly! Did you make a peep of protest last night when Vibhishana's folly forced me into a life-threatening position against my will?"

"That was different."

"How?!"

"That was an accident, Eleanor! You are consciously thwarting destiny! She will find a way to punish you, to punish all of us!"

"We're already being punished! I'm married to the wrong bloody god! I'm living a life that was never supposed to be mine! Uma picked the wrong bloody girl, and now we are all suffering the consequences!"

I did not, Eleanor. You were the right girl. But you must regain your wits now, before it's too late. You are crumbling under the weight of our burden, and you must not let yourself fall.

"I *am* the wrong bloody girl!" Eleanor gave into tears. Suddenly, two years of pent up anger and frustration at her divine struggles rushed to the surface. "I'm just one of Robby MacLeod's fiery little bastards! I should be cleaning up bedpans in Edinburgh right now, and you should be fulfilling your destiny in the body of some pious brahmin virgin that Hanuman would approve of!"

Kuveni took a seat beside her and began rubbing her back like a soothing mother. Eleanor lost track of time as she cried into Kuveni's shoulder.

"Now, now, Eleanor dearest, calm down. It is natural to be upset when a human you love reaches a senseless end."

"Nothing about this situation is natural. He shouldn't have even left Bombay, and *you*, Uma, should not have used Shakti's power to weaken his life-force. We could have used medicine to save him, and now it's too bloody late! Whose fault is that?! There is nothing natural at all about this!"

Kuveni startled and glanced down the stairs.

"They're here. My dear girl, you still have time to change course. Send them away, and I will fetch Jyoti and Amit to say goodbye to Jaap Sahib."

Eleanor's tears morphed back into sobs, and she collapsed into Kuveni's arms. "It isn't bloody fair! Why did I ever think it was fair?! I more than anyone know how bloody unfair life is! But it's this power, Kuveni. It made me think for one glorious moment that I could make a difference, but I can't! I was such a bloody fool!"

"Now, now, Mistress Eleanor, there is nothing wrong with having hope. You have made such a wonderful impact on so many people's lives. Do not ignore your glorious triumphs just because you have reached the boundaries of your divinity. None of us, not even Vibhishana, are omnipotent."

"Uma?!" Hanuman called. He peeked inside the open door of the servants' quarters and spotted their position in the room at the top of the stairs with the door open.

Eleanor took a deep breath and wiped her puffy eyes, annoyed at herself for giving away her emotional state so obviously.

Rama followed Hanuman up the stairs, and they both coughed as the stench from the bathroom reached their noses. Hanuman positioned himself between Rama and Jaap Sahib.

"Stand back, my lord." He threw Eleanor and Kuveni a wildly disapproving look. "How could you summon Lord Rama to a dangerous errand like this?!"

"Dangerous?" Eleanor asked as she sniffled. "How is it dangerous? This man is dying."

Hanuman humphed and hawed as he struggled to put together polite words through his anger.

"My lady, I am human. I am susceptible to human illnesses," Rama replied.

"As am I, my lord." Eleanor wiped the tears from her cheeks and paused to regain full control of her wits. "You needn't worry. I have been a nurse for twenty years, and it is clear as day that he has cholera. Wash your hands thoroughly with warm water and soap, and you will be perfectly fine." Hanuman humphed again angrily, while Rama softened his demeanor. "I am sorry, though. I summoned you on a fool's errand. Jaap Sahib has been a loyal servant for years now, and he has a wife and child waiting for him at home. I planned to beg you to heal him, but I will not burden you, my lord. It was a selfish summons, for which I must apologize now that I have my wits back."

Rama approached her, and Hanuman sighed his disapproval as Rama took a seat beside her.

"You needn't apologize. I know the urge to help them out of their misery very well myself. I often give in, even when it is thoroughly unwise."

"I cannot imagine your burden," Eleanor admitted. "It must be so agonizing when you refuse, as if you are killing them yourself."

"I am killing them. Every decision I make kills someone. If it is not the one before me, it will be the next. The one whom I'm too weak to heal."

Eleanor put her hand gently on his and squeezed it. "I'm sorry to have added to your burden. If you will leave us, I will use the power of Shakti to ease his suffering. Kuveni, will you please fetch Jyoti and Amit?"

Rama squeezed her hand and let go, and then rubbed his hands together until the divine silver light of his healing power emerged.

"My lord, you must not!" Hanuman exclaimed. "You are already weak from healing Eleanor last night! You will be too vulnerable!"

"Really, Rama..." Eleanor wanted to protest as she envisioned Edmund enduring the same excruciating choice, but she stopped herself as she envisioned Jyoti and Amit going about their daily business with no idea that their beloved husband and father was fleeting second by second from their lives.

Hanuman began pacing back and forth, muttering to himself as Rama placed his glowing hands on Jaap Sahib's sweaty chest. Kuveni continued dabbing his forehead with the damp cloth, and Eleanor called forth Shakti's glowing power, carefully relegating the morbidity that Uma had summoned for her dark chore. She rubbed Rama's back soothingly as he shook more and more violently, taking in shallow breaths and then gasping as he absorbed Jaap Sahib's suffering into himself. She caught him before he collapsed onto Jaap Sahib, and instead let him rest his face on her chest, holding him like a sleeping child.

"Thank you, Rama," she whispered into his ear. "I will not ask you to do this again. I should not have asked you this time."

He shivered as she rubbed his back with Shakti's power and rocked him, while Hanuman only watched them with some combination of jealousy and anger.

After many minutes, Rama finally took in a gasping breath, and opened his eyes.

"Shiva's wrath, that was painful," he whispered.

"I'm sorry," Eleanor reiterated. "I will not ask you to do it ever again."

"I am certain that this will not be my last time in this position; although, perhaps, it will be the last time I recover in your arms, my lady."

"Let's hope so," Eleanor smiled.

Rama rubbed his eyes and sat up. He glanced down at Jaap Sahib, who was now sleeping soundly, and then over to Hanuman. He looked down at the floor as he prepared himself for his own great folly.

"My lady, I must ask that you repay this kindness... with that which I have been requesting for too long. It really is only fair..."

"Rama?!" Hanuman exclaimed.

"This is *folly*, my lord," Kuveni hissed.

Uma took his hand. *You are better than this, my lord.*

"I am not," Rama sighed. "I am a truly desperate fool. Now tell me my destiny. Lord Vishnu commands it."

Eleanor felt the familiar queasiness as the room turned green all around her.

"I can't stop it," she squeaked as the Oracle scratched its way to the surface once more.

"Please, Most Holy Oracle, tell me where Sita is," Rama implored. "Tell me how to kill Ravana once and for all!"

"*Upon the eve of the ultimate apocalypse, as the greed of kings and men drags the worlds into darkness once more, chaos will reign. The Lord of Light and the King of Darkness shall strike their final blows in silence, and the destruction of the worlds shall be inevitable.*"

"The destruction of the worlds? Are you saying that if I kill Ravana, the worlds will be destroyed?!" Rama asked in a panic. "But it is my sacred duty to slay him! It is what I was born to do!"

"*The ultimate incarnations of the Preservers of the Universe shall lead the world into darkness.*"

"The ultimate incarnations? Do you mean me and Sita? We will be together? Tell me where she is, I beg you!"

"*Your time has passed, Lord of Light. You and Sita will never be one in this life. The Prince and Princess of Darkness will reign as the divine emperors of the reborn worlds.*"

"The Prince and Princess of Darkness?! What do you mean?! Indrajit? Ravana's son?! He will marry and have a wife and *they* will rule the world? How can this be?! Lord Vishnu must save the world! It is written in the stars! It is *I* who must lead humanity into the light. That's why I'm a weak, worthless human!!!"

Eleanor collapsed into Rama's arms, and re-awoke with a start.

"No! You didn't tell me anything I asked for! Only darkness and lies!" Rama exclaimed.

"Uma warned you," Eleanor rasped. She wiggled out of his arms, and he jumped up and began frantically pacing, holding his head in his hands as if he were in physical pain.

"My lord, how many times did Uma tell you to leave the Oracle alone?" Kuveni reiterated. "It is evil. All it does is create misery."

"But what am I bloody doing here on Earth?!" Rama wailed. "Sita and I will never be one in this life?! I've lost her for good?! Darkness will reign?!!! It can't be true!!! Lord Vishnu cannot lose!"

Uma stood up and took Rama's hands into hers.

Old friend, the prophecies are not literal. You must not let them destroy you. The Oracle is a meddling fiend. It phrases its riddles in the most misleading of ways. You must look into yourself, and let Lord Vishnu's light guide you out of this darkness.

"Why?!" Rama exclaimed. "What's the bloody point?!"

"Rama, calm yourself," Hanuman whispered as he put his hand on Rama's shoulder. "We all knew this was a bad idea, and the Oracle has reiterated why."

"Damn that bloody wicked Oracle!" Rama shouted. "And damn you, Uma! The lot of you! If I had a celestial weapon, I'd use it right now!"

Eleanor called forth her divine trident and stood up. She pointed it at his chest in a feigned challenge. "My lord, would you really unleash the wrath of Durga in your frustration?"

His posture deflated. "It would be exceptionally unwise."

"Good. That means you're regaining your senses." She dissolved the trident and took his hand. "Do not let this folly grow, Rama. Now let Hanuman guide you the rest of the way, and when you are ready, you must move forward and listen to Lord Vishnu's voices within you as they guide you back onto the path of light."

As Jaap Sahib sighed and turned over, Rama pulled away from her, and in a final burst of anger, he kicked a hole in the wall, screamed with frustration and pain, looked around at his unamused observers again, and rushed down the stairs, past the zoo, out onto the lawn, and wailed.

"Is he always like that?" Eleanor asked Kuveni. *No wonder Padma doesn't want to confront him...* Kuveni shrugged, and Eleanor readdressed the question to Hanuman.

"He is not," Hanuman said as he made his way to the door. "He is the greatest hero the world has ever known. But he has been desperate and alone for too long, and the Oracle has only fed his spiraling darkness. I will see him through his grief, like I always do.

Please do not think too much of it, my lady. He should not have put you in that position."

Uma took his hand. *Take with you Shakti's blessings, old friend, and share them with your lord.*

Eleanor noticed Hanuman's talisman on the floor by the bed, and she reached down and picked it up. "Please, take it with you. The temptation was already too much for me to bear, and I've only had it for twenty-four hours. I have just come to fully realize how much of our divine burden is defined by avoiding temptation."

She closed it into his hand, and he did not protest. He offered her a stoic nod, and then rushed down the stairs after Rama.

"My lord, come on. Let's go work out our energy with some target practice!" he called.

As Eleanor sat back down beside Jaap Sahib and gathered her wits, the ring of the telephone in the hallway startled her.

She jumped up to answer it, pushing back a wave of foreboding anxiety.

"Eleanor?" Edmund's voice quivered with emotion. "Eleanor, dearest?"

"What's wrong?" she asked as she felt the blood drain out of her face.

"It's Leo. He's dying."

"Darling, you must tell me what his symptoms are." Eleanor worked harder than she ever had to stay calm.

It's starting! The great misery from my folly! The Oracle is punishing me!

Do not jump to conclusions, my child. Human suffering is natural.

If you say that one more time, I'll gouge my own eyes out!

That would be a grave overreaction, my child.

For god's sake, Uma, haven't you ever met a Scot! We live in hyperbole!

My child, you are the first Scot I ever encountered. Don't you remember how odd I found your coloring?

Yes… I suppose I do…

"Eleanor? Eleanor, are you there? You just cut out. I've been trying to reach you all night. Is everything alright? Please, dearest, tell me everything's alright!"

"Darling, I'm perfectly fine. Please do not worry about me. I was out celebrating Dasara last night. The village had a communal feast in honor of the Goddess. Now, tell me what is wrong with Leo. Did he have symptoms of cholera?"

"Cholera?"

"Diarrhea, dehydration, vomiting…"

"I know the symptoms of cholera, Eleanor. I lived through the nineteenth century."

"Well, is that it then? Is Leo deathly ill with it?"

"No, nothing of the sort… He collapsed at the conference yesterday, and he swore it was nothing, but during dinner… he… he began coughing up blood, Eleanor. He almost choked to death on his own blood… and then I smelled it!"

"Blimey," Eleanor murmured.

"I smelled death, Eleanor! It is wafting off of him now! I don't know how I missed it before! I knew it was there, but I convinced myself it was the tobacco from his bloody cigarettes! If only I'd recognized it sooner!"

"I did think he was looking a bit pale recently. I assumed it was the incessant fog… and he's lost so much weight, but I thought that was the spicy food! I should have realized… Darling, where is he now? He must stay away from the Bidkars. If he has consumption, he might be contagious."

"He claims it isn't consumption. I'm at the hospital with him now. The doctors have been doing tests since yesterday afternoon. He says… he says it's lung cancer."

"*He* says it's cancer? How does he bloody know?!"

"He won't say!"

"Blimey."

They both waited for a commotion in the hospital hallway behind Edmund to calm down before continuing. His voice returned to an emotional quiver.

"I should have realized, Eleanor. I should have smelled it months ago when he could have gone to doctors for help, but the scent of death is much stronger now. It's…" He trailed off and swallowed hard. "It's too late."

"Perhaps there is still something to be done. I will leave for Bombay straightaway, and I will help you talk to the doctors, alright?"

140

"Thank you, dearest... I'm sorry to ruin your lonely holiday."

"Darling, do not think about that for one tiny second, you hear? I love Leo as much as you do. If there is anything that can be done, we will find it."

They paused again as another commotion behind Edmund distracted them.

"Eleanor, dearest, why did you ask about cholera?"

Eleanor's mind raced. She was too tired. Too much happened. She did not want another web of lies, but as she remembered the implications of Jaap Sahib's illness, she forced herself to connect with the responsible nurse that still lived somewhere inside of her.

"Darling, Jaap Sahib came down with cholera. He was in a dire state yesterday, but he is doing much better now. I think he will make a full recovery."

"You went out to a festival last night while Jaap Sahib had cholera?"

Eleanor cringed. "I didn't realize he had it, darling. He stayed in the servants' quarters to give me my privacy. I only discovered his condition when I noticed that Pliny and Ovid were not hovering about."

"I suppose those dogs are good for something other than begging."

Eleanor found his harsh tone disconcerting. "Really, darling? Do you mean that?"

Edmund paused as he got his emotions under control, but a subtle sniffle gave away the tears he was battling. "No, I don't mean it. They are wonderful companions, and I love them much more than any distinguished soldier should. I'm just... overwhelmed. I need Leo, dearest. He has brought me back from the darkness too many times to count."

Eleanor worked hard not to let Edmund's emotions crack through her well-practiced shell. "I will call in the staff to continue caring for Jaap Sahib until he is fit to travel, and I will leave first thing in the morning for Kochi. In the meantime, keep an eye out to make sure that none of the others come down with the symptoms of cholera, and let Ravi and Shruti help you sort things out for Leo."

"I don't want to lose him," Edmund whispered.

"I know, darling. Neither do I. We will be in this together, alright?"

"I love you, Eleanor. You're always so strong."

"I love you, Edmund. You are stronger than you think. I will see you as soon as I can. Goodbye!"

She clicked down the phone, backed up against the wall, took in a deep breath, and let her flood of tears burst through the dam.

Kuveni walked calmly to her side and gathered her into her arms. "Now, now, Mistress Eleanor. Cry all you want. Your spying butler has been a venerable ally and a worthy friend."

Eleanor buried her face in Kuveni's warm shoulder. "What was I to do, Kuveni? Should I have saved my favor from Rama? Should I have saved it for someone who mattered more than that virtuous husband and father who's sleeping soundly in there? Who am I to decide who lives or dies?"

"My dearest girl, it is not your divine burden to make this decision. It is Lord Rama's, and someday it will be Edmund's. For now, you have wisely returned Hanuman's talisman, so you can focus on using your own unique skills to help ease human suffering."

"I will not let Uma kill Leo to end his suffering!" Eleanor exclaimed.

"I didn't mean that you would, Eleanor. You have many skills. Now, let's think carefully before I pop you over to Bombay, about what *can* be done for our virtuous spying butler."

Eleanor wiped her tears and sniffled. "You can't just pop me up to Bombay, Kuveni. Edmund knows it takes a solid two days to get there from here in the best of circumstances."

"Not if you fly."

"He doesn't know any of you can fly."

"We will take 'Lord Blakeney's plane,'" Kuveni winked.

Eleanor took in a deep breath and worked to get her emotions under control. "Even a plane would take several hours."

"My dear girl, stop seeking barriers. Edmund is with Leo at the hospital. Don't you think it would be wise to get Shruti's account of the incident while they are away? You can relax with her sage advice and come up with your plan."

"Yes, you're right."

"Of course I am." Kuveni smiled and pulled Eleanor into a motherly hug. "Now, hold on tight. I will pop you over to Shruti's side, and then I will return here to tend to Jaap Sahib. When he is ready, I will pop him back up to Bombay to join you. If you need anything in the meantime, whisper my name and I will be there in the blink of an eye."

Eleanor squeezed Kuveni. "I love you, Kuveni." She fought back tears. "You are a much better mother than mine ever was."

Kuveni squeezed her back. "Oh, Mistress Eleanor, how I love you."

She dissolved herself around Eleanor, and as Eleanor let herself sniffle one last time, they left two very disappointed dogs behind.

"*Jinn!*" Babri screamed as she threw her sewing supplies up in the air and scrambled into the corner of Shruti's bedroom, whispering prayers to Allah.

Shruti sat up from her lounging position on her bed and put down the book she was reading on the nightstand.

"For god's sake, Babri, what is it now?" She trailed off as she noticed Eleanor standing in front of the closed door. Kuveni had already returned to Jaap Sahib's side, creating the distinct impression that Eleanor had appeared by magic inside the bedroom.

"Eleanor!" Shruti exclaimed. She rushed out of bed and kneeled before her. "My lady, by the grace of Shakti you've come!"

Eleanor guided her back to her feet and hugged her affectionately. As Babri recognized Eleanor, she stood up, gathered up her sewing supplies and sat back down in position to continue on with her project, muttering to herself. "Busty doll is a jinn… How is Babri supposed to make the right clothes for a jinn? Mistress will not be pleased, she will not be pleased at all…"

"Babri, you don't need to make me any clothes," Eleanor called.

"Busty doll wears only a kurta, and still she claims she needs no clothes… strange *firang* jinn, strange, strange, strange…"

Eleanor looked down at her scandalous dress and shrugged. "I suppose Babri has a point." She lowered her voice. "Kuveni, can you please pop along a sari for me?"

The green Mysore silk sari she'd worn the day before at the temple appeared neatly folded on Shruti's bed, along with two fresh strands of jasmine. Shruti helped Eleanor button her blouse and fold her pleats into the petticoat as she changed from her thin western dress into the sari.

"You are such an expert now. I think you must have been Indian in your former life," Shruti said approvingly as Eleanor draped it in the southern style and clipped the jasmine into her hair, offering the other strand to Shruti.

"Some part of me certainly was. Unless Uma was born somewhere else?"

I was born in my temple on Elephanta, my child. Back when there was a colony of Vanaras living there. It was before the Portuguese ran us out of our holy city.

Shruti watched with subtle piety as Eleanor's eyes glowed with the otherworldly green of Uma's presence.

"She says she was born on Elephanta, before the Portuguese ruined it," Eleanor translated.

She clipped the jasmine into Shruti's hair, and Shruti bowed her head in pious thanks and whispered a quiet prayer, accepting Eleanor's offering as a blessing.

"Busty jinn doesn't need Babri's clothes anymore… Busty jinn has magic clothes instead… How can Babri make clothes better than magic clothes?" Babri muttered dejectedly to herself.

"You may make me whatever your heart desires, Babri. I will cherish it always," Eleanor suggested.

Babri's eyes lit up, and she dropped her current project on the floor and skipped into Shruti's closet, chattering to herself happily as she began digging through bolts of new silk.

"There is something peaceful in her simplicity, isn't there?" Eleanor asked wistfully.

"I find it rather calming myself," Shruti admitted.

Eleanor sat down on the bed and gestured for Shruti to sit beside her.

"Tell me, Shruti. Please tell me everything you know about what happened with Mr. Valov."

"I'm so glad you're here," she reiterated. "It was horrible, Eleanor. It started with a row when he and Edmund came home early from the conference yesterday. Edmund insisted that your butler go straight to bed, but he argued that he just needed something to eat. I had the servants make him all the British food we had—eggs and toast and canned beans and that wretched marmite, but he couldn't stomach any of it. He begged us not to tell Edmund, and we didn't know what to do. But as soon as my father got wind of it, he went straight to Lord Kalki, as you would expect, and piously reported Mr. Valov's disobedience."

"Blimey."

"Edmund was more concerned than angry, and Mr. Valov finally conceded and went to bed. But by dinner, he was back, attempting to serve the wine. Edmund told him to go straight back to bed, and then Father insisted that he obey his lordship (which annoyed Edmund and Mr. Valov equally for different reasons), but before the disagreement could escalate, Mr. Valov began coughing. He dropped the tray of wine, and he sounded like he was choking, but Edmund's eyes turned black as he rushed to help him, and

Father panicked and sent all of the other servants away, shouting at them as if he were commanding an army away from a surprise attack! Mr. Valov collapsed on the floor, and as Edmund held him and tried rubbing his back to soothe him, his coughs became even more violent, and he could barely breathe, and that was when he coughed up the blood. Oh, we were all in such a state, Eleanor! It was a wonder the house didn't explode with the energy of our ruckus!"

"How much blood was it?"

"It was a lot, Eleanor. Poor Edmund had to leave him on the floor and walk away from it. I was afraid his spikes would emerge right then and there, but by the grace of Shakti (or perhaps Vishnu?), he somehow kept them under control. I gathered up Mr. Valov and told Edmund to take in the fresh air of the garden, and then I sent my father to get him some water. As soon as they were gone, Mr. Valov thanked me for my service, told me he was dying, and begged me not to tell Edmund. But how am I supposed to lie to Lord Kalki again, Eleanor? I am at my wit's end lying to him under your orders—I can't start lying to him whenever it's convenient for your human *firang* butler!"

"You needn't worry about it anymore, Shruti. Edmund knows. He can smell death, and Leo has already admitted to him that he has lung cancer. Did he tell you how he knew he was dying?"

"He didn't tell me anything else, Eleanor."

"No... no, I suppose he isn't in the habit of oversharing... but if he knew, why wouldn't he have told *me*? Surely he should have asked my advice long ago when he suspected something was wrong..."

"What are you going to do, Eleanor? Is there anything you or Edmund can do about it?"

"Not for another hundred years, give or take..."

"A hundred years?"

"Never mind… I suppose I've been relying too much on Shakti recently. Eleanor MacLeod would start by getting to the truth about Leo's condition, although Eleanor Marriner has to figure out how to keep Edmund from knowing I'm here for another several hours. He doesn't know that Kuveni can transport us in the blink of an eye, and we are going to tell him that Lord Blakeney flew me in his plane… Speaking of which, I suppose I should loop Lord Blakeney into this plan…"

Eleanor squeezed the green sapphire pendant on her necklace until it erupted into an eerie glow. *Mélusine, please come.*

With a gentle breeze, Mélusine was standing across from her. For this Yakshini entrance, Babri didn't even blink from her position sewing in the corner, as she was already solidly focused on concocting her next offering for busty jinn.

"*Mon dieu*, Eleanor?! What in god's name happened last night?!" Mélusine swept her up into a motherly hug. "You had us all worried sick! Sheranee was going mad with fear, and don't get me started on that poor young maharani. The girl was simply beside herself! Not even a mountain of ice cream could distract her from your disappearance!"

Eleanor couldn't help but laugh. "Did you produce an actual mountain of ice cream in the palace garden? That must have given the servants a run for their money."

"It was not a literal mountain, ma chérie, only a heaping feast of it in the ballroom, but you skillfully evaded my question. Have you been taking lessons from your spying butler?"

Eleanor's momentary good humor dissolved. "He has been an excellent teacher." Mélusine raised her eyebrows, refusing to let Eleanor get away with a second evasion. "Durga was transported accidentally through the sacred fire. I showed up… er… at another party. A similar one. It was very disorienting, actually. It took me quite some time to figure out what had happened, but eventually Kuveni came to my rescue."

"*Quelle horrible!* For a goddess to be summoned like a common genie!"

"That's what I said!" Eleanor exclaimed.

"Remind me later to teach you some techniques for ignoring these unwarranted summonses. It is a problem Yakshas have combatted for millennia."

Eleanor paused momentarily to contemplate the implications. "Mélusine, the genie lore is not based on Yakshas, is it? Like fairy lore is?"

"We are not genies or fairies," Mélusine said testily.

"That wasn't my question."

Mélusine glanced suspiciously at Shruti. "Humans have misinterpreted what we are with many names, those two are some of the most widespread, and the most offensive."

"I will keep that in mind." Eleanor forced herself to stop procrastinating. "I called you here because I need your help in a little farce. Edmund called me about an hour ago to tell me that our virtuous spying butler is dying of lung cancer."

"*Mon dieu.*"

"It was a surprise to all of us. Now, I must get to the bottom of what is actually going on, and you must tell Edmund that you flew me here from Munnar in your plane, otherwise we'll have to wait two days for me to have plausibly arrived by train."

"If I must." Mélusine sighed and wiggled herself into the form of Lord Blakeney.

Shruti gasped. "It's you! You're really a woman?"

Mélusine laughed. "Were you wondering who I was while we carried on our banter? Why didn't you ask? This is your house, isn't it?"

"It is not my place to question Eleanor's divine guests."

"You are very wise, ma chérie. Eleanor has excellent judgment. So, tell me, Eleanor, what is your plan?"

Eleanor closed her eyes and tried to focus on the rational part of her that had nursed humans to health for decades before she had any inkling that there was an entire world of supernatural shenanigans afoot.

"I would like to take Leo to see an expert." Suddenly, an uncomfortable idea crossed her mind. She chastised herself for being selfish and added it to her plan. "I know a cancer expert who keeps a practice in London. I believe I can get Leo in to see him at short notice, if someone can distract Edmund."

"It is still afternoon in London," Mélusine pointed out. "Why don't we go now?"

"Edmund is by his side in the hospital."

Mélusine wiggled herself into a feminine form that was not dissimilar to her normal form, but with plain features, grey eyes and straight, inconspicuous short brown hair, clad in a nursing uniform.

"Very convincing!" Eleanor exclaimed.

"I know. Now, I will gather our spying butler up for a private appointment. Edmund will not be invited. I have quite a bit of experience sneaking people out from under a watchful human's nose, and Edmund is not particularly watchful. Wait here. I will collect him, and then Kuveni will bring you to meet us."

Mélusine closed her eyes, whispered some quiet mantras, and dissolved.

"I didn't realize he was a woman," Shruti murmured. "Didn't Edmund think that Lord Blakeney was his brother?"

"Edmund thinks all of them are his relatives in one form or another. I'm sorry I won't be around to see it when they can all be honest with each other."

"How do you know you won't, Eleanor?"

"I know too much about some things… and not enough about others. It is a wicked game. Just when I think I know enough, destiny surprises me again."

"You mean Shakti."

"Yes, I suppose I do."

A pleasant breeze interrupted them as Kuveni appeared before her in the form of Kate, clad in a modern British winter pant suit.

"What is this Mélusine tells me about a trip to London with Leo?"

Without waiting for Eleanor's response, she tapped her finger on Eleanor's sari, and suddenly Eleanor was wearing a stylish grey winter wool dress with a heavy fur-lined coat and a matching hat.

"How can Babri compete with magic clothes!" Babri wailed from her position in the corner. "Sew faster, Babri. Sew faster!"

"Darling, please don't try to race Kuveni. You can win the contest with originality instead… with something utterly unique," Eleanor instructed her.

"Utterly unique…" Babri repeated. She dropped her project on the floor and rushed back into Shruti's closet.

"I'm certain you will see something utterly unique when she's done," Shruti whispered. "You are very kind to indulge her, my lady."

"I hope she isn't ruining your favorite silks," Eleanor whispered.

"Think nothing of it at all."

"My dear girl, where are we going? Mélusine is almost ready for us," Kuveni brought them back to the point.

"We are going to the office of a doctor I knew during the war. He has studied the use of x-rays for treating cancer for years now. It is across from Hyde Park, down a little alleyway in Marylebone."

"Lady Mélusine is ready for us. Come along, Eleanor dearest. We mustn't keep Lord Blakeney waiting in the rain. He will get very cross." Kuveni winked and then dissolved herself, and with a moment of lightheadedness, Eleanor felt her body dissolve once more.

She shivered as they rematerialized in the craggy bushes of Hyde Park. A dark autumnal rain storm had left the park conveniently unpopulated, and Kuveni materialized an umbrella and handed it to Eleanor as they stepped out of the foliage and onto a muddy path.

"God, it's cold here!" Eleanor exclaimed. "And it's only October! I think I've lost my tolerance for home! How am I ever going to go back to Scotland?"

"Never you fear, Mistress Eleanor. You will get used to it in no time."

The setting really did feel foreign, not like home at all. Eleanor paused for a moment to contemplate exactly how much she'd changed since she'd met Edmund. The magnitude overwhelmed her.

Mélusine appeared beside them in the form of Lord Blakeney, clad in an uncharacteristically understated grey suit, with Leo propped up, leaning heavily against her arm and wearing almost exactly the same suit. She held a large black umbrella that sheltered both of them.

"There is no point, Eleanor," Mr. Valov rasped. "I've been a goner for months now, probably years. I saw a doctor in Bombay when I was on leave six months ago, and he told me that I'd be dead by now unless I stopped smoking. I smoked a pack on the way out of his office."

"Why didn't you tell me?!" she exclaimed.

"There was nothing to be done, Eleanor. You would have done exactly what you are doing now, clawing at false hope for a man who deserves no mercy, and the agency would have realized that there was something wrong. They would have insisted on replacing me immediately. This was the only way I could hold out in your service as long as I did."

"Leo, you could have gotten treatment! Maybe you'd have many more years to live with us!"

"Eleanor, I have been smoking two packs a day even after I started coughing up blood. There is no treatment on Earth that can save me from myself."

"That's very nihilistic, you know."

"I'm a spy, Eleanor. We're all nihilistic. It's a requirement of the job."

"Well, I'm not giving up yet. Follow me… if you can."

He wheezed and coughed as Mélusine propped up his weight and walked with them out of the closest park gate and onto the streets of London.

Eleanor held Kuveni's hand, and Kuveni kept a watchful eye on Mélusine and Leo as they pushed their way through the grumpy, wet crowd. The route felt interminable as Eleanor racked her brain, forcing herself to keep her bearings and remember the street plan that she had once traversed regularly for a few months shortly after the war when she'd paid a number of social visits to their expert. The experience felt so distant, so far in the past, that it was almost like another life entirely.

When they finally reached a door with a glass window with the words, "Doctor Theodore Faraday, Radiation and Cancer Expert," painted across it, she took a deep breath, relegated her nerves, and guided them inside, up a dark staircase, and into a windowless waiting room.

An elderly receptionist in a nurse's uniform looked up at them unamusedly from a magazine in her lap and sighed with annoyance. "Doctor Faraday is done for the day, and he sees no one without an appointment."

"He will see me," Eleanor replied. "Go tell him that Ellie MacLeod is here."

The nurse scowled. "I said he's done for the day."

"And I said tell him that Ellie MacLeod is here. If you'd like, you can add that Lady Eleanor Marriner, Countess of Easton has some important business." The nurse looked slightly more interested at the aristocratic moniker, but then returned to her scowl. "I have my orders."

Kuveni moseyed up beside Eleanor and reached forward with several large bills rolled up between her fingers, affectedly offering them to the nurse as if they were a cigarette. "Dear girl, there is more in it for you after you obey the reasonable request of the Countess of Easton."

The nurse unrolled the bills and counted them, with her eyes widening as she realized the colossal sum of money that had just landed in her hand. "This is just for me?"

"It is, my friend. Now go fetch Doctor Faraday."

The nurse pocketed the money and stood up without a word of agreement. She trudged down the hallway to the farthest door, rolled her shoulders, and then knocked.

"I told you to leave me alone!" a strict male voice with a cockney accent yelled through the door.

"Doctor Faraday, some countess is here to see you."

"Tell her to get in line like everyone else! I swear, these lords and ladies think their lives are worth more than the common folk. It sickens me, just sickens me..."

The nurse shrugged, ready to give up, but Kuveni held up another wad of bills and began casually counting them. The nurse grimaced and pushed on.

"She says her name is Ellie MacLeod, and she insists on seeing you now."

The door swung open, and a bald, frightfully thin man with thick glasses propped on the very edge of his angular nose peeked skeptically into the hallway, looking past the nurse into the waiting room. All four of them looked back at him, and Eleanor smiled and skipped up to greet him.

"Teddy, you are a sight for sore eyes!" she exclaimed.

"Ellie?" He squinted at her as he emerged from his office. One of the sleeves of his white lab coat and his suit underneath was entirely missing, revealing his exceptionally pale, wrinkled skin underneath.

She took both of his hands and reached forward to kiss both of his cheeks. He found the gesture confusing, and then he looked her up and down again, squinting as he took in her greener eyes, larger bust, and exceptionally expensive-looking outfit.

153

"Is it really you, Ellie? Time has been kinder to you than it has been to me... and what is this countess business?"

Eleanor looked down self-consciously as she noticed his eyes wandering down to a peek of cleavage Kuveni had snuck into her outfit, and then to her glistening green sapphire pendant that had settled into the nook.

"It is me, Teddy. I'm the same fiery old Ellie MacLeod who's more trouble than she's worth... now more than ever. A lot has happened." She took a deep breath as she prepared herself for the revelation she'd been dreading most. "I'm a married woman now."

He glanced down at the enormous blue sapphire of her wedding ring, and his posture deflated. "I'm happy for you, Ellie. I really am. I'd always thought you weren't the marrying type, but I suppose you were just letting me down easy."

"I wasn't the marrying type, Teddy. I promise. It was as surprising to me as anyone that it seemed like a good idea."

"I see it's made your life... richer."

Eleanor straightened her posture. "I didn't marry for money, Teddy. I married for love. The details were a coincidence that I learned about after I fell in love with a shell-shocked colonel. He was awarded the Victoria Cross for honor in the war."

He sighed with disappointment. "Sounds like you found the whole package, Ellie. I'm happy for you." He glanced past her. "Is that him then?" He cleared his throat, looked down at his white arm, and sighed with resignation as he ignored his uncouth appearance and walked towards Mélusine with his arm out in greeting. "Welcome to my practice, Mr.? Or should I call you 'my lord'? Or perhaps colonel?" He suddenly spoke with an educated Oxbridge accent, and Eleanor smiled. She'd admired his trick for years, as he'd hidden his working class eastender origins from his snobby patients with his posh dialectical impression.

"I am Lord George Blakeney, Viscount Cornbury." Eleanor could hear Mélusine working hard not to use the affected foppish accent that usually went along with her character in favor of a more subdued impression of Edmund's.

Eleanor ran after Teddy. "He's not my husband, Teddy. Neither of them are. And there's no need to put on airs."

"I am… er… Eleanor's husband's cousin," Mélusine explained. "And this is Mr. Valov, Eleanor's butler."

As Teddy reached their position, he glanced at Mr. Valov and sighed again with disappointment. "I should have known that this wasn't a social call. You were the only one who ever paid me social calls, Ellie, and I suppose that time has passed now too. Come with me, I'll see you in the x-ray room. Nonny, go on home. I'll see you in the morning." He dismissed the nurse with a flippant hand gesture as he guided them into the office from which he'd originally emerged. Kuveni slipped the wad of bills into Nonny's hand, and the woman grabbed her coat and ran for the door before her employer could see, but Teddy didn't pay any attention to her at all.

He gestured to the bed, and Mélusine helped Mr. Valov onto it. Teddy propped up his glasses and unceremoniously began poking and prodding Mr. Valov, quietly noting the various pained whimpers and humphs that his movements were eliciting. He held up his stethoscope, and as Mr. Valov attempted one deep breath, he burst into a mad coughing fit, and Teddy calmly gathered up a clean handkerchief from a stack in a drawer and handed it to him.

"Lung cancer, very advanced, but you knew that, I reckon."

As a fresh batch of red blood filled the handkerchief, Mélusine subtly placed her hand on Mr. Valov's wrist and pushed a hefty dose of euphoria into him until his coughs subsided.

"Thank you," he whispered.

"Don't mention it, mon chéri."

Teddy shrugged. "There's nothing that can be done. I'd tell you to stop smoking to buy yourself a few weeks, but honestly, it won't even be worth the effort. Those weeks would be very unpleasant. Go somewhere nice and say your goodbyes."

Eleanor felt like he'd just kicked her in the stomach. "Teddy, how can you be so callous?!"

"I've done this for too many years, Ellie. It would be callous for me to give him false hope. Would you rather I tell him to go about his business so that he can drop dead, or worse, collapse into a semi-vegetative state to be cared for night and day by a patient nurse like you?"

"You tried, Eleanor," Mr. Valov rasped. "I told you there was nothing to be done."

"What about radiation?" she pushed.

Teddy shook his head. "It doesn't work on its own, Ellie. It's only useful for certain cancers, usually when paired with removing a tumor, and I have come to recently realize that it isn't a perfect cure…" He held up his arm. "Too much of it causes cancer. I've got it too now from my years of testing my machines on my arm."

"For god's sake, aren't there any ordinary humans left who aren't dying of something horrible?!" Eleanor exclaimed.

Kuveni threw her a look of warning, and she cringed as she realized she'd used precarious verbiage.

"I'm sorry… it just feels like everyone I love is dying," she whispered.

Teddy smiled sadly. "I always loved you too, Ellie, but you knew that. I might as well tell you now that I have nothing to lose." He threw an apologetic look towards Mélusine. "No offense meant towards your full package of a husband… or his cousin."

Eleanor hugged him. "I did know, Teddy. Your fourteen marriage proposals took a lot of the guessing out of it." She winked.

"Was it really fourteen? I thought it was twelve."

"There was the time in the ambulance in Reims when we barely dodged the land mine, and the time we were drunk in the back of the cargo van. I don't know if you were sober enough to remember."

"Doesn't matter now, I suppose." He returned his attention to Mr. Valov. "I'm sorry I don't have better news for you. If I were you, I'd finish up my business and go somewhere nice with my family… if I had a family. If you'd like, I can connect you with a solicitor who specializes in wills… I have a lot of patients who need one."

"I have one, thank you." Mr. Valov slipped off of the bed, and almost collapsed into Mélusine's arms.

Eleanor fought back a ball in her throat, and Teddy noticed her watering eyes. "I'll leave you for now. Come on out to the waiting room when you're ready."

She watched him go, and then buried her face in Kuveni's shoulder. "Now, now, Mistress Eleanor, it was a good idea."

"Thank you, Eleanor," Mr. Valov whispered. "You didn't have to do this."

She sucked up her emotions. "Well, what do we do now?"

"I will have to make an Irish exit, and the Secret Service will send a replacement. I already have my eye on a couple junior officers who should be trustworthy replacements, but you will need to manage them very carefully, Eleanor. They shouldn't know what I know… not even close."

"You will not!" Eleanor exclaimed. She felt a wave of her fiery temper working its way to the surface, mixing dangerously with her sorrow. "There will be no Irish exits, you hear? Now, where do you want to go for your hospice? Shall we go visit your father in York?"

"I don't need to see him ever again, Eleanor. We said our goodbyes decades ago when I joined the Secret Service."

"Then what? Shall we go to a tropical island somewhere? Mauritius is supposed to be lovely, and I'm sure Kuveni can accommodate us. Can't you?"

"Eleanor, I can't go hopping about the earth in the arms of a Yakshini. The agency is already highly suspicious of the many magical shenanigans I've been covering up. My lies to them have had to become very creative, but if they get wind that I am somehow in York… or London for that matter… I don't know how I will explain it."

"You will be dead, Leo. It won't matter."

"That's very nihilistic of you." He winked, and she finally let his friendly jab relax her nerves. "My top priority is you, Eleanor. You and Edmund. We must keep the agency's awareness of your true power as minimal as possible. It will be an even more difficult problem to solve when I'm gone."

"Well, we can't just go home to Munnar and sit around waiting for you to die. You don't even like India."

"Not for a lack of trying."

"You needn't defend yourself, Leo. Tell me what you want. We must have a plan to propose before we return to Edmund."

He sighed with resignation, and then his eyes teared up. "You should have seen him, Eleanor. He was so bloody devastated when he smelled the death on me. I was waiting for him to notice it for months, and still I wasn't prepared when he finally realized."

"He loves you, just as I love you. You are a part of our family, Leo."

He wiped his eyes and sniffed self-consciously as he fought back a rumbling bout of coughs. "It is my duty to recuse myself when I am incapable of service. The agency is not going to let me just stay with you until the end."

"They will. We will insist. And if they try to stop us, we will kidnap you and take you to the far reaches of the earth where they won't be able to find you," Eleanor replied matter-of-factly. "We are the gods, Leo. And whisking you away so you can die where you want is one of the powers we do have… at least with the help of our loving allies."

He swallowed hard as more tears pushed their way to the surface. "I just want to be with you, Eleanor. You and Edmund. I want to be with you until the end. But you must believe me when

I tell you that I do not deserve to have my wishes met. I have done so many horrific things, I lost count."

"Well, it isn't time for your dying confessional yet, so let's figure out where we're going to go."

They each thought carefully until Mr. Valov moved to speak and then thought the better of his suggestion.

"What? Tell us," Eleanor coaxed.

"We never managed to make that trip down to Perth. I would feel more comfortable with my transition if you and Edmund were in the presence of trustworthy allies like the Helmsworths."

Eleanor's eyes lit up. "That is the best idea I've heard in my life!"

Mr. Valov smiled. "I doubt that, but it solves a lot of our problems."

"Is it where you want to die, Leo?"

He stopped to consider the harsh reality of the question. "It is."

"Then let's get started. We have no time to waste."

She took Kuveni's hand and led her into the waiting room, and as Mélusine escorted Leo more slowly, Eleanor pulled Teddy into a parting hug. "Thank you for everything."

He hugged her back for slightly too long for comfort.

"I didn't do anything, Ellie."

She eyed his thin body and his sleeveless arm with newfound awareness, and a wave of melancholy washed over her. "You did what you could. Now, take care of yourself, will you?"

As Mélusine and Mr. Valov reached the waiting room, Eleanor wrestled with a momentary fancy and then gave in. She squeezed Teddy's hands.

Take with you Shakti's blessings, my friend. May they bring you peace and comfort in your final transition.

She let go, and he shivered.

"What was that, Ellie?"

"I'm a goddess, Teddy. I was blessing you. I might as well tell you now that I have nothing to lose."

He smiled. "You could always pull my leg, Ellie."

She grinned and called forth her green glowing trident and her golden crown, bringing them slowly so he could watch. Mr. Valov shook his head with defeated disapproval. "What the hell are you going to do when I'm gone," he muttered. "The whole bloody world will know your secrets."

"Blimey," Teddy whispered as he reached forward to touch the crown. "No wonder you bewitched me."

She hugged him one last time. "Goodbye, Teddy."

She dissolved her trident and crown and then nodded to Kuveni and Mélusine. "Shall we return to the hospital in Bombay?"

"*On y va.* We'll pop back into the broom closet where we left," Mélusine agreed.

Mélusine and Kuveni took hands and encircled Eleanor and Mr. Valov into a Yakshini vortex.

"Goodbye, Ellie. It was nice knowing you," Teddy whispered tearfully.

And with a flash of light, all four of them disappeared.

CHAPTER 12 – UNINVITED

As soon as they rematerialized in the broom closet, Mélusine helped Mr. Valov back onto the stretcher she'd left there upon her initial stealthy kidnapping an hour earlier. She wiggled herself into her nurse disguise.

Kuveni tapped Eleanor's arm and transformed her winter dress into a pair of fashionable white linen pants with a flowing silk blouse that was more appropriate for the warm weather, albeit a bit more revealing than Eleanor would have liked with her copious cleavage bursting out of the camisole underneath the sheer blue silk. Kuveni transformed her own outfit into a more conservative modern summer dress with flowing lavender silk that almost reached the floor with an asymmetrical cut that highlighted her unusual height.

"Ma chérie, you wait here while I take him back to his room. Then I will fetch you and switch back into Lord Blakeney so we can approach Edmund together."

Mélusine pushed open the door, and Eleanor hid as several nurses questioned her about why she'd taken a patient into the broom closet. With a few stealthy deflections from Mr. Valov and some feigned idiocy on the part of Mélusine, they were on their way, and Eleanor was left with her nerves.

"We are playing a dangerous game, Kuveni."

"Now, now, Mistress Eleanor, it is a wretched situation and we are making the best of it. That's all we can do."

"Do you really think Edmund is going to believe that Lord Blakeney flew me here in his plane?"

"My dear girl, what alternative is there in his mind? That she flew you here with her own wings? Or popped you over like a Yakshini? We have given him a plausible explanation, the *only* plausible human explanation, so why would he question it?"

Mélusine rushed back into the closet and shut the door behind her.

"Mr. Valov's return awoke our beloved Edmund, the poor boy. He must have been awake all night sitting up by Leo's side." She wiggled back into the form of Lord Blakeney, this time returning to her familiar foppish purple suit. "I hate this farce more than any." She took Eleanor's hand and listened at the door for the hallway to be clear. "*On y va.*"

Kuveni followed them as they charged authoritatively through the busy hallways.

Eleanor took a deep breath as they reached Leo's room. "Well, aren't you a sight for sore eyes," she said as she knocked on the doorframe, as if she'd just arrived.

Edmund scrambled up out of his chair. "Eleanor, dearest, how did you possibly get here so quickly?!"

He pulled her into a desperately passionate kiss. As he let go, Mélusine and Kuveni stepped into the room.

"I should have guessed." He shook Mélusine's hand, holding on to take in the warmth of her familiar divine power until she gently pulled away. "Thank you for bringing her here."

He hugged Kuveni, and she couldn't help but squeeze him for an extra-long motherly moment.

162

"You needn't thank us, my dearest boy. It is our pleasure as always to be here with you when you need us most."

Edmund swallowed hard as he battled a ball in his throat. "I hope you didn't travel far? Surely you must have been close by to get here so quickly."

"It was nothing, Edmund. Please do not think of it at all. Lord Blakeney and I were taking in the sights and sounds of the Dasara parade in Mysore when Eleanor called us with the sad news."

Eleanor approached Mr. Valov's bed and sat down on the edge beside him. "I talked to the doctors, Leo. They said that there is nothing to be done."

Mr. Valov shrugged. "I told Edmund as much, but he still won't believe me."

"Darling, one of the foremost cancer researchers in the world just saw Leo for almost an hour. Even he says there is nothing to be done."

The grimace on Edmund's face broke her heart.

"Is there…" He glanced at Kuveni and then Mélusine. "Is there anything you can do for him?"

"Mon chéri, this kind of problem is beyond our power."

His miserable frown only grew. "I'm sorry, I shouldn't have asked."

"You should have, mon chéri. I'm sorry I couldn't give you a better answer."

"Darling, the doctors suggested that some fresh, warm sea air might ease Leo's symptoms. It occurs to me that we owe Oz and Yvie a visit anyway. What do you think about heading down to Perth?"

Edmund took in a deep breath, relegating his emotions, and joined her on the bed by Mr. Valov's side. "Would you like to go to Perth, Leo? Or do you have relatives in Europe we should visit instead?"

"You would travel all the way back to Europe for me?" Leo asked, giving away his emotion.

"I wouldn't think twice about it."

Mr. Valov let a rogue tear escape. "Thank you for the offer, Colonel, but Perth sounds just wonderful to me."

Edmund squeezed his hand. "Then it's settled. We'll leave as soon as we can gather our belongings. I reckon we'd better pack for a long trip, and we'd better telephone Oz and Yvie with a warning to be expecting us. I hope we won't be imposing on such short notice, but I'm sure there are plenty of hotels in Perth if we become a bother."

"Dear boy, leave the details to us," Kuveni suggested. "I will call Oz and Yvie as soon as we're back at the Bidkars, and Percy can manage your staff to pack up your trunks and your dogs and send them along after you."

"The dogs!" he exclaimed guiltily. "Eleanor, what about the dogs?! I forgot all about them, the poor buggers!"

"They are being well taken care of already, mon chéri," Mélusine reassured him. "I will reunite them with you as soon as humanly possible."

"And in the meantime, darling, I'm sure Shruti can help us scrounge up a few outfits that will be good enough for our journey," Eleanor added for good measure. She relegated her own sense of guilt at having forgotten about their loyal companions twice in two days.

Edmund pulled her into a tender kiss. "Thank you, dearest. You're so wonderfully strong." Mr. Valov cleared his throat awkwardly from his position right beside them in the bed. "And thank *you*," Edmund said sheepishly, as he ripped his attention away from Eleanor and returned it to Kuveni and Mélusine.

"It is our pleasure, dear Edmund. Now, let us help you and Mr. Valov get back to the Bidkars'. There is a car waiting for us."

Mélusine closed her eyes, and Eleanor wondered if she'd simply conjured a full-sized Rolls Royce on the curb outside. She decided not to worry about it.

Edmund helped Mr. Valov up, and Mélusine flanked him as they guided Mr. Valov right into the hallway. Eleanor was grateful that their trip to London had already clothed Leo appropriately for their escape, and she hoped that none of the nurses would notice their hasty exit. She was grateful that Edmund knew so little about hospitals that he didn't realize that simply getting up and leaving was not a normal way for a patient to make an exit, and as they passed through the double doors onto the dark, muggy boulevard across from the Victoria Terminus station, she made a mental note to remember to pay the bill before they left for Perth. She sighed with stress and sadness that Leo wouldn't be around anymore to help them manage the details that they hadn't had to think about themselves in years.

As they made their way down the stairs, scores of rickshaws that were packed onto every inch of the road lunged towards them eagerly, shouting their offers of a very good price in several different languages. However, right in the middle of their pack, a sleek, black car with an exceptionally handsome blond male driver dressed in the formal uniform of a British chauffeur awaited. He looked vaguely annoyed, and Eleanor wondered which Yaksha ally he was. She had never seen the form before.

"Right here, into Mr. Marlowe's car." Kuveni shooed Edmund into the car and helped Mélusine ease Mr. Valov into the back seat.

Eleanor and Kuveni squeezed into the front seat beside the driver, who headed into traffic as soon as the doors were closed. Eleanor watched him intently. She was certain that she knew him, but she would not dare to guess in front of Edmund.

They all sat in silence, watching the ebb and flow of Bombay's nighttime traffic for what felt like many hours. Eleanor glanced every so often in the rearview mirror to spy Edmund holding Leo's hand, as if Leo were his son, while they both stared pensively into space. As she forced herself to bury her emotions, a pang of remnant burning sensation tingled in her wrist, and she was reminded of the divine chaos that she had narrowly escaped just moments before diving right into her newest farce.

When they finally arrived at the Bidkars' palatial residence, Ravi rushed outside to greet them, followed by Shruti. Jaap Sahib followed more slowly, with his baby son in his arms and his wife by his side.

"Father, wait!" Shruti called. "Give them some space!"

As Eleanor stepped out of the car, Ravi stopped for a moment, processing the meaning of her presence, and then he bowed his head piously and whispered, "Welcome back to our home, Holy Mother. It is an honor to be in your presence."

Eleanor hugged him and whispered into his ear. "That will be the end of divine honorifics until we leave for Perth, Ravi. Do you understand? I am Eleanor, Edmund's ordinary human wife."

"Yes, Holy Mother."

Eleanor threw him a strict look of disapproval.

"Yes, Eleanor."

"That's better."

"Eleanor…" Ravi trailed off as he thought the better of his question.

"Yes, Ravi? If you have something private to ask, do it now before Edmund steps out of the car."

"Is it true that Lord Rama healed Jaap Sahib from a deathly illness?"

Eleanor's heart almost exploded. She did not have the energy to extend her web of lies to another branch of their pantheon.

"Who told you that?"

"Jaap Sahib did, my lady. He told me so after your Yakshini servant delivered him back from Munnar just a few minutes ago."

Eleanor glanced over at Kuveni. "She is not my servant. She is my ally, and she should be treated as a member of our family and yours."

"Yes, my lady! But... but... my lady..." Ravi lowered his voice as he repeated the question he knew he shouldn't ask. "What happened to Jaap Sahib?"

She eyed Jaap Sahib, who bowed his head in pious acknowledgement. "Well, I suppose he was more cognizant than I realized in his altered state. You will not breathe a word of this to anyone, Ravi, especially Edmund. Do you understand? You will maintain total silence on this topic. Shakti commands it."

"But, my lady, does that mean then that Lord Rama... Lord Rama lives?"

"Take from the story what you will, Ravi. I have more important problems to occupy my mind..." She trailed off into a hiss of pain as the burning sensation in her wrist erupted into a more powerful wave.

"Is something wrong, my lady?"

"Only that you insist on calling me, 'my lady.' Really, Ravi, you must work on being more obedient."

"Yes... Eleanor."

"Eleanor, what can we do to help?" Shruti interrupted.

Eleanor was grateful for the reprieve. "I'm quite sure that Edmund could use a hot meal. All of us could."

Ravi clapped his hands, and several servants rushed from their corners to bow before him and receive their orders.

"Prepare for a full dinner at once! And bring out a full case of the Margaux! And make some of that bland English food for Mr. Valov."

"Sri Bidkar, how many shall we prepare the meal for?" the head servant asked.

Ravi finally noticed Mélusine flanking Mr. Valov alongside Edmund, and Kuveni chatting quietly with their mysterious chauffer. He watched Kuveni's particularly familiar demeanor with Edmund and paused for a moment as he observed her unusual height and similar features. As the wheels began turning in Ravi's head, Eleanor regretted her choice of words in suggesting that

Kuveni should be treated as a member of their family, and she sighed with stress.

Ravi took her sigh as annoyance at his slow response. "Make it for ten! Include Jaap Sahib and Jyoti, and Lord Marriner's honored guests... including his... sister?" He looked to Eleanor expectantly for confirmation.

"You will get no further intel from me, Ravi. Why don't you ask them yourself."

"Set the table at once!" Ravi boomed to the servants. They bowed obediently and scampered away.

Without another word to Eleanor, Ravi rushed over to engage Kuveni in conversation, and Jaap Sahib discreetly made his way to Eleanor's side.

"My lady, I must beg your forgiveness." He averted his eyes, but strategically avoided a pious bow.

Eleanor felt her entire body stiffen with stress. She didn't need yet another detail to cover up in her web of lies. "For what?"

"When Kuveni delivered me here, Sri Bidkar mentioned Mr. Valov's illness, but I thought that he was referring to my illness. I gave away many divine secrets in one foolish response. Please tell me how I can make up for this inexcusable failure."

Eleanor relaxed. "Sri Bidkar can ensnare the best of us, Jaap Sahib. You are one of the most discreet and loyal allies we have, and one slip of the tongue does not change that."

She took his hand in her right, and Jyoti's in her left.

Make the most of the second chance that the gods have given you. Take with you Shakti's blessings and share them with the world, my children.

"Yes, my lady," they whispered in unison.

As Amit began wiggling with boredom, Jaap Sahib handed him over to Jyoti.

"My lady, how may I serve you now?" he whispered.

"Are you feeling up to it? Perhaps you should rest. You were remarkably close to death."

168

Jyoti sighed with some combination of stress and relief at the reminder, but said nothing as she bounced Amit up and down in her arms and kissed his hand.

Jaap Sahib lowered his voice. "I haven't felt this good in years, Holy Mother. Lord Rama's gift was truly divine."

"Yes... I know exactly what you mean... Well then, Jaap Sahib, I have the perfect task for you. You can keep a close eye on Sri Bidkar for me, and when you see him considering a moment of indiscretion on behalf of our divine secrets, you can remind him of his solemn vow to me."

"Yes, my lady."

Without another word, Jaap Sahib made his way to Ravi's side.

"This is precarious, isn't it?" Shruti whispered as she stood beside Eleanor and watched her father joke jovially with Kuveni and Mélusine.

"You have no idea," Eleanor murmured.

They watched as Kuveni laughed heartily and then pulled Ravi into a motherly hug, while the chauffeur watched them with a disapproving raised eyebrow. When Ravi turned his attention on the chauffeur, he demurred awkwardly several times, until Ravi pulled him into a hug against his will and laughed loudly, indicating that he'd attempted one of his classic introductory jabs in an effort to loosen the man's spirits.

"Good lord." Eleanor laughed as she realized who he was. "Mr. Marlowe indeed."

"Come, all of you!" Ravi clapped his hands. "We are already preparing a late dinner for you."

"No, really, we shouldn't stay," Mélusine protested.

"Nonsense! You've all had a busy day of travel. Stay with us tonight, and you can leave in the morning."

"That is not necessary," Mr. Marlowe reiterated.

"Oh, but it is!"

As Mr. Valov began coughing, Edmund whispered something into his ear and escorted him straight past Eleanor, towards his room.

Edmund's voice was tired and his posture haggard. "We will join you when Leo is settled in."

"As you wish, my lord." Ravi bowed his head piously, and Jaap Sahib readied himself to fulfill his most recent assignment, but before Ravi let himself slip any further, he refocused his piety on action. "Come!" he yelled at a few lingering servants. "You must set the table at once!"

He followed them into the dining room barking orders, and Eleanor took a deep breath from the release.

Shruti took Eleanor's hand. "Come, we will get you some wine. I hate to ask, but perhaps you can show one of the servants how to use the corkscrew? Mr. Valov is the only one who has ever served wine in this house."

"I can," Eleanor agreed. "Although, Monty over there can too."

He glanced over at her as he heard his name, and she winked.

She guided Shruti over to greet him and lowered her voice. "Shruti, I'd like you to meet Mr. Montero. He is a loyal Yaksha ally. Monty, Shruti is my sister in arms and in secrets."

He offered her a polite *namaste* and then returned his attention to Eleanor. "My lady, I have other matters to attend to. I came because Lady Mélusine summoned me with an urgent request, but I do not have time to dilly dally here until morning. The Patels are still struggling with the aftermath of Lord Vibhishana's little show last night."

"Vibhi put on a show last night?" Mélusine interrupted.

Mr. Montero was not pleased with his unintentional revelation. "The dandiya party got out of hand like it always does. There were some Rakshasa talents on display that should not have been."

Eleanor admired his skilled discretion.

"What could have enticed Vibhi into that? He has kept the Patels' secrets safe for centuries!" Mélusine exclaimed.

"Even the best of us can lose ourselves in the moment from time to time," Kuveni interjected.

"Still, Vibhi of all people? That's not like him at all."

"Shruti, let me show you how to open the wine," Eleanor said in an attempt to extricate herself as she contemplated the unpleasant idea of weaving Mélusine's ignorance about Vibhishana's divine identity into her exploding web of lies. "Monty, now is your best chance to make an exit. Edmund and Ravi are both fully occupied."

"Thank you, my lady."

He bowed his head, tipped his hat, and dissolved, leaving the Yaksha car behind.

"We should be going too. This spiraling farce is ripe for disaster," Mélusine humphed.

"If we leave now, my beautiful boy will feel like we've abandoned him. He thinks that we're here to support him in this trying time, and I will not ruin that," Kuveni countered.

Mélusine looked questioningly to Eleanor, and Eleanor found the deferral strange. It was the first time since they'd met that Mélusine had treated her as an equal, or even a superior.

"It's up to you. I'm sure you're a comfort to Edmund, but our farce is getting more and more precarious by the moment. I'm already up to my ears in my own web of lies, and I will cover for you if you want to leave."

"Please stay. Our home is your home. I will bring you some wine," Shruti offered.

"Don't bother, ma chérie." Mélusine snapped her fingers, and a dusty old bottle appeared in her hand. "Do you have a sitting room?"

Eleanor smiled. She was grateful for Mélusine's choice. "I'm quite sure they have ten."

"It's only eight," Shruti corrected her. "Please follow me."

Mélusine sighed with ambivalence as she and Kuveni followed them through several airy open marble hallways, past several verdant tropical gardens, and finally into the music room.

Eleanor plopped herself down on a silk brocade chair and suddenly realized how utterly exhausted she was.

Kuveni and Mélusine sat down next to each other on a matching brocade divan, and Mélusine snapped her fingers again, producing three large wine glasses on the intricately carved wooden table between them.

"Won't you join us?" Eleanor asked Shruti, who was waiting politely by the door for her divine guests to settle in.

"I will see to the preparations for dinner, and make sure that my father doesn't do anything unwise," Shruti demurred.

She offered them a subtle bow of respect and left them alone.

"That dear girl is a valuable ally," Kuveni sighed.

"*Oui, d'accord.* She is a rare breed, indeed. I have encountered more virtuous, trustworthy humans since Eleanor came into our lives than I have in centuries… millennia, in fact."

"Perhaps you haven't given humans enough of a chance, my lady," Kuveni jabbed politely.

Mélusine shrugged. "Every time I try it, it comes back to haunt me. Perhaps Eleanor just has better luck than I do. Or better judgment."

"I do have excellent judgment," Eleanor admitted.

As she reached forward to grab the generous glass of wine Mélusine had poured, she hissed with pain as another burst of burning energy traveled up her arm from her wrist.

"What's wrong, ma chérie?" Mélusine asked concernedly.

"My travel through the sacred fire last night seems to have left some residual burning sensations," Eleanor replied with a skillful half-truth.

"How strange… I suppose it is not normal for a human to travel in sacred fire at all. I'm surprised it worked."

"So am I," Eleanor agreed truthfully.

She held up her glass in a toast. "Thank you for being here. I'm sure it means a lot to Edmund, and it is a great relief to not be facing these tribulations alone."

"You are most welcome, my dear girl," Kuveni replied as she clinked her glass.

As they took their first sips, Mélusine sat up with her ears perked, and Kuveni dissolved herself, dropping the glass of wine on the persian carpet.

"Be on guard, ma chérie, someone uninvited just landed in the garden."

Eleanor put down her wine and called forth her glowing trident as she stood up.

"*Mon dieu!*" Mélusine exclaimed.

In a blur, Vibhishana was standing beside Eleanor in his gentle Lankan form with a similarly defensive stance.

"What are you doing here? Edmund is hovering about!" Eleanor hissed.

"You're not in danger?" he asked as he threw a questioning look to Mélusine. "Melysium, I didn't expect to see you here."

"Likewise, my lord."

He held out his arm, showing her a glowing violet symbol that Eleanor found hauntingly familiar, but she couldn't remember from where. He reached forward and coaxed her into presenting the wrist that had been burning all evening, and as he touched his wrist to hers, the symbol exploded into a momentary flash of light and burned itself into her skin in the same color of green as Shakti's divine power. She hissed as a burst of electrical energy rushed into her from the point of their connection, down her spine, and into the center of her being. She looked down, but the burning sensation was gone, and her skin was smooth and human, as if nothing had happened at all.

Vibhishana shivered and took in a deep breath of relief, rolling his shoulders and looking around the room more soberly.

"What the hell was that?" Eleanor tried to shake off the unsettling feeling.

Vibhishana glanced nervously at Mélusine. "The Oracle inside of you summoned me, Eleanor. I am its guardian. I cannot resist its summons, but I just released myself from its control by proving to it that I'm here. In five thousand years, the Oracle has only ever summoned me when its host is in grave danger. If you are not in grave danger, I do not understand what I'm doing here."

"That meddling fiend," she whispered.

"Lord Vibhishana?!" Ravi exclaimed. "What an honor it is to have you in our presence!"

Vibhishana looked past Eleanor, through the wide-open door into the hallway beyond, where Ravi stood with a tray of wine. Vibhi blurred to Ravi's side and covered his mouth.

"My friend, you must learn to be more discreet." He removed his hand. "Where is Edmund?"

"He's still tending to Mr. Valov. I thought the Holy Mother might like some wine..." His posture deflated as he spotted the open bottle. "I can see that Lord Blakeney has beaten me to it."

"Thank you for the offer, Ravi, but we can tend to ourselves for now. Perhaps you can leave us for a bit?" Eleanor suggested.

"But..." He moved to protest and then thought the better of it. "As you wish, my lady. My lord, it would be an utmost honor for you to join us for dinner."

Vibhishana moved to argue, and then he gave in. "As you wish, Sri Bidkar. I will only require hot milk."

Ravi's eyes lit up at his acceptance. "I will tell the servants at once!"

"What an excellent idea," Vibhishana agreed as he relieved Ravi of his tray.

Ravi watched curiously as Vibhishana returned to Eleanor's side with the fresh bottle, but when Vibhishana noticed his attention, he subtly shooed him away.

174

"Set another place!" Ravi shouted to no servant in particular as he clapped his hands and rushed down the hall, back towards the kitchen.

"Vibhi, you're not actually going to stay, are you? I thought you were keeping your distance," Mélusine asked.

"The Oracle brought me here for a reason. I must find out why."

Kuveni materialized beside him and returned to her seat, subtly dissolving the stain from her red wine on the carpet, and then refilling her glass. "Well, if you're going to tempt fate, I don't see why I shouldn't either, my lord."

He moved to argue, and then he shrugged his acceptance. "I do not understand how so much is changing so fast. Destiny is in motion, but it isn't time yet."

"Perhaps you misinterpreted the prophecies. It has been known to happen, even to the best of us," Mélusine suggested.

He poured himself a tall glass and refilled Eleanor's, taking a seat across from her, as far as he could reasonably be without giving away his responsible desire to put distance between them. "I have been obsessing over that possibility for quite some time, but it still doesn't add up. Just this morning, the Oracle delivered another prophecy reiterating the expected timeline…" He trailed off as he realized his mistake.

"Just this morning?" Mélusine asked astutely. "Which Oracle was that? Were you visiting the Rakshasa Oracle without me?"

"I'd best not say," he evaded.

"Vibhi?!" Mélusine exclaimed. "We agreed to interpret the prophecies together a thousand years ago!"

"This prophecy came unexpectedly," Vibhishana replied as he threw Eleanor a guilty glance. "It was only intended for my ears."

"Perhaps destiny is in motion because you have set it in motion, my lord. By doing all sorts of things that you know not to do," Mélusine humphed.

"Perhaps…"

She did not expect him to agree with her.

"My lord, what have you been up to? What is this I hear about a public display of Rakshasa talent at the maharaja's palace last night in Baroda?"

He could not hide his distaste for the topic. "The party got out of hand, like it always does."

"So I hear."

Shruti rushed into the music room and practically fell over as she spotted Vibhishana, trying to slow down her pace on the slippery marble. She attempted to play off her ungraceful movement as a pious bow.

"My lord?! What are you doing here?"

"I am asking myself that same question," he admitted flippantly.

"Edmund is coming!"

Vibhishana relegated a moment of panic back into his smooth expression, and with a subtle wiggle, he sat in a clean-shaven, short-haired version of his ancient Christian form, clad in a tasteful western suit.

"*Mon dieu!*" Mélusine exclaimed. "Of all the forms to choose! Something *has* gotten into you!"

He looked down sheepishly. "I suppose it was on my mind."

Eleanor hated that she found him strikingly handsome.

"Why don't you just use the form he knows?" Eleanor asked.

He thought carefully about the reasonable question. "I don't want Edmund to begin expecting me to show up at every turn. He must learn to stand on his own, fully and completely, and if he believes that I will come at the drop of a hat, it will undo the progress he made suffering alone in the trenches."

Eleanor snorted. "I wouldn't call acute, debilitating shell-shock and Rakshasa bloodthirst progress."

She realized as she spoke the words that it was the first time she was addressing Vibhishana directly on his choice to let Edmund suffer.

"Enduring exceptional pain is a requirement of growing up, Eleanor. You know it as well as I do, and it is even more important for the gods. We must know human suffering intimately, so that we can make the right divine decisions when it matters most."

Eleanor subtly wrapped her hand around the green sapphire bangle he had given her as his talisman.

Careful, D.H. That was a dangerous plural you just used in front of Mélusine.

Shiva's wrath.

Indeed.

Eleanor continued as if they had not just shared a silent exchange. "Then why are you here now? You can see I'm not in danger, and even if I were, would that suffering not be natural? A requirement of my divine position in the pantheon?"

Vibhishana glanced at Mélusine again and chose his words carefully. "Not all suffering is necessary, Eleanor. Lord Shiva and Parvati manage the natural cycles of destruction and rebirth. You must be able to manage these things until your heir is born, and as the guardian of the Oracle, I can't leave here until I understand why it brought me here." He glanced around the music room again. "Speaking of which, why are we at the Bidkars'? Weren't you in Munnar a few hours ago? How does Edmund think you got here?"

"We flew in Lord Blakeney's plane," Eleanor shrugged.

"And that's why you're here?" he addressed Mélusine. "To support that farce?"

"*C'est vrai.*"

"Mr. Valov is dying," Eleanor explained. "That is why we're all here on such a conspicuous timeline."

"I'm sorry. Trustworthy human allies are a rare treasure indeed." He glanced at Shruti.

"Shruti, was there something else you were going to warn us about?" Eleanor asked as the thought occurred to her. "You were in quite a rush."

"I was going to warn you that my father had invited some unknown entity to dinner, but I think I understand what's happening now."

"I am the unknown entity," Vibhishana confirmed. "That is a slight relief, I suppose."

"Speak for yourself," Eleanor muttered.

"Dearest?" Edmund called.

"At attention," she hissed to all of them as she stood up and scampered to greet him in the hallway.

"Darling, come join us for some wine." She guided him into the music room, and he immediately landed his attention on Vibhishana.

Vibhi stood up and offered his hand in greeting.

"Darling this is... er... Doctor Carpenter. He came by from the hospital to discuss our preparations for Leo in Perth."

Edmund shook his hand. "That's very kind of you to come all this way on such short notice."

"Think nothing of it. I am glad to be of service," Vibhi said as Edmund held on just a little bit too long.

"Do I know you? You feel strikingly familiar, but I can't place from where," Edmund asked.

"I was a medic on the western front in Belgium during the war. Perhaps you saw me there?" Vibhishana suggested.

"Yes... perhaps that was it... Are you staying for dinner? Please do. You are most welcome. The traffic up from the hospital must have been insufferable."

"I have already accepted Sri Bidkar's invitation," Vibhishana agreed.

"Come, darling, sit. Let's wait for dinner together in here."

Eleanor guided him to a divan and sat down next to him, cuddling up in a slightly overcompensatory manner, while Shruti seated herself in Eleanor's vacated chair.

"I see you've already met Lord Blakeney and Kate Marriner?" Edmund asked. "They are my relatives of some form or another."

Eleanor almost snorted at his unintended pun.

"Yes, they have been filling me in," Vibhishana replied.

The room fell into awkward silence.

"It should be quite lovely to see Mr. and Mrs. Helmsworth again." Shruti attempted to break the tension. "I hope they are doing well?"

"To be honest, I haven't talked to them in months," Eleanor admitted. "I really should have been better about keeping up. I hope our visit isn't too much of a surprise for them."

"They did say to come any time," Edmund reassured himself.

"I'm sure they will be perfectly accommodating. I have missed them so much," Eleanor added.

"Perhaps I will call them now," Kuveni suggested. She stood up. "Shruti, dear, can you direct me to the telephone?"

"Of course, please follow me."

Kuveni followed Shruti down a dark hallway and disappeared.

Edmund glanced at Mélusine and Vibhishana, and then chose his topic. "So, Doctor Carpenter, what are your recommendations for Leo's situation? Unless you've already finished your conversation with Eleanor. Don't repeat yourself for my sake."

"He was just suggesting that we find some help," Eleanor replied on Vibhi's behalf. "In fact, he was suggesting that we hire a nurse, which I think is a fine idea. I'm sure Yvie can connect us with some qualified applicants as soon as we arrive in Perth."

"Yes… yes, I suppose that's wise. It isn't fair for you to be left with nursing him, dearest. I know that you never wanted to be a glorified nurse wife, and being one for our butler sounds especially unbearable."

"To be honest, darling, I don't have the emotional distance to care for Leo medically. It will be good to have an unbiased helper."

"Yes… yes, of course."

Shruti returned alone from the dark hallway. "The servants tell me that dinner will be ready in a few minutes. They have warmed up our leftovers from dinner earlier, and they made an English breakfast for Mr. Valov."

"How kind," Edmund murmured sadly. "Leo said he wanted to join us, so I suppose I will go collect him now."

"Do you need help?" Mélusine offered.

"No, I will be perfectly fine. Thank you."

Edmund stood up and trudged haggardly back down the dark hallway.

"He's going to need a good night's sleep," Eleanor sighed.

Shruti lowered her voice and bowed her head to address Mélusine. "My lady…" Vibhi raised his eyebrows at Shruti's awareness of Mélusine's preferred form. "I didn't want to say so in front of Edmund, but the servants have served us their dinner. I was wondering if you might be so kind as to give them something to eat when they are finished serving us? I did not want my father to know that you could do such a thing."

Mélusine smiled. "Think nothing of it, ma chérie. I will feed them a Yaksha feast when Edmund and your father have gone to bed."

"Can you tell them that you ordered it in?" Eleanor suggested.

"Yes… that is a good idea," Shruti agreed.

As Eleanor moved to stand up, she suddenly felt faint, and the burning sensation in her wrist exploded, traveling from the spot where Vibhi had connected, all the way into her gut where Shakti's power and the Oracle brewed. She gasped, but felt like she was drowning, and just as she had twice in the last twenty-four hours, she felt the Oracle clawing its way to the surface.

As the world turned green, Vibhishana blurred to her side and collected her into his arms, but this time, instead of the dark, booming voice from beyond, Eleanor's mind was bombarded with a flood of images.

"Eleanor?" Shruti asked nervously. "Are you alright?"

"*Mon dieu*, what's happening?" Mélusine's voice sounded distant, more distant than when Eleanor had been sucked into the sacred fire.

The roar of Sheranee echoed in the distance, but Eleanor did not have the wherewithal to worry about what her uninvited presence would mean for her web of lies.

"Eleanor? Eleanor, hold on. Focus on me," Vibhi's voice called.

"The Oracle's inner eye. It's manifesting!" Mélusine panicked.

Eleanor felt Sheranee lick her feet, but the physical sensation could not break her out of her seizure. Millions of images complete with scents, sounds, and feelings of too many people who were not her... of all people... everywhere... filled her head, and her consciousness began to wane. A calming darkness began to take hold.

"A human can't handle its visions directly! They'll drive her mad, or they'll kill her!" Mélusine exclaimed. "My lord, we must stop it!"

"Eleanor?!" Vibhishana called. "Stay focused on me. Do not let the Oracle tear you apart."

She was barely conscious of her body convulsing, as Vibhishana squeezed her up against him.

Eleanor? His voice boomed in her head.

Vibhi?

Eleanor, stay focused on me. I must take the Oracle's burden into my consciousness, or it will kill you. I am going to infuse you with my energy, and you must infuse me with yours. That is the only way we can transfer its visions.

I don't know how.

Uma does. You must let her.

Eleanor released control of her body, and Uma cuddled up into Vibhishana's arms and slammed her glowing wrist onto his. Even relegated to the secondary sensory position in her body, Eleanor gasped as a wave of pleasure unlike anything she'd ever felt in her life pumped through her. She wasn't coherent enough to worry about the marital mess she would be in if Edmund were to observe the exchange.

As Eleanor gave into the increasingly sinful bursts of ecstasy, the images began to disperse, until her consciousness emerged from the darkness, into the silence of the room. She took in a deep, gasping breath, and the green tint of the world around her finally dissolved.

She looked up into Vibhi's eyes, and his gentle Lankan form looked back at her and smiled. She basked in his relief as it infused their connected consciousness.

Are you more relieved that you avoided revealing Lord Shiva's form to Mélusine, or that you saved me from that fiend like a proper white knight?

I am relieved that you are alive and sane, Eleanor. No human has ever manifested the Oracle's inner eye and lived to tell about it. The only humans who survived at all became soulless, empty creatures.

I suppose I owe you one, D.H.

This was why... This was why the Oracle summoned me. It was a warning.

That was polite of the fiend.

It was. I will have to carefully consider what it means.

"Eleanor?" Mélusine interrupted their unspoken exchange. "Are you alright? What in god's name did you do, Vibhi? I've never seen anything like it!"

"I helped Eleanor release herself from the Oracle's damning visions," he replied vaguely. "I wasn't sure it would work, but I had to do something. I have returned them now to the depths where they belong."

"*Incréable.*"

Eleanor took in another gasping breath as she relegated Uma back into her rightful position. She sat up, and Sheranee growled.

"Now, now, no need for that, my love. I'm fine now."

Sheranee turned her attention to the far door of the music room. There, Babri stood beside a brown-haired, properly tuxedoed teenaged bloke with grey eyes, soft features, and an expression of utter disbelief plastered across this face.

Babri clapped and laughed. "Hurrah, busty jinn! What a show, what a show! I have brought you my offering!"

She rushed into the room and bowed as she presented a purple outfit made up of poufy, sheer silk pants underneath an open-front skirt with a long train made up of especially finely beaded silk, along with a blouse that was so low-cut that it even exceeded Kuveni's lax standards of modesty. Hanging from the back of the beaded blouse was a long, sheer black cape that flowed into the train with a surprisingly natural look. Eleanor had never seen any design like it, although it did vaguely remind her of what she'd imagined Scheherazade to be wearing when her father had read her the *Arabian Nights* as a lass.

"How unique," Eleanor said as she took it and inspected the fine craftsmanship of the beading.

"It is! It is!" Babri exclaimed. "It is perfect for a jinn flying in the sky!"

Eleanor smiled. "Yes, darling girl, I reckon it is."

Sheranee paid no mind to Babri, and growled again at the uninvited guest. But, before they could ask him who he was, or what he was doing there, Kuveni materialized beside them in a panic.

"Master Edmund is on his way! My lord, you must return to your other form!"

As Eleanor scrambled guiltily out of Vibhishana's arms, he closed his eyes, and with significantly more concentration than he normally required, he returned himself to the form of Doctor Carpenter.

The expression on the face of the uninvited guest transitioned from disbelief to astonishment.

Babri clapped and cheered. "Hurrah, hurrah! It is a family of jinns! Babri must make more clothes!"

She dropped the outfit on the floor, patted Sheranee on the head, and skipped cheerfully out of the music room, right past the uninvited guest, as if nothing strange had happened at all.

"Dearest?" Edmund called. He peeked his head into the door of the music room. "Dearest, I've already seated Leo at the table…" He trailed off as he noticed Sheranee.

Eleanor gulped and threw a desperate look to Kuveni, who threw a desperate look to Mélusine, who threw a desperate look to Vibhishana, who found himself at a rare loss for words.

"Oh, Edmund, have you met Sheranee?" Shruti asked casually as she hopped up and scratched Sheranee's ears. She purred approvingly. "She is our pet tiger. The vet just delivered her home after her grooming appointment."

He stared at the familiar tigress with puzzlement. "When did you procure a tiger, Shruti? It is very unwise to keep her in your home. They are dangerous beasts, even if they seem tame."

"I promise, Edmund, Sheranee is the tamest tigress in the world. Durga herself could depend on her." Shruti threw a sideways glance to Eleanor as she reassured him.

Ravi came up behind him. "Come, my lord, dinner is served…" He trailed off as he spotted his daughter communing with the tiger.

"Father, can you believe Edmund hasn't met Sheranee, our pet tiger? How have we kept her such a secret?!" Shruti exclaimed. Sheranee licked her hands affectionately, playing her role in the farce like the expert mount that she was.

"I have no idea…" he murmured.

Ravi stepped aside as Mr. Valov approached from behind him. "Leo! We had you all settled in!" Edmund protested as he gathered up Mr. Valov's weight and let him lean against him.

"I'm not a completely crippled invalid yet, Colonel. I had to come see what all the ruckus was about. Good lord…" He spotted Sheranee, but as his eyes wandered around the room, all the color drained out of his face as he spotted the uninvited guest. "My reckoning has come."

As Edmund noticed the young man, he straightened his posture, and as Ravi noticed Edmund's stance, he readied himself to call for the guards.

"Who do you think you are, young man? Coming into my home uninvited?" Ravi demanded.

"Oh wonder, how many godly creatures are there here…" the uninvited guest murmured to himself as he glanced around at every magical person in the room, landing his gaze on Leo. "I… I… I…"

"Well, spit it out!" Ravi boomed.

"Do explain yourself," Edmund added more calmly.

The boy looked at his feet and then mustered his courage. "My name is Mr. Abernathy, sir. I am Mr. Valov's replacement."

"You are *what?*" Edmund worked to hide his unfocused displeasure. Eleanor could hear the emotions itching to burst out of her overly-tired husband, but he did an admirable job of keeping himself under control. "Leo, did you know about this?"

Mr. Valov couldn't hide the devastation in his expression. "I did call around to find a replacement, Colonel. I am no use to you as a butler in this state. But Mr. Abernathy here is not the one I sent for." He threw Eleanor a desperate look of warning.

Mr. Abernathy cleared his throat. "Still, sir, I am the one they sent."

Eleanor couldn't believe that the boy was the Secret Service's choice. His voice hadn't even finished dropping.

"Well, this is utterly absurd," Edmund grumbled. "Eleanor and I will decide who is accepted into our household, and we have no need of a butler in the present moment. Now go right on back to where you came from."

Mr. Abernathy glanced at Mr. Valov questioningly, but Mr. Valov looked away and muffled a pained cough, refusing to step in on his behalf.

"Was there something unclear about my orders, boy?" Edmund's tone became sharp, as if he were commanding an insubordinate cadet.

"No, Colonel." Mr. Abernathy glanced at Mr. Valov. "Shall I escort you to the car, sir? It's waiting outside."

Edmund's expression only darkened. "And why would you do that, Mr. Abernathy?"

"To... er... take him to get his treatment," Mr. Abernathy lied unconvincingly.

"There is no treatment," Eleanor stepped in. "He has already seen several of the world's leading cancer experts. Now, we are going to take care of Mr. Valov throughout his hospice, and you can tell your agency that they may consider sending a replacement for him when he is dead and buried. Then, and only then, will we consider adding a new member to our staff, and have no doubt that *we* will be the ones who decide whom to accept into the position. Understood?"

"But..."

"Leave!" Ravi shouted. "If you don't find your way out, the guards will find it for you!"

Sheranee growled her agreement.

"Please, Colonel," Mr. Valov rasped. "Let me have a moment alone with Mr. Abernathy."

"Leo, you're weak. You must eat and rest," Edmund argued.

"I will, Colonel. I promise. But first, I must finish up some business with Mr. Abernathy. Eleanor, perhaps you can join us? Sri Bidkar, do you have a private room where we can talk?"

"But... but..." Ravi glanced at Edmund as he protested.

"Please," Mr. Valov reiterated.

"It will be perfectly alright," Eleanor chimed in as she stood up and approached them, taking Mr. Valov's weight onto her arm.

"Edmund, darling, I will help Leo sort things out, and then we will meet you in the dining room. I'm sure it will only take a few minutes to send Mr. Abernathy on his way."

"Are you sure, Eleanor?" Edmund asked.

"I'm certain, darling. Now, your stomach is growling louder than Sheranee. Why don't you guide our patient guests into the dining room. It's already very late for dinner, and I'm sure Percy and Jaap Sahib are starving after our long flight. Besides, I suspect that at this hour, the servants are hoping to get their own meal in before they head to bed. It's best for everyone if we don't delay any longer."

"Yes… yes, I suppose," he conceded begrudgingly.

"Mr. Abernathy, you will follow us," Eleanor ordered sharply. "Somewhere private, Ravi," she whispered.

"Yes, my lady."

Ravi reached under Mr. Valov's arm and took on the other half of his weight as he obediently guided them past several sitting rooms and finally into the library. Eleanor helped Mr. Valov sit down on the couch, and then dismissed Ravi.

"Shall I wait outside, my lady?" he asked hopefully.

"Please don't, Ravi. Edmund could use your company in this trying time."

"Yes, yes, of course, my lady!"

Ravi bowed and closed the door behind him.

Eleanor glanced skeptically at Mr. Abernathy again, and he straightened his bowtie.

"*Thou shan't remain here whether thou wilt or not*," Mr. Abernathy murmured to himself. Then he cleared his throat and readied himself to address Eleanor. "Ma'am, I really must insist on taking Mr. Valov with me."

Eleanor raised her eyebrows. "Cadet, you are not in any position to insist on anything."

"Cadet?" he asked confusedly.

Mr. Valov looked like he might pass out from the strain of the stress, but Eleanor would not let him manage the situation himself. She was, after all, the one who was going to be stuck managing the delicate education of his replacement.

"Is that not the lowest rank in the Secret Service? It is a military organization, is it not? And as you appear to be all of twelve years of age, I cannot fathom you having earned a higher rank than that. Now tell me, Mr. Abernathy, were you even born yet when the Great War started?"

Mr. Abernathy's eyes widened with surprise, and then he glanced accusingly at Mr. Valov.

"Oh, don't get your knickers in a knot. Leo didn't reveal his cards. You all must think we are the biggest dullards on the planet to not notice a spy hopping about right under our noses. It only took weeks for me to figure it out, but it took me years to prove it." She threw Mr. Valov a challenging look. "Did you think you could fool me, Leo?"

A look of subtle recognition of her game worked its way into his expression, followed by a hint of pride.

"I... I... I... don't know what to say, Eleanor," he stuttered. "I'm just your loyal butler!"

"Then if I go out there and interrogate the driver of this so-called butling agency's car, I will not find him to be a spy?"

"Of course not!" he exclaimed.

"And which agency did you say he was from?" she asked Mr. Abernathy. "Which agency did Mr. Valov call from his hospital bed in Bombay to arrange an immediate replacement? That was rather forward thinking of him, was it not? Given that his dire prognosis was just given three hours ago?"

Mr. Abernathy only stared at her, struggling desperately for a response.

"What is your driver's name, boy?!" she demanded.

"It's... it's... George!" Mr. Abernathy squeaked.

Eleanor raised her eyebrows skeptically again. "George is it? George what?"

"George Smith!" Mr. Abernathy exclaimed.

Mr. Valov shook his head with dismay at his woefully unprepared replacement.

"Well, we are in quite a precarious position then, aren't we?" Eleanor continued confidently. "Leo, you've been lying to Edmund since he accepted you into his household seven years ago, and Mr. Abernathy, you have been lying since you rudely intruded on Sri Bidkar's private home. What do you have to say for yourselves?"

"The mohammedan simpleton let me in!" Mr. Abernathy exclaimed.

"I see. And so you saw fit to take advantage of the kindness of a simpleton and sneak around a private household into which you had not been invited, rather than announcing yourself like a real gentleman's gentleman? You chose to begin your relationship as our so-called butler with blatant reconnaissance and lies?"

"Explain yourself, boy!" Mr. Valov added for good measure.

"I… I… I… didn't mean any harm!" Mr. Abernathy looked like he might cry.

"Mr. Abernathy walked in on us during a rather delicate moment, in fact." Eleanor explained to Mr. Valov. "What exactly did you see, Cadet?"

"I didn't see anything," he whispered.

With one burst of green, glowing power accompanied by a gust of wind that set the papers on Ravi's desk aflutter, Eleanor conjured her trident and slammed it against Mr. Abernathy's chest, cornering him up against a bookcase.

"There will be no more lies in my presence!" she boomed.

"Oh, for god's sake, Eleanor…" Mr. Valov murmured.

Mr. Abernathy glanced over at him, noticing that Mr. Valov was not surprised by the development, but as Eleanor tightened her hold on the trident, pushing it slowly into his chest until he could barely breathe, he whimpered.

"Tell me what your mission is."

"I have no mission!" he squeaked. "I'm just a butler!"

"Cadet, you will tell me your mission, or you will not leave this room alive."

As the trident burst into another wave of divine flames, Mr. Abernathy wet himself.

"I'm waiting!" Eleanor reiterated.

"I am here to report back on Colonel Marriner's movements to the Crown!" he confessed.

Eleanor threw Mr. Valov a satisfied glance.

"And why is the Crown so interested in Colonel Marriner's movements?"

"I... I... I don't know!" Mr. Abernathy exclaimed. "They said it was because he might be a subversive element in the army, but now I have no bloody clue!"

Eleanor laughed. "Boy, he hasn't even been active in the army in two years. Did you do no research at all? He's an unimportant colonial magistrate in an unimportant corner of the Madras Presidency."

"I... I... I didn't have any time for research! I got off the boat from England three days ago! This is my first assignment!"

Mr. Valov shook his head with dismay. "How can they be so bloody stupid, sending a green little schoolboy for this mission?"

"Ah ha!" Eleanor exclaimed. "So you admit you're a spy, Mr. Valov?! I bet that isn't even your real name!"

He shrugged. "I admit to nothing, unlike greenie over there, who has given himself away in the first five minutes of his first mission." He switched into his natural British accent as he spoke, and Eleanor threw him a subtle wink.

"I... I... I..." Mr. Abernathy stuttered.

"Yes?" Eleanor pushed.

"I have nothing to say," he whispered.

"Well, that is a fine start. Now, Mr. Abernathy, tell me your name."

"*A nose by any other name would smell as sweet...*" he murmured.

"A nose?" Eleanor couldn't help but laugh. "Methinks you should study your Shakespeare, boy, before you try to use his quotes as a distraction. Now tell me your real name."

"That is my real name!" he exclaimed.

Mr. Valov shook his head again with disappointment. "For god's bloody sake..."

Eleanor looked into his eyes, and shook her head with bemusement. "That really is your name, isn't it? You didn't even come up with a pseudonym before you came over here to infiltrate our household for an indefinite period of time?"

"No one told me I needed a pseudonym!"

He suddenly looked even more desperate as he realized that he'd just given away more intel.

Eleanor laughed. "Cadet, you are an undercover spy. The days of your superiors telling you exactly what to do are over."

"I don't have any bloody idea what is happening here," he admitted.

"You are in over your head, greenie." Mr. Valov chuckled, but his laugh dissolved into a pained cough.

"What is your first name, Mr. Abernathy?" Eleanor asked as she loosened the grip on her trident, but kept him pinned up against the bookshelf.

"It's... er... George."

Eleanor smiled. "If you're going to come up with a false name, you should come up with something slightly more interesting, my friend. At the very least, you should say it with more conviction."

"John?" he proposed questioningly.

Mr. Valov looked pained at his exceptional incompetence, but some part of Eleanor was beginning to feel sympathy for the boy. "Alright, boy, how about we call you Geoffrey from now on?

Geoffrey Abernathy. The next time you speak to your superiors, you will tell them that that is your new pseudonym."

"Eleanor…" Mr. Valov moved to protest, but Eleanor threw him a commanding look of disagreement, and he gave in.

Eleanor released Geoffrey from her grasp and dissolved her trident. She straightened his bowtie, and let him rub his sore shoulders.

"You've seen too much, I'm afraid."

"Please don't kill me!" Geoffrey begged.

Eleanor smiled. "My young friend, we will put off your untimely death for now. I reckon that Leo has been quite helpful in covering our tracks. I have often wondered how our magical shenanigans have gone unnoticed by the wider world, and I have a sneaking suspicion that you have something to do with it, Mr. Valov?"

"You're right, my lady," he agreed. "I have been secretly helping you for years. Do you remember the time Sheranee rescued you from that wanton American thief in Agra?"

"I do."

"I am the one who cleared her name and yours after she ate the bloke and left his carrion in the hotel swimming pool."

Geoffrey gulped. "That tiger eats people?"

"Only my enemies," Eleanor replied nonchalantly.

Geoffrey did not find the qualification reassuring.

"My lady, that is only one of many examples. It has been my duty to cover your tracks for years now," Mr. Valov explained.

Eleanor paced back and forth with feigned displeasure. "I knew you'd been spying on us for years, but I could never figure out why. What is in it for you? For Britain?"

"Because it is in the best interest of the Crown and the Empire to keep your power under wraps, my lady. The world is not ready to know about what you and Edmund and your… er… special relatives can do."

She sighed with resignation. "You have been a loyal friend and ally, Leo. We have needed your help, haven't we?"

"You have, my lady."

"But, I reckon you've been very skilled in how you've gone about it?"

"My lady, I came to you with decades of experience, and still your assignment challenged me unlike anything I'd ever imagined. It changed everything."

They both reveled in the tidbit of truth in the middle of their farce. They both knew too well how dearly Eleanor and Edmund had needed Mr. Valov's help, and how dearly they were going to miss it.

She caught a look of confusion on Geoffrey's face. "Is there something you'd like to ask me, Geoffrey? By all means, we'd better start getting to know each other. You will eventually become a member of our household, after Mr. Valov educates you in how to be a better spy."

Geoffrey was overwhelmed by her direct question. "Why… why is he calling you, 'my lady,' ma'am?"

Eleanor smiled. "Because I'm a goddess."

"A goddess? Like Venus or Aphrodite? How absurd!" Geoffrey became somber when he realized he'd already spoken out of turn again.

"And what did you think I was… all of us were… after that debacle you witnessed upon your covert entry to Sri Bidkar's home?"

"What exactly did he witness?" Mr. Valov asked with sudden concern.

"Yes, Geoffrey, what exactly did you witness? Answer me truthfully this time. Your trousers do not need another stain."

He looked back and forth between them, and then attempted to choose his words more carefully. "You were in the midst of some sort of spell of feminine hysteria…" Eleanor and Leo both raised their eyebrows at the offensive characterization, but

Geoffrey continued, unaware of their disapproval, "and then the tiger just appeared in the hallway... and then that man changed into another man... and then that woman appeared out of thin air... It was like something out of *The Tempest* or *A Midsummer Night's Dream.*"

"It sounds like the one suffering from hysteria is you, boy," Mr. Valov chuckled.

"I wasn't! It was all true! I saw it with my own eyes!" Geoffrey looked at both of their unamused expressions and calmed himself. "Unless... unless I was bewitched, like Lysander... or like Bottom!"

Eleanor laughed. "As far as I can tell, you don't have an ass's head yet, at least not literally." Mr. Valov did not understand her reference, and Eleanor glanced over to explain. "In *A Midsummer Night's Dream,* the fairies give Mr. Bottom the head of an ass. It is one of Edmund's favorite scenes. He laughs hysterically every time."

"The night's still young. Kuveni may still indulge us," Mr. Valov winked, and Eleanor was grateful that he was allowing himself a moment of good humor.

Geoffrey did not find their exchange humorous as he glanced around the room for an escape.

"So your professional opinion on behalf of the Crown is that we are fairies?" Eleanor re-engaged him. He avoided eye contact with Mr. Valov at the outrageous suggestion, but he did not disagree with her. "Are you a Shakespeare man, then?"

"I studied Shakespeare at Oxford, before I joined the Service."

"You must have been a baby genius!" Eleanor laughed. "Perhaps you should go study the plays again now that you're almost full grown. I think perhaps you've forgotten some of the details."

Geoffrey blushed with embarrassment. "I'm twenty-two, ma'am... and I've played the lead in fourteen Shakespeare plays. It was a lot to memorize… too much, sometimes… but I tried my best, ma'am."

"I see. So you are a man old enough to be called a man, but too young to have become a man in the war. You are a man young enough not to realize yet that sometimes his best isn't good enough."

"I would have fought if I'd been old enough," he sulked.

"You should thank the gods every night for the rest of your life that you escaped that hellish fate, my young friend. But perhaps you will come to that conclusion yourself when you spend more time with Edmund. Tell me, though, what on earth possessed a Shakespearean actor to join the Secret Service? It wasn't for your skilled deception, that's for sure."

"I'd rather not say, ma'am."

"Suit yourself. I'll needle it out of you soon enough. You are not very good at keeping secrets. Mr. Valov has been a member of our household for seven years without admitting to his treachery, and you didn't last five minutes."

Geoffrey looked down at the floor in shame. "I'm sure that my replacement will be more skilled."

Eleanor laughed. "My young friend, you will not need a replacement. You will do just fine. Mr. Valov will train you up, and you will serve us loyally."

"My loyalty is to the Crown, ma'am."

"Then you will have no problem at all! Edmund is King George's son."

Mr. Valov's eyes bulged at her revelation.

"But… but… Edmund and King George are the same age!" Geoffrey argued.

"No, my young friend. He is George IV's son. He was born in 1818."

"But that would make him over a hundred years old!"

Geoffrey looked to Mr. Valov, who sighed with resignation. "It is a long story that we will tell you only when you earn the right to know it."

Geoffrey straightened his bowtie. "It is my duty to recuse myself now that I have given away my mission."

Eleanor found his simplicity equal parts endearing and aggravating. "My young friend, you have given away the Secret Service's entire game. Do you think we would accept any other butler and believe for one second that he is anyone other than one of your agents? I am resigned to accept your help, if you can prove yourself worthy, and you must commit to fulfilling your duty in this most difficult of assignments."

Leo glanced at Eleanor and switched into Czech. "I hope you know what you're doing. He's the worst cadet I've ever seen. He must be related to someone important to have become an officer at all, but the name Abernathy is not familiar to me."

"He is virtuous and malleable, and he has no idea what he's doing. He is a perfect candidate for you, Leo," she replied in Czech using Uma's divine linguistic talents. "And he's a Shakespearean scholar, which makes him a perfect candidate for Edmund."

"This situation makes me very nervous, Eleanor. They should not have sent a schoolboy for this mission. There is something very wrong up the chain of command."

"Then we'd best get Geoffrey solidified on our side before his superiors show up to see our shenanigans for themselves, don't you think?"

"You have always been wonderfully shrewd, Eleanor."

"Don't remind me." She glanced at Geoffrey who was watching their exchange with puzzlement. She switched back into English to address him. "We were speaking Czech. You don't speak an obscure language, do you?"

Geoffrey's posture perked up as he finally had some good news to share. "I speak Breton, ma'am. It is one of the most obscure languages left on the planet."

198

Eleanor smiled and replied in perfect Breton. "Perfect! That will be most useful."

"Ma'am, might I ask how you speak Breton?" Geoffrey asked as curiosity joined his growing compilation of emotions.

Eleanor returned to English. "It is one of my many divine talents, greenie, and watch your tongue. Edmund can also speak every language."

Geoffrey snorted. "Every language?"

"Every single one," Mr. Valov reiterated.

"*Oh brave new world that has such creatures in it...*" Geoffrey murmured.

"Might I ask how *you* speak Breton, my friend?" Eleanor asked.

"I grew up in Bretagne, ma'am. In a village near Saint-Brieuc. I lived there until I went to boarding school in England."

The town sounded familiar, but Eleanor couldn't place from where, and she pushed back a rumble of foreboding at the odd coincidence of his arrival with the Oracle's fiendish attack. But, as she looked into his eyes, she was certain that his poor entrance was due to incompetence rather than malice. She was certain that with the right training, she could mold him, and as Leo sat back and gave into another bout of violent coughs, she reminded herself that the wicked clock was ticking.

"Now, my young friend, this is what is going to happen: You are going to follow Leo's lead. You are not going to give yourself away to anyone, including Edmund. You are going to do as I say, and you are going to tell your superiors that your infiltration was a success. As a condition of your acceptance into our household, we have insisted that Mr. Valov remain on staff to train you. Do you understand?"

"They are not going to be happy," Geoffrey said nervously as he glanced at Mr. Valov. "They wanted you to resign."

"Welcome to the job, greenie," Mr. Valov rasped as he barely got his coughing under control. "Obeying Eleanor and managing your superiors' disappointment are core tenets of the job."

"But isn't that treason?"

"Greenie, this position was created by Queen Victoria herself. It has been the most important position in the Secret Service for decades. How a buffoon like you stumbled upon it, I can't fathom, but I think you have seen enough already to have an inkling of the magnitude of the assignment."

"I was the only unassigned agent in India," Geoffrey admitted. "When they heard you were in hospital, they assigned me straightaway. I don't think they realized... er... how unusual it was."

"You think?" Mr. Valov coughed out another laugh. "Someone's head will roll for this, it's only a matter of time. In the meantime, I will connect you with G."

"G?" Geoffrey glanced at Eleanor suspiciously.

"My one and only senior officer," Mr. Valov replied, without a hint of concern at Eleanor hearing the mysterious code name.

As the clock began chiming its ten o'clock warning, Eleanor felt the pull of the pantheon dining just down the hall.

"Alright, then it's settled. Geoffrey will be our spying butler's apprentice, I will tell Edmund that he has passed my gauntlet of an interview, and Leo will live long enough to make him into a worthy heir."

"Is that a promise, my lady?" Mr. Valov quipped. "Perhaps that's the key to my immortality."

Eleanor reached forward and took both of his hands.

I will do everything in my power to keep you alive as long as I can.

I truly do not deserve your mercy, Eleanor.

And yet you shall have it anyway. It is my mercy to give.

Mr. Valov swallowed hard as he battled the ball in his throat, and his struggle dissolved into muffled coughs.

Take with you Shakti's blessings, my child.

He bowed his head with respect.

Thank you, Holy Mother.

Eleanor cleared her throat as her emotions encroached. "Now, Geoffrey, help Leo up. The first task of your assignment will be to support him in every way that you can."

Geoffrey obediently reached down and helped Mr. Valov up off of the couch.

"So are you really fairies?" he asked Eleanor. "Or genies like the mohammedan simpleton said?"

"I told you, my young friend. I am a goddess."

"I'm a Christian," he informed her. "There are no goddesses in Christianity."

Eleanor laughed. "And yet there are fairies? I think perhaps I missed that part of the Bible. Was the queen of Elfame there for the birth of Christ?"

"No, ma'am," Stanley mumbled. "There are no fairies in the Bible either."

Eleanor nodded her approval of his concession. Slowly but surely, they were going to make progress. "Perhaps you should sit near Doctor Carpenter at dinner," she suggested. "He has a unique perspective on Christianity that you should take straight to heart. He used to be a vicar, in fact. I suggest you ask him about his opinion of goddesses, and the second task of your assignment is to report back to me on his response."

She grabbed his hand. *Take with you Shakti's blessings, my young friend. You will need them.*

His eyes widened. "What on earth...?"

"Greenie, you have a lot to learn," Mr. Valov rasped.

May Shakti give us enough time to teach him before it's too late, Eleanor prayed.

We will do what we can, my child, Uma reassured her.

But will it be enough?

It will have to be.

PART TWO
EASTWARD AND DOWN

CHAPTER 14 – A COINCIDENCE?

Eleanor awoke to the sound of Edmund grumbling to himself in the closet of their opulent suite on the P&O steamer as it chugged along eastward towards the port of Fremantle.

They'd already been on board for six long days, chasing the horizon south and east as the water became bluer and warmer and then cooler again until it felt like their elusive target was taunting them from beyond the sky itself, like the end of a rainbow... or perhaps Heaven. She had always thought of Heaven as a con of sorts, an illusory dream for those foolish enough to believe the earthly lies of proselytizing priests or the recruitment posters from His Majesty's Armed Services.

Now, despite her elevated position in the pantheon, she knew just as little about it as she had long ago as an ordinary human nurse, and she relished her ignorance. She wondered if the Oracle's damning visions would have given her all the answers... the answers that would have eliminated every final drop of humanity she had left, and she stretched, wiggling her toes and twiddling her fingers, enjoying the corporeal nature of the sensation with a newfound appreciation that she had only come to recognize while enduring the secondary position in her own body.

A loud clomp and a hissed tirade of curses emanating from the closet broke her out of her meandering thoughts. She had hoped when she went to bed early many hours before that an extra-long night of sleep might make the final hours of their journey more bearable, and she had not expected her gentle husband to awaken before her. He'd spent every other night of their journey making up for the sleep he'd lost sitting by Leo's side in the hospital, and she found his restlessness unsettling.

"Can't bloody find anything on my own... like a bloody spoiled prince with servants at his beck and call... just a lazy bloody lout, not worth the fabric of his breeches..."

"Darling? Are you alrigh?"

She sat up and turned to watch him standing naked in the closet with a hat in one hand and a sock in the other.

Edmund turned around to face her, and he looked like he might cry.

Eleanor hopped out of bed naked and scampered across the room. She took the hat and the sock out of his hands, dropped them on the floor, and then stood on her tiptoes, put her arms around his neck, and kissed him. He pulled away.

"I'm like a spoiled child, Eleanor. I can't do anything for myself anymore. I've become so dependent on Leo that I can't even dress myself. What am I going to do when he's gone?"

She took his hand and guided him back to the bed. She sat him down and took a seat next to him, gently tickling the soft, cold skin of his arm until he shivered.

"Darling, it isn't healthy for you to redirect your anger at Leo's tragedy onto yourself."

"What do you mean?"

"Are you really a lazy bloody lout, not worth the fabric of your breeches? How many decades has it been since you've even worn proper breeches?"

A rich red blush rushed into his cheeks. "I thought you were still asleep."

"I was, until you woke me with your tirade against yourself. You're being rather harsh, don't you think? You don't even have your glasses on, it's no wonder you can't find anything."

He glanced at his glasses on the bedside table, but her observation did not ease his concern, in fact, he looked even closer to tears. "Glasses or not, I should be able to fend for myself without being coddled."

"Darling, I haven't been able to find anything in these trunks either. Ravi's staff packed them in a most annoying way. I don't think they understood how an English wardrobe works. Why don't you come back to bed? We can lie in each other's arms for a while longer, before we have to get up for breakfast."

"I'm sorry I woke you, dearest. I've been awake for hours, and I thought I'd go check on Leo. With that worthless schoolboy caring for him, who knows what trouble he's in."

"Geoffrey has a lot to learn, I agree, but he is eager, and he is young enough that if we can train him up, he can be your right-hand man for decades."

Edmund scoffed. "That boy is utterly untrainable. I trained thousands of cadets in the army over the years, and he is clumsier than all of them combined."

"I will admit, I have seen more graceful butlers."

"Besides, I'll have to re-set myself at some point. I'm already much older than I was when we met. I need my glasses all the time now."

"But you almost never wear them!" Eleanor exclaimed. "Why don't you just wear them, darling?"

"Because soon enough, I'll be a blind and hunched-over scrooge, hobbling everywhere with a cane. Neither of us needs a reminder of that. It will only make me grumpy, and we both know what you think about me being grumpy."

"Darling, you are allowed to be grumpy sometimes."

"I don't like myself when I'm in a mood, and I don't blame you one bit when you don't like me either, Eleanor."

"Darling, I think you are making too much of this. Wearing glasses is hardly putting a foot in the grave. Children wear glasses, for god's sake!"

"I only need them when I'm old, Eleanor. It is the first step in a long series of humiliating, painful unpleasantries."

Eleanor couldn't help but laugh, and Edmund humphed angrily at her flippant reaction and pulled his arm out of her grasp. Eleanor let him have his space.

"Darling, you are describing the human condition. The only difference between you and me is that at the end of the humiliation, you will be a gorgeous, virile young cad again, while I will be a wrinkled old corpse."

Edmund grimaced. Eleanor knew that she should steer clear of a reminder of her mortality, but he had aroused a passion in her that she couldn't ignore.

"Darling, all I am saying is that you enjoy a luxury that no human has. Perhaps you should try to appreciate what you do have in common with the rest of us. Mr. Johnson doesn't age at all, and I don't think he understands humans nearly as well as you do. In some ways, your ability to age naturally is a gift."

"Are you saying that I should enjoy descending into a grotesque cadaverous state because it is a curse that you and Leo and Edward Rutherford and everyone else I love will also suffer? That's so bloody perverse!"

Eleanor caught a hint of desperate despair in his eye that immediately extinguished her fiery temper.

"I'm sorry, darling. I didn't mean it like that. I know that it is very painful for you to worry about the mortality of those you love.

It is a position I can't imagine being in myself. It must make you feel very alone."

He looked at the floor. "It does."

"You aren't alone now, darling. I'm here, and I'm going to be here for a very long time. And you have Mr. Johnson now, and Kate, and Percy, and who knows who else? You will never be alone again."

Eleanor took his hand back and returned to gently stroking the soft skin of his inner forearm until a wave of goosebumps erupted across his skin.

"None of the others need glasses," Edmund humphed. "It is as if I have the maladies of both of my people. I have the dark urges of my father's people and the wretched weakness of my mother's."

Eleanor was taken aback by his reference. "Dark urges?"

"Mr. Johnson told me on our wedding day that everything that I struggle with is normal. That he, and Percy, and others, struggle with it every day. He told me that the madwoman who attacked us lost her struggle. I constantly worry about becoming a monster like her, or a crippled old miser like I was in 1895."

"Is there anything I can say to convince you that you don't have to worry about becoming either? You have so much more control than you realize, darling."

"You have too much faith in me, Eleanor."

"I told you the day that we met that I have excellent judgment," she countered. "Perhaps you should trust me."

Her statement yanked him out of his combative mood. "I do trust you, Eleanor. I trust you more than anyone I've ever known."

Eleanor sighed sadly. "I know you do, darling." She decided to move the topic along before it depressed her too much. "I think for now, though, you do not need to worry about imminently becoming a monster or a scrooge. How old were you physically the last time you needed a cane?"

"About seventy-five, give or take."

"So you have about twenty years left before that happens?"

"It is not long enough, Eleanor. You deserve to have a capable lover and husband. It is absurd for you to care for me in an aged state that neither of us needs to endure."

"So don't!" Edmund sighed his disagreement, and Eleanor hunkered down for a wifely lecture. "Darling, I am the only woman on Earth whose husband can pop himself back to being a virile young cad at the drop of a hat. Can't you trust that when the time comes, we will make a good decision together? Then we can hop over to our homestead in New Zealand where nobody knows us, and you can pleasure me until..." She trailed off as another reminder of her mortality almost spilled out. "Until I tire of you and find myself a younger, more vigorous lover." She winked, but he was not amused.

"There are many problems with that plan, Eleanor. We will need help, and Leo won't be around to offer it."

"Darling, Leo would have stayed with us through thick and thin, but we must accept that it is not his fate to live to a ripe old age by our side. We must start working on an alternative, and right now, Geoffrey is our most viable option. For all we know, someday he will be trustworthy enough to truly walk in Leo's shoes. He already quotes Shakespeare, you know."

"I don't need a fool at my feet to quote Shakespeare, Eleanor, and those quotes just spill out of him in the most irritating way. He doesn't even get them right!"

Eleanor took his hand. "Darling, is it possible that you are finding him especially irritating because you do not want Leo to be replaced?"

Edmund considered the suggestion for an extended moment before conceding. "It is theoretically possible."

Eleanor smiled and leaned over to kiss him on the cheek. "I love you, darling. We will get through this together. Now, shall I help you dress?"

"I should be able to dress myself, Eleanor."

She skipped over to the closet and bent down, sensually running her fingers up her bare leg and then her breast as she collected his hat off the floor. She put it on and winked. "But what fun would that be, darling?"

He finally let a smile break through. "You're right. It wouldn't be as much fun."

She began pulling all of his clothes out of the poorly packed trunk one by one, spreading them across the already-messy floor.

"Dearest!" Edmund protested half-heartedly.

"Leo should teach Geoffrey how to repack our trunks anyway. I'm doing half the work for them. Ah ha! I've found the other sock! We shall not lose you again, my friend…" She put it on her hand as if it were a puppet and continued on with her sexy show until the floor of their room was completely covered in clothing. She spied the first sock, put it on her other hand, and skipped back to him, straddling him playfully.

"This is all you needed, right, darling? Socks and a hat? I think they'll be very stylish together, don't you?"

She licked his lips, and as he gave into a burst of excitement that neither of them had felt since Leo's tragic news took the wind out of their sails, she wrapped her legs around him and sighed at the delightful sensation of two avatars becoming one.

She moaned with pleasure for a wonderfully long engagement, as his vigor and his attention to detail grew with every thrust until she felt her third orgasm approaching and nibbled on the soft skin of his ear, pulling him right over the edge with her.

"I love you, Eleanor," he whispered as the last of his tension was released. He kissed her again, this time more tenderly.

"I love you, Edmund." She kissed his forehead, then each of his cheeks, and then returned to his lips.

As the relief of their shared catharsis began settling in, the door to their room flew open. Eleanor scrambled off of her husband and under the covers with a squeal, and Edmund's eyes turned black.

Geoffrey stood in the wide-open doorway, staring at them as if he'd never seen anything of the sort in his life. "*The beast with two backs...*" he murmured.

"What are you *doing*?!" Mr. Valov exclaimed angrily as he approached from behind. "You never, ever barge inside without knocking! *Never!* Were you born yesterday, boy?" He trailed off into a pained cough, but ignored his struggle as he pushed Geoffrey into the room and slammed the door shut behind them.

"But... but... but the door was unlocked!" Geoffrey stuttered.

Edmund's black eyes returned to their human hazel as a deep red blush took over his entire face. He looked frantically around the floor for anything he could use to cover himself. Still coughing, Mr. Valov reached down and gathered up a black silk robe that was underneath a crumpled suit jacket and handed it to Edmund.

Edmund wrapped himself up and then guided Mr. Valov to the edge of the messy bed, sitting him down in almost the exact spot where they'd been enjoying their time together (only a few feet from where Eleanor was still lying naked under the covers), and offering him a decorative silk handkerchief from the bedside table. His eyes returned to their demonic black as Leo's violent coughs filled the handkerchief with blood, but as Geoffrey watched Edmund nervously and moved to say something, Eleanor threw daggers at him with her eyes.

"*The prince of darkness is a gentleman...*" he murmured to himself instead.

Eleanor found the reference disconcertingly similar to the language of the Oracle, but as she began panicking, wondering if their bumbling spy might actually be some greater enemy in a well-executed disguise, Edmund identified the true source of the quote.

"*When we are born, we cry that we are come to this great stage of fools!*" Eleanor, Leo, and Geoffrey were each startled by his odd outburst for different reasons. "This is no time for *King Lear*, boy! Shall I quote the bard back to you every time you butcher his words from now on? Now find something useful to do!"

Geoffrey tripped over a silk dress as he attempted to make his way through the mounds of clothes to the bathroom, and as he landed on the floor with one of Eleanor's modern bras under one hand and a discarded pair of panties under the other, he scrambled up, accidentally bringing them with him, and dropped them back onto the floor with a squeal, desperately scoping the room for any reasonable place he could escape to without causing more embarrassment.

Edmund shook his head with dismay as he rubbed Leo's back soothingly.

"Darling, perhaps you should go out onto the balcony for some fresh air and get yourself back under control. I will see to Leo," Eleanor suggested.

Edmund moved to protest, but as Leo wheezed and nodded his support of the suggestion, he shrugged and gave in. Without a word, he stood up and walked outside.

"Fetch me that robe, boy," Eleanor said sharply as she pointed across the room to a kimono that was crumpled in the corner. Geoffrey stood still, distracted by watching Edmund as he paced back and forth on the balcony whispering his mantras.

"Do it, boy! Don't be daft!" Leo rasped.

Geoffrey startled, and then rushed to follow Mr. Valov's orders, tripping over several more items of clothing before making his way to the corner.

"Greenie, you will be the death of me," Leo muttered.

Eleanor grabbed the kimono as Geoffrey awkwardly presented it to her in a messy clump. "Turn your back so I can get out of bed, greenie. Don't move until I tell you to."

He turned around and covered his eyes like a child counting in a game of hide and seek, while Leo politely (and more naturally), kept his gaze locked on Edmund on the balcony as Eleanor scampered out of bed and wrapped herself up, tightening the belt of the robe, and then loosening it as she noticed the thin silk hugging her breasts too revealingly.

As soon as she was covered, she walked around the bed and checked on Leo's condition, feeling his clammy forehead with the back of her hand and examining the dangerous amount of blood in the handkerchief.

"We're going to need to get you a proper nurse as soon as we arrive in Perth," she whispered in Czech. "And I'm going to ask Mélusine to pop by once a day to help you manage your pain."

"Eleanor, that's really not necessary..."

He wheezed as he struggled to speak, and she raised her eyebrows skeptically as she rubbed his back.

"You're making my arguments for me, Leo."

"I'm sure that she has much better things to do with her time, Eleanor."

"I agree, but it will only take her a few minutes a day, and it may buy us some time so that you can double down on your training of greenie over there. That will be in everyone's best interest, including Mélusine's. None of us need that bumbling buffoon of a spy reporting back misunderstood half-truths about us to the Crown."

She glanced over at Geoffrey as he remained obediently facing the wall with his eyes covered.

"What are we going to do with him? You can't send him back for someone better, can you? He already knows too much."

"No, I can't send him back. I talked to G as soon as we boarded the steamer. Greenie is very well-connected, and his assignment was not an accident. It appeared to be a routine backfill to the midlevel commander who sent him over to the Bidkars' without a word of warning, but there was a far more strategic plan afoot, a plan that Geoffrey himself is not aware of yet."

"Do tell. I can't fathom how his presence here could possibly be intentional."

"It's better if you don't know yet, Eleanor. Please trust me."

214

"You could drop dead any minute, Leo. You know that, right? The era of secrets is over. You must tell me everything I need to know to manage this mess when you're gone."

"I will, Eleanor. I promise. But please let me do what I do best for just a little bit longer? I'm not dead yet."

She sighed her begrudging agreement, and glanced back over at Geoffrey. "Greenie, you can turn around."

He turned around sheepishly and glanced over at Edmund, who was still pacing back and forth, although his mantras had morphed into another round of muttering self-castigation.

"Ma'am, might I ask what exactly the ailment is that…"

Eleanor practically dove across the bed to pummel Geoffrey into silence. She slammed her hand over his mouth and threw him up against the wall.

First rule of the household, greenie: Say nothing about Edmund's ailments. Got it?

Geoffrey's eyes widened as Eleanor's voice boomed in his head.

Got it?

"Yes, ma'am."

Don't respond out loud, greenie!

But how else am I supposed to respond?

Exactly like that. Respond like that.

You can hear the thoughts in my head?

Yes. I can.

He shifted uncomfortably.

Only when we're making physical contact, greenie. And only the thoughts on the surface. Your other meandering fantasies are safe locked up in the back of your mind.

He relaxed slightly.

How is this possible? You can read my thoughts? Like a psychic? Is that why your eyes are glowing like that? Shakespeare's fairies can't read minds.

I told you, greenie. I'm a goddess.

I'm a Christian, ma'am. Remember?

What did Doctor Carpenter say about goddesses?

He said that God manifests in many beautiful ways, and that those who are too attached to one notion are to be pitied for depriving themselves of connecting with divinity. I told him goddesses were just remnants of the pagan past.

And what did he say to that?

Our very eyes are sometimes like our judgments, blind.

That was rather poetic of him.

It was a Shakespeare quote, ma'am. From Cymbeline.

Eleanor laughed. *D.H. sure does know how to speak to his audience...*

'D.H.,' ma'am?

Not an acronym for you to know, greenie. You have not proven that you are worthy of knowing anything else about us. For now, you will keep your mouth shut. Got it? Leo will tell you what you must know when you must know it.

But, ma'am, is the colonel... is he alright?

He's fine, greenie. He's just shell-shocked from the war. His eyes manifest his struggle when his adrenaline is unleashed. He doesn't know that his eyes are black, and it is going to stay that way, got it? He doesn't need another problem to worry about.

But, ma'am, doesn't it frighten people?

Sometimes it does. It is Mr. Valov's job to make sure that their fear does not cause problems for us or for the Crown. And now, it will be your job too.

But how would it cause problems for the Crown, ma'am?

Leo will tell you when you're worthy. Now, Edmund is coming inside. Not a word of any of this, got it? He doesn't know that I can do this. He doesn't know that I can do anything unusual, and it is going to stay that way. Got it?

Eleanor pulled away and closed her eyes, relegating the last of Shakti's power back into the core of her being.

"Darling, you're looking much better!" She skipped over to his side and kissed him gently on the lips. "I was just giving greenie

216

over there a little lecture on etiquette. He won't be barging in on us again, locked or unlocked. Right, greenie?"

"Yes, ma'am."

"Now, greenie, Edmund and I are going to get dressed and go to breakfast. You will repack our trunks following Mr. Valov's instructions to the letter, got it?"

"Yes, ma'am." She threw him another look of disapproval as she caught a hint of sulking in his tone. "You may start as soon as I have collected our wardrobe for the morning."

She tiptoed around the room, gathering up wrinkled outfits for herself and Edmund, and then she guided Edmund into the bathroom and shut the door behind them.

She dropped the clothes on the floor, put her arms around his neck, and kissed him. "We will get through this, darling." She pulled the loose end of his belt until his robe fell open, and then she ran her finger along his nipples until they hardened. She slowly and sensually moved her fingers and her lips downwards.

"Eleanor!" he whispered with equal parts embarrassment and excitement. "They're just through the door!"

"Since when did that stop us, darling? Leo has slept in the room beside ours for years."

She slammed him up against the door playfully and continued on with her skilled stimulation.

"But, dearest, that's different…" Edmund trailed off with a sigh of pleasure, but worked to continue on with his point. Eleanor enjoyed their little game immensely. "Leo is a consummate gentleman's gentleman… He is discretion itself… That boy in there not only knows nothing about service, he doesn't appear to even know what sex is, other than through a bloody… Shakespearean… reference…"

"Darling, he's not a boy anymore. He's twenty-two. By the time I was twenty-two, I'd been a nurse for four years, and I'd already had my fair share of lovers." She distracted him from the unpleasant fact with a particularly enticing stroke of her tongue.

"If he's twenty-two and he's still this innocent, he'd better learn fast, because I will not spend the rest of our married life worrying about that boy's opinion of our marital activities. Do you want to give this up because our boy butler can't handle the world of grown-ups?"

As Edmund moaned with pleasure, Eleanor let her argument rest in favor of more pleasant activities, until she'd elicited a fully satisfied response from her husband.

"That was... very good, Eleanor..." he murmured as he worked to catch his breath.

She winked. "I'm glad you enjoyed it, darling."

She ran the bath and didn't wait for it to warm up before beginning her hasty hygienic routine. They both hopped around the bathroom getting themselves ready, while Mr. Valov's muffled barked orders at greenie made their way through the door.

As soon as Eleanor finished buttoning up the sides of a low-waisted sage green lace dress with a stylish asymmetrical hemline that looked very reminiscent of the one Kuveni had worn to dinner at Ravi and Shruti's, she tied Edmund's tie, checked that her pendant from Mélusine and the bangle from Vibhishana were both in position, and kissed him on the lips one last time.

"Hello, what's that there?" Edmund asked as he noticed the bangle. "It is strikingly similar to the pendant I bought you in Turkey."

Eleanor's heart almost exploded as she held up her arm nonchalantly. "Oh, this?"

"Why are you scared, Eleanor?"

She felt his heart begin racing as he picked up on the burst of anxiety that she hadn't been able to hide. Her mind raced... what lie could she tell him that wouldn't make him ask more questions?

"To be honest, darling..." Suddenly the truth began burrowing out of her. "You didn't buy me the pendant." She was almost as shocked as he was as the words came out of her mouth. "It was a gift from Kate, as was the bangle. That is why they match.

218

She'd asked me to lie about it in Turkey, because she didn't want you to know she was there, and by the time she revealed her presence, I'd forgotten all about the lie. I'm sorry."

Well, it was mostly true… partially true… she wished so dearly that it was true… *Your divine husband gave it to you,* her mean inner monologue screamed. *You are wearing another man's gift. Another husband's gift! A gift from the man he thinks is his bloody father!!!*

You did not agree to marry Lord Vibhishana, Eleanor. His presence in your life is my curse on you. Do not be so harsh on yourself, Uma reassured her. *You have shown exceptional restraint in the face of my shameful weakness for him.*

As Uma's words calmed down Eleanor's self-castigation, Edmund sensed her relief, and attributed it to her half-truth.

"She should not ask you to lie to me. None of them should."

"I know, darling. But they all think it's in your best interest. I can see the pain in their eyes when they refuse to give you the answers you seek. Wouldn't you rather know them as they are, without the full truth, than not know them at all?"

Eleanor hoped that he would agree with her, as his answer would, she had to admit dismally, apply to his relationship with her as well.

"I wish I wouldn't have to choose between two imperfect options," he humphed.

"I do too, darling. But you and I both know that life isn't fair. We must often pick the best of imperfect options."

"I suppose," he conceded. "I suppose I do feel better knowing that Kate and Lord Blakeney or Percy or whatever his real name is are around. It makes me feel less alone."

Eleanor kissed him gently on the lips. "That's what I thought, darling. You are a wonderfully rational and patient man. The best I've ever known."

He put his strong arm around her back and pulled her into a deeper kiss.

"I love you, Eleanor."

"I love…" Eleanor trailed off as a loud clomp distracted them, and Mr. Valov began another cough-filled tirade against Geoffrey.

Edmund shook his head. "That boy is a daft fop if ever I've seen one."

"He still has a lot to learn," Eleanor agreed. "Darling, let's have a leisurely breakfast with Leo, and before we know it, we'll be in Perth with Oz and Yvie, and we will have their staff to help us fill in the gaps left by Geoffrey's incomplete education."

"I have missed them mightily," he admitted. "I suppose with Leo's bad news, I haven't let myself think about the happy reunion."

"Me neither, darling. But things are looking up. Now, shall we?"

She pushed open the door. Leo was still sitting on the bed, while Geoffrey stood beside him, leaning over a crumpled mound of their clothing. Several failed attempts at folding their laundry were laid out on the bed beside it.

"Now fold in the corner all the way to the edge. No, not like that!"

Leo looked up at them, and Geoffrey blushed as he stopped what he was doing to greet them.

"Colonel, ma'am, it appears you're finally clothed? Ow!" Leo kicked him in the shin. "I mean, how may I assist you while you are enjoying your breakfast?"

Eleanor looked around at the mess. "Geoffrey, you may stay here and continue folding our laundry. At this rate, it will be a miracle if you're done by the time we pull into port. Leo, you're coming to eat with us."

"But, ma'am… when will I eat?" Geoffrey asked.

"Like a bloody child…" Edmund muttered.

"You will eat when you are done with your task," Eleanor informed him.

"Eleanor, I'm not properly dressed for breakfast in the first-class dining room," Leo whispered. "And neither is Edmund."

Eleanor glanced at the relaxed linen suit she had selected for him and sighed with annoyance. She'd never really gotten used to the excessive formality of British first-class accommodations. "Do you think they'll disallow us from entering?"

"I suspect the status of Lord and Lady Marriner, Earl and Countess of Easton, will be enough to earn their grumbling forgiveness."

"Earl and Countess of Easton?" Geoffrey interrupted. "You never said the colonel was a lord!"

Edmund made no effort to hide his annoyance. "I'm not. It is just a silly misnomer concocted by Ravi Bidkar and perpetuated by too many lemmings who do not check their sources."

Eleanor leaned down to gather Leo's weight onto her arm, and Edmund swooped down and followed her lead, pulling him up nimbly.

"Then we'll go as we are," Eleanor decided. "Dressing up for breakfast is a stuffy tradition anyway. The Americans can always wear whatever they want, and no one ever says a peep."

"That's because they're barbarous cowboys without a hint of taste, Eleanor," Leo rasped. "The world has given up on their manners."

She laughed. "Then we'd all better get used to it, because we're headed down under to another land of barbarous cowboys, if Oz's tall tales told us anything about the wild west of Australia."

She let Edmund take on the brunt of Leo's weight and rushed in front of them to open the door. Some part of her had hoped that Geoffrey might notice the need and do it for her, but he only stood dumbstruck, watching them from his position by the pile of laundry. She shooed Edmund and Leo through the door before either of them could be annoyed by the oversight, and then slammed it closed, leaving Geoffrey behind.

"What time are we supposed to pull into port?" she asked casually as she guided them both down the hallway and onto the elevator.

"It was scheduled for two o'clock, but the captain said we'd be a bit early," Leo rasped. "Greenie had better pick up his pace, or your trunks will still be empty by the time we disembark."

"I'm sure we can manage it," Eleanor replied. "Please don't worry about these details anymore, Leo."

"I'd much rather worry about them than about other things, Eleanor."

At the sad thought, they all dissolved into pensiveness while the elevator worked its way up to the first-class dining room.

When they stepped off, into a vast foyer with an enormous chandelier, several waiters rushed to greet them.

"Three of us will be dining together," Edmund informed them.

"Yes, Colonel! Please come this way!" One of the waiters gestured for them to follow.

But, as they made their way across the crowded dining room, towards a lovely table situated beside the open french doors out onto the balcony where the fresh sea air was rustling the white lace curtains, Leo stopped, and all the color drained from his face.

Eleanor and Edmund both followed his gaze to the neighboring table where a lone man sat reading a newspaper by himself with a cup of coffee. As Eleanor grabbed Leo's wrist, Edmund grinned happily.

Who is that, Leo?
What the hell is he doing?!
Who?!!!

Mr. Valov pulled away from her as the man stood up to greet them. He was elderly but distinguished, with a full head of perfectly placed white hair and military posture that rivalled Edmund's, wearing a very expensive and well-fitted grey wool suit, similarly inappropriate to their attire in comparison to the other diners in the otherwise unreasonably formal venue.

He walked nimbly towards them with his arm out in greeting. Eleanor knew him, but she couldn't place from where.

222

"Fancy seeing you here, Colonel!"

"Lord Grimby?!" Edmund exclaimed. "What a wonderful surprise to see you here! Have you been on board since Bombay? How have we never crossed paths?"

He shook the man's hand.

"Lord Grimby?" Eleanor murmured as she tried to place the name. "You came to our wedding in Basingstoke, didn't you?"

"It's a wonder you remember!" he said jovially as he shook her hand. "You had quite the audience to entertain that day, but what an occasion it was. The most beautiful wedding I've been to in decades. I was happy to see you off on your honeymoon, at least in spirit."

"You did get my card, thanking you for loaning us your plane?" Edmund asked. "We couldn't have had a better welcome from Norwenn. She's doing well, I hope?"

"Norwenn!" Eleanor exclaimed as she finally placed the name. "I'm so embarrassed! I should have remembered who you were, Lord Grimby! We had such a nice time at your holiday home in Bretagne!"

"It was my pleasure entirely, Mrs. Marriner. My pleasure entirely. I owe your husband a great debt of gratitude, for his service to our empire, and to my son."

Edmund looked down at the floor self-consciously, and Lord Grimby noticed his reticence.

"Come, join me! I've been locked away ill since I disembarked from the steamer in Bombay, and I'm finally ready for a fine English breakfast. I should have known the spices would do me in, but every time I'm there, I simply can't resist that fried bread. What do they call it, Colonel?"

"Puri," Edmund replied.

"Yes! That's it! With those chickpeas… oh how delicious, but they get me every time."

Lord Grimby gestured for them to sit at his table, and the waiter didn't blink at the change.

"Lord Grimby, I'm not sure you've had the pleasure of meeting our butler, Mr. Valov." Edmund gestured for them to shake hands. "He has recently taken ill (nothing contagious, mind you), and we are taking a little trip down under to visit some dear friends in the hope that the warm sea air will do him some good."

Leo looked pained as he shook Lord Grimby's hand. "Pleased to meet you, sir."

"It's a pleasure," Lord Grimby replied as he shook Leo's hand. "Please, do sit. You do not look well."

As soon as they were seated, the waiters rushed to pour them coffee.

"So, Lord Grimby, what brings you to this obscure corner of the Empire?" Edmund asked cheerfully.

Lord Grimby leaned in confidingly. "Retirement, Colonel. I've got my eye on a vineyard down in Margaret River. Some Aussie diggers I met during the war talked my ear off about the lovely winemaking soil down there, and I've come to scope it out. I could use some warm sea air myself these days."

"They are growing wine by the sea?" Eleanor asked with genuine curiosity. "Is that normal?"

Lord Grimby laughed. "I'll believe it when I see it. They say the geography is different than France, but similar enough in the ways that matter. Sitting back on a porch overlooking the ocean with my own grapes growing all around me sounds too good to be true. I was thinking of orchards too, come to think of it. Norwenn's brother in Normandie has a recipe for calvados that is sure to be a winner on our side of the pond, with proper marketing, that is."

Eleanor finally let herself relax, despite noting Mr. Valov's uncomfortable posture. She simply didn't have the energy to think about his continuing deterioration. She'd been thinking about it for days on end. Instead, she sat back and listened as Edmund and Lord Grimby engaged each other in a lively conversation about colonial farming techniques and the French brilliance at winemaking, until the coffee from breakfast turned into an aperitif before for lunch.

"Have we really been sitting here that long?" Edmund asked with good cheer for the first time in over a week as the waiters delivered them each a glass of champagne. "It feels like we just got here! I suppose we should get ready to disembark soon. Our worthless butler-in-training has probably dropped all of our clothing off the balcony at this point."

"We still have a few hours to go," Leo rasped as he glanced at a pocket-watch. "Fremantle is the last stop for this steamer before it begins its return voyage. We will have plenty of time to disembark."

Eleanor held up her glass in a toast. "To better times."

Edmund clinked it sadly as his cheer dissolved, and Leo held in a bout of coughs as the bubbles tickled his throat.

Lord Grimby sighed nostalgically. "I remember the days of training my young staff. One poor girl ironed holes into three of my suits before we reassigned her to the garden. At least then she couldn't break anything precious… or so I thought. My wife was horribly unhappy when she smashed our prize-winning roses, but in the end, she found her stride. We had her with us for thirty years. She was really very loyal… and perhaps she knew that she couldn't get another equivalent position with her shortcomings. It made her more loyal, I think."

"I suppose that is one silver lining of excessive incompetence…" Edmund muttered. The loud crash of a tray hitting the floor and glasses shattering distracted them, and they each looked over to the source. "Well, speak of the devil…"

Geoffrey stood dumbstruck in the foyer. Several angry waiters yelled at him to get out of their way as they rushed to clean up the mess all around him, but his attention was entirely focused on Lord Grimby.

As one waiter gruffly pushed him out of the way, he darted between tables, bumping almost every lady and gentleman he passed and ignoring their increasingly vehement chastisements as he worked his way towards their table.

"Dearest, can we please sack him?" Edmund implored as the boy knocked a feathered hat off of an elderly woman and then stepped on it as it landed on the floor at his feet. "Surely we can find a replacement in Perth whom Leo can train? Anyone! How about that waiter chap over there? He's been competent at carrying a tray all week!"

As Geoffrey reached their table, he looked at each of them with puzzlement. *"If the shadows have offended, think ye this and all is mended..."* he murmured.

Lord Grimby reached out his hand. "Colonel, I reckon this is your buffoon of a new butler? You may call me Lord Grimby, boy."

Geoffrey only stared at Lord Grimby's hand with puzzlement. "But, Uncle Chester, we've already met. It's me, Stanley!"

CHAPTER 15 – STANLEY

Lord Grimby squinted and pulled a pair of glasses out of his front pocket. He carefully cleaned them with a handkerchief and then put them on and looked Geoffrey up and down again.

"Why, Stanley, it is you!"

Lord Grimby grabbed Stanley's hand and shook it jovially.

"What the hell are you doing on a steamer to Australia, boy? I thought you were off to Canada to join the Royal Canadian Shakespeare Company or some other such nonsense." He leaned in confidingly to Eleanor. "He drove my dearest sister positively mad when he told her he was leaving England to make his own lonely way in the world... and as an actor, of all frivolities! She fainted right then and there at the dinner table when he delivered the horrific news... on her birthday, no less!"

"Sounds like him..." Edmund grumbled. "Why did you lie to me about your name, boy?"

"I... I... I..." Stanley stuttered. "I didn't want anyone to know who I was!" He looked too proud of his lie. "You know, because being a butler is such a lowly calling!"

Eleanor snorted, and Mr. Valov coughed at his loud, uncouth declaration. Several other hovering butlers of distinguished passengers looked over and eyed him disapprovingly.

Edmund straightened his posture. "I'll have you know, boy, that Mr. Valov has been utterly invaluable. He has saved my life and many others' too many times to count, and he still had time to make me breakfast. You can't even fold a bloody shirt. You'd be lucky to be half the man that he is."

"That isn't what I meant." Stanley began looking desperate again.

"Really? Then what did you mean? You'd best say what you mean, boy."

Eleanor squeezed Edmund's thigh. "Darling, you don't need to berate him."

"Don't I? This boy has been wasting our time, *Leo's* precious time when he needs to be focusing on his health, all as some sort of childish game. Do you think it's funny to disrespect a respectable profession, boy?"

"No, sir." Stanley glanced at Mr. Valov, who did not offer him any encouragement.

"Then what explanation do you have to offer?" Edmund demanded. "What in god's name are you doing here? Meddling in our lives for sport?"

"I'm here to become a man," Stanley mumbled.

"Speak up, boy. I couldn't hear you," Edmund ordered like the military commander that he was.

"I'm here to become a man," Stanley repeated as he glanced at Lord Grimby. "Like Uncle Chester told me to be, before I left England to follow my dream. He said actors aren't men, they are leeches, and that I'd best find you, Colonel, to learn what a real man looks like… So I did… and I did."

"You did what?" Edmund asked.

Stanley looked at the floor. "I learned what a real man looks like… and a real woman, for that matter…"

An intense blush exploded in Edmund's cheeks as he realized that Stanley was referring to his earlier intrusion on their marital activities. Eleanor, on the other hand, didn't have the foggiest idea how to manage the situation. She knew that some aspect of Stanley's explanation must be true, given what a wretched liar the boy was, and she hoped that his first successful half-truth was a miniscule sign of improvement on his part, especially after several increasingly idiotic moves in a row.

"Well, now that you've had your show, you can go on your merry way," Edmund said with annoyance. "No offense to you, General, but as our stories all morning have demonstrated, your nephew is the worst excuse for a butler I have ever laid eyes on."

"No offense taken, Colonel. It's a wonder to me that he lasted as long as he did. Six days, you said? I wouldn't have given him five minutes."

"Neither would I," Edmund grumbled.

"It was my decision to keep him on," Eleanor interjected, as she noticed Lord Grimby's confusion at Edmund's offhand comment. "He seemed like he had... er... a hint of potential, and we needed some help immediately with Mr. Valov in his current state."

As an annoyed waiter carrying a wide silver tray with the first course of lunch struggled to get around Stanley, Stanley helped himself to an open seat beside Lord Grimby, and put his napkin in his lap as if he had been invited.

Edmund worked hard to hold in his annoyance at the gesture as the familial relationship with his friendly superior officer now complicated his otherwise scathing opinion of the boy.

"So, Stanley, instead of getting on the steamer to Québec that you told your mother about, you boarded a steamer all the way to India, just to find Colonel Marriner?" Lord Grimby asked as he threw Edmund an apologetic glance.

Stanley glanced at Mr. Valov as he considered his response. "I decided to make something of myself, so that you and Mum could be proud of me. You said that if Colonel Marriner could make a man of Reggie, then he could make a man of anyone."

"Reggie is my son," Lord Grimby informed Eleanor. "He goes by Reginald outside of the family. Your husband commanded him for three long years in the trenches, and saved his life on more than one occasion."

"Reggie was a fine officer," Edmund said as he fought back dark memories. "I was sorry to see him lose his arm."

"He would have lost a lot more if you hadn't carried him out of harm's way, Colonel."

Edmund fell into silence, and Eleanor squeezed his leg, hoping to pull him out of it. Edmund returned his attention to Stanley. "What I don't understand is how someone with as little sense as you managed to find us in the first place."

"Well, I... I knew you were in India, because Uncle Chester and Mum had been talking about you..."

Edmund raised his eyebrows.

"I was using your retirement as an excuse for my own, Colonel," Lord Grimby interjected. "Your descriptions of the tea plantations in Munnar in your letter almost made me want to move there, but my sister pointed out that I have never had the stomach for India. That is how I got started on the path that led me to the idea for the Margaret River vineyard."

"If you're not careful, before you know it, you'll find yourself waking up one morning as the local magistrate," Edmund winked, momentarily forgetting his many woes.

"The thought has crossed my mind, Colonel. And I must admit, it doesn't sound like the worst idea—keeping my mind occupied a bit while I watch the grapes grow, eh?"

"You'd make a fine magistrate, General."

"Well, let's see first if the legends of the Elysium of the Southwest coast are even true. I'm half expecting to step off the boat straight into the desert, to hear the big city journalists go on and on about the woes of the Group Settlement projects. But that's enough politics for now, I reckon."

Edmund returned his attention to Stanley, slightly less testily than he had been before. "So, Stanley, you knew I was in India, you hopped on a steamer to Bombay, and then?"

"Well, sir, when I got to Bombay, I found myself without sufficient funds. I didn't know what to do, so I signed myself up for the first opportunity that came about... and then I was assigned to you by the butling agency. I could hardly believe my luck! It was like God answered my prayers!"

He looked back to Mr. Valov, who was not impressed by the ending of the otherwise decent start to his cover story.

"Well, it was right rotten luck for us," Edmund muttered.

"But, Colonel, I've been trying my best!" Stanley whined.

Edmund shifted uncomfortably as he glanced at Lord Grimby and then prepared himself for conflict. "Sometimes your best isn't good enough, boy."

Stanley looked genuinely disappointed by Edmund's admonishment for the first time since he'd shown up at the Bidkars'. "I learned how to fold your shirts, Colonel. They're all folded on the bed upstairs," he sulked.

"You mean you didn't pack them into the trunks?" Eleanor asked.

Stanley cringed. "I forgot that I was supposed to pack them."

Lord Grimby sighed with resignation. "Stanley, why don't you go on up to my room. I'm in suite number four on the fourth floor. Mr. MacAllister is there, and he will teach you what you need to know."

"Mac?! You want *me* to work for Mac? But, Uncle Chester, he's... he's... he's *our* butler!"

"And now you are Colonel Marriner's butler," Lord Grimby said sharply. "Now go, before I change my mind."

Without seeking Edmund's permission, Stanley stood up and slinked away. Everyone at the table watched him go, and Eleanor had a sneaking suspicion that they each had a slightly different distaste for him in their expressions. Personally, she found his whining, childish demeanor in the face of the most important assignment in the Secret Service (an assignment that he certainly hadn't earned), to be especially reprehensible. Somehow, despite all he'd already seen, he didn't have any inkling of the true power that now surrounded him. The power of life and death, of gods and angels and demons... of beings far more interesting and complicated than fairies or genies or whatever other penny dreadful ideas were swimming around in his head.

As soon as Stanley was out of the dining room, Lord Grimby sighed again. "Colonel, I must apologize. I had no idea that Stanley would take my offhand comment so literally. To be honest, I'm rather impressed that he found you at all. He isn't the most competent boy."

"We've noticed," Edmund shrugged. "But you must understand, General, we need to seek a competent replacement for Mr. Valov. He does not need the strain of training an untrainable fledgling like Stanley. As soon as we arrive in Perth, Stanley will need to go along his merry way, and we will hire someone more capable."

Lord Grimby took a long sip of his champagne, and as Eleanor remembered hers, she did the same.

"Colonel, that is certainly your prerogative, and I don't blame you one bit. I'm sure you have had the patience of Job to put up with him for as long as you have. He has always been... er... shall we say... a special lad. But, I must confess something..." He lowered his voice and leaned in. "There is more going on here than meets the eye."

Eleanor was only more intrigued as she noticed the subtle surprise in Mr. Valov's expression.

"Colonel, we have known each other for a long time, I should say. How many years is it now?"

"Fifteen," Edmund replied. "Since I got you and Lord Curzon out of that mess in Ayodhya."

"Exactly… I'd almost forgotten about that… A right bunch of fools we were back then, the lot of us! Except for you, of course, Colonel, and that Rutherford chap… but that is all beside the point. My point is, Edmund… may I call you Edmund?"

"Please do, Chester," Edmund winked. "It has been too long since someone has requested to use my first name. The trend has gone in the most infuriatingly opposite direction."

"People are asking to call you Colonel?"

"People are insisting on calling me 'my lord,' after an old friend of mine decided to perpetuate a rumor that I am, in fact, the Earl of Easton, wherever that is."

Lord Grimby smiled. "I find it tiresome myself these days. Back when I was a young, egotistical chap with a freshly inherited title, I loved the ring of it, but age teaches us many things, doesn't it, Edmund, old boy? Most importantly, it teaches us what really matters."

"I could't agree more."

"Good. I thought you would, which is why I must offer you a solemn confession, a confession so scandalous that only a handful of people in the world know about it."

Edmund looked around the crowded dining room. "You would like to confess something scandalous here? Amongst this crowd? Wouldn't you prefer to come to our room after lunch instead?"

Lord Grimby chuckled. "That's very thoughtful of you, Edmund. It is almost as if you are no stranger to the confession of scandals."

Edmund shifted uncomfortably. "I have exchanged my fair share of private information."

"As I suppose most men of your age have," Lord Grimby replied nonchalantly. He lowered his voice. "This crowd is not paying any attention to us at all, Colonel. I reckon it would take quite a loud interruption to distract them from Dame Nellie Melba, who is just over there at the corner table."

Eleanor glanced over to where Lord Grimby was pointing, and he was indeed correct. Everyone in the dining room was watching the glamorous opera singer as she graciously signed autographs for a waiting queue.

"Has she been on this ship since we embarked in Bombay?" Edmund asked.

"She's been on this ship since Southampton!" Lord Grimby laughed. "And a right scene she's caused at every port as a new entourage of adoring fans notices her presence. I can't blame them, though. Even at her age, she's a right beautiful woman, if I do say so myself, and I haven't even heard her sing!"

Edmund didn't share his enthusiasm. "How tiresome it must be for her. Can you imagine throngs of people following you everywhere you go? Worshipping you as if you're some sort of idol?"

"Darling, it may have its benefits." Eleanor relegated a memory of the waves of intoxicating power that washed over her at her Dasara appearances. She had to admit, some part of her, not just Uma, had liked it. "She has inspired many thousands of people. Perhaps she finds her elevated position worth the sacrifice."

"I'd rather be anonymously watching from the corner, thank you very much." Edmund drank down his entire glass of champagne in one gulp. "I don't see how anyone could enjoy themselves with an ogling crowd watching their every move."

Lord Grimby followed Edmund's lead, drinking down the rest of his champagne. "I agree with you, Colonel. But now I mustn't let us be distracted any longer. I must confess that Stanley is not really my nephew."

Eleanor glanced over to Leo, who coughed into his handkerchief, hiding his reaction.

"He seemed to think that he was," Edmund pointed out.

Eleanor wondered how Edmund's dubious familial connections with their many dishonest loved ones would affect his reaction to wherever Lord Grimby's confession was going. She couldn't decide whether she'd rather he be more or less inquisitive.

"The truth is... Stanley is my son." Lord Grimby eyed Edmund's reaction, and then Eleanor's. "I had an affair many years ago... twenty-three years ago to be precise, while Rosalind, my wife, and I were living apart... and... well... I've endured a twenty-two-year-long reminder of my folly."

That was not what Eleanor thought he was going to say.

"That is a rather unpleasant way of referring to your own son. It wasn't his fault that you were philandering about," Edmund countered.

Eleanor squeezed his hand under the table. She felt his empathy for Stanley blossoming.

"Truer words have never been spoken, Colonel. But to be completely honest, I wasn't philandering about. I was in love with someone... with a woman who was in love with me. She and I... er... never really lost the spark, even after Stanley was born... or after Rosalind died... but, you see, that's where it gets rather complicated..." Lord Grimby paused to observe their reactions. "You see... Rosalind was never a very happy woman, and when her lover left her..." He paused again... "We had been separated for years at that point, of course... When he left her, she took her own life... and so, you see, it was never really appropriate for me to acknowledge Stanley or his mother after that... and God, what a unique woman she was... she is... because she insisted, just *insisted* that we do what we could for Stanley to have a life worthy of Lord Grimby's son, no matter what it meant for her... and you see, my sister, Louisa, having no children of her own and a rather reclusive husband, agreed to raise Stanley as her own, which was really a wonderful gesture for which I will owe Louisa forever. None of us realized at the time exactly what she was signing up for, as Reginald had been a rather easy child... loud and rambunctious as boys often are, but predictable… but Stanley… Stanley has always been in a world of his own."

"It's no wonder. He doesn't even know who his real parents are," Edmund muttered.

Lord Grimby gestured to the waiter, who swooped in to serve them each another generous pour of champagne.

"I will accept the blame, Colonel, although I don't think that his upbringing is the whole problem. He has been… er… a bit odd since he was a very small child, when his mother was raising him up together with my sister in Bretagne. He had both of them mothering him like you wouldn't believe, until it became clear that he needed a bit more… er… discipline if he was going to make something of himself. That was when I used every connection I had to get him admittance to boarding school in Cambridge, but as you can see… we were too late."

"Perhaps taking him away from his mother at a vulnerable age was the problem, General," Edmund replied. "If I had had a family at that age and I'd been sent off to boarding school, I don't know if I'd ever recover."

Eleanor noticed Edmund cringe slightly as he realized his mistake in admitting his own dubious familial origins, but Lord Grimby didn't take the opportunity to press him.

"Perhaps," he sighed with resignation instead. "Who knows. But Norwenn was very insistent that he not enter a life of service. She wanted more for him, and I couldn't blame her."

"Norwenn?" Eleanor asked.

Lord Grimby cleared his throat. "Yes… Norwenn is Stanley's mother, and she and I are… er… still an item. That is why I fly to Bretagne so frequently. You see, one of my many motivations for this little excursion to Margaret River is to see if the place is sufficiently remote for Norwenn to join me… permanently, without the cream of the crop raising eyebrows left and right. I was hoping that perhaps we might even find a little remote church where we could christen our relationship properly, like we should have done as soon as Rosalind was gone… it was just… I wasn't ready to give up my rank at the time, and a scandal like this would have been a recipe for career and societal suicide. Still, though…" He trailed off into unspoken nostalgia… or perhaps regret.

"So you are planning on marrying Stanley's mother, and still you are lying to him about who his parents are?" Edmund pushed. Eleanor understood exactly why he was so disturbed by the idea.

Lord Grimby pulled himself out of his thoughts. "Well, the boy is already a mess. Informing him that he is the bastard son of a maid rather than the distinguished son of a lord's sister would be rather harsh, don't you think? Besides, if Reggie has no children, the title could still go to Stanley as my sister's son. We do not have any others in line. As my bastard, he will be removed from contention."

"He should know his father," Edmund countered. "He should know who you really are to him. How else will he ever know himself?"

"If I didn't know any better, I'd say you speak from experience, Edmund."

Edmund drank down his entire glass of champagne. "I have a lot of experience, General. More than meets the eye."

Lord Grimby chuckled. "Don't we all, Colonel. Don't we all. Well, I will take your advice under serious consideration, and in the meantime, I must ask you to entertain an idea. Lord knows that I haven't been able to make Stanley useful, but you, Colonel… You made so many boys into men over the years. I must implore you to consider trying your hand at Stanley."

Edmund raised his eyebrows skeptically. "You want *me* to mentor *your* unacknowledged son?"

"I suppose I do," Lord Grimby agreed sheepishly.

"As my butler?" Edmund added.

"Well, Colonel, he's failed at everything else in life. Perhaps he'll find his calling in service. Norwenn would be furious, though, if she heard me say so. She kept him away from every household chore just to make sure he'd be a gentleman… that is, perhaps, part of why he is so wretched at his job so far. But he can learn, Colonel. He is bad at many things, but he is very good at repetition. If you give him a few months, we will both know if he can improve himself."

"General, this task would be too much to ask of us in any circumstance, but Mr. Valov is dying. His delicate health cannot take the strain of managing idiocy on an hourly basis."

Lord Grimby cringed at the insult, but held his ground. "I understand, Colonel, and I of all men, owe you too much already. But, as I step into utter shamelessness on behalf of my son, might I offer you an alternative? While we are both in Western Australia, I will loan you the services of my butler, Mr. MacAllister. He is a loyal and capable man's man with thirty years of experience by my side. He will teach Stanley what he needs to know to be a good butler, and you may supervise and command both of them as you see fit. Simply having a man with your nobility of character to observe will be more than Stanley has ever known, Colonel, because lord knows he didn't get it from me, nor Louisa's tippling recluse of a husband. In some ways, it is a wonder that Stanley is as good as he is with the poor examples of conduct he's grown up with over the years… and that boarding school… oh, don't get me started on the ridicule he suffered there… I hate to think of it…"

Edmund sighed loudly with ambivalence and looked to Eleanor. "Dearest, what do you think?"

Eleanor looked to Mr. Valov, whose expression was completely unreadable as he stared pensively at his mostly full champagne glass.

"I think it is worth a try, darling. Stanley has already made some strides, and if we can train him up, he could become a useful member of our household. Besides, we both have quite a bit of sympathy for those who aren't born into the best of circumstances, don't we?"

"I suppose," he grumbled.

"Then it's settled!" Lord Grimby exclaimed. "Let's celebrate over lunch."

As three waiters served their soup course in unison, Mr. Valov began coughing. With greater and greater urgency, he coughed into the handkerchief until it seemed like he was struggling to breathe, although mercifully there was no blood.

"Leo, are you alright?" Edmund asked concernedly as he patted his back.

Eleanor stood up and rushed to his side, taking his wrist into hers to measure his pulse.

Be careful, Eleanor. The game just became more dangerous, Leo's voice boomed in her head as soon as she made contact with his skin.

Eleanor closed her eyes and feigned counting his heartbeats. *Why didn't you say something a minute ago, before I agreed?!*

What could I say, Eleanor? In front of both of them?

I don't know?! Anything! Who is this MacAllister?

You needn't worry about MacAllister, Eleanor. He has been mute since the war.

Mute? Really? How will he teach Stanley how to be a decent butler?

He will find a way like he always does. It's not as if Stanley responds well to spoken commands.

Then what?!

I was sure you'd realize the connection without me having to spell it out for you.

Well, I didn't! So tell me now! I must look like a dullard counting your pulse for this long!

It's Lord Grimby you have to worry about, Eleanor. He knows nothing of your power, only Edmund's. I've kept him completely in the dark about you.

I don't understand. You told him about Edmund's power?

For god's sake, Eleanor. He already knew. He's G!

"Dearest, are you having trouble finding it?" Edmund couldn't mask the panic in his voice.

Eleanor took in a deep breath, relegating Shakti's power back into the core of her being, and opened her eyes. "Finding what, darling?"

"His pulse."

Eleanor let go of Mr. Valov's wrist, and he took in a shallow breath and stopped coughing.

"No, darling, everything is fine. I was just making sure that it was stabilizing after Leo's coughing fit. You're fine now, Leo, aren't you?"

Mr. Valov nodded his agreement and swallowed a final cough with a sip of water.

Eleanor sat back down and took a sip of her soup, and at her signal, the rest of them did the same.

"Lovely weather they're having down in Perth, I should think?" she said casually. If she had learned one thing in the company of Edmund's aristocratic colleagues over the years, it was that returning the conversation to the weather would bring a swift halt to any more interesting subjects. "Is it spring there? I think I've lost track of the seasons in our little refuge in the foggy mountains."

"I've heard that the weather has been horrid, actually," Lord Grimby replied, taking her pass and running with it, although not in the direction she expected. "Sizzling hot one day, freezing cold the next. Six Group Settlements have folded completely in the last month. I've been asked by Premier Mitchell himself to look into it once I've settled in."

"What exactly is a Group Settlement?" Eleanor asked, only with vague interest. She needed some time to contemplate the implications of Lord Grimby's position as Mr. Valov's one and only superior officer.

"Ah, I'm glad you asked! It used to be called the Soldier Settlement Scheme, right after the war. The gist of the whole idea was to give land to soldiers who were willing to resettle in Western Australia, you know, to fill it up a bit. But a right disaster it's been so far. There's a rumor that half of the farms have already been abandoned! And by soldiers, no less! Fine men, ready to make their mark on the world! There's something strange going on, and I'm going to find out what."

Eleanor wondered subtly if the statement was a hook, a mystery designed to lure Edmund into some sort of shared quest.

"Sounds like you'll have your work cut out for you, General." Edmund did not take the bait, and Eleanor was grateful. "Leo, would you like something else?" Edmund glanced down at Mr. Valov's untouched soup.

"I don't have much of an appetite, Colonel," he said dismally. "Perhaps the next course will be more appealing."

Edmund sighed sadly, and Lord Grimby let the mood stand, as they ate the rest of their meal in polite conversation about the unique culture of Bretagne with which, it turned out, Lord Grimby was especially well-acquainted.

242

By the time the dessert course was over, Edmund and Mr. Valov looked equally haggard, Mr. Valov having worked his hardest to swallow a few bites of chocolate mousse, and Edmund having implored with increasing fervor at each rejected course to ask the chef for something more palatable. Lord Grimby watched their back-and-forth curiously without comment, and Eleanor was ready for a break.

"Darling, I think we'd better get back to our room. We're arriving in Fremantle soon, and we have our work cut out for us repacking our trunks on our own."

"Yes, dearest. You're right." Edmund stood up, but as he leaned down to help Leo up, Lord Grimby rushed to intervene.

"Please, Colonel. I will help Mr. Valov back to his room. You go. It's the least I can offer on behalf of Stanley's deficiencies."

"Go, Colonel. I'd rather not worry about your trunks," Mr. Valov reiterated.

Edmund moved to protest, and then he gave in. "We'll come by your room on our way out. I will ask the porters to collect our luggage so Stanley doesn't leave it on the boat." He reached out his hand to Lord Grimby. "It was a pleasure catching up with you, General. I suspect we'll be seeing more of each other in the future."

"Thank you again, Colonel." Lord Grimby held onto Edmund's hand for slightly too long as he shook it profusely.

"Goodbye!" Eleanor called as she escorted Edmund across the dining room, past the line of Nellie Melba's fans, and into the foyer.

Edmund stopped and looked back into the dining room. "There is something odd about this whole situation, Eleanor."

"Really, darling? What?" Eleanor was both proud and stressed by his correct observation.

"Lord Grimby spent twenty-two years doing everything he could to keep Stanley out of service, then the moment the boy decided to join up, he was assigned to me, the exact person he had traveled across the world to find? Just like that? And now Lord

Grimby has no qualms at all about disobeying Norwenn's wishes for their son's future, even though he loves her and intends to marry her? There is something here that doesn't add up."

"Darling, I think you are absolutely right. What do you think it is?"

Edmund paused as he thought through the details, and then he sighed with annoyance. "I have no bloody clue. I'm really a daft detective, dearest. You know that better than anyone."

"Well, I suppose we will just have to keep our eyes and our ears open for more clues, darling. In the meantime, we'd better get cracking."

She squeezed his hand as she guided him through the long hallway, down the lift, and finally to their suite. As she pushed open the door, she stopped with surprise to observe its pristine condition. Their trunks awaited them fully packed in the center of the room, each with a perfectly pressed outfit laid out for their use. Eleanor loved the Roman styling of the flowing periwinkle dress awaiting her, and she made a mental note to thank Kuveni for her intervention later.

"Jolly good on... Mr. MacAllister?" Edmund said questioningly. "Stanley sure as hell didn't do this. Maybe Lord Grimby's plan won't be so doomed after all... at least for our butling needs..." He sighed sadly. "Leo isn't well. His life is fleeting faster by the day. I think... I think I've finally given up hope for his magical recovery. It's a wretched feeling."

Eleanor rubbed his back, and then leaned onto her tip toes to kiss his cheek. "I know, darling. It is wickedly hard to watch. But I suppose we at least have this time with him, and knowing that his life is fleeting so quickly, we can appreciate him while he's still alive."

"I suppose."

As a deep, resonating horn announced their impending arrival at port, he unceremoniously began stripping off his clothes, and she followed his lead, changing into her new dress without any of the romantic teasing that they had enjoyed earlier in the morning. But, as she rushed into the bathroom to fix her hair and throw on some semblance of makeup, she noticed the copious cleavage that Kuveni had chosen to highlight with her design, and she sighed with stress. Yvie had not seen her since her divine transformation.

With everything else going on, she annoyed herself with her self-consciousness, but she couldn't relegate the base feeling. She had always hated change, especially to her physicality, so much so that she had managed to make it all the way to the autumn of 1924 without cutting her hair short, like every other woman on the planet had (except, of course, for her mother...). And her breasts... for god's sake, she was thirty bloody nine! She was too old for such a change to have naturally happened, but what other explanation was there? She hadn't had to think about facing old friends in a while, except, perhaps for Mae, who hadn't been a particularly close friend to begin with, and who didn't need to dwell on Eleanor's bustline when so many other divine shenanigans had been on display instead. Jesus Christ himself had been there to distract her!

At the memory, Eleanor worked to push back all of her fear and guilt about every aspect of her relationship with D.H., and then Mr. Valov's dire warning echoed in her head.

Lord Grimby is G... Leo's spying boss is here on this ship, inserting himself into our lives... He doesn't bloody know! He knows nothing about Shakti or Uma, and who knows what he knows about Sheranee or Mélusine, or Kuveni, or Monty, or Vibhi... There are too many people to protect! And what am I going to say to Yvie?! It's been too bloody long!!!

Relax, my child. All will be well. Yvie is a worthy confidante. She is the Preserver of your Tridevi, remember? She and Oz will be there to support all of us, and the spies will do what they do.

They almost handed over a ship with seven-hundred innocent civilians to a party of bloodthirsty pirates, just to catch Edmund in an act of heroism.

There is nothing we can do to stop them, Eleanor. All we can do is give them our blessings, so that when the time comes, they can make the right choices on behalf of our entire pantheon. In the end, humans must choose to support us, and it is our sacred duty to guide them to the path of light.

Easier said than done.

Yes, but not impossible. Where there is Shakti's will, there is a way.

Do you really think so? Is there still a way to save Leo?

My child, he is unworthy of our mercy. He has been a great help to you and Edmund, and you are both very generous with your love, but he has done many horrific things. Things that he will pay for mightily when his cycle continues.

How do you know?

The Oracle knows all, my child.

You mean those visions, the ones Vibhi stopped?

Yes, my child. The visions that would have driven you mad. Vanaras have always had a stronger temperament for the Oracle's power than humans have. Vibhishana was right to spare you. Knowing too much is a burden that no one should endure.

I already know too much…

Eleanor took in a deep breath and began smoothing out her frizzy curls into calm ringlets. As she finished up her routine, Edmund called through the door.

"Come look, dearest, we're pulling into port now!"

Eleanor scampered out of the bathroom and joined Edmund on the balcony as the rich cerulean water of the Southern Indian Ocean gave way to sprawling industrial shipyards and docks where workers and machinery chugged away at the port's daily churn of cargo processing.

"Welcome to Oz, dearest."

Edmund coaxed her into a romantic dip, and she laughed with the thrill. It felt like it had been ages since they'd had such a romantic impromptu moment, and despite everything, she reveled in it.

When he let go of her, he sat down on one of their lounge chairs and patted his lap encouragingly. She plopped herself right into his lap, draped her arms around his neck, and kissed him again. They both sighed with contentment.

"I am excited to see Oz and Yvie again," she sighed. "With everything that's going on, I keep forgetting about that important detail."

"To be honest, I've been a bit apprehensive about our reunion," Edmund admitted.

"Really, darling? Why?"

"I suppose some part of me is worried that they were too good to be true. It is so rare for me to encounter people who are so accepting of my many quirks, I suppose I'm afraid that my memories of them are a bit played up into legend. It's really not fair to them for my expectations to be so high."

"Oh, darling, you have wonderful memories of me, and they're all true, aren't they?" She hated that the real answer was no.

"Well, dearest, I have the privilege of a daily comparison for you, to make sure your pedestal never falters."

Eleanor laughed. "Except last year when I almost set the kitchen on fire frying a pie for your birthday."

"I love your faults as much as I love your attributes, dearest. They remind me that you're real."

"I must say the same for you, darling. Wholeheartedly."

He moved to argue, and then he stopped himself. She was grateful that he had learned enough during their nearly two years of marriage to avoid arguing with her about her love of his faults. Instead, he worked his hand naughtily up under her dress, and she sighed happily as they spent the next many minutes teasing each other, until another call of the horn coincided with a polite knock at their door, and Edmund removed his hand.

She hopped up and straightened her dress. "We'd better wash up."

She squealed as he beat her to the bathroom in a blur. "Darling, I haven't seen you do that in almost a year! I wasn't sure you could even still do it!"

"I wasn't either," he admitted as he rinsed his hands in the washbasin, absorbing the water into his skin.

Eleanor washed her hands and then reapplied her red lipstick, using the towel to clean off the copious lipstick that was still smeared across Edmund's lips.

"Aww, I was saving that as a trophy!" Edmund whined.

She was elated that his spirits had soared high enough for him to joke.

"We will just have to play another match later," she winked. "Winner takes all."

He squeezed her bum naughtily as they walked to the door, and then they both straightened their posture and readied themselves to face their project.

As Edmund swung open the door, Stanley stood beside a man who looked about the same physical age as Edmund, with thinning sandy blond hair peppered with streaks of white. Burn marks covered his lower right jaw, leading into an ugly scar on his neck that disappeared into his starched tuxedo collar.

"You must be Mr. MacAllister," Edmund said as he reached out his hand in greeting. "It is a pleasure to meet you. I assume Lord Grimby has recruited you willingly into our little butling school of sorts? Please be honest with me if you'd rather make your escape now. I wouldn't blame you one bit."

Mr. MacAllister shook Edmund's hand with a reassuring smile.

"You look very familiar," Edmund said as he gazed more observantly at Mr. MacAllister's features. "You were with me on the front, weren't you? You were with Reggie and my unit during the first mustard gas attack, when I..." Edmund trailed off with a grimace. "I remember now. I thought you were a goner, but Reggie insisted on going back for you. He was burned carrying you back to the trench, and he couldn't make it all the way on his own..."

Mr. MacAllister shook Edmund's hand more profusely.

"The shrapnel got his arm and your throat before I could get to you…" Edmund looked at the floor, and then he took a deep breath and looked right into Mr. MacAllister's eyes. "I'm sorry. I should have listened to Reggie. I should have collected you myself when Reggie suggested it the first time. You'd both be unscathed."

Mr. MacAllister nodded his disagreement. Then he reached into his pocket and handed him a pre-written note.

You saved my life, Colonel. I am at your service. ~Mac

Edmund sighed with stress, and Eleanor took his hand. "Darling, let him be grateful. You couldn't save everyone, and you made the best choices you could make at the time. If you'd left him out in the line of fire, he'd be dead."

Mac nodded his agreement and reached out to shake Eleanor's hand. She smiled and shook it back.

"We will be grateful for your help getting Stanley here up to snuff. You have your work cut out for you."

Mac laughed and patted Stanley on the head like he was a young child. Stanley threw him a look of adolescent disdain at the embarrassing gesture.

Edmund took in a deep breath and tried his hardest to obey Eleanor's suggestion. "Well, Mac, we must already start thanking you, I reckon. These trunks are impeccably packed. Have you already called for the porters, or shall we?"

Mac looked slightly confused at his statement, and Eleanor suddenly realized the great benefit of Mac's enforced silence. She knew in that moment that Lord Grimby and Mr. Valov must have recognized it too. The truth of the situation began blossoming in her mind. Mac wasn't simply Lord Grimby's butler… by the grace of Shakti, *he* was the new agent actually given the most important assignment in the Secret Service. Brilliant! Finally, they were back to a man who had actually earned his assignment and then some, *and* he was already loyal to Edmund! Her heart sang with relief at the most positive development in their spying games in weeks. Finally, someone had done something right!

"I will call for them," Stanley stepped in. His insertion annoyed her as it broke her out of her secret celebration.

"I reckon Mac here would have a hard time doing it himself," Edmund pointed out.

Edmund's comment filled in more color to the canvas quickly developing in her mind... yes... of course! With his disability, Mac couldn't do *all* of the tasks required, he would need some help... He would need a lackey capable enough to follow his orders but not so independent as to go off and do something foolish on his own! A lackey who wouldn't tell the bloodthirsty bastards at MI-5 a single peep, and if he did, they wouldn't even believe him! Genius! Pure genius! Stanley could be loyal, she was convinced, as long as tight reins kept him aware of the boundaries, and that was where she would come in... and Leo while he could still do it... and even perhaps Lord Grimby himself...

"How many porters shall I call for, Colonel?" Stanley pulled her out of her thought-stream.

As Edmund sighed with annoyance at the basic question, Mac held up his hand, indicating four.

"Four... yes, four... of course..." Stanley mumbled as he rushed across the room to the telephone.

"Mac, you are a godsend!" Eleanor exclaimed.

She kissed him on the cheek, and he blushed and looked to Edmund apologetically. Edmund winked mischievously at her, and then leaned forward and kissed Mac on the other cheek.

"I second my wife's declaration, Mac."

Stanley's eyes bulged at the scene, while Mac didn't look particularly pleased about it himself, but the concierge on the other end of the line wouldn't let him get too distracted.

Mac took both of their hands and pushed them out the door, waving and smiling as he indicated that he would manage the rest of their logistics alongside Stanley.

"Darling, don't take this the wrong way, but I think I'm in love."

250

"I know exactly what you mean, dearest. Now, I believe we have a butler to escort and some wonderful friends to reunite with."

"Come on!"

Eleanor skipped down the hallway to the lift, but as it reached Mr. Valov's floor, they didn't need to fetch him. He stood in the hallway leaning heavily on a cane, waiting for them with a more contented look on his face than Eleanor had ever seen.

"The Helmsworths are waiting for us at port, Colonel. Mac will help Stanley see to the details."

Edmund moved to take Mr. Valov's weight onto his arm, but Leo brushed him off.

"If you don't mind, Colonel, I'd like to walk on my own. A man needs to feel self-sufficient, and you have a beautiful wife who doesn't need an old coughing butler to come between you."

Eleanor wrapped her arm around Edmund's. "Let us know when you want our help, Leo."

"As you wish, Countess," he winked at Edmund tauntingly as he said it.

"I daresay, Mr. Valov, you are an accomplice in a very annoying prank that seems to have stood the test of time," Edmund complained only half-jokingly.

"I would not dare to deny it, Colonel."

They walked slowly side by side down the hallway to the gangplank. As soon as they reached the sun, Mr. Valov took in a deep breath. Eleanor noticed (while Edmund did not) that it was Mr. Valov's first deep breath in over a week.

"The warm sea air will do me some good, I think," he sighed. "And there, Colonel, I believe, are some very worthy friends."

He pointed to Oz and Yvie who stood at the bottom of the gangplank, pointing and waving happily.

"Good lord," Edmund murmured.

Eleanor was bombarded with a flood of mixed emotions as she spied Yvie's pregnant belly prominently visible through the flowing silk of her stylish dress.

"What wonderful news!" Edmund exclaimed.

Eleanor pushed back her emotions. "Yes... it really is wonderful."

As they reached Oz and Yvie, Eleanor noticed a hint of timidity in their expressions, the same hint of timidity she was certain that Edmund was sharing with her, and she finally relaxed.

"Welcome to Oz, mates!"

"Congratulations!" Edmund pulled Oz into a brotherly hug. "Why didn't you tell us?!"

"We thought it would be a better surprise in person!" Oz exclaimed.

"It was." Edmund squeezed him again.

Eleanor leaned forward and carefully hugged Yvie, but Yvie leaned in and squeezed her. "I'm not going to break, Ellie."

Eleanor hugged her tighter. "You're right, of course. I just wasn't ready for the wonderful surprise."

"It was a surprise to us as well... five months ago, that is. I am almost at eight months now. I am keeping my head down and my fingers crossed every minute... but that is enough of that talk for now." Yvie pulled away and looked Eleanor up and down as she eyed Eleanor's cleavage and a wide smile spread across her face. "Do you have news, Ellie?"

Eleanor felt like she'd just been kicked in the stomach. "Not the news you think."

She grabbed Yvie and pulled her into another hug so that Edmund couldn't see her glowing eyes.

I'm not pregnant. I am a goddess. I inherited Uma's power in the cave in Elephanta, and her measurements were part of the package. Surprise?

CHAPTER 17 – ACTS OF GOD?

"*Mon dieu!*" Yvie whispered. "*C'est vrai?*"

"*C'est vrai,*" Eleanor agreed. She continued whispering in Yvie's ear in perfect French. "I can do everything Uma could do… and more."

"Dearest, Oz says the train is leaving straightaway!" Edmund interrupted them.

"The train? We aren't taking a car?" Eleanor asked. "I thought Fremantle was right next to Perth?"

Oz prepared himself to deliver the potentially disappointing news. "Well, you see, we aren't actually living at our house in Perth at the moment. We've been living down in Margaret River. Yvie has been working on establishing a cognac distillery for almost a year there, the first in Australia! But Kate mentioned that you were seeking a house by the sea with warm air for Mr. Valov, and our house in Margaret River has just that, so we told her to send you on down. I reckon she didn't tell you about the change in plans?"

"She did not," Edmund said testily. "She has a bad habit of withholding valuable information."

"Well, as long as it suits you, we're mighty glad to host you, Colonel. We have a lot of tall tales to catch up on!"

"*Viens*," Yvie said as she took Eleanor's hand. "Come. We don't want to miss the train. There isn't another train down to Mandurah until tomorrow."

Eleanor let Yvie lead her, basking in relief that she'd already managed to get her most uncomfortable revelation out of the way. The Helmsworths seemed just as friendly and trustworthy as they'd always been, and as Eleanor glanced over at Edmund, who was chuckling jovially at Oz's first punchline, she could see that he was reveling in the reality of their reunion too.

Mr. Valov walked beside them silently, focusing on using his cane to keep up with their brisk pace. Eleanor was surprised by his competence at the task after almost a week of watching him becoming winded just hobbling across their room.

They rushed past several docks to an imposing passenger train station that looked not as dissimilar to the Victoria Terminus in Bombay as she'd expected. It lacked the gothic detail and the crowded chaos, but its red and brown brick intermixed with a smattering of Victorian flourishes created the distinct look of a grand colonial railway station.

As a whistle blew, Oz guided them swiftly onto the closest train, and Edmund reached down and pulled Mr. Valov up the stairs with one nimble tug.

"Are you alright, Leo?" he asked as Mr. Valov coughed and wheezed, leaning over to catch his breath.

"Perfectly fine," he rasped.

Eleanor took his pulse, while Oz stepped in to assess his coloring. "You're not looking perfectly fine, mate, and I'm an expert now. After Ellie kindly pointed out that I seemed like a fine specimen of a doctor back on the steamer, I took her advice to heart. I finally stopped procrastinating, and just last month I finished up the medical program I'd started before the war. I'm a full-fledged doctor now."

Edmund smiled and pulled him into another brotherly hug. "Congratulations, mate."

"I was so proud of Ozzy," Yvie whispered. "His brothers razzed him the whole time about shirking his duties out on the ranches, but he didn't even do that. He took a term off and went out past the black stump like he always does, and he still finished on time."

"I'm not surprised at all," Eleanor said as she offered Oz a congratulatory smile.

As Leo coughed some blood into his handkerchief, they returned their attention to him. Oz reached forward to poke and prod him with a minor examination, but Leo shooed him away.

"Don't bother with that, Doctor Helmsworth. I am as fine as a dying man can be," Leo reiterated.

Edmund sighed sadly, and Eleanor changed the subject.

"What is our itinerary?" she asked, before Edmund could contemplate Leo's words too deeply.

Oz gestured for them to follow as he glanced at the numbers of each compartment.

"It'll be a long journey, I'm afraid. It's only three hours to Mandurah, but then it will be five hours to Bunbury, where we will spend the night, and then another three hours to Margaret River in the morning. It's not so far to travel, but the train stops in every town with a population greater than ten... they're what we call big cities down here at the edge of the world," Oz winked.

"You came all this way, a two-day trip, just to greet us?" Edmund asked.

"We would have done it a million times to greet such bonza mates, Edmund," Oz reassured him.

Edmund patted him on the back. "We're grateful for the privilege, mate."

"It is our pleasure, really," Yvie chimed in. She pointed at an empty compartment. "Ozzy, perhaps Eleanor and I should take this one, and you men can catch up next door."

Eleanor glanced through the glass of the compartment's closed door into the space that was big enough to seat at least eight people.

"If I didn't know any better, I'd say you were trying to get rid of us!" Oz countered jovially. "Are we too loud for you, Yvie?"

"It will be better for you, Ozzy. You won't have me around to cast doubt on the dubious details of your stories. Besides, Eleanor and I have a lot to talk about." Yvie looked down at her pregnant belly. "A lot of things that you don't want to hear."

Oz became more serious and nodded his agreement. "Come on by if you need anything. We'll be right next door."

Yvie pushed open the door and gestured for Eleanor to sit next to her on the bench facing the men's compartment. Yvie smiled and waved as Edmund helped Leo into the next compartment and disappeared inside, and then she lowered her voice.

"Eleanor, I am so glad you're here. Both of you. You are like a godsend..." She became solemn. "I suppose you *are* a godsend. What a coincidence that your man fell ill when he did. We've needed your help for months now."

"Really?" Eleanor couldn't hide her surprise at the development. "What's wrong?"

"Everything!" Yvie blurted.

"That sounds serious," Eleanor replied with a hint of cheek.

Yvie smiled. "I suppose not *everything*. But things are not going so well in Margaret River. There have been very strange happenings all over town that feel... just... wrong, and Oz's mother has been living with us since his brother's wife kicked her out last year, hounding us incessantly night and day, hemming and hawing over everything she disapproves of, which is *everything*! Oh, Eleanor, she is such a..." she glanced towards the men's compartment and dropped into a whisper, "she is a petty, manipulative, jealous woman! She resents me for stealing Ozzy away from her, and she does so many small, mean things to hurt

256

me. She even knows all sorts of secrets that I've only ever told Ozzy. He swears he hasn't told her, and I don't think he's lying, but when I tell him she must be spying on us, he steadfastly refuses! It is like she enjoys putting a wedge between us! And I'm scared to death that something is going to go wrong with the baby, and she says so many little things to make me more scared, as if I'm not strong enough to be a good mother, and then I wonder if she's right! It's all just piling up!" Yvie's eyes teared up.

Eleanor took Yvie's hand and squeezed it. *Take with you Shakti's blessings, my child, and all will be as it should.*

Yvie sniffled and wiped her eyes with a handkerchief. "I'm sorry, Eleanor. Here I am going on and on about these trivialities, when you and Edmund must have overcome so much since we saw you last. You are an angel now too?"

"I am a goddess," Eleanor corrected her. "I am an avatar, just like Edmund is. Although, I don't have his speed or his strength, and most importantly, I don't have his immortality. I have to be very careful. We had a nice break from trouble finding us, but I think it's back now. It's been a wild week."

"I hope it isn't us."

"You?"

"Eleanor... I prayed for you both to come. I hope we haven't inconvenienced you by summoning you against your will?"

Eleanor smiled. "I don't think it works so literally... at least not when humans do it... I'm sure it's just a happy coincidence."

"Perhaps... It's just..." Yvie trailed off.

Eleanor put her arm over Yvie's shoulder like an old girlish pal. "It's just? You don't have to be shy around me now, Yvie. I'm the same person I was before... at least I feel like I am when Uma is keeping her thoughts to herself."

"You hear Uma's thoughts?"

"When she chooses to share them. It's mostly like having an old friend inside my head, chiming in with her opinion when she fancies it."

"How bizarre," Yvie murmured. "I would say it is unbelievable, but I have seen too much. I had forgotten just how odd your lives are. I hope it doesn't offend you that I say so?"

"Why would it offend me? Our lives are so strange now that I can hardly remember what it was like to be normal. Now tell me what you were going to say."

"I was going to admit something that Edmund won't like."

"Then it's a good thing you got rid of him, isn't it?" Eleanor smiled reassuringly.

Yvie hunkered down for her confession. "The thing is… I couldn't get pregnant, Ellie. For years and years, we enjoyed all the pleasures that being man and wife had to offer, but nothing ever came of it. We weren't sure if it was him, or me, or us, but after five years, we'd given up on the idea of having our own children. Then, five months ago, I started showing, and I had the worst morning sickness! It was horrible! The only thing I craved was cheese, but the Aussie cheese is just wretched, Ellie! I couldn't stomach anything in this godforsaken outback! I lost five pounds before I gained any weight… it was terrifying. I was sure any day it would all fall apart. But now I'm feeling better, and we are getting closer to the finish line."

"But why would Edmund not like this story?"

"Once it seemed like it might actually work out, Ozzy and I talked quite a bit about why it would happen now, after so many years of longing… and we thought that perhaps Edmund had something to do with it… or Kate, or Percy… and now, I suppose… perhaps you did?"

Uma took her hand. *Shakti's blessings are very powerful, my child. Eleanor and I both blessed you in our own ways. I'm glad that you are able to show Eleanor the fruits of our labor.*

"So it was you…" Yvie murmured.

"I see. *That* is the assertion that Edmund wouldn't like… You're right. He wouldn't. You must keep this between us, Yvie. Edmund knows nothing about Uma, and the whole thing is more complicated than you can imagine. It is sooooo, so bloody complicated."

"I will do whatever you ask of me, Eleanor," Yvie vowed. "I never told Oz what happened in that cave, no matter how many times he asked."

"I was lucky that Edmund was distracted enough by his encounter with Ravi to forget that I hadn't given him a good explanation for what we were up to. I suppose he must assume that we were trying to get out. He usually gives me the benefit of the doubt... it makes it easier to lie to him."

"I hated lying to Ozzy," Yvie admitted. "Even just that little lie. I'm sorry you must endure so much, Eleanor."

Eleanor shrugged. "Apparently, it's my destiny. We can't fight destiny, right?"

"*Peut-être...*"

"You say that when you politely disagree." Eleanor switched into perfect French. "I used to think that was literally what the words meant."

"Your French is perfect."

"Languages are one of Uma's most useful talents. I can hear the words coming out of my mouth in French, but in my head, they are still in English. What I don't understand is how she decides which dialect to use. What dialect of perfect French am I speaking?"

"You are speaking my family's dialect, from the well-educated people of Reims. It sounds exactly as if you're my sister."

Eleanor switched back into English. "Hmm... I wonder how she decides which one to use if there are multiple dialects in the room... I hope I'm not using a posh British accent with Edmund accidentally!"

"You sound the same as always in English, Ellie. Lyrical, like a ballad storyteller."

"That is a very flattering description of Scots English," Eleanor winked. "Perhaps too flattering."

"*Peut-être.*"

"Ah ha! You said it again!"

Yvie smiled and continued on in French. "I suppose it is the easiest way to avoid conceding without an argument. Ozzy can argue a rock into the ground if you give him enough time. It is often not worth the effort."

"Edmund probably feels the same way about me."

"*Non!* Certainly he doesn't!"

Eleanor chuckled. "You're probably right. We rarely argue, actually, even when he should be pressing me on all sorts of things that don't add up... I hate it. I wish he would notice all my lies and call me on them." She sighed with resignation. "Do you really believe that you can fight destiny?"

Yvie hissed with discomfort and looked down at her belly. She took Eleanor's hand to feel for a tiny kicking foot.

"I will withhold my judgment until this child is alive and well in my living arms," Yvie replied. "Only then will I decide what to believe."

Eleanor paused to feel as the baby did a somersault.

"It hurts when he's moving around, but it is such a relief that I don't care. I feel like there is a ticking time bomb inside of me that could go off any second. I don't know how other women can be so calm. I'm scared for him, and for me."

"I know what you mean. I'm bloody terrified of what would happen if I got pregnant. I haven't had the heart to tell Edmund so, because he will think that it's his fault." Eleanor realized as she spoke the words that she'd never admitted the truth to anyone before.

"Surely *you* would have nothing to worry about, Ellie?"

Eleanor sighed. "I wish that were true, but I'm still mortal."

"Still, plenty of women survive and have healthy children. It is a fact I must remind myself of every day."

"Edmund's father wasn't human. His mother died giving birth to him, and apparently, the trend is the same for other human women who carry children of Edmund's... er... species."

"Species... what an odd word to use to describe him. He seems so human most of the time."

"I agree. But you have seen the violet plasma that heals him. It is conspicuously not human."

"*C'est vrai.* And I couldn't believe it that day when we returned from the yacht, and he was standing there like a university schoolboy by your side!"

Eleanor laughed. She hadn't thought about the memory in ages. "I couldn't believe it either. I still can't believe I managed to distract him long enough that he changed back without noticing it himself."

"It sounded like you both enjoyed your distraction all afternoon," Yvie winked.

"Youthful vigor and skill are a delightful and rare combination," Eleanor winked back.

Yvie sighed as she returned to seriousness. "Many of the women in my family have died in childbirth, including my own mother when she gave birth to my youngest brother. Oz knows, because I wanted him to be as scared about it as I was, but I regret telling him now. He's become very protective... too protective, for a modern sheila like me."

"That's why I've avoided telling Edmund about the real risks. He brings up the idea of children every few months now, testing the waters. I keep telling him that I'm just not ready for what it will mean for our relationship if we're distracted by the demands of a child, but he's accepting my argument less and less. He thinks it's because I'm scared of having a child like him, and it breaks my heart. But I can't bring myself to tell him the truth."

"Ellie, might I ask *why* Edmund thinks it's a choice? Certainly you aren't using protection every time as a married couple?"

Eleanor snorted a laugh. "You're right. To be honest, we've never used anything. Not once. Edmund's guardians informed me the first time we ever talked that there is some sort of telepathic element to the process for them—his people can't conceive unless we both want it to happen. I've been very careful to keep my opinion solid on the matter, since he is surely longing for a baby every time we're together, and so far, it's worked."

"But he doesn't know very much about his people, does he? Does he know that? Did Kate or Percy tell him?"

"No. He doesn't even know that. They don't tell him anything about himself. Instead, they tell me, and I get to come up with the lies. I told him the first time we were together that I was on a magical pill that would keep me from conceiving."

"A pill!" Yvie exclaimed. "That would be magic!"

"Edmund usually doesn't know enough about the real world to challenge my lies, especially around women's issues. The first time we met, he asked why any woman would be expected to give up her job upon marriage."

Yvie laughed. "No wonder he stole your heart."

Eleanor took in a deep, relaxing breath. "God, I've missed you, Yvie. We shouldn't have waited so long to visit."

A young steward who looked about as old as Stanley pushed a beverage cart up the aisle to the door and knocked. Yvie waved him in.

"Afternoon tea will be served at three o'clock in the dining car, Mrs. Helmsworth," he informed them with an Aussie accent even thicker than Oz's. "Would you like to start the afternoon off with an aperitif?"

"An aperitif before tea?" Eleanor laughed. "I think we've come to the right country!"

"I will have Perrier, please," Yvie said as she glanced down at her belly. "But my friend here will have a brimming glass of your finest cognac."

"I should've guessed that any friend of yours would have good taste," he said approvingly as he poured Eleanor a glass of cognac so large that it looked almost like a fish bowl.

"Ned, this is Mrs. Marriner," Yvie introduced them. "She is the wife of the distinguished colonel who is laughing with my husband in the compartment next door. Ellie, Ned and I know each other well, from all our travels to and fro between Perth and Margaret River."

"The best darn customers I've ever had!" Ned replied. "Although, it's no wonder, with them being such classy people. I reckon, Mrs. Marriner, that you and Colonel Marriner must be fair dinkum classy too."

A wave of mischief washed over Eleanor. "Actually, my husband is Lord Marriner now. He is the Earl of Easton, and I am the Countess of Easton."

"*C'est vrai?*" Yvie asked with surprise. She dropped into French. "That is a story you must tell!"

"*Peut-être*," Eleanor winked.

"Lord Marriner..." Ned murmured as he thought about the name. Eleanor couldn't tell what about it was interesting to him. "It's like the whole royal family is heading on down to Margaret River! I didn't think it was that important of a place..."

"The whole royal family?" Eleanor asked.

"There's another lord just down the hall," he pointed. "Lord Grumble or something. He's so important that he has *two* butlers!"

"Oh yes... him," Eleanor muttered.

It suddenly occurred to her that Lord Grimby's cover story had been concocted long before they stumbled upon him in the dining room at breakfast. He had uncovered through his network of spies that the Helmsworths were no longer residing in Perth, and he had known that they were headed for Margaret River before they did. He had seamlessly planted his excuse for tagging along beside them before even Mr. Valov knew that's what he was doing. Leo was right. The game had just become more sophisticated.

"So you know him?" Ned interrupted her thoughts. "I should have figured you'd all know each other."

"He and my husband served together in the military," Eleanor explained to Ned and Yvie simultaneously. "His name is Lord Grimby, not Lord Grumble, and those two butlers are actually ours." She leaned in confidingly and whispered in French to Yvie. "I will tell you the whole story later."

She was glad to put off concocting another web of lies to keep Oz and Yvie in the dark about the burgeoning unit of the Secret Service that was descending upon all of them in perfectly civilized silence a few compartments away.

"Hooley-dooley, then you must be fair dinkum important too," Ned said as he topped off Eleanor's cognac to the very brim of the glass. She giggled at the outrageous size of the pour.

"You have no idea... Now, Ned, when you pop by the compartment next door, be sure to serve Lord Marriner a similarly generous pour of the cognac... In fact, give him the rest of the bottle, care of Lady Marriner, and give them a second bottle to share between the three of them."

"Doctor Helmsworth will be sure to appreciate it!"

"I see you've built up quite the reputation," she winked at Yvie.

"You know Ozzy. He always loves chatting up everyone who matters, like Ned here. And Ned has been kind enough to go out of his way to order our favorite spirits from France. We travel so often, they have a special stash just for us."

"It's our pleasure, Mrs. Helmsworth. Not every railway company gets to serve the head of Helmsworth Ranches."

"*C'est vrai,*" Yvie winked. "It is true."

Ned leaned in confidingly. "Did you know that Dame Nellie Melba herself is on the train today? She's heading all the way down to Albany to do an opera recording in a cave! Can you imagine? Seems like it would be mighty dreary for a dame like that to have to sing in a cave, but she seems to think it's a fine idea. Something about the acrostics."

Eleanor laughed. "I think you mean the acoustics."

"Do I? Whatever it was sounded fair dinkum scientific to me."

"*C'est vrai?* Nellie Melba?"

"I saw her with my own two eyes!" Ned confirmed. "She even ordered melba toast!"

"She was on our steamer from Bombay. Apparently, she'd been on it since England," Eleanor added.

"*Quelle surprise.* This will be perfect for Ozzy's surprise birthday! I'm planning a nice family dinner for the Saturday after next. I wonder how much we would have to pay her to come and sing. Surely she must have a price."

"I didn't realize it was Oz's birthday!" Eleanor exclaimed.

"Thirty-two! Another reason for the impeccable timing of your arrival. Oh, Ellie, it will be wonderful to have you there with us to celebrate." Yvie took a sip of her Perrier and then paid Ned with a generous tip. "If you have the time, Ned, please send Nellie Melba our best. There will be more in it for you if you can get her to come on by our compartment for a little chat. Tell her Lady Eleanor Marriner, Countess of Easton requests it."

"Yes, of course, Mrs. Helmsworth!" Ned agreed.

"And don't forget to give Lord Marriner his cognac!" Eleanor added.

"I won't, Lady Marriner, I won't! Have a right bonza day, ladies!"

As soon as Ned left them, Yvie clinked Eleanor's glass with her dainty glass of sparkling water. "I'm so glad that you're here, Ellie. You couldn't have chosen a more perfect time."

Eleanor took a long, savoring sip of the cognac, working not to spill it on her dress.

Yvie laughed. "Ned is a bit too enthusiastic sometimes. Perhaps you can drink what you'd like and give the rest of it to Edmund. It would be a shame to waste it."

"Don't worry about me. It turns out Uma's temperament is unaffected by alcohol, and so neither is mine these days. There has been more than one occasion when I've wished dearly that I could get blurry-eyed, but it hasn't happened. I don't even feel tipsy anymore."

"I've missed it myself these last many months. Oz's mother keeps telling me to drink to settle my nerves, but I can't stomach it at all. I don't think alcohol is good for pregnant women. Do you?"

"Probably not. Anything that makes you sick when you're not pregnant should probably be avoided when your body is working so hard."

"Thank you, Ellie! I have had no voice of reason to stand by my side this whole time, and Ozzy doesn't count. He's agreed with me on absolutely everything since we realized I was pregnant, and I can tell that he doesn't actually agree with me when he says he does. It has made it impossible to have a real conversation when all of these strange things are happening!"

"Tell me about them. I will be as rational and honest as a goddess can be. It will be a nice change for me too."

Yvie squeezed Eleanor's hand affectionately. "Thank you, Ellie. It all started... well, I don't really know when, actually. I suppose in some ways it was already going on when we bought our vineyards in Margaret River. The prior owner had given up on his plan to make a winery. He lost his shirt on the project, I think. He left for Melbourne the day we signed the papers, which was a bit foreboding... as if he wanted to be out of town when we discovered the truth of it all. We learned after we'd signed that the weather had become much more unpredictable in the last few years, and that he hadn't been able to grow enough of a crop to pay for the lovely house he'd built... and it is a lovely house, Ellie. You'll love it. It is two stories and has a shaded porch that wraps all the way around it. The whole house is made of local karri, which is a lovely hard wood, really very unique. The aborigines believe it's sacred—something about their ancestors' spirits inhabiting the trees. If I'd known about their beliefs, I wouldn't have used it, but the house was already there, so Oz convinced me to just enjoy it."

"It sounds like our house in India. We bought it to preserve the jungles beyond the tea plantation, and it is also made of a beautiful local wood that should not have been cut down. I suppose I shouldn't be surprised that we share the same taste."

"No, neither of us should. I have always envied your fashions, and this one is just as lovely as the others." She felt the silk of Eleanor's skirt.

"Perhaps we should ask Kate to make you one," Eleanor winked.

"Kate made this? It makes sense now… I'd wondered how you'd gotten such fine silk in post-war Turkey. Is it real silk? Or did she conjure it like the Roman armor?"

"I don't think those two things are mutually exclusive, but perhaps we can ask her how it works when we see her next, which, if I know her, won't be too far off."

"I hope you weren't mad at her for not warning you about my condition."

"Did you tell her when she called?"

"She saw for herself when she popped into our bedroom in the dead of night to inform us of your plans to visit."

Eleanor chuckled apologetically. "She doesn't have the same sense of modesty (or manners) that humans have. I hope she didn't give you too much of a fright?"

"To be honest, it was a huge relief that it was her. I've been very jumpy for months now, not just because of the baby. At first I was afraid that she was Miro."

"Miro?"

"He is the local aboriginal witchdoctor, for lack of a better term. He is really more of a priest, but I can't say that in front of any of the white people. They are certain that everything he does is for show, just to scare us."

"But you think that it isn't just for show? You think he has real power?"

Yvie sighed. "I don't know. I don't dismiss it as easily as they do. How could I? I have seen what you and Edmund can do. There is a lot of power in this world that isn't discussed in the Bible."

"And a lot of the Bible is actually about us." Eleanor felt a pang of anxiety at the risky revelation, but she let her positive experience with Mae, and her confidence in Yvie pull her along.

"*C'est vrai?*" Yvie asked. "It is interesting…"

"I probably shouldn't discuss the details. There are a lot of secrets that aren't mine to tell."

"That isn't so much what I meant… you see, I was thinking about what it means for the things that have been happening here… There have been too many acts of God, Ellie. That is what the white people and the aborigines have both been calling the disasters. First, there was the tidal wave last autumn."

"A tidal wave?!"

"*Oui.* It hardly even made news outside of Australia. Out of nowhere on a fine, warm day, a huge wave came and killed twelve people who were playing at the beach down below the cliffs. It was a beautiful beach, with soft, white sand… and now everyone has been too afraid to go back."

"I don't blame them."

"Me neither. We haven't been back either. That day, we watched the tide go out too far, too fast, almost to the horizon. There were fish just flopping around on the empty seabed. It was very surreal, very unnatural. Like someone had opened the plug of the bathtub, and the sea was just draining away. We could see it all from the house, which overlooks the sea. We knew something was wrong, but we didn't realize what it meant until it was too late. If only we'd known… seven of the deaths were children."

Eleanor squeezed her hand. "You couldn't have known."

268

Yvie shrugged. "I tell myself that, but it doesn't help. It only makes me more worried about the baby, as if God will come for him for payment of those children's lives we should have saved."

Eleanor looked her in the eyes. *God doesn't work like that, Yvie. I promise.*

Eleanor brushed Yvie's hair out of her eyes, and Yvie sighed with relief. *I'm so glad you're here, Ellie.*

Me too. Eleanor smiled reassuringly. "Now, tell me what happened next. That was not the only disaster?"

"A couple months later, just last winter, there was a fire in the karri forest. It was an ancient forest, Ellie. It had been there for thousands of years, but when a Group Settlement went in right beside it, the next week the forest caught on fire. It burned for weeks. The local council blamed the settlers for having done something foolish to set it, but they swore up and down that they hadn't done a thing. In fact, they weren't even there! They'd gone to the cattle fair in Busselton, and I saw them there! It couldn't have been them."

"Forest fires do happen down here, don't they? I read about the forest fires in New South Wales last year."

"They don't usually happen in winter," Yvie explained. "And it had otherwise been a very wet season. It didn't make sense that it would burn like that. In fact, the following weeks were ravaged by storms, and by the end of August, just this last August, there were terrible floods. I thought we might lose all of our vineyards when Margaret River flooded, and I was ever so grateful that the investment was more of a hobby than a necessity."

"Really? You moved all the way down here for a hobby?"

"You sound like Oz's mother," Yvie humphed. "She thinks that I should have stayed in Perth, knitting and waiting by the window for Oz like a lost puppy."

"She and my mother have a lot in common. We shouldn't introduce them," Eleanor winked.

269

"The truth is, the whole endeavor has been Oz's kind effort to keep me busy while he has to go off and see to the cattle. He goes away all summer, every summer, while I am left to sit around alone waiting for him. It was compounding my boredom and sorrow at not having any children to keep me company. This way, at least I have something to focus on, and it is something that I always dreamed of doing that I never would have been allowed to do on my own in France as a woman. I even hired a man whose family has made cognac for centuries and brought him over here to help me. I treated it like a real business, but, I suppose like the bloke before us, I haven't been able to make it work."

"Yet," Eleanor corrected her. "You haven't been able to make it work *yet*. How long has it been? It hasn't even been two years since we saw you last."

"We signed the papers a little over a year ago, and the weather has been wild ever since. So, I suppose you're right that my expectations were too high. It can take decades to get a distillery established, and there are no grapes to buy, so we can only distill what we are able to grow... it was perhaps a foolish idea to begin with. Still, I'm not sure what we're going to do now with the baby coming. Ozzy still needs to talk to his brothers about it, because it is his turn to go out to the ranches in December, but neither of us want him to go. The town needs him more than ever now, too, because the doctor quit and moved back up to Perth after the tidal wave, so Ozzy has been filling in unofficially ever since. I was helping out until my feet were so swollen I couldn't stand long enough to tend to the patients."

"I'm sure something will work out. You are both very resourceful."

"I suppose... but that wasn't even the end of the disasters, Ellie. Thirteen people have died in the last month alone from spider and snake bites. It makes the whole thing feel doomed."

"Thirteen people? In what vicinity?"

"Just in Margaret River!"

"What's the population of Margaret River?"

"About a hundred."

"Blimey."

"I suppose it's seventy-five now after the two disasters…" Yvie trailed off pensively but then caught herself. "It is not unusual for someone to occasionally have a problem. Australia has more poisonous snakes and spiders than one can count, and they are common enough that the locals all know what to watch out for. I almost got right back on the boat when Oz gave me my first tutorial on how to identify a redback and warned me never to sit straight on the dunny in case it climbed up from inside to bite me, but in five years living here, I'd never known anyone personally who'd been bitten… until a month ago. Oz thinks that the trend is because of the weather—that somehow the fire and the floods brought the buggers out of hiding, and he might be right, but it just feels… wrong."

"Thirteen people does seem like a lot."

"It isn't just the number. You see, Miro's mother, Darana, was an aboriginal priestess, and she died suddenly about six months ago… not long before the tidal wave, now that I think about it. A horse threw her, not far from our house, on the dirt road between two of our vineyards. The aborigines were very upset about it, and I think they blamed us, although I'm still not sure what they thought we did to get an old horse to throw her."

"Sometimes people just need someone to blame for a tragedy."

"Yes, that is what we thought as well. And the whole situation was made worse because the aborigines worshipped her a bit, as a connection to Heaven or something of that nature. They believed that she had a lot of power… power to control the weather to give them good crops, power to connect them to their ancestors through rituals, and all sorts of other things that I don't really understand myself. She was a very important person. When she died, we offered to give her a Christian funeral, but Miro wouldn't have any of it. He organized the other aborigines to help him put her body up in a very tall karri tree, and they just let the vultures devour her."

"That sounds very… unusual."

"It isn't so unusual for the aborigines. The white Christians of Margaret River were up in arms about it, but I told Oz that if the Hindus who are as civilized as Ravi Bidkar can burn their dead, then leaving a body in a tree isn't that different, and we shouldn't be the ones to judge."

"That was very enlightened of you. But how do you think this is connected to the spiders and the snakes?"

"This is where Oz disagrees with me but he won't say so," Yvie admitted. "When Darana died, Miro inherited his mother's title as priest, but whereas she had been very discreet about her role in the aboriginal community, which was wise, since many of the white people in town wanted them to be relocated farther inland anyway, Miro was just the opposite. He began walking about town covered in body paint in a very native-looking feathered loin cloth (none of the other aborigines in the area wear traditional clothing anymore, so it looked odd, even to them), and he would do things… strange things… like following people around whispering chants and banging painted sticks together… that quickly made everyone in the village—white and aborigine— uncomfortable. Oz thinks he was just doing it to scare us, as some sort of prank, or perhaps as a way of trying to get us to leave the area, but I think it was more than that. Three of the people he followed were bitten, two by redbacks, and another by a death adder."

"Does Oz really think it isn't related? That seems rather close-minded of him."

"Well, six of the people who were bitten had no encounter with him at all (at least that we know of), and he's been doing this little ritual for months now. He tried it on me and Oz once a few months ago as we were strolling in the vineyards, until Oz threatened to punch him in the nose. He slinked off like a scolded puppy, which is part of why Oz thinks it's all just a show. He pointed out that if Miro were really some sort of witchdoctor, he wouldn't have cared about Oz's minor threat."

"Was there any other connection between you and the others that you've seen him bothering?"

"None! Other than that we mostly knew each other, but everyone knows each other in a small town like this, and one day he even followed a Portuguese migrant who had come into town looking for work. The man had absolutely nothing to do with our town at all. Another day, only shortly after my priest had arrived from Perth, he followed the poor boy around for hours, until he became so uncomfortable that he went back to the church and grabbed his Bible so that he could use it to dispel any evil. I don't think the poor boy realized that he'd signed up to be a missionary in the bush."

"You have a priest?" Eleanor asked with surprise.

Yvie blushed. "I hope it doesn't bother you? Or Edmund?"

"I suppose I just hadn't thought of you or Oz as particularly religious. Usually, religious people aren't so accepting of people like us, especially people like Edmund."

"Those people do not follow the right scripture. Jesus himself said to love thy neighbor. I have told Oz the same many times, since he is not particularly fond of religion, but it is not really a choice for me. My great-grandmother promised God that she and her children would remain Catholic if she survived the revolution, and my family has not forgotten her promise. I suppose it was just ingrained in me, and with three of my brothers killed in the war, I felt like I understood how she'd felt when she'd made that promise."

"I know someone who would be quite glad to know that his scripture is being used in such a positive way."

"*C'est vrai?*" Yvie suddenly became self-conscious, and Eleanor realized that with the new intel, she needed to be more careful about what she shared.

"Perhaps I will introduce you at some point, but don't let me distract you from your story. Your priest went back to the church to get his Bible to fight off Miro's witchcraft?"

"Yes, that is how Father O'Donnelly described the situation as well. Oz was not pleased at all when he used the word, and neither were the other villagers. It reiterated their belief that Catholics are too superstitious."

"The other villagers aren't Catholic?"

"Not one! Not even Monsieur Guy, the man I brought from France to manage the vineyards. Even he is a protestant! I had to petition the church three times to send a priest down from Perth, because Margaret River wasn't big enough to have a Catholic parish, but when I paid for a church to be built, they finally sent us the youngest priest they had. He is practically a schoolboy still, fresh out of seminary in Ireland, ready to save the world. He is a blessing and a curse, but he drives Oz's mother positively mad, since she doesn't consider Catholics Christian (and tells me and Oz so often), and so I invite him around for dinner as often as possible."

Eleanor smiled. "That sounds like something I would enjoy doing to my mother."

"You will get to witness the theatrics for yourself. He is around for dinner almost every night now, not just to torment her, but to keep my nerves at bay about the baby. I hate to prove them all right about my superstitions, but it all still feels... wrong."

"You have good instincts, Yvie. Perhaps there is something strange going on. When we get to Margaret River, I will keep a hawk's eye out for trouble. Maybe together we can figure out what's actually going on."

Yvie pulled her into a tight hug. "You are a godsend, Ellie."

A light tapping at the door of their compartment pulled them out of their moment. A regal woman in her mid-sixties, dressed to the nines, stood outside their compartment, eyeing them curiously.

"Do you know her?" Yvie asked.

"That, *mon amie*, is Nellie Melba."

"*C'est vrai*?! Nellie Melba?!"

Eleanor pulled open the door.

"Are you Lady Eleanor Marriner, Countess of Easton?" she asked.

Eleanor blushed. She hadn't really been prepared for someone so famous to refer to the aristocratic moniker that Mr. Valov had secretly legitimized for her during her honeymoon. "I am."

"I don't know you, do I? I'd remember a head of hair that ginger. Is it natural?"

Eleanor smiled. "It is. It has been quite some time since anyone has asked. In India, people were so overwhelmed by it, they didn't know what to say."

"You lived in India?"

It was the first time Eleanor had heard the phrase in the past tense, and she realized at that moment as a flash of her Dasara celebration rushed through her mind, that it was going to stay that way. Shakti had found a way to keep Edmund from learning her secret.

You must trust in her plan, Eleanor.

Eleanor fought back a moment of melancholy as she focused on Nellie Melba's question. "Yes, I've lived there for two years, in a lovely hilltown near Munnar in the south, surrounded by tea plantations."

"Then we don't know each other?"

"I'm afraid not, but we know you, Dame Melba. I'm sure that's a common occurrence for you."

"Yes, yes. That is always how it is when I travel. I'm a diva, after all. Are you alone?"

"We are," Eleanor replied, more intrigued by the woman's unreadable demeanor.

"Do you mind if I take a seat?" She sat down across from them without waiting for their response. "It's wonderfully quiet here. My compartment is a zoo at the moment. Some lordship and his two butlers insisted on joining my entourage, and the younger of the two men simply wouldn't stop talking. That kind of chaos is bad for the voice, and for my temper."

"Lord Grimby?" Eleanor asked.

"How did you know?"

"We're acquainted," Eleanor explained. "My husband served with him in the military, and also commanded his son on the western front in Belgium."

"Oh, I'm sorry."

"Yes, it was quite bad for him. The shell shock was unbearable, like it was for most."

"Was he killed in action?"

"No... er... he's in the compartment next door, actually. It has been too long since Yvie here and I caught up, just us girls, and so we left the men to themselves. Is there something we can do for you?"

She laughed. "This silence is enough for now. That boy steward insisted that I come and say hello to the Countess of Easton, and as it has been ages since anyone has dared to insist that I do anything, and as that young butler couldn't stop butchering Shakespeare's sonnets, I decided I'd oblige him."

"It is a pleasure," Yvie chimed in as she reached out her hand for a friendly shake. "I'm Yvie Helmsworth."

"Helmsworth?" Nellie Melba replied with an eyebrow raised. "So you're the French tart who seduced Australia's most eligible bachelor?"

Yvie looked down at the floor, struggling for a response, and Eleanor reeled from the surprising insult.

"I haven't heard that phrase in many years," Yvie replied with such grace that Eleanor's respect for her soared. "That article was published the day my youngest brother was killed in action... fighting alongside an Aussie regiment. Oz and I got the telegram while the newspaper was still wide open on the dining room table taunting us."

Nellie Melba reached forward and patted Yvie on the knee. "They only say such things because their lives are so empty. They only wish they were you... or me. If I had listened to every tirade thrust upon me by a jealous opponent, I never would've become who I am. I didn't mean to offend you. I remember the article because it was published alongside one of the most scathing reviews of my repertoire I've ever read. I kept it for posterity."

"Oz almost bought that newspaper just to fire the editor. I convinced him that there were much better things to do with his money... with our money. We'd only been married a week when the article came out. That was when I realized what I'd really signed up for."

"Notoriety is the bedfellow of fame, and neither are very good lovers," Nellie Melba informed her.

"Perhaps that's why we got along from the get go, Yvie," Eleanor said as she took in another long sip of her cognac.

"Are you notorious as well?" Nellie Melba asked curiously as she noticed the outrageous size of Eleanor's drink for the first time. "I don't think I've ever heard of you."

Eleanor smiled. "No. But we share a distaste for bad lovers."

They all laughed, and with the tension broken, Nellie Melba moved the conversation along. "Well, I'm in fine company. Who would've thought on a train down to the bush, I'd enjoy the companionship of a Scottish countess and an Australian queen. Perhaps my manager wasn't as foolish as I thought he was, concocting this cockamamie cave recording idea at the very edge of the civilized world."

"A queen?!" Yvie snorted.

"You're as close as we get down here, Mrs. Helmsworth. Why do you think every woman in the country was so jealous of you?"

"A few days with me in Margaret River would cure anyone of that misconception. Speaking of which... I hate to ask... but if you happen to still be here week after next, it is my husband's birthday, and it would be a wonderful surprise for you to oblige us with a song or two. We used to listen to your records all the time on the gramophone in the field army hospital. It kept everyone focused on something beautiful in the face of such horrific gore."

"You were in an army field hospital? The papers conveniently omitted that fact."

"Yes. We noticed. I was a nurse, as was Ellie. Oz, my husband, was a medic; that is how we met. He spent more time carrying injured men from the front than actually treating them inside the hospital, since he wasn't a licensed doctor yet, but we all saw our fair share of carnage."

"I simply can't fathom it. I did several benefit concerts at recovery hospitals in England during the war, and those men were in brutal condition after they'd already been cleaned up."

"They looked much better by the time they got to England," Yvie confirmed. "When they came into the hospital in Reims, some hardly looked human anymore."

"Those men owed you their lives, I reckon."

"Some of them probably did," Yvie agreed. "But not just us. It took many people to keep them going. Edmund... Eleanor's husband... and men like him did more than their fair share too. Colonel Marriner was awarded the Victoria Cross for valor."

"He doesn't like to talk about it," Eleanor jumped in. "Please don't mention the war to him. He can only think of the men he didn't save."

Nellie Melba sighed. "Such tormented, honorable men make opera characters seem so flat. When is your husband's birthday?"

"Saturday after next."

"I'll be there. I will tell my manager to expect my return to Perth a few days later than scheduled."

"*C'est vrai?!*" Yvie exclaimed as she clapped her hands excitedly. "Oh, Dame Melba, you must stay with us! Our home is much nicer than the local inn. Please say that you will!"

"I'll discuss it with my manager when I arrive in Mandurah. I'm giving a concert there tomorrow evening."

"*C'est parfait!*"

"Now, tell me, as I rest my eyes, which of my arias did you listen to in the army hospital, and which ones did the poor injured men like most."

"*Mi Chiamano Mimi* was everyone's favorite," Yvie began.

Eleanor sipped her cognac and sat back, listening to Yvie's lyrical descriptions of her time in the army field hospital intermixed strangely with her commentary on various opera plots, and as she accepted a wave of comfy satisfaction at her lovely reunion with a wonderfully worthy friend, she closed her eyes and dozed off to the gentle rumbling of the train.

A mystery at the edge of the world awaited.

CHAPTER 18 – THE BUGGERS

Edmund squeezed Eleanor's hand on one side and Mr. Valov's on the other as their final train ride of the long journey screeched into the hamlet of Margaret River. As the chug-chug of the steam engine came to a belabored halt, a few red brick colonial buildings that had somewhat failed at their aim to emulate the twee look of various historical villages back in England, with gingerbread flourishes slapped onto what were otherwise square blocks, were lined up along the railway tracks, flanked by dirt roads that had been spruced up at some point with rose bushes which had since grown out beyond their manicured intention and then dried out and collapsed into pathetic thorny corpses. Eleanor found the evidence of their failed struggle both beautiful and disconcerting. She didn't like that Uma's affinity towards death and dilapidation had worked its way into her taste.

It is a natural requirement of life in our universe, my child. Someone must manage it.

I don't have to like it.

Suit yourself.

The journey had remained mercifully uneventful, with Nellie Melba taking her leave at their first stop in Mandurah, and Lord Grimby stepping in to rescue them from Stanley's jibber jabber, insisting instead that Mac take the empty seat in their six-person compartment for the long journey to Bunbury and thence, finally, to Margaret River after a night spent tossing and turning in an uncomfortable bed (about a foot too short for Edmund) at a small inn right next to the station, for which Oz and Yvie had profusely and proactively apologized.

"Welcome to our bustling metropolis, mates!" Oz declared. "I warn you, there's too much going on for any one man to handle. You'll have to choose what you want to do, and then resign yourselves to missing out on a flurry of other fun activities." He winked.

As the train finally stopped, only three empty, dusty cars awaited them outside of the one-room brick station. There wasn't a person in sight, and a tumbleweed blew past them in the bluster of the train's wake, finally catching itself in the craggy arms of one of the dead rose bushes. Across from the station was a small, cracked-earth plaza that would have been cute if anything other than dirt had adorned it. Beyond it, a small white chapel in a distinctly French, incongruently flourished style marked the edge of town. It stood before a thick row of eucalyptus trees, which waved their branches in the warm breeze in languid movements that almost looked like they were swaying kelp flowing with the underwater tides. Beyond it, only dried grass in empty flat fields dotted with bleating sheep stretched to the hazy horizon. It looked much hotter than Eleanor had expected it to be in spring, and Uma sighed with satisfaction at the delightful twist.

Lord Grimby barreled up the aisle and opened the door to their compartment without asking. He pointed out the window. "I reckon one of those cars is mine. I will be heading over to a house I rented by the sea now. I've given Mac the address and the

telephone number. Give me a ring if you need anything…
including a swift lashing for Stanley here."

He laughed, but Stanley did not find the comment funny in
the slightest as he stood behind his father in the aisle with his
shoulders collapsed in defeated posture, staring at the floor.
Eleanor glanced at Edmund. He also didn't find the comment
funny.

"I reckon you must be Stanley?" Oz said, standing up to shake
the boy's hand. "I hear you'll be staying with us while Mac trains
you up to be Mr. Valov's replacement? You've got some big shoes
to fill."

"Yes, sir. So I hear," Stanley sulked.

Oz patted him on the back. "Don't worry about it. We all start
out as a young pup at some point. The first time I tried to ride a
horse, I fell right off the back of her. My father wasn't sure I'd ever
get the hang of it, but slowly and surely, she and I mended our
fences. We were together for twenty years working on the ranch,
and now she's chomping away in our pasture as we speak enjoying
her retirement."

Stanley's posture improved slightly. As the train came to its
final stop, Edmund helped Mr. Valov up and positioned his cane
for him. Mac swept in to balance him, and Eleanor was once again
grateful for his presence.

Oz helped Yvie, who threw Eleanor a knowing glance at his
coddling posture, and Eleanor took Edmund's hand.

"Westward ho!" she declared jokingly as they piled off of the
train.

Oz guided them to the second of the three waiting cars, but
as Eleanor looked around the empty streets for a chauffeur, she
realized there wasn't one.

"Colonel, I reckon you can drive this beaut?" he asked. "We
have three cars for when my brothers visit. That way we don't fight
over who gets to drive, although only two of these are ours. The
other's back at the house."

"I'm keen. It's been too long!" Edmund agreed. "Have these been sitting here since you left for Perth? It's a wonder they're all still here!"

Oz laughed. "Welcome to the bush. We just leave the cars parked right here at the station when we travel. Since we're the only ones in town who own a car, it's pretty clear whose they are. It works out unless the local boys get it in their heads to take a joy ride, but usually they get them back in fine condition."

"We really are at the edge of the world, aren't we?" Eleanor murmured.

"*C'est vrai,*" Yvie whispered. "More than you know."

"They've never had such crowded company, General!" Oz laughed as Lord Grimby poked his head into the window of the third car, which was noticeably less interesting than Oz's matching Fords.

"They just left the windows wide open!" he exclaimed. "The inside looks like it's been through a haboob!"

"What's a haboob?" Yvie whispered to Eleanor.

"I think it's a dust storm, like they have in the deserts of Africa."

Oz shrugged. "It would've looked like that eventually. Probably the dust flew in when the bloke you hired drove it down from Bunbury. It's been so hot this spring, he probably had the windows open for the cool air. You're down under now, General. Nature works its way into every little crevice of everything you consider civilized and then some. You'd better get used to the dirt."

Lord Grimby rolled his shoulders. "I will take that under advisement, Lieutenant. I'm sure that after mastering the Sudan and the Thar desert, Western Australia shouldn't be a problem."

Oz laughed. "Famous last words, General."

Lord Grimby saluted only half-jokingly, and then pulled open the door, sat right down in the drivers' seat, and pulled a small key out of his breast pocket. Eleanor watched curiously as he opened the locked dashboard, but as he reached inside, he squealed like a schoolboy and scrambled out of the car, flailing his hand about.

"General? Are you alright?" Edmund asked as he approached.

"Something bit me!" he exclaimed. "And it really bloody hurts!"

"*Mon dieu*," Yvie whispered. "See what I mean, Ellie! Danger at every turn!"

Oz, Yvie, and Eleanor all approached Lord Grimby as he danced around, wiggling his fingers.

"What do I do?!"

He looked genuinely concerned for the first time since she'd met him.

"Calm down, General. It was probably a redback. You should never reach right into a dark compartment like that. They love to hide in nooks and crannies."

"Good lord," Lord Grimby murmured. "Those almost *were* my last words!"

Oz patted him on the back. "It's going to hurt like hell, but with proper attention, we can hopefully keep you alive. You'd better come with us, though. You shouldn't be alone. We'll give you some ice when we get back to our house, and then I will keep an eye on you until the symptoms pass."

Edmund left them and walked around the car, leaning in the opposite window, and sticking his hand right into the glove compartment.

"Darling?!" Eleanor exclaimed. "What are you doing?!"

He gathered the spider onto his hand and held it up before his eyes, looking straight at it. Yvie gasped, and Eleanor held in a squeal. It was not a redback.

"Strewth," Oz whispered as he went over to take a look at it. "That's the biggest tarantula I've ever seen!"

Stanley collapsed unconscious onto the ground. Mac kneeled down, slapping his face.

"I've got good news for you, General," Oz said matter-of-factly. "Tarantulas look worse than they are. I don't think they even have venom. They're just fair dinkum ugly, and their fangs are sharp."

"I don't know, I think she's rather sweet," Edmund said as he walked the tarantula up to the closest tree and released her onto the lowest branch. Eleanor felt a burst of love that she hadn't known in quite some time at his surprisingly calm reaction to the entire episode.

As Stanley awoke and sat up, Lord Grimby looked down at him and sighed. "Remember what I told you, boy. Colonel Marriner is a real man. You should follow his lead. Now, if I'm not under doctor's orders, I'll be happy to take my leave now."

He sucked up his pain and nerves and sat back down in the drivers' seat.

"General, don't you have any luggage?" Oz asked.

"It's coming in two days," he grumbled. "Stanley failed to get it onto the train this morning. That goes for your trunks too, Colonel."

Edmund sighed with annoyance, but as he looked down at Stanley's miserable state—brushing the dust off of his dirty butler's tuxedo and stumbling around in a feeble effort to stand up, while Mac watched him struggle without even offering a helping hand––Edmund's anger dissolved. "I'm sure we'll make due."

Lord Grimby muttered a hasty goodbye and sped off, leaving a cloud of dust in his wake.

"Shall we?" Eleanor suggested. "I'm starving."

"We'd better get going then. Our cook is in the hospital in Perth, so I will be our chef for now," Yvie said with a resigned sigh. "Oh, and our butler and housekeeper have stayed with her, so I suppose I will also be our maid."

"Oh no! What happened?" Eleanor exclaimed.

"When she wakes up, hopefully she'll be able to tell us," Yvie shrugged. "We found her passed out on the kitchen floor four days ago, and since we were coming up to greet you anyway, we decided to take her up to the best hospital in Western Australia instead of the smaller one in Bunbury."

"Well, we'll all help out in the kitchen, and if we're really lucky, none of us will burn it down," Eleanor reassured her, only half-jokingly. "Let's keep Edmund away from the stove."

"Someday, I might be a master chef." He lowered his voice, "perhaps with a few hundred years of extra practice."

Edmund held open the door to Oz's second car for Eleanor, and she slipped inside, but as he made his way around the car, Eleanor squealed.

"Edmund?!" she called. "Edmund, please come quickly!"

He slipped into the driver's seat, and she felt his heart skip a beat. "Dearest, why are you scared?"

"Look!"

She pointed at the center consul, upon which an enormous redback was sitting, looking right at her.

In one swift move, Edmund scooped it up, but before he could offer a humane position for it on the tree branch beside the tarantula, his eyes turned black, and he smashed it in the palm of his hand. Gooey white venom oozed out of its carcass.

"Thank you, darling. Perhaps you can check the car for any others?"

Edmund glanced around, and then ran his fingers along the floor of the back seat, then the cushions, then all around the front seat, until he was satisfied that the danger had passed.

Oz moseyed on up to the window, and paused nervously as he noticed Edmund's black eyes.

"Everything alright, mates?" he addressed his question to Eleanor.

"My white knight just saved me from the wildlife. You'd better check your car too before Yvie gets inside," Eleanor suggested as Edmund held up the smashed spider.

"This place is just plagued with the buggers now," he muttered. "Yvie! Don't get in the car yet!" he called as he rushed to stop her from opening the door.

"Darling, take a deep breath and get yourself under control." Eleanor stroked Edmund's back soothingly. He wiped the spider carcass on the outside of the car door, and then he reached into his pocket for a handkerchief.

Before he could take another calming breath, Mac pulled open the door behind him and pushed Stanley inside, and then walked around to take the seat behind Eleanor.

"Darling, *now*," Eleanor hissed. "Say your mantras."

Edmund whispered his mantras, pausing as Oz borrowed Mr. Valov's cane and began smashing it into the passenger seat of his own car.

"Blimey, I think he must have found one too," Eleanor whispered.

Mr. Valov approached them slowly, each step more belabored than the one before it. He leaned on the car as he addressed them through the open window. "Stanley and Mac, you will ride with Oz. I will ride with Yvie in the back seat of this car."

Oz broke the news to Yvie simultaneously, and Eleanor watched as a moment of annoyance quickly morphed into acceptance as Oz pulled another redback carcass out of the car on the end of Mr. Valov's cane.

Yvie rushed as fast as her heavily pregnant state would allow to catch up with Mr. Valov, while Mac dutifully got out of the car and then pulled open Stanley's door to ensure his compliance with Mr. Valov's orders. He gestured to Stanley to go ahead, and then he saluted to Edmund and escorted Stanley over to Oz's side. Stanley shivered and whimpered as Oz wiped the spider carcass on the ground.

"*Mon dieu*, it is like we are living in a penny dreadful," Yvie muttered. Mr. Valov helped her into the back seat and then hobbled around the car to sit beside her. "*Allons-y, Edmund.* Let's go home."

As Oz got into the car behind them, and Mac pushed Stanley into the back seat as if he were a prisoner being arrested, Edmund pulled out onto the empty road.

"Do you know how to get there?" he asked Yvie. As he glanced at her in the rearview mirror, Eleanor, Leo and Yvie cringed together as they noticed that his eyes were still black.

"I do, Edmund. Go straight onto the western road out of town. You will drive five miles on it before you need to turn." Eleanor loved her even more for her skilled overlooking of his frightening malady.

"Darling, everything is okay now. Why don't you try to relax a bit," Eleanor suggested as she rubbed his back.

"I can't shake this odd feeling," he admitted.

"What feeling, darling?"

He glanced at Leo in the rearview mirror. "It's too silly to admit, even in friendly company."

"Darling, we all love you. Please, tell us what you were going to say."

"It was as if... it was as if the redback was hunting you. I was going to rescue it, as I had the tarantula, but then... it felt as if that wouldn't do the trick. I *needed* to kill it to keep you safe."

"It was just a spider, darling. It wasn't a man. You have nothing to feel guilty about. Look at what a beating Oz gave to his!"

"It is not guilt I'm feeling... it is hard to explain. It is as if I am still on alert. As if the danger hasn't entirely passed."

Yvie threw Eleanor a nervous look.

"But, darling, you searched the car already for more spiders."

"No, it isn't another spider that worries me... I mean... I suppose it could be, but the fear isn't so specific. I just feel... I feel as if there is someone or something watching us. Something evil." He glanced back at Yvie in the rearview mirror. "I'm sorry, Yvie. I hope dearly that we haven't just brought some great evil down upon you. There are some people like me who aren't good like I am."

Eleanor put her hand on his as he shifted gears. "Darling, I promise you, the woman from Hyderabad is not here. She wouldn't dare attack us again."

"You said yourself, and Mr. Johnson confirmed, that she is still alive, Eleanor. This feels… similar. It feels similar to how it felt when I was… er… trapped in that dungeon and she was doing the evil things that she did." He glanced self-consciously at Yvie.

"A dungeon? How horrible!" she said supportively.

"Do you think that there is someone following us right now?" Eleanor asked.

She worked hard to keep her own anxiety under control, as Edmund had never once in all of their time together given into his instincts in such a way. She closed her eyes, and let Uma momentarily come forward.

Do you know what he's talking about?

I do not, my child. I feel nothing out of the ordinary, except your fast-beating heart. Do you feel anything unusual?

Eleanor paused and took in a deep breath. *I can feel Yvie's fear and Mr. Valov's impending death. Both of those sensations are very strong. Maybe they are masking what Edmund is feeling.*

Perhaps. We should be very careful, Eleanor. We must protect ourselves, and our allies.

Agreed.

"I don't know." Edmund finally took in a deep breath, and his eyes dissolved back into their human hazel. "I suppose I might just be tired after the long journey. Everything seems a bit more overwhelming when I'm too tired."

Eleanor squeezed his hand. "We will all keep on guard for anything unusual. You don't have to do it alone, darling."

He finally relaxed. "Yvie, have you picked out a name yet for the baby?"

She and Eleanor were equally startled by the question. "We have agreed not to do it until the baby is born. It is just a silly superstition, but I will feel better following it all the same. But tell me, Edmund, how is it that you went from commanding the Household Cavalry to being a colonial magistrate in India? Eleanor didn't have time to tell me the story, all she said was that you quickly tired of being a retired artist."

Eleanor loved her skilled deflection.

"Well, that is an interesting story, actually…" Edmund began.

Eleanor threw Yvie a look of gratitude in the mirror and sat back, listening to Edmund tell his overly-modest rendition of the tale, until they finally pulled up to a long driveway entirely surrounded by fledgling vineyards with only the tiniest hints of spring grapes beginning to grow.

"It's lovely, Yvie," Eleanor murmured as they pulled up to the wide, green lawn of a beautiful colonial house that looked strikingly similar in architecture to their house back in Munnar, but with a beautiful marbled brown hue to the unpainted wood. Eleanor loved the gingerbread details of the awnings that looked much more at home than the similar ones had back at the brick train station. "How did you get the lawn so green? It's like a desert oasis!"

"The well has been very generous," she explained. "After our wet winter, I couldn't bear to watch the beautiful green grasses whither, so we we've been watering the lawn almost every day for the last month."

"Hello, what on earth?" Edmund murmured as they pulled around the side of the house.

Eleanor almost snorted as she spied the largest private plane she'd ever seen, and then she gasped with excitement as Ovid and Pliny barreled across the lawn to greet them.

Edmund almost hopped out of the moving car, but he threw on the break as he remembered his passengers.

"Eleanor, how did they possibly get here so fast?!"

Eleanor grinned as Kate Marriner and Lord Blakeney rushed out of the back door of the house and down the stairs to greet them. She didn't even care what a dangerous game they'd chosen to perpetuate.

"Welcome to Oz, my darlings!" Kuveni exclaimed. "What took you so long?!"

CHAPTER 19 – CHEZ HELMSWORTH

Edmund jumped out of the car and kneeled onto the grass as Ovid and Pliny pummeled him, licking his face and barking excitedly.

"You missed me? Well, my friends, the feeling was mutual!" He rubbed their ears and laughed as they continued on with their voracious licking.

Kuveni and Mélusine rushed to greet them, and as Eleanor helped Mr. Valov out of the car, Mélusine swooped in and steadied him. She grabbed his wrist, closed her eyes, and he gasped in a deep breath of relief. Kuveni hugged Eleanor, blocking Edmund's view of the exchange.

"Thank you," Mr. Valov whispered to Mélusine. "The last dose wore off hours ago. The pain has been almost unbearable."

"Don't mention it, mon chéri," she replied. "I will be staying close by for now."

"That isn't necessary," Mr. Valov protested. "Surely someone with your power has more important things to be doing."

"You are not wrong, but I am not staying here for you. There is something wrong here. I can feel a dark energy brewing, but I haven't been able to identify the source. I will stay until it is sorted."

"Edmund noticed the same."

"Did he? His instincts must be improving. Eleanor, did you or Uma feel it?"

Eleanor pulled away from Kuveni. "Neither of us can feel much of anything at the moment. The energy of Leo's impending death is too distracting."

He glanced over at Edmund and sighed sadly. "I'm sorry, Eleanor. I wish I could have stayed with you longer."

"Don't waste your energy with regrets." Eleanor took a deep breath, pushing back her emotions.

As Kuveni noticed Yvie's uncomfortable ascent from the back seat on the other side of the car, she rushed around to help her up.

"Now, now, Yvie dear, you only have a few short weeks left before your load will be lightened. Hang in there, my girl. I applaud every human who can stand carrying for nine whole months."

"Do your people not carry so long?" Yvie asked curiously.

"We can't fathom nine months," Kuveni confided. "It is why we so rarely pair up with humans. Sometimes hybrid children require a human gestation period, and none of us wants to do that."

"How long is your... eh... gestation period?"

"Usually a few hours," Kuveni replied nonchalantly.

Yvie laughed and then threw Eleanor a questioning glance as she worked to decide whether or not Kuveni was joking.

"Blimey, that isn't true for Rakshasas, is it?" Eleanor whispered to Mélusine. "You must have had time to get Edmund's mother out of the palace?"

Mélusine glanced over at Edmund, who was still engaged with the dogs, and then lowered her voice. "Six weeks is normal for full Rakshasas. Hybrids can take anywhere between six weeks and nine months. The longer the gestation, the less Rakshasa the child will be, or so we have come to believe. Hybrids are very unpredictable."

"What an odd word to describe people… as if they're peas in some science experiment."

"Is there another word in English, ma chérie? Sometimes my language is too literal."

"I suppose most of the words are derogatory," Eleanor admitted. "That word is better than most."

"*Attention*," Mélusine whispered as she noticed Edmund approaching them.

"I must thank you again for reuniting me with my loved ones," he said as he shook Mélusine's hand and then pulled Kuveni into a hug. "Did you really fly these dogs all the way from India in that plane?"

Kuveni laughed. "What else would we have done, dear boy?"

"I suppose not much else could get you here so fast. Is this the famed plane I've heard so much about?" Edmund walked over to inspect its unique design. "It is quite different from anything I've seen the military use. Did you design it yourself? It must be wonderfully spacious for its passengers."

"And it is temperature-controlled," Mélusine replied as she ran her hand along the smooth, cold metal of the shell. "I had to add some of my own inventions to make it up to my own high standards. I studied the latest technology, and found it to be too limited for my ambitions."

"So you're an inventor?" Edmund asked with genuine curiosity. "I suppose I haven't thought much about what you do with your time when you aren't rushing to my rescue."

"I suppose you can say that," Mélusine replied. "I've acquired quite a bit of engineering expertise over the years."

"Yes… yes, I suppose you must have… It was your brilliance that modernized my house in Basingstoke, I reckon?"

Mélusine was startled by his astute observation, but she relegated her reaction instantly. "Yes. You provided quite a challenging project, but I was glad we could get it done in time."

Edmund patted her on the back. "Thank you, Percy. I never told you how grateful I was for all of your help with our wedding. It made the day perfect, even with that freak storm. Both of you were positively indispensable."

"It was our pleasure entirely, Edmund." Eleanor could see a hint of relief in Mélusine's expression to have the little truthful exchange couched amongst their many lies.

"I've been wondering, actually..." Edmund paused as he glanced between Kuveni and Mélusine. They both stiffened in preparation for his next question as he moved to speak several times, stopping himself before the words spilled out.

"Please, mon chéri, speak your mind," Mélusine encouraged him.

"It was a silly question," he demurred.

"There are no silly questions with us," Kuveni reassured him.

"I was going to ask... if you two are an item."

Eleanor guffawed, and Mélusine didn't appear to know what he meant with his euphemism. Kuveni, however, grabbed Mélusine's hand and planted a wet kiss on her cheek.

"My dearest boy, you have caught us red-handed!"

"An item?" Mélusine asked. Kuveni whispered in her ear, and Mélusine threw her a look of fierce annoyance. "You're saying we're lovers, Kate?"

"There's no point in denying it, Percy," Kuveni pushed the farce along. "Edmund has noticed that we argue like an old married couple. Is that what gave us away, my dear boy?"

"You are always together... and you have a certain familiarity."

"You are not wrong." Kuveni put her arm around Mélusine's shoulders. "We know each other very well, Percy, don't we?"

"I know more about you than I care to think about," Mélusine replied with an eye roll. "And I have no doubt that you know too much about me."

Oz's arrival in the second car distracted them from their banter. Stanley's eyes bulged as he spotted the plane on the lawn, and Mac leaned his head out the window to take a long look for himself. Next to Oz in the front seat, sat a very young priest with strawberry blond hair and freckles.

"No wonder it took them so long. They must have picked up Father O'Donnelly on the way," Yvie murmured, more to herself than to anyone around her. She approached the car and greeted the priest with a handshake as soon as he stood up, while Oz rushed out of the driver's seat and whisked them both swiftly away from it.

"What's wrong, Ozzy?" Yvie asked nervously.

"There was another redback! He almost got my hand when I was shifting. Father O'Donnelly here saved my life when he smashed it dead with his Bible!"

"*Mon dieu*, it really did ward off evil!"

Oz leaned in. "I'll admit, Yvie, it's starting to feel like the buggers are after us."

"God will protect us," Father O'Donnelly reassured them. "*The lord is my shepherd, I shall not want...*"

Oz gave away a hint of embarrassment as he glanced at Edmund and then interrupted the psalm. "Uhhh... Father O'Donnelly, you haven't met our distinguished guests yet!" He guided him right up to Edmund. "This is Colonel Edmund Marriner, and his wife Eleanor. They are some very special friends... *very* special."

Edmund shook his hand politely. "This, uh, father, is my cousin Kate, and her... er... husband, Percy," Edmund introduced them.

Eleanor almost snorted at his lie. She hadn't anticipated having to support a web of lies from Edmund! She worried her brain might finally lose track of all of the many untrue details.

"What brings you here, father?" Kuveni asked casually.

"I've come by for lunch, and to give mass to Yvie, since she missed it with her travels this morning. Would you like to join us?"

"Oh, no thank you. I take my preaching directly from the source, and only when I'm in dire straits. But, Yvie dear, be sure to collect one of the cases of Margaux that we stocked into your cellar for your communion. The blood of Christ should have an excellent nose and a fine finish."

Father O'Donnelly was speechless.

"Thank you, Kate," Yvie said self-consciously.

"Come!" Kuveni clapped her hands. "Lunch is ready. Percy and I prepared it just over there under the ancient karri tree."

"You helped prepare lunch?" Father O'Donnelly asked Mélusine as he eyed her muscular male form sporting her flamboyant purple suit.

"Yes, mon chéri. In our household, we do not care very much about human gender, do we, Kate? We find it unnecessarily constraining."

"There are many things about humanity that we find too constraining," Kuveni agreed.

"I see... a *modern* marriage..." Father O'Donnelly looked like he was working hard to hold his tongue, and Eleanor found this particular farce refreshingly entertaining to watch.

"Modern is a word rarely used to describe us, but to each his own." Kuveni offered him a friendly wink and moved the conversation along. "Now come, my darlings, before the spiders find their way into the silver platters. I do love dining outdoors, don't you? Especially on a fine day like this one."

As they followed Kuveni to the shade of a massive eucalyptus tree just on the edge of the dusty, fledgling vineyards, a thin woman with blonde hair tied back into a bun, clad in a conservative navy

298

blue dress, came around the deck from the front of the house and waved.

"Welcome to Margaret River!" she called. She looked about Edmund's age, and as she walked spryly down the steps, Eleanor wondered momentarily if it was possible that she was old enough to be Oz's mother.

She walked straight up to Eleanor and greeted her with a friendly handshake. "You must be the Mrs. Marriner I've been hearing so much about. I am Mrs. Helmsworth, Jackie's mother…"

"It's Oz, Mum," Oz hissed with annoyance. "No one calls me Jackie anymore."

She didn't acknowledge him at all and kept talking, "… but as I have been deposed from my throne by the younger Mrs. Helmsworths, you may call me Sheila."

"Pleased to meet you, Sheila. Please call me Eleanor," Eleanor said politely as she shook the woman's hand. She noted the subtle jab against Yvie thrown in alongside the cheerful tone.

"I'm Colonel Marriner, but you can call me Edmund." Edmund offered her his hand to shake, and Sheila loosened her wrist into a gesture intended to be dainty, but that instead came across as a classic limp fish.

Edmund winked mischievously at Eleanor, and then pulled Sheila's hand into the archaic Victorian hand kiss that had puzzled Eleanor the first time they'd met. "It is a pleasure to meet you, Sheila. Now we can see where Oz got his golden hair."

Sheila looked equally confused and flattered by his odd greeting. "A lucky bloke my little Jackie was, too. His brothers got his father's hair—dirt brown like the floor of a dunny."

"Mum," Oz hissed.

"Hello, Father O'Donnelly," she said as she brushed off her son's protestation like he was still a little boy. "Warding off evil again, I take it? Shall we light some incense and chant in Latin?"

"Bloody oath, he is," Oz replied on the priest's behalf. "He just smashed a redback in the car with his Bible."

"Oh posh, we've had spiders in Oz since before Captain Cook."

"There were three waiting for us in the cars when we got off the train, two redbacks and a tarantula," Yvie joined in.

"Jackie, how many times have I warned you not to leave the cars parked out in the open like that. It's a wonder they weren't filled to the brim with death adders and a family of wombats!"

"Yvie, my dear girl, was that your stomach growling?" Kuveni interrupted. "Come, my friends, we must give this woman some food!"

She guided everyone to the dining table.

"Where did this come from?" Sheila asked with puzzlement.

Kuveni laughed affectedly, as if the question was unreasonable. "Never you worry. We will take care of everything while your cook is indisposed. Percy and I are gourmets."

"But the table?!"

"Can you believe the bloke renting Lord Grimby his house didn't want it? He said it was too big! Now, in my personal experience, there is no such thing as too big of a table, but his loss is our gain. We collected it this morning when we went out to the market," Kuveni explained without missing a beat.

"How long have you been here?" Edmund asked.

"Oh, since yesterday morning," Kuveni replied. "We wanted to have enough time to unload the items we brought for you from Munnar. Besides, your dogs were going mad without you. The change of scenery seems to have done the trick."

Edmund looked down and patted Ovid's head as the dogs trailed right behind them.

"How lovely," Yvie whispered as they approached the banquet table. A white linen tablecloth fluttered in the breeze, held down by massive silver platters and formal place settings.

"You did this too?" Sheila asked.

"All in a day's work. What fun is dining if it isn't an experience?" Kuveni replied.

Kuveni lifted up the closest lid to reveal a rich orange burbling curry that looked very familiar.

"What the hell is that?" Sheila's impressed tone at the formality of the banquet morphed into disappointment.

"It's curry," Kuveni explained. "Edmund, dear boy, this is your favorite, is it not? It is the one Percy instructed the staff to make for your wedding. We thought it would be nice for everyone here to taste it."

"Smells scrummy to me," Oz said as he sat right down at the head of the table. "We'd better eat while it's still hot."

The group followed his lead, with Yvie taking the seat beside him, and his mother taking the seat at the opposite end of the table. But as Stanley moved to take a seat beside Mr. Valov, Mac grabbed him by the shoulders and redirected him into a standing position up against the tree. Stanley moved to argue, and then stopped himself and settled in looking miserable.

"You are a godsend, Colonel, to bring your staff," Sheila said as she put her napkin on her lap. "We've had no help since Mrs. Jenkins carked it in the kitchen four days ago."

"Mum, she didn't cark it," Oz whispered. "Be respectful. She's worked for us for years."

"She just hasn't carked it *yet.* There is a plague in Margaret River!" She waved her finger melodramatically as she spoke. "That is, at least, what the Catholics at the table think, isn't it? Always looking for a plague to bring god-fearing protestants back to the gilded old church of yore."

Yvie threw Eleanor a knowing glance.

"Well now, what makes better lunchtime conversation than plagues?" Kuveni said cheerfully. "But we must be eating to enjoy a lunchtime conversation, don't you think?"

She lifted up several more lids, revealing a steaming biryani, stacks of roti, and a huge mound of spiced sautéed vegetables.

"When did you make all of this?" Sheila asked. "Have you been slaving away silently in the kitchen all day? I didn't hear a single pot slam! Perhaps it's a blessing that Mrs. Jenkins isn't around."

"Mum!" Oz hissed.

"Percy is the most graceful chef on Earth," Kuveni replied. "And Edmund, there is more of everything back in the house, so there's no need to be shy. I know that you and Oz like to compete for the most platters consumed."

"Ready, set, go!" Oz declared jovially as he dug right into the biriyani. "We're among family now, so I reckon there's no need to pretend we're in a stuffy British first-class dining room. Don't you think, mate?"

"I couldn't agree more," Edmund said happily as he relaxed and began serving himself up an inhuman portion of vegetables.

As Eleanor served herself, Father O'Donnelly stared at the foreign food with puzzlement, and Kuveni lifted up the lid to the silver platter before Mr. Valov, revealing a full English breakfast.

"Eat what you can, Leo," she whispered. "But our dearest Edmund will notice if you don't eat a single bite."

Mélusine worked her way around the table to Yvie's side and whispered into her ear in French. "Ma chérie, a little birdie told me that you have been missing a taste of home. If the spicy food is too much for you in your weakened human state, I thought perhaps you'd prefer something more familiar." She lifted up the one remaining silver platter, and Yvie gasped.

"*Mon dieu*, how did you know?! You have answered my most selfish, silly prayer!"

Five huge hunks of French cheese awaited her, alongside two full baguettes that still smelled as fresh as baking bread. Yvie ripped off the end of the closest baguette, grabbed the cheese knife, and spread an oozing, aromatic blob of soft cheese until there was more cheese than bread in her bite, and then she sighed with pleasure as she chewed it. Oz's mother watched her and then moved her attention to the burbling curry, both of which produced a grimace of disapproval.

"How did you get stinky French cheese here?" Sheila asked.

"We have friends in high places, ma chérie," Mélusine replied as she took the empty seat beside Yvie and helped herself to her own bite of oozing cheese. "It is best to just accept our many offerings. Asking too many questions will produce unsatisfying answers, just ask Edmund."

"Their lips are sealed," he agreed as he finished off his first serving and moved immediately along to the next.

"Colonel, I think you left your manners in India," Sheila said as she watched him scoop up a bite of curry with a roti in the graceful style of his childhood in Hyderabad.

Edmund was unbothered by her observation. "If I'm going to win the contest against your son, I must be able to use all of the tools at my disposal. Eating Indian food Indian style is quite an advantage, don't you think?"

"Then eat as you will, Colonel. We're all friends here. Even Yvie has decided to entertain us by eating like a child," she said as she watched Yvie pop another bite of bread into her mouth.

"It is the traditional French style," Yvie replied.

"Well then, it's lucky I will be around to teach this child some old-fashioned manners."

"Mum," Oz hissed. "Not another word."

Father O'Donnelly coughed as he took his first bite of spiced vegetables, and then Mr. Valov whispered something into his ear. Father O'Donnelly nodded gratefully, and began scooping portions of Leo's eggs and beans onto his plate. Edmund eyed the transaction, but Oz re-engaged him in a friendly race through a plate of biriyani.

They settled in, and Eleanor finally relaxed as Kuveni skillfully engaged Oz's mother in a conversation about why Australia was the best of the British colonies, throwing in details every so often about her castle in Somerset that she was just dying to return to, and about her husband Percy's many silly forays into invention. Eleanor was grateful that the meal's web of lies wasn't hers, and she had to concede a hint of respect to Oz's mother as the woman dutifully ate the spicy curry with only a few muffled coughs here and there.

Kuveni finished up her lunch and skipped into the house to bring out another heaping, steaming platter of biriyani for Edmund, but as she returned with a heavy silver cauldron in both hands, the loud crack of a gunshot echoed in the distance.

Both dogs went wild barking.

Boom.

"Was that a *shotgun*?" Sheila exclaimed.

Boom.

Boom.

"Three shots," Yvie whispered. "Who would be shooting?"

Edmund's eyes turned black, and Oz hopped right out of his seat.

Eleanor grabbed Edmund's thigh under the table and whispered into his ear. "Darling, close your eyes and say your mantras."

As Edmund followed her orders, Mac approached Oz and silently offered his help in accompanying him to investigate.

"Sshhh!" Eleanor hissed at the dogs. She threw them both a commanding look, and they whimpered and crawled under the table beside Edmund, licking his hands.

"This might take three men," Mélusine said as she stood up and placed her hand on Eleanor's shoulder. *Stay here, ma chérie. Make sure Edmund's malady remains a secret, and protect these defenseless lambs. Call Sheranee if you must. We will tell Edmund we brought her in the plane.* "Edmund, stay here with the wives and children."

"There aren't any children here," Stanley pointed out.

"I meant you and our boy priest, mon chéri."

As Mélusine joined Oz and Mac at the edge of the closest vineyard, the crunch-crunch-crunch of frenzied, running footsteps approached them.

Boom.

Oz ran down the path towards the fourth shot, and Mac and Mélusine followed.

Frantic shouting in French between Mélusine and an older man ensued, followed by Oz shouting at someone else.

Boom.

"Are you a bloody drongo?" Oz exclaimed angrily.

The shuffling of footsteps came closer. As the men returned from the pathway, Mélusine carried a shotgun in one hand and escorted a skinny, elderly man clad in dirty overalls with the other. The two of them were arguing in heated French whispers.

Oz and Mac flanked a young aboriginal man as they escorted him, dressed exactly as Yvie had described him in a colorful feathered loin cloth paired with body paint on his bare chest and arms, back towards the group under the karri tree.

The old man began shouting again, this time as an entreaty to Yvie.

"Who was shooting?" Sheila demanded.

"Guy? Were you shooting at Miro?" Yvie asked as she slowly stood up and approached him.

"It's him! He's evil! You were right, Yvie!" he implored in French. "The plagues are all him! I was walking in the vineyard, and a death adder charged right at me! I shot that bastard, and it still kept coming! It took three shots before it would stop squirming, like the bloody Devil himself! And then Miro followed! He whispered his chants, and another adder came right up behind me! He's a snake-charmer!"

"What's he saying, Yvie? Looked clear as day like he shot at Miro," Oz said as he let go of Miro's arm to address her.

"He says he was shooting at an adder... at two, in fact. He says all the shots were aimed at snakes attacking him... and that Miro was controlling the snakes."

"Did you see any snakes?" Oz asked Mac and Mélusine. Mac nodded in the negative.

"No, mon chéri. There were no snakes." Mélusine glanced around, observing the vineyards with more scrutiny.

Eleanor stood up and joined the men, while Mr. Valov took charge of helping Edmund control his nerves.

"What are you doing here?" Eleanor whispered to Miro.

"Revenge, revenge, revenge," he hissed in a strange, distant tongue.

"Revenge for what?"

Oz and Mac glanced at her with confusion.

"Why do you want revenge? For your mother's death? It was an accident, Miro. Just a tragic accident."

Eleanor took his free hand into hers as she turned him away from the rest of the group, hiding her glowing eyes from their view.

My child, you must let go of this hatred. It is useless. It will only lead you to ruin.

Revenge. Revenge. Revenge.

Eleanor let go as he began to shake.

"I believe he's seeking revenge for his mother's death. I can't seem to get through to him. Has he always been so single-minded? Or does he speak coherently sometimes?"

"He was a perfectly normal young bloke when we first arrived in Margaret River, but he's been like this for months," Yvie whispered. "Since his mother died."

Oz lowered his voice. "I didn't realize you shared Edmund's talent for languages, Ellie."

Eleanor glanced over at Edmund. "It is a complicated story that I'd rather not discuss, and it should not be discussed with Edmund either. Understand?"

Oz nodded, throwing Yvie a nervous look at the unexpected development.

Eleanor sighed with stress. "I don't know how to deal with him. Do you have any ideas? He seems like he's working himself into some sort of base hysterical state, probably as a result of the mental anguish from his mother's death. If he were a mental patient, I would have him committed and observed, but we're a far cry from having that option out here."

"I have no bloody clue," Oz shrugged. "Most of the aborigines won't allow themselves to be treated by white doctors anyway."

"Ellie, do you think he's dangerous?" Yvie asked.

"I honestly don't know. He feels human to me, and I usually have pretty good instincts for identifying... er... special qualities in people."

She took his hand again, feeling for any inkling of godly power, Rakshasa frigidity, or Yaksha warmth—every special quality that she had become so attuned to identifying. He felt entirely human.

Miro, you must let go of your pain. Shakti commands it. Can you feel my power? I am a goddess, and I am ordering you to let go of this futile quest for vengeance. The person you're hurting most is yourself.

She pushed a wave of Shakti's calming power straight into him, and he shivered and then collapsed onto the ground, writhing and screaming.

"Revenge, revenge, revenge!"

Eleanor stepped back and watched as Miro rolled around in the dust and his screams dissolved into mantras.

"Strewth, Ellie, what did you do?" Oz hissed.

"Apparently, I did something wrong," she said as she threw Mélusine a nervous look. "But I don't sense any dark power emanating from him. Do you, Percy?"

"It is here, ma chérie. I can feel it. But it is not concentrated. It is as if it is all around us," Mélusine whispered in French.

"He's evil!" Guy interrupted.

"That's enough! I have half a mind to send you back to France right now. What possessed you to think that you were welcome to Oz's shotgun?" Yvie snapped.

Guy gasped with offense and continued their argument in French. "You expect me to walk around this monster-infested bush without any protection?! It's lucky for me and for you that I had it! I would have been killed by those bloody adders. You were the one telling everyone that Miro was controlling them. How dare you blame me for believing you!"

Yvie moved to argue, and then she gave in. "You're right. I'm sorry. There is too much happening."

"Might I remind you that I never agreed to live in the bush? You told me this was a civilized place when I agreed to come from France. I'm not a bloody missionary," he continued.

"It was civilized when I brought you here." Yvie looked like she might cry. "Everything has fallen apart." She sucked in a calming breath and relegated her emotions. "Ellie, what do you think we should do?"

"Percy, help me calm him," Eleanor suggested.

"It is a bad idea, ma chérie. Your use of your unique talent already made him worse. Mine may do the same."

"Do you have any calming drugs?" she asked Yvie. "He needs some help snapping out of whatever this is."

Yvie leaned in to whisper. "Oz's mother has a sleeping tonic." She switched back into English. "Ozzy, will you go fetch the sleeping tonic?"

He moved to argue, but Mélusine stepped in. "I will manage the situation. *Allez.* Go!"

Oz jogged past them back up the stairs into the house. The dogs ran inside after him barking, and Eleanor sighed with annoyance.

"I'll add dog training to our list of activities."

As she watched them disappear into the foyer, Stanley started screaming like a schoolboy. Before anyone could chastise him, Oz's mother followed suit, and then Father O'Donnelly joined the chorus.

Kuveni reached down calmly under the table. With one excruciating crunch, she pulled a dead, grey-striped snake up off of the ground and examined it.

"Good on ya, Kate," Sheila murmured as she poked at its cool skin. "You're a braver woman than I am. Like a born and bred bushie."

Edmund turned away from them as Mr. Valov rubbed his back and he continued his mantras.

"That snake should not have attacked like that," Yvie said as Kuveni walked its carcass over to the other side of the tree and lay it neatly on the roots. "Death adders are camouflaged hunters. They don't just slither onto a crowded open lawn."

Oz rushed back down the stairs and kneeled down beside Miro. He lifted his head and fed him a sip of the tonic.

"Drink up, mate."

Miro fought back, writhing and gyrating more and more aggressively, until suddenly he gave up and collapsed unconscious. Oz checked his pulse and his breath, and then stood up and put the bottle of tonic in his breast pocket.

"*Attention!*" Yvie exclaimed.

As Eleanor debated summoning her trident, the dead death adder slithered towards Mac. He danced around, almost knocking Yvie over in his effort to scramble to the other side of Miro, using the unconscious boy as a barrier between the serpent and his feet.

"Yvie, get behind me!" Oz exclaimed as he grabbed Yvie and pulled her to the other side of Miro, standing in front of her and blocking her with his arms. He threw Mac a look of disgust at his ungentlemanly conduct. "A lot of help you are, mate."

Mac would not be distracted from watching the scene unfold as Mélusine swooped down and gathered the snake right up into her arms, holding it up so she could address it face to face. She stared at it intensely, in what Eleanor assumed was a silent conversation. After a long exchange, the snake went limp in her arms. She looked around, considering her options, and then she ripped its head right off and tossed it far into the vineyard, dropping the rest of the carcass at her feet.

"That's one way of making sure it's dead," Oz murmured.

"I'm sure it was dead the first time," Kuveni said as Oz kept Yvie's hand locked tightly in his and walked over to join Mélusine on the far side of the karri tree, away from the rest of their audience, who was still gathered at the banquet table.

Edmund was paying no attention to them at all as he continued whispering his mantras, while Mr. Valov was keeping one eye on Edmund and one eye on Eleanor. Stanley, all the while, had taken a seat beside Father O'Donnelly, and was hungrily eating down the rest of Mr. Valov's English breakfast, while Sheila was sitting with her arms crossed with a look of unfocused sour disapproval on her face.

Mélusine glanced over at their audience and lowered her voice into a barely audible whisper. "It has been dead since you killed it, Kate. This movement wasn't from its life-force. Its body was reanimated." She turned her attention to Eleanor. "It is a very difficult thing to do. I have only ever seen it one other time…" She trailed off as she considered an idea. She leaned down and placed both hands on Miro's chest, but after many seconds of effort, she pulled away and furrowed her brow. "I do not understand what is happening here. He is entirely human."

Sheila stood up and joined them. "For god's sake, we may seem like we're out past the black stump, but we don't have zombie snakes down under. You must have just stunned it before."

Mélusine addressed Yvie and Eleanor in French. "It was dead. I must figure out what it means." She closed her eyes, took in a deep breath, and snapped her fingers. "Mes chéries, do not despair.

I have put up a barrier around the house. No creatures shall pass uninvited, alive or dead."

"Isn't that just like the frogs, switching into gibberish to keep the rest of us in the dark," Sheila muttered. She sat back down and stole the final sausage off of Mr. Valov's plate with a humph.

"What in god's name are you talking about? Invisible barriers? Re-animated snakes?" Mr. Guy interrupted, still in French.

"Nothing that concerns you," Mélusine replied.

"Nothing that concerns me? But I was just attacked by two evil snakes at once! The Devil's after me! It's that Miro! He thinks I shod his mother's horse that threw her!"

"Did you?" Eleanor asked.

"Maybe…"

"You didn't tell me that!" Yvie exclaimed. "What else have you lied about, Monsieur? Tell me now!"

"Nothing! I swear! The horse was clomping down the road with its shoe half off, and that Darana woman said she didn't have the money to fix it! So I brought her over here and did it for free! It was an act of kindness! Now, see what I get for helping out one of those savage natives? I should have just let that horse get blistered up until he couldn't walk, and then they'd have no one to blame but themselves…"

"That is *enough*," Yvie hissed. "You have spouted enough hate for one day, Monsieur."

Mr. Guy moved to argue, and then he looked down at the headless body of their reanimated snake and held his tongue.

"Thank you for helping us, Percy," Yvie whispered as she pulled Mélusine into a hug and gave into tears. "*Merci, merci, merci.* I will sleep well for the first time in months."

Kuveni kneeled down to check on Miro. "Perhaps we should let him rest inside."

Sheila's eyes bulged at the suggestion. "Inside the house?!"

Yvie leaned in to whisper in Eleanor's ear. "You are certain that he isn't dangerous, Ellie? I trust your judgment."

311

Eleanor thought about her potential answers. Was she certain? No. There was obviously something unsettling about the whole thing. But her gut told her that Miro wasn't the problem. Now… that the problem was connected to him? Of that, she was certain. She glanced down at him again. He looked like a boy, even younger than Stanley. He must have been seventeen or eighteen by her guess, and he was suffering from a natural emotional break over the senseless death of his mother. She thought about Edmund's many frightening maladies, and her own morbid power that Uma had unwisely used on Jaap Sahib to bring swift and silent death to anyone she fancied, and she let herself give into pity.

"I don't believe he's evil, Yvie. But we should still be careful. Vengeance is a powerful motivator, especially for a young man of his age who doesn't have much else of a future to think about. Percy and Kate will be able to keep him under observation, though, until he's fit to go home. Won't you?"

"It will be done, ma chérie," Mélusine agreed.

Yvie squeezed her hand. "Bring him in. Let him sleep in the downstairs guest room until the tonic wears off. When he wakes up, we will offer him food and water and then send him on his way."

"*Allons-y,*" Mélusine agreed as she lifted him up into her arms and carried him into the house.

Mac clucked with subtle disgust as he watched Percy carry the sleeping boy into the house, and Eleanor noticed a certain harshness to him for the first time. She wasn't sure if it was just the ugly scar and the coldness that always went with such a tragic disability, or if it was something deeper. She didn't have the energy to add him to her worries. Instead, she skipped over to Edmund to observe his recovery. He smiled weakly at her with his hazel eyes, and she sighed with relief.

"I'm glad you're feeling better, darling."

"Yes, I feel as if a weight has been lifted. That foreboding feeling just disappeared after Percy killed the snake. I don't know what it means. Something, I reckon."

"I'm sure it means something, darling. Shall we think on it during an afternoon tipple? Kate offered to open the Margaux, if I'm not mistaken?"

"I'll see to it. My dears, why don't you go settle into the comfort of the shaded porch?" Kuveni suggested cheerfully as she skipped into the house behind Percy and disappeared.

As they all climbed the stairs and seated themselves on the comfortable padded wicker furniture, Mac followed, taking a butling position behind them, while Stanley remained the only one sitting at the banquet table.

"Leo? What am I supposed to do?!" he called.

"It's time for you to learn how to clean dishes, greenie," Mr. Valov rasped.

Stanley looked down at the piles of dirty plates and serving platters caked with drying curry, and then down at the snake's dead, headless carcass.

"*We know what we are, but know not what we may be,*" he muttered.

"Amen to that," Eleanor murmured as she cuddled onto the couch beside Edmund.

She took in a deep breath as she let his pulsating power reverberate through her. It felt closer to Rama's strength than she'd ever felt from her husband before, but as he kissed her gently on the lips, she settled in and relished his innocence. Someday, soon enough, he would know what his powerful instincts truly meant, and in the meantime, she finally let a tiny part of herself accept that her painful role in perpetuating his ignorance was a gift.

For the moment, the danger had passed, but as she gazed out over the pastoral sun-drenched vineyards, she was certain it would return, stronger than ever.

As it turned out, she wasn't wrong.

PART THREE
UNLEASHED

CHAPTER 20 – SPORTSMANSHIP

The following days passed by uneventfully. Miro awoke glassy-eyed from his deep slumber and stumbled home without more than a few whispered mantras, with no mention of the hospitality they'd offered or the divine power that Eleanor had used to accidentally push him over the edge.

With his exit, the entire household began breathing easier. After a few Yakshini meals cleverly prepared in the kitchen, which the rest of the household was barred from entering so that Kate and Percy could focus entirely on their 'gourmet genius,' and after a few days without a single spider or snake anywhere in sight, Eleanor and Edmund finally began settling in and enjoying their joyful reunion with two of the kindest people they'd ever had the pleasure of meeting.

Each day, Mélusine snuck several doses of Yakshini euphoria into Mr. Valov, noting privately for Eleanor the subtle increase in frequency required to keep him functioning. He took to sitting peacefully on a swing on the porch with Yvie, watching as all of the other adults, even Sheila, gave into childlike giggling as

Edmund attempted day after day to teach Stanley how to play cricket.

The poor boy was hopeless, but his spirits improved along with everyone else's as the food and the relaxation began to sink in. Eleanor realized on the fourth day of their efforts that Stanley had probably never enjoyed the simple pleasures of being an innocent child in a happy family, just like Edmund hadn't, and so her patience for his incompetence grew, especially with Mac around to fill in the wide gap left by his many clumsy mistakes.

On the fifth day, Lord Grimby telephoned during breakfast with an intriguingly vague yet cheerful invitation for all of the able-bodied members of their household to join him at his rented property as soon as they could manage it. And so, as the sun rose high into the sky, bringing the temperature high enough to rival a steamy Indian summer day, Eleanor sat beside Edmund and Kuveni in the back seat of one of Oz's cars, while Oz drove, and Mac and Stanley squeezed into the front seat beside him. Neither of their butlers looked remotely pleased about their uncomfortably close quarters.

"I reckon it's going to be a scorcher today," Oz said as he drove towards the heat mirage emanating off of the dusty road before them. "In Perth, it usually doesn't get this hot until December."

"What do you think Lord Grimby has in mind?" Eleanor asked, hiding her pleasure at the wonderful heat as she rolled down her window and held her hand out into the warm breeze.

"Something painful," Stanley muttered. "And undoubtedly humiliating."

Every ounce of cheer that had blossomed in the boy over the last several days had dissolved, and his hunched over posture made him seem even more miserable than his dismal assertion did.

"Aw, now, Stanley, my boy. Buck up. You've been making steady progress at cricket and at butling," Edmund encouraged him. Eleanor smiled at the tone that gave away his years as a

318

commander of bright-eyed young troops. "What's most important is that you haven't given up."

"If you say so," Stanley mumbled. Mac threw him a disapproving look. "Sir," he added as an afterthought.

"It is going to be hot today, isn't it?" Edmund said as he looked out the front window and changed the subject. "Our lovely little corner of the Western Ghats has been a wonderful escape from the scorching temperatures elsewhere in India. I'm not used to the heat anymore."

He glanced down at the dry skin of his hand nervously, and Eleanor took it and kissed it. "Just stay hydrated, darling. I'm sure Kate will help us collect all of the cold water that Lord Grimby's house has to offer into some lovely carafes."

Kuveni took his other hand, and Edmund shivered as she subtly pushed a wave of cooling Yakshini energy right into him.

"Don't worry, Edmund darling. You'll be perfectly fine no matter what mother nature throws at us today."

He relaxed, and Eleanor nestled her head against his shoulder as the car turned around another bend, onto a particularly bumpy section of the road. Stanley's face turned slightly green, and he stuck his head out the window, gritting his teeth together as he worked to keep his motion sickness at bay.

"These bumpy roads do me in sometimes myself," Oz said encouragingly as Mac shook his head with annoyance.

When they finally pulled up a gravel drive, leading between two vast vineyards to a beautifully manicured green lawn around a white wooden house that didn't look dissimilar to Oz and Yvie's in style, Stanley pushed open the door of the moving car and hopped out, slamming it closed again as he rushed away from them and finally lost his battle.

Oz stopped the car, but Stanley waved him on. "I'll walk the rest of the way," he rasped.

"Are you sure?" Oz called.

Stanley waved them on desperately as he bent over for another round.

Oz drove on, and as they pulled up onto a lawn that was even larger than Oz and Yvie's, Eleanor's heart raced with unexpected excitement as she spotted six beautiful, saddled thoroughbreds waiting in the shade of a tall karri tree.

"Crikey, look at those beauts!" Oz exclaimed.

Eleanor hopped out of the car with almost as much haste as Stanley had, and Edmund followed her swiftly as she skipped right over to the horses.

"G'day, mates. How did Lord Grimby get you here all the way from Heaven?" Eleanor joked.

"I bought them three days ago up in Perth. They're all trained polo ponies, freshly immigrated from Argentina," Lord Grimby replied as he approached down the wooden stairs of his porch, clad in a full polo riding uniform of baggy knickerbockers tucked into tall leather boots, a gold-buttoned coat, and a round, pointed helmet, all in a dark tropical khaki that made him look almost like he was wearing a colonial army uniform from many decades earlier. "I just couldn't help myself when I saw how much this lawn resembled a polo field. There's a nice set of stables out the back of the house, and I figured I'd start putting them to some use."

"What a wonderful idea," Edmund said as he stroked the mane of the svelte spotted mare beside him. "I've missed having horses mightily in India, but the terrain just wasn't suitable to their grazing needs, and the effort it would have taken to bring in the hay wasn't worth the trouble with our motorcar being useful enough for our travel needs."

"Are you going to care for them yourself?" Eleanor asked curiously. He hadn't struck her as the type to shovel the manure of six horses all on his own.

"I've already hired the local boys to do it for me," Lord Grimby said with a hint of pride. "You know, give them some real work, so they know how to become men..." He trailed off as he spied Stanley stumbling up the gravel drive. "I've come to realize it is not a step to be taken for granted."

As soon as Stanley noticed his father's clothing and the horses, he began shaking his head and muttering unhappily.

"Are we here to play polo now?" Edmund asked with enough enthusiasm to make up for Stanley's void as he took another look at Lord Grimby's outfit. "I thought maybe you were ready to hop up to Delhi for the Durbar!"

Lord Grimby laughed, but Eleanor could tell that he didn't find Edmund's friendly jab particularly funny. "We're civilized men wherever we go, Colonel, and I reckon we should dress like it."

Edmund looked down at his perfectly fitted beige summer suit. "I feel civilized enough, General, although, if I'd known we were coming to ride, I would've worn my riding clothes."

Eleanor was suddenly suspicious of Lord Grimby's motives as she forced herself to remember that *he* was the Secret Service mastermind in charge of their fate. She hoped that this friendly game wasn't just some ill-conceived scheme to ogle at Edmund using his Rakshasa abilities, and she hated that after so many days of not having to hide their secrets around Oz and Yvie, she was being forced back into her defensive position.

Lord Grimby chuckled, ignoring Edmund's comment. "Well, Colonel, I've thought for quite some time that you might be an admirable opponent on horseback. The king thought so too after noticing your work with the Household Cavalry."

"The king?" Edmund snorted. "You have always known how to pull my leg, General. I'm sure that between his tea with the Emperor of Japan and his meeting with the prime minister, King George was discussing my aptitude for equestrian with his generals."

Lord Grimby smiled and patted Edmund on the back. "I have always admired your humility, Colonel. Now come, you won't be left improperly attired. I took the liberty of acquiring a few more uniforms for the occasion." He eyed Eleanor and then Kuveni.

"Although, I must admit that I didn't anticipate the ladies joining us when I rang up with my request for all of the able-bodied men in your household." He glanced at Stanley, but quickly relegated an expression of disdain, and then addressed Oz. "You don't have a butler of your own? Or perhaps a valet? Or a cook? Or a chauffeur?"

"Our entire staff has been up in Perth since last week," Oz replied. "But I reckon that these two modern sheilas here will give you a run for your money." He winked at Eleanor, and she smiled. She knew exactly why Yvie loved him so much.

"You needn't worry about me," Kuveni chimed in. "You'll need an umpire if you plan to have a fair game." She reached out her hand for an affected handshake. "General, I'm not sure we've had the pleasure. I'm Kate Marriner, Edmund's cousin from Somerset."

Lord Grimby eyed her resemblance to Edmund questioningly and forced a smile. "I have no doubt you're doing us a great service, Miss Marriner. Even the best of us can lose our senses from time to time in the heat of the game."

"Well, without the bottom of the barrel of Oz's staff, I guess you'll need me to even up your numbers," Eleanor pointed out. "My father was a thoroughbred trainer. Surely I will be less of a liability to the game than Stanley is?"

She regretted her insensitive comparison as soon as it came out of her mouth as she watched poor Stanley's posture deflate even more. She was annoyed at herself that she'd let her instinct to fight Lord Grimby's sexist attitude get the best of her.

"Have you ever played polo before, dearest?" Edmund asked with a combination of curiosity and concern.

"Yes," she lied. "Shall we?"

"You never cease to amaze me," Edmund swooned. "Oz, perhaps you and Eleanor can be my numbers one and two?" He glanced at Stanley. "A fair enough pairing of handicaps, I reckon?" he suggested to Lord Grimby.

Lord Grimby glanced at Stanley, whose coloring was still off from his battle with motion sickness, and nodded his agreement. Eleanor chose not to dwell on the fact that Edmund believed her to be Stanley's equal on horseback, although, she also had to admit that she had never actually swung a mallet while riding.

Don't worry, my child. Polo was the game of Indian royalty long before the British Empire existed. Let me play for you, and we will show Lord Kalki what our real handicap is.

She was glad that she'd worn the sunglasses Yvie had loaned her as she continued her silent conversation. She was equally excited by Uma's contribution to her skill, and by Uma's burst of competitive enthusiasm.

We mustn't give away our divine power to Lord Grimby.

We will be discretion itself, my child. The only thing that will shock him is our aptitude.

"I'm not sure any of the uniforms will fit you, Eleanor," Edmund interrupted her silent commune.

She looked down at her stylish white linen pants, flowing green silk blouse, and her cute, matching leather loafers. "If I'd had some warning, I would have brought my own riding clothes, but I've ridden in worse. Perhaps we should all just play in what we're wearing? It's just a friendly game, isn't it?"

"Are you sure, dearest?" Edmund asked concernedly.

Eleanor tied the ribbon of her wide-brimmed white sunhat securely under her chin. "Since when did I ever let my inappropriate clothing stop me from doing something worth doing? I seem to remember a moonlit ride side-saddle in a lehenga to the Taj Mahal?"

Edmund stole a kiss. "You were perfect that night, Eleanor, in every possible way."

"I reckon I'll feel more comfortable dressed as I am," Oz interrupted before they could get too distracted. "I've never liked those stuffy English riding boots."

"General, you certainly don't have a uniform that will fit a man of my height just lying around," Edmund added. "Let's just get on with it, shall we? It's getting hotter by the minute, and I should avoid the height of the midday sun. It bothers my skin, even when I'm wearing a hat."

Eleanor caught a subtle expression of panic as the minor mutiny foiled some aspect of Lord Grimby's plan, and she was satisfied to see it. Although, as she noticed Stanley throwing Mac a commiserative glance at the prospect of playing in their starched butlers' tuxedos (a glance which Mac returned with a snide cluck and the straightening of his own stilted militaristic posture), she once again regretted being so thoughtless in her approach.

Lord Grimby relegated his emotion and smiled. "As you wish, Colonel. Choose your mount."

As Edmund inspected each of the horses, pausing at the one who engaged him most enthusiastically, Eleanor placed her hand on the forehead of the mare next to her and conveyed her silent message.

Will you do me the honor?

The mare neighed her agreement.

Lord Grimby hopped onto the largest black steed, and Oz and Mac took the ones closest to them, leaving one unsure black mare in the back, who eyed Stanley skeptically.

"Boy, go get the mallets and the ball," Lord Grimby ordered. "And you'd best get a helmet for yourself, if you know what's good for you."

Stanley sighed loudly and stomped up the stairs into the house like a rebellious adolescent throwing his father a bone of obedience. After several loud bangs and clomps, he returned with a helmet placed loosely backwards on his head, his hands full of mallets, and a white leather-bound ball protruding precariously from his pocket.

Without a word, he handed each player a mallet, popped the ball out of his pocket and handed it to Kuveni, and then scrambled ungracefully onto his horse, who neighed with disapproval and pain as he held onto her mane for support.

"Do not pull on her like that," Edmund said sharply. "She is your partner, not your slave. Do nothing to her that you would not willingly endure yourself."

Stanley scrambled off of her.

"Are you daft?" Lord Grimby exclaimed.

Stanley looked genuinely confused.

"What are you doing?" Edmund asked. "There will be more appropriate times to practice mounting her."

"Sir, I was just following your orders." Stanley gulped, and Edmund nodded for him to continue. "You see, I wouldn't willingly endure someone riding me."

Mac snorted, and Lord Grimby turned red with anger. As Stanley noticed their reactions, he scrambled back up onto the horse, doing his best to use the saddle, rather than the horse's mane, to support his weight.

"Greenie, you have a fair point," Edmund conceded. "But I daresay that she has been bred to like her position, as long as you treat her right. I can see that all of them have quite a bit of energy pent up. Shall we begin?"

Stanley looked down at the ground where his mallet was lying in the dirt, but as he cringed and looked around for any option that wouldn't require a third dismounting, Kuveni graciously collected it and handed it over to him. He passed it into his left hand, and Lord Grimby cleared his throat.

"You will play right-handed, boy. You are not a deviant."

Stanley grimaced and returned the mallet to his right hand.

"You're left-handed?" Eleanor asked.

"I'm not a deviant," Stanley mumbled.

"No wonder you've been so bad at cricket! You've been playing right-handed all week! Why didn't you just play with the hand that felt natural?" she needled.

"I am not a deviant, ma'am," Stanley repeated as he glanced over at his father.

"You'd better not be, boy. Now, shall we begin?" Lord Grimby pushed forward.

He rode out into the middle of the sunny lawn without looking back, and Mac lined up next to him. Eleanor relaxed and let Uma work her way into her limbs, while Stanley struggled to control his horse with only one hand. Edmund rode alongside him, and Oz followed, offering him tips and correcting his form as they rode around in a wider circle, until Stanley looked like he might at least be able to stay afloat.

When Stanley finally lined up beside Mac, Edmund and Oz lined up beside Eleanor, and Edmund offered her a wink.

Kuveni stood along the sideline of the field, noting, no doubt, as Eleanor did, that Lord Grimby's planning for the occasion had included all of the necessary markings being outlined in white powder along the ground. He had even installed imposing wooden goal posts to mark each goal at the ends of the field.

"Ready…" Kuveni tossed the ball up into the air, "Go!"

She blew a whistle, and Mac lunged forward, capturing the ball with one swift, graceful move. He was off, charging down the field, hitting the ball with his mallet as he went.

"I'm beginning to understand the appeal of this game!" Eleanor exclaimed as she raced at her top speed alongside him.

She ripped off her hat and let it float away behind her, and with another swift movement, she pulled the ribbon out of her hair so her long tendrils could flow free in the wind, like they had when she was secretly racing her father's thoroughbreds as a lass.

As Edmund flanked Mac, riding him off the line of the ball, Eleanor felt Uma's competitive enthusiasm erupt, and with one swoop, she captured the ball and sent it careening down to the opposite end of the field.

326

"What in god's name just happened?" Lord Grimby exclaimed as he watched the ball soar through the air, and then slowed down and circled to stare at Eleanor. Mac shared his unhappy surprise.

"Dearest, you're a natural!" Edmund exclaimed.

"Looks like our modern sheila just raised her handicap," Oz laughed as he picked up her pass and ran with it. As her shocked opponents gathered their wits, she sped off with Edmund in a heated race to the other end of the field.

Lord Grimby yelled angrily at Stanley, and then charged up beside Oz, slamming his mallet against his in an effort to break off his control of the ball, but just as Lord Grimby succeeded, pulling Oz out of contention and into a circle to keep his horse balanced, Eleanor felt Uma's excitement growing again, and she leaned forward and captured the ball. Edmund rode up beside her, blocking Mac from riding her off, and with one graceful swing, Eleanor shot the ball straight through the goal posts.

"Good on ya!" Oz exclaimed. "Bloody brilliant, Ellie!"

"Dearest?! I don't even have the words!" Edmund exclaimed.

She rode up next to him. "Save your enthusiasm for later, darling. We will celebrate my victory together in private."

"What in the bloody hell is wrong with you?!" Lord Grimby shouted as he rode back at his top speed to Stanley, who was approaching midfield from the opposite goal. Mac followed, surrounding Stanley from the other side, in a formation that Eleanor found disconcertingly threatening.

"I thought I'd be most useful as number four, waiting for a pass by the goal."

"Number four?!" Lord Grimby boomed. "Do you see four players here, boy? Don't be bloody daft! Your orders are to play in the bloody game, you hear?"

"Yes, sir," Stanley mumbled.

"That language is hardly necessary, General," Edmund chastised like a stern father as he rode up beside them. "The boy can hardly keep control of his horse. He shouldn't be riding alongside skilled players. It isn't safe for him or for us."

"He isn't going to learn if he never tries," Lord Grimby shot back. "Don't you want to be a man, boy?"

Stanley thought about his answer for too long, and Mac poked him in the back with his mallet.

"Yes, sir," Stanley mumbled.

"One for us," Oz declared as he rode up beside them.

Eleanor flanked him, and as Kuveni approached them with the ball in her hand, they lined up, readying themselves for another go.

"Watch me, boy," Lord Grimby hissed. "And play the bloody game."

"Ready... set... go!" Kuveni called as she threw the ball into the air again and then rushed out of their way at her fastest approximation of human speed.

Eleanor did not like the glint of competitive desperation in Lord Grimby's eye as he smashed the ball with his mallet and charged past her, swinging his mallet around and slamming Edmund's as he went.

Edmund was ignited with friendly sportsmanship as he chased his opponent up the field, and he laughed happily as Oz joined him, flanking Lord Grimby and riding him off until Lord Grimby lost control of the ball.

A long series of epithets spewed forth from Lord Grimby, beginning with muttering, and growing in intensity until he was shouting like a madman, but as Eleanor smashed the ball the opposite direction, taking control, there was no one else to catch it. She leaned in and raced as Mac charged forward beside her, reaching his mallet out and aiming for hers in an effort to slow her down.

Uma anticipated his move, and rather than fighting against it, absorbing the brunt of his blow with her bare arm, she swung her mallet around along with his, throwing him off balance.

328

In a split second, Mac lost control and careened off of his horse, landing on the ground with an ominous thud, but before Eleanor had a chance to stop and help, Lord Grimby charged up alongside her, riding her off, away from Mac's position and back towards the ball.

"Play!" he commanded. "It is a man's game, and men's games don't stop when a fool falls down."

His comment ignited her, and she leaned in and raced him up the field, laughing as she galloped past him. She knew better than anyone that a tiny, light, strong woman could beat a heavy old man in a thoroughbred race any day, and he had chosen the biggest, burliest horse, which she was now realizing was a decision made purely out of vanity.

She slammed the ball forward, and Edmund rode up beside her.

"You're a goddess, Eleanor!" he declared as he took her pass and ran with it.

With one graceful swing, Edmund slammed the ball through the goal posts.

Oz cheered as Edmund slowed his horse to a trot and followed the ball to politely knock it back up to the center of the field.

"Where the hell were you?!" Lord Grimby shouted at Stanley. "It's like I'm bloody playing alone!"

"I was waiting to make sure Mac was okay." Stanley's voice was flat and resigned, and he looked down, anticipating his father's next tirade.

"Mac is a man! He survived the trenches for three bloody years. He can bloody take care of himself!" Lord Grimby shouted.

Mac sat up and brushed himself off. He looked pained as he leaned on his mallet and stood up.

"Are you alright?" Edmund called as he rode up beside him. "That was quite a spill you just took."

Mac gave him a thumbs-up as he hobbled towards his horse, who had obediently slowed himself down and waited for Mac's orders, but as he climbed back up onto her back, Eleanor could see that Mac was about as happy about the outcome of their first two rounds as Lord Grimby was.

By the time they'd all lined up again, Lord Grimby's team was looking rather dismal. Stanley had returned to his common expression of fighting off tears, while Mac's upper lip was so stiff it was quivering as he forced himself into a rigid posture that his bruised back was clearly not encouraging. Lord Grimby looked like he was ready to rip someone's head off at the slightest provocation, and the horses seemed well aware of their feelings as they neighed and whinnied unhappily.

"With that injury, mate, it might be more fair if I switched sides for this chukka," Oz suggested. "Although, I reckon the fairest trade would be our modern sheila for your injured man, but I wouldn't dream of putting our perfect pair on opposite sides."

"No, I wouldn't dream of it either," Lord Grimby grumbled. "Go."

He gestured for Mac to switch with Oz.

"My friends, it is only a game," Kuveni reminded them.

She waited for Mac and Oz to settle into place, and then she threw the ball up in the air, and Lord Grimby whacked it like a tennis serve, while it was still well above his head.

Kuveni blew her whistle. "Foul!" she called. "We will not bend the rules of safety because of your sour mood, General."

Lord Grimby looked like the vein in his forehead might burst, and Edmund rode off dutifully and collected the ball, bringing it back to the center for Kuveni to restart the chukka.

She threw Lord Grimby a commanding look. "I expect to see sportsmanship worthy of His Majesty's officers, General."

She threw the ball up in the air and skedaddled out of the way as Edmund sniped Lord Grimby's position and whacked the ball halfway down the field in one shot. Eleanor leaned in and raced him to it, laughing with the thrill as she rode like a jockey, gaining speed against him.

As she took possession, Mac rode up beside her and tried to steal it.

"You're on my team now!" she called.

He didn't respond. He hit the ball backwards, as if he were still playing on Lord Grimby's team, but as Edmund flanked him, moving him away from her with a look of fierce protectiveness in his expression, the ball slammed Stanley in the eye and knocked him right off of his horse. His helmet went flying, and he squealed as he hit the ground with a thud. His horse kept running.

Lord Grimby rode over to him and poked him with his mallet.

"Get up, boy! Be a man!"

Oz rode up between them and knocked Lord Grimby's mallet out of his hand. "That's enough."

As Mac circled, slowing to a trot, and Oz dismounted to tend to Stanley, Eleanor rode at her top speed to join them.

She hopped off her horse and kneeled down beside Oz as he examined Stanley's eye which was already black and swollen shut.

"I'm a doctor, mate. Let me look at it. We've gotta do what we can to make sure you don't lose your vision with a shiner like this one."

Tears streamed down Stanley's face from the uninjured eye as he held his arms in front of his face, blocking everyone's view of him.

"Leave me alone!" he cried.

"Hey," Eleanor gently coaxed his arms out of the way so she could look at his wound. "Let me see it. I'm a nurse, remember?"

"Whimpering little child," Lord Grimby muttered as he took off on his horse to the other end of the field without looking back.

Mac scrambled off his horse to join Eleanor. She was grateful to see that he looked concerned. He pulled a small notebook and pencil out of his breast pocket and began scribbling in shorthand.

I didn't mean to hit him. I thought Edmund was behind me. I was trying to help. I swear.

Mac pushed it in front of her as she ran her fingers along the edge of Stanley's injury, and he whimpered with the pain.

"You can discuss your explanations with Edmund. I'm busy," she said sternly.

Edmund hopped off of his horse, as Kuveni reached their position on foot.

"My dear boy, that looked wretched!" she exclaimed as she kneeled down. "Is there a term for a game-ending foul?"

"I believe the term you're looking for is overly-competitive wanker," Edmund said as he kneeled down beside them. "That was exceptionally bad form, Mac. I didn't take you for a cheater, or a bully."

Now Mac looked like he might cry. He frantically scribbled while Kuveni placed her hand gently on Stanley's wound. He took in a deep breath as she pushed a dose of Yakshini warmth right into him.

"Dear boy, when you're ready, we will help you back to the house and get you all cleaned up. I'm sure a lovely steak will have you feeling better in no time."

"I'm not hungry," Stanley sobbed.

"My dear boy, I meant for your eye."

Eleanor leaned forward to inspect Stanley for additional injuries from his fall as Mac pushed a note into Edmund's hand.

Colonel, I swear I didn't mean to hit him. I was attempting the Stewart Maneuver. I thought you'd know it? It was invented at the Calcutta Polo Club. It was the favorite of the Indian Army officers I played with before the war. Number Two hits the ball backwards to Number Three so he can break away from the opponents' defensive line. I didn't think Stanley would be anywhere near us. He'd been holding back the whole time.

Edmund's defensive posture deflated slightly at Mac's reasonable explanation. "It must be quite frustrating for you to have to write out your thoughts like this, mustn't it? It's my fault you can't just speak your mind."

Mac began scribbling again.

"How many fingers am I holding up?" Eleanor asked as she held three fingers above Stanley's good eye. He had to wipe away his tears before he could answer her.

"Three."

"What is your name?"

"Stanley Abernathy."

"Where were you born, Stanley?"

"Saint-Brieuc."

Mac stopped his scribbling to throw Stanley a disapproving look.

"Well, greenie, you took a bad fall, but I don't see any broken bones, and I don't think you have a concussion. You'll need plenty of rest, though, and we will need to keep that ugly wound clean so it doesn't get infected."

Mac threw another note at Edmund and kept scribbling.

Colonel, my condition is not your fault. You didn't start the war. You weren't the Krauts attacking us. You did what you thought was best, and you saved seventeen men while you thought I was dead. I'm grateful to be alive, and it is thanks to you.

"Come now," Kuveni said as she helped Stanley sit up.

"Go slowly," Oz advised. "Don't push yourself. You should rest for the rest of the day and night. If you have internal bleeding, we don't want to aggravate it."

Stanley whimpered. "You don't think I'm going to die, do you?"

"Mate, I think you'll survive just fine," Oz said as he patted him gently on the back. "In the meantime, I reckon you'll have quite a blokey tale to tell about how you got this shiner. The bushies down at the pub will buy you a round for it."

Stanley looked mildly proud of himself, but then he grimaced with pain and looked to Eleanor for affirmation.

Eleanor smiled reassuringly. "You aren't going to die, greenie, but I do think that polo isn't your sport."

"I know it isn't," Stanley muttered. "And so does Lord Grimby. I've been daft at it since I was a boy."

"This wasn't your first polo match?" Edmund asked.

Stanley chuckled, and then whimpered with the pain. "This was my fortieth match, Colonel. I'm hopeless. You don't need to say so, and neither does Uncle Chester."

"Good god," Edmund murmured. "Why didn't you just refuse to play?"

Stanley sighed with pain and resignation. "Have you met Uncle Chester?"

"Hrm, I see what you mean," Edmund agreed. "Well, next time you don't want to play, why don't you tell me, and I will make your excuse for you?"

Mac's eyes bulged at the assertion, and he threw Stanley a piercing look.

Stanley cleared his throat. "That's very kind of you, Colonel, but I can handle myself just fine. I'm a man, after all."

He gathered himself up and leaned on Edmund for a woozy moment before he caught himself and let go. He brushed off the dust and looked around for his horse.

"I guess I shouldn't ride her back?"

"No, greenie. You shouldn't ride her back. Why don't you lean on Kate, and I'll guide your mare back to the stables alongside mine?" Eleanor suggested.

He leaned on Kuveni, and she put his arm around her shoulders, whispering motherly support into his ear as she guided him across the field towards the house.

"I reckon we'll get you out of the midday sun right on time, Colonel. This was the shortest polo match I've ever played," Oz sighed. "It was fun, though. I could go for a cold one right about now. Too bad the pub is miles and miles away."

"Uncle Chester keeps a chest of beer in the stables," Stanley called. "They aren't cold, though. He's too British to like them cold."

"And you aren't?" Edmund asked curiously.

Stanley turned back and glanced nervously at Mac. "I told you I was born in Saint-Brieuc. I'm a Breton at heart."

As Mac wrestled silently with his response, Eleanor glanced up as she heard a whir coming towards them. Edmund and Oz looked up too, and as Mac glanced up to see what they were all looking at, the polo ball smacked him in the eye, and he tumbled backwards and collapsed onto the ground.

The ball bounced a few times and rolled away.

"That general is a bloody menace!" Oz exclaimed. "You'd think he'd never lost a match in his life!"

Eleanor and Edmund looked around, but Lord Grimby was nowhere to be seen. Eleanor kneeled down to inspect Mac's wound, and in the distance, she saw Lord Grimby coming down the stairs of the house from inside.

"Stanley, I've got a steak for your eye!" he called. "The rest of you ought to come in for a pint!"

Eleanor found his cheer confusing. She found his location even more so. There was no way any human could have thrown the ball so far.

Oz noticed her reaction and then, as he assessed the distance between Lord Grimby and Mac, even Edmund noticed.

"Where did the ball come from?" Edmund asked with puzzlement.

"Kate, did you see where it came from?" Eleanor called to Kuveni.

"I am as puzzled as you are, my dear girl. It is as if it came from the Heavens!"

Oz laughed. "It looks like God had it in for you, mate." He kneeled down next to Mac and examined his wound. "It looks about as painful as Stanley's. Coincidence? I think not."

He brushed off his hands and sprung up jovially. "Colonel, I reckon we should take Lord Grimby up on his offer? I'm getting thirsty."

Edmund leaned down and offered Mac his hand, but Mac refused, woozily standing up on his own. He saluted rigidly to Edmund, and then marched past Stanley, across the vast lawn, and finally up the stairs, leaving his horse behind without even a nod.

"I must admit, I have no idea what just happened," Edmund said as he gathered up the reins of Mac's attentive horse and hopped up onto his own.

"I believe the Hindus call it karma, darling," Eleanor quipped as she hopped up onto her mare, keeping the reins of Stanley's in her left hand. She did not want to admit that she was just as puzzled as Edmund was, and she made a mental note to ask Kuveni what had really happened when they were alone in private later. As she watched Kuveni support Stanley's weight on her arm, she had a sneaking suspicion that Kuveni had, perhaps, used her Yakshini talents to be their angel of vengeance.

Oz hopped up onto his horse with five of the mallets in his left hand, and he joined them as they trotted up to Stanley and Kuveni.

"Come meet us in the stables when you're feeling up to it," Edmund suggested. "You've earned a schooner or two, I reckon."

"Sir, what's a schooner?" Stanley asked reluctantly.

"What's a schooner?!" Oz exclaimed. "We'll need to start you some lessons in Strine, mate. Come on over to the stables and we'll show you."

Stanley suddenly looked suspicious. "I don't need any more humiliation today."

"My dear boy, it is a beer," Kuveni whispered. "You are in kind company now. None of us find your suffering the least bit entertaining."

Stanley sighed with relief. "If this is what it takes to earn a schooner, I think I've earned forty." They all laughed at his joke, and then he smiled as he realized he'd made one. "Thank you, Colonel. I think I will."

Kuveni rubbed his back and waved them on.

"There's hope for that boy yet," Edmund whispered. "And that means there must be hope for us all."

"Amen," Oz winked.

Eleanor gave into the relief of a match well-won, but she couldn't ignore an ominous feeling deep in the pit of her stomach.

All will become clear in time, my child. Enjoy yourself. You must be fully rested when the time for battle comes.

Battle?!

I've said too much.

And with that, Uma settled in and began her silent wait.

CHAPTER 21 – CURRENTS

Three days passed by uneventfully, with the exception (or not) that Kuveni maintained steadfastly that she had no idea who the perpetrator was who'd given Mac his karmic black eye. Eleanor had to admit that she wasn't entirely certain how karmic it was, as Mac had been exceptionally repentant for days, running ahead of Stanley and offering to do his work, while using every excuse to help Edmund and Eleanor do the most miniscule tasks, until they tired of his hovering presence and asked him to follow Oz around instead.

She loved Edmund for his sympathy for Mac's plight, and his acceptance of Mac's excuse for his unsportsmanlike conduct, although she wondered how much of Edmund's quick forgiveness was rooted in his misplaced sense of personal responsibility for Mac's disability. Still, it turned out that the Stewart Maneuver that he had used as his excuse was, in fact, a common polo play, corroborated by a late-night visit Kuveni payed to the Calcutta Polo Club's illustrious (and rather uncooperative) president, and so she forced herself to forgive him for his treachery, which she begrudgingly admitted wasn't treachery at all.

Both of their injured butlers' eyes began healing slowly but surely, although Stanley's had a running start, as Kuveni had secretly provided him with a pouch of Mélusine's Roman remedy, while conveniently overlooking Mac's ailment. Eleanor was grateful, and slightly guilty, that Kuveni must have felt the same unfocused distaste for Mac that she did after the incident, although she did appreciate that her sympathy for Stanley had grown, and with it, her acceptance of his continuous bumbling, which was, she had to admit, as bad as it had always been, if not worse.

On the Saturday morning exactly a week before Oz's birthday, the Marriners and the Helmsworths sat fanning themselves on the shaded porch as they waited for Stanley and Mac to serve them a late breakfast, produced, no doubt, like all their other meals with an unobserved snap of Yakshini fingers in the off-limits kitchen. The weather was the steamiest it had been since they'd arrived in Australia, even more sweltering than it had been for their polo match, and while the others were markedly oppressed by the thick, heavy air, Uma and Eleanor were finding it delightfully infernal.

As soon as Stanley carried out a huge silver tray with tea and water, Edmund helped unload it from his shaking arms before he dropped it straight onto the wooden deck (as he had twice already throughout the week). Stanley took a moment to catch his breath and rub his pained triceps, to the clucking disapproval of Mac who followed him out with another tray heaped high with French pastries and fresh fruit, while Edmund uncouthly poured himself a tall glass of water and guzzled it down in one Rakshasa gulp before offering any to the others. Sheila watched his impolite gesture with unspoken disapproval, but as Eleanor noticed a thin layer of his skin flaking off, she was grateful that he'd let his need for hydration outweigh his Victorian manners. After all, shedding his human skin like a snake was one of the most grotesque things she'd ever seen his body do. It was more grotesque, now that she was used to his many alien traits, than anything involving his violet plasma.

"Perhaps you should go fetch us more water, Stanley," Eleanor suggested. "*Lots* more water."

Stanley wiped the sweat from his forehead with a yellow handkerchief and miserably headed back into the house to follow her orders. Mac bowed melodramatically, in a style that seemed almost unctuous, and then followed him right back inside. Eleanor once again found his demeanor unsettling, although she couldn't articulate why.

Edmund poured himself another glass of water, and then glanced at his audience and politely poured them each their own.

"*Il fait trop chaud,*" Yvie humphed as she took hers. "I can't imagine Hell could be any hotter, and it isn't even summer yet."

"This is nothing compared to the outback," Sheila pointed out. "Real bushies relish the heat."

"Mum," Oz hissed.

"I never claimed to be a real bushie." Yvie shot back. "I don't understand why you think it's a positive term. Living out in the middle of nowhere with no education or medicine, eating God-knows-what to stay alive, and drinking dusty water if you're lucky enough to find water at all, who wants to live like that?"

"True blue Aussies, that's who!" Sheila's tone became shrill. "Folks who don't need to be coddled and pampered all the bloody time!"

"Coddled and pampered! I was a *nurse*, Sheila, for ten bloody years! I was in the bloody VAD! Do you have any idea what kind of gruesome things I did every bloody day? You wouldn't last ten seconds tending to the wounds of wailing men whose arms had just been blown off. Not *ten* bloody seconds!"

"Oh please, they were all cowards, the lot of 'em! I know plenty of bloke's blokes who came back perfectly fine. Look at my Jackie, here! He's as ace as ever! Those whiners just weren't strong enough! Now, if they'd been reared out past the black stump, maybe they'd have been just fine..."

"Mum, that's enough!" Oz shouted.

Edmund and Eleanor threw each other a commiserative look at their awkward witnessing of the family spat, which only became more awkward as Stanley and Mac approached slowly, having listened in on Sheila's small-minded rant.

"My brother lost his arm in the war," Stanley said quietly. "And he was the blokiest bloke of them all. It was bloody awful, and he still hasn't recovered."

Mac threw him a fiercely disapproving look, but Stanley refused to look at him. Edmund looked down at the ground, lost in regretful thoughts.

"I saw thousands of strong men suffer more than you can imagine, Mum. You're only making yourself sound like a yobbo by yabbering on about things you don't understand."

Sheila looked like Oz's comment had slapped her in the face. She stuttered for a response, threw Yvie a livid look, stood up, and huffed away, back into the house, stomping her way up the stairs and slamming her bedroom door like a chastised teenager.

"I'm sorry, Colonel. I didn't mean to bring up old wounds," Stanley said as he painstakingly put down another tray of water carafes on the low coffee table.

"I'm sorry I didn't rescue Reggie when I had the first chance." Edmund looked up at Stanley and then at Mac. "Hindsight is 20/20, I suppose."

"He's alive, Colonel. That's what matters most, and he has you to thank for that," Stanley said as he began handing out white cloth napkins and silverware.

Mac kicked the foot of an empty wicker chair until Stanley noticed him and got out of his way so that he could put down another heavy silver tray heaped high with scrambled eggs and bacon.

"Well, now, this looks scrumptious!" Kuveni said cheerfully as she began piling bacon and eggs onto her plate. "Percy has outdone himself again!"

Eleanor took a canelé and some fruit, pouring herself a hefty cup of coffee, and finally, Edmund broke himself out of his melancholy to unenthusiastically fill his plate to the brim.

They ate in pensive silence while Stanley and Mac stood by the door, awaiting their next orders, until Eleanor spied several figures approaching up the driveway, almost like a mirage through the waves of heat wiggling in the still air.

"*Mon dieu*, I completely forgot!" Yvie exclaimed. "Oh, he shouldn't have brought them so far in this heat! You don't think they walked all the way from town, do you? Ozzy, can you go greet them? They must be parched!"

Oz hopped up dutifully and grabbed his hat from its peg just inside the door to skip down the driveway and greet Father O'Donnelly who was dripping sweat from his completely red face as he escorted several tan teenaged boys up to the house. They all had similarly wavy, unkempt hair yellowing from the sun, and they wore ragged old knickerbockers and shirts and shoes that had seen many better days. The boys looked only about thirteen or fourteen, but their eyes already had the same crow's feet that Oz's had from years of squinting in the powerful sun. Eleanor made a mental note to ask Kuveni to conjure them some hats before they returned home.

"Father O'Donnelly suggested that some of the village boys might be interested in learning about viticulture, so I invited him to rally a posse to come talk to Monsieur Guy," Yvie explained. "I thought it might keep them out of trouble, but they shouldn't stand around in the sun in this heat. They're going to burn right up!"

"I'm sure they won't feel it, if they're *real* bushies," Eleanor winked mischievously.

"*C'est vrai*, bushies have an extra layer of skin, you know, to shield them from all of their woes," Yvie replied snarkily as she glanced back over to where Sheila had made her exit. As she returned her attention to Eleanor, she noticed Edmund poking at the flaking skin on his hands. She blushed with embarrassment at her unintentional jab, but he was too distracted by his own thoughts to hear her.

She leaned heavily on the chair as she stood up and then waddled to the edge of the shaded porch, holding her pained lower back as she waited for their guests to arrive.

"G'day, mates!" Oz called to them as he shook their hands and then guided them towards the house.

"Top o' the mornin', Doctor Helmsworth." Despite his cheerful tone, Father O'Donnelly looked pained as he took off his black felt hat and nodded in greeting. "I've brought along Mick, Mickey, Jimbo, and... Dazza? Is that really your name?"

"Bloody oath, it is!" Dazza exclaimed.

Oz laughed. "It's a Strine nickname for Darren," he explained to Father O'Donnelly. "What's your first name, if I might ask, father?"

"Colin," Father O'Donnelly said reluctantly after glancing at Yvie.

"Fair dinkum," Oz winked. "Your Aussie name will be Cozza from now on." When Father O'Donnelly looked sufficiently flustered by the suggestion, Oz slapped him jovially on the back. "Don't worry, father, I was just taking the piss out of you. We've gotta do something to keep ourselves entertained out here at the edge of the world. Come on up, and we'll get you sorted."

"*Bienvenue*, all of you. Come!" Yvie reiterated. "Get into the shade, and have something to drink! I'm Mrs. Helmsworth, and this is Colonel and Mrs. Marriner, and Colonel Marriner's cousin, Miss Marriner."

"That won't be confusing," Eleanor winked. "Please call me Eleanor."

"And you may call me Kate," Kuveni suggested. "We were just finishing up our leisurely breakfast. We're a bit slow today in this incessant heat."

The four village boys' eyes widened as they noticed the heaping remnants of their feast.

344

Yvie smiled. "Are you hungry? Come! Eat! I'm afraid Monsieur Guy will not be willing to walk you around the vineyards in the sun when it's this hot, but perhaps you can have something else to make your infernal walk worth the effort."

"Do you really mean it?" Mickey asked.

"*Mais, bien sûr*! I never say things I don't mean!" Yvie said as she shook Father O'Donnelly's hand and gestured for the boys to sit down.

"Crikey, have you ever seen this much food in one place?" Jimbo whispered to the others.

"At the Bunbury Cattle Fair!" Mick exclaimed. "Right bonza, it was!"

"Eat up, darlings, there's more where that came from," Kuveni encouraged them.

Father O'Donnelly tsked with admonishment as Mick and Mickey reached their dirty hands out to grab pastries from the pile and stuff them into their mouths in one bite.

Yvie winked reassuringly to Father O'Donnelly. "We don't stand on ceremony here. We're about as far from Buckingham Palace as one can be on Earth."

She poured Father O'Donnelly a cup of tea, and as Kuveni caught him eyeing a canelé, she picked one up off of the pile and placed it on his saucer. "Try it, father. It was invented by a very clever monk."

His eyes widened with surprise as he took his first bite, and Kuveni smiled approvingly and placed two more on an empty plate in front of him before the village boys could devour the entire collection.

"Ace! This is the scrummiest cake I've ever had!" Jimbo declared.

"It is called a *pain au chocolat*," Yvie explained. "It's from France, where I'm from."

"Sounds pretty fancy," Mickey said as he grabbed one and stuffed it into his mouth.

"It just means 'chocolate bread.' Everything sounds fancy when it's in a foreign language, don't you think?" Yvie smiled as they began more enthusiastically digging through the remaining pastries.

"That would be *aran seoclaid* in Gaelic," Eleanor pointed out. "I think it sounds fancier in French."

"It's *panis scelerisque* in Latin," Edmund finally joined the conversation. "The French still sounds best."

"I'm glad we all agree," Yvie winked.

"Strewth, Edmund, do you think we look like that when we're eating?" Oz asked good-naturedly as he watched the boys scarf down the last of the pastries and turn their appetites and their fingers towards the remaining bacon.

Edmund chuckled. "I reckon from time to time we look far more like pigs gobbling from a trough than they do now."

"You're much more graceful," Eleanor reassured him.

"You're not," Yvie countered as she stuck out her tongue at Oz.

"No one can deny that we have an honest household here," Oz laughed. He grabbed what was left of the pastry on his plate and stuffed it into his mouth in one bite. "I really look like this in the first-class dining rooms?" he asked with his mouth full.

"Oh, Ozzy, you're such a tease!" Yvie giggled.

"Perhaps you can tell the lads a wee bit about growing grapes," Father O'Donnelly suggested. "That was the original reason for our visit, wasn't it, lads?"

"If you say so," Mickey agreed unconvincingly.

"Don't sound too enthusiastic," Eleanor teased them. "Why did you really come?"

The boys looked to each other guiltily.

"Well, spit it out!" Oz encouraged them. "You've got nothing to lose now that we've already fed you!"

"I thought Doctor Helmsworth might let us drive his car," Mick admitted.

346

"I thought we might get to try some wine," Mickey added.

"I thought maybe we could see inside the grand house," Dazza confessed.

"My mates told me to come along," Jimbo concluded.

"Well, I'm glad we have a team of bright-eyed and bushy-tailed future viticulturists at our beck and call," Oz laughed. "Do you blokes want to pick some grapes for money when the harvest comes next fall?"

"Yes!" they all declared in unison.

"We're going to be richer than kings!" Jimbo exclaimed.

"Can we pick your grapes and watch Lord Grimby's horses?" Dazza asked more pragmatically. "We already told him we'd muck out his stables and feed them every day."

"What about school?" Edmund asked.

"We'll go after school," Dazza explained.

"What about homework?" Eleanor pushed.

"Homework! That's for chumps!" Mickey exclaimed.

"He said that if we're really good, we might even be able to have the horses for ourselves!" Mick added. "That'll be worth way more than money!"

"He isn't going to pay you for your work as you do it?" Eleanor asked.

"He said that real men don't talk about money," Mickey informed her.

She threw Edmund a look of disapproving surprise at Lord Grimby's apparent plan to take advantage of the naiveté of the local bumpkin blokes for their free labor.

"Real men pay a fair wage for honest work," Edmund corrected him. Eleanor noticed Mac grimace subtly as Edmund contradicted Lord Grimby's unscrupulous plan. "I'll have a talk with him the next time we run into each other, and in the meantime, none of you should ever shy away from asking what you'll be paid to do a job before you do it. Agreed?"

"Aye, aye, Captain!" Jimbo said with an exaggerated salute.

"I'm actually a colonel," Edmund winked. "But you can call me Edmund."

The boys finished up every last morsel of food on the table, and then sat back, rubbing their bellies with satisfaction.

"Thanks, Mrs. H, this was grouse!" Dazza said.

"What'll we do now?" Jimbo asked.

"It's too hot for cricket," Edmund said disappointedly. "I suppose you boys aren't interested in reading quietly in the shade?"

"Reading? On a Saturday?! I'd rather dig out a dunny!" Mickey confirmed.

"Don't be a wally," Dazza hissed.

"Aw, you're just a wowser, Dazz," Mickey shot back.

"Don't knock it till you try it, mates," Oz laughed.

"If you don't mind, I'd prefer to wait until the heat of the day passes before I walk another marathon home," Father O'Donnelly interjected. "I'm afraid my Irish temperament has reached its limit. I'm surprised that you're doing so well, Mrs. Marriner."

"I had a few years living in India to get me accustomed," Eleanor replied, not untruthfully. "I've come to love the heat, even more than my husband does, and he grew up in India."

"Really?" Father O'Donnelly asked curiously. "How did that come to be? Was your father in the Colonial Army, Colonel?"

"It's a long story," Edmund demurred.

Eleanor regretted putting him on the spot when he was already distracted with his war memory malaise.

"I can drive you back to the rectory," Oz offered. "And, for that matter, I can drive you blokes back home when you're ready."

"Ace!" Jimbo agreed.

Dazza and Mickey, though, nodded their disagreement.

"Trying to stay fit as a fiddle?" Oz asked them.

"No, we're going to the diving rock," Dazza replied. Mickey kicked him in the shin. "What? He's a bloke's bloke! You aren't going to tell our parents we're going, are you, Doc?"

"Why don't they want you to go?" Eleanor asked.

"They're all afraid of the beaches now, after the tidal wave killed half the town," Dazza explained.

"It wasn't half the town," Mickey countered. "It was only thirteen people."

"*Only* thirteen! Everyone in town knew someone who was down there," Dazza argued. "It might as well have been the whole town. Everyone's still too bloody scared to go to the beach, but it's almost summer! Summer isn't summer without the diving rock! We're all gonna die of heat if we don't have anywhere to swim!"

"A nice swim does sound delightful," Edmund chimed in.

Eleanor was so surprised by his return to cheer that she couldn't help but take his interest and run with it. "I'd be up for a swim myself!"

Yvie did not like the direction of their conversation, but Oz refused to notice her disapproving cues. "Can you blokes tell us how to get to the beach you have in mind?"

"Ozzy, no!" Yvie exclaimed.

"Don't worry, my dear girl. All will be well with the angels by your side," Kuveni reassured her.

Father O'Donnelly threw Kuveni a questioning look. "I didn't volunteer to go to the beach," he replied, misunderstanding Kuveni's meaning. "I'm already so sunburned my Mam wouldn't even recognize me."

"There's shade!" Dazza exclaimed. "There's big tall trees right there on the beach!" Mickey kicked him in the shin again. "What? The more the merrier! It'll be like old times!"

"The breeze from the ocean will make the temperature in the shade much more bearable than it is here," Oz said to Yvie. "Come on, Yvie, we could all use a break."

"Is it a hike down to the beach?" Yvie asked skeptically.

"It's easy!" Dazza exclaimed. "Come on and just give it a burl!"

"I will help you," Kuveni offered.

"What is the foolish plan that's taking hold?" Mélusine asked as she followed Stanley out the front door to join them. Eleanor couldn't decide if she loved or hated that Stanley had gone to Mélusine for intervention.

"Oh, come now, Percy, we could all use some cheer," Kuveni argued.

"I'm cheerful," Mélusine countered unconvincingly.

"Indeed," Kuveni laughed. "As cheerful as an exiled Roman."

"Well, I'm ready for a dip," Edmund said as he glanced down at his flaking skin and moved his hands out of view to under the table. "The sooner the better."

"It isn't a good idea, mon chéri," Mélusine reiterated.

"Why not?" Edmund asked with genuine concern.

"I can't say," Mélusine conceded. "It's just a feeling."

"I've been feeling it too," Edmund admitted. "There is something odd in the air all around, but surely that would be the same whether we're here or there? Perhaps an escape from the empty curses of that aboriginal chap is just what we need?"

"*Peut-être*," Mélusine replied.

"Come with us," Kuveni urged her. "We'll all go together and have a lovely picnic by the sea."

"Leo's still asleep, and we shouldn't leave him alone," Mélusine argued. "And none of you should go anywhere without me."

"My mum's here," Oz pointed out.

Yvie humphed. "He'd be better off alone."

"Someone with more empathy would be advisable," Kuveni added more diplomatically.

"Mac can stay," Eleanor suggested, although she wasn't entirely comfortable leaving Leo with him either.

Mac couldn't hide his annoyance at her suggestion, but as he gestured to Stanley to protest on his behalf, Stanley refused to step in. "I'll come with you, Colonel. I assume there's going to be some heavy packs to lug?" he suggested instead.

350

"We can lug our own supplies, but you are welcome to join us," Edmund replied. "Still, someone who can call for help should stay with Leo." He cringed guiltily, looking away from Mac as he said it.

"I'll stay," Father O'Donnelly volunteered. "I've had enough of the great outdoors for a lifetime."

"Then it's settled!" Kuveni clapped excitedly. "My darlings, why don't you go put on your bathers, while Percy and I pack up a picnic for later."

Dazza winked to the other boys triumphantly.

"I reckon you didn't plan on getting the royal treatment for your secret jaunt to the diving rock, did you, mates?" Oz asked amicably.

"No, sir!" they agreed. Even Mickey seemed satisfied with the conclusion.

"Do you have bathers?" Edmund asked them.

"That's why we wore our old knickerbockers!" Dazza exclaimed.

Edmund laughed. "If only I had some of my own! Alas, I'll have to wear real bathers instead."

The thought of a dip in the cool sea did sound pleasant as the idea took hold, and Eleanor hopped up and skipped into the house, assuming on her way to their bedroom that Kuveni had conjured her a stylish swimsuit for the occasion. But, as she stepped into her closet and noticed the little black number hanging neatly right in front of the mirror, Eleanor suddenly realized that she had never, not once since her divine transformation, pranced about in a skin-tight swimsuit.

She decided to hold off her judgment until she had it on, but after several awkward minutes of hopping around on the dressing platform, squeezing it up her legs and over her large breasts until a hefty curve of cleavage was prominently on display, she sighed and shook her head.

"Kuveni, what are you trying to accomplish? Those poor adolescent lads aren't going to be able to think straight if I'm wearing this," she whispered.

As she stood on the platform staring at herself, debating momentarily whether to leave her green sapphire pendant and bangle behind for safekeeping, but then deciding to keep them on, Edmund joined her. A pang of arousal annoyed her as she looked at her own curvy figure.

"Blimey, dearest, if you wear that, you'll drive all the chaps wild. I don't know if I'll be able to control myself!"

"I know. I'm not going to wear it." She sighed with annoyance. "That is, if I can ever get it off."

"I didn't mean it like that," Edmund said as he reached around her naughtily to cop a pleasant feel. She felt him perk up with excitement.

"Yes, you did, and you're not wrong," she said as she turned around and kissed him. "Even I'm getting hot and bothered by it."

As they almost lost themselves in the moment, Oz knocked on the bedroom door.

"Train's leaving the station, mates, and you'd better be on it!" he called.

Edmund blushed. "He knows us too well." He glanced around the closet and then dug into a drawer, pulling out his own bathing costume that looked several years out of date. "I don't like mine either. For the first nine decades of my life, a man wouldn't have dared to wear anything so revealing in public, even to the beach."

As he stripped and then hopped around putting on his tight shorts and pulling the straps over his shoulders, Eleanor loved him even more.

"I suppose this won't be as embarrassing as it was the first time I wore it on the busy beach in Brighton. I was down for a day trip with some of the chaps from the barracks, and I almost packed up and went straight back to London before anyone saw me. They convinced me to stay, and I hated to admit that I found it useful for swimming... I reckon I need to swim today, before I start shedding like a lizard. Even the water at breakfast wasn't enough."

He blushed with embarrassment as he looked at both of them in the mirror.

"The Nizam would've had our heads if we'd worn anything like this in Hyderabad."

"Queen Victoria wouldn't have even known what to say," Eleanor winked.

She pulled on a low-waisted white cotton dress. "Maybe I can limit my embarrassment outside of the water."

He pulled on some white linen pants and a buttoning shirt over his swimsuit, and then pulled her into a romantic dip. "You're always a bastion of reason, dearest."

Oz banged on the door again, and they scampered guiltily to meet him.

He laughed as they opened the door. "I'm glad I'm not the only one who didn't want to prance around in just his cossie." He was also wearing some summer trousers with a buttoning shirt over his bathing suit. "I reckon that means I'm an oldie."

"We'll be oldies together," Edmund winked. "Welcome to the club."

As they headed for the stairs, Leo emerged from his room dressed in a silk bathrobe over his pajamas, balancing heavily on his cane. He was paler than he had been throughout the prior week, with a morbid grey tint to his skin, and Edmund's eyes turned black at the scent of death wafting off of him.

Leo eyed all three of them, stopping for a moment too long on Eleanor's cleavage that was still peeping out of her low-cut dress, before looking away.

"Have a good day at the beach," he said. "I'll hold down the fort."

"Do you want to come?" Edmund asked. He closed his eyes, whispered his mantras, and reopened them with his senses back under control. He'd had so much dastardly practice combatting the increasingly repulsive scent of Leo's decline, that he didn't even acknowledge his struggle anymore. "It should be lovely weather in the shade. Even Yvie's coming."

Leo moved to protest, but then he stopped to think about it. "Do you think it will be cooler there?"

"It will, mate," Oz replied. "It's always much cooler at the beach than it is inland if you can find some shade. The temperature of the ocean keeps it nice, especially in spring."

"Are you sure I won't be any trouble?"

"Sure as day!" Eleanor said cheerfully. She took Leo's arm, and at her cue, Edmund took his other, and they escorted him down the stairs.

As they helped Leo onto the porch, the boys, along with Mac and Stanley, were gathered around two of Oz's Fords that were parked right out front.

"Doctor Helmsworth, please can I drive?!" Mick begged.

"I reckon Colonel Marriner here will drive one car, and I'll drive the other," Oz refused. "And you'd best learn how to drive before you offer to drive other people around, Mick. I don't want to be called up to treat some ghastly injuries after a foolish accident. I saw enough gore in the war for a lifetime."

"Yes, sir," he sulked.

"I still don't think this is a good idea," Yvie whispered to Oz.

"You don't have to come, Yvie."

"And let you go alone?!"

"It is an option."

"*Non*! If you go, I go. But I still don't like it."

Oz took her aside and whispered into her ear. "Yvie, if you really don't want to go, I'll stay back with you, but Edmund and Eleanor are going, and Percy and Kate are going. If you're really worried about whatever superstitious mumbo jumbo Miro is up to, don't you think that we'll be safer if we stick with those who have special talents to keep us safe?"

Eleanor approached them and took Yvie's hand as she hugged her gently.

Is there something specific that has you worried?

Yvie's eyes watered. *Non! Ellie, I don't know why I'm so worried! It all just seems too benign! It feels how it must have felt before the others went to the beach and then drowned on a lovely sunny day!*

I know why the contrast is jarring. But if it really is just your imagination getting the better of you, thinking about those doomed people, don't you think that going to the beach and having a good experience will help you get over your nerves? You live by a beautiful ocean, Yvie. It would be a shame to fear it forever, and you'll never have a safer trip than with four angels keeping watch.

Eleanor pulled away and wiped Yvie's tears like a doting mother.

"*C'est vrai*," Yvie conceded. "*Allons-y.*"

Eleanor squeezed her hand. "Why don't you ride in our car. Oz, why don't you take Stanley and the lads, and Edmund will take the ladies and Mr. Valov."

As Mélusine approached the passenger door of Edmund's car, Eleanor hoped that no one had noticed the detail of her self-identification as one of 'the ladies.' In the meantime, all four boys pushed and shoved as they piled into the back of Oz's car, and Yvie watched their adolescent ruckus with her concern unabated.

Oz kissed Yvie and then nudged her to go with Eleanor. "Go with the angels, Yvie. I'll go in front, and you can keep an eye on me the whole time."

Kuveni helped ease Leo into the back seat, and when she was done with him, she helped Yvie get comfortable, and then wiggled herself in beside her. As Edmund took his spot in the driver's seat, Eleanor squeezed in next to him, and Mélusine begrudgingly sandwiched her in. Mac watched the whole affair with growing fury.

"There's room here to squeeze in next to Stanley if you want to come, mate!" Oz called.

Mac considered the option, but as Ovid and Pliny came barreling across the lawn and hopped into the empty seat, he turned around and stomped back into the house. Stanley squealed as he nudged the golden retrievers off his lap and onto the floor, and then he barely managed to reach around them to pull the door closed. Eleanor and Edmund both laughed as their view of Stanley and Oz was obscured by two very pleased, panting dogs sticking their heads out of the open window.

Father O'Donnelly waved them goodbye, and then with a screech of the tires, Oz sped off, and Edmund followed.

"I hope this isn't a big mistake," Yvie muttered.

As it turned out, Yvie's instincts should not have been ignored.

CHAPTER 22 – GODS V. MONSTERS

For over an hour, they drove on a narrow gravel road down the coast past thick karri forests and vast sand dunes until Oz pulled over, and his wards raced each other out of the car. Ovid and Pliny won. They bounded around in wide circles jumping on the boys, and then Oz, and then Stanley, as Edmund drove slowly in a concerted effort not to hit them.

"Perhaps we should work harder on dog training in our spare time," Edmund said as he watched them almost knock Stanley over.

"They weren't particularly used to visitors in Munnar," Eleanor explained to Yvie. "And they never went out of the yard. I suppose we really should work harder on helping them navigate these new circumstances if we're going to be here a while."

"I hope you will be," Yvie said as she squeezed Eleanor's shoulder affectionately from the back seat.

Eleanor hopped out of the front passenger's seat after Mélusine and helped Yvie up while Mélusine helped Leo.

The boys were already stripping off their shirts as they ran down a path carved into some grassy dunes that led down a softly undulating hill. Beyond it, a canopy of several large eucalyptus trees popped up from the beach below, and beyond them, the deep cerulean of the Indian Ocean sparkled in the bright, mid-afternoon light. The air was thick and still, and the sea looked almost like a glassy lake. The leaves of the eucalyptus hardly rustled; in fact, Eleanor had never seen the thin, paper-like leaves move so little.

She took a deep, calming breath. Despite the ominous silence of the day's odd weather, she was glad they'd come. It was one of the most beautiful beaches she'd ever seen, and the childlike excitement of the boys was contagious enough to help her quell her unease caused by Yvie's nerves.

Kuveni opened the boot of the car and collected two massive picnic baskets, by far the biggest Eleanor had ever seen. Kuveni put one on each arm, and then skipped off to follow the boys down the path.

"Come along, my furry friends!" she called to the dogs. They ran in circles around her, barking and leaping with joy as they followed her.

"Should I help you carry those?" Stanley asked less as a genuine offer and more as a halfhearted courtesy.

"Posh, Stanley, my boy. You're still injured! Why don't you go help Yvie and Leo," Kuveni suggested. "I'll go scope out our playground."

Oz rushed to Yvie's side, while Stanley joined Mélusine to support Leo. Eleanor took Edmund's hand, and together they set off on the path.

"Are you alright, Yvie?" Oz asked as the sandy route quickly steepened.

"I don't like it, Ozzy." She tightened her grip on his arm.

As they probably should have anticipated, Dazza's teenaged perception of its difficulty was not particularly suited to an eight-month pregnant woman or a dying man's needs, so Eleanor took Yvie's other arm, and Edmund followed Mélusine and Stanley, ready to catch Leo if he slipped. Together, they meticulously worked their way down the hill, into the eucalyptus forest.

"Don't forget to watch out for the drop bears, mates," Oz said as he looked up into the canopy.

"Do I want to know what a drop bear is?" Stanley asked nervously.

"Oh, they're just carnivorous koalas who drop out of trees to eat unsuspecting foreign butlers," Oz replied nonchalantly.

Yvie wasn't amused. "There are enough real dangers as it is, Ozzy. You don't need to make up silly stories."

"*Say vray*," he shrugged.

"Good thing I'm not a tasty specimen anymore," Leo joined in the facetious game. "I'm sure they'll finish you off before they bother with me, greenie."

Eleanor smiled, grateful that he was feeling well enough to joke.

"They aren't real, though, are they?" Stanley asked. He flinched as a loud crunch resonated behind them.

Eleanor turned around and sighed a long sigh of annoyance as she spied Mac and Lord Grimby running to catch up, followed by Father O'Donnelly huffing and puffing as he trailed behind them. As Stanley spotted them, his already waning posture deflated even more.

"Don't worry, mate, now the drop bears will have someone else to eat first," Oz whispered. "Mac'll keep them full for at least a few days."

Stanley finally smiled. "I wouldn't have tasted good anyway. I'm just skin and bones."

"There you are!" Lord Grimby exclaimed as he barreled awkwardly down the sandy path to reach them, almost tripping over a rogue tree root. "Fancy seeing you here!"

Edmund eyed Mac and Father O'Donnelly. "It hardly seems like a coincidence, given that your two companions watched us hit the road."

Eleanor was glad that Edmund wasn't letting him get away with his obviously false premise.

Lord Grimby laughed awkwardly. "You've got me, Colonel. I stopped on by the Helmsworths' to say hello just after you headed out, and Mac was so enthusiastic about taking a dip, I couldn't bear to disappoint him."

Mac smiled a toothy smile and bowed apologetically.

"I thought you didn't want to come?" Eleanor asked Father O'Donnelly.

It was only at that moment, as she considered the priest joining them for their sojourn, that the precarious position Edmund had put himself in swimming in front of so many strangers occurred to her. She grasped onto the comforting idea that he had done it before, even in Brighton with a group of army chaps, and no one had noticed that he didn't look the least bit wet... She hoped that that would be his only foreign quality on display.

"I didn't," he said as he pulled off his white priestly collar and unbuttoned his sweat-stained black shirt a bit further than he probably would have thought respectable in front of a rectory mirror, revealing a hint of his freckled chest and orange curly chest hair. "Mac asked for my help in calling up Lord Grimby for a ride, and then he insisted that I come along to help him communicate."

"Why didn't you just say no?" Eleanor asked.

"Priests aren't in the habit of refusing requests for help from crippled veterans," Father O'Donnelly replied. He cringed with embarrassment as he realized how offensive the statement had come out, but he was too flushed to blush and too haggard to correct himself.

"I thought you said that you stopped on by of your own accord, General?" Edmund addressed Lord Grimby. Eleanor could not have been prouder that he'd noticed the inconsistency, and that he'd been willing to push on it openly.

Lord Grimby laughed awkwardly again. "Well, now, I suppose you've got me again, Colonel. Mac didn't want to seem too desperate to join the party, but I guess the cat's out of the bag now. He rang as soon as you headed out, and I happened to be sitting around just down the road with nothing better to do, so I thought it would be a charitable endeavor to indulge him after the extra work he's been up to training Stanley, which I'm sure we can all agree is a thankless job, managing constant inane clumsiness and flagrant idiocy."

"Perhaps, General, if you let Stanley go about his business without insulting him in front of everyone, he'd gain the confidence to do a better job," Eleanor replied.

There was something about Lord Grimby's blatant verbal abuse of his son that reminded her of the many mean jabs her mother had showered upon her throughout her life.

Lord Grimby laughed, but Eleanor could see that he was not remotely happy with her challenge. "When Stanley here does a decent job for once, I'll have nothing left to insult. Real men rise up when they're challenged instead of cowering like a chastised child."

"Real men don't abuse those who are weaker than them to make themselves feel powerful," Edmund countered. Eleanor found his assertive tone to be mildly arousing. "And while we're on the topic of real men, they also don't lie to unsuspecting youngsters, tricking them into doing hard manual labor for a far-off carrot that they don't ever intend to give."

Lord Grimby looked questioningly to Mac, and then angrily at Stanley. "I don't know what you're talking about, Colonel. You'll have to fill me in."

"The village boys mentioned that you enlisted them to clean your stables and tend to your horses every day in perpetuity for no monetary pay, only the promise that maybe someday you'll give them one of the polo ponies. Were they lying?" Edmund asked innocently.

"Well, I don't see it that way at all!"

"How do you see it, General?"

"I offered them the opportunity to learn and grow! Consider it an apprenticeship! They'd never have the chance to touch a horse so grand if I hadn't come to town! I can't believe those little scoundrels went running to you to complain! Clearly they need to grow their spines if they're going to become real men."

Eleanor could feel Edmund's passion building, and she shivered as a subtle wave of power wafted off of him. "They didn't come to me to complain. They excitedly asked Doctor Helmsworth whether or not they'd be able to accommodate their work for you when he offered them paid work picking grapes in the fall. They were ready to turn down his offer in the false belief that you'd give them a pony for their troubles. Now, I've never met a real man in my long life who's taken advantage of enthusiastic children for his own gain, let alone a man with the extensive means that you have, *Lord* Grimby. Quite frankly, I don't know what to think of the whole matter, but I'm not thinking particularly highly of it at the moment."

Eleanor noticed Leo tense at Edmund's confrontation, while Mac's face turned red with anger, and Lord Grimby once again looked like the vein in his forehead might just explode.

"I will not apologize for those bogan country bumpkins misunderstanding our arrangement," Lord Grimby replied haughtily. "Now, if they have a problem with their apprenticeship terms, they can take it up with me."

"Perhaps I will ask them if they know what an apprenticeship is," Edmund countered, "because I'm quite sure that they will tell me that it is a job paid for in ponies."

"Pah," Lord Grimby muttered. "Those little artful dodgers will take what they can get, ponies or no ponies, if they know what's good for them."

"I suppose then, I will explain to them the real terms of their unpaid apprenticeship, and we will see where their true expectations lie. I reckon that's a fair enough arrangement, not dissimilar to one I determined in court last year as the colonial magistrate in Munnar."

"You are a magistrate, Colonel?" Father O'Donnelly asked, attempting to move the conversation away from the uncomfortable confrontation.

"Yes. I planned to retire when Eleanor and I moved to India after our honeymoon, but I found that I simply couldn't sit on my hands when I was witnessing various forms of injustice. So, I carved out a little niche for myself back in India as a magistrate in our rural cantonment. I suppose it must be ingrained in me, because here I am, unable to sit on my hands again on behalf of some bright-eyed bumpkin blokes."

Lord Grimby clenched his jaw. "Perhaps, Colonel, you should practice recognizing when fighting a battle over others' trivialities is or isn't in your own best interest."

Eleanor didn't like Lord Grimby's sharp, threatening tone one bit, and neither did Leo, who coughed several times, leaning on Mélusine and wheezing until she squeezed another dose of Yakshini euphoria into his hand.

Edmund moved to rebut, and then he thought the better of it. "Perhaps."

"I'm ready for a swim," Oz changed the subject.

Leo hobbled forward, and the group followed his cue to continue on.

By the time they emerged onto a small beach flanked by rocky, volcanic bluffs on both sides, the boys were already jumping off of the closest cliff.

"Take a squiz at this!" Dazza exclaimed as he hopped right off the ledge, holding his legs up in a cannon ball. His splash engulfed Mickey and Jimbo, who were already swimming in the water, and as he popped up, they ganged up on him with a rogue splash attack. They all laughed and hollered as Mick waited impatiently for them to get out of the way.

"I'm coming in, whether you're there or not!" he called.

They scrambled out of the way, and he jumped right in with his own glugging, blooping splash.

Eleanor loved watching them. They reminded her of her carefree days as a lass, swimming in the chilly North Sea with her sisters and her Da while her happy mother cheered them on from their picnic blanket on the rocky shore. She pushed the melancholy of the memory away, letting herself hold onto the fleeting moment when her mother was smiling, and their innocent life was beautiful.

She flipped off her sandals and wiggled her toes in the fine, white powdery sand, and then she spied Kuveni, who had already set up a shaded area with a large picnic blanket in front of a log bench that Eleanor suspected was a new Yakshini addition to the otherwise wild terrain. There were several sweating carafes of water, iced tea, and watermelon juice laid out alongside two large ice buckets, one with three bottles of champagne, and another with adorable little stubbies of beer. But, other than several collections of purposeful glasses for each beverage, nothing else had been removed from the picnic baskets, which remained closed on each side of the log bench. Eleanor was curious to watch how Kuveni planned to go about her Yakshini magic unobserved. The dogs, all the while, lay in the sand beside Kuveni, each chomping away happily on a juicy bone.

Eleanor and Oz helped Yvie sit down, while Stanley and Mélusine helped Leo, and as Edmund noticed a layer of skin from his neck break lose and flurry to the ground, she smacked his bum playfully.

"Go, darling! Go take a nice dip! I'll follow you in a minute."

As Mélusine took a seat beside Leo on the bench, squeezing his hand to secretly push another dose of Yakshini euphoria into him, Edmund hastily ripped off his clothes and ran right into the sea until all she could see was his head as he treaded water against the unusually gentle, lapping waves. They were almost like the waves of a Highland loch on a perfectly still summer morning.

364

"What a bonza day to come out. I've never seen the waves so smooth," Oz said as he stripped off his clothes and dashed across the sand in his tight cossie to join Edmund in the water.

As Stanley began unbuttoning the shirt of his absurdly formal butler's uniform to join them, Mac nodded his profuse objection, followed by Lord Grimby throwing him a furious look.

"Greenie, you can't strip down and go frolicking about in the water with the blokes," Leo said as he patted the bench next to him. "You're the butler, remember? It's your duty to serve, not to pretend you're a member of the family. Come sit down and wait for your orders. When Kate and Percy are ready to serve up lunch, you should be here to help them."

Stanley looked like he might cry as he watched Mac take a seat next to Lord Grimby on the sand in the shade of another tree, where both of them could keep a hawk's eye on the scene. Eleanor noticed in passing that neither of them had bothered to bring bathers, towels, food, or water. She wondered what about the situation had warranted such a blatant spying intrusion, and why they'd insisted that Father O'Donnelly come along for the ride. For a moment, she considered the unpleasant idea that he too was a Secret Service agent, but as he walked right past them, muttering unhappily and wiping sweat from his red face, she relegated the unlikely scenario into the back of her mind with the many others that bombarded her constantly.

"We don't stand on ceremony here," Yvie reminded Leo. "No one will mind if you go cool off, Stanley. If I weren't about to burst, I'd even consider it myself, it's so infernal in this heavy, hot air."

Leo glanced over at Lord Grimby and lowered his voice. "Don't push your luck, greenie. You already left Mac behind once, and you don't want to incur their wrath."

Stanley crossed his arms in a decidedly adolescent manner, and Leo looked away as Father O'Donnelly timidly eyed them, hoping for an invitation to sit on their comfortable bench. As Father O'Donnelly glanced at Mac, who seemed to have no problem communicating as he passed notes back and forth with Lord Grimby, he shook his head with resignation.

"Glad I could be of service," he muttered.

"Take my open seat on the bench, father," Eleanor suggested. "I'm headed into the water anyway."

Father O'Donnelly sat down next to Stanley, and as the boys scampered out of the water, racing each other to the top of the rock for another round of cannon balls, Eleanor took a deep breath, relegated her nerves, and ripped off her dress.

Leo patted Stanley on the back as she scampered towards the water.

"Don't pout, greenie. You're not the only one who has to settle for admiring the tantalizing view from afar. Men like us don't get what others have. We've just got to take the yoke of our destiny and bear it alone, like God intended."

"Amen," Father O'Donnelly murmured.

She wished that she hadn't heard them, but she ignored their comments and dove right into the lovely cool sea, shedding her self-consciousness as she went.

Edmund dove down under the water, and in a mischievous blur that Eleanor hoped wouldn't be noticed by their spying audience, he reached her in a split second and gathered her into his arms for a wet kiss. She couldn't help but straddle him for a naughty hello, but as she noticed Oz dutifully looking away and then all the others watching with interest, she splashed him playfully and wiggled out of his arms for a friendly and publicly appropriate game.

"Here, my darlings!" Kuveni called. She reached into one of the picnic baskets and pulled out a cricket ball.

"Ace!" Oz exclaimed as she tossed it to them. Edmund caught it effortlessly. "Good thinking, Kate!"

Edmund tossed the ball to Eleanor, and she was grateful that she caught it. Having proved her prowess, she smiled, ready to thoroughly distract herself from all of her intense stressors, and she tossed it to Oz. He dove down to swim into position and catch it, and thus, their friendly game of water catch began.

They played for hours, splashing and laughing and ignoring the incessant, hounding sun in their eyes as its light turned from white to yellow, and it edged its way across the clear, blue sky. Often, she glanced over to watch her beloved audience sitting on their shaded bench chatting and laughing, sipping iced tea and eating baguette sandwiches.

Throughout the afternoon, the men slowly released themselves from their stifling clothing, first with Leo's robe and Stanley's jacket tossed aside, then with their pants rolled up to their knees, then with their shirts fully unbuttoned and sleeves rolled up, until they were all sitting around in undershirts and makeshift knickerbockers. As the humans made their changes, Mélusine dutifully followed suit, creating a modern undershirt for Percy on the fly. Eleanor wondered if the others had noticed that his style was exactly the same old-fashioned Irish priestly cut as Father O'Donnelly's, but as she watched them seamlessly interact, her respect for Kuveni and Mélusine only grew. She would never have guessed just by looking at them that they were exceedingly ancient, powerful beings sitting relaxedly, telling jokes that even a Catholic priest could laugh at.

Mac and Lord Grimby, all the while, sat alone together silently scowling and passing more notes. Eleanor was glad to see that after their unpleasant interaction, no one from her camp had apparently felt the need to offer Lord Grimby or Mac a sandwich, and they, in turn, had not been willing to ask for one. If she hadn't found them so unlikeable, her medical sensibilities would have worried about their imminent dehydration, but instead, as she watched them become angrier and thirstier, she felt petty satisfaction at their self-imposed plight. Each time she dove back into her game, she relished the humanity that her silly spite represented. She had no doubt that there was nothing divine about it.

After hours of athletic exercise, her stomach began to rumble, and she tossed the ball one final time to Edmund.

"I think I could finally use a sandwich… or two, or three," she called to Edmund and Oz. "I think Kate probably has a few left for us. Should we take a breather for a bite and a tipple?"

"A tipple?!" Oz exclaimed. "I'm in!"

Eleanor laughed. "Kate, is there any champagne left?"

"Champagne and stubbies!" she called back.

"Is there more?!" the boys called from the diving rock.

"There's plenty!" Kuveni called. "But the booze will be for oldies only."

"Aww," Mickey whined.

"Don't whinge!" Dazza chastised him. "When was the last time you had a right bonza sheila lug a bag of tucker to the beach for you?"

"Never," Mickey admitted.

"Bombs away!" Jimbo shouted as he jumped into the water.

With one glance of group solidarity, the other three boys flew off the ledge in formation, blasting the water up into the biggest splash of the day with the power of three synchronous cannon balls.

"Why, I think they're ready for the Olympics!" Oz laughed.

Edmund sighed happily. "I don't know if I've ever been so carefree in my life. It's lovely to watch."

Jimbo dove down to join his mates under the water, but as the adults watched and waited for the boys to reemerge, quickly their cheer dissolved.

"That seems a bit too long, doesn't it?" Oz said as he began swimming towards their position.

He dove down under the water.

"Ozzy?" Yvie called nervously.

"Wait here, all of you," Mélusine ordered as she ran to the edge of the water. She closed her eyes, scrunched her nose, and took in a deep breath, listening intently.

"*Sacre bleu*, something's wrong. Kate, go fetch Vibhi. *Now!*"

The dogs began barking, and then they dove under the bench to hide, whimpering with fear.

Edmund dove down, and a second later, Eleanor felt it too.

Something grabbed her feet and pulled her under. It wasn't a voluntary dive—it was a wicked trap.

What followed happened so quickly that Eleanor could barely keep track of the order of things.

She struggled to open her eyes in the salty ocean water, but in the distance, she spied Edmund and Oz flailing against an unseen force. She looked down at her own ankles, expecting to see some sort of animal, but all she could see was water. It was like the North Sea rip currents that her mother had worried so much about when she was swimming as a child, but unlike those, this current had unquestionably conscious movement.

She felt like her heart might explode as a burst of panic erupted from her gut.

Uma, do you know what's happening?!

This is bad, very, very bad.

D.H.! Come now! Something's wrong!

She let her body go limp instead of wasting her energy and her oxygen fighting against the current. She felt the remnant breath in her lungs disperse, but she fought her instinct to breath in a lungful of water with all her might.

Just as she felt her head hit the sandy bottom, and her lungs felt like they were going to burst, in a blur, a black tentacle ripped her up and shot her through the water. She felt battered and faint as it dragged her through the heavy currents that tore viciously at her hair, pulling her back.

But, just as she was about to lose consciousness, Vibhishana was there, ripping her out of the tentacle's grip.

She gasped as he burst them up out of the water and into the sky above. He was using the clean-shaven, short-haired version of his ancient Christian form, clad in a bathing suit that looked just like Edmund's, creating a bizarre contrast as his beautiful golden falcon wings sparkled in the sunlight. She didn't have the wherewithal to worry about the divine show their audience was witnessing.

"Get Oz," she rasped. "He's still trapped down there! Vibhi, you have to save all of them! There's four young boys, plus Edmund and Oz!"

He soared to the beach and laid her down gently on the sand. Without a moment wasted, he dissolved his wings and blurred back into the water.

Yvie and Kuveni rushed to her side, while Stanley paced around frantically, debating whether or not to dive in himself.

"Stay put, Greenie," Leo rasped. "The angels don't need another human to rescue."

"He's right," Kuveni reiterated. "Stay here where *I* can keep you safe."

Father O'Donnelly stayed glued in position on the bench, squeezing his rosary and whispering heated prayers, while Mac and Lord Grimby argued with each other with exaggerated gestures. Grimby was forcefully poking Mac in the shoulder, and Mac was poking him back on his upper arm. Grimby threw the notebook at Mac and huffed away, and Mac picked it up and ran after him, poking him in the back with the same systematic style until Grimby turned around, and Mac began using his pencil to tap more patterns on the cover of the notebook.

Eleanor recognized it. "Brilliant," she murmured. They were using Morse Code.

"Ellie, what happened?!" Yvie sobbed as she crouched down by her side. "Is Ozzy okay? Please tell me he'll be okay!"

At her cue, Mélusine popped up out of the waves and delivered Oz onto the shore. With only the frenzied splash of a merman's tail, she disappeared back into the water. Father O'Donnelly's prayers only hastened.

"What are you doing?!" Stanley shouted as Mac ran into the water and Lord Grimby followed.

"We're going to be men!" Lord Grimby declared. "Men don't stand by and watch other men drown!"

"Kate said not to!" Stanley called. They ignored him.

As they waded into the sea and then dove under, Stanley paced even faster, arguing with himself in Breton as he debated what to do.

"Wait *here*," Kuveni ordered the rest of the group with her eye on Stanley as she ran over to Oz and dragged him across the sand, placing him in the shade next to Eleanor.

"Ozzy?!" Yvie screamed. "He has water in his lungs!"

She began beating his chest, throwing all of her weight against him until he coughed and gagged. Eleanor turned him over so he wouldn't choke on the water that had just come up. He gasped and then turned over to hold himself up as he wretched.

"Yvie?" he rasped as soon as he was done.

"Ozzy?!" She cried. "I thought you were dead!"

"So did I," he said dazedly. "Until... uh... Percy came to the rescue. He... uh... wasn't entirely himself, but I reckon he'll want me to leave out mention of the tail when I tell the tall tale."

"He'll be grateful never to hear a single word about it," Kuveni agreed distractedly as she watched the water for signs of life.

"It's just as well. I never liked stories about mermaids. They were too far-fetched..."

He sat in the sand and pulled Yvie into his arms as she sobbed. Eleanor leaned heavily on Kuveni to stand up and survey the scene. Vibhi and Mélusine had now been under too long themselves.

"Can't you do something?" she asked Kuveni.

"I can't!" Kuveni whispered with dismay. "We can control the tides and the currents, but it isn't working! Mélusine can't do it either!"

"Can't you go help them dive for the others?"

Kuveni was visibly annoyed. "Do you think I'd just be sitting around here if I could?!" She lowered her voice. "Yakshinis don't do well under water! It is very difficult for us to stay solid, and we can't disperse ourselves like we do in the air! Whoever chose this form of attack *knew* this weakness, Eleanor! It is someone from our world!"

"Blimey."

As a black tentacle whipped up out of the water, Vibhishana burst into the sky with Mick in one arm and Mickey in the other. He flew them in a blur to the beach beside Eleanor, and didn't look at his audience as he blurred back into the water.

Eleanor began pressing against Mick's chest, while Oz took Mickey's. They breathed air into their mouths in precise intervals until the boys gagged and choked, releasing the water from their lungs. The boys gasped in breaths of fresh air, but didn't wake up.

"I'm sorry, ma'am, I have to go!" Stanley squeaked. "Uncle Chester and Mac have been under too long!"

"Greenie, no!" Eleanor called.

"I'm sorry!"

He ran to the water and dove in, and Eleanor could only shake her head. As she glanced over at Leo, he was smoking a cigarette, even though every wheezing breath was paired with a pained cough and blood dripping down his chin. Despite the grotesque sight, Father O'Donnelly was now sharing Leo's pocket ashtray as he too sucked in long drags. They were whispering to each other, and as Father O'Donnelly's eyes widened, she was grateful that Leo was still around to manage the discretion of their witnesses.

Mélusine delivered Dazza to the shore, revealing her merman form again for a split second before diving back in, and Eleanor and Oz ran out to tend to him. But, as Edmund finally popped up, gasping in a deep breath, a black tentacle whipped up out of the water behind him.

"Watch out!" Eleanor and Oz screamed in unison.

Edmund looked up and blurred out of its path as it slammed down into the water, while another tentacle ripped Jimbo's unconscious body up, tossing him into the air. As that tentacle slammed down, the creature's wake sucked Edmund under again. Eleanor's only solace was that Edmund's tolerance for being stuck under water was, as she should have guessed, far better than any human's.

Vibhishana burst into the sky, catching Jimbo before he hit the water again. He soared to the shore beside Eleanor, and put the boy down. Oz immediately began pounding on his chest.

"Who's left?" Vibhi asked.

"It would've been just Edmund, but now we have another troop of fools to rescue," Eleanor muttered. "Grimby and Mac went in, and then Stanley went after them."

Vibhishana shook his head with annoyance, and then dissolved his wings and dove back into the water. As Eleanor kneeled down to help Oz tend to Jimbo, Stanley swam up with Mac unconscious in his arms.

"Blimey, greenie, I didn't expect you'd be the one to defeat the kraken!" Eleanor exclaimed.

Stanley let go of Mac. "I swam in the channel my whole bloody boyhood, and those currents were just as wicked. I'm going back in."

Without waiting for her approval, he waded back in and then dove back under.

Eleanor began pounding on Mac's chest while Oz finally got Jimbo breathing again, but as Mac coughed up the water in his lungs, and Stanley pulled Lord Grimby up to the surface several meters out, Lord Grimby, fully conscious and seemingly unscathed, began yelling at him and pounding against him, trying to get out of his grip.

They both looked up with horror as a black tentacle reached out of the water and loomed over them. Stanley let go of Lord Grimby and scrambled away with the grace of a seasoned swimmer, but the tentacle slammed down, capturing Lord Grimby and pulling him under.

"Get away from it!" Eleanor called to Stanley. "Let the others save him!"

Stanley refused. Instead, he dove down again.

Edmund finally surfaced again. "Did we get everyone?!" he called to Eleanor.

"Everyone but Grimby," she called back.

He looked torn, but before he had the burden of deciding his next move, the black tentacle slammed Lord Grimby's body onto the water's edge with a thud. The water lapped around him, darkened with clouds of blood until it soaked into the sand and circled back into the waves.

He wailed with pain, and Eleanor and Oz raced over to examine him. He was alive and breathing, but deep gashes were carved into both of his cheeks.

"The kraken stung me!" he yelled. "It bloody stung me on the face!"

Something about the odd circumstance felt unsettlingly familiar.

Stanley popped up. "Does anyone see him?!"

"He's here!" Eleanor called back. "Get yourself out of the water, all of you!" *That goes for you too, D.H.*

Edmund swam over to Stanley at a tired human pace to escort him back to shore, but as Mélusine and Vibhishana both popped their heads up, the kraken screeched with pain.

Its black tentacles flailed around in the air as an ominous hot gust of wind rustled Eleanor's salty, sandy, tangled tendrils. Suddenly, colorful tropical fish of every imaginable variety floated dead to the surface of the water.

"*Gast,*" Stanley murmured as he looked around at the gruesome sight. A putrid scent bombarded her, and all of the Rakshasas' eyes turned momentarily black before they could get themselves back under control.

374

With one final piercing screech, the kraken blurred out to sea. Stanley swam at an admirable, athletic human pace through the stinking carnage back to shore, and Edmund looked pained as he struggled to keep up. Vibhishana and Mélusine followed, foregoing their mythical features now that Edmund was watching. All three Rakshasas were grotesquely flaking as they emerged from the water, which now had a visible layer of white crust forming amongst the dead fish.

"Father, please come with me. I need your help tending to our heroes," Kuveni addressed Father O'Donnelly.

She reached into one of the picnic baskets and pulled out a large stack of towels.

He glanced at Leo as she dumped them into his arms, but Leo only shrugged. "The Secret Service thanks you for your cooperation. Remember, not a word about what you just saw to anyone, including Colonel Marriner. We'll be in touch later today with compensation for your silence."

"I don't need compensation," Father O'Donnelly murmured as he couldn't pull his eyes off of Vibhishana. "If silence is the Lord's will, it will be a privilege to serve Him."

"It is," Kuveni confirmed.

She reached into the other basket and pulled out four carafes of fresh water, and then rushed across the beach, offering the first to Vibhi. "Drink this, before you flake into oblivion."

Edmund glanced questioningly at Vibhi as he drank down his water in one Rakshasa gulp, but he thirstily followed her orders before indulging his curiosity. Vibhi, Percy, and Edmund each self-consciously wrapped their completely dry, flaking bodies in the towels as Father O'Donnelly stared at them, while Stanley stood in his sopping pants and undershirt sipping his water at a human pace.

While Oz tended to their injured wards, and Mac, now returned to some semblance of strength, engaged Lord Grimby in a heated silent debate, Eleanor rushed over to her husband to manage the fallout.

Yvie met her halfway, awkwardly lugging the picnic basket that had produced the water carafes towards the angels' position.

"Thank you," Eleanor whispered as she took it from her. It felt empty, and she smiled. Of course Kuveni had only used it as a mechanism for hiding her magic.

Yvie nodded tearfully. "You saved us again. I knew something was wrong. I just knew it!"

Eleanor patted her on the back. "It's over now, and the angels triumphed again. Don't you feel better knowing that together we could defeat a sea monster?"

Yvie smiled as she wiped her tears. "*C'est vrai.* You're right, Ellie. I should have had more faith."

Eleanor was not about to reveal how close to failure they'd come. Dazza and Jimbo were still unconscious, and she was quite sure that no one had the slightest idea what unseen enemy had actually ensnared them. As her memories of the action rushed through her mind on repeat, an unpleasant idea burrowed its way to the surface: The kraken was not the culprit. That creature's tentacle had pulled her up out of the deadly current, and then it had done the same for Jimbo...

"Dearest!" Edmund ran to her and pulled her into a salty kiss. "Thank god, you're alright! I thought as I was trapped in the rip current that I wouldn't be able to save you!"

"Don't worry, darling. We had all the help anyone could pray for, I reckon." She looked at Father O'Donnelly as she said it, and then she moved her gaze to Vibhishana, opening the door for Edmund to ask what she knew was already running through his mind.

"Doctor Carpenter?" He took her cue. "You're one of Father Johnson's agents?"

Vibhishana nodded, grateful that Edmund had offered up an explanation that he could run with. "I came to check up on how Leo was doing, and it looked like you could use some help."

"You came all the way from India to check up on my butler?" Edmund pushed.

"I did, my boy. Loyal allies are treasures to be cherished." He looked right at Father O'Donnelly.

Father O'Donnelly looked down at his feet with timid piety, and Edmund sighed with stress. "Did you see us do something odd, father?"

Father O'Donnelly now looked startled at the direct question, but as he glanced at Vibhishana, Vibhishana gestured subtly for discretion. "No, Colonel. Nothing at all out of the ordinary."

Edmund held out for a final glance at each of his unhelpful allies, and then he shrugged his concession. "Well, Doctor Carpenter, I'm glad you were here to help. Do you know what happened? It was like the rip current came out of nowhere... but it wasn't a normal rip current. It was..." He glanced self-consciously at Eleanor. "It felt a bit as if it was evil. I don't normally believe in evil incarnate, so it is an odd thing to admit, but then, I suppose, I don't often encounter sea monsters, either."

"I felt it too," Mélusine agreed. "It was the same feeling as when the snake attacked us last week, but it was stronger this time. My power wasn't enough to stop it."

"Perhaps, father, you should go ask Oz if he needs any help?" Eleanor suggested.

"I'll go too," Yvie volunteered.

"There is more water in the other picnic basket," Kuveni suggested. "The other victims will need to drink up before we hike back to the cars."

Eleanor offered her a grateful smile as Yvie escorted Father O'Donnelly away.

"I'll help too," Stanley said as he noticed Edmund eyeing him.

As he turned to walk away from them, Edmund grabbed his wrist. "You did well today, greenie. You were brave and calm and a wickedly good swimmer."

"I didn't follow my orders. Kate and Leo both told me to stay out of the water."

"You knew you could help, and you were right," Eleanor argued supportively. "We should have had more faith in you. It's not like you go around claiming that you're good at everything."

Stanley smiled. "There wouldn't be any point. It's already painful enough when you expect me to mess everything up and I do it. I don't need to add surprise to that mix."

"Stanley?!" Lord Grimby shouted. "Stanley Abernathy, you get over here now, or I'll have your head!"

Stanley's posture deflated, and he cleared his throat. "Thank you for your praise. It's the first I've ever gotten in my life."

"STANLEY?!"

"I'm coming, Uncle Chester," Stanley called.

He handed his half-drunk carafe to Eleanor, and ran off to tend to his cantankerous father. She took a few sips, realizing for the first time how dehydrated she was after her hours in the sun and salty water, and she couldn't stop herself as she chugged down all that was left. As she noticed the Rakshasas watching her, she handed the picnic basket to Kuveni, who reached in and pulled out another set of full, sweating carafes of wonderfully cold, fresh water.

"Drink up, my loves. It's going to take much more than this to get you back into shape in this heat."

"It wasn't just the heat," Vibhishana said as soon as he'd finished his second helping. He politely collected the others' carafes and stacked them in the empty basket. "The salinity of the water changed. In a split second, it became utterly unbearable. That's what killed the fish."

"What kind of creature has the power to change the salinity of the sea?" Edmund asked nervously.

"I don't know," Vibhishana replied. "The details don't fit together. Do you have any ideas?" He addressed Mélusine.

"A few," she said as she glanced at Edmund. "Perhaps we can discuss them later in private, *Doctor Carpenter*."

Eleanor closed her eyes. *Do you know, Uma?* Uma didn't respond.

"If you know what did this, you must tell us!" Edmund exclaimed. "Look at all the innocent people who almost died! Did you know this could happen, Percy? Did you let us bring Leo and Yvie and a group of young boys to the beach knowing that some creature might try to pull us down into the depths?!"

Mélusine couldn't hide her annoyance. "No, mon chéri, I didn't know that a kraken would come up from the depths to drown all of you. If I had known what form our enemy would take, I would have defeated him myself without an audience of interested humans along to watch our every foreign move. But, if you will all remember, I told you it was a bad idea to come here, and you didn't listen to me. What else should I have said to convince you?"

Edmund sighed with self-castigation. "It was my fault. I should've listened to you."

"That isn't what I meant, mon chéri," Mélusine said with a softer tone. "Everyone but Yvie wanted to come on this little excursion. We all deserve some blame, but blame isn't going to fix our problem. The evil power that caused this is still in the air, I can feel it."

"Do you think we should leave?" Eleanor asked. "Should we all just pack up and drive to Perth?"

"The thought did occur to me," Mélusine admitted. "But what happened today was an important test. We are quite far from Margaret River now, and the evil still found us. I don't believe running away will help. If anything, it will put more innocent people at risk if we bring it to a more populated area… No, we must figure out what it is and how to defeat it here."

"We should send Oz and Yvie away then," Eleanor suggested. "And Leo, for that matter. We can stay and combat whatever this is ourselves."

"What makes you think that it didn't follow them, ma chérie? It was plaguing the whole town long before we arrived, *n'est pas*? If we send them away, and it goes with them, they will not have our protection."

"I suppose splitting up is always a terrible idea," Eleanor humphed.

"It is," Mélusine agreed.

"You don't think that there is something real about Miro's curses, do you?" Eleanor asked.

"Curses are only real in fairy tales and folklore, ma chérie," Mélusine scoffed.

"Just like mermaids, and angels, and krakens?" Eleanor shot back. "Just because humans don't understand what they're seeing, it doesn't mean that there isn't a grain of truth to the claims."

"Mermaids?!" Edmund laughed. "Dearest, did a whole fairy tale unfold while I was trapped in the current?"

His momentary cheer dissolved as another hot breeze blew the scent of dead fish at them.

"I agree, mon chéri, the idea is absurd," Mélusine muttered.

Eleanor didn't have the energy to perpetuate her web of lies. "I just used the example to make a point."

Edmund mistook her reaction as offense at his flippant remark. "I'm sorry, dearest. I didn't mean to belittle you. I can imagine why you'd be open to preposterous ideas when you're surrounded by odd creatures like us all the time."

Eleanor was now annoyed by his patronizing tone, and she rolled her eyes. "Oh, can you? I'm glad you've let your imagination stretch its wings, darling."

Vibhishana shifted uncomfortably at her reference, while Edmund sensed her degenerating mood and changed his tactic. "I agree that something odd did happen here. There was something unnatural about the rip current, and then there was that giant squid making everything worse. Both of them seemed to have a bit too much consciousness for my comfort."

"You don't think they were one and the same?" Vibhishana asked. "You don't think the sea creature caused the rip current?"

"I suppose I didn't think too much about it," Edmund admitted.

"I don't," Eleanor interjected. "I've been thinking through the memory since escaping from the water. I think the squid was trying to help. It pulled me out of the rip current, and I think… I think it was clumsily fighting against the same force."

"If I hadn't caught that boy that it flung into the air, he would've broken his neck when he hit the water," Vibhishana pointed out.

"Yes, but you were there to catch him. Maybe the creature knew that."

"How did you catch him before he hit the water?" Edmund asked astutely.

"I was lucky," he replied vaguely.

"Well, mes chéris, I think we can agree that all we can do now is help our victims recover and head back to Margaret River." Mélusine swiftly moved the conversation along. "It will be better not to drive in the dark, and sunset is not too far off."

"What an excellent idea," Vibhishana agreed. "I'll go check if Doctor Helmsworth could use my help."

Without giving Edmund an opportunity to protest, Vibhishana left them, and Mélusine followed. Edmund sighed with frustration at their obvious deflection, but without any recourse, he let it go.

"Someday, I won't be a child trapped in the dark."

"Someday, my dear boy," Kuveni said with her own sigh of resignation. "I am awaiting it as impatiently as you are."

She picked up the basket where Vibhishana had left it and carried it back to the bench beside Leo.

"So much for your relaxing excursion to the beach," she said apologetically as she reached into the empty basket and offered him a freshly conjured glass of cold water.

"I'm glad to be here. It might be the last time I'll ever be useful to anyone."

Kuveni squeezed his shoulder, and then reached into the basket to gather some cold glass bottles of water for the dazed boys who were now all sitting up, staring pensively at the low sun glittering on the sea. She handed the bottles to Father O'Donnelly to distribute, while Yvie helped Oz check the boys' cognition with a series of motor tests. Vibhishana joined in, skillfully mimicking Yvie's style as he dove into his farce as a doctor.

"Where's Stanley?" Eleanor asked as she guided Edmund over to them and noticed that Stanley, Mac, and Lord Grimby were nowhere in sight.

"Lord Grimby wanted to have a word with him," Oz replied as he helped Dazza drink down some small sips of the fresh water. "I think they went back towards the road."

Eleanor didn't like it, and as Edmund sensed her concern, he squeezed her hand. "Let's go check on our boy butler, dearest." He tightened the towel around his waist as he led her into the eucalyptus forest.

Vibhishana noticed their plan, and he left Yvie's side to follow them at an inconspicuous distance.

They walked and they walked, farther than it had seemed on their leisurely trip down, until they heard the crunch of feet on the dried eucalyptus leaves, followed by Stanley whimpering, and Lord Grimby hissing with a tone that reminded her far too much of her mother's scariest parental rebukes over the years.

"Do you think it's funny to disobey me, boy?! Do you think this is a game? Grow up, you pansy, or I'll have you thrown in jail so fast, you won't know what hit you! Don't you think for one second that I won't do it, you hear?!"

"But I… I… I… I saved Mac!" Stanley stuttered. "He was drowning!"

"You put your hands on him one more time, and I'll cut them off, you hear? Then you can join Reggie in his namby-pamby classes for crippled cowards."

As they approached, Mac was holding Stanley pinned up against the trunk of a particularly massive tree, while Lord Grimby was pushing down on the bruise around his black eye. Fresh bruises were already showing in several spots along his upper arms, and on his jaw.

"What in god's name is going on here?!" Edmund demanded.

He left Eleanor behind as he ran to intervene, and she ran to catch up with him. Mac let go of Stanley as Edmund reached them, and Stanley wiped the tears from his eyes. His hands were shaking.

"Answer me!" A wave of power wafted off of Edmund. "What in god's name is going on here?!"

"Nothing that concerns you, Colonel. Just a bit of familial discipline for an unruly child," Lord Grimby replied as he turned away from Stanley and Edmund, pacing into the forest.

"All I see is two bullies attacking a boy after an act of heroism," Edmund countered.

Lord Grimby's face was red with rage as he re-approached Edmund, and a fresh layer of blood was oozing from the scratches on his cheeks imparted by the kraken.

Edmund's eyes turned black, but he didn't begin his mantras. Mac backed away as he noticed Edmund's demonic trait, but Lord Grimby held his ground.

"What are you going to do to me, Colonel?" he baited him.

Edmund didn't answer. Instead, he squinted as he looked more carefully at the wounds. Eleanor joined him, and after a few seconds of staring at them herself, she realized that they were symbols.

"What is going on?" Vibhishana asked as he joined them. As soon as he saw the symbols, his eyes turned black. "Shiva's wrath."

Without an explanation, he ran at his fastest approximation of human speed straight into the forest and disappeared.

"What? What is it?" Lord Grimby seemed genuinely concerned for the first time.

"Nothing," Edmund lied.

"For god's sake, tell me!" Lord Grimby demanded. "I know that look, Colonel. I know what it looks like when a powerful man is humbled, and I don't believe for one second that you're humbled by my presence."

"Loathsome traitor," Edmund whispered.

Mac relegated his fear and approached him with a threatening stance. Now it was Stanley's turn to back away from the confrontation.

"I beg your pardon?" Lord Grimby now looked outright scared, despite his commanding tone.

"That's what the scratches on your face say," Edmund explained. "They say *loathsome traitor* in a foreign tongue. I can't tell you which one."

"Maybe it's written in kraken," Eleanor quipped under her breath, even though she knew that the situation was sufficiently dangerous that she shouldn't joke. As she stared at the symbols and let Uma rise up to the surface, suddenly she could read them too, and she realized why Vibhishana had left with such haste.

Blimey, they're written in Rakshasa...

This is very, very bad.

"Well, that's... that's... that's preposterous! Are you trying to tell me that a giant squid stung me on the face, leaving words that you can read carved into my flesh?"

"I suppose that is what I'm saying," Edmund replied.

"Preposterous!" Lord Grimby repeated. He grimaced as he felt the scratches with his fingers. Eleanor could tell that with his elevated position in the Secret Service, he knew enough about Edmund's mad world not to discount the occurrence as flippantly as he was pretending to.

384

"I agree," Edmund shrugged. "Still, you should have a doctor in Perth take a look at those. I hear squid venom can leave nasty scars, and I don't think Doctor Helmsworth is an expert."

As many footsteps approached along the path to the road, Edmund closed his eyes, whispered his mantras, and returned completely to his humanity. He put his arm around Stanley's shoulders, and even though Stanley hissed with pain at the pressure, he didn't pull away.

"Come on, greenie. Let's get you home. I think we could all use some rest."

Eleanor took Edmund's free hand, and walked with them back to the path. Kuveni and Father O'Donnelly were flanking Leo, while Oz was helping Yvie, and Mélusine was escorting Dazza and Jimbo, who stumbled clumsily alongside Mick and Mickey, who were leaning on each other.

"Well, Yvie, turns out you were right," Oz sighed dejectedly. "We shouldn't have come."

"What do you mean?" Dazza asked. "This was grouse!"

"Fair dinkum, it was," Jimbo agreed.

"This story's gonna be good as gold. We'll get a round of schooners every time we tell it down at the boozer for the rest of our lives!" Mickey added.

"That's because you're alive to tell the tale," Yvie countered. "You shouldn't take your fortune for granted."

"Fortune favors the bold," Mick informed her.

"Can we have dinner at your house?" Dazza asked.

"Being bold?" Eleanor chuckled. She liked the boys' enthusiasm, and she liked even more that they seemed just as carefree as they were before they almost met their maker.

"I'm not taking my fortune for granted," Dazza winked. "Just like Mrs. H said."

"I think we could all use a feast," Kuveni agreed.

As they reached the cars, Father O'Donnelly helped load Leo into the back seat of Edmund's car, and then he took Eleanor aside. "Mrs. Marriner, do you mind if I ride with you? If there's room, that is?"

"Come, father. Join us," she agreed. He squeezed in next to Leo.

As Yvie switched cars to sit next to Oz, Eleanor took a seat in the front, and Ovid and Pliny came barreling up the path, hopping right into Eleanor's lap in the front seat. Stanley ran after them. "Is there room for me too?"

Leo scooted into the middle and patted the empty seat. "Come along, greenie, the more the merrier."

Stanley squeezed in beside him, but as he awkwardly scrunched up against Leo, making room for Kuveni, she closed the door behind him.

"Don't worry about me, greenie. Percy and I will ride with Doctor Carpenter. His car is parked at the top of another path farther down the road. We'll see you when you get home."

"How are you going to beat us home if you have to walk down the road to his car?" Edmund asked.

"He knows a shortcut, my dear boy, and we'd better get back as fast as we can if we're going to have a banquet ready to feed our hungry heroes." She took Mélusine's hand, and they started down the road at a quick jog until they made it around a bend, out of view.

Edmund straightened his posture as he approached Mac, who was passing another set of notes with Lord Grimby. "Mr. MacAllister, I reckon you should help Chester here get up to see a doctor in Perth straightaway. Don't worry about us. We'll do just fine without your help from now on." Mac moved to protest, but Edmund shook his head. "Chester needs you."

He left them at Lord Grimby's car without another word, and slipped into the driver's seat.

"Is everyone accounted for?" he asked as he watched the last of the boys climbing into Oz's back seat.

"Aye, Captain," Eleanor winked.

"Then let's get the hell out of here."

And with a screech of the tires, the gods and their wards headed home, ready for an escape from their excursion.

CHAPTER 23 – BASED ON THE EVIDENCE

By the time they reached the house, Edmund's stomach was growling. As they pulled up the drive, a squeaky-clean silver Rolls Royce was parked right in front, and meaty smoke was billowing from the garden behind the house.

"My father's agents must be exceedingly well-compensated," Edmund said as he pulled up behind the new car. "If I didn't know any better, I'd think he was a maharaja…" Edmund trailed off, contemplating the idea.

Stanley moved to ask a question, but Leo pinched his knee, and he held his tongue.

As soon as Oz pulled up behind them, the boys tumbled out of the Ford and ran to inspect the Rolls Royce.

"Crikey, Doctor H, is the Queen of England visiting?" Mickey shouted.

"It's only natural for her to pay homage to the Queen of Australia," Eleanor joked as she opened her door and the dogs tumbled out, running in wide circles around them and barking with excitement.

She followed Edmund as he joined the boys to inspect the car.

Edmund looked at himself in the side mirror, blushing slightly with embarrassment as he noticed how exposed he was in his tight bathing suit, and then grimacing as he noticed that his skin was still grotesquely flaking off in long, translucent strips.

"Blimey, Eleanor. I think I left my clothes at the beach."

"I'm sure Kate and Percy collected all of our mess, darling. The boot of this car is probably full of our stuff, unless they already unloaded it."

He glanced through the window into the empty boot, and then ran his finger across the top of the car. "It looks brand-spanking new. How do you think Doctor Carpenter got it this clean after driving around on the dusty roads? Surely if they took a shortcut through the bush, it should have been even dirtier?"

Eleanor was glad that he was thinking so critically about it, although she didn't have the energy for more lies.

"That sounds like an excellent question to ask them, darling."

"Come along, my darlings, the barbie's already fired up!" Kuveni called as she peeked around the edge of the house and gestured for them to join her. The boys raced each other, while Father O'Donnelly helped Stanley dutifully escort Leo into the house.

"I think I'd better wash up," Edmund said as he looked down at his flaking skin.

"Me too, darling."

Eleanor was glad that the action of the afternoon had sufficiently distracted her from her self-consciousness about her tight bathing suit. She dashed up the stairs ahead of him, giggling as Edmund spanked her mischievously.

She ran straight to the bathroom and turned on the water to begin filling the bath, and Edmund followed her in and locked the door behind him.

"I suppose I could have just taken a long, cool bath this morning, and then we wouldn't have put ourselves in danger," Edmund said guiltily.

"Hogwash, darling. You wanted to swim, and so did I. Oz, and Stanley and the boys wanted to go, and even Leo was happy with the excursion. It was a lovely day overall, don't you think?"

"Except for everyone nearly drowning."

Eleanor didn't like where his mind was headed, and she pulled off his shoulder straps, peeling off his bathing suit to distract him. It didn't work.

"I don't know how, but I feel like it's all somehow my fault," he admitted.

"Darling, it wasn't your fault. These odd occurrences were plaguing the town for months before we arrived. Think of how lucky they were that you were there to help."

"A lot of help, I was," he humphed. "I didn't rescue anyone. Not one person. If it hadn't been for Doctor Carpenter and Percy and even Stanley, all those boys would've drowned. I couldn't even save myself."

Eleanor pulled down her top, sighing with relief as she released her breasts from the tight fabric, but even her enticing move couldn't distract him.

"You seemed perfectly fine in the end, darling. Don't you think?"

She kissed him gently on the lips, but he pulled away and began slowly pacing.

"I didn't save myself, Eleanor. I was too distracted by the frenzy to think about it clearly earlier, but you were right about what you said to Doctor Carpenter. I think that the giant squid was trying to help. I couldn't free myself from the current. As I fought harder, it pushed me down deeper. It was like I was trapped in a heavy net that was squeezing me tighter and tighter until I thought I might implode, but then that squid ripped me out of it. I felt something from the squid when I was in its grip... it wasn't the same lurking evil that has been bothering me, but it was still familiar and frightening… I can't explain it."

Eleanor finished peeling off her bathing suit and stood before him naked.

"Perhaps we discovered an unexpected ally, darling. That should be cause for some cheer, don't you think?"

He finally wrapped his arms around her, cupping her bum and licking her tongue.

"I suppose through my bumbling, I did manage to escape without showing off my foreign talents to the others. That must count for something… although…" He trailed off.

"Although?" Eleanor coaxed.

"It's silly, I shouldn't even say it."

"Why not, darling? You can tell me anything."

"What did you really mean earlier when you were talking about mermaids and angels and krakens, darling?"

"Why do you ask?"

He went to the bath and dipped his toe in, watching as the fresh water absorbed into his skin, eliminating the flaking.

"I assumed that my mind was playing tricks on me while I was drowning, but I could have sworn that I saw… and then when you said it… but it was too absurd… no, I'm not even going to say it."

Eleanor joined him by the bath and urged him into the water. He lay down under the running faucet and sighed with relief as the fresh water soaked into his parched body. When he looked like his flaking was finally under control, she climbed in on top of him, straddling him playfully.

"Say it, darling. I promise not to laugh."

He sighed a long sigh of concession. "I could have sworn I saw Percy swimming about with a merman's tail."

"A merman's tail?" Eleanor asked innocently. She refused to derail his honest confession.

"I told you it was absurd."

"I'm not laughing, am I? Tell me about it, darling."

She began gently massaging his chest, pushing the water from the sides of the bath onto it and watching it absorb right into him as if he were a sponge.

"At one point, Percy was pulled down in the current not too far from me, fighting against it just like I was. Just as I thought we might both be goners, I could have *sworn* I saw his trousers and then his legs turn right into a fishtail. That was when he broke away from the current and shot through the water away from me. I was afraid I'd already drowned and the whole thing was a dream, but then the squid pulled me out of it, and I seemed to be perfectly awake. I'm sorry, dearest. I shouldn't have belittled you for sharing the idea earlier. It was a rather brutish thing to do after what I thought I saw... I just... I didn't want to think about what it might mean."

Eleanor kissed him gently on the lips, and then turned her head under the faucet to catch several mouthfuls of delicious fresh water.

"What might it mean to you, darling?"

Eleanor was genuinely curious about where his mind was after the unusual occurrences of the past week. After all, it was the first time in his life he'd ever admitted to feeling something in the air all around him that he couldn't explain.

"I don't really want to think about it."

Eleanor didn't push. Instead, she continued with her gentle massage as he drank in several liters of water from the faucet in one long Rakshasa gulp.

"I can't deny that my people have an unusual affinity for water," he finally spoke. "We all drink like fishes, we like to sleep in the bath, we relish the rain and fog and humidity as if the water in the air itself is nourishment, and when I'm resting in water, I feel at home in a way that is perhaps more primal than when I'm walking about on land like an average human... and then there is the flaking when it's too hot and dry, as if we aren't really meant to be in such conditions at all..."

"What do you think it all means?"

"I haven't really thought of these details in this context before, and I don't like doing it now… It's too fantastical… I don't want to be some fairy tale creature… I don't want fairy tale creatures to exist at all… but then that kraken was conscious, I'm sure of it… It was as if it knew me, like we were brethren…"

"Are you saying, darling, that you think your people are mermaids?"

He blushed. "I'm glad you said it like that, dearest. It sounds even more preposterous out loud than it sounded in my head. No. I don't think my people are mermaids… No. They aren't. No way. There must be some other more reasonable scientific explanation for how these things fit together."

He reached up to gently squeeze her breasts, and as he perked up with excitement, she invited him into her and sighed with satisfaction.

"Well, darling, no one can deny that you have more pleasure at your disposal than a merman does. I don't see how a merman could have any fun at all, let alone reproduce…"

He smiled, and then sighed as she nibbled his nipples. "You are a bastion of reason, my dearest thistle. Thank you for indulging my whimsical imagination."

"All in a day's work, Colonel."

She moaned as he indulged his human urges, and they set about enjoying his return to confidence and his freshly hydrated vigor.

An hour later, Eleanor's skin was distinctly prunelike as she lay on top of him in the cool water. Edmund was fighting to stay awake. The last rays of golden sun had long dissolved, and laughter echoed from the lawn below. Eleanor smiled as she noticed two perfectly pressed summer outfits hanging on the hooks on the inside of the door for them.

"Darling, I think it's time for a feast, don't you?"

He grunted unenthusiastically, but then his stomach growled. "I reckon I could use a dinner or two."

Eleanor climbed out of the bath and dried off with a freshly folded towel from a stack on the counter, but as Edmund stood up, looking down at his fully hydrated body, he sighed with stress.

"Are you still worried about flaking, darling?" Eleanor asked cheerfully as she slipped on some panties and a low-waisted green cotton sundress without one of Kuveni's modern bras to constrain her.

"No… no, I think I should be alright now that the height of the day's heat has passed… no, it's just… I feel so much better, Eleanor. I feel as if the water was really all the nourishment I needed."

"Your growling stomach disagrees," she pointed out as she handed him a pair of loose grey summer trousers.

"I suppose…" He distractedly hopped around putting on his clothing, finishing off his outfit with a white buttoning shirt that he didn't bother to button up all the way, or to even wear over an undershirt. Eleanor ran her fingers through his salt and pepper chest hair teasingly.

"They all saw my chest all day anyway. I suppose I have nothing left to hide," he shrugged.

"Really, darling, nothing?" She copped a pleasant feel, breaking him out of his stress. He grabbed her bum, and they licked each other's tongues until they almost lost themselves again, and she pulled away. "Let's go join the party. That barbeque smells delicious, and I'm famished after our long day in the sun."

She took his hand and led him down the stairs. "Now, do you think that mermen would or wouldn't want to eat shrimp?"

"Humans eat all sorts of meat on land," he pointed out.

"Ah, so I think then that they would eat shrimp. Now, how do you think it would come out of them when they're done with digestion?"

Eleanor regretted the question as soon as she said it. He stopped and leaned up against the wall, refusing to look at her.

"I have asked myself that question about myself since I was a boy, dearest. I don't know where the gobs of food I gobble down go. It all just seems to disappear... I'm sure you've noticed that I don't... er... need to do any... er... ablutions... ever."

"Darling, I have noticed, but isn't it nice not to have to worry about where you're going to find facilities? Let me tell you, as a woman, it's wickedly uncomfortable to travel without a decent toilet anywhere in sight."

"I won't deny that it has its perks, but, dearest... you don't think... you don't think it's more evidence, do you?"

"More evidence that you're a merman?" Eleanor asked. She was finding his assertions more and more difficult to combat. His guardians' obsessive refusal to tell him anything real about himself had sent him along a train of thought that was now rationally leading towards a fairy tale explanation that was far more absurd than the truth they were hiding... or, at least, equally absurd...

"Darling, I think that there are plenty of other explanations for your unusual characteristics. But I can see that it's bothering you, so why don't you just ask Percy?"

"Ask him if he's a merman? He already laughed heartily at the idea. I don't need him thinking that I'm still a foolish child, looking for fanciful explanations for the perfectly natural world around me. If I'm not careful, they'll all just pack up and leave again, and then I'll be further from the truth than ever."

Eleanor sighed with frustration. His concern was not unwarranted after the many experiences he'd had with them. Every time Kuveni had revealed too much, they'd all followed Vibhi's orders and pulled back, leaving Edmund with an ever-growing list of questions without answers. But she knew her husband, and she knew that he wasn't ready to know the truth, not because Vibhishana, or the prophecies, or some godly Oracle from their strange world had declared it, but because Edmund himself had admitted it, not five minutes earlier.

She decided to use a tactic that had worked several times before.

"Darling, what would happen if you went right down to the garden, took Percy aside, and demanded that he tell you whether or not you're actually mermaids, and he said, 'Well, mon chéri, it looks like you've figured us out. Shall I show you how to make your tail?'"

He looked annoyed. "I don't need you to mock me, dearest. I already know how ludicrous the whole thing sounds."

"I'm not mocking you, darling. Some part of you is taking this question seriously, and I don't blame you. You know that you aren't entirely human, but you don't know any more than that. It is perfectly natural for you to want to know more about yourself, and now you've been faced with an absurd explanation that fits with the evidence. You should think about what you would do if you turned out to be right."

Now he looked nervous. "Dearest, Percy didn't tell you something in confidence, did he? He didn't tell you that we *are* mermaids?"

"Darling, he has steadfastly refused the notion that your people are mermaids."

She was grateful it was true, even though she knew that Mélusine's protestations were based on technicalities, just as her assertion that Yakshinis weren't fairies was based on a rather nuanced definition of the term.

"So, purely hypothetically, think about what you would do if he turned right around and admitted that he'd been lying. Really think about it, darling."

He finally turned around to face her. "I'd probably run away and convince myself that it was all just a cruel prank."

"And if you then woke up one morning in the bath with a fishtail instead of legs?"

He finally cracked a smile. "I'd be glad that I still had a tongue to please you, dearest, although it would be rather dismal for me."

Eleanor smiled and kissed him gently on the lips. "I love you, Edmund. I love all that you are. Angel and demon and merman, artist and lover and husband, champion of the downtrodden underdogs and the bright-eyed bogan bumpkins, and an extraordinarily ordinary almost-human man."

He fought back a ball in his throat. "I love you, Eleanor. I don't know how you manage to make everything seem okay."

"All in a day's work," she winked. She went in for another kiss and squeezed his bum. "I'm sorry that this guessing game is so unpleasant for you. Perhaps the greater meaning in all of it is that before you wake up with a tail or some similarly fantastical condition, we should enjoy all that your humanity has to offer."

She took his hand and guided him down the stairs, but as they reached the open front door and a hot breeze rustled her hair, she noticed Father O'Donnelly sitting in the parlor with a rosary in one hand and a Bible in the other.

A flurry of butterflies erupted in her gut at the prospect that he had just overheard their conversation. She didn't have a great sense of what exactly he'd witnessed on the beach, other than that Leo and Kuveni had already demanded his silence, but as he looked up at them, and Edmund grimaced as he took in a whiff of his fear, Eleanor knew that he'd seen enough.

"Oh, hello, Colonel," Father O'Donnelly squeaked. "I didn't mean to… I mean… I was just so tired of being outside, and after I helped Mr. Valov to bed, I just needed a few minutes of silence after all that happened today… I hope I haven't offended you?"

"By sitting in the parlor?" Edmund asked. Eleanor could tell that he was similarly concerned by Father O'Donnelly's jumpy demeanor.

Father O'Donnelly stood up and awkwardly bowed his head. "I'm sorry, Colonel. I didn't realize… I didn't mean to listen… If

I'd realized I could hear... er... private conversations, I never would've sat here."

Edmund cleared his throat awkwardly. "Well, my friend, it would seem you stumbled upon a private romantic moment between husband and wife. We always enjoy a bit of role playing, don't we, dearest?"

"Aye," Eleanor agreed.

She was grateful that he wasn't overly flustered by the intrusion, although, perhaps his composure was rooted in not understanding all that Father O'Donnelly had witnessed earlier in the day.

"I assume private moments between husband and wife that reinforce the sanctity of our holy union are permissible in your religion?"

Eleanor was slightly turned on by his dogmatic description of their naughty moment.

"Er... they are?" Father O'Donnelly agreed.

"Good. Now, Eleanor and I are going to go enjoy this lovely evening in the garden."

"I hope I won't offend you if I stay inside for now?"

"Please don't apologize for relishing your time alone. I know myself how daunting it can be to spend a long day amongst strangers; although, I reckon with our little excursion today, you're beginning to feel a bit more at home in Margaret River? I know I am."

"I suppose I am," Father O'Donnelly agreed. "It's certainly more interesting than I thought at first. I think... er... God has more of an eye on it than I realized when Mrs. Helmsworth called me down from Perth. I'm finally grateful that she did, even if she is the only Catholic in town... er... at least self-professed Catholic... I don't want to make any assumptions, and all are welcome, of course..."

He looked hopefully at Edmund, who shrugged and looked to Eleanor.

"We worship in our own way, father. Remember?"

"Aye," he agreed, working to hide his disappointment.

"I'm sure, like all good people, we have a lot in common no matter how we describe ourselves," she added more encouragingly.

"Aye, Mrs. Marriner. Saint Francis and many others would agree with you."

"Do *you*?" she asked.

He looked nervously at Edmund. "Who am I to disagree with those who are older and wiser?"

"Think for yourself, my friend," Edmund replied. "The time will come when scripture won't give you the answers you seek, and when that happens, you'll need your own conscience to fall back on."

"But what if I'm wrong, Colonel?" Father O'Donnelly asked with genuine puzzlement.

"That is a question that plagues the lot of us, my friend. When you have the answer, let me know." He winked, but Father O'Donnelly looked a bit overwhelmed. "Don't worry too much, father. I've come to realize over the years that we can only do our best and hope that it's good enough. That's about as universal a truth as I've ever stumbled upon."

"Aye, Colonel, I'll keep it in mind."

As Father O'Donnelly sat back down and returned to his reading, Edmund breathed in a deep sigh of relief, and Eleanor guided him out onto the porch and around the back of the house to the garden where Kuveni and Stanley were barbequing, while the boys were using rocks to smash massive lobster shells, and Oz and Yvie were more politely using metal shell crackers.

"Come, join us!" Stanley called to them cheerfully. "Kate managed to find us a cooler full of freshly caught seafood! It's like a Breton summer!"

He was standing barefoot on the grass, wearing a familiar flamboyant purple hat with a long peacock feather sticking up into the air along with a pair of bright blue knickerbockers and a loose purple button-down shirt buttoned halfway down, revealing a white undershirt that matched Father O'Donnelly's priestly style. He was using his left hand to manage several rows of odd sea creatures on the grill, while drinking a sweating stubby of beer with his right. Kuveni was boiling a cauldron of lobsters over a roaring bonfire and mixing a hefty potato salad in a large bowl. They both looked surprisingly at ease.

"Freshly caught seafood, you say?" Edmund asked with a raised eyebrow. "Where's Percy?"

"Oh, he and Doctor Carpenter are off investigating the kraken," Kuveni said nonchalantly. "You know these wild Aussie animals; they always seem right out of the pages of a penny dreadful."

"Looks like he let you raid his closet, greenie," Eleanor laughed.

"He did," Stanley smiled. "Actually, Kate did. It's nice to get out of that stiff butler's tuxedo... not that I mind wearing it, Colonel, it's a perfectly fine uniform..."

Edmund patted him on the back. "Don't worry, greenie. Mac isn't here to smack you around anymore. Why didn't you just tell us that he was a bully?"

Stanley's cheer dissolved. "That's how everyone treats me, Colonel. I bring it upon myself."

Edmund took him by the shoulders and looked straight into his eyes. "I'm just going to say this once, and you have to believe me, my boy: There is nothing you could do that would warrant the type of wanton, petty abuse I saw earlier today. Do you understand? *Nothing.* I don't know what bee Grimby has in his bonnet, but it isn't your fault. Got it?"

Stanley's eyes watered. "Thank you, sir."

Edmund smiled, and Stanley wiped his eyes.

"Now, tell me what you've got going on here? Is that a sea urchin? I didn't realize those were edible, which I suppose means that I am not, as it turns out, a merman."

Stanley threw Eleanor a questioning look, but as Edmund laughed amicably, he straightened his posture and began explaining how to eat the wide variety of sea creatures.

Eleanor grabbed herself a beer from one of several iceboxes beside the grill, and sat down next to Oz and Yvie to relax.

"How are you?" she asked Yvie.

Yvie took her hand and placed it on her belly. The baby was turning somersaults, and through her grimace of pain, Yvie smiled. "All's well that ends well." She squeezed Eleanor's hand. *I hadn't felt him move since yesterday morning. I didn't want Oz to know that's why I was nervous. I thought it was all related, and maybe it was. He woke up during all the action on the beach, and now he hasn't stopped moving.*

I'm sorry we didn't listen to you. You were right. We shouldn't have gone.

Who knows, Ellie. Maybe something else would have happened if we'd stayed home. What I've learned living here through all of these natural disasters is that we can't start letting fear dictate our lives—it will only drive us mad, just like during the war. When we start thinking about all the things that could go wrong, we only make things worse for ourselves. It was true then, and it's true now.

You're very wise, Yvie.

Peut-être.

Yvie let go of Eleanor's hand as Stanley delivered a heaping platter of tiger prawns to the middle of the table. The boys slapped each other's hands digging in, but Oz reached down and calmly placed his hands on top of theirs to stop them.

"I reckon we oughtta let the colonel have a bite, don't you? Eleanor and Stanley might want a shrimp or two themselves."

The boys politely pulled their hands back as Edmund took a seat across from them and gathered up a plate for himself from a stack at the end of the table. He started with one, but as his stomach growled, he lost his manners and gathered a heaping pile onto his plate.

"No worries, mates. I'll make more." Stanley took one prawn off the top to taste. "Mmm, *c'est bon.* Just like Maman's," he whispered to himself.

Eleanor was glad that Stanley was feeling good about something, and she realized that all of her distaste for him that had emerged throughout their unpleasant introductory days had dissolved. He still wasn't a particularly good butler, and he was a wretched spy, but she could see something else in him now, a spark of life that had been ignited without the overbearing presence of his father or Mac to keep him down.

He winked at Kuveni as he reached into an icebox next to the beers and pulled out a hefty second serving of raw, fresh sea creatures to load onto the grill. He pulled off two spiked sea urchins to make room for more shrimp and placed them on the picnic table in front of the boys. "The bloke who can figure out how to eat these will earn himself an extra lobster tail, I reckon."

The boys began poking at them, and Eleanor took in a deep breath of relaxation. A gust of hot wind rustled her hair, and she took a long sip of her beer. Somehow, despite everything, she felt more content than she had in months, since long before Leo's illness had forced them to take the trip that they should have taken as soon as their honeymoon was over. It wasn't a fair thought, she admitted, since they'd both loved their life in India, and their time there together had allowed them to perfectly settle into the joys of their mostly mundane marriage. But still, sitting next to Oz and Yvie in the garden and reveling in a wonderfully honest friendship was more fulfilling than she'd let herself imagine.

"This shrimp is scrummy!" Edmund exclaimed. "It's sweet and salty at the same time! Jolly good, Stanley, my boy!"

"Thank you, Colonel, but I think the prawns did most of the work."

"The high salinity of the water made them nice and salty," Kuveni admitted.

"Do you think it's safe to eat them?" Edmund asked.

Yvie spit out the prawn she was chewing before Kuveni could answer.

"Why wouldn't it be, my dear boy?"

"Do you know what caused the salinity to change?"

Kuveni smiled reassuringly to Yvie. "It doesn't matter now. Everything is back to normal, and Percy and I both made sure that every tidbit we harvested was perfectly safe to eat. We're proper experts in these matters, my boy. You must trust our judgment."

"Well, I suppose then, I'm glad your unusual underwater expertise allowed us all to enjoy what mother nature offered up," he said, eyeing her suspiciously.

"All in a day's work." Kuveni took a handful of prawns and ate them until Yvie relaxed. "We're helping clean up by eating as much as we can tonight before these unfortunate creatures' carrion disrupts the fragile ecosystem, so don't hold back, my boys. Especially you, Edmund dear. This is a perfect night for your voracious appetite to be put to good use."

Oz cracked his knuckles. "That's some advice that I can take to heart!"

"And to your stomach," Yvie teased as she fed him a shrimp.

"Is there some reason that you'd think I'd like seafood more than other foods, Kate?" Edmund asked as he ate several prawns in a row.

"Because it's delicious?" Kuveni replied.

"And why I'd care so much about the fragile ecosystem of the sea?"

"Because it's important to maintaining the delicate balance of life on Earth. Don't you care about that?"

"I suppose." He popped several more into his mouth and then waited to finish chewing before continuing. "I was just thinking, though, about some things I saw earlier today while I was trapped in the current… things that seemed to… er… fill in some gaps that I hadn't noticed before about myself."

Kuveni muttered something under her breath, and then smiled, relegating her visible concern at the turn of the conversation.

"Edmund, my dear boy, perhaps we should discuss matters of a personal nature later in private." She glanced at the boys who were still working on how to crack open the urchins.

He sighed with resignation. "I suppose you're right."

He reached over and cracked open one of the urchins for the boys with one swift Rakshasa movement.

"Whoa!" Mick and Mickey exclaimed.

"Ow!" Jimbo added as he poked himself trying unsuccessfully to copy Edmund's technique with the other urchin. The other boys followed his lead, sucking on their pricked fingers in their failure.

"I suppose I'm just a natural," he shrugged.

Uma stirred, and Eleanor stood up to grab another beer from the cooler, handing one to Edmund and another to Oz as she pushed down the fluttering anticipation in her gut.

"Edmund, my boy! You're looking better!" Vibhishana called, still in the form of Doctor Carpenter, as he and Mélusine approached from the front of the house.

They were both wearing tasteful light summer evening suits, and they too had a relaxed, fully rehydrated glow to them. Eleanor wondered if they'd just been taking a dip in the Sacred Well or some other Rakshasa bed in the far reaches of the globe, perhaps in Smyrna or Baroda or Basingstoke or Bath…

"Yes, a nice long bath seemed to refresh me," Edmund replied as he watched carefully for their reactions. "It looks like you benefitted from a nice long dip yourselves?"

Vibhishana looked down at himself and then at Mélusine. "Yes, I must admit that we did. We were terribly dehydrated from the high salinity of the water, but that too seems to have dissipated."

"Did you find our cousin?" Edmund asked.

Vibhishana glanced at Mélusine questioningly.

"Which cousin, mon chéri?"

"The kraken," Edmund replied nonchalantly. "Did you find him?"

"No, my boy. We didn't. We gave up our search for now."

Vibhishana collected two beers from the cooler and handed one to Mélusine. They sat down next to Oz at the picnic table, and began drinking with an admirable approximation of human speed, hiding their concern at the cheeky tone of Edmund's questions. They could tell that he was fishing for something.

What did he see, Eleanor? What is he really asking?

Eleanor relegated her annoyance at Vibhishana's sudden intrusion in her head. She closed her eyes.

He saw Mélusine transform into a merman. It turns out a lot of your foreign traits support the cockamamie idea that you're really mermaids.

Mermaids?! But we have legs! HE has legs!

You like sleeping in water, you're always thirsty, you're unusually absorbent, you dry out when it's too dry, and he felt a kinship with your cousin, the kraken... and, he <u>saw</u> Mélusine transform into a merman!

Blimey.

Exactly. I'll leave the damage control to you.

"Eleanor, are you alright?" Edmund asked as he noticed her sitting with her eyes closed.

She smiled and looked up at him. "Perfectly fine, darling. I'm just enjoying the feeling of this hot wind in my hair. It's wonderfully refreshing after a long day in the sun."

As Kuveni delivered a heaping platter of lobsters, Edmund took one right off the top and cracked it open with his fingers.

Oz laughed as he took one onto his plate and used the metal cracker. "Someday you'll have to teach me your technique, mate."

"I'm not sure you'll be able to do it," Edmund said truthfully. "It takes one with special, innate skills, I reckon."

He devoured the meat of the entire lobster tail in one bite.

Vibhishana sipped his beer slowly as he watched him.

"Don't you want to try it?" Edmund asked him.

"I don't eat shellfish," Vibhishana replied.

"Really, why not?" Edmund pushed.

Vibhishana glanced at Eleanor. "Because I'm a Jew."

Eleanor almost spit out her beer. That was not what she thought he was going to say. Her divine husband in all of his Rakshasa glory had just initiated the next step of a farce that she hadn't remotely expected him to perpetuate.

"Really?" Edmund asked as he stopped eating to assess him more closely. The boys whispered to each other with intrigue, while Oz and Yvie politely pretended not to listen.

"Why does that surprise you, Edmund? I look rather Sephardic, don't I?"

Edmund thought about the idea for an extra-long moment. "I suppose you do. I've never really thought of my father's agents as having a religion. If anything, I thought they would be Muslim, or Hindu, or perhaps Christian... and at one point I thought perhaps Zoroastrian. He's kept me guessing for so long, I've lost track of all my theories."

"Couldn't Mr. Johnson's agents be of many different religions, or of no religion at all?"

"Yes, I suppose they could. I suppose I should have considered that you wouldn't all be the same, but I was hoping that finding a pattern could give me another clue about my origins. I've become rather desperate to know... too desperate. I've been wrestling with the most preposterous idea as of late, but I think perhaps you've just cured me of it."

Vibhishana couldn't hide a look of great sadness in his expression, and then he leaned in and whispered confidingly. Eleanor took a moment with Uma's help to identify the language, and then she smiled at his apropos choice. He addressed Edmund in Hebrew. "There are many preposterous truths about this world, my boy. Far more than you know of right now. But I promise you with complete and utter honesty, that your native home is not in the sea. Mr. Johnson will feel dreadful when he learns that our lies have led you to such a fanciful false conclusion. It is his fault entirely for drowning you in lies, and he will find a way to remedy it."

"You aren't going to tell me the truth, are you?"

"No, my boy. It isn't the right time."

Vibhishana squeezed Edmund's shoulder apologetically, and then finished his beer. Kuveni handed each of them another, and as Eleanor went back to eating her lobster, Oz patted his stomach with satisfaction and then reached for another lobster, gesturing to the boys that they were welcome to join him.

"Show me how you cracked it with your bare hands, mate," he asked Edmund, bringing his attention back to their relaxed evening feast. "Let's see if I can manage it. I can almost outpace you at the pub, and this is a much more useful skill."

Edmund smiled gratefully at his return to mundanity and began showing Oz his technique, but at the sound of a car pulling up the drive, Eleanor felt Edmund tense.

As it parked and turned off its headlights, Stanley ripped off Percy's hat and threw it into the darkness, frantically buttoning his shirt all the way up. He switched his tongs into his right hand as he began muttering angrily to himself.

"*Gast ahas*. You should've realized they'd come for you, you bloody fool. It's your own bloody fault for thinking something you did might turn out alright, you wicked, doomed, hellbound chump… *What fools these mortals be!* You're the most idiotic mortal of them all! Stupid, stupid, stupid, stupid, Stanley…"

Kuveni wrapped her arm around his shoulder and whispered into his ear. "Stanley, my dear boy, don't let them get into your head like this. You are worth more than the vapid insults they use to harass you. You're a kind, loving soul, and that's what matters more than anything else."

"It doesn't matter, Kate. I'm bloody doomed, and I always have been."

408

Eleanor turned around to watch Mac and Lord Grimby approaching across the lawn. The dogs ran out from under the table to greet them, circling them while barking and then jumping up on them. They were not amused by their enthusiastic furry welcome.

Mac was wearing a freshly pressed butler's tuxedo, and Lord Grimby was wearing a formal white-tie dinner tuxedo, as if they'd been planning on crashing a banquet at Buckingham Palace, or, perhaps, at the home of the Queen of Australia. She could see that Lord Grimby was flustered as he observed their relaxed outdoor barbeque, landing his attention on the piles of shrimp shells in front of the dirty children without even a plate or a bin to contain their rubbish.

"Fancy seeing you here!" Lord Grimby called cheerfully.

She found his use of the same phrase that he had used every other time he was dropping in uninvited to spy on them odd. In fact, she found it downright condescending, as if he thought they weren't smart enough to notice that it was a harbinger of lies. But, as he approached with his hand out in peaceful greeting, smiling his overcompensating toothy smile that looked strikingly similar to Mac's, she realized that the phrase was not a dropped gauntlet, but a tick that he didn't even recognize was noticeable to the trained observer. It meant that he knew that he wasn't in control, and he hated it.

She smiled to herself. Leo would've been proud. She had just noticed a weakness in one of the most senior Secret Service officers in the world. Now, if she could just make it useful somehow...

Edmund stood up unenthusiastically to shake his hand. "General."

"I thought you were going to see a doctor about those nasty cuts on your face," Kuveni said as she walked right up to Edmund's side.

"Well, the next train up to Perth leaves bright and early in the morning. I figured a real man wouldn't sit around and pout." He eyed her. "You wouldn't know much about that, I reckon."

"No, General, I have no experience whatsoever with real men, only fake ones," Kuveni replied.

He smiled even wider, clenching his teeth as he worked to control his temper. "Colonel, the truth is, I think we parted on poor terms, and I wasn't feeling good about it. Mac and I came on by to apologize to you and to Stanley. I don't think we had a full picture of what was going on, and I must admit, I didn't give Stanley the benefit of the doubt. Mac would like to thank him for saving his life, and I need to commend him for trying to save mine. If it weren't for that giant Aussie squid, I reckon he'd have swam me to safety too."

Stanley watched them suspiciously as they walked around Edmund to greet him.

"Thank you, Stanley. I already called your parents to tell them all about your heroic day. They send their best wishes from the retreat in Brighton, and your mother wanted me to tell you that your father's treatment is going well."

"I'm glad to hear it. Maybe one of these days he'll kick the bottle," Stanley muttered.

The vein on Lord Grimby's forehead bulged with rage, but he held his tongue, eying Stanley's colorful outfit disapprovingly, and then pulling him into an awkward hug.

Mac stood behind Lord Grimby, as if he was waiting for his turn, and then he pulled Stanley into his own hug. Eleanor could see beads of nervous sweat break out on Stanley's forehead as Mac whispered something unfriendly into his ear.

"Cooking up a storm?" Lord Grimby asked him with a hard slap on his back that pushed him forward almost a foot.

"Shrimp on the barbie. It's a local Aussie custom," Stanley replied flatly as he clumsily poked the shrimp with his nondominant right hand. A whole row fell right through the grate into the ashes, and Eleanor's heart went out to him.

"Perhaps, Mr. Abernathy, you would do a better job if you were wearing something respectable," Lord Grimby muttered.

"Like a chef's hat?" Stanley asked. Eleanor couldn't tell if he was being cheeky.

"Or your uniform," Lord Grimby forced an awkward laugh. "But dressing like a teenager seems to be par for the course tonight."

"I borrowed clothes from Percy because mine were all dirty." Stanley cringed as he watched his father's judgmental reaction to the intel. "Kate was kind enough to oblige me with a trip to Percy's closet while he was off investigating the incident with Doctor Carpenter."

"Well, I suppose in the bush we can't expect anyone other than Mac to keep up a semblance of propriety." Lord Grimby moved his attention to the picnic table. "Would you mind terribly if we joined you for a bite, Colonel?"

"It's Doctor Helmsworth's home. You should ask him if you are welcome to join his dinner party uninvited," Edmund said, popping another lobster tail into his mouth.

Eleanor couldn't believe that her husband was taunting Lord Grimby to such a degree, and yet, she knew him well enough to spy the twinkle of impertinent mischief in his eye.

Lord Grimby could barely speak through his clenched teeth. "Doctor Helmsworth, do you mind? We don't have much food back at my place. I haven't been able to convince a quality chef to make the move down from Perth yet, but I reckon I'll find the right bloke at the right price with a bit of perseverance."

"Haven't found anyone willing to work for a barrel of future lobsters yet?" Edmund asked him snarkily.

Even though Eleanor knew his baiting wasn't wise, she couldn't fault her husband for doing it. After all, one of the first things he'd ever done that demonstrated that he wasn't a typical army sycophant was insulting the drunken, abusive heir apparent of the Baron of Heathfield on her behalf. Now, with Lord Grimby as his military superior, she found Edmund's brazen attitude even more captivating.

Lord Grimby refused to dignify Edmund's rude comment with a response, and he sat himself down on the picnic bench next to the boys. Mac collected an empty beer box from beside one of the coolers, and using his pristine white-gloved hand, he collected all of the crustacean shells, even the spikey sea urchin, into the bag. He placed it on the ground at the end of the table, and then smiled as he gestured to the boys to use it. Despite his seemingly friendly demeanor, there was something about Mac's forced cheer that struck Eleanor not only as false, but as creepy—as if he were a devious clown with a smile painted on his face, using his disguise to get away with something sinister.

Lord Grimby eyed the remaining pile of lobsters and shrimp, and then he turned his attention on Vibhishana and Mélusine.

"I don't think we've been properly introduced. I'm Lord Chester Grimby, Marquis of Clarence."

Vibhishana shook his hand politely. "Doctor Jacob Carpenter."

He turned his attention on Mélusine, who begrudgingly shook his hand.

"Lord Percival George Blakeney, Viscount Cornbury."

"Viscount Cornbury?" he asked with a raised eyebrow.

"I don't believe in titles either, mon chéri. I've seen them bestow unwarranted hubris upon malevolent miscreants too many times in my long life. I'm sure you wouldn't know anything about that."

Eleanor was both grateful and wary that her entire pantheon seemed to dislike him as much as she did, and that they were making their feelings known.

"Not enjoying the lobster feast?" Lord Grimby asked them. "Maybe Stanley could use some tips in how to make his sea monsters edible to anyone but starving yokels."

Eleanor was glad that the boys didn't know what a yokel was, and as she watched Lord Grimby size up Vibhishana's reaction, she wondered if he'd seen enough during the afternoon's skirmish to recognize that they were Rakshasas, and, perhaps more disturbingly, if he was intentionally jabbing at their typical lack of human appetite that Edmund fortuitously didn't share.

"I made the lobster, and I stand by my cooking," Kuveni stepped in.

"And I think that everything is scrumptious, lobster and prawns and urchins and all," Edmund declared.

"Amen to that," Oz said, working hard to lighten the mood. "These shrimp on the barbie are good as gold, and I've had gobs in my life to compare them to."

"Don't share the colonel's cosseting opinion of Stanley's cooking, Doctor Carpenter?" Lord Grimby needled.

"I don't eat shellfish," Vibhishana repeated.

"Don't have the stomach for it?" Lord Grimby pushed with a bit too much of a satisfied sneer.

"It is accurate to say that I don't," Vibhishana agreed.

"Perhaps a liquid dinner would be more suitable," Lord Grimby suggested.

Vibhishana smiled smoothly and held up his beer in a toast.

"You must be hungry, Doctor Carpenter," Yvie chimed in with genuine concern. "Can I get you something else to eat? We don't have anything kosher, but I've been craving baguette and cheese all day. Would that be enough to entice you to eat? I think we have some époisses in the kitchen left over from dinner last night."

He moved to protest, but at her thoughtful accommodation, he smiled. "That would be very kind of you, Mrs. Helmsworth. Thank you."

"Please call me Yvie, everyone does."

"Not us, Mrs. H!" Dazza corrected her with his mouth full of shrimp.

"All the oldies, that is," she smiled.

Eleanor hoped Yvie's hospitable deflection would stand, but alas, Lord Grimby had come for one reason, and one reason only... to make trouble.

"A stomach for stinking French cheese and not for fresh lobster?" Lord Grimby needled. "You might be the only one, Doctor."

"I'm not," Vibhishana replied.

"He's a Jew," Yvie said quietly, trying to keep her tone calm. "Perhaps you shouldn't make such loud commentary about his eating habits, General. There are plenty of people in this world who follow religious rules, and in this house, we respect them."

Lord Grimby looked like he'd been slapped in the face, and his surprise morphed into antagonistic fury. "Who knew that even the bankers had their own angels? By all means, let's celebrate the chosen people with a song! Something about reclaiming Zion, I reckon? Stanley, perhaps you should start us off with a monologue from the *Merchant of Venice*. Shylock was an aspirational specimen, wasn't he? Making a good profit from others' misfortunes?"

As he stared Stanley down tauntingly, Stanley glanced at Kuveni, and then at Vibhishana. Eleanor was proud to see a twinkle of adolescent rebellion in his eye.

"Hath not a Jew eyes? Hath not a Jew hands, organs, dimensions, senses, affections, passions..." Lord Grimby looked like he might explode with rage at Stanley's choice of monologue, and as Stanley watched his satisfyingly irate reaction, he cleared his throat and doubled down with his drama. *"Fed with the same food, hurt with the same weapons, subject to the same diseases, warmed and cooled by the same winter and summer as a Christian is? If you prick us, do we not bleed?"*

"If we prick you, will you bleed, Doctor Carpenter?" Lord Grimby interrupted.

414

Stanley kept going. "*If you tickle us, do we not laugh? If you poison us, do we not die?*"

"If we poison you, will you die, Doctor? Or, perhaps all we need is a bit of salt?" Grimby needled.

"*Ça suffit!*" Yvie hissed. "You will stop it this instant!"

"*AND, IF YOU WRONG US, SHALL WE NOT SEEK REVENGE?!*" Stanley shouted as he held up his tongs like a sword ready for battle. Kuveni offered him a supportive wink, and he returned the tongs to his left hand, took a sip of his beer, and went back to competently turning the shrimp.

"*That* we shall," Vibhishana said quietly as he threw a look of such powerful silent fury at Grimby that even Eleanor shivered.

Grimby's face turned white with fear, but then he cleared his throat and forced a chuckle. "No need for threats at a friendly garden barbeque, Doctor."

Oz lowered his voice. "Bloody oath, mate, you're being a right pommie bastard. We don't need any more trouble tonight. I've kicked much bigger blokes than you to the curb after a rotten night at the boozer. Don't make me do it again tonight."

Vibhishana sat quietly, sizing up Lord Grimby and sipping his beer with feigned calm. Eleanor could feel Lord Shiva's heightened emotions rumbling deep in her core, and she could tell that he too was overwhelmed by the sheer impudence of the attack. This man who knew more about Edmund and Rakshasas than any human on Earth (who wasn't in their pantheon's inner circle) was trying to rile them up, seemingly for sport. The cool, collected general who'd intercepted them on the steamer had been replaced entirely by the petty loser of their polo match. She wondered how he'd made it so far in life with such a mercurial temper, ready to explode at the slightest provocation; and yet, there he was, staring down a man he'd watched using angel wings to rescue innocent humans, taunting him about his foreign nature in front of the very people he'd saved.

Lord Grimby was flustered as everyone stared him down, awaiting his response. He was too obstinate to back down.

"Fed with the same food, eh, Doctor?"

Oz shook his head and Yvie sighed with annoyance as he grabbed a lobster and placed it on the table in front of Vibhishana, and then took another one for himself.

Vibhishana only watched silently as Lord Grimby grabbed the shell and tried to rip it open with his hands, to no avail. Edmund glanced over at Eleanor, and then at Oz and Vibhi and Mélusine. Kuveni put her arm over Stanley's shoulder, and they all shared a satisfied smirk at his struggle.

The boys began snickering, and Lord Grimby's face turned red, highlighting the bloody scars that were settling into his cheeks. As the sight became more and more awkward, Mac grabbed the metal cracker and stepped in, cracking the lobster shell for him and then stepping back to his butling position with his arms crossed like a bodyguard.

With a subtle wink, Oz used the technique Edmund had just taught him, cracking his lobster successfully with his hands. The boys offered him high fives, and then Mélusine picked up a lobster and cracked it open with a graceful pinch of her fingers. Edmund joined in with the humiliation, returning to the platter to take another for himself, and as he cracked his open with just his fingers, Kuveni urged Stanley to pick up the one in front of Vibhishana. It cracked right open as soon as he touched it. Stanley hid his surprise at his easy triumph and ate the meat of the tail in one flourished, slurpy bite.

Lord Grimby growled, refusing to look at them as he dug the meat out of the shell and settled into merciful silence.

"I'll go get the époisses, Doctor Carpenter," Yvie said as she leaned heavily on Oz to stand up.

"I'll get it," Eleanor said as she hopped up and urged Yvie to stay seated.

"Ellie, you don't have to do that," Yvie protested, even though Eleanor could see that she was grateful for the reprieve. "I'm the lady of the house."

"I don't want to usurp you, but I thought I might see if any of that chocolate mousse was left over from last night. Do you mind?"

Yvie winked. "Perhaps you could bring back two?"

"Or three!" Oz added.

"Or four!" Edmund joined in.

"There should still be enough for everyone, ma chérie," Mélusine said as she finished up her beer and collected another round from the cooler for the group, conspicuously leaving Lord Grimby out along with the teenaged boys.

"I'll be right back," Eleanor said as she headed towards the house.

As soon as she was in the kitchen, she leaned up against the wall, glad to be away from the social battlefield.

She glanced around the empty counters, and then opened each and every cupboard, certain that Mélusine had secretly conjured her requested items with a covert finger snap.

"Ah ha!" she declared triumphantly as she opened the last cupboard.

On the bottom shelf, there was a full tray of fresh, glistening chocolate mousses each in a delicate crystal coupe, topped off with fresh raspberries and a dollop of whipped cream. On the top shelf, there was a beautiful cheese plate covered in fragrant, ripe, oozing french cheeses interspersed with fresh grapes and dried fruit. A heaping basket of fragrant baguettes appeared on the floor beside her.

But, as she carefully pulled out the tray of mousses, the door to the back porch opened and slammed shut. As she turned around to see who it was, her heart jumped into her throat.

There, in a grotesquely flaking black niqab, stood Surpanakha.

CHAPTER 24 – THE KRAKEN IN THE KITCHEN

Surpanakha kneeled on the floor in prostration before Eleanor, blocking the door.

This is very, very bad.

"Please forgive me, Your Eminence."

Eleanor concentrated all of her energy on containing Uma's fear. She approached Surpanakha slowly, with exactly the feigned calm that she'd used for twenty years with her most unstable patients.

"What have you done that needs to be forgiven, my child?" Eleanor asked.

"I know that you ordered me to stay away, but when I discovered that your human lackey was dying, I thought you could use my help throughout this trying time... so, I followed you."

"How have you been helping us, my child?"

Surpanakha looked up at her. Her skin was flaking just as much as her veil and her robes were, but her large brown eyes were still beautiful. In her calm state, a hint of the woman she had been so long ago peeked through.

"I haven't killed one human in your name, Holy Mother, *not one!*" she exclaimed. "Even though that horrid human tyrant and his minion deserve to die!"

Eleanor reached down and took Surpanakha's clawed, freezing hand, coaxing her into a standing position. Surpanakha shuddered at the physical contact, but she did not pull away.

As Eleanor noticed the white layer of salt caked on her skin, one of the day's biggest mysteries suddenly became clear.

"You're dehydrated. You should drink something."

Eleanor walked calmly to the sink and collected a glass from the cupboard. She filled it to the brim and offered it to Surpanakha, who stared at it with disbelief.

"You're offering me water, Your Eminence?"

"Drink," Eleanor reiterated. "The salinity of the ocean was brutal for all of the Rakshasas. It was brave of you to intervene in our battle with your younger brother so close by."

Surpanakha only stared at the full glass, struggling to comprehend Eleanor's praise.

"That was you, wasn't it? Our mysterious kraken ally?"

"I thought... I feared... I was sure... I was absolutely certain you would think it was I who'd attacked you, Your Eminence!"

"Trust in me, my child. The Holy Mother knows how to see deeper truths. Drink. That small glass won't be enough to quench your thirst. Once you drink, I will get you more."

Surpanakha lifted her veil with her clawed fingers and drank the water down in one Rakshasa gulp, but instead of handing Eleanor back the glass, she whipped out her clawed hand into a familiar black tentacle, returning the glass to the counter and switching on the faucet. She held her tentacle underneath the flowing water, moaning with relief as her body perked up like a freshly sopped sponge, and the salt on her surface cracked off and fell to the floor.

Eleanor watched the phenomenon curiously, pushing Uma's fear down even deeper. She found Surpanakha's tendency towards

420

non-human forms to be fascinating in its deviation from the other Rakshasas. She wondered if she had always been that way, or if whatever tragedy had maimed her had driven her to a special commune with the beasts.

"You look better already," Eleanor said as Surpanakha dissolved her tentacle, morphing it back into her skeletal hand.

"Thank you, Holy Mother," Surpanakha said with her eyes averted.

"Now, tell me, my child, why are you here right now? I assume you didn't disobey my orders to come apologize for disobeying my orders?"

"I thought… I needed… I feared… I couldn't leave it alone! I couldn't have you believing that I was a blasphemous fiend, Your Eminence! That it was I who'd attacked you and Young Edmund!"

"I believe you," Eleanor said simply.

"I didn't think you would. I thought I would have to prove it to you." She reached into her robe and pulled out a handful of matted, curly black hair. "That belonged to the demon's human lackey, Your Eminence. I found him in the forest after you left the beach."

Eleanor took it and held it up to the light. It was certainly human, and unsettlingly familiar.

"What did he look like, my child?"

Surpanakha closed her eyes. Her niqab dissolved, melting into the male, aboriginal body of Miro in his ceremonial loin cloth. The ugly gap where her nose belonged was still the defining feature of her face, but otherwise, her impression looked exactly like the young man who'd paid Oz and Yvie a disconcerting visit earlier that week.

"Did you kill him?"

"No, I didn't, Your Eminence! I swear it! I let him go so I could follow him and learn more about his master, but then my meddling brother came sniffing around with Melysium, and I had to leave before they realized I was there! He ruined everything!"

"What would've happened if you'd revealed yourself to him in peace like you've just come to me? Couldn't you have worked together for a shared cause?"

Surpanakha morphed into her most natural human form, the mutilated Indic woman with long, silky black hair clad in a flowing lehenga covered in iridescent black dragon scales. It was the same form Eleanor had seen once before, the form that was beautiful except for the gaping wound she couldn't hide. Eleanor observed it for a longer moment than she'd been able to before, without the distraction of Surpanakha's battle with Vibhishana in the Nizam's tower in Hyderabad after she'd tortured Edmund as a twisted birthday gift and kidnapped Eleanor, not realizing which avatar she'd ensnared.

There was something familiar about Surpanakha in her calm, humanoid state—something about her mannerisms that she shared with Vibhishana, and even Edmund. Eleanor found the family resemblance fascinating. It made it harder for her to think of Surpanakha as the soulless monster that everyone in their world, even Uma, feared.

Eleanor gestured for Surpanakha to sit at a small table in the corner with two chairs, and Surpanakha once again looked confused by the personal gesture.

"You wish me to sit, Your Eminence?" She kneeled on the floor, but Eleanor gently took her arm and coaxed her up.

"No, my child, I do not want you to prostrate yourself at my feet. I just want you to sit with me for a bit. Would you like some chocolate mousse? Mélusine made it. It's wonderfully rich with a perfect hint of bitterness."

"I don't eat, Your Eminence. The process of digestion distracts me."

"Suit yourself." Eleanor grabbed one of the mousses from the tray and a spoon from the closest drawer and sat herself down at the table, reiterating her gesture for Surpanakha to join her.

Surpanakha watched her skeptically, as if it was a trap, but as Eleanor ate her first bite, she took a seat across from her, placing her clawed hands on top of each other on the table where Eleanor could see them.

Eleanor snapped her fingers. "I know what we need!" Surpanakha was startled, and her eyes turned black. "Don't be afraid, my child. This isn't some sort of devious ploy to ensnare you." Eleanor waited for Surpanakha's eyes to return to their soulful brown. "There is a bottle of Mélusine's cognac in the cupboard above the sink, just there." Eleanor pointed. "You may grab it, or I will do it myself, whichever you prefer."

"Why do you want to sit here and sip cognac with a fiend?"

"Because, my child, you are better company than those two human wankers who just crashed our leisurely party out in the garden... That is *not* an invitation for you to kill them."

"They deserve to die," Surpanakha hissed as her eyes turned black at the vengeful thought. "They're traitors, my lady. They are collecting information about our people for the British government to use against us."

"And what do you think will happen if it becomes clear to their superiors that they were brutally slaughtered by a Rakshasa, my child? How will that help?"

"Do you have a different plan to stop them, Your Eminence? They will not acknowledge your divinity. They're selfish, greedy, blasphemous fools. I know the type only too well, and the only fate they deserve is a painful, karmic death."

Eleanor thought carefully about what to reveal. "I do have a plan, my child. I have already infiltrated their chain of command with a spy of my own. He will feed them false information about us, while helping us use their resources to cover our tracks, just as Leo did."

Surpanakha scrunched her forehead as the contemplated the idea. "Your dying human butler was a double agent?"

"He was."

"Loyal to you?"

"As loyal as anyone could possibly be."

"And that waifish boy who fought off the current with just his flailing legs today is his replacement?"

"He is. His superiors disrespect him enough that all of his misinformation on our behalf will be considered ineptitude if he gets caught. He will be able to serve us loyally for decades now—long enough to stay with us throughout Edmund's transitions."

Eleanor took another bite of her mousse, focusing on the flavor instead of her nerves as Surpanakha grimaced, thinking through Eleanor's intel. She hoped that she hadn't just fed the beast.

"Please forgive me, Your Eminence. I shouldn't have questioned you. You are as wise as you are forgiving."

"And I am as forgiving as I am thirsty," Eleanor quipped. "Shall I get the cognac myself?"

Surpanakha eyed her, still on alert for some form of deception, but as Eleanor calmly ate another bite of her mousse, Surpanakha blurred up and grabbed the cognac and two glasses. Eleanor poured them each a hefty taste, and then clinked Surpanakha's glass.

Surpanakha only stared at it as Eleanor took in a long, savoring sip.

"Thank you, my child. This is just the distraction I needed after today's theatrics."

"I do not understand how you aren't afraid of me, Your Eminence. Everyone is afraid of me, especially with my disgusting wound on display."

"I am the Holy Mother, my child. I see all that you are, not just your faults, just as a mother should."

"My mother saw nothing but my wickedness." Surpanakha stared down at her glass and then took a small sip.

"So did mine," Eleanor admitted.

"My mother was right," Surpanakha countered.

424

"Mine wasn't." Eleanor took another sip. "I don't believe yours was either. I see a woman before me now who risked pain and humiliation earlier today to help her goddess, the nephew she loves, and even some simpleton humans."

Surpanakha's eyes turned black as she battled another wave of madness.

"Release yourself from your pain, my child. Focus on my voice. It is Shakti's will."

"Love is folly," Surpanakha said as she reopened her eyes, barely holding back her demon. "It ruins anyone who feels it."

"Has Edmund's love for me ruined him? He's much stronger than he was when I met him. I'm sure you know him well enough to see his transformation."

"He will be ruined when you're dead, Your Eminence. He will be a worthless, whimpering weakling, ripe for the slaughter."

"Who will slaughter him? Not you, I assume?"

"Of course not! I love him! I'm his Auntie Surpanakha!"

Eleanor smiled. "That's what I thought. So, who else are you worried will slaughter him? His wicked father?"

"If the King of Darkness discovers that Edmund is his son, Edmund will wish he'd died a quick death. My brother will torture him endlessly as punishment for the treachery of his mother."

"So, is that what you're afraid of? Ravana torturing him?"

"If he is weak, he is vulnerable, Your Eminence. Any enemy could slay him, even a human one! He isn't strong like I am! His humanity has infected him!"

Eleanor couldn't help but chuckle. "He is half human, my child. He cannot be infected by being who he is."

"He is a demon, and he should act like one. It is the only way he'll be safe."

Eleanor didn't like the dark glint in Surpanakha's eyes as she said it. "You must protect him from your own dark tendencies, my child. You must let him develop on his own. It is Shakti's will."

"But, Your Eminence, how can you not see that he's too weak? He couldn't even rip himself from the current today! There is a dark enemy stalking you, and its power is growing, and he isn't ready to fight it!"

"Do you know what it is?"

"I don't!"

That was the first time since Eleanor had revealed her divine throne to her repentant nemesis that Eleanor heard true fear in Surpanakha's voice, and that, more than anything, revealed the magnitude of the danger that was lurking. She took a long, distracting sip of her cognac to keep herself calm.

"Your Eminence, I thought I was well-acquainted with all of the dark beings left living on Earth, but I don't know who or what is here now. It feels familiar, but I don't know from where. It knows our people's weaknesses, and yet it doesn't suffer from them itself. I thought, at first, it was a pesky old Yaksha making trouble, but if that was all it was, it would not have been able to ensnare my beautiful Melysium like it did. I have never seen her forced to humiliate herself like that in battle before. It was disgusting!"

Eleanor smiled. "I suspect she felt the same way."

"She should have used her demonic form. She wouldn't have needed my help. My little brother's sniveling sense of self-righteousness has weakened her, just as it weakened Edmund. But will he admit his own fault?" Surpanakha drank down the rest of her cognac in one long sip. "Never!"

She slammed the glass onto the table with a flourish that reminded Eleanor too much of the exaggerated melodrama she'd used as the dragon while tormenting her in the Nizam's tower, but Surpanakha took in a deep, calming breath, barely keeping her madness at bay.

"When my beloveds suffer senselessly at the hands of their evil foe, my self-righteous little brother won't even realize it was all his bloody fault. *Destiny*…" She rolled her eyes with a gesture that looked distinctly like Edmund, "he'll blame *destiny* for their pain, when all they needed to do was use the power God gave them in the first place."

Eleanor was glad that her odd mood had led her to engage Surpanakha in the friendly chat. She was mad and unpredictable, yes, a victim of her own bloodlust and a thousand painful blows over the millennia, but she was not completely irrational. In fact, Eleanor couldn't deny that she had made a perfectly fine point.

Be careful, my child. Do not encourage her. She will twist your words into fodder for more evil deeds.

Surpanakha noticed Uma's presence in Eleanor's glowing eyes, and mistook its meaning. "Your Eminence, please forgive me! I didn't mean to speak out of turn!"

Eleanor reached forward and squeezed Surpanakha's skeletal hand. "I forgive you, my child."

Her eyes turned black, and then Eleanor heard it too: heavy footsteps slowly making their way up the back-porch stairs.

Surpanakha's eyes darted about like a cornered beast's, but Eleanor refused to let go of her hand. As she spied Yvie approaching through the window's lace curtain, she brought forth her divine crown, and with it, her godly glow.

"Be calm, my child. She is a friend."

"I can't be seen here! I'll ruin everything for you and Young Edmund! They'll see what monsters we really are!"

"Let me show you something, my child. Something that you need to see. Stay exactly as you are. It is Shakti's will."

Eleanor stood up, keeping Surpanakha's hand in hers as Yvie pushed open the door. "Ellie? Ellie, do you need help carrying…" She trailed off as she noticed them.

"*Mon dieu*," she whispered. Her eyes wandered from Eleanor's crown to Surpanakha's mangled face. "I'm so sorry, Ellie! I didn't realize you had… er… company."

"An unexpected ally came to offer us some intel about our invisible foe," Eleanor explained.

Yvie reached out her hand to Surpanakha, looking her in the eye, without giving away a hint of disgust at the ghoulish hole where her nose belonged. She shivered slightly but said nothing as Surpanakha stood up and wrapped her skeletal, clawed fingers around her hand.

Yvie smiled. "I'm Mrs. Helmsworth, the lady of the house, but you may call me Yvie."

Eleanor worked to control her nerves as Surpanakha held on too long for comfort, watching Yvie's calm reaction with puzzlement.

"I was just leaving," Surpanakha replied.

"You don't have to leave. Anyone of virtue is welcome in our home, human and non-human alike, although, it might be wiser to stay inside for a few more minutes. Edmund is having a final word with our uninvited guests. They should be leaving momentarily. Can I get you something? We have red wine and cognac and tea and hot milk, and some of the others have been enjoying beer for a change tonight. I was almost tempted myself to indulge, but the little one wouldn't let me get away with it."

Surpanakha finally pulled her hand away, looking down at it, almost as if she was making sure that it was still as ghoulish as she thought it was.

"I've already had all that I needed to drink, thank you," Surpanakha replied. She bowed her head and averted her eyes. "Thank you, Holy Mother, for your generous counsel. I will endeavor to serve you as best I can within the restrictions you've given me. Please be careful, and gather your strength. You will need all of your divine power to fight on behalf of those who are pointlessly weak around you."

"Thank you for your help today, my child. Take with you my blessings."

Surpanakha morphed back into her niqab, but as she opened the back door, Vibhishana was coming up the stairs.

"Brother!" she hissed.

428

"*You!*" he hissed back.

They took one ferocious look at each other, and with a whoosh and a draft, they both disappeared into the dark vineyards.

Leave her alone, D.H.! She isn't the enemy today!

You were just talking to her? Willingly? Eleanor, she could have killed you!

And yet she didn't. She's here to help, Vibhi, and you should let her.

She's devious, Eleanor! She lured you into a false sense of security so she could strike!

Do you think I'm that dense? Do you really think I can't tell when I'm being misled?

Eleanor, she's lured brilliant victims to horrifically violent deaths for thousands of years!

That isn't what she was doing here. You should believe your divine wife. We have another shared enemy, and we need her help, just like we needed it today. She was the kraken. She was helping earlier, and she's helping now.

SHE LIES, Eleanor!

You'll only bring misery on us all if you pursue her. We have bigger fish to fry. It is Shakti's will!

Do not confuse the divine voices inside of you with your own, Eleanor.

Ditto.

I'm sorry. I have to follow my instincts. I must keep her away from you and Edmund and Kuveni. She must stay away!

Eleanor sighed with extreme annoyance.

As you wish, D.H. I'll prepare to fight our unseen enemy alone. May Shakti give me the power I need to triumph when it matters most.

He didn't respond.

"Ellie, are you alright?" Yvie asked.

"Perfectly fine," Eleanor lied. "Let's get these mousses out to our guests before they spoil."

"Ellie... your... eh... crown is still on your head... and you're... eh... still glowing."

Eleanor smiled. She closed her eyes and released her divine features. "You have no idea how helpful you just were, Yvie."

"That visitor wasn't a friend, was she?" Yvie said as she glanced out the back door to where they'd disappeared. "There was something fierce about her, beyond her foreign physicality."

"Normally, she's quite a villain," Eleanor agreed. "But she loves me and Edmund, and we needed her help today. She saved almost everyone. I'm hoping that acknowledging a hint of light in her might help it grow."

Yvie hugged Eleanor. "You're an angel if ever I've seen one, Ellie."

As Yvie pulled away, her face turned white, and Eleanor turned around to see what she was looking at. Father O'Donnelly was standing just inside the swinging kitchen door to the dining room, staring at them with his rosary gripped tightly in his hand.

"Can I help you, father?" Yvie asked nervously.

"I'm sorry! I just... I didn't... I mean, I was just coming in for a cuppa!"

"The angels don't appreciate eavesdropping," Eleanor informed him.

He dropped to his knees. "I didn't mean any harm! With God as my witness, you must believe me!"

Eleanor looked into his eyes and observed his genuine trembling until he looked down and began whispering the *Ave Maria* over and over again. She released him from her gaze, although there was still something that was bothering her about his guilty demeanor.

"Leo and Kate already explained to you the need for discretion?" she asked sternly.

He nodded, closing his eyes as fearful tears ran down his face.

"The angels command your silence on our behalf." Eleanor guided him back to his feet. "I think, father, you've seen quite enough divinity for one day. Perhaps you can ask Oz to drive you home."

"He's going to take the boys in a few minutes anyway," Yvie suggested. "They convinced him to wait until they got some chocolate for the road."

As Eleanor sighed, readier than ever to be over with the day's drama, she picked up the tray of chocolate mousses, but Father O'Donnelly rushed to help her.

"Please let me take those, Your Eminence!"

At his use of Surpanakha's chosen honorific for her, Eleanor's Celtic temper erupted, and as she refused to let him take the tray out of her hands, it fell right onto the floor, shattering the crystal dishes.

"No!" he squealed fearfully. "I'm sorry!"

"Do you know how lucky you are that that demon didn't know you were spying?!" she boomed.

"I... I... I... I was just coming for a spot of tea!" he repeated. "But then I heard you... and I heard her... through the door, and I had to know if... if... if... if I was being asked to lie for mermaids or angels! Lying's a sin, you see, and I had to know if it was truly God's will!"

Eleanor rolled her eyes so hard that they hurt, and then she called forth her divine glow, her crown, and her trident all in one flash of bright green light. He dropped to his knees again as she pointed the trident at his chest.

"If that demon had caught you spying, she would have ripped out your spine and eaten it, do you understand? This isn't the dark stone hallways of some Irish country seminary, ripe for your eavesdropping on schoolboy drama, *father*. These are matters of divine significance. They are *biblical* in scale, and you will not distract us from our sacred duties again to feed your own petty curiosity. Do you understand?"

"Yes, Your Eminence."

"Stop calling me that. It is Eleanor or Mrs. Marriner. That's an order straight from the Holy Mother, got it?"

"Yes, Mrs. Marriner," he agreed.

"Now, go start working on improving your judgment, father, just as Edmund suggested. I can see that you still need some practice."

"Yes, Mrs. Marriner... but... but... but... how can *you* be the Holy Mother? How is it possible? Isn't the Holy Mother in Heaven?"

"She comes down from time to time to help on the earthly plane. This time around, she's taken up residence inside of me. Any more questions?"

"No," Yvie answered on his behalf. "Father O'Donnelly has already learned more than enough information that wasn't his to know. Haven't you, father?"

"Yes, Mrs. Helmsworth."

"I'm sorry, Ellie," Yvie whispered with a deep red blush. "I won't invite him around again."

"It's not your fault, Yvie, and you needn't apologize for someone else's poor judgment. But I meant what I said. Our visitor would have relished imparting a wickedly ghoulish punishment on him if she'd realized he was spying."

"She isn't the evil that's been stalking us, is she?"

"No. There's some other dark power far more dangerous behind it. She came to warn me, but she didn't know exactly what it was either."

Yvie sighed with stress and rubbed her belly, and Eleanor hugged her reassuringly. "Don't worry, my child. All will be well with the angels by your side."

"I just shook the hand of a demon in my kitchen," she whispered. "An *evil* one! And that wasn't even the most perilous moment of the day!"

Eleanor smiled. "You were perfect, Yvie. You showed her your exceptional virtue and helped me plant a seed of light in her. If you see her again, you must reiterate the exceptional kindness and acceptance that you showed her just now, and everything will be okay. Now she knows that you aren't her enemy, and as long as you keep your head on straight, you'll be able to keep it that way." She looked down at Father O'Donnelly. "There is a battle brewing, father, and everyone will need to support our band of angels if we're going to win."

She closed her eyes and dissolved her divine features once more.

With his shaking hands, Father O'Donnelly crawled across the floor and collected a mop from the corner to clean up the spilled mousses.

"That's a fine start, father," Yvie said sharply. "I'll ask my husband to come get you when he's ready to take you home."

"Yes, Mrs. Helmsworth. Thank you, Mrs. Helmsworth."

Yvie took Eleanor's arm. "*Viens*, Ellie. The temperature is quite pleasant outside now, and our brutish guests are leaving any minute."

As Eleanor followed her down the stairs, she heard Edmund's voice echoing from the side of the house. She squeezed Yvie's hand, indicating for her to go on without her, and then she tiptoed along the wrap-around deck, peeking around the corner.

"Good god, man, what in the hell has gotten into you?!"

Edmund loomed over Lord Grimby, who was backed up against the wall. Edmund's eyes were black, and Lord Grimby's chest was puffed up in defiance, despite the fact that he was trembling.

"I... I... I don't see how you can be so ungrateful after everything I've done for you, Colonel!" Lord Grimby stuttered.

"Lending me your plane and your holiday home for a weekend excursion on my honeymoon does not give you the right to be an abusive brute in my presence."

"Do you really think that's all I've done for you?" Lord Grimby shot back.

"I don't care if you saved my life, General, nothing between you and me gives you the right to abuse your son, or to invade my friends' home uninvited and submit an unassuming stranger to an anti-Semitic tirade."

"That man claiming to be a Jew is preposterous!"

Edmund was taken aback. "Why?"

A look of cheeky mischief crossed Grimby's face. "Because he didn't have horns."

Edmund leaned in, uncomfortably close to Grimby's face. "Do you think this is funny?"

"I think you're a bloody fool, Colonel." He gulped with fear as he pretended to stand his ground. "You're so bloody quick to jump to arms over a Jew and a gawky, deviant little pansy. For what? They mean nothing to you! Don't you realize what kind of power you could have with a man like me helping you? Even now, you'd have nothing if it weren't for my help!"

"What help?! You mean that incident with Lord Curzon in the catacombs under the mosque? You were both bloody lucky I was there, or more men would have died from your arrogant, foolish folly!"

Eleanor could feel Lord Grimby just itching to reveal everything. She hoped he would, and they'd be done with one of her most infuriating farces.

Lord Grimby lowered his voice into a furious hiss. "You have no idea what I've done for you, Colonel. No bloody clue."

"Enlighten me, General. You sure as hell didn't help when I needed it most."

"What are you talking about?" Lord Grimby sounded humbled for the first time.

Edmund lowered his voice. "I asked for your help *seven* times to get me out of the trenches after my bloodlust made me a danger to my men, and you did *nothing*, General. You kept me there, fighting against ghoulish shell-shocked urges for another year. Do you have any idea what could have happened if I'd lost control?"

"I made you stronger, Colonel. I proved to you that you were a man!"

434

"No, General, all you proved to me was that bathing in enough blood could unlock a ghastly, vicious monster from deep inside of me. You have no idea how dangerous that realization was to me and to everyone else around me."

"Is that why you're coddling Stanley like he's a whimpering babe in arms?"

"I trained thousands of cadets in the Indian Army. Do you think that I don't know how to bring out the best in my men? You didn't seem to have a problem with my leadership when you were sending scores of fresh bodies to be blown apart every bloody day in the trenches."

"Pah. The ones who didn't survive weren't strong enough to begin with! It's good for Britain that they're gone! It's simple evolution, Colonel, the survival of the fittest!"

"Your son and Mac wouldn't have survived if I hadn't rescued them. Did they deserve to be wiped off the face of the Earth for not running away while their lungs were burning with mustard gas?"

"Yes, Colonel. They did."

Edmund finally let go of his threatening stance as he turned away. "I can see that we have nothing in common anymore, General. Doctor Helmsworth asked me to inform you that you are no longer welcome in his home, nor is Mac. If I were you, I'd stay in Perth after you have a doctor look at those nasty cuts. There won't be much left for you down here."

"Is that a threat?"

"It's the truth, General, pure and simple. You already think the locals are worthless bogans, and you won't be getting any more social invitations from us or the Helmsworths. I reckon you'll have a better time making your mark elsewhere."

Grimby straightened his bowtie. "You'll regret this, Colonel. Mark my words, you don't know what kind of gauntlet you dropped today, but you'll live to regret it!"

"I'll live a lot longer than you will, General. At some point, nothing you do now will matter anymore, to me or anyone else, and you'd best remember that when you're wasting your breath conjuring up more ideas for petty mischief."

"You'll regret it," Grimby muttered. "Mac?! Go start the car!" he called in no particular direction.

Eleanor startled as she felt someone touch her arm. Leo was standing beside her in his pajamas and his robe, leaning heavily against the house. His lips were grey, and there was still blood on his chin from his last bout of coughing. He took her hand.

This is not a fight he should have picked, Eleanor.

You should have seen it, Leo. Grimby was a Class-A wanker today.

It doesn't matter, Eleanor. G has more power than he should. With one phone call, he can make things very difficult for both of you.

I'm used to life being hard. We'll figure out how to make things work, no matter what he throws at us.

I hope you're right.

So do I.

As Edmund noticed them, Leo let go of her hand.

"How much of that did you hear? I hope we didn't disturb you, Leo?"

Leo forced a smile. "I didn't like him anyway, Colonel."

Edmund didn't look reassured. "So you did hear it…"

"We heard enough, darling." Eleanor kissed him on the cheek. "Now, say your mantras. Grumpy Grimby's leaving, and he's not coming back."

Edmund closed his eyes and brought himself back under control, despite Leo's horrid state.

He took Leo's arm. "Come on, my friend. I think there might still be a few shrimp left. If not, I'm sure Stanley can make you more."

Leo moved to protest, but then he gave in. "Thank you, Colonel. I don't mind if I do. If my last seafood feast is half as good as the last beach trip of my life, it will be worth the effort of coming down the stairs."

And with that depressing, mundane truth, the gods and their allies set off to finish out their harrowing day, less ready than ever to face the brewing battle with their unseen enemy.

CHAPTER 25 – LORD KALKI'S TRIUMPH

The rest of the week passed by uneventfully, although Surpanakha's dire warning made the silence feel more sinister than ever. Vibhishana didn't return, and Eleanor only became more annoyed at him as she summoned him every morning to make sure he wasn't locked in some dungeon deep below the earth, or some other such fairy tale nonsense that had become a real potential danger in the absurd world around her.

His response was always some version of: *I'm fine. Let me do what I need to do, Eleanor. It is my sacred duty to keep all of you safe.*

She felt like snarkily responding with a version of his own reminder that he should be careful to separate his own voice from the divine voices within him, but she knew at this point that it wouldn't do any good. He was a god on a mission.

Throughout the week, the heat settled down to a pleasant, sunny spring warmth, and as Oz's birthday approached, a buzz of excitement began to grow. A familiar woman rang on Friday night asking for the Countess of Easton or the Queen of Australia, whomever was in closer proximity to the telephone, and Yvie joined Eleanor to receive the call from Dame Nellie Melba, who had changed her plans to return two days earlier than planned on Saturday from her recording project in the cave, just in time for Oz's birthday… as long as they were able to offer her a home-cooked meal and a comfortable bed. They cheered silently, and then accepted Dame Melba's request with reserved positivity. "Yes, of course, if that's what you'd like to do, Dame Melba…"

But, after the household awoke late on Saturday morning, the excitement quickly morphed into panic as the group was enjoying a leisurely Yakshini breakfast out under the shade of the karri tree.

"Mum, you invited everyone in the whole town over for my birthday? Why in all of carnation did you do that?! We don't even have a staff!" Oz exclaimed as soon as his mother dropped the detail casually into the conversation while reading out the newspaper's uninteresting weather report.

"Jackie, this town needs a little cheer after all we've been through," she argued. "And what better way of solidifying our position in the community than to show them all a good time."

"We were supposed to have an intimate family gathering," Yvie countered, "where we could all relax and be ourselves."

"We can do that every other night of the year," she shot back. "Besides, Freddy and Billy should be back from the ranch any minute, and they deserve a ripper of a bash after all of their hard work."

"Mum, they deserve a ripper of a nap," Oz sighed. "Where are we going to get all the supplies? Or the food?! We don't have enough food for a hundred people, do we?" He looked to Kuveni.

"Oh, dear boy, never fear. We will pop right up to Perth and get everything we need," Kuveni replied nonchalantly.

"It's too late for you to go up to Perth. It took us two days by train to get here," Edmund reminded her.

"A train? How archaic!" Kuveni laughed.

"I remember when trains were the height of modernity," he humphed.

440

"You will get used to times changing soon enough, Edmund dear. There are many benefits of the world moving forward, and today we will use one. I will fly up to Perth in a jiffy and get us everything we need. Percy's plane has been gathering too much dust anyway." She stood up. "Percy, do you want to come, or shall I go alone?"

"*You* know how to fly that plane?" Sheila asked with surprise.

"Of course! It's just like riding a bicycle. In fact, it's easier without those pesky pedals getting in the way."

"I'll stay," Mélusine replied. "I'm needed here."

"I thought you might say that. Shall I check in on your convalescing staff while I'm in Perth, Yvie?" Kuveni asked as she stood up.

"There's no need," Oz interjected. "I telephoned up to Perth last night, and Mrs. Jenkins is doing well. The rest of the staff has also decided to take some extra time to relax away from the poisonous critters. I thought with Stanley and Percy's generous help, we could let them enjoy their reprieve a bit longer... and they were scared of coming back."

"Scared? Why?" Eleanor asked.

Oz looked at Yvie, and then looked away. "Mrs. Jenkins was bitten by a redback in the kitchen."

"What?! You said she'd had a heart attack! Ozzy?!" Yvie exclaimed. "You swore you weren't lying!"

"I didn't want to worry you."

"I'm much more worried that my husband finds it so easy to lie to me."

"I did it for your nerves, Yvie. And for the baby."

"You should let me decide! You didn't think it was important for me to know that the redbacks had made their way into the house? What if there had been one in our water closet in the middle of the night? If I'd known they were in the house, I would have turned on the lights to look!"

Oz looked to Edmund, then Eleanor, and then down at his half-eaten pancakes.

"Ozzy?! The baby and I could both die from a redback bite!"

"I'm sorry, Yvie. I wasn't thinking."

"*C'est vrai*," Yvie humphed.

"What a way to treat your husband on his birthday," Oz's mother muttered.

"Mum!" Oz hissed.

"Well, I'd better get going," Kuveni interrupted. "I'll be back by mid-afternoon with all of the supplies. In the meantime, Percy, perhaps you can figure out where to get some banquet tables in town."

"There are some old wooden tables and folding chairs in Uncle Chester's storage shed." Stanley interjected from his butling position by the karri tree. "I found them when I was looking for more hay for the horses yesterday."

"Is that where you've been disappearing to every day?" Edmund asked.

Stanley looked down at his feet nervously. "Yes, sir. When he left for Perth with Mac, he just left the ponies assuming those local boys would tend to them, but I had a suspicion that they weren't going to do it after you told them they wouldn't get paid for their work, and I was right."

"Why didn't you just tell us? We would have been happy to help!" Edmund asked. "Eleanor and I are both consummate professionals when it comes to mucking out stalls."

"Don't forget me, Colonel! I was practically born on the back of a horse," Oz added.

"The back of a horse would've been more pleasant than the dreadful bushie bed I was strapped to when I birthed you," Sheila scoffed. Then she moved her attention back to Yvie. "But did I whinge on and on about it to my hubby like a no-hoper? Not on your life, I didn't."

"Mum," Oz hissed angrily.

442

"I… er… didn't want to cause any more strife, Colonel," Stanley attempted to move the conversation along. "You're all finally rid of Grumpy Grimby, but I'm still stuck with him… you know, as family and whatnot… and I figured it would just be easier to keep you out of it."

Edmund gestured for Stanley to take a seat on the bench beside him. "Stanley, my boy, you don't have to take the whole world on by yourself. You're in the Marriner household now, and we do things differently."

Edmund handed him a plate and stacked several pancakes onto it.

"I can see that, sir." Stanley's eyes watered.

Edmund patted him on the back. "Good. Now, tell us more about these tables. Are they big enough for our hundred guests?"

"I think they are, sir. At least they will be, if we line them up right."

"I'm sure they will be," Mélusine chimed in. "We're clever enough to make it work."

"Jolly good!" Edmund said cheerfully. Eleanor appreciated his attempt to lighten the mood. "Now, shall Percy and I go fetch the tables after breakfast?"

"No, sir. I can do it. Uncle Chester and Mac aren't supposed to be back from Perth until tonight."

"Are you suggesting we borrow them without his permission?" Eleanor asked with feigned concern.

"Yes?" Stanley admitted guiltily.

"Excellent plan, greenie," Eleanor winked. "Kate, can you collect some nice big table cloths in Perth?"

"But, of course! Don't worry about a thing, any of you! We will have an epic bash for our beloved Oz's birthday."

"See, Jackie. I told you it was a good idea," Sheila needled.

"Don't be late, Kate," Mélusine said with a husbandly tone that made Eleanor smile. "We must have the supplies in time to cook everything before the crowds arrive. Which is at what time?" she addressed Sheila.

"Six o'clock," she replied.

"Bloody oath, Mum, you didn't give us much time," Oz muttered.

"Six o'clock is the appropriate time for an evening to begin," she argued.

"Yeah, in the civilized world," Oz argued.

"Civilization exists because we make it so," she countered.

Kuveni laughed. "I think for once you've said something wise, Sheila!"

Before Sheila could rebuke her insult, Kuveni skipped down the stairs and across the lawn, pulled open the latch of the heavy hatch door underneath the fuselage of 'Lord Blakeney's plane,' and pulled herself up the five-foot gap without the help of a staircase. Kuveni blew them a kiss as she closed herself inside.

Eleanor was excited to watch the take-off, as she hadn't actually believed that the plane could fly. For two weeks as it had sat idle on the lawn, she'd subtly assumed that it was just a prop Mélusine had concocted to support her farce.

"Is it really going to work?" Eleanor asked.

"Why wouldn't it?" Mélusine replied.

"Touché."

Eleanor glanced at Edmund as he watched the entire episode with just as much curiosity as everyone else. Kuveni took her place in the pilot's seat, and with a roaring start followed by a loud sput-sput of the propellers, she started the engines and bumped the plane along the grass to the dirt road in front of the house.

"Is that road really wide enough to be a runway?" Edmund asked Mélusine.

"It is what we landed on when we arrived. Kate will do what's necessary to make it work," she replied.

Sure enough, the plane sped up, and with a few precarious pops and clanks, it was gracefully taking off, buzzing away into the clear, sunny sky.

"These modern sheilas sure can do everything these days!" Oz laughed.

"Kate is niftier than most modern blokes, as you Aussies would put it," Mélusine replied. "Is my slang improving?"

Eleanor smiled. "Sounds like Strine to me."

"*Bon.* Now, Stanley, I will go with you to Grumpy Grimby's storage shed. We should start now, in case it takes longer than we expect."

"Just you?" Stanley asked. "I mean, your help is always welcome, of course, sir."

"Don't worry, mon chéri. Between the two of us, we should have plenty of manpower."

"You aren't offering to help just because I'm daft, are you?"

"Mon chéri, you are a child. Children are not daft just because they have much still to learn."

"I'm twenty-two," he mumbled as his posture deflated.

"As I said, mon chéri, you are still practically a babe-in-arms. When my son was twenty-two, he was still a mischievous little rapscallion."

"You don't look old enough to have a twenty-two-year-old child," Sheila interjected.

Mélusine shrugged. "I look good for my age."

"You have a son?" Stanley asked.

Edmund glanced at Mélusine with piqued interest. "You have a son?"

Mélusine sighed with sadness. "I did, mon chéri. He has been gone for a very long time now. Now, *allons-y.* It will take us more time than it should to do this the hard way."

"What's the easy way?" Edmund asked.

"Someday I will show you, mon chéri, but not today. In the meantime, perhaps you should all rest up. We will have a lot of work to do when we get back. Stanley, I will take the front car, you take the back car. We will work twice as fast with twice the hauling capacity."

She trudged across the lawn towards the two dusty Fords without waiting for his agreement. He chased after her. He looked around nervously as he stood at the driver's door without pulling it open.

"*Que'est-ce que c'est?*" Mélusine asked. "You *do* know how to drive this thing, don't you? If you don't, we will need Oz or Eleanor to help so Edmund can stay back and keep an eye on things."

"I do know how to drive." He looked annoyed at himself as she stared him down, waiting for his explanation. "It was the spiders, sir. I was worried there would be more spiders. The little buggers make me want to crawl out of my skin."

Mélusine leaned into the car. "It's all clear, mon chéri. Do you trust me?"

"Yes, sir. I trust you with anything and everything. It's a strange feeling for me. Usually, I'm afraid someone's going to pull me into a painful prank."

"There will be no petty human cruelty today, mon chéri; I've seen enough of it myself for many lifetimes," Mélusine reiterated as she patted him on the back.

Stanley nodded and got into the car. As Mélusine sped off in the front car, Stanley stalled several times, and then in a cloud of dust, he sped off after her with a screech.

"Well, I'm going to take Percy's advice," Yvie said as she struggled to stand up and Oz rushed to help her. "A nap seems like a nice idea."

"Shall we, darling?" Eleanor asked. "We should prepare our outfits for the party later tonight anyway. We probably won't have much time to make decisions between setting up and guests arriving."

She took Edmund's hand and nodded a polite goodbye to Leo, who had been sitting silently in his pajamas at the foot of the table, nursing a glass of cognac as a liquid breakfast.

"Shall we help you to your room, Leo?" Edmund asked concernedly.

"I will be just fine resting where I am in the fresh air. Thank you anyway, Colonel. Enjoy your post-breakfast nap." He winked, and Edmund blushed. Eleanor offered him a friendly wave as she took her husband's hand and led him up the stairs.

As soon as they were inside, she flipped off her shoes and began unbuckling Edmund's belt. He smiled and slipped her dress off over her head, kissing her breasts as soon as he unsnapped her bra. He threw it into the corner triumphantly, and she raced to unbutton his beige summer suit's vest and then his shirt, but with a mischievous wink, he ripped them both open, popping the buttons off and shooting them across the room.

They took turns removing the last of each other's underwear, and then they lay down naked, facing each other on the bed. Eleanor ran her finger along Edmund's skin that still pulsated with warmth from the coffee at breakfast.

A wave of goosebumps erupted, and he sighed with satisfaction. "It's nice being here, isn't it? I think perhaps we were a bit lonely in India, and we didn't realize it."

"I know exactly what you mean." She moved her gentle strokes downward.

"I was thinking…" He trailed off.

"Yes, darling? Don't be shy," she stroked him playfully, and he sighed with pleasure.

"Never mind."

He pounced on top of her and straddled her, and she giggled with the thrill of his spontaneity. She sighed with satisfaction as he entered her, and then she let her mind go blank, reveling in the simple pleasures of two avatars becoming one.

She sighed louder and louder as he channeled his vigor into waves of powerful and gentle thrusts, bringing her to the tantalizing edge and pulling back, until she couldn't stand it anymore, and she gave in and brought him along with her.

They moaned together and then collapsed into each other's arms.

"I love you, Eleanor," he whispered as she lay in the nook of his arm and put her head on his shoulder.

"I love you, Edmund."

She began running her fingers along his chest in gentle patterns.

"What were you going to say before?" she asked.

He paused to think through his words. "I was thinking... I was debating whether to propose that we stay here for a while... regardless of how long Leo... er... needs to be here."

Eleanor couldn't deny that the thought had crossed her mind throughout the past several days as well. Even with the many odd challenges since they'd arrived, the place felt more like home than anywhere she'd ever lived. It gave her a little taste of the life they could have lived in Baroda, if destiny hadn't sullied their beautiful honeymoon domestic life with two of the cruelest romantic love triangles in history.

"It's not that I didn't love our life in India..." he added nervously as she didn't respond.

"I've been thinking about it too, darling. I think it would be quite nice to be close to Oz and Yvie. Perhaps you could be the local magistrate."

"Unless Grumpy Grimby wants the position. He outranks me."

"I have no doubt that you would be doing the district a great service by displacing him."

Eleanor had momentarily managed to banish Grumpy Grimby from her list of many worries, and Edmund's reference brought back the unpleasant elephant in the room. She had no idea what his long-term game was. She wondered suddenly if he'd had a plan to follow them across the globe all along, with a specific agenda in mind that they'd already thwarted without even realizing it. She found the contrast between her initial affection for the man who had loaned them his holiday home for their honeymoon and the petty bully he'd now become to be disconcerting, much more so, even, than when Leo had dropped his Czech cover story and revealed his natural British intonation for the first time. Surrounded by shapeshifters, she'd come to see past distracting externalities to identify the souls of her companions, and she didn't like the idea that there was anyone in her midst, human or otherwise, who was actively disguising their true selves so thoroughly that she, of all people, couldn't even recognize them.

A particularly annoying paranoid thought bombarded her. Could Mac's and Grumpy Grimby's bullying of Stanley be entirely a farce? A well-calculated ploy to endear Stanley to them through sympathy, just as Mr. Valov's Czech sob story had been? Eleanor mulled over the idea momentarily, and then she let it go. She had preternatural judgment, and she was sure that Stanley's misery and fear in the presence of his father was real. The boy was many things, but he was not, she was absolutely certain, a believable actor.

"Shameful," he muttered. "It's just shameful."

"What is?"

"Norwenn. Stanley. His harsh attitude towards his dead wife, and Reggie, his crippled son… and even Mac! Bully or not, Mac is one of the most loyal butlers I've ever encountered. He even gives Leo a run for his money! And yet here goes Grimby, prattling on as if the lives of the people who matter most to him are worth nothing. I used to think of him as a bit of a role model, even when he steadfastly refused to help me escape from the trenches, but now I see that he has always been just a selfish, uncaring brute. I should have realized it sooner."

Eleanor kissed him gently on the lips. "You give people the benefit of the doubt, darling. I love that about you. For every brute it invites in the door, it makes it possible for other beautiful relationships to blossom. Just look at Stanley! No one would have given him the time of day, and in just a couple weeks, you've helped him become a new man!"

"Hardly, dearest. You're the one who's really been helping him. I've just been throwing him some slow bowls in cricket."

"Yes, darling, that's all you've done for him," Eleanor winked teasingly.

Eleanor hopped up and scampered to the en-suite water closet. She went about her mundane hygienic requirements, pausing for a moment to smooth out the frizzy wild waves of her hair into soft tendrils, and then scampered back into bed with two large glasses of water. As she handed one to Edmund, his eyes turned black.

"Darling, what is it?"

He put the glass down on the side table as his eyes darted around the room. He got up and looked out the window, squinting into the distance, and then he examined the curtains and the windowsill with great scrutiny. He continued on his quest, pulling every drawer out of the writing desk, lifting up the cushions of the divan and the rocking chair in the corner, until finally he'd completed a circle.

Just as he was getting ready to change tactics (or give up, Eleanor wasn't sure which), he dove under the bed in a blur and ripped another death adder right out from underneath her.

With a flash of demonic ferocity, he ripped its head right off. He threw the carcass out the open window as far as his Rakshasa strength would carry it, deep into the vineyards beyond, keeping the head in his hand like a ghoulish trophy.

He examined it just as Mélusine had examined the other one on the day they'd arrived in Margaret River, looking around the room at the conspicuous lack of blood from the gruesome injury

450

he'd imparted. As he stared into its glassy, black, lifeless eyes, the head dissolved into sparkling black dust.

He kneeled down and picked up a pinch of the dust, putting it into the palm of his hand, and then he held it up to the light streaming in through the window.

"Have you ever seen anything like this before?" he asked.

"No. Never. Have you, darling?"

He scrunched his nose as he thought carefully about his answer. "Yes. Once. In some underground ruins, under the city of Ayodhya in India."

He held his hand out the open window and let go of his sample, watching it sparkle momentarily as it blew away in the warm breeze.

"Was there anything similar about that situation?"

Edmund furrowed his brow. "The only similarity was that Grimby was around."

That was not what she thought he was going to say, and she didn't like it one bit. She'd been assuming without question that Grimby's only role in the shenanigans around them was as Leo's Secret Service superior. Was it possible that he was more connected to their world than he'd let on? It would explain his change in behavior since their cheerful first meeting, although, Stanley didn't seem particularly surprised by his abuse…

She sat down on the edge of the bed and gestured for him to join her. "Tell me about it, darling."

He took a seat, but he didn't relax. He was still too troubled as he stared at the black powder littering the floor.

"I was commanding the special forces of the Colonial Army at the time. There were rumors of a treasure buried beneath the Babri mosque in Ayodhya, and Lord Curzon and Grimby insisted that we go down into the catacombs to investigate, even though the locals were up in arms about it. It was a site sacred to Hindus and Muslims alike, and all of their religious leaders came along to voice their protestations, but no matter how much I protested on their behalf, Grimby pulled his rank and ordered me and my men to climb down into the depths to look for buried treasure, just as if we were common pirates. Edward Rutherford and another chap, the Scottish one I told you about, Captain Ferguson, almost got themselves killed while we were down in the catacombs below, and another bloke, a young lieutenant from Wales, lost his life. He was the first death under my command…" Edmund trailed off pensively as the dark memory settled in.

"That must have been very traumatic, darling."

He sighed with regret. "By the time I got there, the deed had been done. He'd fallen down a chasm and cracked his neck. We couldn't even get him out for a proper burial. Edward was a mess for weeks after that. I was afraid he'd never come out of it."

"Was Grimby there? Do you think he could have had a more active role in whatever happened?"

"No, he was up in the mosque above, making trouble another way. By the time we came back up, he was holding off a riot of unhappy protestors with half the British troops in the province by his side. It took me almost an hour to secure our peaceful exit, and afterwards, he wouldn't admit his own fault in it. I was promoted to the rank of major shortly after that, and I took the promotion as an apology of sorts, but now that I see who he really is, it's clear that it was more of a bribe for silence than an acknowledgment of my wisdom in the matter."

"His bribe was Britain's gain… and India's for that matter. Having someone like you in command was probably useful for keeping similar incidents from happening more often."

"It was."

She was glad he was willing to acknowledge his own merit on the topic.

"But, darling, how did the black sparkling powder fit into the story?"

"The ground around Edward Rutherford and Captain Ferguson was covered with it when I found them. Edward was shaking, staring down into the chasm at Lieutenant Llewellyn's body, while Captain Ferguson leaned up against the cave wall, refusing to look at the carnage at all. At the time, I thought he was being rather cowardly, but now I realize he was protecting himself from more trauma. Neither of them could tell me any more about it than I can tell you now."

"Was there a snake involved?"

"I didn't see one, but those men were in such a horrid state that I could only focus on getting them out of there. Perhaps I should have pressed them more."

"Do you think Edward would tell you now? Maybe we should telephone him, if it would give us a clue about this dark force that's lurking?"

Edmund thought about the idea for almost a minute. "No. I don't want to ask him. He's still a bit fragile in some ways, just as I am. Every time I've tried to bring it up, he's gone a bit batty."

Eleanor made a mental note to ask Kuveni what she knew about the story later, but she was certain of one thing: If Edmund had seen the substance before, then it and whatever happened to Edward Rutherford and the poor dead soldier was directly connected to the divine shenanigans of their pantheon. *How* was another question.

She closed her eyes.

Do you know, Uma? Have you seen this black dust before?

A great evil has been vanquished, my child.

A great evil? Just like that? Edmund smashed our nemesis with his hands in one second while standing naked by the bedside?

He is Lord Kalki, my child. Lord Vishnu's power is exceptional. He has thousands of years of experience vanquishing evil.

Yes, but surely this seems anti-climactic? Surely there should have been a bigger battle?

Do you wish that there had been?

I suppose not. I just don't feel like the whole thing could be over so easily.

You are right to be cautious, my child. We are mortal, and we must take care. But the black dust does indicate Lord Kalki's triumph.

"Eleanor? Dearest? Are you alright?"

Eleanor relegated Shakti's power and opened her eyes.

"Yes, darling. I was just thinking about the implications. I think we should ask Percy and Kate what they think it all means."

"It is nice having them here," he admitted.

"And you haven't even become a lazy lout," Eleanor teased, glad for a change in subject.

"Not yet, at least. It feels like finally I'm not alone anymore. I hope they don't have to go anytime soon, but I keep telling myself not to get my hopes up. They must have very busy lives. Can you believe the brilliance of Percy's airplane? The military must be drooling to get their hands on something so innovative. I suppose there must be a reason he hasn't offered it up to them, Grumpy Grimby's temper aside."

Eleanor felt a pang of anxiety at his accurate observation. Could assessing Yaksha technology have been part of Grumpy Grimby's agenda? He had, after all, witnessed the divine transformation of Edmund's property in Basingstoke before their wedding. She *knew* they should have been more careful...

"We've all witnessed the military's poor judgment several times now. That steamer incident alone probably made it clear to Percy that the British military shouldn't have access to technology that they weren't smart enough to invent themselves."

"I agree with him. In fact, he and I have a lot in common..." Eleanor could see Edmund's mind wandering. "Do you think... do you think that he might be my brother? I know that he said that he isn't, but I simply can't shake this unusual sense of familiarity. It is similar to the feeling I get when I'm with Mr. Johnson. Although... Doctor Carpenter feels very familiar too... it couldn't mean... No, I don't think so... no."

"He said that he isn't your brother," Eleanor reminded him.

"Yes… I know. They all say that, and yet here they are, staying by my side as I care for my ailing butler. Why else would they be here? Because Mr. Johnson is paying them to come down to the edge of the world to look after his hundred-year-old bastard son? I don't believe it. Even Doctor Carpenter, whom I've hardly spoken to a few times, has a demeanor that is too familiar, familial almost… It makes sense, now that I think about it…"

"What does, darling?"

"I don't have the same sense of familiarity with Kate. She is effusive and loving, but she doesn't feel connected to me in the way that Percy and Doctor Carpenter do. It makes sense, if she is my sister only through marriage."

"But Doctor Carpenter looks nothing like you, darling, and for that matter, Percy doesn't either."

"Well, my father is clearly a skilled liar. Perhaps he's a cad, and they are my half-brothers. They could both just look more like their mothers."

"So, your father is a cad whose children from other women have traveled to the ends of the earth to look after you? Their kid brother?"

"If I had a kid brother, that's what I'd do. I wouldn't think twice about it. In fact, if my cad of a father disapproved of my plan, I'd probably lie about who I was! Maybe that's it!"

Eleanor sighed with resignation. It was both sad and beautiful that Edmund's desire for family had led him down this path, and she couldn't deny that the theory was far more realistic than his merman one.

"I think it sounds like a perfectly logical theory, darling."

He lay back and began stroking her naked back with his cool fingers. "I wonder what happened to Percy's son. Do you think the boy was his son with Kate?"

"I highly doubt it."

"Did he tell you so? Did you know he had a son? To be honest, I always took him as a bit of a dandy... I suppose I was too quick to judge... That boy would be my nephew, if I'm right."

"He did mention a son a while back."

"Do you know what happened?"

"He didn't want to talk about it."

"I don't blame him. If my child died, I would die along with him." He furrowed his brow. "You don't think that his son was alive during my lifetime, do you?"

"I honestly don't know, darling." Eleanor was finding his inquisitive stream to be particularly tiring.

"If his son was alive during my lifetime, perhaps I could have met him. Instead, they're all hopping about secretly without telling me a damn thing. I hope I didn't miss meeting the only nephew I have."

"Darling, if you really think that Percy and Doctor Carpenter are your brothers, and you just met them recently, what makes you think that you don't have other siblings?"

Eleanor regretted the words the moment they came out of her mouth.

"Do I? Do you know if I have other siblings? Have they told you?"

"No, darling. They haven't told me one word about any siblings." She was grateful that the statement was an honest one.

He took her hand. "Dearest, please tell me honestly if they did. I know they ask you to lie to me, but I really must know."

Eleanor looked him straight in the eye. "Edmund, I swear to you, they have never mentioned one word about you having siblings. And Percy has insisted to me exactly what he has insisted to you, that he isn't your brother, and Kate isn't your sister."

He sighed with disappointment. "I suppose I should stop chasing rainbows. It will only drive me mad not catching them."

"It is natural for you to want to know more about yourself, darling. You've lived a long time amongst secrets. But I trust their

456

judgment now. I've seen their wisdom too many times to discount it."

"I suppose they have many centuries of experience… it is strange, though…"

"What is, darling?"

"I suppose I'd just assumed that anyone related to me would be hearty, like I am. If Percy's son is dead, I wonder if there is some mortal blow from which I can't recover."

"That sounds like a good question to ask Percy."

"I did wonder during the war what would happen if I was blown to bits. I mostly managed to keep my mind away from the question."

"I'm glad, darling. It's not something I'd like to think about either."

"What do you think we should do now? It feels silly twiddling our thumbs while we wait for Kate and Percy to return, but I don't know what else to do. My anxiety has passed now that the snake is dead."

"Perhaps we should reanimate another snake, darling," Eleanor said with a teasing lick of his lips as she stroked him enticingly. She laughed with her triumph and climbed on top of him.

"I'm defeated," he sighed happily as they became one.

And so, they both pushed back the unsolved mystery from their minds, and gave in completely to a second round of pleasure in their post-breakfast nap.

CHAPTER 26—TOM OR SHEILA?

"My darlings, it's time to wake up!" Kuveni's voice echoed through the closed door of their bedroom. "Our dearest Oz is only turning thirty-two once!"

Eleanor stirred, and then resettled into the cool nook of Edmund's arm. It had been ages since she'd allowed herself to fully give into a lazy afternoon relaxing naked in his sleeping arms. But, as a gust of wind slammed one of the shutters closed with a crash, Edmund startled and sat up, looking around the room with black eyes for a culprit.

"That was hardly necessary, Kate," Eleanor muttered.

"It wasn't me!" she called through the door. "These gusts have been picking up all day. It took all of my effort to land the plane safely! Now, chop chop, my darlings. Yvie would like your help in the kitchen, Eleanor, and Edmund dearest, Oz would like your help setting up outside."

Edmund rolled out of bed unenthusiastically, and as Eleanor slapped his bum playfully, his eyes returned to their human hazel, and he began looking around for his underwear. He paused momentarily as he noticed the pile of sparkling black powder that remained on the floor where he'd left it after his earlier triumph against the adder, but as the echo of Oz shouting at Stanley traveled up from the lawn below, he ignored the unsolved mystery and blurred to the closet to pick out his outfit for the party.

"You don't think I have to wear a tuxedo do you, dearest?"

"Oz said to wear your favorite summer suit!" Kuveni called through the door.

Eleanor giggled and joined Edmund in the luxuriously spacious walk-in closet, sifting through the piles of silk dresses Kuveni had conjured for her. She settled on an emerald green silk flapper dress with one of the many Roman stylings of billowing folded fabric brought together flatteringly with golden ties around the low waist. She loved most of all that she could get away with wearing it without using one of Kuveni's modern bras.

She climbed a step up onto the formal dressing platform before the tall mirror (a convenient set-up that she was sure Yvie must have brought with her from France), and as she slipped on the dress, Edmund noticed her liberated state in the mirror and swooped in for a naughty squeeze. She felt him perk up with excitement, but as she kissed him deeper back, another gust of wind ripped at the shutters, breaking them out of their moment.

"Sounds like Scotland in spring. I suppose we were lucky that there weren't so many storms in Munnar. I'd forgotten how unpleasant the wind can be."

Eleanor was glad that Kuveni had finally taken Vibhishana's orders against Yakshini meddling to heart, although, she was rather surprised that Kuveni had managed to muster her rare self-control on such a special occasion.

"I hope it doesn't throw a damper on Oz's party," Edmund said as he finished tying his tie.

"He seems like he can enjoy himself in all weather conditions."

"He's a jolly good bloke to be around," Edmund agreed. "One of the best I've ever met."

She threw on her matching earrings (the same earrings she'd managed to keep safe since she borrowed them from Shruti on their honeymoon), and then she checked that Mélusine's pendant and Vibhi's bangle were in place before slipping on some emerald-encrusted sandals.

"Those are lovely," Edmund said as he noticed them. "The design is so interesting, almost Moorish. I've never seen anything quite like them."

"They were a gift from Kate," Eleanor replied truthfully. "Come on."

She locked the door, placing the small key in her hidden pocket, and took his hand to lead him down the stairs, noting that despite Kuveni's input on their dressing choices, she was nowhere to be seen.

"No, not like that! Be careful! The rope will cut you if you hold it like that in a gust!" Oz exclaimed from the lawn as they approached the foyer, where the front door was held wide open with two hefty wooden hutches pushed in front of them to keep them steady against the gusts of wind. A thin layer of dust had already gathered across the wooden floor. "The whole tent will blow away like a parachute!"

As Oz rushed to Stanley's side to instruct him in how to safely tie down the tent, a set of tumbleweeds blew past them, nestling up against the deck, which now looked like the color of beach sand, rather than the rich dark marbling of the karri wood underneath. Stanley squealed as he slammed his thumb with a hammer, and Oz calmed himself and set about showing Stanley how to use it.

"I reckon you'll do a better job if you use your left hand, mate."

Stanley looked around, and then guiltily switched hands, hitting the nail perfectly on the first go. But, as Oz patted him encouragingly on the back, Mac rushed past them carrying a case of wine, and Stanley swiftly switched the hammer back.

"What the hell is *he* doing here?" Eleanor blurted.

Kuveni walked up behind them from the direction of the kitchen. "He followed Stanley and Percy back from Grumpy Grimby's house."

Mac didn't even acknowledge Edmund or Eleanor's presence as he carried the heavy box out onto the deck and around the back of the house.

"He cornered them while they were loading the tables and chairs into the cars, and practically scared the living daylights out of poor Stanley. He claimed that Grimby had sent him back early from Perth, and then he insisted that it was his solemn duty to help us prepare for Oz's birthday."

"Why didn't they just say no?!" Edmund exclaimed. "I couldn't have made it clearer that he and Grimby aren't welcome here."

"Poor Stanley was too afraid to protest, and I'm afraid Percy wasn't in the strongest position either, after getting caught in the act of petty thievery. We've been assigning him the tasks that Stanley and Oz don't want to do, so I suppose it isn't a total loss."

Oz watched Mac disapprovingly as Mac returned empty-handed from his task, eyeing Stanley with a threatening frown as he walked along the wooden deck back to the front door. He didn't seem to notice their presence. Instead, he was singularly focused on intimidating Stanley from afar. As Oz nodded at him disapprovingly, another gust whooshed across the yard, whipping up the untied tent until it was billowing precariously in the wind, held down only by the one successfully executed stake.

Stanley slammed the hammer onto his thumb again and teared up, and Eleanor urged Edmund to rescue him.

"Looks like your help isn't coming a moment too soon, darling."

Edmund nodded, squeezed her bum, and then headed down onto the lawn to join the men.

"My boy, it might be easier if you hold the corner down there while Oz and I get these other stakes in…"

"Come, Eleanor dearest, we can use your help in the kitchen," Kuveni said as she put her arm over Eleanor's shoulders.

Eleanor took a moment to swoon at her husband's kind approach to fathering Stanley, and then as another gust of wind almost ripped the tent right out of the ground, she let Kuveni guide her to the kitchen.

As they reached the swinging door, Mac rushed up behind them. Kuveni maneuvered her off to the side so that they could watch Mac execute whatever his ill-advised plan was.

He was clad in his full butler's uniform with white gloves and a tailed-tuxedo, and his arms were shaking slightly as he carried a heavy silver tub of ice. He looked somewhat haggard, especially with his black eye from the polo match still prominently visible, and as he leaned the glistening wet tub up against the door to the kitchen, he almost fell over as the door refused to budge.

He looked equally confused and furious, and he leaned in with all his weight against the door for a second go. Still, it wouldn't budge. Eleanor felt Kuveni snort with subtle satisfaction.

"Maybe we can help?" Eleanor suggested. "That is, if you're willing to debase yourself by being helped by a woman?"

He rolled his shoulders, working to hide his annoyance, and his toothy, sinister smile returned as he bowed his head in unctuous agreement.

She pushed on the door with her index finger. The door swung right open, and Mac fell into the room. He dropped the ice tub, spilling its contents all across the floor and falling right into the wet mess in a move that looked distinctly like something Stanley would do.

Yvie and Mélusine whispered to each other about his uselessness from their position standing at the large center island, which was covered in bowls of rich, red ratatouille, each with a subtle difference in color and consistency. Mr. Valov watched the ungraceful gaffe from his position seated in a rocking chair in the corner with a blanket over his lap and a glass of cognac in his hand. He glanced at Eleanor, and she loved the smirk on his face as he watched Mac struggling to stand up on the slippery ice.

Eleanor noticed a glint of the same competitive desperation in Mac's eyes that she had seen on the polo field as he contemplated Mr. Valov's prestigious position inside the room that he had been unable to enter himself.

Mr. Valov held up his cognac glass in a feigned toast. "As your employer has told Stanley too many times to count, the real test of a man is failure, Mr. MacAllister. Now get on up from your fall and get some more ice from the icebox in the pantry. Stanley would have been up and running by now."

Mac's face turned red with rage, and he slipped and slid, grabbing onto an empty chair by the kitchen island to pull himself up. Mr. Valov sat sipping his cognac languidly as he watched him struggle.

"Mr. MacAllister, didn't I tell you that you were to complete your duties out there?" Kuveni asked him when he was finally standing again. His uniform was soaked, and his white gloves were dirty from the water mixing with the dust on the floor. "One must always remember that there are consequences for bad behavior. Now, I will clean up this mess, and you will continue setting up the bar in the dining room, understood? There are more cases of Margaux in the pantry, and then you can move on to the champagne, which is chilling in the icebox."

Mac eyed Mr. Valov again, and then moved his attention to the rest of the room, taking some sort of mental notes. He reached into his breast pocket for his notebook.

"Were my orders unclear?" Kuveni asked sharply. He nodded in the negative. "Then off with you!"

She practically pushed him out the door, and then slammed it shut behind him, whispering a quiet mantra.

"That man has been trying to barge his way in here all afternoon," Mélusine said with annoyance. "He's up to something, and I don't like it."

Kuveni glanced at Yvie's nervous expression. "Petty human connivance is of no concern to us today, Percy. We have defeated far greater enemies than him and Grumpy Grimby, and we will do it again if we have to." She snapped her fingers, and all of the water and ice disappeared. "See? Good as new."

"You should not underestimate their importance," Mr. Valov warned.

"Posh," Kuveni scoffed, a bit too forcefully. "Now come, Eleanor dearest, and watch the kind of genius that can be unleashed when humans and angels join forces."

With Mac's distraction out of the way, Eleanor took a moment to get her bearings. The kitchen was pristine, with neat baskets of uncut fresh vegetables in one corner, an untouched cutting board and stove along the wall, and an empty oven in the corner behind Mr. Valov that had been gathering dust since Kuveni and Mélusine's arrival.

"You look lovely, Ellie," Yvie said with a wink. "A perfect choice, made by those with only the best taste."

Eleanor laughed as she noticed that Yvie was wearing almost exactly the same dress as she was, a gift, she was sure, from Kuveni.

"It looks like we shop at the same store," Eleanor winked at Kuveni. "It looks better on you, Yvie."

Yvie laughed. "*Ce n'est pas vrai.* I look like I'm a balloon about to burst."

"You look lovely and happy and fashionable," Eleanor countered.

"*Peut-être,*" Yvie winked.

"Shall I change your dress for you now, Eleanor dearest?" Kuveni asked.

465

"No. I actually have another one in mind that's hanging nicely in my closet. I'll go change when I'm done in the kitchen, just in case I catch something on fire. I must admit that I can't be of much use to you here. You should all know by now that I'm a wickedly bad chef."

"Now, now, there are many jobs in the kitchen," Kuveni corrected her. "And right now, all we need are some tasters."

"How's that?" Mélusine asked as Yvie took a bite of a particularly chunky ratatouille from a ramekin.

Mélusine snapped her fingers, producing two more cute tasting bowls of the same ratatouille complete with tiny spoons, and handed one to Leo and the other to Eleanor.

"It's just as scrummy as the last," Leo said after he struggled to swallow a small bite.

Eleanor paused for a moment, glanced at Yvie, and then back at Leo. He had just used his natural British voice, free from the fake Czech accent he'd used as his cover for years.

"You're not the only one enjoying an honest week with the Helmsworths," Leo said as he noticed Eleanor's observation and glanced at Yvie. "Yvie and Oz have known about my position in the Secret Service since I helped clean up the mess on the Orient Express. They have been discretion itself."

"I'm sorry I didn't tell you, Ellie," Yvie said self-consciously.

"Think nothing of it at all. If I couldn't forgive others for their white lies, then I'd be the biggest hypocrite on the planet."

"How is it, ma chérie?" Mélusine asked as she waited for Eleanor to taste the ratatouille.

"About a hundred times better than anything I've ever made."

"Ma chérie, that may not be high enough praise."

Eleanor was surprised by the cheekiness of the jab, until she realized that Mélusine had meant her statement seriously.

"What do you think, ma chérie?" she turned her attention onto Yvie.

"*C'est bon.* The garlic is perfect now. Perhaps, though, the tomatoes should be ever so slightly sweeter, with just a pinch more salt."

Mélusine closed her eyes, and another bowl appeared right before Yvie. Eleanor glanced over to the pile of vegetables on the far counter, where the selection of tomatoes had just dwindled.

"And that?"

"*C'est parfait,*" Yvie winked. "I think the local tomatoes make all the difference."

"*Ça va,* one more item down," Mélusine agreed.

"You're using real tomatoes this time instead of just conjuring them?" Eleanor asked curiously.

"Real ingredients always taste better," Kuveni confided. "And since I supposedly went to Perth to get groceries, I decided to collect the best produce that Western Australia had to offer for a more authentic experience."

Mélusine snapped her fingers, and a massive bowl of ratatouille appeared on the butler's counter by the door, alongside several steaming, golden brown chickens served upon a mountain of roasted vegetables, a cauldron of coq au vin, a platter of duck confit with a heaping side of peach compote, an aromatic pile of fresh baguettes, and four deliciously stinking and oozing cheese plates.

"They had French cheese in Perth?" Eleanor asked.

"French cheese is far too delicious for the backwards Australian palate," Mélusine scoffed. "Those cheeses came straight from the Périgord, from a supplier whose family has been making them since France was Gaul. They have been a reliable source for millennia, even when the Normans were pillaging the countryside for sport. Now, shall we move on to *les haricots verts* or *pommes landaises*?" Mélusine asked Yvie.

Yvie clucked her tongue with regret. "We should have done the *pommes landaises* alongside the duck, so we'd still have a palate for the richness of the duck fat."

Mélusine snapped her fingers, and another plate of duck confit appeared on the counter.

"Let's refresh your memory, ma chérie."

As Yvie reached forward and used her fingers to pull a morsel of confit off the bone, Eleanor followed her lead.

"Blimey, that's good."

Eleanor reached in for another piece, while Kuveni took one and fed it to Mr. Valov with her fingers.

"I'm not an infant," he protested. As he tasted the rich flavors, he gave in and ate the rest of the bite. "It's the best thing I've tasted in years. Perhaps I should have asked for a supply of this while Edmund and Eleanor were guzzling down their absurdly spicy curries."

"Live and learn," Kuveni winked. She brought him the rest of the plate. "Eat what you can, Leo, dear."

"Now, ma chérie, let me pop over to our cellar in France for a minute. We still have some excellent potatoes stored from 1836. It was an excellent year for potatoes." Mélusine disappeared.

"What a marvelous idea, to be able to save the best of the best ingredients across thousands of years," Yvie said with wonder.

"If you remember after your beautiful boy joins us in the world, we will serve you some French wine from before the blight. It tastes remarkably different," Kuveni offered.

"Do you know for sure it's a boy?" Yvie asked. "We had to pick a pronoun to talk about him, since English is so restrictive, and I felt like 'he' was right, but I would love so much to have a girl too. Any healthy baby will be a blessing." She glanced self-consciously at Eleanor.

"It's a boy. Percy's never wrong," Kuveni confirmed. "You'd better start thinking up names."

"A boy… *un fils*…" Yvie murmured. "Oz will be so happy."

Mélusine reappeared with a huge basket of tiny golden potatoes.

"These will be perfect," she said as she left it in the corner and rubbed her hands together in anticipation.

She closed her eyes, snapped her fingers, and a plate with a few crispy, steaming, golden brown potatoes appeared on the counter before them.

"Leo should do the honors. No one knows potatoes better than the Czechs," Kuveni suggested as she picked one up and walked it over to him.

"It's hot!" he exclaimed as she tried to feed it to him. She blew on it like a mother feeding a baby, and then popped it into his mouth. "It's the best potato I've ever eaten."

"That is high praise coming from you," Kuveni winked.

"Are you really Czech?" Yvie asked casually. "I assumed that you made that up as part of your cover."

"I'm half Czech, through my mother," Leo replied.

Kuveni snapped her fingers, and a plate of steaming hot, golden brown potatoes appeared in her hand.

"Eat up, dear man. Eat all that you can stomach and more. I haven't seen you eat this much in weeks. If I'd known French cuisine would be the key to your stomach, I would have tried it sooner, but I thought you were quite committed to your bland British palate."

"So did I. I suppose there are a lot of things I didn't try when I had the chance, and now it's too late."

"Now, now, my dear man, don't despair. I'm sure you will try all sorts of things on your next go."

"My next go?"

Kuveni cleared her throat. "In your next life, but we shouldn't speak of such complicated things on a happy day like today. Tell us, Leo, what was the most entertaining thing that has ever happened to you?"

"Entertaining?" he asked as he took another bite of potato. "My life has been dangerous and stressful... and not particularly entertaining. I'm not anything like the spies in the fictional novels cooked up by bored moneyed housewives in the countryside."

"Surely there must be something?" Kuveni pushed.

"I suppose there was the time when I mistook the famous Czech opera singer, Emmy Destinn, for a prostitute I was trailing outside of the Royal Opera House... It was excruciating for me, one of my most embarrassing blunders, but the story is probably quite entertaining for you."

"Do tell!" Kuveni clapped with excitement.

He glanced at Eleanor. "I will tell, if you promise not to judge. You must save your judgement for later, when I tell you all of the stories that aren't fit for polite company."

"Please, Leo, I would love to hear it," she reiterated.

"I suppose I was about Stanley's age..." He trailed off with a wistful sigh. "In many ways I was less foolish than he is. I was more competent, I think, and more coordinated, but I was an arrogant little bastard. I was assigned to infiltrate the London brothels, to capture Czech spies who were using them to smuggle information back to the Austro-Hungarians." He chuckled at the memory. "Assigning an arrogant, virile young man to the task was about the worst idea my commanders had ever had, and I proved exactly how bad a choice it was immediately, when I fell for the wiles of the madame at Le Moulin Bohème and gave away my mission within the first week. They almost sacked me right then and there, but someone must have seen my potential, and I was given a second chance..."

Mélusine and Yvie continued on with their cooking while they listened, finishing up the potatoes and moving on through the green beans, until they reached the final dish, a meaty white fish in a delicate white wine sauce. It was easily the most delicious fish Eleanor had ever tasted, with a subtle natural sweetness and none of the bland gamey flavor that was so common in the cheap, cold-water fish she had known her whole life.

"Now, ma chérie, what shall we do for your husband's birthday dessert?" Mélusine asked when Leo had finished up his story, and their cooking session was reaching its end.

The light had taken on a particularly golden afternoon hue as the wind continued to batter the house, whipping up dust that danced in the rays of sunlight streaming in through the sheer curtains on the back window.

As Eleanor watched the peaceful scattering of the dust particles in the light, a shadow through the closed curtains of the kitchen door out to the porch caught her eye, and her heart began racing.

"What is it?" Mélusine asked as she blurred to Eleanor's side. "Eleanor, why are you scared?"

"It's probably nothing," she said as she looked around the kitchen again with more scrutiny. She suddenly noticed that a painting next to the oven was crooked. She was quite certain that it hadn't been when she'd first entered the room.

She walked casually over to it and pulled it off the wall. "Yvie, has there always been a hole in the wall here?"

She put her eye up to a peep hole that had been carved into the wall and peeked through it into the pantry.

"There shouldn't be any holes!" Yvie exclaimed. "We inspected everything when we moved in!"

"I suppose we know what Mac's really been up to then," Eleanor said as she worked to push down her panic.

A flood of annoying questions rushed through her mind… How long had Mac been using the peephole? Did he know how much of Leo's cover had been blown? Had he seen Mélusine's magical approach to cooking? God, what had they said in that kitchen that he might have overheard? Too much! How much of it did Grimby already know?

Her heart jumped into her throat.

Could he have been lurking when Surpanakha was there? When the Goddess called forth her divine power, and along with it her shimmering trident and crown? What would Grimby do with that information, other than have a temper tantrum? What *could* he do with it? As if anyone would believe him! She envisioned him presenting the news of a Hindu goddess on Earth to the other generals. Surely, all it would produce was a hearty round of laughter, which would only make him angrier... so then who would suffer? How would he use the power that he had to make them pay? To punish all of them for keeping him in the dark about the true depths of their power?

"Blimey, we've been too sloppy. Leo, you've been compromised."

"Eleanor, you needn't worry about me, remember? I'm dying," Leo said as he gave into a bout of coughs. She could hear the panic through the feigned calm of his tone.

She ripped open the door to the porch, and then ripped open the perpendicular door to the pantry. Everyone but Mr. Valov followed her.

The shelves were all filled with dusty canned goods. In the farthest, darkest corner, the large modern icebox hummed, while in the front of the pantry, baskets of dried goods and root vegetables on the floor alongside several crates of fine Bordeaux made the scene look distinctly French. Beside the crates, though, an incriminating stool was readied for its occupant to sit right at the peeping hole. Yvie picked up a women's magazine that was stuffed onto the shelf between some suspiciously un-dusty cans of beans, while Eleanor noticed a recently used kerosene lamp nestled behind them on the shelf.

"*Sacre bleu, quelle putain!*" Yvie hissed.

"What? What does all this mean to you?" Eleanor asked nervously.

"It's *Sheila's* peeping hole! Oz's mother has been spying on me in the kitchen!" All the color drained from her face. "That means she's been spying on all of us."

472

"Let's not panic," Eleanor said unconvincingly. "We didn't *see* the hole from inside the kitchen. She can't see anything with the painting blocking it. That means she's only been able to listen, not to watch, so she hasn't seen anything magical."

"But we've been chatting all week about all sorts of secret things!" Yvie exclaimed. "You thought our conversations were in confidence, but I'd accidentally set a trap for you!" She grabbed her head with her hands and growled. "First Father O'Donnelly, and now this! It's shameful!"

"Now, now, my dear girl, don't worry about us at all. Surely a woman with as little imagination as Sheila must think that we are either mad or speaking in code," Kuveni reassured her.

"Yes, but we have a bigger problem," Mélusine informed them as she glanced out the door, moving their attention to Mac, who was returning from his task with an empty wooden wine box. "There are four cases of Margaux still here. Only one has been carried over to the dining room. That means that our unwelcome butler has only managed to transport one case of wine while we've been chatting away in the kitchen."

"Blimey," Eleanor whispered. "Whether he made the hole or not, he's been using it."

As Mac noticed them hovering around the scene of the crime, he stopped in his tracks. He looked around guiltily for his escape options, and then he straightened his posture and approached them.

He put down the empty wine box and picked up the next, and Eleanor sighed with annoyance. His choice to completely ignore the situation and hope that they didn't notice represented a level of disrespect for their intellect that irked her.

"You owe us an explanation for your slow progress," she demanded.

He reached into his pocket and pulled out his notebook to scribble his answer.

I asked Stanley to help me. He said he would come after finishing the tent, but he never showed up.

"I didn't ask Stanley to set up the bar, did I?" Kuveni challenged him. "I asked you to do it."

I thought it would be good exercise for him. My back was hurting after the fall from the horse.

"You didn't have to help us at all," Eleanor chastised him. "You're the one who insisted on coming over here, and now all you've done is intimidate our butler and spy on us. I have half a mind to call up the Bunbury constable and have you arrested for trespassing."

He clenched his teeth and almost broke his pencil as he wrote his response.

You can't host a party for a hundred guests with only Stanley to help you. The idea would be absurd even with a competent butler. I'm not the villain here.

"Really, so you weren't using this peephole to spy on our conversation?" Eleanor said as she pointed at the light flowing through from the other side, now that the painting had been removed.

The color drained from Mac's face. He backed away from them, eyeing his options for escape once more, but as Leo's coughs echoed through the peephole, Eleanor lost her fiery Celtic temper and grabbed Mac's hand.

You will not spy on us again. You will say nothing of the secrets you stole that weren't yours to hear. Not to Grimby nor to anyone else. Do you understand? Shakti commands it. You will stop meddling with powers you don't understand.

His eyes widened, and Eleanor let go. She brushed the dust off of her hands and rolled her shoulders.

"It looks like you're behind in your work, Mac. We need the bar set up now, before the guests start arriving."

He nodded his agreement, much jumpier than before, and collected two cases at once.

474

As Eleanor watched him run with them around the porch to the front door by the dining room, she sighed with stress.

"If that man's back hurts, I'll eat my hat," she muttered.

"You didn't just do something unwise, ma chérie, did you? He's too close for comfort now."

Eleanor glanced at Yvie's nervous expression. "Of course not. I think we whipped him into shape, don't you?"

She guided them back into the kitchen. Kuveni snapped her fingers, covering up the hole in the wall, and then replaced the painting.

"You do need to be more careful, Eleanor," Leo rasped. "I shouldn't have been so foolhardy myself. Now he knows that I've blown my cover, not just to you, but to Edmund's guardians. My treachery is a threat to Britain and to Grimby that I've managed to keep secret for two years. I don't know what will happen when Grimby learns of it. Treason is a capital crime."

"Treason!" Kuveni exclaimed. "Hogwash! Edmund is the son of George IV! He has a more rightful claim to the throne than King George V does!"

"He does?" Yvie asked.

Leo and Mélusine both threw Kuveni looks of annoyance at her shouting of the important secret.

"He doesn't," Mélusine corrected Kuveni. "Edmund's father had no valid claim to the throne, and you know it, Kate."

"Nothing will happen, Leo. I promise," Eleanor reiterated calmly.

"Don't make promises you can't keep, Eleanor. It's not your style."

"I promise," she reiterated. "Trust me." She hoped she wasn't lying.

He took a long sip of the cognac and held in a cough as he returned to rocking.

"Now, I think that ice cream would be a nice novelty out here in the bush, don't you?" Kuveni suggested.

As Yvie rubbed her belly and sighed subtly with pain, Eleanor let Kuveni's return to cheerful mundanity stand.

"*Peut-être,*" Yvie replied.

Eleanor smiled as she noticed her polite disagreement. "Perhaps you have something better in mind, Yvie?"

"Ozzy's favorite dessert in all the world is pavlova. It is an Aussie specialty of soft meringue, topped with whipped cream and fruit."

Mélusine closed her eyes and concentrated, and then snapped her fingers, producing her first attempt.

"The meringue is too hard," Yvie said as soon as she saw it.

Mélusine snapped her fingers again, replacing it with another one.

"There isn't enough fruit."

Mélusine snapped her fingers again, and they were off and running. Eleanor relegated her many concerns and focused on the fun of watching Yvie teach Mélusine her recipe, a process she hadn't fully appreciated throughout the years she'd taken for granted all of the delicious food Kuveni had produced with a snap of her fingers. She wondered if Miriam had done the same thing to teach them her recipe for carpenter's pie, and then she pushed away a passing thought about where Vibhishana was at that moment. She didn't want to care.

As a thin layer of high clouds and dust shrouded the yellow afternoon sun until it was a disconcerting color of dark golden brown, Eleanor went to the back window and peeked around the curtain to look out. The first locals were just arriving by foot, carrying homemade bouquets and plates of freshly baked cookies up to the last of several large, perfectly-shaped canvas tents that Oz and Edmund were just finishing up in the back garden.

"Thank you kindly, mate!" Oz said as he brushed the dust off his hands and tasted a cookie.

"How lovely. We've worked up quite an appetite!" Edmund exclaimed as he brushed his dust onto Oz's dirty sleeve and took two cookies at once.

The old woman who'd offered them up was pleased by their reaction, and she tsked her husband as he took one for himself while Oz went in for seconds.

Yvie joined Eleanor at the window to watch.

"I do like the rural life here," Yvie admitted. "They are so sweet. We must seem like gods to them living in this big house with the money to buy anything we want, and yet they brought us what they could muster. It would not happen in France like this. The villagers would be too intimidated to come to a party at a stately home… or perhaps too offended by its existence to even consider the invitation… and it would be exceptionally rare for them to receive an invitation in the first place…"

Eleanor smiled. "I like it here too. To be honest, Edmund and I were considering whether or not we should stay longer… perhaps, indefinitely."

"*Mon dieu*, it would be wonderful!" Yvie squealed. She hugged Eleanor. "Please do! We know such wonderful builders in Perth. We will ring them tomorrow to give you ideas for a house! You could live next door!"

Eleanor laughed. "Perhaps that's moving a bit too fast."

Yvie blushed. "I'm sorry, I get ahead of myself sometimes."

"It's a lovely idea. We will think carefully about it," Eleanor reassured her. "I think that our time in India has officially come to an end."

As a larger group of guests approached Oz and Edmund out on the lawn, Eleanor looked down at her dress and Yvie's.

"I'd better go change. I have a lovely crimson dress with beadwork and gemstones embroidered into the fabric that I've been looking forward to wearing."

"Do you think the gemstones are real?" Yvie asked.

"Do they count if they've been conjured?"

"I think they should count more than the ones mined by children in Africa."

"Touché."

"Don't be too long." Yvie squeezed her affectionately. "Nellie Melba will be here any minute, and Oz doesn't know she's coming. I don't want you to miss the surprise!"

"I'm sure Kuveni won't let me."

Kuveni glanced over from her position inspecting some freshly conjured napkins in five different colors.

"Go, Eleanor dearest. I will pop right up to get you when the festivities begin. With Edmund preoccupied, I don't see a reason for you to take too long."

Eleanor skipped out of the kitchen and up the stairs. As she dug through her pocket for her key, she noticed that the door was already cracked open. She was certain that she'd locked it in anticipation of the many guests milling about unsupervised... She relegated a burst of anxiety as she pushed it open, readying herself to attack any intruder. The room was empty, but then she heard the rustling of fabric coming from inside the closet.

She noticed the light on under the crack of the closed closet door, and she shook her head with extreme annoyance.

"Mac, I swear to god, if you're rifling through my things, I'm going to kill you right here and now," she muttered.

She hoped he hadn't just found her pistol in its locked box in her steamer trunk...

Readying to use the element of surprise, she rushed straight to the closet and ripped open the door.

"AH!"

"AH!"

She screamed in unison with Stanley.

"Blimey," she murmured.

Stanley tumbled down off of the dressing platform and crawled under Edmund's neatly hung suits to hide himself away from her.

478

"Please don't tell anyone!" he begged.

She kneeled down to examine his surprising state. She moved the bottoms of Edmund's hanging trousers out of the way to take in Stanley's made up face with her red lipstick and rouge applied quite neatly, giving his youthful features a surprisingly natural feminine look. He was wearing the odd genie-inspired outfit that Babri had made for her back in Bombay, although the pants and skirt were on backwards, so that the long, embellished train was trailing down in front of him. The blouse was also on backwards, buttoned only by one button in the middle of his chest, revealing her bra stuffed with handkerchiefs and stretching precariously around his masculine rib cage. Her tallest, most sparkling set of heels were barely strapped onto his larger feet, and his shaggy brown leg-hair and large, hairy toes made the effect rather ungraceful.

She offered him her hand, but he nestled deeper into the closet, like a guilty dog hiding from the punishing hand of his master.

"Come on out, greenie. Let's have a little chat, woman to woman."

CHAPTER 27 – THE CLOSET OF NO SECRETS

Stanley hid his face, and Eleanor reached forward and wrapped her hand around his wrist.

Come out, my child. I'm not going to hurt you.

I can't! I can't! I can't!

You must. Shakti commands it.

She gently tugged at him, and he finally gave in.

He tripped and scrambled, trying to get up from his awkward position in the unfamiliar fabric and uncomfortable shoes, and Eleanor steadied him as he finally balanced himself and glanced in the mirror.

"*Oh, I am fortune's fool,*" he murmured.

She sat down on the edge of the dressing platform and gestured for him to sit next to her.

"Please don't tell my father," he whispered.

That was not what she thought he was going to say.

"Your father?"

"Grumpy Grimby. He told me if he ever caught me being a deviant again he'd have me thrown in jail, where they'd really make a man out of me. He'll do it this time, I'm sure of it."

Suddenly, Lord Grimby's obsession with "making a man" out of Stanley took on a whole new meaning.

"What are you doing?" Eleanor asked, even though she had a pretty good idea of the answer.

Stanley looked down at himself. "I'm being a deviant, ma'am. Everyone was busy preparing for the party downstairs, and the colonel asked me to lay out a suit for him to change into, but when I came in here, and I saw all of your lovely silk clothing hanging so nicely, I couldn't help myself. I had to see how they'd look on me, and I wanted to imagine what it would be like if I looked... er... like you."

"And the bra?"

Stanley blushed.

"And the makeup?"

"I'm a deviant, ma'am. Please don't tell my father you caught me. He's crueler than ever now that the colonel insulted him."

"I'm not going to tell Grumpy Grimby a thing, Stanley. Do you really think I'd do that? I thought we'd already proven to you that not everyone in the world is an abusive wanker."

Stanley's eyes teared up. "On the rare occasions when people are nice to me, it always dissolves when they realize I'm a deviant. *Always.*"

Eleanor took his hand and squeezed it reassuringly. "Not anymore. You're in the kind company of friends now."

Stanley lost his battle with tears, and his mascara began running down his cheeks in black streaks as he worked hard to keep himself from devolving into sobs.

"The deviant bastard son of Lord Chester Grimby doesn't deserve any friends."

"I didn't realize you knew he was your father. Why are you still calling him Uncle Chester?"

482

"Didn't you already know? He told me he told you!"

"He told me that he didn't tell *you*."

"He didn't. Not at first. He was too much of a selfish coward."

Through the makeup and his poor placement of her clothing, Eleanor saw more of the earnestness that had begun to peek through as he'd started to let his guard down throughout the week.

"My mother told me the truth on my eighteenth birthday, but she said I had to keep calling him Uncle Chester or we'd be ruined." As he spoke, he let his voice become softer and lighter than she was used to, as if the whole time she'd known him, he'd been doing an impression of the deepest voice he could muster. "I was happy that my drunkard Uncle Arthur wasn't my father, until I realized how disappointed my real father was in me. I wished afterwards that she hadn't told me. He'd always been so gruff and unforgiving, and I'd always just thought it was because he was an army general. It turned out he'd been secretly pulling the strings my whole life."

"I suppose that arrangement must have come quite naturally to him."

Stanley snorted. "Tormenting people from afar is one of his favorite pastimes, me most of all. My mother finally admitted after he went off on one of his tirades a few years ago, that the horrific boarding schools I'd been sent off to as a boy weren't because of Uncle Arthur's addiction to the bottle. It turned out my father had taken me away from my mother and Auntie Louisa because he said they'd coddled me into being a pouf. I don't know how my mother can still love him."

"Blimey," Eleanor murmured.

She was annoyed at herself for not recognizing the obvious explanation for the well-practiced bullying from Lord Grimby and Mac, and the fearful self-castigation that Stanley was unleashing against himself.

"I'm not a pouf," he clarified quickly. "I've never done anything with anyone."

"If you had, it would be no one's business but yours."

"That's not how my father sees it. Or the church. Or the government. I'd be thrown in jail, and then I'd go straight to Hell."

"That doesn't sound like a very pleasant fate."

"It's bloody awful!" Stanley exclaimed. "But I can't change! I've tried so hard! I'm such a bloody daft wanker, because I'm so bloody scared everyone's going to find out! When I'm alone I can do all sorts of things just fine, but when there are people watching, I'm clumsy and distracted because I'm trying so hard to be someone I'm not... someone right-handed and manly enough that the boarding school chaps won't want to strap me naked to a tree and leave me out for the birds to peck all weekend. They're going to see that on the inside, I'm really..."

Eleanor rubbed his back soothingly as he gave into another round of tears.

"You really are?" she coaxed.

"I don't know. I'm something. I'm not a bloke's bloke like my brother is. My father said that all the chaps' abuse at school was my own fault because I wasn't acting like a man. He even hired a diction coach to teach me how to speak deeper, but I hated every minute of it. It felt like someone else's voice was coming out of my mouth, but then at Eton, it got the blokes to stop beating on me. Sometimes I think God made a mistake... or a cruel joke. I think that I was supposed to be born a girl."

Eleanor thought for a long time about her response, and then, as she contemplated how wholly unpleasant Stanley's fate had been as he'd worked so hard to hide who he was while traversing the unforgiving human world without any allies to confide in, a thought occurred to her. There was someone very close who would understand his plight better than she did.

She squeezed Mélusine's pendant. *Mélusine, please come. I need your help with a delicate matter.*

With a pleasant breeze, Mélusine appeared by her side, freshly returned to her preferred feminine form with her long tendrils of blonde fairy hair, clad in her flowing white medieval dress with her copious cleavage conspicuously on display.

Stanley scrambled back into his position hidden behind Edmund's suits.

"*Qu'est-ce que c'est?*" Mélusine asked as she glanced at his feet sticking awkwardly out into the room.

Mélusine took a moment to recognize who Stanley was, and then she glanced at Eleanor and realized what was happening. She kneeled down just as Eleanor had.

"Come out, mon chéri. You needn't keep secrets from me."

She reached in and helped him out, and then took a seat beside him on the platform, sandwiching him in next to Eleanor.

"Your skirt is on backwards," she pointed out. "I have trouble figuring out how to put on human clothing myself. It's much easier to just make them as part of my form."

She switched her dress into a modern violet beaded flapper dress.

Stanley reached out to touch the fabric of her frilly sleeve. "That's a neat trick. Like something Ariel or Puck could do."

Mélusine snorted. "Puck could make much better clothing than this. He was better at making his own fashions than I was, and he was very skilled at making human clothing, just as Kate is. I've never been able to get the dimensions right for anyone but myself. It's shameful, really, given how skilled I am at other kinds of engineering."

"I don't understand," Stanley admitted.

"Puck was my son," Mélusine explained. "He died many centuries ago. That wretched writer slandered his reputation and mine with that asinine play. It made us all look like petty fools."

"You knew Shakespeare?" Stanley asked.

Eleanor noted that he was already so used to their magical world, that he wasn't even distracted by her casual reference to living hundreds of years ago.

"I did, mon chéri. He was an opportunistic little worm. You would know me as Titania from the play, but my real name is Mélusine."

"*Ill met by moonlight, proud Titania,*" Stanley whispered.

"*C'est bon, mon chéri.* I think you got the line right this time."

"I've played fourteen leading roles. I studied Shakespeare at Oxford because I learned at Eton that men got to play women's roles. I've only ever played the heroines... and I was always distracted by... er... other worries when I was learning my lines. I was afraid someone would notice how much I liked the costumes, or how natural I sounded in the roles when I wasn't forcing my voice to be manlier." He cringed as he waited for some sort of backlash from his confession. When none came, he glanced at her again, and then self-consciously reached out his hand. "My name is Stanley. I'm a daft Secret Service officer who's doing a shameful job of masquerading as Eleanor's butler."

Eleanor laughed at his unabashed admission, and Stanley suddenly seemed concerned. "You said I needn't keep secrets?"

Mélusine smiled. "You're right, mon chéri, I did. And as we're being perfectly honest, I must admit that we already know each other."

She morphed into the form of Percy in her flamboyant purple suit.

"*Gast,*" Stanley murmured. "I wondered if you were queer like I was. My father was certain you were, and he told me if he caught me alone with you, he'd whip my hide right off and have you hanged. He could do it, too. He's the most powerful man in the Empire. He probably has more real power than the king does."

"Your father?"

"Grumpy Grimby," Stanley humphed. "I'm not supposed to tell anyone because he's ashamed of his dandy bastard of a son."

"Ah, I see. That explains a lot, actually. My father was a villain too." Mélusine glanced at Eleanor. "I understand now why you were so acutely afraid when Mac walked in on us taking the tables.

Why did you agree to go over there alone with me if you were so afraid of getting caught?"

Stanley looked down at his hands. "I thought… I thought maybe you invited me because… Never mind."

"Ah. I'm sorry I disappointed you, mon chéri. You will find someone to be with someday."

"No, I won't. I'll be alone forever. That's why my father was so pleased when the assignment as a butler came up… and with Colonel Marriner, nonetheless. He had no doubt Edmund would keep me in line. He said so over and over again. He thought all his prayers had been answered when Leo coughed up a lung… the bastard. My father doesn't care about anyone but himself."

"Most humans are selfish fiends," Mélusine informed him. "It is a great miracle when we come upon a human like Eleanor who isn't."

"I thought you were a goddess?" he asked Eleanor.

"I thought you were a Christian," Eleanor shot back cheekily.

"I have no bloody clue what I am," Stanley admitted dismally. "I'm doomed, that's all I know."

"Aww, mon chéri, we all feel like that sometimes."

Mélusine rubbed his back like a doting mother, and he leaned into her embrace and took a deep breath. He caught himself and pulled away when he noticed his pleasant position cuddled up in her male arms.

"Which body is the real you? Are you Percy or Titania?"

Mélusine thought about her answer carefully. "I suppose it depends on how you define that." She wiggled again, into the male form that Eleanor had seen once before on Dasara when Kuvcni had tried to pressure her into using it. She wiggled again, into a white silk Roman tunic with delicate golden details woven into the fabric. "This is who I was born to be."

"You look more like Oberon than Titania," Stanley said as he felt the fabric.

Mélusine smiled. "I do actually look quite a bit like he did at the time, although Oberon always had an English look about him. All of my forms have been Roman. He never knew this form of mine, though. I decided to be female almost two thousand years ago, and by the time I had Puck, I had become so native to the form that I was able to be his mother. Oberon never knew that I was born male."

"Was he Puck's father?" Eleanor couldn't help but ask, now that they'd stumbled upon the topic.

"He married me after Puck was born as a bit of a charity. I probably should have refused him in retrospect, but *c'est la vie*. He wasn't Puck's father. I never told anyone who Puck's father was." Mélusine glanced around and then lowered her voice. "His father was the pope."

Eleanor laughed, but Mélusine did not. "Really?" Eleanor asked. "Was he really the pope?"

"*That*, mes chéris, is a story for another time." Mélusine wiggled back into her feminine form in her white medieval dress. "I only use male forms now when it's necessary for the task at hand. Being female is still inconvenient when I need certain bloke's blokes to take me seriously. They're so consumed with lust and misplaced chivalry that it gets in the way."

Stanley thought about the idea silently for a long time. "I wouldn't need to switch back and forth, I think. I would be happy being a woman all the time. All I've ever really wanted to be is a wife."

Mélusine sighed with resignation. "I'm sorry, mon chéri. These things are harder for humans than they are for us."

"You can't… you can't change me, can you?" he asked. "I'd do anything you wanted me to! I'd be your slave!"

She looked even sadder. "No, mon chéri. That is beyond my power. And you should never, ever offer to be a slave. I was enslaved as a child, and it is a trauma I haven't fully recovered from in two thousand years."

His posture deflated. "I'm sorry. I didn't mean it like that. I'm bad at saying what I really mean. I offend people so often, I've come to expect it. At least then they hate me because of something I've said instead of who I am."

"Mon chéri, perhaps you can make a life for yourself where people don't hate you at all."

"I'm a deviant," he whispered. "I deserve to be hated."

Eleanor put her arm around his shoulders. "Greenie, I've known many men who deserved to be hated, and you aren't one of them. Stick with us, and you can be who you really are."

"I can't, ma'am."

"Oh for god's sake, greenie, call me Eleanor."

"Eleanor, I can't. I can't answer the door of your house wearing high heels and a dress. It will bring ridicule upon me and upon you. We will all be in trouble."

"That's very thoughtful of you. I didn't realize you cared so much about us."

Stanley looked at the floor. "I didn't. I wanted out of this mission. I was so desperate to escape from you that I blew my father's cover on the steamer. He threatened to have me shot for treason."

"I see. So you weren't actually as daft as you seemed?"

He shook his head. "I'm an absurdly bad officer. My father only gave me this assignment because he needed someone loyal to him on the inside, who wouldn't be swayed by... you, Eleanor. It was the one time in my life when my deviance was a benefit... at least to him."

"Swayed by me?" Her interest was piqued.

"He thought that Leo's judgment had been compromised by his love for you."

"I see. But now we're bringing you into our family. Did he think that wouldn't happen? That Edmund and I wouldn't care for you as much as we cared for Leo?"

489

"He didn't think you'd accept me. I'm positive that's why he lost his head after Edmund defended me on the polo field, and then again at the beach. That's why he was so mad at me for rescuing Mac, the bastard. He wanted me to let Mac drown so Edmund would save both of them while I stood by like a lazy dullard watching. It was the only heroic thing I've ever done, and it still turned out to be bad."

"It wasn't bad," Eleanor corrected him sternly. "Don't ever let him make you think otherwise."

"Well, it was bad for him. He expected my bumbling to bring you closer to *him*, as you commiserated about how worthless I was. I heard him saying so to Mac on the steamer, and then I ruined all his plans, like I always do."

"Huh…" Eleanor thought through the implications. She'd certainly met enough egomaniacal men in her life to see the pattern in Grimby, going *off his heid*, as her mother would say, when his best laid plans had gone awry. "I will admit that at first we weren't impressed, but I understand you now, greenie. I have no doubt we'll love you as much as we love Leo someday, if not more."

"No one has ever said anything like that to me, Eleanor. Not ever, and certainly not when I was dressed like a deviant." Stanley teared up again at the idea, and Eleanor put her arm around his shoulders. "But that isn't what I meant. I meant that he knew that I wouldn't give into your wiles. He knew that I wouldn't fall in love with you like Leo did."

Eleanor didn't like hearing the assertion spoken out loud. She'd known, of course, since her divine transformation on her honeymoon, that Leo had been working hard to hide his feelings every time he stumbled upon her in her slinky morning robe, but it wasn't just that. Her exceptional knack for reading human emotion had picked up on a certain type of familiarity in his demeanor that was not purely professional, nor platonic. Every time she'd confided in him about her divine struggles instead of her husband, she'd felt the familiarity grow, and yet she'd ignored

490

it. He'd done such an exceptional job of controlling himself, a better job, she had to admit, than Vibhishana had, that she'd hoped he might make it to his grave with his most guarded secret intact. She was sorry for him that he hadn't.

"I didn't think it was such a well-known secret."

Stanley cringed. "I shouldn't have told you. Leo will skin me for it."

"I won't tell him you said it. We're in the closet of no secrets, remember?" Eleanor reassured him as she relegated her complicated emotions on the topic.

"My father was wrong, though."

"Don't tell me that my wiles have seduced you after all? As a goddess, I suppose I need to be more careful about leaving a trail of broken hearts in my wake."

Stanley finally smiled. "No, ma'am... I mean Eleanor. I'm still," he looked down at her handkerchief-stuffed bra on his hairless flat chest, "as queer as I always was. I meant that my father was wrong about my loyalty. I've already seen that you and the colonel are far better people than he is. My loyalty is to you... that is, as long as I'm also loyal to the Crown. I am a British officer, after all, even if my father made me one out of pure self-interest."

"I think we can live with that," Eleanor smiled. "In the meantime, we will ask Kate to make you a wardrobe of your own. You can wear it whenever you want in private, and we won't tell a soul."

"Do you really mean it?" Stanley looked like he might cry again as he hugged her, but then his posture deflated, and he pulled away. "I can't. My father will find out. He *always* finds out."

"But what would he do about it? He wouldn't dare come snatch you out of Colonel Marriner's distinguished household, would he? He'd give himself away *and* Edmund would go after him, and no matter what he says to the contrary, he's scared of Edmund now. I can see it in his eyes."

"My father cares more about his position than anything else, and I mean *anything*, Eleanor. If there's a conflict, he will choose himself every time, and you need to be more careful than ever. I can see that he's desperate now after things didn't go his way these last couple weeks, and he still doesn't know anything about your power. He'll go even madder if he realizes that Leo and I knew about it, and that neither of us said a peep to him. It could be the end for all of us."

Eleanor sighed with annoyance, pushing down a burst of self-castigating anxiety. "He will now. I revealed some of my power to Mac, although I'm not sure what he made of the encounter. He made something of it…"

"I'll try to steal his report before he hands it in," Stanley suggested.

"His report?"

"Mac reports everything to my father, and I mean *everything*, Eleanor. Last week he reported when he heard you flushing the toilet at 12:04am, and then again at 1:08am. He reported that you and the colonel were enjoying yourselves despite it being the time of your… er…" Eleanor scoffed with disgust. "Never mind."

"I knew I hated him." Eleanor sighed with frustration as she thought through the many nights of pleasure they'd relaxedly enjoyed since their arrival. She didn't want to think about Mac lurking just outside the door taking notes in his grubby little notebook. "Will stealing his report get you shot for treason if you get caught?"

"I'll tell my father that it had something bad about me in it that I didn't want him to see. There will be something bad, because there always is, and he might just think I'm being a petty child, like always."

"You're better at this game than I realized, greenie. That's an impressive feat."

Stanley looked down again. "I've been hiding who I am my whole life. I guess I've had some practice."

"Eleanor?" Edmund's voice called as the bedroom door swung open. "Eleanor, dearest, are you in here? Nellie Melba just arrived!"

Mélusine dissolved, and Stanley scrambled into his hiding place under Edmund's hanging trousers.

"Please don't tell him! I'm not ready!" he squealed.

"There are no secrets in the closet today, greenie."

"But he's an army man! He won't understand!"

"He will, Stanley. Trust me."

"But I don't want to lose him, Eleanor!" Stanley's tears returned. "He's been so nice!"

Eleanor's heart broke watching the poor boy crying at the thought of losing one of the only people he'd ventured to trust.

"Stanley, Edmund knows what it's like to live in fear that the people he loves will turn on him when they learn his secrets. If any straight man on Earth can understand your plight, it's him."

As Edmund went to the en-suite bathroom to look for her, Eleanor rushed to greet him, closing the closet door as Stanley unenthusiastically crawled out of his hiding place.

"Oh no!" she laughed.

Edmund was absolutely covered in dust from head to toe.

"It's like a bloody cyclone out there!" he exclaimed. "Oz and I are changing our clothes while Kate and Percy move the party inside. Nellie Melba is going to sing. Can you believe it? What a wonderful surprise!"

Edmund charged towards the closet, and Eleanor grabbed his arm to slow him down. "Darling, when I came up here to change my dress, I found Stanley in our closet. He was... er... experimenting with my wardrobe."

She gently pushed open the door, and Stanley was standing on the dressing platform staring nervously at his feet.

"Good lord," Edmund murmured. He looked Stanley up and down, and Eleanor watched as the implications settled into his expression.

"Darling, Stanley has confided in me that he feels more natural this way… that on the inside he feels more like a woman than a man."

"That's what it was all about…" His eyes turned black, and Stanley whimpered. "Is *this* why Grimby and Mac have been slapping you around, boy?"

"Yes, sir… and because I'm daft at everything I do…"

"I'm going to *kill* those brutes!"

That was not what Stanley thought he was going to say.

Eleanor took his hand. "Darling, we don't need to stoop to violence right now. Now say your mantras."

He closed his eyes, whispered his mantras, and got himself back under control.

"Now, darling, as you can imagine, this has been weighing heavily on Stanley's mind. He was afraid that we would turn on him if we found out."

"Turn on him?!" Edmund exclaimed indignantly. "Stanley, my boy, we aren't all heartless brutes!"

Stanley gave into another flood of tears. Edmund approached him and invited him into a hug, but Stanley resisted.

"You really want to touch me, Colonel? You're not afraid that I'll… er… lust after you?"

Edmund stopped to think about it. "Will you?"

"No, sir." Stanley cleared his throat. "You aren't really my type."

Edmund smiled. "You're only human, my boy. And if we didn't mind years of Leo lusting after Eleanor, I don't see why it wouldn't be the same for you, even if I were your type." Eleanor and Stanley were both surprised to hear him describe Leo's plight so blatantly. "I assume you have an appropriate amount of self-control?"

"No one assumes that," Stanley whispered. "They're all afraid I'm going to try to cop some perverted feel. Mac was so convinced I'd molest those teenaged boys at the beach that he admitted he'd lost track of me to my father, just so they could come chase me down and keep me in line. But they were wrong. I'm not a pervert, and I never have been. I just wanted to swim because I was hot, and it reminded me of being home in Bretagne with Maman."

"Well, my boy, I have faith in you, and from now on, your personal business is your own. How does that sound?"

Stanley squeezed him. "It sounds like a dream come true, Colonel. Really, I never thought… I never dreamed…" He began sniffling again. "Thank you, Colonel."

As he pulled away, a string of beads from Babri's genie-inspired outfit caught on one of Edmund's vest buttons and popped off, tinkling as they spread across the wooden floor. Edmund lifted up the purple sleeve of the blouse to inspect its intact beadwork.

"Is this yours, dearest? It's quite an odd thing, isn't it?"

Eleanor smiled. "Babri made it for me. I had to pack it up and bring it. Besides, it does have a bit of a Scheherazade look to it that I thought we might enjoy together some time."

Stanley and Edmund blushed simultaneously.

"Darling, I promised Stanley that we would keep his secret, and that when he's at home in private, he can dress and act however he wants. I suggested he begin filling a trunk of his own so he won't have to borrow my clothes."

"Right. Well, I suppose then, we'll have more secrets to keep in our house. My boy, I daresay that your secrets aren't even the most scandalous under our roof."

Stanley hugged him again, and then blushed as Edmund glanced down at Eleanor's scarf-stuffed bra.

"I hate to break it to you, my boy, but my wife's bra looks better on her."

Stanley laughed as he wiped his eyes. "I had no delusions about that, Colonel."

As another gust of wind shook the house, Eleanor realized that they were dilly-dallying too long.

"Stanley, why don't you change back into your uniform in the bathroom and wipe off my makeup? It's probably best to keep up appearances with the whole town watching," Eleanor suggested. "I assume you want to see Nellie Melba perform?"

"I don't really care," he admitted. "I was only chattering on at her on the train to embarrass my father. I've never really found opera appealing. It doesn't have the depth that Shakespeare has."

"I agree with you," Edmund said as he collected Stanley's discarded tuxedo from the floor and handed it to him. "Perhaps some time when we aren't so busy, we can discuss our favorite plays, man to man."

"Thank you, Colonel," Stanley said as his eyes watered again. "I'd like that."

He scampered into the bathroom and slammed the door.

"Good lord," Edmund murmured. "So *that's* the bee in Grimby's bonnet. He sent his son to learn how to be a man from me, and instead, I thoughtlessly let him be himself. What did he think I would do? Beat it into him? Surely he must have known that I wouldn't. Surely…"

"You trained thousands of army cadets over the years, surely you dealt with some who had similar inclinations to Stanley? I've run into plenty in the army hospitals over the years."

"I always sent them home," he admitted. "I came up with some excuse for an honorable discharge and shipped them right back to Britain. If they'd been caught by anyone other than me, they would've been shot."

"Shot? Really? I assumed Grimby was using that as an exaggerated threat."

Edmund shook his head. "Death is the penalty for deviance in the army. It's so draconian that it feels almost Roman, but I wasn't in a powerful enough position to change the rules myself. I suppose that means I did a good enough job of disguising my ulterior motives for the discharges that Grimby didn't figure me out."

496

"I think there is a lot more to him than meets the eye, darling. Stanley knows Grimby's his father, by the way. Norwenn told him. He said he wished afterwards she hadn't."

"Huh…" Edmund grunted pensively.

"What?"

"Nothing. It was an unpleasant thought."

"Yes, darling?" Eleanor put her arms around his dusty neck and enticed him into a kiss.

"What if the secrets that I keep needling Kate and Percy to tell me are things that I'll regret knowing as soon as they tell me?"

"What if they are?"

"I suppose I should enjoy my lighter burden and stop needling them for answers."

"Is that what you want?"

She squealed as he pulled her into a surprise twirl.

"Right now, I just want to kiss you, dearest. You are so kind and forgiving and open. Look at that poor boy! He must have been terrified when you caught him, and now he's as giddy as a schoolboy."

"Does he remind you of you?"

"I suppose in some ways he does. I've lived my life terrified of someone catching me being who I am, and then you rescued me from my fear. You were my white knight, Eleanor."

"You still owe me some custom armor. Shall we fit me for it now?"

Eleanor kicked closed the door and pushed him up against the wall, ripping off her dress as he hastily removed his dirty suit.

And so, as the raging winds shook the house and their young butler stretched and whimpered as he attempted to unsnap her modern bra, Edmund and Eleanor snuck in one more secret round of delightfully dirty pleasure inside the closet of no secrets.

CHAPTER 28 – AGAINST THE RAGING WIND

By the time Edmund and Eleanor had washed up and re-dressed themselves after their steamy sojourn in the closet, the house was shaking against the assault of continuous violent gusts of wind outside. Inside, however, it was bustling with the laughter and merry banter of the entire town, who had shown up in droves for the very special party hosted by the King and Queen of Australia. Eleanor loved the coziness of the contrast between inside and out, like the Christmases she'd spent as a wee lass when the Scottish winter gales pounded their stone house, and her father's contagious cheer had kept them all happy and safe and warm.

Instead of pushing the memory away like she usually did, Eleanor took a deep breath and let it in. With it, a subtle wave of love for her father snuck in with it, a love she had trampled down with all of her might for almost thirty years.

Let it be, my child. You can love him and hate him at the same time.

A troop of giggling children ran past them towards the attic stairs as they snuck guiltily out of their bedroom, and Eleanor let herself relegate her conflicted thoughts and return to the reality before her.

"Doctor Helmsworth says there's a dollhouse!" one girl exclaimed.

"And a box of boomerangs!" another added excitedly.

"Last one upstairs is a rotten egg!"

Eleanor saw a hint of wistful longing in Edmund's expression as he watched them, and she took his hand and led him downstairs, but as he spied the large crowd dressed in their Sunday best, which was markedly less fancy than his own distinguished wool suit, he paused to consider their options.

"I think we're overdressed, dearest," he whispered as he eyed his well-fitted formal suit, and then fingered the glittering rubies sewn into delicate patterned clusters along the borders of her floor-length, crimson, slinky silk gown. She had to admit, she'd still been a bit aroused when she'd chosen the exceptionally low cut option, although she'd been wanting to wear the matching beaded hairpiece since she'd seen it mysteriously appear on her vanity several days earlier. "Should we go up and change?"

Stanley, looking more distinguished and confident than he ever had before in his formal butler's tuxedo, rushed to greet them.

"You look magnificent, Eleanor," he whispered. "Did Kate give that to you?"

"She did."

"She's rather generous, isn't she?" Edmund commented nonchalantly.

"She is," Eleanor agreed.

Stanley noticed her discomfort and changed the subject, and her heart soared at his newest demonstration of competence in the unpleasant quest to keep Edmund in ignorance.

"Nellie Melba is going to begin her concert shortly in the conservatory by the piano. Leo has saved seats for you beside Doctor and Mrs. Helmsworth in the front row, and Kate and Percy asked me to tell you that they are managing the crowd." Eleanor noticed as he spoke with his natural soft voice that he was also still wearing her mascara and a tasteful hint of rouge. She winked, and he smiled with relief. "Come, I'll show you to your seats."

Edmund threw Eleanor a look of impressed surprise at Stanley's noticeable improvement in butling now that he was no longer fully distracted by hiding his secrets, and he squeezed her bum naughtily and put his arm over her shoulders to follow Stanley into the makeshift concert hall.

"I love you, Eleanor," he whispered into her ear as Stanley informed Oz and Yvie of their arrival, and then took his place against the wall, ready to step in and help. "Look at what a few minutes with you has done for that boy."

"I didn't do it alone, darling," she whispered back as she stole a kiss on his cheek.

"*Venez!*" Yvie said as she waved them over. "We were afraid you'd miss it!"

"I hear you were a culprit in planning this surprise, Ellie." Oz squeezed her hand. "Thank you kindly."

Eleanor squeezed him back and then put her arm over Yvie's shoulders. "We make a good team, don't we?"

"The best," Yvie agreed.

"You are looking lovely tonight in that gown, Eleanor," Leo rasped. "And you're quite dapper in that suit, as always, Colonel."

Eleanor couldn't ignore Stanley's unintentional reminder of Leo's true feelings. She sighed and reached over Edmund to squeeze Leo's hand. *Thank you, my friend.*

The buzzing audience fell into silence as an elderly man in a tuxedo entered from the library, followed by the dame clad in a floor-length silver ball gown that sparkled in the twinkling light of the crystal chandelier above. Even her arm-length white opera gloves shimmered in the gentle light.

"Spectacular," Stanley whispered.

Kuveni entered the room and took a standing position next to Stanley. She leaned in to whisper into his ear. "I hope you're keeping a list of your requests for our special project, my dear boy. We will get you all squared away with a trunk of your own tomorrow."

Stanley pulled her into a tight hug, and then let go and straightened his bowtie as he noticed several people watching him.

Nellie Melba waited for her accompanist to take a seat at the large Steinway grand, and then took her position at the front of the room beside it.

"Tonight's concert is dedicated to our countrymen who sacrificed so much during the war." She glanced at Edmund and Oz. Eleanor squeezed Edmund's hand as she felt him sigh with discomfort. "And to the women who are so rarely remembered for their pivotal roles nursing our fallen soldiers back to health." She glanced at Eleanor and Yvie. "It was my privilege to encounter some of these remarkable blokes and sheilas right here in Western Australia on the train down from Perth, and I couldn't think of a better use of a blustery Saturday evening like this one than to pay homage to their courage on Lieutenant Jack Helmsworth's birthday. I will start tonight's concert with my signature aria, *Mi Chiamano Mimi*, a piece I am told by Mrs. Helmsworth was the favorite of the injured men in the twenty-fourth field hospital in Reims, where she and her husband were tending to the gory treatment of our fallen soldiers for three years of the war to end all wars."

Eleanor caught a subtle grimace on Sheila's face from her position in the back corner of the room, and she relegated a burst of distaste for the woman. Then she moved her attention over to catch Oz squeezing Yvie's leg as he wiped a tear from the corner of his eye. Yvie kissed his wet cheek.

"I love you, Yvie," he whispered.

"*Et je t'aime, mon amour.*"

He worked his hand up under her dress. "You know I can't resist your *français*, Yvie."

"*Bientôt*, Ozzy. Patience."

502

She guided his roving hand to her pregnant belly. He sighed with contentment, and Eleanor felt a burst of love for both of them, and for the authenticity of the love that they shared. They were the only other people she'd met in her life who could compete with how she felt for Edmund.

She was startled as the concert began, not with the piano, but with a simple, lyrical hello. *"Si, mi chiamano Mimi, ma il mio nome è Lucia… Yes, they call me Mimi, but my name is Lucia…"* Eleanor sat back and listened to the soft, pleasant, surprisingly youthful quality of Dame Melba's voice intermingling with the rich, harmonious piano accompaniment.

What a novelty to know what the words mean. Thank you, Uma.
You're welcome, my child.

The audience sat in enraptured silence through a full-length concert of all of Nellie Melba's favorite arias, even as she paused twice and restarted when gusts of wind shook the house, distracting her pianist, who apologized and worked increasingly hard to hide his discomfort with the weather.

When they reached the finale, the drama was fitting as Dame Melba's delicate voice sang the ominous warning from the doomed Desdemona's most famous aria from Verdi's *Otello*, a Shakespearean reference that she was sure Edmund and Stanley were both greatly appreciating.

"Il salce funebre sera la mia garlanda…The willow will be my funeral garland…"

"Salce, Salce, Salce… Willow, Willow, Willow…"

As the entire room sat mesmerized by the quiet fear that Dame Melba's sweet voice was conveying through the music, the front door flew open, sending a dusty draft right through the foyer and into the concert room, strewing the pianist's sheet music all over the floor.

Edmund's eyes turned black, and the entire audience turned around to watch as Percy slammed the door shut, muttering to himself, and, as Eleanor recognized, whispering quiet yet heated mantras. Kuveni casually made her way to Mélusine's side, and they engaged each other in a silent conversation.

As the poor pianist scrambled around collecting the music, and then cracked his knuckles and restarted the section of the aria, Nellie Melba returned to her mark with an air of dramatic madness as if nothing had happened at all.

"*Salce, Salce, Salce… Willow, Willow, Willow…*"

Eleanor wrapped her hand around Mélusine's pendant and closed her eyes.

What's happening? Are we in danger?

Something is very wrong, ma chérie.

Can you make the wind stop?

I can't! I'm too weak! It is like my power is just evaporating! The harder I try, the worse it gets! This has never, ever happened before! I don't understand what it means!

Edmund's eyes are black. He senses something too.

The dark force is stirring. It is as if it is feeding off of my power. But who could do that?! No one! I know of no one with that kind of power!

I thought Edmund vanquished the enemy already…

What do you mean, ma chérie?

Earlier today, Edmund killed an adder in our room. Its head dissolved into black sparkling dust, and Uma said that Lord Kalki had triumphed.

Mon dieu! Why didn't you say anything?!

Eleanor suddenly felt foolish. *It slipped my mind. Uma was convinced that the danger had passed.*

Well, it hasn't! Mon dieu, what could it mean?! Who could it have been? I know of no one whose companion is an adder! Are you certain it wasn't a Rakshasa? Did you see it change form?

It didn't change form. Edmund ripped off its head. There was no blood, but no plasma either.

Mon dieu… what could it mean?!

Mélusine began pacing back and forth, and Kuveni watched her nervously.

Should we evacuate all the guests? Oz? Yvie? We must keep them safe.

504

I don't know where they would go, ma chérie. It is dangerous for humans to travel outside in a storm like this. They won't be able to breathe, or to see in the dark.

Can Kuveni help you secure us in the house?

She's already trying. Her power isn't strong enough either. This is very, very bad. I have lost control of the perimeter.

What about Monty? Can you call him for help?

He isn't answering my summons. He <u>always</u> answers my summons, Eleanor. If he isn't answering, something must have happened to him.

Blimey.

Let me focus, ma chérie. I will pull power from our communal Yaksha reserves that we keep stored in the Sacred Well.

Is that dangerous?

Yes, ma chérie. We are all in grave danger, and I don't have a solution yet. You must stay calm, and be my ally. I will need you to keep these humans under control so I can do what I need to do... whatever that is...

Eleanor grabbed Edmund's hand. "Take a deep breath and concentrate on your mantras, darling," she whispered into his ear.

Dame Melba's voice forced Eleanor to attention as she reached the climactic high note of Desdemona's desperate last words.

"Ah! Farewell, Emilia, how my eyes itch! Is it the tears? Goodnight, Emilia. Farewell!"

She found the relevance of the line disconcerting, but as Dame Melba took her final bow and the crowd burst into a standing ovation, Eleanor focused on managing the mundane aspects of the silently spiraling situation.

She launched herself up from her seat into a position beside Nellie Melba.

"Thank you, Dame Melba. What a glorious gift you've given all of us. Now, everyone, without any further ado, please help yourselves to the dinner banquet laid out in the dining room. You may take a seat or stand anywhere you find a spot, but please stay away from the doors and windows. If I didn't know any better, I'd think we were weathering a highland gale. Bon appetit!"

She clapped and smiled as the villagers charged out of the room towards the food.

"It really was a wonderful evening, Dame Melba," she whispered, as if there wasn't a raging disaster unfolding. "Thank you so much for indulging us."

"It was my pleasure. If you don't mind, though, I'm simply starving. I haven't eaten anything worth eating in a week."

"Please enjoy yourself! Yvie worked with Percy and Kate here to bring a taste of Oz's French favorites down to the edge of the world. There is coq au vin, duck confit, ratatouille, a mountain of stinky cheese, and free flowing Margaux."

"Crickey, I will join the stampede!" she laughed.

Eleanor shooed Nellie Melba away, and then took a deep breath and looked around, deciding on her next task.

Sheila rushed over to Oz. "Jackie, your brothers! Your brothers must be stuck in the storm! Mr. Guy went out hours ago to collect them from the station!"

Oz looked around at the seemingly calm situation. "Mum, they know how to handle themselves. We've survived the westerlies since we were ankle-biters. They can probably teach Mr. Guy a thing or two about surviving in the outback... and Margaret River is hardly the outback."

"Mr. Guy went out to the station *four hours* ago!" she argued. "The storm has only gotten worse! Jackie, we need to help them!"

Yvie grabbed Oz's arm. "Don't leave me, Ozzy," she whispered. "Something's wrong. I can feel it."

"Jackie, they're your *brothers!*" Sheila screeched in an emotional panic that Eleanor hadn't realized the cold woman could muster. She wondered if the entire episode was just a gambit to test Oz's loyalties.

"Mum, they're adults. If I go out in the haboob to look for them, I will be in just as much danger as they are. They know how

506

to find shelter and wait it out. We do it all the time out on the ranches."

"This is because of *you*!" She pointed accusingly at Yvie. "My Jackie used to care about his family, and now he's just a whipped little pup, worshipping his French tart!"

"Mum!" he shouted. "Yvie *is* my family! She's my wife, and she comes first!"

"I just don't know you anymore, Jackie!"

"French tart?" Yvie whispered. Her face turned red with rage. "You told the editor of that newspaper to write that article, didn't you? The article about me stealing Ozzy away from all of Australia! The article that was published the day Jean-Michel was killed in action!"

"I... I... I..." Sheila stuttered.

"Mum?" Oz asked with shock.

"Are you going to lie about this like you've been lying about spying on us?"

"Mum?" Oz repeated more vehemently.

"I don't know what you're talking about!" Sheila exclaimed with feigned offense.

"*C'est vrai?* You don't know anything about the hole that was carved into the wall from the pantry so you could spy on us in the kitchen? That was your *Women's Day* magazine crumpled between the cans, wasn't it? You're the only one here who reads it!"

Oz suddenly looked angrier than Eleanor had ever seen him. "Mum? Is that how you knew Yvie was pregnant before we told you?"

"I... I... I... deserved to know! No one tells me anything about my own children anymore!"

"I can't believe you did that, Mum. Those secrets weren't yours to know! Did you spy on Anna and Freddy in their house last year? Is that why they really kicked you out?"

"I... I... I... deserved to know! Jackie, you can't blame me!" Sheila implored.

"Bloody oath, I can."

Sheila took one last look at them, and then ran out of the room in tears.

"*Putain,*" Yvie muttered.

"Yvie… I'm sorry." Oz took in a deep breath, trying to control his own rage. "I didn't realize she had a kangaroo loose in the top paddock."

"You didn't publish the article, Ozzy. At least now you know that what I've been saying about her for years is true."

"*Say vray,*" he admitted dismally.

Eleanor skillfully hid her panic at the unsolved catastrophe unfolding around them, and as she noticed that Edmund's eyes were still trapped in their demonic black, Leo also noticed the problem, and he shifted into gear, throwing Stanley a subtle nod of engagement to ready himself.

Unlike every prior time, Stanley leaned forward and addressed Edmund, ignoring his black eyes while simultaneously addressing Mr. Valov with a level of expert deception that Eleanor hadn't fathomed existed anywhere within him.

"What are my orders, sir?"

"I need some air," Edmund said as he stood up and looked around the large crowd with growing panic.

Leo gestured for Stanley to step in, and pointed emphatically towards the door to the library.

"Colonel, I can see that you aren't feeling well. Come with me." Stanley escorted him swiftly into the library and shut the door behind them. Leo watched them go with a combination of puzzlement and concern.

"Did you replace greenie with a Yaksha duplicate?" he asked only half-jokingly.

"It turns out that Stanley is more competent than he let on. I think I've found the key to his potential now."

"You truly are a great goddess, Eleanor." He said the statement lightly, but Eleanor could see that he meant it.

He dissolved into pained coughs until blood began filling his handkerchief. Eleanor rushed to his side and rubbed his back, but she knew that the gesture was futile. The storm had blown in enough dust to bother her lungs, and she was certain that his dying lungs had no tolerance left.

"Is Mélusine around?" he rasped. "I missed my last dose of her… er… help with my pain."

"She's occupied with whatever is happening that has Edmund's adrenaline aroused." She grabbed his hand. *It is very serious, Leo. She doesn't know what's happening, and her power isn't working as it should. She hasn't been able to reach reinforcements, and we're all trapped in the house by the storm.*

Can't she stop the storm?

She's tried. Her power isn't working. She's scared, and we should be too.

Mr. Johnson. Summon Mr. Johnson. He is the most powerful of all of them, isn't he?

He won't be able to get here in time. Rakshasas can't travel instantly like Yakshas can.

Have Kuveni bring him.

You're a genius.

Eleanor let go of his hand. *Kuveni! Kuveni, come now!*

Eleanor waited impatiently for several seconds.

"Kuveni?!" she hissed. "Kuveni!" she shouted.

Kuveni ran at human speed from the foyer.

"It doesn't work!!!"

Eleanor's heart almost exploded as she saw a grimace of acute terror in Kuveni's expression that she'd never once seen before.

"What doesn't?"

"My power!!! I can't do *anything*! I'm trapped in this corporeal form! This has never happened before, Eleanor! Not once in six thousand years!"

"Blimey. Does that mean you can't collect Vibhi for me?"

"I can't do *anything*, Eleanor! I'm changing!"

She grabbed a pin out of Eleanor's hairpiece and stabbed it into the center of her hand. Eleanor cringed as Kuveni pulled it out. They both watched as a gooey black substance oozed to the surface, filling the wound, but not healing it.

"Is that Yakshini plasma?"

"There's no such thing!!! I don't have any bloody clue what it is, Eleanor! We're not supposed to have corporeal reactions like this! When we're injured, we dissolve—*that's what we are*! Our most natural form is to be dispersed! I don't know what the hell is going on!"

Eleanor pulled her into a tight hug.

We will figure it out, Kuveni.

Kuveni gave into tears, and Eleanor held her tighter for a second hug.

I love you, Mistress Eleanor. At least your power still works.

It does! My power still works! We must figure out how to use it!

Eleanor let go of Kuveni and looked around. She looked down at her gown, and around the room at the party guests who were making circles with the chairs as they pleasantly chomped away at the birthday feast without a hint of the danger encircling them.

As she began pacing and rubbing her forehead, trying to force herself to think, Vibhishana's bangle knocked against her nose.

She grabbed it with her left hand and closed her eyes.

Vibhi, where are you? You must come now!

I can't! I'm already on my way, but I'm too far to get there in time! My wicked sister led me right into a trap!

I told you so.

You weren't right, Eleanor. She led me astray so that you would be left vulnerable. She did exactly what I said she would do, just not in the form I anticipated. She's outwitted me again!

How do you know she did this to get at me? Did she tell you so?

We don't have time to bicker, Eleanor!

So, she didn't.

No, Eleanor. She swore up and down that she was only trying to help. But she lies! She __always__ lies!

She wasn't lying about the great darkness that's rising. Everything she warned me about is coming true, and now thanks to your hubris, you aren't even here to help.

She knew the words were harsh, but she didn't have the energy to soften them for his feelings. His silence immediately bothered her.

I do believe that we might be having our first divine marital spat, D.H., and we don't have time for it. Have you learned any more about what the darkness is that's rising?

The better question is who it is. And I don't know. But I can feel its power growing. What do you know of it? What's happening?

We're trapped in the house, and Mélusine and Kuveni's powers aren't working. They're trapped in their corporeal forms, and Edmund's demon is aroused, but he doesn't know what's happening. Oh, and he killed a snake that turned into black sparkling dust when he ripped its head off.

This is bad. Very, very bad…

That's what Mélusine said.

She's right. You must stall, Eleanor. It will still take me time to get there. At least several hours.

Several hours?! Where the hell did Surpanakha lead you?

Lanka.

Blimey. Do you have any idea at all who our unseen enemy could be? Tell me everything you know! I don't think we'll be able to wait several hours!

Only a few ancient demons can steal the power of Yakshas like that. As far as I know, they've all been vanquished!

Eleanor's heart almost exploded as the distinct scent of burning wood wafted down the stairs.

"Kuveni, is that smoke?"

Kuveni closed her eyes and scrunched her nose with excessive effort. Black tears oozed from her eyes as she looked up the stairs. "Mistress Eleanor, I'm useless."

Eleanor squeezed her hand. "We're in this together. Vibhi's already on his way from Lanka."

"Lanka?! But it will take hours for him to get here with his Rakshasa wings!"

"We will do what we have to do. You've been through worse, haven't you?"

"Never!"

Eleanor sighed with stress.

"Dearest?"

"Colonel, wait!"

Edmund came charging towards her from the library as Stanley chased after him. Eleanor turned away from him.

Vibhi, please get here quick! The house is on fire, and Kuveni and Mélusine won't be able to stop it! There are people everywhere, and Edmund's eyes are black!

Eleanor, don't worry at all about keeping our secrets, not even from Edmund. A great battle is at hand. Your only priority is to keep yourself safe. The rest of us are immortal, and we will deal with the fall-out of our witnesses later.

But the whole bloody town's here! Literally, Vibhi, there are a <u>hundred</u> humans watching.

My orders stand. Save yourself, Eleanor, and let them see what they see.

Your orders?

Fine. My husbandly suggestions. Please keep yourself safe, for all of us who love you.

"Dearest?!" Edmund exclaimed as he reached her. She closed her eyes and relegated her power. "Do you smell smoke?" He glanced at Kuveni. "Can you help us?"

"I can't!" she exclaimed. "None of my power works! Edmund, this is very unusual! I don't know what's happening!"

"Bloody hell," Edmund murmured. He began whispering his mantras.

Eleanor glanced out the window at the storm. "Darling, are the tents you put up earlier still standing?"

Edmund glanced out the window, squinting to see through the dark, dusty night.

"They are, sir. I can see the one in the front yard just there," Stanley chimed in.

"Fire!" an elderly man shouted as he dropped a plate of pavlova on the persian carpet.

"Fire!" his wife seconded as she pointed up the stairs.

Golden flames flickered, illuminating the hallway.

Screams erupted as the crowd burst into a panic.

"Where are we going to go?!"

"There's nowhere to go!"

A woman ripped open the front door, and a wall of sand blew inside. Mac rushed over to slam it closed, throwing all of his weight against it to shut it against the raging wind.

"The storm has whipped up the dunes!"

"The Yeagarup dunes?! Those are hundreds of miles away!"

Mac gestured for them to calm themselves, but no one paid him any mind.

"Where are we going to go?!"

"There's nowhere to go!"

"God really does want to punish us! But why?!"

"God isn't punishing you. You must stay calm," Father O'Donnelly interrupted. Just as it seemed his declaration was helping, the electric lights flickered.

"We're all going to die!" a woman screamed.

"STOP!" Stanley shouted with a shockingly high pitch. He took a deep breath as he relegated his surprise that they had all stopped to listen to him. "We will evacuate to the closest tent in an orderly manner. Choose a partner, and stick with him. When you are in the tent, look for people who might be missing, and report them to... er..." He looked around... "Father O'Donnelly!"

"You heard the man," Nellie Melba declared as she approached from the dining room. "Let's go!"

She took the hand of her accompanist, rolled her shoulders, held her breath, and lead the way as Mac opened the door.

Father O'Donnelly followed, coaxing the crowd out the door along with him, but as the surprisingly orderly evacuation commenced, Sheila rushed down the stairs, holding her arms out as she blocked the flames from her face.

"The children!" she screamed. "The children are trapped in the attic!" She ran up to Kuveni. "Please! Please don't punish them! Punish me!"

"Punish you?" Kuveni asked.

"For spying on you! On Yvie! For lying! For every wicked thing I've done! I thought you were mad as hatters, the lot of you! I thought you were foolish, superstitious Catholics making up stories of angels and demons all week. I didn't realize you were real!"

"After everything you overheard, you believe that we would burn down a house full of innocent people to punish *you* for spying on Yvie?" Kuveni asked with scornful disbelief. "Get over yourself, mate."

"I'm sorry!" Sheila exclaimed. "Please help us! Help the children!"

"As foolish as your conduct was, none of this is my doing," Kuveni replied. "I have as little control over it as you do."

"Please!" Sheila begged again.

Oz rushed into the foyer with Yvie from the dining room, pushing their way through the crowd. As another gust of wind shook the house and blew more sand inside, the electric lights went out. Suddenly, the house was only illuminated by the eerie red glow of fire.

Mélusine rushed out of the second-floor flames, but stopped at the top of the stairs to call down. "Kate?! There are people trapped in the second-floor rooms! I can't get the doors open! *C'est un disastre incroyable!*" She snapped her fingers to no avail, and then ran back into the flames swearing.

"Ozzy!" Yvie whimpered. "I knew we were doomed!"

"Oz, the children are trapped in the attic!" his mother reiterated. "Kate claims she can't help them!"

"I will get the children," Edmund declared. Mac stepped forward to volunteer his services. Edmund hesitated, and then chose the most mature response. "Right. Mac is with me. Oz, take the rest of the group out to the tent."

"I will help you, Colonel," Oz countered.

"No!" Yvie cried.

"I will help the people who reach the foyer," Stanley volunteered. "Oz, why don't you help people go from the house to the tent?"

Oz moved to protest, but as Yvie squeezed his hand, he gave in.

"Come," Kuveni whisked Yvie to the door. "We must get you and the baby to safety. I will stay with you, and Oz will be out in a minute."

Edmund looked up the stairs, and then at the crowd.

"Where's Leo?" Eleanor asked as she noticed his absence. She ran back into the smoky concert room, and Edmund, Mac, and Stanley followed. Leo was passed out on the floor.

"Jackie, no, you need help!" Sheila screamed as Oz ran up the stairs towards the attic flames.

"Edmund, go after him!" Eleanor screamed. "I'll get Leo out! Go save Oz and the children!"

"I'll help you, Eleanor," Stanley said as he squatted down to gather Leo's weight onto his arm.

"Darling, go! Do what you have to do!" Eleanor shooed Edmund away.

Edmund took one self-conscious look at Stanley and Mac, and then he disappeared in a blur. Sheila backed away, out into the storm, muttering prayers to herself.

Stanley ignored Edmund's supernatural showing and doubled down on his efforts to lift Leo. Mac was more distracted by it.

"Mac, be a bloody man and go help them! Eleanor and I have Leo covered!" Stanley shouted as Mac returned his attention to them. "Go!"

Mac hesitated.

"GO!" Eleanor commanded.

He ran up the stairs into the flames.

"Eleanor, I don't know how to lift him," Stanley said as he dropped Leo's limp arm back onto the floor. "I'm not strong enough to just throw him over my shoulder like a sack of flour."

"I'm not either, but I've been able to lift patients up into bed for twenty years. There's just a bit of technique to it. Watch me do it, and then you do it for the other side of him. We'll get him up, with each of us on a side, and then we'll flank him as we drag him out."

Eleanor kneeled down and showed him how to do it, and he followed her instructions admirably.

"And, up!"

They stood up with Leo. Eleanor held her breath and closed her eyes as they dragged Leo against the wind into the raging storm. Eleanor's eyes itched and watered, and her nose began running as the sand beat against her skin, but Stanley pulled them along until they reached the flapping canvas door of the tent. It beat her in the face as she passed.

As soon as they were inside, they lay Leo on the ground, and Stanley rushed to re-strap the door, leaving it loose enough for people to easily open it, but tight enough to keep the wind from ripping it.

"Good thinking, greenie," Eleanor said as she kneeled down beside Leo to take his pulse. It was weak. Weaker than it had ever been. She could feel his life-force fading, but as the eerie glow of the red flames illuminated the tent, she wouldn't let herself give into her emotions.

"I used to manage the tents for the summer Shakespeare festival at Oxford. That's where I learned how to evacuate a theater

516

too. I guess I did learn something useful at university," Stanley whispered.

"I'm sure you learned many important things. I can't wait to see what they are now that you aren't so distracted by hiding your secrets."

"Me too," he admitted, and then he caught himself before he became too distracted with the idea. "What are your orders now, ma'am?"

"Where's Oz?" Yvie asked as Kuveni escorted her to Eleanor's side.

"He's still inside."

Yvie whimpered.

"I'll go check on them. Greenie, you're with me. Yvie and Kate, please do what you can to help Leo!"

Stanley opened and reclosed the tent flap with a few swift moves, and then he grabbed Eleanor's hand as they braved the sandstorm together.

When they reached the front door, the wind had blown it shut, and smoke was pouring from every window crack. Stanley grabbed the handle and pulled, but the door wouldn't budge. Eleanor tried it herself, but it was utterly steadfast, like pulling against a boulder.

This is very, very bad, Uma murmured.

Eleanor wouldn't let her dire declaration distract her.

Sheranee, please come. We need your help!

Eleanor summoned her trident, but it appeared much more slowly than normal, as if its particles were fighting a battle with the swirling sand and wind to come together.

"By the power of Shakti, I command you!" Eleanor shouted.

As her trident burst into the green flames of her power, she aimed it at the door.

"Open Sesame!"

She gasped with surprise that the silly phrase had worked as flames shot forth from the three tips of her weapon and the door flew off its hinges, into the foyer, landing beside Oz and two teenaged couples who were crouched, shivering with fear in each other's arms on the floor.

"Mickey?" Eleanor said as she recognized one of the boys.

"Mrs. M?" he asked.

"You're an angel too?" the other boy asked.

She realized he was Jimbo. She hadn't recognized him with his face covered in soot.

"Yes! Now come!" Eleanor exclaimed. "Get yourselves to safety! This smoke is wickedly bad for your lungs!"

Mélusine was standing behind them, shielding them from the flames that had now spread downstairs into the dining room and kitchen, but the air was so thick, Eleanor could hardly take a breath.

"*Mon dieu*, thank the gods, Eleanor! We were trapped!" Mélusine exclaimed.

"Strewth, Ellie, I should have realized you were an angel too," Oz murmured.

Mélusine whisked them up and pushed them past Eleanor, out the door. "*Allez*! Go, mes chéris! Get out while you can!"

"Go!" Eleanor reiterated to Oz. She dissolved her crown and trident, but he only looked more surprised. "I'll explain everything later. Yvie's worried sick, and you need to support her, got it? Your most sacred duty right now is to be the husband that your pregnant wife needs. We'll help everyone else!"

One of the teenaged girls screamed and then choked on the blowing sand as Sheranee bounded through the gale, right into the foyer. Oz glanced at her with puzzlement, and then dutifully dove out into the storm.

"My love, I'm so happy to see you," Eleanor said as she planted a kiss on the top of Sheranee's head.

Mélusine pushed forward. "Edmund is still upstairs trying to get the door to the attic open."

"Is that everyone left in the house?" Eleanor asked.

"How should I know?!" Mélusine exclaimed. "I don't know *anything*, Eleanor! I'm trapped in this form! What if I can't ever get out of it?! I'll be stuck for eternity as Percy bloody Blakeney!"

Eleanor placed her hands on Mélusine's shoulders and looked straight into her eyes. "You will not be stuck in this form, my child. Now calm yourself, and we will stop this catastrophe together."

Sheranee licked Mélusine's hands soothingly, but Mélusine pulled away as she rolled her shoulders and gathered her wits.

"I do not need to be comforted, ma chérie. I need to be on guard, and so do you."

As she spoke, Miro stumbled into the front door and collapsed on the floor. His eyes were glassy. He was naked, and his body was covered in dust.

"Too late. Too late. Too late," he whispered feverishly in a distant, ancient tongue. It was not the aboriginal tongue he had been mumbling when she'd first encountered him.

His ceremonial stick clanked as it hit the ground, but he kept it clenched in his hand.

"It's *you*!" Mélusine hissed. "But *how*? How is a measly human doing this?!"

Eleanor kneeled down and gently slapped his face. "Miro? Miro, wake up!"

As she tried to wrestle the stick from him, she gasped and stepped back. She knew that feeling.

"Qu'est-ce que c'est?" Mélusine hissed.

"Touch it!"

Mélusine wrapped her hand around the stick, and her eyes turned black with rage.

"What have you done?!" she boomed as she stepped back and looked at the boy with unabashed disgust. "How dare you enslave a Yaksha! What was it for? Revenge? Power? It has consumed you, you fool! You've brought ruin on us all!"

She burst into her female demonic form and blurred into a straddling position above Miro, ripping the stick from his hand. Stanley stumbled backwards away from them with a squeal.

"Thank god, you changed your form!" Eleanor exclaimed. "Mélusine, do you have your power back?"

Mélusine paid no attention to her as she lifted up Miro and slammed him against the wall. "Tell me how you're doing this! Tell me how you've captured my power! You will give it back to me now, or I will rip you from limb to limb!"

"Too late. Too late. Too late."

"I am the Sacred Rakshini of the Roman Millennium! I am the Guardian of the Yaksha people, and I will make you *pay* for what you've done!"

His mantras stopped, and his eyes closed. She let go of him, and he fell limply to the floor.

"Did you kill him?" Eleanor asked as she rushed forward to take his pulse. "He isn't dead."

Mélusine looked at the stick in her hand. "I'm such a fool, Eleanor. I didn't sense the power from him because it wasn't his. It was a Yaksha's! This selfish human has been harnessing the power of a Yaksha who has been enslaved into the stick. He has been using our power for his own petty revenge!"

"Can you free the Yaksha?"

"I can't! Only a very powerful deity has the power to release a captured Yaksha!"

"Then I'll do it!"

"Oh, ma chérie, you are a godsend!" Mélusine handed Eleanor the stick.

"What do I do?"

"I don't know, ask Uma."

Uma, how do I free a Yaksha?

Uma didn't respond.

Uma? Hello?

"She's not responding."

520

"Ma chérie, we must make all of this stop. We must take all of our power back from this unworthy boy!"

Eleanor dissolved her trident and took the stick into both of her hands. She closed her eyes and felt for the depths of Shakti's power emanating from the core of her being.

"By the power of Shakti, I release you."

The stick exploded into black smoke and disintegrated. Eleanor almost fainted as an unfocused wave of acute terror overcame her. The house rattled as another gust of wind assaulted it, and the sand and dust swirled into the indistinct shape of a fanged, spiked, demonic Rakshasa face.

Sheranee growled and leapt up, snapping futilely into the air.

"Mua ha ha…" Evil laughter boomed from all around them. "Revenge shall be mine!"

"*Mon dieu*, what have I done?" Mélusine hissed.

"What have *I* done?!" Eleanor panicked.

"Tonight, Lord Vishnu shall die!" their nemesis declared.

"Hari?!" Mélusine hissed. "You're dead! Narasimha slayed you! I saw it with my own eyes!"

"It's Haranyakashipu to you, slave!"

"Hari, stop it this instant! The Sacred Rakshini commands it!"

The booming voice laughed louder. "Fools! You're all such fools. It isn't even a pleasure to defeat you!"

Mélusine closed her eyes and concentrated, and a golden staff appeared in her hand. She aimed it at the creature.

"To the ether with you for eternity!" she declared.

But, as a silver bolt of lightning shot forth from her staff, a sparkling red spear materialized from the swirling sand and stabbed her right through the belly. She looked down with shock, and violet plasma oozed out of her mouth and down her spiked chin.

"NO!" Eleanor screamed.

The golden staff disappeared. Mélusine dissolved into a puddle of violet metallic plasma and disappeared in a blur. Sheranee whimpered and ran behind Eleanor for protection.

Uma, what do I do?!

Eleanor dreaded the silence in her head.

Uma, please! How do I defeat him?!

She grabbed her bangle.

Vibhi?! How do I win?! Someone named Hari just slayed Mélusine!!! For god's sake, answer me!!!

In a cloud of smoke, Vibhishana appeared, crouching in the flames of the raging fire that was spreading into the foyer from the dining room.

"Vibhi?!" Eleanor rushed to his side. Sheranee pounced on top of him and licked his face.

He looked around confusedly, and his wings flapped as he looked down at his handsome Lankan form clad in a tasteful western suit, and then up at Eleanor. He communicated only through her bangle.

You must have summoned me through the sacred fire, Eleanor! Like I summoned you on Dasara! Thank god we've found a good use for it! Who is our foe?

Haranyakashipu? Hari? Do you know him?

Shiva's wrath. He should be dead.

Well, he's not.

This is very, very bad.

Tell me! Tell me everything!

He nudged Sheranee gently out of his way so he could look at Eleanor unencumbered for their silent conversation. She reached down her hand and pulled him up, but he wouldn't let go after he was steadied in her arms. He held on tightly as he answered her.

He was a powerful, evil Rakshasa. One of the worst! He made my evil brother seem like an amateur, Eleanor.

Great... But you killed him, and he came back? Like your brother did when Rama slayed him?

I wasn't the one who killed him. He was immortal against all men and beasts. Lord Vishnu came to Earth as a hybrid avatar, as a half man half lion, and he slayed him. But that was almost two thousand years ago, Eleanor. He should be dead! Do you know anything about how he's here now?

524

Mélusine thought he was a Yaksha, trapped in a ceremonial stick by a foolish, vengeful boy. She thought if we freed the Yaksha, we'd solve the problem, so I freed him, and now he's here!

But I still don't understand. Rakshasas can't be enslaved in an object. It simply doesn't happen!

Well, he's here now, and he came out of that damned stick! What do we do?!

I can't slay him, Eleanor. He is immortal against blows from all men and beasts, even me. We must think!

Is he immortal against blows from women?

Vibhishana looked past her to the disembodied form of their foe, and she liked the subtle smile that worked its way onto his face.

So, that is what the prophecy meant... That is not what I thought at all... But it wasn't supposed to happen this way, was it? How could I have been so wrong?!

"Lord Vibhishana?" Their foe's voice boomed all around them. "What a pleasure it is to see that you've joined Lord Vishnu for his demise. I see your loyalties have remained as stagnant as your form all these years. How disappointing. Do you even remember how to be a demon anymore?"

As the house shook with demonic laughter, Vibhishana burst into his demonic form. Eleanor found the contrast with his sparkling golden wings to look strangely natural.

You're right, Eleanor. You are the key. You will slay him. That's what the prophecies meant... You must harness the full power of Durga. Don't hold yourself back, and let her guide you. She will know what to do. She defeated a demon of this strength before when she slayed Mahishasura.

He ripped a familiar sword out of a hidden pocket in his form. It was the same curved ancient sword he had used when he'd come to rescue her from Surpanakha on her honeymoon. The laughter only echoed louder as he removed the red sparkling blade from its leather sheath and held it poised.

Eleanor, you must be very clever. I will weaken him, and then you must take him by surprise as soon as he slays me. And do not, under any circumstance, reveal to him that I am Lord Shiva.

You're going to let him slay you? Why?! Come up with a better solution, D.H.! You've got five thousand years of wisdom to choose from!

Don't falter, D.W. Be who you were meant to be. No matter what happens, you MUST defeat him.

NO! Uma's voice finally emerged. *Vibhi, don't do it!*

Eleanor, don't let her distract you. You know what you need to do.

He lunged towards the creature, and it solidified into the form of a fierce, spiked Rakshasa twice the size of Vibhishana, but still made entirely of sand.

"Now shall we have some fun, my lord?" It laughed. "Or has it been so long since you've fought a real battle that you've forgotten how?"

It summoned its red sapphire spear up off the floor and aimed it at Vibhishana.

In a blur, Vibhishana slammed the blade of his sword against the spear deflecting it, and then he pushed his nemesis out into the raging winds of the storm.

What happened, Uma? Where have you been?

I was trapped, my child. I couldn't crawl my way to the surface of your consciousness. It was as if Shakti herself demanded my silence.

Great.

My child, you must triumph. This is why Shakti chose you. You will not waver like I would.

Sheranee followed Eleanor as she approached the doorframe and squinted to look out into the night. Illuminated in the eerie red glow of the burning house, Eleanor could see the enraptured, fearful faces of Oz and Yvie as they held handkerchiefs up against their mouths and noses, watching the battle from just inside the cracked-open flap of the tent.

"Blimey," she whispered.

526

Vibhishana and Hari's red sapphire weapons slammed against each other in a whirlwind combat almost too fast for her eyes to see or her brain to process.

Vibhishana laughed with a moment of triumph as he captured Hari's spear. He broke it over his knee and threw it off to the side, but his foe only grinned devilishly and threw himself at Vibhishana, encompassing him with his massive arms.

"Ma'am, what are your orders?" Stanley squeaked as he emerged from his corner to take a position beside her. He offered her a handkerchief as he held one against his mouth and nose.

"I'm going into battle, greenie. No matter what happens, you have to make sure that Edmund gets out of this house alive. Got it? Edmund first. If he gets burned beyond his ability to heal, the world will end sooner rather than later, and that will be a very bad ending for everyone."

"Aren't you scared?"

"I'm bloody terrified."

Vibhishana threw Hari against the house, and every window shattered.

As Vibhishana raised his sword and went in for his final, weakening blow, the house shook with laughter.

Vibhishana stabbed him straight through the belly, but the blow had no effect at all, other than throwing Vibhishana off balance as he pulled his sword out of the swirling sand of Hari's form.

Vibhishana stepped back, and Eleanor did not like the fear she heard in his voice. "How have you done this? How have you made yourself invincible? Every Rakshasa can be disarmed by the Patel sword, even me!"

"You're even more blind than you were two thousand years ago, *my lord*! Can't you see that I'm not a Rakshasa anymore? I've evolved!"

"How?! No god would ever give you a boon!"

"Are you certain, my lord?"

"Yes."

Eleanor felt a burst of divine power waft off of him.

Careful, D.H., don't give yourself away.

Hari grinned. "I didn't need a god to give me a boon. I took it! I took what was mine! I dove into the Sacred Well while your worthless guardian was distracted, and I drank in the power of ten Yakshas! I am the ultimate Yaksha! I am unstoppable!"

"Melysium would never let you into the Crystal Cave. You're lying."

He burst into booming laughter. "She was too busy sharing your sister's bed to stop me, my lord. If I hadn't killed her already, I'd suggest you ask her! Now both of you will die, Lord Vishnu will parish, and I will take my rightful position in Indra's place, the god to rule all gods!"

"You will never be a god," Vibhishana scoffed.

Suddenly, the sky above them cleared entirely, while the screeching winds and raging dust of the haboob continued all around them.

"I already am," he declared. "And now, Lord Vishnu will pay for what he did to me. He will pay for the centuries of formless life I endured in the dead desert sands after he banished me to the other side of the planet! He will pay for the decades I spent enslaved in the pocket of a weak human witch!"

"I see. So the ultimate Yaksha still suffers from the greatest weakness of his species? Perhaps you should have thought more carefully before you dove into the Sacred Well to steal power that wasn't destined for you. I've told you many times that great misery stalks those who thwart destiny."

Even through his demonic features impeded by the swirling sand of his form, Eleanor could see a grimace of unabashed hatred in Hari's expression.

"*I've* been in control for months," he hissed. "I enslaved the meagre human heir to that witch as soon as he touched my vessel. It took *nothing* for me to twist his petty rage at her pointless death

528

to my own ends. With no effort, I enslaved the spiders and the serpents! I endowed my most devoted follower with more power than any Rakshasa could dream of. I made him so powerful that he almost defeated Lord Vishnu himself! I enslaved the sea, and even Varuna didn't dare to challenge me! And now I have enslaved the sky! I am not a Yaksha slave. I am God!"

Both pieces of the broken spear levitated up from the ground, reforming back into a solid weapon.

"Watch out!" Stanley screamed.

Vibhishana looked back, but it was too late.

Eleanor grabbed Stanley's arm and held her breath as the spear slayed Vibhishana from behind. Sheranee roared with horror.

"It is God's will that you die, you traitor!" Hari declared.

NO! A wave of Uma's despair washed over Eleanor, but she pushed it away.

Violet metallic plasma oozed from Vibhishana's mouth, down his chin, and just as Mélusine had, he dissolved into a puddle of liquid and disappeared in a blur.

Hari laughed as he collected Vibhishana's red sapphire sword into one hand and his spear into the other. "Lord Vishnu thought that a Rakshasa avatar would stop me? The god who triumphed over death itself? He's as arrogant as he always was."

"It's time for my reckoning," Eleanor muttered as she climbed onto Sheranee's back. "Remember my orders, greenie. You're my number one handmaiden now. Do the position justice."

"Yes, my lady," he agreed with a solemn nod.

Maa Durga, I am your vessel. Please guide me.

She felt her heavy golden crown materialize on her head as her flaming green trident appeared in her hand. Sheranee growled, and as Eleanor dug in her heels, just as if her loyal mount were a noble steed, she felt her own posture straighten and her limbs stiffen as an intoxicating burst of power, infinitely more euphoric than what she had felt on Dasara, infused every cell of her being.

The red reflection of the house's flames morphed into an eerie green as she glanced one last time at Oz and Yvie watching her.

"Hya!"

Sheranee roared.

Eleanor rode her mount into the storm with her trident poised. Hari's laughter dissolved as he watched her approach.

"Durga?!" he hissed. "No! It can't be! Lord Vishnu can't be married to Durga! You're supposed to be Padma! The worthless Avatar of Lakshmi, a pretty little princess ripe for the slaughter!"

He hurled the spear at her. As Eleanor aimed her trident at it, she felt a familiar weight pull her back, and she struggled to stay balanced on Sheranee's back. She looked up to see one of Durga's extra arms twirling a noose up above her head. In one swift move, she captured the spear and dissolved it. Eleanor laughed as another rush of power infused her. Her head swam.

"We are told too often what we cannot be," Durga replied, echoing the words that Uma had spoken the fateful day Eleanor had first met her in the cave in Elephanta... the day Eleanor had become a goddess.

Hari grinned devilishly at her challenge, but as he held out Vibhishana's sword before him and charged at Sheranee, another of her arms reached out with a shield, smashing against the sword and knocking it to the ground.

He backed away to get his bearings, and then with a ferocious look of renewed vigor, he morphed his clawed Rakshasa hands of swirling sand into two perfect copies of Durga's noose and whipped them out to ensnare her extra arms. As Eleanor felt him rip at Durga's form, two more arms loomed above her. Hari didn't have time to pull away before she severed his grip with a serrated, flat circular discus in one hand, and her own sparkling, curved red sapphire sword in the other.

He wailed with pain. *Ah ha!* Durga had found his weakness. Her divine weapons *could* inflict pain on his semi-corporeal form.

530

She braced herself as the weight of Durga's divine form stiffened. Several more arms loomed over her. As Hari backed away, Durga positioned a bow and aimed a sparkling red sapphire arrow right at his forehead.

Pew. Pew. Pew.

In a split second, three divine arrows struck him, sticking grotesquely in his form. The same black goo that had oozed out of Kuveni's hand dripped out of the wounds on his forehead, his chest, and his belly.

Hari's surprise morphed into terror, and he screamed as he looked down.

"How have you done this?! I am a Yaksha! Yakshas cannot be trapped in their forms!"

"There are consequences for meddling with powers you don't understand, my child!" Durga boomed. "And like an insolent child, it is time for your punishment."

Eleanor held up her flaming trident and another burst of green flames engulfed her. Hari threw himself onto the ground in prostration.

"Your Eminence, I beg your forgiveness! Please, spare me! I have triumphed over death itself. Surely I can serve you faithfully! You will not find a stronger servant!"

"How many innocents have you killed for sport, my child? It is time for your reign of terror to end."

He stuttered, and Eleanor realized he was buying time.

Slay him, Eleanor. He's lying. Slay him before it's too late. Vibhishana's weak voice resonated in her head.

As their foe reached down to grab Vibhishana's sword, Sheranee roared, engulfing his hand into her mouth. It dissolved into sand, and as she coughed and spit it out, he cackled, and his hand reformed.

"I've triumphed over death! You think I won't triumph over you?! A weak human avatar?!"

In a blur, he ripped the sword up from the ground, but as he swung straight for Eleanor's waist, she gave in completely to the euphoria of Shakti's power. She sunk back into the secondary position in her body and watched as Durga dodged his blow and thrust her flaming trident straight into the belly of the beast.

He looked down with shock and wailed with pain.

"Not man nor beast, the Goddess has defeated you once and for all!" she declared. "Haranyakashipu, you shall repent in Naraka! Shakti commands it!"

He exploded into a puff of black, sparkling powder, and the wind dissolved.

Suddenly, the night was still. Everything was covered in a fine layer of dust and sand, while drifts of miniature dunes were nestled into every corner. The only sounds that echoed in the night were the crackling of the house burning and the gasps of her audience watching from the tent.

Sheranee huffed and puffed as she paced around in a circle, spreading the black sparkling powder around.

As the weight of Durga's form lifted, Eleanor dissolved her trident and her crown, and hopped off of Sheranee's back. She ran straight back into the house.

"Eleanor?" Stanley asked timidly when she reached the front door where he'd watched her entire battle. "Are you alright?"

"I'm fine, greenie, but the fun isn't over yet. We have to help Edmund! Edmund?!" she called.

He didn't answer.

Eleanor, we must stop the fire. Vibhishana's voice echoed in her head.

How? Are you alright? That was an ugly injury. I'm quite sure Uma thought you were dead.

I am immortal, Eleanor. Truly and completely. But I am weak. I can't hold a humanoid form yet.

Where are you?

I'm in the parlor. Leave the boy behind.

"Cover my tracks, greenie," Eleanor hissed. "Keep everyone else away!"

"Yes, ma'am." He took his position guarding the front door.

Sheranee followed as she ran into the parlor, coughing as the smoke of the raging fire bit at her lungs.

"Where? Where are you?!" she called.

I'm resting… in the ice bucket.

She looked around, and then spotted a buffet table with a soot-blackened white table-cloth. A massive silver ice bucket holding several open bottles of champagne still sweated. She ran up to it, and lo and behold, on the surface of the melted ice, there was her divine husband, resting as a thick layer of violet metallic plasma.

Blimey. You really are very foreign, aren't you? That's all of you?

It is an embarrassing state to be seen in, Eleanor. But it doesn't matter now. You must stop the fire.

How?

You can absorb the flames into your being. It is one of your divine powers as the Transformer of the Universe.

Will it burn my human skin?

Shiva's wrath. Uma didn't burn, but you might…

We need a plan, D.H. Edmund isn't answering me. He's still upstairs trying to get the trapped children out of the attic.

Stop the fire, Eleanor. I will protect you.

The violet metallic liquid oozed and folded. Eleanor watched curiously as it struggled to morph into a cohesive shape.

Put your hands in the water, Eleanor.

She dipped her hands into his plasma, and shivered as the icy water and his frigid plasma engulfed her skin, creating the bizarre impression that she was wearing her divine husband like he was a pair of opera gloves.

I will protect you, Eleanor. We will absorb the flames together.

She pulled her hands out of the ice bucket, and shivered again at the oddly pleasant sensation of feeling his smooth plasma against her skin.

Hold your breath, Eleanor, and go towards the worst of the flames with your hands and my plasma in front of you.

She followed his instructions and walked up the stairs, fighting the burning smoke in her lungs until she reached the raging second floor fire. She hissed with pain as the flames bit at the many unprotected parts of her body.

Vibhishana expanded his form, molding his plasma over her dress and her hair and even her feet, until every part of her was covered with a thin layer of his silky plasma. She tried not to think about how outrageous the alien sight must have looked, but as Vibhishana's energy connected with hers, the heat of the fire morphed into something greater, something wonderful… and something guilty. As she focused entirely on absorbing the flames––on doing what she had to do to save *Edmund*—Uma moaned with pleasure at her uninhibited connection with her other half.

As the heat flowed through her, warming her from the inside out while feeding into itself until she couldn't hold herself up any longer, Eleanor gave into the all-encompassing ecstasy of the fire mingling with his energy and hers. In that moment, she was utterly and completely something and someone else. Eleanor MacLeod was, and always had been, just a means to an end. Every part of her—even the jaded, austere human nurse who'd staunchly supported her struggling sisters and mother for decades—finally believed that she *was* the Avatar of Shakti.

As the flames dissolved all around her, she collapsed onto the floor, gasping for air. The bitter smoke filled her lungs, and she coughed violently. Uma moaned as one final wave of pleasure washed over them, and Eleanor scratched her way back to her humanity. Her prior thought-stream suddenly felt like a dream, but the truth of the epiphany stuck in the back of her mind.

It is done, Eleanor.

She opened her eyes. Sheranee licked her feet. The flames were gone. Lingering smoke still filled the air. Vibhishana's plasma oozed off of her onto the floor, and Eleanor looked down. Other than a thin layer of soot that had settled onto her before her epic battle, her dress, her hair, and all of the skin he had protected showed no sign of the fire and brimstone she'd absorbed.

Thank you, D.H.

I must go regain my strength. I'll help you deal with the witnesses when I'm presentable again.

Go. I'll deal with them. I already have plenty of practice.

Eleanor sat up dazedly, struggling to breathe with her irritated lungs, and then she heard the clomping of footsteps emerging from the floor above.

Edmund blurred down the stairs with three children carefully secured in his arms and stopped just short of running her over. His entire body was black with soot, and his violet metallic plasma oozed at the surface of gaping wounds all up his arms. Eleanor gratefully noted that his eyes had already returned to their human hazel, and that his burns didn't appear to be bad enough for his body to entirely re-set. All of the children were unconscious as he kneeled down and carefully released them from his arms.

"Dearest, are you alright? Are you injured?" He trailed off as he suddenly processed Sheranee's presence. Sheranee bowed regally.

"I'm fine," she rasped. "Just a little smoke inhalation. What happened to your arms?"

She reached over and took the children's pulses and felt for breath.

"I couldn't get the attic door open... I went a bit mad beating myself against it." He looked around. "Is the fire out completely?" Eleanor nodded. "Thank god. There are more children still upstairs. Are these ones alright? They were unconscious by the time I beat down the door. The ones still upstairs are in a similar state."

"They're fine. They will probably have some trouble breathing, but they're alive. I'm sure their parents are worried sick."

She gave into a bout of coughs, and Sheranee licked her face.

"What is that tiger doing here, Eleanor?"

"Darling, she is Kate and Percy's companion. Shruti lied about it back in Bombay, because they asked her to."

"They flew a tiger down here in an airplane? Alongside our dogs? Our dogs! Eleanor, where are the dogs?! I haven't seen them since we let them out into the garden this morning to play!"

"Darling, first things first. I'm sure they hid in the barn down the road or something similarly intelligent when the brunt of the storm hit. They never wander too far from us anyway. Sheranee, will you please go find Ovid and Pliny?"

Sheranee humphed her dutiful agreement and leapt down the stairs.

Edmund watched her go. "She is a very obedient tiger… and her English is superb."

"Darling, the children need rest, and their parents must be worried sick. Why don't you take them out to the tent? The wind storm has finally stopped."

He looked down at the oozing plasma on his arms. "Do you think I should wait until my foreign ailments have disappeared, now that the danger has passed?"

"Darling, I think that if a single person here doesn't think we are angels or demons, it will be a true miracle. Perhaps letting them see you saving the children in all your foreign glory will help us keep their fears abated."

He moved to argue.

"Darling, we must give them some explanation. They've witnessed many strange things tonight."

"Like what? What did they see, Eleanor? Did Kate and Percy do something odd? There wasn't any water around…"

"Darling, many people did many things to help out during this unfortunate situation. Now, angels in disguise has worked well as an excuse in the past, don't you think?"

"I suppose… just don't expect me to discuss liturgy with that priest."

"I wouldn't dream of it, darling."

With a resigned sigh, he re-secured the children in his arms and blurred down the stairs and out the front door.

Eleanor noticed Stanley watching them from the bottom of the staircase. He stared as he watched Edmund reach the tent. Joyful wails mixed with gasps as he reunited the children with their parents.

Stanley climbed up the stairs to join her. "I wondered what it would look like… It's stranger than I expected."

"His speed or his purple blood?"

"His purple blood," Stanley admitted. "When Leo described it, I thought he was pulling my leg, even after Mac smacked me upside the head for laughing at the idea. I thought at first that all of it was just a mean prank cooked up by Mac and my father… until I saw Edmund's black eyes on the steamer. I thought even that might be a prank at first, until you popped right into my head. I suppose I should thank you for doing that now, it helped me take everything more seriously."

"Mac!" Eleanor exclaimed at the reminder. "Where's Mac? Have you seen him? He was with Edmund, wasn't he?"

Edmund returned to her side in a blur. "There are four more children upstairs, and their parents are right behind me." He glanced self-consciously at Stanley, and then down at his hands as the last of his plasma disappeared into his freshly-healed skin. "I told you that your secrets weren't the most scandalous under our roof."

"I'm better at keeping secrets than I let on, Colonel. I've had a lifetime of practice. I'll keep yours as if they were my own."

Edmund patted him on the back. "I expected nothing less, my boy."

"Colonel, do you know where Mac is? Is he back in the tent?"

"I haven't seen him. Was he in the house?"

As a troop of parents charged up the stairs, Eleanor scrambled out of the way, and Stanley and Edmund both offered her their hands to help her up. She smiled and let them each support her as she woozily stood up. She was still lightheaded from the entire ordeal, and she held back a bout of coughs that were itching to burst forth.

"Go, darling. Lead the parents to their bairns. I will help Stanley look for Mac."

Edmund blurred back up the stairs, and as several burly, dusty men barreled past her, Stanley noticed her continued weakness and reached under her, using the technique she had shown him to support Mr. Valov.

"I'm not that weak, greenie, just give me a minute." She maneuvered out of his arms and leaned on the soot-covered wall. "We really do need to find Mac. Why don't you open every door on this floor and look inside? He won't be able to call out to us."

"I can't see very well, ma'am. It's too dark."

Eleanor called forth her flaming trident.

"That's one way of doing it," Stanley whispered.

"We might as well use what we have available. Don't you think?"

"That's what my brother, Reggie, always says too. It drives my father mad. My father would watch a man die if rescuing him would make him look improper."

"Well, it's a good thing your father isn't here then, isn't it?"

"In so many ways, Eleanor, I can't even count them."

She patted his back and then followed him as he opened the doors to every room until they reached the farthest one, Oz's study.

"Mac!" Stanley exclaimed.

538

Mac was collapsed in Oz's leather chair with his head on the desk and the telephone receiver still in his hand. Eleanor took his pulse, but she knew it was pointless. She knew only too well what fresh death looked like.

As she put his hand back down, she noticed an unfinished note scribbled directly onto the blotter, but instead of handwriting or shorthand, it was only spelled out in a series of dots and lines. She stared at it for an extended moment, letting Uma's linguistic talent emerge.

"It's Morse Code," Stanley said as he squinted at it with concentration. "Mac used it to communicate with my father by phone. He would always plan out his messages before he'd make his reports. He claimed it was for clarity, but I think he wasn't very comfortable with the code."

"He seemed pretty comfortable with it when he was using it to argue with your father on the beach."

"I told them if they weren't careful about that someone would notice. They thought you'd all be too stupid to recognize it. But the language they use in person is all very simple. Mac wasn't very good at languages, so writing complex sentences in the code was hard for him. He would never admit it, though."

"Well, it looks like he left quite a paper trail for us to read. Do you think he left it on purpose, hoping we'd read it?"

"I doubt it. He never thought very highly of women's intellect, and he thinks I'm an idiot too. I never saw fit to correct him." Stanley smirked. "I've been reading his notes for years."

She ran her fingers across the smooth penciled lines. She could read it herself with Uma's help, but she let Stanley have his moment.

"*Countess as powerful as Colonel X. Mind control possible. Extreme caution advised. Colonel X more powerful than reported by Agent C. Displays speed and strength of Subject S and Subject P. Suspicions re: Subject P and Subject K confirmed; spontaneous creation of matter observed. All subjects are possible source of invincible armor and advanced airplane design. Source of*

539

aeronautics expertise still unknown. No evidence of British military engineering in design or function. Mechanism simple enough for female Subject K to pilot. Additional manpower for observation required. Agent C fully compromised. Readying for ordered termination. No confirmation on Subject P's deviance. Agent A... He stops there. Agent C is Leo, Agent A is me. Subject P is Percy, Subject K is Kate, and Subject S is Doctor Carpenter."

"Subject S?"

Stanley rolled his eyes. "For Shylock."

Eleanor shrugged, and then squinted to re-read the message.

"Ordered termination? Of Leo?" Eleanor felt her Celtic temper erupting. As the heat of the flames she'd absorbed forced their way to the surface, she leaned on Stanley, taking several deep, calming breaths until she had them barely contained. "Do you think Mac started the fire as a cover for executing Leo?"

"Yes."

"That bastard! How could he do that?! There were a hundred innocent people in the house!"

"One hundred innocent lives are well within the acceptable casualty standard for the termination of an acute risk to the Empire."

"What is this, bloody Rome?"

"Our empire is bigger than Rome ever was, Eleanor, and my father and Mac don't have any delusions about how it got that way—with an iron fist. Leo's sharing of state secrets to Edmund's guardians was treason, which is a capital crime—a crime that I am committing now too by helping you."

"Blimey."

Stanley shrugged. "I should be in jail anyway for who I am. I might as well do what I think is right."

"Do you think he sent the message? Or did he pass out from the smoke while he was writing his draft?"

"I don't know." Stanley looked nervous. "It will be very bad if he managed to send it. My father is already just itching for an excuse to make it seem reasonable for him to arrest you, and treason is the best reason in the book."

Eleanor sighed with stress.

"When he returns from Perth, I'll try to find out if he got the message. He'll be so outraged by Mac's death, that he probably won't be able to keep the intel a secret."

"Greenie, I don't think I realized until now how lucky we really are to have you."

"Does that mean you'll stop calling me greenie?"

"You don't like it? We meant it disparagingly at first, but now I find it kind of endearing. You are still at the beginning of your journey, you know."

Stanley thought about it. "I suppose it's the kindest nickname I've ever been given."

"We can call you something else if you don't like it."

Stanley shrugged. "Nah. How about I earn my way into another nickname?"

"Excellent plan."

"What should we do now?"

Eleanor pried the phone from Mac's dead hand and listened for a dial tone. It was blank. "I think we shouldn't worry about the message for now. The wind probably disconnected the line hours ago."

Eleanor examined his body for evidence of foul play, but just as she was ready to wash her hands of it, she noticed a hint of fresh blood on Mac's white shirt sleeve sticking out of his formal butler's coat.

"Help me get his clothes off."

Stanley blushed. "Are you sure? Mac wouldn't like it if I took his clothes off. He told me if he ever caught me checking him out, he'd knock my teeth out."

"How did he tell you that?"

"I was thirteen. It was before he lost his voice in the war."

"Blimey, you've lived a painful couple of decades, haven't you?"

"You have no idea."

"You're right. I don't. But my father was unmasked by the *Edinburgh Register* as a polygamist when I was ten, and we lost everything when he shot himself, so I'm no stranger to childhood pain."

"*Gast*, Eleanor. I'm sorry."

Eleanor sighed. "There's enough sorrow in this world to go around, greenie. Now, Mac is dead. His bullying doesn't matter anymore, and your orders are to help me strip him."

"Yes, ma'am."

They both flailed awkwardly against the dead weight of Mac's corpse as they unfurled his tuxedo jacket, and then set about unbuttoning his vest and his dress shirt.

"I've always dreamed of unbuttoning a beautiful man's shirt," Stanley admitted as he struggled to unbutton the top button. "I suppose this is some sort of practice; although, Mac is one ugly dead wanker."

"Inside and out," Eleanor winked.

She unbuttoned the rest with the speed of an expert, and then pulled it off to reveal his bare arms.

"*Ma doué*, what happened?" Stanley whispered as he held up Mac's heavy left arm.

There were words scratched into it in a very foreign tongue, but Eleanor was relieved, despite her distaste for him, that the lack of fresh blood indicated that the deed had been done after he was dead.

"Do you think that's a language?" he asked. "The strokes look familiar, but I don't know from where. They don't even look like runes."

Eleanor closed her eyes and reopened them, blinking several times as she focused on understanding the meaning rather than the strokes. "It is the language of Edmund's people."

"Demons have a written language?"

"You mean that angels do, greenie."

"If you say so."

"I do."

Eleanor squinted to read the message:

Forgive me, Your Eminence. He was a blasphemous traitor. A petty eye injury was not sufficient punishment.

She lifted up the other arm where the message continued.

Tell our boy Stanley to serve his masters well. I'll be watching.

"Blimey," Eleanor whispered.

"Can you read it?"

"It's a message from our kraken. She's apologizing for disobeying my orders not to kill, and is suggesting that you should serve me well."

"Is that a threat? Do I need to worry that she'll do something like that to me?"

Eleanor patted his shoulder. "Everything she says is a bit of a threat. If she wanted to hurt you, she would've already done it. She let you rescue Mac in the water. She was very impressed by you, in fact. Stay loyal to us, and you'll be perfectly fine."

"No one has ever been impressed by me."

Eleanor thought about the development, wrestling with a realization at the tip of her tongue. "Blimey... *that's* where Mac's black eye came from. That woman has the weirdest priorities."

"The kraken hit Mac in the face with a polo ball?"

"She is as mad as a hatter."

"Figures she's mad if she thought I was impressive."

"Don't be so down on yourself, greenie. You're already finding your stride."

"If you say so."

"I do. Now, we must focus on the positives. This is one of the sanest things I've ever seen her do."

"Murdering a man and scratching a message into his arm is one of the sanest thing she's ever done?"

"I suppose turning into a sea monster and scratching a message into your father's face was slightly saner...." Eleanor sighed with stress. "I can't let myself think about it, we have too much else to do. She's not here now, and there's no point in stewing about it. We need to hide the evidence. We don't need your father getting hold of any proof that we had anything to do with Mac's demise."

"Amen to that... But how do we do it? My father's going to notice that there's a message scratched into Mac's arms. Even I noticed it."

Eleanor paced back and forth as she thought about their options, and as she coughed with the painful burning in her lungs, a morbid idea crossed her mind.

Use the fire, my child. Use the flames that you absorbed. They are yours now to use as you see fit.

"Greenie, I'm going to need you to stand back."

"Why?" he asked nervously.

"I have our plan."

She guided him to the door and nudged him behind her. She took in a deep breath and called forth her trident. She relaxed and let the flames she'd already been fighting so hard to contain work their way into her fingertips, and as she felt her skin begin to burn, she concentrated with all her might on channeling the flames straight into the weapon. With a burst of intoxicating power that overwhelmed her human pain, earthly fire erupted from her trident alongside the green flames of Shakti's power, igniting everything in the room.

After almost a minute of raging conflagration, a wave of hot nausea washed over her, and Eleanor collapsed. Stanley caught her as she felt her power retract back into her. She dropped her trident, but before it hit the floor, it dissolved, returning to its divine perch to await her next summons. She looked down and wiggled her fingers. She couldn't have been more grateful that they weren't burned.

She leaned on the doorframe and coughed at the remnant smoke as she took in the results of her work. The entire room was charred, and the ghoulish scent of burned flesh from Mac's barely recognizable body mixed grotesquely with the smoking remnants of paper and fabric and wood. She felt slightly guilty about the inconvenience her actions would cause to Oz and Yvie with their important papers burned, but she was certain that Lord Grimby having fewer excuses to meddle in their lives would be enough of a blessing for everyone to warrant the loss.

Eleanor stumbled into the room and covered her nose with the fabric of her dress as she leaned down to examine what was left of Mac's body. Even with her hearty temperament, the sight and the smell were almost too much to bear, but she didn't regret it. All evidence of Surpanakha's message had disappeared with Mac's melting flesh.

"He was already dead, greenie. We should always remember that when we think back on how horrific this looks," she said woozily.

"You really are a great goddess, Eleanor," Stanley murmured. He gathered her weight onto his arm. "Let me help you downstairs. We shouldn't let anyone see us here. As soon as he finds out Mac's dead, my father will start asking a lot of difficult questions."

"Hold on, greenie." She wiped a line of melted mascara off of his cheeks and onto her ruined dress. "You've been an exceptional handmaiden this fine evening, but if you're going to wear makeup every day, you're going to have to learn how to deal with its limitations."

"Will you teach me?"

She smiled. "I'd be glad to. But first I have to face my firing squad. It's one of your most difficult tasks to help us manage the crowds after they've witnessed a wild show like this one. I honestly don't know how Leo did it."

"I don't either," he admitted. "Leo was the best officer in the service, and everyone, including my father, knew it."

He helped her down the stairs, and out into the clear night. The temperature had become pleasant, although, as the crowd milled about, the dust tickled her nose, which was already raw and irritated from the smoke.

Kuveni rushed to greet her, pulling her into a motherly hug so tight that Eleanor couldn't breathe.

"The Goddess triumphed tonight," Kuveni whispered into her ear. "It was a privilege to watch, for me," she glanced back at the crowd of villagers, "and for everyone else. Even with the tent flaps closed, they could see the silhouette of the entire battle illuminated by the flames of the house. I don't know what they make of it yet. They don't seem to be gathering their pitchforks; although, perhaps they just don't have any handy."

Eleanor glanced over self-consciously at the many curious eyes watching her, but no one had the courage, or the audacity, to approach her. Nellie Melba, Sheila, and Father O'Donnelly distributed water and blankets from a pile in the middle of the tent, avoiding eye contact with Eleanor and Kuveni. Stanley kneeled down as he noticed Leo sleeping soundly on the ground.

"He doesn't look well, Eleanor."

Stanley was right. Leo's lips were grey, and his skin a pale, ashen white. Eleanor kneeled down and took his pulse. Present but weak. She stroked his forehead and sighed sadly as she stood up.

"I think that tonight is the night."

Kuveni hugged her again. "I'm sorry, Mistress Eleanor."

"Where did the supplies come from?" she changed the subject.

"They're all that I've been able to conjure since you defeated that bastard of a demon. When Mélusine is deposed like this, we all suffer. Our collective reserves of power have been depleted. It is a very unfortunate situation…" she glanced over at Yvie, "and we are going to need you to be the Goddess a little bit longer tonight, I'm afraid."

Oz noticed their attention and gestured for them to come over to where he was sitting beside Yvie, holding both of her hands in his.

"What's wrong?" Eleanor asked as she kneeled down before Yvie and noticed her face wet with tears. "Did you lose someone? So far the only death we've noted is Mac."

"Mac? I suppose I'd be a heartless brute to say good riddance, so I'll keep the idea to myself…" Oz said.

Eleanor didn't let Mac or Oz distract her. "Yvie, what's wrong? I hope you're not… er… worried about what you saw us do? We're all really very normal."

"*Ce n'est pas vrai*," Yvie countered. "You are not normal at all. But, Ellie, it's not that."

Eleanor took her hand. *Just tell me, Yvie. Spit it out.*

"It seems like a trivial thing after what just happened, but I'm really, really scared," she sniffled.

"Why?" Eleanor asked as she wiped the tears away.

"Ellie, I'm in labor!"

"Blimey. When did your water break?"

"About fifteen minutes ago… but something's wrong, Ellie. It's too soon!"

Eleanor rubbed her back. "A month early is still okay. My nephew was born a month early, and he and his mother were perfectly fine."

"We don't have anywhere clean to go," Oz whispered with the calmest voice he could muster.

"Ozzy's mother suggested we go to the barn. We aren't bloody Mary and Joseph!" Yvie exclaimed.

"I didn't even know you had a barn!" Eleanor exclaimed. "We could have taken the villagers there!"

"It is a ruin down the road on the other side of the vineyards that we haven't gotten around to fixing," Oz explained. "And it's full of distillery equipment at the moment. There's nowhere for Yvie to lie. We don't even keep hay for livestock."

Eleanor looked to Kuveni.

"I can't do it yet!" Kuveni said with dismay. "I can't even transport myself, and I can't convert anything into a sterile labor room. I don't have the power!"

Yvie let another round of tears flow. "I knew we were doomed! Even the angels can't help us!"

A group of crying women swarmed the front flap of the tent as Edmund returned with the final group of children and their fathers.

Father O'Donnelly began muttering prayers as Edmund put down the youngest boy gently on the ground and his mother crouched down and gathered him up into her arms.

"He's alive, but you should take him to a doctor in Bunbury in the morning. Let us know if you need funds; we are happy to help you pay for the treatment." It was clearly not the first time that Edmund had made the same offer.

"Are you an angel?" she asked. Edmund nodded his reluctant agreement, and she grabbed his hand and kissed it. "Thank you, thank you, thank you…"

He pulled it gently away, and Eleanor admired his attempt to hide his discomfort. "I'm sorry I couldn't have done more," he said as he stood up. "As you can see, I'm not all-powerful, and I'd like you and the others to remember that. Please do what you can to save yourselves next time?"

"Yes, Your Holiness."

"Please call me Edmund." He sighed with stress as he looked around at the wide eyes watching him. "I'm really very ordinary most of the time," he addressed the wider crowd.

Eleanor held her breath as Father O'Donnelly approached him. The priest rolled his shoulders, gathering his courage, and then glanced momentarily up at Edmund before averting his eyes.

"It is very kind of you to help them pay for their medicine, Colonel. Most of the people here can't afford a train ticket to Bunbury."

"It's nothing for us. We don't deserve any special thanks," Edmund brushed off his praise. "If I'd gotten them out of the house sooner, they wouldn't need to go to the doctor at all. It's my fault that they're in this dreadful state."

"I didn't realize you were the one who set the house on fire?"

Eleanor was surprised, and rather impressed, by the boy's audacity. She wondered if the time he'd spent thinking through Edmund's advice after their encounter with Surpanakha had actually gotten through to him.

"I didn't," Edmund said sternly.

Father O'Donnelly looked genuinely puzzled himself, and Eleanor realized that his cheek hadn't been intentional.

"Forgive me, Colonel. I might be a bit daft, but how is it your fault that these people are suffering from the smoke of a fire that you didn't cause?"

Edmund paused for a long moment. "I suppose you have a fair point, father."

"Thank you, Colonel." He looked down, gathering his nerves. "May I ask you just one question?"

"You may ask, if I may refuse to answer."

Father O'Donnelly cleared his throat. "Do you remember what Heaven looks like, or did you forget when you came to Earth?"

Edmund sighed with resignation. "I know as much about Heaven as you do, my boy."

"How sad," he murmured.

"On the contrary. What I can tell you is that Heaven could not possibly be as wonderful as my life is with Eleanor right here on Earth. I don't need to covet greener pastures in the afterlife, my boy, and neither do you."

"YOU!" Oz hissed.

Eleanor looked over to see what had elicited his reaction, but before she could process what was happening, Oz barreled across the tent and threw himself on top of Miro, who was standing just inside the doorway, still naked and covered in dust.

Oz punched him in the jaw, and the boy didn't fight back.

Edmund blurred over to them and pulled Oz away. Oz squirmed to get loose, but Edmund held him steadfast.

"It was YOU, you mongrel!" he shouted at Miro. "You caused all this misery! You burned down our house, you hurt the children, you killed a man, and now you've hurt Yvie! I'm going to kill you, you bastard!"

"It was my fault. I couldn't control it," Miro whispered in perfect Aussie English. "I was an unworthy heir of the talisman."

Eleanor approached them. She put her hand gently on Oz's arm, as she had often done to calm Edmund when he was in a similar state.

"Oz, your wife needs you. We've had enough death and despair for one day. It's time to focus on birth now."

Edmund looked down at her. "What do you mean?"

"Yvie's in labor. We have to figure out where to take her. She shouldn't have a baby right here. It will be dangerous for her and for the baby to be out in the elements."

"We can take her to my father's house," Stanley suggested. "There's plenty of room, and the evening train probably didn't arrive on time with the storm."

"I will not let my wife give birth right under Grumpy Grimby's nose!" Oz exclaimed.

"Would you rather she give birth in a dirty tent, in front of the entire village? Or perhaps inside the freshly smoldering remnants of your home?" Eleanor didn't have the energy to temper her cheek at his annoyingly impractical attitude.

Oz growled with frustration and squirmed to escape from Edmund's arms, and Edmund let him go. He began pacing as he considered their many unpleasant options.

Miro looked up at Eleanor. "My mother thanks you for defeating Julana."

552

"Julana?" she asked.

"The sand demon. The priestesses of my family kept the world safe from him for centuries, but I couldn't do it. He was too strong, and I wasn't ready."

"Do you mean the haboob?" Edmund asked.

Miro stared at Eleanor. "I mean Julana. He used me for months for his own evil ends. I didn't even realize what he was doing at first. I didn't realize until it was too late, until someone much more powerful than I am needed to step in." He bowed his head in subtle deference to Eleanor. "I'm grateful that my ancestors sent you, Miss."

As Edmund moved to ask a follow-up question, Eleanor interrupted him. "Darling, let's let it all pass. We must help Yvie."

"I'm leaving town, and I won't come back," Miro said as he wiped the blood off his chin. "I'm sorry."

He stumbled out into the night, and Eleanor felt a pang of pity for him.

"Come on. We have more important things to do," she said as she guided Oz back to Yvie's side. Stanley and Edmund followed. "Yvie, we'll take you to Grimby's house. It will be clean and comfortable, and it isn't too far."

Yvie moved to protest, but then she nodded tearfully. "Ça suffit."

Sheila approached them. "Jackie, your brothers are still missing."

"Mum, I'm not leaving Yvie's side. I'm ashamed of you for even suggesting it."

"Men should never watch their wives give birth," she humphed. "It isn't proper. She isn't a cow."

"Oz, I will go look for your brothers," Edmund offered. "You think they're near the road from the station in Margaret River?" he addressed Sheila. She nodded. "Where's Mac? I'll take him with me."

"Darling, Mac is dead."

Edmund cleared his throat, hiding his ambivalent emotions. "What happened?"

"He burned to death in the fire. We left what was left of him where we found him in Oz's office. Perhaps we can ask Father O'Donnelly to arrange a proper Christian funeral."

Sheila humphed disagreeably at the suggestion.

The priest looked up as he heard his name, and then nodded his agreement. "I will do whatever you need of me."

Yvie moaned as a contraction began, and Kuveni kneeled down and squeezed her hand. "Breathe, dear girl. Take in a deep, calming breath. All will be well with the angels by your side tonight."

"Go, Edmund, and take Sheila with you. You know the road, don't you, Sheila?" Eleanor suggested.

"But, Jackie…" Sheila glanced at Oz, and Yvie, then Eleanor, who threw her a strict look of disapproval at her absurdly selfish ploy to keep Oz's attention away from Yvie. "Yes, I'll go."

"What about the rest of these people?" Edmund asked as he glanced around the crowded tent.

"I'll see to them, Colonel," Nellie Melba volunteered. "It's the least I can do." She glanced at Eleanor. "Tonight I've realized that I'm not the greatest diva in the world. It has been a humbling experience."

As Yvie's contraction dissipated, Eleanor urged them into action. "Darling, can you collect Leo and bring him to our car? Stanley will drive, and I will sit with Leo in the front seat so that Oz and Yvie and Kate can ride in the back. When you've found Oz's brothers, come on by Grimby's house. I'm sure Sheila can show you the way. Is everyone accounted for?"

"Yes, Captain," Edmund agreed with a facetious salute. He reached into his pocket and handed Nellie Melba a huge wad of cash. "For the doctor's visits tomorrow. Give it to anyone who needs it."

"Yes, Colonel." She saluted without any of the joking tone that he'd used for his.

He reached down and spryly gathered Leo's unconscious body into his arms, but he paused for a moment as his eyes turned black.

"He's dying, Eleanor."

"I know, darling. I know."

He moved to rethink their plan, but Eleanor stopped him. "Darling, you know what he would have wanted you to do. We will help the living, and then we will say goodbye."

Edmund blurred Leo to the car, and Eleanor shooed everyone else into action. As soon as Oz and Kuveni had Yvie safely flanked in the back seat, Eleanor squeezed into the front seat beside Leo, and Stanley started them off down the road in a cloud of dust.

Eleanor turned around to watch Yvie and offer her moral support, while Kuveni held Yvie's hand. They both calmly guided her breathing through her contractions, but she sighed with pain as Stanley hit unseen bumps in the dark road that was littered with fallen branches and long strips of eucalyptus bark that had been torn off by the strong winds.

"I'm sorry!" he called out each time. "I can't see them until it's too late! But you don't want me to go slower, do you?"

"No!" they all answered in unison.

"Oh, thank the gods!" Kuveni exclaimed as they turned around a particularly perilous bend, only to discover a massive downed karri tree blocking the road.

"Blimey," Eleanor whispered. "This is a disaster."

Kuveni disappeared.

"Oh, thank god!" Eleanor exclaimed.

"Why?!" Yvie exclaimed.

"Where did she go?" Oz asked as he looked around.

"If she can disappear, her power is returning!" Eleanor exclaimed.

"Thank god," Yvie whispered.

"Can Edmund do that?" Oz asked.

"There are many things that Kate and Percy can do that Edmund can't. It's important that he doesn't know about them yet, and for that matter, it's important that you don't tell him what you watched me do tonight. He doesn't know that I'm anything more than his ordinary human wife, and it must stay that way."

"What are you really, though?" he asked.

Eleanor suddenly felt self-conscious at the revelation, as if some aspect of telling Oz was a proxy for telling Edmund. "I am a goddess."

"Strewth," Oz whispered. "I reckon you are."

In the blink of an eye, the tree blocking the road disappeared completely, leaving the road wide open.

"Ha! That isn't what I thought they were going to do with it." Eleanor found herself feeling giddy as another wave of adrenaline washed over her. Finally, things were looking up.

"Lady Mélusine is going to take my seat." Kuveni's disembodied voice echoed. "She would like me to warn you that she isn't back to her full self yet, and she would like you to refrain from screaming."

"*Mon dieu, pourquoi?*" Yvie asked.

"*C'est pourquoi.*" Mélusine materialized in the empty seat beside Yvie in her female demonic form.

"Strewth," Oz gasped.

"I know, mon chéri, I don't like it either. It is the only form I can muster at the moment. Give me more time to recover, and I won't be so ugly."

She wiggled her fingers, scrunched her nose, and sighed with relief as she managed to make one of her clawed, spiked hands back into a smooth human one.

Yvie flinched but said nothing as Mélusine reached her hand over to feel her belly.

"He is not positioned correctly yet." She pulled her hand away. "I will help him relax, and when we arrive at your labor room, I will help him into position."

"Are you sure you know what you're doing?" Oz asked.

"Mon chéri, I am Saint Mélusine. I have helped thousands of human women give birth."

"I'm not familiar with her, only with the witch Mélusine," Yvie said timidly.

Mélusine looked down at her body and shrugged. "Yes, well, I'm sure you can see why they were confused."

She closed her eyes again in concentration, and her face returned to her spritely human features, leaving only her left arm still trapped in her colorful, spiked demonic form.

"Did Kate call you here to help me?" Yvie asked. "I hope you weren't too busy."

Mélusine smiled. "Ma chérie, you already know me. I'm Percy. You saw me stabbed by a bastard of a demon a few hours ago. That's why I'm so weak right now."

"*You're* Percy?" Oz asked with disbelief. "But how?!"

Mélusine scrunched her nose with concentration, and with an ungraceful flail, she morphed into the form they knew, and with it, the last of her demonic features dissolved. "That's how."

"Strewth," he repeated. "Is that how you made the... er... fishtail?"

"*C'est vrai*, mon chéri. We can take many forms, human and otherwise to meet our ends. Edmund doesn't know that we can do this yet, and you will not tell him. Understood?"

"Whatever you say... Percy."

Mélusine wiggled herself back into her female form and took in a deep, calming breath. "My power is returning faster now. It's a good sign." She closed her eyes. "I've asked Kate to prepare a room in Grimby's house for us. She will be waiting for us when we arrive. We're almost there."

"I don't like it," Yvie muttered. "What if he's there, and he refuses to let us inside? Or worse, if he wants to watch?!"

Mélusine squeezed Yvie's hand, pushing a calming dose of Yakshini euphoria into her. "All will be well with the angels by your side tonight, ma chérie. A petty human brute is the least of your worries. I'll transport him to the top of Mount Kailash if I have to."

Yvie teared up. "*Merci.*"

They sat silently as Stanley traversed the rest of the road without a single bump, until they drove up the gravel drive. In the distance, all of the lights were on in the house, creating a welcoming yellow glow. The drive was significantly smoother than Eleanor remembered it, and she had never been more grateful for the subtle ways in which Kuveni made hers, and so many others' lives easier.

"Come, ma chérie. I will help you." Mélusine and Oz helped Yvie out of the car and up the stairs to the wide-open front door of the house. There was no dust anywhere.

Stanley helped Eleanor get Leo out of the car, and they followed Oz and Yvie inside.

"My father only uses the bedroom at the top of the stairs. You can use any other bedroom you want," Stanley offered.

"Come, come!" Kuveni exclaimed as she rushed towards them. "I've prepared a perfect little nest."

"What about Grimby?" Oz asked.

"He's not here," Kuveni replied. "I don't know where he is, and right now it doesn't matter. Now, come!"

As Yvie moaned with another contraction and Kuveni led her to the room at the far end of the hallway, Eleanor followed Stanley into the closest bedroom, just across the hall from Lord Grimby's at the top of the stairs, and they lay Leo down on the bed. Eleanor was satisfied with the gentle light produced by the flickering fire torches that Kuveni had used to illuminate the room.

"Greenie, stay with him, and come tell me if his breathing gets worse, got it? Come get me at the first sign of trouble."

"Yes, my lady."

Stanley took a seat beside the bed.

"There is drinking water in the kitchen, and there are some towels in the bathroom that my father uses. Feel free to ruin all of them," Stanley suggested.

"Thanks, greenie. But I think Kuveni will have us covered from now on."

"Eleanor... you did a bang-up job tonight. I never dreamed of seeing anything like that. You were a true warrior queen."

She smiled and left him alone, dashing towards the loud moans coming from Yvie's birthing room. Oz was pacing back and forth outside the closed door, and as he saw her approach, he dropped to his knees.

"Ellie, please promise me that Yvie will be okay. I'll do anything for you. *Anything.*"

Eleanor reached down and coaxed him back into a standing position. She ran her hand along his cheek, and then pulled him into a hug.

You don't need to beg or pray, my child. I love her as if she were my own sister. I'm not omnipotent, but whatever power I do have, I will use it to keep her safe.

As she pulled away, tears were streaming down his face. "It was fair dinkum good trot that we met you, wasn't it?"

Eleanor smiled. "Likewise. You are the most wonderful people I've ever met, and I'm quite sure Edmund feels the same way. Now, why don't you go in there and be by Yvie's side?"

"She won't let me," he said with a sniffle as he wiped away his tears. "Turns out she agrees with my mum on this one. She said she didn't want me to think of her as a patient."

Eleanor rubbed his back. "Do you want me to wait with you out here?"

"No, Ellie. You should be in there, watching over her."

But as Yvie moaned, Stanley rushed down the hall. "Eleanor, wait! Leo just woke up. He said it's time for his final confession. Do you know what he means?"

Eleanor squeezed Oz's hand reassuringly. "I will keep Yvie in my thoughts from just down the hall. She is in the best hands in the world right now. She is under the protection of Saint Mélusine."

She took Mélusine's talisman off and handed it to Oz, closing it into the palm of his hand. "When you can't stand the wait anymore, squeeze the pendant. Ask Mélusine to send Kate out to give you an update."

Oz squeezed it as if it was a rosary, and as Leo gave into a violent bout of coughs that echoed down the hallway from his open door, she rushed back to his room, and Stanley followed.

"Greenie, please keep Oz company. I think he'll go a bit mad by himself in the hallway."

Stanley nodded and followed her orders, but as he moved to close the door behind him, she stopped him.

"Leave it open. I want to stay connected to Yvie down the hall. Managing a birth and a death simultaneously is not something I have enough experience to do properly."

Don't worry, my child. I will focus on Yvie. You focus on our darker task.

She took a seat by the head of Leo's bed. He could barely open his eyes to look at her. She unbuttoned his starched collar, and then ripped open his sweat-stained undershirt to reveal his clammy chest.

As he struggled to speak, she took his hand and squeezed it.

No need to waste your energy on that. We must keep you alive until Edmund returns. He won't forgive me if you die while he's gone.

He smiled weakly. *We must keep the peace between the gods, mustn't we?*

Eleanor smiled. *We will be in it together, my friend.*

He coughed up a mouthful of blood, and Eleanor wiped it away gently with a handkerchief.

Eleanor… I don't know how long I can hold on. The pain is unbearable. I feel like I'm drowning. I don't want Edmund to see me like this.

When the time comes, I will use my power to help you go peacefully, but you must say goodbye to Edmund.

I didn't think it would end this way. I was absolutely certain I'd die a valiant death in the line of duty. I've been wishing for months that I had… until this week. Thank you, Eleanor. Thank you for showing me how beautiful life can be.

Perhaps you should be thanking Edmund instead. I've only really learned how beautiful the world can be since I met him. He brings out the best in people—you and me both… except for our colossal web of lies.

Speaking of our lies, Eleanor, I must tell you something I have been keeping to myself since you met the Helmsworths.

Please don't tell me that they're spies or cons or murderers.

They aren't, but you will be surprised by their connection to you.

Leo, please don't build so much suspense. You could die any second, and I will be left very unsatisfied.

He smiled. *I knew that Yvie's name sounded familiar, and so I did some digging into our secret case files. The Comtesse de Saint-Cyr, who escaped to England during the French Revolution only to return a few years later to marry a general in Napoléon's army, wasn't the rightful comtesse. She claimed the title after her older sister fell in love with an even more powerful man and disappeared with her false name into English society. The rightful Comtesse de Saint-Cyr died giving birth to Edmund on April 26, 1818.*

Blimey. It never even crossed my mind that Edmund could have human family.

I planned to tell you a few times, but there was always a distraction. It was better this way, though. It is more important than ever that Edmund does not know this connection.

For god's sake, how could this information possibly be detrimental?

Eleanor, you must be more careful than ever about protecting your secrets. Edmund has made an enemy of Grimby now. I've done what I can to involve

General Kettering as an alternative ally for you, but you do not want Grimby knowing that Yvie is any more of a weakness than she already is.

A weakness?! She is a strength! Reliable human allies are our greatest strength!

Grimby will systematically eliminate your allies to ruin you, Eleanor. It is a classic Machiavellian move that he knows well. That is how true power works.

Paw. That is how petty human power works.

You still live in the human world, Eleanor. You must respect its power structures. You will not have me to be a buffer anymore, and I don't know how willing General Kettering will be to help you. He has his own political considerations. You must stand on your own, and you must be more clever than you've ever been, because Edmund is too open, too trusting, and too brazen. He needs you to be his white knight in all sorts of battles that he isn't prepared to fight himself.

I suppose at some point I should get that fitted armor he keeps promising me.

Leo did not find her quip funny. *You will need it, Eleanor, but it must be invisible. G looks for weaknesses he can exploit, so that he can always remain the most powerful man in the room. If he learns of the true extent of your power, he will be very dangerous. He has never liked how difficult it is to keep women under control.*

Eleanor laughed. *I think he'll have to get in line with that one.*

You're right, Eleanor. You have made me rethink many ideas I had about women... perhaps all of them.

All in a day's work.

As he cringed with a painful, bloody cough, Eleanor noticed a conspicuous stack of handkerchiefs alongside a fresh, steaming water basin on the bedside table, and she made a note to thank Kuveni for it later. She took the top handkerchief from the stack and dabbed his sweaty forehead.

There is something else I must tell you, Eleanor, before we descend down the dark path to my overflowing cache of unforgivable sins.

Eleanor braced herself. *You can tell me anything, Leo.*

I can, but I shouldn't.

You have nothing left to lose.

He reached up and gently intercepted her hand before she could dab his forehead with the wet handkerchief again.

I do not deserve to say so, Eleanor... but I love you. I have loved you since the moment I stopped hating you. I have been utterly, shamefully in love with you since the moment you burst uninvited into our lonely lives.

She put the handkerchief down in the water basin and took his other hand.

I know.

No, Eleanor. I don't think you do.

I told you a long time ago that I am an excellent judge of character. Shakti has only made my instincts sharper.

He thought about her point for a long, pained moment.

I'm sorry, Eleanor.

I forgive you.

Edmund shouldn't. I have coveted you biblically, if you will forgive the term. I know he wouldn't.

My friend, he already has. Over the years, I've realized that we mustn't confuse him being discreet with him being unobservant. He had no delusions about your feelings, and neither did I. We both chose to forgive you anyway, just like angels should. Eleanor smiled. *I will admit that the Good Book did turn out to be a better representation of humanity than I gave it credit for.*

Perhaps. But this sin has been very painful for me... perhaps the most painful. When I tell you what else I've done, you'll know what a horrible person I am for caring most about this triviality... the triviality of loving you and betraying him. Seeing the two of you together was like a glimpse of the beautiful life that would never be mine. I knew from the moment I saw the love in your eyes for him that Edmund deserved it so much more than I did, but I couldn't stop myself from wanting it... from wanting you... from longing so desperately for that love to be for me. It has been a shameful secret, but a secret I thought I'd managed to keep to myself all the same. But, in the end, it seems I failed at that too.

It was a doomed proposition, Leo. I know far too much about too many things. You shouldn't blame yourself.

I should, Eleanor. I'm a grown man. I should have had more self-control on this and so many other matters... horrible matters. If you really knew all the ghastly things I've done, you wouldn't be so forgiving.

Try me. I'm here for your confession, aren't I?

I don't know if I'm ready...

Better now than never, Leo.

I'm not so sure...

We can sit here singing hymns if you'd prefer? I wonder how many I'll remember. My mother always translated them into Scots as a nationalistic nod, so I probably don't know any of the right lyrics...

Leo chuckled, and then his laughs degenerated into another round of bloody coughs. Eleanor gave him another handkerchief, and then returned to dabbing his forehead.

I love you, Eleanor.

It is a privilege to be loved by a man who has seen so much, Leo, and I don't mean that facetiously.

Eleanor, I truly don't deserve your praise. I've done so many horrible things... things that I'm sure I'm going to think about very carefully when I'm burning in Hell. I don't want you to know them, but I feel this odd compulsion... it has been growing for weeks now. I feel like I must tell you. Is it your divine will that I'm feeling?

Leo, I don't have any desire to hear what you don't want to say.

Then I suppose the compulsion must be my own... it was easier to think you'd insisted upon it... What's that?

They both startled as the window squeaked and wiggled open, but as Eleanor felt Uma stir, she knew exactly who the culprit was. She watched as an animate blob of violet metallic liquid oozed across the window pane and down the wall to the floor. It gathered itself into a puddle, and then settled down for another moment of static rest.

We have a visitor, whom I believe we both know quite well.

Has the Devil come for me?

564

Oh yes, she came, but she's already left. Surpanakha sends you her best.

He grimaced. *That joke is too irreverent, even for me.*

I wasn't joking. She killed Mac earlier tonight as he was drafting a message to send to your boss about our secrets. She must have been watching him.

Did she kill him before he got the message through?

I think she did, but I don't know for sure. The phone lines were down when we found him.

You need an ally, Eleanor.

We have one now. Stanley will do just fine. By the grace of Shakti, he made it to competence in time for your exit, even with a few hours to spare.

How did you do it? That boy was untrainable.

Training wasn't his problem. He's been too distracted by hiding his homosexuality to focus on anything else. I feel rather sad for him, actually. The world is very unforgiving of people in his position.

Mac warned me that he was a pouf. If that had been his only vice, I would have thought the choice to be rather strategic, given the weakness I've had for you, but that boy is as dull as a doorknob and as stubborn as a bull.

I thought you'd warmed to him!

I didn't like watching them torment him, but he's still a dreadful butler and an even worse spy. You need to be careful, Eleanor. With G after you and Stanley your only ally, you're sitting ducks.

He's more than meets the eye, just as you are, my friend.

I'm glad to hear it, but you should still be careful. He could be a loose cannon, and he is G's son. You can't depend on his loyalty.

I have faith in him. More faith than his father does, and I'm prepared to offer him something he doesn't get from anyone else.

And that is?

Freedom to be himself. I've already told him that he can be whoever he wants to be in the privacy of our home. Lipstick and silk stockings included.

For god's sake, Eleanor. When I'm dead, your lives will be a bloody circus.

My friend, our lives are already a circus, with or without you. In some ways, poor Stanley will fit better into our lives as secret outcasts than you do.

I will take your word for it. Please be careful, for my sake and for Edmund's. The game you're playing is getting more dangerous by the minute. G will be furious if he discovers that Stanley has been using his elevated position to gallivant around like a glittery little can-can girl.

We will just have to make sure that G doesn't catch him. We've already added it to our long list of secrets.

You shouldn't have, Eleanor. You have enough to worry about as it is, and Stanley does not deserve your support.

I have it on good authority that you don't either, Leo. And yet, here we are.

Leo wheezed and coughed as he glanced up. The violet metallic liquid slowly formed into the shape of a man, and then solidified into Vibhishana's handsome ancient Lankan form, clad in the same tasteful western suit he'd been wearing earlier in the evening when Eleanor had summoned him through the sacred fire.

"I'm sorry. I didn't mean to interrupt your silent commune with such an alien show, but I'm still struggling to hold my forms after our battle." He looked down at himself self-consciously. "Eleanor, I came to thank you for defeating our foe, and to say goodbye before I leave for Baroda."

She stood up to greet Vibhishana, and he squeezed her hand. Uma sighed as their energy connected, but Eleanor pulled away.

"Vibhi, Leo is dying. You've come just in time for his deathbed confessional. He's not allowed to expire before Edmund returns from rescuing Oz's brothers."

"I'm sorry." He turned back towards the window. "I'll leave you two. It was a pleasure fighting by your side, Eleanor, as always."

"You don't have to rush!" Eleanor didn't like the urgency she suddenly felt to keep him there. "Perhaps you can share some words of wisdom with Leo before... er... his end."

"I don't believe we've had the pleasure," Leo rasped as he let go of Eleanor's hand and reached up to greet Vibhishana.

Vibhishana shook Leo's hand with both of his. "It is not every day I can ooze into a room and still have a perfectly amicable conversation with a human. You have been a worthy ally for all of us."

"Despite my many faults, I must agree that I have. But which of you are you, if I might ask?"

Vibhishana smiled. "I'm Mr. Johnson." He morphed into the handsome British form that Edmund and Leo both knew, and then he morphed into his ancient Christian form. "And Doctor Carpenter."

Leo smiled. "A vicar and a Jew, eh? What's next, a Hindu demigod? Lord Vibhishana, the virtuous immortal demon, I think it was?"

"You have it right, my friend. I'm glad you've been such a trustworthy ally," Vibhishana replied without any concern or surprise about Leo's knowledge of his true identity. "I am at your disposal, if you'd like a father confessor to join Eleanor for your remaining wait. I'm somewhat of an expert."

"I should have realized who you were after the incident on the beach. I knew there was something familiar about you."

Vibhishana smiled. "You are very perceptive. I suppose it's a good trait for a spy. This is actually my ancient Christian form. I used it when I was exploring human life as a Jew preaching in Jerusalem… during the Roman era."

Leo's eyes widened. "Then Hell is real. I guess my number's up."

"There is a Heaven and Hell of sorts, but it isn't as simple as that. You will be cleansed of your sins and rewarded for your rectitude before you're reborn back on Earth. The process is more hellish for those who have inflicted more pain on others."

Eleanor felt Leo tense. "Then I shouldn't tell you what I've done."

"You will suffer for your sins whether you tell me or not, my friend. It is a natural process that even I can't put asunder. I can, however, help you go into it with a peaceful heart, if you'd like. Confessing to me and Eleanor will put your soul at ease, which will help you get through the pain."

Eleanor squeezed his hand supportively. *It's up to you, Leo.*

Eleanor, I'm not proud of what I've done. I don't need Jesus Christ himself to cringe at my sins.

"He's concerned that he'll shock you with his sins," Eleanor translated.

Leo threw her a disapproving look, but she wasn't going to let him deprive himself of a father confessor out of fear.

Vibhishana smiled reassuringly, and then with a subtle wiggle, he morphed into his demonic form.

Leo coughed with surprise, and as his coughs morphed into wheezing alongside silent tears at the unbearable pain, Eleanor rubbed his chest. She pulled away as Uma brought forth Shakti's green glowing power.

Uma, you will not kill him yet.

I understand our mission, my child. We will wait for Lord Kalki to return before we end his suffering.

His wheezing morphed into belabored shallow breaths.

"I promise you, my friend, nothing you've done can compare to the crooked path I've walked for five thousand years," Vibhishana said as he took a seat across from Eleanor on the other side of the bed. "Would you prefer to confess to a demon, or to a god?"

Leo took one long look at him. "The demon and I have more in common."

Vibhishana reached forward and took Leo's hand, carefully maneuvering to keep his spikes from scratching Leo's skin. The image of his colorful, spiked hands and black clawed fingers around Leo's greying human ones was strangely beautiful to Eleanor, and she didn't think it was just Uma's taste on the matter. "Tell us what you've done, my friend. Eleanor and I will begin your transformation together."

568

Leo took in one belabored, wheezing breath, and then he began.

Perhaps we should start with the sins I've committed during our acquaintance, Eleanor.

You may start wherever you want, Leo. Tell us everything that has been eating away at you.

My first murder after I met you was the gatekeeper at the Maharaja of Gondal's estate, neighboring Ravi Bidkar's in Bombay. The agency demanded a culprit for the assassination of the two British officers in Ravi Bidkar's garden, and they had already signed the death warrant for Ravi. But there was one more man who could take the fall. The only man who'd been in the area during the crime without an alibi… the next-door neighbor's guard. I attested to his guilt myself as a witness, and he was arrested within the hour, but by the time Surpanakha's next grisly murder came to pass, the proud man had already killed himself in prison. He wasn't supposed to be a victim… not like that. He was supposed to just buy us time…

He stared stoically at the ceiling.

I made so many ugly choices like that. Too many to count. I made another one a few days later, in the town where the thieves attacked the Maharaja of Gwalior's children… The boys down at the pub were an even easier target to frame than the guard had been, but their deaths did not come at their own hands. I assume now that their bloody dismemberment came from Surpanakha, but those boys had nothing to do with the crime. Nothing… Only what I made up… They had mothers and sisters and some even had wives… But I'm procrastinating, Eleanor. I'm avoiding the murders I committed with my own two hands. I will have to go back to the beginning of the list… to the first of the 162 people whose lives I took willingly…

They lost track of time as Leo worked his way back through the many gory details of the inglorious things he'd done to protect Edmund, and before that during the war, back to his time in MI-2 in Bohemia and even into his childhood, when he'd started off on the path he would eventually follow by killing the man with greasy hair and grubby hands who came to take his mother kicking and screaming back to her evil father in Bohemia. She'd told him then how proud she was that he was strong enough to pull the trigger, and that sometimes one had to kill to live... It was a lesson he had absorbed perhaps too readily, but that had proven itself true too many times after that.

With each confession, Leo's expression became slightly less pained, and Eleanor was certain that it wasn't just Shakti's soothing power that was chipping away at his burden.

Finally, as Yvie's intermittent moans and screams and sighs dissolved, the sound of a car pulling up the gravel drive marked the end of Leo's wait, and of his demon-confessor's visit.

Vibhishana positioned himself behind the lace curtain as he morphed back into his gentle Lankan form and looked out the open window to spy Edmund hopping out of the car alongside two men, both with Oz's stocky, muscular build, Sheila, who wouldn't let go of their arms as she escorted them inside, Mr. Guy, who muttered to himself in French, and finally Lord Grimby, who looked rather dazed with his scarred cheeks and tattered suit, as Ovid and Pliny barreled out of the car behind him, barking with excitement as they circled Edmund, naughtily jumping up on him and demanding his attention. They were all covered from head to toe in dust, and in the distance, the roar of a tiger indicated that Sheranee had not yet seen fit to return to her divine perch without Eleanor's explicit orders.

Vibhi returned his attention to Leo and kneeled down beside him. He placed his right hand on Leo's forehead, and his left hand on his chest.

"We will be with you in spirit, my friend. Do not fear the trials to come. Your rebirth has already begun, and when your penances are complete, your path will be clear for a better life."

As footsteps clomped up the front stairs, he glanced at the cracked-open door, then at Eleanor, and then at the window. In a blur, he was standing above her. He kissed her forehead, and then whispered in her ear.

"*Jai mata di*. Tonight you were glorious, Eleanor. A true Avatar of Light. Revel in Edmund's arms, and I wish both of you all of the love I have to give."

As Uma swooned, Vibhishana didn't give Eleanor the chance to debate how to respond. Instead, he morphed into the form of a falcon and soared gracefully out the window, into the dark, starry sky.

Leo stared for an extra-long moment to where Vibhishana had disappeared, and then he glanced at Eleanor.

He loves you, you know. Even more than I do.

I know.

I knew there was a queue, but I didn't realize I'd be standing behind more than one god... It seems fitting for you, though, Eleanor. You deserve to be loved more than any other woman in the world, more than Venus herself.

Eleanor squeezed his hand and returned to dabbing his forehead. *Get all of that sentiment out before Edmund makes his way up here, my friend.*

Leo weakly maneuvered her hand to his mouth and kissed it.

I've been wanting to do that for a long time.

The front door squeaked as it swung open, slamming against the window beside it and shaking the house.

"Jack?!" A man's voice that sounded strikingly similar to Oz's shouted from the foyer. "Jackie boy?! Is he here yet?!"

"I'll go manage Grimby. Don't worry about him bothering you," Stanley whispered as he and Oz approached the top of the staircase, just outside the half-open door to Leo's room.

"Are you a father yet?!" a very similar voice boomed.

Loud clomping echoed through the house as they rushed up the stairs. One man pulled Oz into a hug, while the other tried to maneuver him into a brotherly headlock. Oz grabbed his brother's wrist and defeated him without any enthusiasm, but his brothers didn't take his stern cue.

"Jackie boy, you won't believe it! That bloody haboob got us good! It was like we were way out past the black stump in a cyclone!

None of us could see a bloody thing, and Mr. Guy drove us off onto the wrong road, and with one gust of wind, we thought we were done for! It knocked the car right into a ditch, and Billy and I couldn't get any of the doors open, even with the help of Mr. Guy and that pommy Grimby bloke!"

The other brother took over the story. "That's not the most important part, Freddy! A bloody tiger came to our rescue! Can you believe it?! We thought we had a kangaroo loose in the top paddock! She came with those two bonza goldies who followed her like she was their nursing mum! She pulled us each out of the car without hurting a hair on anyone's precious head..."

"Except that Grimby chap," Freddy corrected him. "He kept beating against her like she was trying to eat him alive! She nipped him in the neck just like a dog mum getting her pup in line!"

Billy shook his head at the memory. "You should've seen him, Jackie. He was going bloody bonkers trying to get away from her, going on and on about how he'd told her to leave him alone, and he knew she was a monster!"

"A kraken!" Freddy laughed. "What kind of animals does he think we have down here?! A tiger was bad enough, but a kraken? I asked him if he needed a unicorn to come to the rescue, but his pommy sense of humor wasn't having any of it."

"He fell right back into the ditch in the dark, and it took both of us to pull him out," Billy added. "We thought about leaving him there till morning so he could get his head back on straight, but Mum wouldn't let us leave an important *lord general* all alone in the dark..." He rolled his eyes. "With generals like that, it's a wonder we won the war at all."

"How did Mum even find you?" Oz asked.

"That's the craziest part!" Freddy exclaimed. "While we were trying to get that pommy bastard to calm down, the tiger sent the dogs to the main road, just like she was a true blue military commander! And what do you know? The storm passed, and onward came Colonel Marriner and Mum to pick us up like we'd just stumbled legless out of a rotten night at the boozer!"

"I'm glad you're all okay," Oz replied more reservedly. "I'd have come myself, but I've got more important things on my mind than rescuing your dusty hides."

"Right... Jackie. Right..." Billy calmed down as he considered the gravity of the situation.

"Is Yvie alright?" Edmund asked concernedly as he hugged Oz.

"Kate says she's taking her time because it's too early... She's a bloody month too early... They're doing everything they can for her... for both of them, but I'm going out of my mind waiting out here."

"Well, now you've got our ugly company to feast your eyes on," Freddy declared with a brotherly flourish.

Leo choked on his own spit and exploded into another round of bloody coughs, and as Eleanor ran her soothing hands across his chest, Edmund peeked his head in.

With one whiff of the putrid scent of death filling the room, Edmund's eyes were black. He closed the door behind him and took Vibhishana's vacated seat. He took Leo's hand and squeezed it.

"Eleanor promised you'd be around for me to say goodbye, and I'm grateful that she always tells the truth. How are you feeling, Leo?"

"Like a dead man," he rasped.

Edmund reached forward and brushed the stringy hair out of Leo's eyes like a doting father.

"Leo..." He trailed off as his throat closed up, and he worked hard to keep his emotions under control. "Leo, you've saved me from myself. There are no words to thank you for what you've done. If you hadn't been how you were... so kind, and patient, and forgiving of my many horrific secrets... I would never have recovered as much as I did from the war, and I never would have met Eleanor. Everything that is good in my life, I owe to you."

"You give me too much credit," Leo whispered. "But it has always been my pleasure to help you, Colonel. You are the best man I've ever met. It has been the happiest time of my life to watch you and Eleanor be in love. You've shown me something I didn't know was possible."

"I didn't know it was possible either. But we owe so much to you, Leo. More than you know." Leo coughed, and Edmund's tears began to flow. "I wish we could have spent more time together. Decades more."

"You don't need me anymore, Colonel, and I've always known the best time to make my exit."

Edmund laughed through his tears. "You know I've never liked melodrama."

"Perhaps that's why we got along so well..." Leo's rasping speech dissolved into more violent coughs.

Edmund closed his eyes and cried silently as he tried to get himself under control, and Leo grabbed Eleanor's hand as tears streamed down his face.

Please, Eleanor. Make the pain stop. I'm ready.

Eleanor took a deep breath and let Uma begin her work.

She held his hand as she felt her most morbid power work its way up from the center of her being, into her hands, and then into Leo's. It was cold, like his clammy skin, but not frigid like Edmund's. It felt entirely natural.

Good luck, Leo. Take with you my forgiveness and Shakti's blessings.

Thank you, Holy Mother.

"I love you both." Leo closed his eyes and took in his last belabored breath.

They both held their breath as they felt the last spark of life dissolve.

"Goodbye, Leo," Edmund whispered as he reached forward to stop the clock by the bedside.

574

Eleanor got up from her chair and took a seat on the bed beside Leo, letting Edmund bury his head in her chest as he cried and cried.

"I hate mortality," he whispered. "It's so bloody cruel and so bloody inevitable. Every bloody time it reminds me how alone I am."

"You're not alone now, darling. Not in any sense of the word."

Until that moment, she'd managed to keep herself together, but as the subtle pulsating power of her husband infused her with his divine sorrow, she finally gave in, and let herself cry along with him.

They cried and cried, until Eleanor felt like she had no tears left, and then the sound of a different cry distracted her.

"Edmund! Do you hear that?!"

The raging screams of a newborn infant echoed through the closed door. She grabbed Edmund's hand, wiped away his tears, kissed him gently on the lips, and then guided him out of the room. Lord Grimby sat alone on a bench in the hallway, seemingly in deep thought. He eyed them as they passed, but said nothing as they skipped over to Yvie's open door, where a crowd had already gathered.

Yvie lay in bed, wrapped up in blankets, holding a tiny swaddled baby boy in her arms and crying with tears of joy.

"Ellie!" she exclaimed. "Ellie, he's perfect! Come look!"

Eleanor took a position beside Kuveni, noting that Mélusine was nowhere in sight, and leaned down to look into the glassy eyes of the little creature who had just made his way into the world. A thin layer of fine fur covered his skin, and a dried white paste was still crusted behind his ears.

"You just couldn't wait to say hello, could you? Impatient, just like your father," Yvie said as she tapped his nose. He smiled, and then burst into another round of screams.

"Sshhh… Sshhh…" Yvie whispered. "Now that they're here, we'll give you your name, *mon fils*." She looked up at Edmund and smiled. "We have decided to name him Edmund. Edmund Helmsworth. After my great-grandfather, and after you, Edmund."

Oz patted Edmund on the back. "It is the namesake of a great inspiration to both of us. It's the name of a hero who never gives up, and who fights every battle with humility and honor. We hope our son will be like you, mate, and perhaps, if we could be so lucky, he may learn all sorts of things from you… that is… if you want to stay in Australia with us."

Edmund looked to Eleanor, and she nodded her agreement.

"It would be an honor to know my namesake," he said as he pulled Oz into a brotherly hug. "And to watch you be a bonza father, mate."

"We'll need a new nickname for you then… so we can tell you apart!" Oz said excitedly. "How about Ned?"

Edmund coughed his disapproval. "I've never been a fan of nicknames."

"Well then, I guess the babe pulled the short stick!" Oz said giddily.

"Ozzy, no! We can't ruin a distinguished name like Edmund with a bushy nickname like that!"

"Mate, I think that your wife gets the final say after the night she's had," Eleanor stepped in.

"*Peut-être*," Oz said with a wink.

"Oh, Ozzy, you are incorrigible!"

Oz swooped over to her and stole a kiss on her lips, followed by a careful kiss on baby Edmund's forehead.

Kuveni clapped happily. "My darlings, you must all be famished. There is a banquet downstairs in the kitchen, available to everyone who doesn't ask anything about where it came from."

"I'm starving!" Freddy exclaimed.

"It's been ages since I've had a home-cooked meal!" Billy added.

576

Stanley approached from the hallway. "Everyone, please follow me. I will escort you down to Percy's fabulous French feast." He pointed with his left hand and spoke with his natural voice as he threw his father a taunting glance.

The crowd milled out of the room behind Stanley, until only Kuveni, Eleanor, Edmund, and the new happy family were left.

"I'm sorry. We didn't mean to put you on the spot like that," Yvie said as Ned whimpered and then calmed himself. "You have no obligation to stay in Margaret River. I don't even know where we're going to live while the house gets fixed up."

"Don't worry, my darling girl, we have ways of making these things easier," Kuveni reassured her. "And as soon as we're finished, I must join Percy and take my leave, Edmund. I have indulged all of us too much. You have a new life here that you should live without our meddling. But first, go and eat! You must be famished!"

"Go," Yvie encouraged them. "I think Neddy is hungry too, and learning how to feed him is not a public affair."

"Congratulations," Eleanor whispered as she kissed Yvie's forehead one last time. *Take with you Shakti's blessings.*

"*Merci*, Ellie. For everything," she whispered.

Oz kneeled down to coo at his son, and Eleanor took Edmund's hand and guided him out of the room. She could feel that neither of them were ready to return to the unpleasant tasks before them. As they reached the bottom of the staircase, Edmund stopped and looked back.

"It is a very strange thing."

"What is, darling?"

"No matter how much power one has, it can never compete with the greatness of the natural order of things. I wanted to help Leo so badly, and yet he's still dead, but now, just down the hall, there is new life sprung entirely from Oz and Yvie's love. It is quite comforting, actually."

"What is, darling?"

"That there is no god to meddle… no one with the power of life and death in the palm of his hand. We must resign ourselves to fate, and sometimes, fate hands us a miracle."

"I didn't think you believed in miracles, darling."

"It was nothing short of a miracle that I met you, dearest. And now we have these wonderful friends with whom I can be completely honest, and it has been so nice to spend so much time with Kate and Percy, and even Stanley seems to be finding his stride… I finally feel as if fate is on our side. It is a lovely feeling."

Eleanor pulled him into a gentle kiss, and then guided him into the cheerful dining room for their impromptu Yakshini feast.

"Ah, it's the star of the hour, the namesake of Jackie boy's firstborn!" Freddy exclaimed as he shook Edmund's hand. "Colonel, we hear you're going to keep our brother company while he's stuck tending to the whims of an ankle-biter? I hope you realize what you've signed up for. As Jackie's son, Neddy's sure to be a wild little bushy!"

"I can't think of anything I'd rather do," Edmund said happily.

"Welcome home, Edmund," Eleanor whispered.

"That is where we are, isn't it?" he asked with wonder. "It finally feels like we're home."

And so, as Leo embarked upon the next stage of his journey with the thoughts and well wishes of the Transformers of the Universe to guide him, and Edmund's namesake took his first taste of all that the earthly human world had to offer, the gods and their wards sat back and let fate embark upon a new chapter of its natural, unimpeded course.

Do you think this peace can last, Uma?

Peut-être, my child. Peut-être.

EPILOGUE

Edmund and Supriya looked up from their position huddled together on a cushy leather couch in the ancient library of Vibhishana's hidden Anglo-Roman estate. They had been waiting for hours for Kuveni to return from her invisible lurking with news on poor Charlie, who had insisted on waiting alone by the bedside for his mother to wake up in one of the many guest bedrooms. But, as the pleasant breeze rustled Supriya's long hair, instead of their dependable motherly ally, Ellie appeared.

"Dad?! Are you alright?! Kuveni told me what happened!"

Edmund stood up and let Ellie engulf him into a loving hug.

"You didn't have to come, Ellie-bean." His voice wavered with emotion.

"You didn't answer my question," she countered.

"I have been better," he admitted. "But how I feel now doesn't matter. It's Charlie I'm worried about."

"He's a good lad, and you were there for him when he needed you most. I'm sure in the long run, that is what he will remember."

Edmund hugged her again. "I love you, Ellie-bean." He looked around as a thought occurred to him. "Where's Kuveni? She brought you here?"

"She said she would return to lurking. How she knew to find me in London is beyond me... She scared the living daylights out of my curator when she popped right into our new gallery space. But, she felt like you both needed a reinforcement, and I agreed."

"She was right." Supriya stood up and hugged Ellie. "Thanks for coming. If you remind me later, I'll give you my next manuscript. I just finished it up a few days ago."

Ellie nodded her agreement, and then returned her attention to her father. "Is the shrew awake yet?"

Edmund nodded in the negative.

"Blimey, it must have been bad if it's taking her this long to wake up."

Edmund sighed resignedly. "She was moments from death. To be honest, my life-force is still struggling to recover from it. It was one of the most painful healing exchanges I've ever endured, and that doesn't count the lifetime of her memories I absorbed in the process. I only have a few glimpses so far, but they are really very unpleasant."

"My love, you didn't say that you were still in pain. You should borrow some of my life-force," Supriya said as she rubbed her hands together to bring forth the silver healing light.

He gently placed his hands on hers to stop her. "I will be perfectly fine. You needn't trouble yourself in the slightest on her behalf. I will bear the full brunt of my responsibility for her involvement in our life."

Ellie threw Supriya a knowing glance. "Dad, we all make mistakes."

He shook off her support. "Ellie-bean, the burden I brought down on you by marrying Grace so foolishly is even more acute now. I should have known... I should have realized that she wasn't worthy of being in our lives. Not then, and not now."

"Woulda-coulda-shoulda," Ellie shrugged. "You're not doing Charlie any favors by stewing about this, you know. He's going to need you to be strong when she wakes up."

As Edmund's posture deflated at the idea, Supriya reached forward and placed her glowing hand on his. He sucked in a hefty dose of her life-force, and then caught her as she collapsed momentarily into his arms. She stood back up and stole a mischievous kiss.

"Problem solved, Colonel."

"I love you, Supriya, but you really didn't have to do that."

"And yet I did."

"Good lord," he murmured. "The memories are flowing now. I rather wish they weren't."

He stumbled back to the couch and sat down as he closed his eyes and focused on uncluttering his tired mind.

"How about some cognac, my darlings?" Kuveni interrupted as she materialized beside them in the form of Kate.

"I'd love some," Ellie said as she sat down in an imposing leather chair at the mahogany desk in the middle of the room.

"Really?" Edmund asked with surprise.

Ellie blushed slightly. "Ever since Mum and I… er… reconnected… I've had a taste for it. I think it's her taste, but I'm enjoying it all the same."

"I know exactly what you mean. Ever since I connected with my prior incarnations, I've had a new appreciation for all sorts of South Indian dishes that I'd found kind of boring before," Supriya reassured her casually as she sat back down on the couch and kissed Edmund, pulling his attention out of Grace's memories and back into the present. He squeezed her hand gratefully for the rescue.

Kuveni snapped her fingers, producing four large crystal glasses, and then poured them each a generous serving up to the brim of each glass. She passed them around and then held hers up in a toast.

"To the triumph of light on another hard night," she declared.

They held up their glasses and then took their first sips.

"This is definitely the Hine 1848," Ellie said matter-of-factly.

"It was your mother's favorite," Kuveni agreed. "Do you like it as much as she did?"

Ellie's eyes flashed a moment of green. "It is still our favorite."

She offered her father an apologetic glance as she noticed the discomfort in his expression.

"So you have a new manuscript for me?" Ellie asked Supriya as she attempted to take her father's mind off of his many unusual problems.

"I do. Although I left it back at the palace in Lanka, actually. Kuveni can pop back to get it for you later if you want. It covers their marital life in India and their move to Australia."

"I can't wait to read about it."

Edmund sighed with nostalgia, and then a hint of melancholy.

"It is not as happy as the last one," Supriya warned her. "But there were enough moments of joy to make it worth the journey... just like life, I suppose."

They all sat in contemplative silence, focusing on the rich flavors of the cognac instead of their other, more unpleasant thoughts, until the shuffling of a tired boy's footsteps on the mosaic floors pulled them back to attention.

"Mum is awake," Charlie said as he rubbed his tired, puffy eyes. "She wants to talk to you, Dad."

Edmund stood up and gathered Charlie into a hug. "I love you, Charlie. Everything is going to be just fine."

Charlie squeezed Edmund tighter. "I already told her that you saved her life, but she still wants to talk to you."

"I'm sure she just wants to thank me, Charlie."

Edmund let Charlie squeeze him until his weak arms gave out.

"Why don't you eat something," Edmund suggested. "It's been hours and hours. Kuveni will make you whatever you want."

"I'm not hungry," Charlie mumbled.

582

"Not even for chocolate chip ice cream?" Kuveni asked as she stood up and joined them.

"No," Charlie reiterated. "I'm not hungry."

"I will talk to your mother, and then will you promise to eat something with us?" Edmund negotiated.

Charlie nodded and stumbled over to Supriya, taking a seat beside her on the couch. Supriya offered him her hand, and he took it silently. He looked up at Ellie, noticing her for the first time, and as his eyes lit up, she made her way to Edmund's former position and sat down beside him, squishing him into a cold Rakshasa sandwich.

"I've missed you, Ellie," he whispered.

"I've missed you too, Charlie." She kissed the top of his head as he leaned it against her shoulder. "We're all in this together now, alright?"

He sniffled his agreement, and Ellie and Supriya both nodded their silent support to Edmund.

He rolled his shoulders, took a deep breath, and prepared himself to face the most challenging opponent he had ever met in his life. Charlie hid his face in Ellie's shoulder as he watched his father go.

Edmund knocked on the door of one of the many guest bedrooms, and when he didn't hear a response, he pushed it open anyway. Grace was sitting up in the old-fashioned bed squeezing her eyes closed as she prayed incoherently. Her prayers resonated distractingly in his head.

"Grace?"

She opened her eyes and took a deep breath. He approached her slowly, as if he were approaching a cornered beast, and then he took a seat in an old rocking chair beside her.

"Where are we?" she asked as she looked around at the bedroom that had not been updated in roughly two hundred years.

"We are in Shambhala." She stared at him blankly. "Lord Vibhishana's Anglo-Roman estate in Bath."

"Bath?"

"Yes, in the Cotswalds."

"Why is it called Shambhala? That sounds… Indian."

"The name is used in Hindu and Buddhist scripture, if that is what you're asking. They believed Shambhala would be in Mongolia, the homeland of the invading Khans. It turned out that Lord Kalki was born in the land of the modern invaders instead. Kuveni named the estate in honor of my birth here."

"You were born here?"

"I was born just down the hall. It will be two hundred years in April."

"Why are we here?"

"Kuveni brought us here so we could escape from the paparazzi who were waiting for us at the hospital."

"Bloody parasites," she muttered.

"I agree."

She shifted uncomfortably, readying herself to ask what she had really wanted to ask in the first place.

"Charlie says that you saved my life," she whispered.

"I did."

Her long pause disarmed him completely.

"Am I… am I still human?"

Edmund worked hard to hide his annoyance at the self-imposed ignorance and irrational paranoia that the question represented. As her memories continued to float about in his mind, he couldn't believe that for all of the unwarranted accusations she'd lobbed at him verbally, there had been a b-movie's worth of silent nightmarish imaginings that she'd thought the better of speaking out loud.

"Yes, Grace. You are still human. We are not vampires, unnaturally feeding dark life into otherwise dead human beings."

He didn't like the unconvinced expression on her face, or the subtle puff of fear that wafted off of her at his poorly strategized reference to one of her many unspoken dark fancies.

"Grace, we are avatars of God. The same god that you worship, more or less... minus the lightning bolts and vengeful flooding and selfish obsession with being worshipped. We heal humans just like Christian scripture says that Jesus did, with no strings attached... at least for you. It's bloody painful for us."

Grace grimaced, but didn't say a word.

"Right then..." Edmund paused as he debated his next move. "Is that all you wanted to say? You wanted to know if you were still human? Well, you are. Please enjoy it. We do not heal most people who stumble across our path. It is bad for humanity to turn to prayer instead of medicine. You all need to keep moving forward with self-sufficiency, or Earth will be thrown back into the Dark Ages."

"Why did you heal me?"

Edmund considered the question carefully, and then he gave into the Age of Truth and offered her his honest answer. "Because it was better for Charlie."

Grace's eyes teared up. "I understand."

Edmund fought back his urge to climb out the window, away from the ongoing torture of their conversation.

"Is that it then?"

He stood up, but Grace grabbed his wrist to stop him.

"Edmund... is it normal for the people you heal to feel things... things that you felt?"

Edmund sat back down. "Not that I know of, why?"

Grace's tears began to flow. "I have these images... these feelings in my head now... memories of how I treated you... of how you felt when I left you and told you that you would never see Charlie again... But it was for him! It was all for him! To protect him from a demon!"

Edmund took a deep calming breath as he worked to keep his temper under control.

"Grace, I will say this once and only once: We are not demons. I have produced ample evidence to support my statement."

"I didn't know it at the time!" she wailed. "You were just this unnatural creature, a monster who had taken the place of my husband, and he was my *son*. I had to protect him!"

"I have never been a monster in front of you, Grace. Not *once*. You haven't even seen my predatory deterrent form in the flesh!"

"I did see it," she argued. "I saw it twice! First when you came to rescue us in Mallorca, and then when you and Ellie gave your speech at Charlie's school."

"Grace, I was not remotely monstrous either of those times! I was rescuing you from a bomb that would have killed you and Charlie, and then I was giving a lecture about acceptance to a group of schoolchildren!"

"That wasn't what you said, Edmund. You said I'd never seen it."

Edmund took several deep calming breaths in a row. "Not once while we were together did I ever give you any evidence that I wasn't human. *That* was why you were so upset when you learned my secret, because it was so much of a surprise!"

"Well, it was!" she exclaimed.

"Because I wasn't a monster, Grace. I wasn't then, and I'm not now. It has taken me centuries to fully accept myself, and your incessant, irrational fear of me doesn't help one bit."

"Then is this my punishment? Do I have your painful memories as punishment for what I did to you? For how I made you feel?"

Edmund stopped to consider the implications.

"So the only memories of mine that you have are of pain? Of the pain that you caused?"

"I didn't mean to cause it!"

"That wasn't my question, Grace."

He felt a subtle wave of divine power emanate from deep within himself, and Grace shivered.

"They are the ones with me... hurting you. There are none of the good times... of our wedding, or our honeymoon, or collecting Charlie at the orphanage."

Edmund shrugged. "I did not do it consciously. We always get the memories of the person we are healing, but I have never heard of someone getting ours. It is possible that Lord Vishnu enacted this punishment through me. I am not always privy to his plans."

"You always get the memories of the person you healed? Are you saying that you have all of my memories now?"

Edmund cringed as he heard the shrill tone of her displeasure working its way into her voice, a tone he knew only too well, and that he was quite happy to never know again.

"I do, Grace. It is not something I can control."

"But they're mine!"

"Would you rather be dead?"

Grace moved to rebut, and then she rethought her words. "It wouldn't be good for Charlie."

Edmund sighed with resignation. "I'm glad we agree on something."

They sat in excruciating silence once more, until Edmund couldn't stand it any longer.

"Speaking of things that are good for Charlie, I will be coming by more often from now on. It is important for him to know me, and to remember that I love him, even with everything else that is going on in my life."

"It is always a media circus when you show up, you know. It lasts for days after you leave."

"I know. I've been considering that problem. I have decided that it is still better for him to spend time with me. I will do what is necessary to keep the circus away. I must ask that you support me on this. Not a word to Charlie that you disapprove of my coming and going. I will stop by whenever I can carve a detour into my schedule."

"Is this my payment? In exchange for my life?"

"Call it what you will. The Preserver of the Universe has spoken."

Edmund stood up and walked to the door, pulling it open slowly to give her one last chance to offer the two words he had been hoping so desperately to hear.

As she gazed at him silently, he shrugged one last time. "You're welcome."

He closed the door, rolled his shoulders, plastered on a fake smile, and blurred back to the library.

Charlie scrambled up off the couch, and Supriya and Ellie stood up beside him.

"I could use a carpenter's pie, couldn't you?" Edmund said cheerfully. "Kuveni, one of these days you'll have to show me how to make it."

Ellie burst into laughter at the outrageous prospect, and Kuveni and Supriya joined her.

Kuveni guided them to the door. "Come, my beautiful boys, I will make it for you straightaway. Do you want to eat under the stars in the orchard? The weather is lovely and warm outside this time of year."

"In December?" Charlie asked.

"It's never December in Shambhala, unless we want it to be," Kuveni winked. "Come, come."

She whisked them through the arched, mosaicked hallways into the open-aired garden in the middle of the estate where huge peaches, pears, and apples were fully ripe and falling off the trees.

"I've been so busy, I forgot to harvest them." Kuveni sighed as she noticed them. "Life is just so full these days in the Age of Truth, don't you think? You boys should eat however much you want right off the trees. I will plant a new crop tomorrow."

Edmund pulled out a wicker chair at the table in the middle of the garden, but instead of pulling out the chair beside him, Charlie sat down on his lap and put his arms around his father's neck, like he had done as a much younger boy.

Edmund kissed him on the forehead and let Charlie hold on. "This was a very hard day, wasn't it?"

Charlie nodded.

"You were very brave. You did just what you should have done, and now everything will be perfectly fine. Your mother and I have agreed that I will come by to see you more often, okay?"

"Will you really?" Charlie asked meekly.

"I will make the time, Charlie. No matter what it takes."

Charlie nestled his head into Edmund's shoulder, and he offered Ellie and Supriya an apologetic glance.

"I think I'd rather eat in the library," Supriya suggested. "Perhaps we should let these two men enjoy the fresh summer air?"

Kuveni snapped her fingers and produced two steaming carpenter's pies along with two carafes of hot honeyed milk.

"Call if you need more, my beautiful boys. I will be just around the corner."

She took Supriya's hand in her right and Ellie's hand in her left and guided them back to the library. As soon as the door was closed, she pulled them into a tight hug.

"My dearest girls, I am utterly beside myself! I feel like I might just explode into a million pieces."

"Why?" Supriya asked nervously as she hugged Kuveni back. She had never seen Kuveni flustered, not even during the hardest moments of their struggle to save the worlds. "Was Grace really that horrible? She didn't call Edmund a demon again, did she?"

Kuveni pulled away and relegated a look of offense. "I wasn't eavesdropping on their conversation, my dear girl. I was with you right here in the library the whole time! How could I have possibly been lurking invisibly when I was trapped in this imprisoning corporeal form?"

"I don't know. I'm still not totally sure how all the Yakshini stuff works." Supriya was getting even more anxious at Kuveni's uncharacteristic temperament.

"No, no, no. That wasn't it at all. Supriya, did Charlie tell you what happened? How Grace was injured?"

"You said she was hit by a car. He didn't say anything about what happened."

"Good… good… then he probably didn't notice… that's something, at least…"

"Kuveni, you're scaring me. What are you not saying?"

Kuveni glanced at the door and lowered her voice. "It was those bloody parasites. One of those bloody, worthless, horrific excuses of a human monster pushed her. She and Charlie were waiting at an intersection for the light to change, and one of those wretched paparazzi pushed her while another one came around with the car. It was a set-up!"

Supriya's eyes turned black with rage, while Ellie's glowed an eerie green.

"Do you know who they are?" Supriya asked.

"Do you know *where* they are?" Ellie added.

Kuveni paused for a moment, debating how far she was willing to take it, and then she nodded her agreement. "I do know. I left a trace on them."

"A what?" Supriya asked.

She glanced guiltily between them and lowered her voice into a barely audible whisper. "Have you ever wondered how I know where you are all the time?"

"Yes?" they asked in unison.

"I leave tiny particles of myself on anyone I need to track," Kuveni confessed.

"Blimey," Ellie whispered. "I'm not sure I wanted to know the answer to that mystery."

"Do not tell the other Yakshas how I do it. They would not approve at all, but you know as well as I do that my techniques are often a necessary evil. Today's case in point."

Supriya pushed back her disgust at the implications, and focused on the more immediate emergency. "We can't let them get away with it. They're probably rolling in the dough already with the pictures they got of the accident!"

"Rolling in the dough?" Ellie asked.

"Sorry, it's an Americanism. Racking in the money!"

"The bastards," Kuveni spat.

"I agree. As of now, their plot worked. They will do it again, and again, and again. It will be bad for all of us, especially Charlie. We must stop the disease from spreading."

"I will do whatever you see fit, my lady."

"What do you think we should do?" Ellie added.

Supriya paced back and forth across the library contemplating the situation and glancing back and forth between Kuveni and Ellie, until her eyes lit up, and she snapped her fingers.

"I have it! Ellie, do you remember what I did to punish Craig?"

"I will never forget it, Supriya."

"Neither will I." Supriya sighed with ambivalence. "So, we will use that as the basis, but we will need to make some changes. His repentance must be complete, but he must be able to communicate to any others not to follow in his footsteps."

"You aren't going to kill him?" Kuveni asked with minor disappointment.

"When I'm done with him, he'll wish he were dead."

They all paused to acknowledge the dark truth of the statement.

"If he's going to stay alive, he should not reap any rewards from what he's done," Ellie pushed forward.

"You're right. We should start with the money," Supriya agreed. "We're going to need a reinforcement for that."

"Are you going to call Shaheen?" Ellie asked. "She should probably not be involved in something like this. It will be bad for her career if she gets caught."

"No. We're going to keep it in the family." Supriya closed her eyes and whispered a summons. "Lady Saraswati, your sister requires your presence."

With a pleasant breeze, Neha was standing before her, clad in her favorite grey t-shirt, tight jeans, and lab coat.

"Whoa... I've never been summoned like that before! Wicked!"

"Did I make you come, or did you come willingly?" Supriya asked curiously.

"Daaarling, do you think you could *make* me do anything? *Me?*"

Supriya pulled her into a hug. "I've missed you."

Neha hugged her back, and then held on for an extra-long moment as she felt Supriya's underlying stress. After a solid, supportive, sisterly embrace, Neha glanced at Ellie, and then dragged her sister back into action.

"So, what's up? What trouble are we getting ourselves into, sis? I just dissolved out of a lecture mid-sentence at MIT for this, so it better be good."

Supriya rubbed her hands together until the divine silver light of the Guardian of Memories burst forth from her palms, and then she placed her right hand on Neha's forehead, transferring all of her memories from the trying day into her mind.

As she let go, Neha's eyes turned black with rage.

"Bloody bastards. What are we going to do? It's time to squash these parasites!" Her eyes returned to their normal sparkling blue. "I'm not really good at killing people, though. It leaves me drowning in guilt, even when they totally deserve it. Are you going to kill them on behalf of all of us, sis? You're good at that, you know."

"It's not a skill I'd like to brag about, but you can leave their final punishments to me."

"Then why did you call me here? Moral support? I'm all about family cheerleading, just tell me what you need."

"First, we're going to start with the money. Do you have your laptop?"

Neha closed her eyes, whispered a quiet mantra, and her laptop appeared in her hand.

She ripped it open and sat down on the couch. Supriya and Ellie sat down beside her, leaning in to watch as she pulled up her terminal while Kuveni paced back and forth watching them.

"Alright. So, first we're going to find these bastards," Neha began. "I'm sure they've already sold the pictures. I will hack into the worst London tabloid's records. That will tell us who they are, and how they've been paid... Yes! Their accounting system has the account numbers for the wire transfers of the money! There were three photographers who were paid today for their pictures of the accident... Accessing all of their accounts now through the banking portals... God, these people are charlatans with their security. It's a good thing we're benevolent. We could wreak havoc on the world financial system in a few minutes if we wanted to..."

Neha's fingers breezed across the keyboard at Rakshasa speed.

"Hacking into the account of the guy who got paid the most for his photos today. Probably he had the best angle, which means he must have been lying in wait; maybe he was even the one who pushed her... God, what an arrogant prick. Does he think we were born yesterday? He transferred money to four accomplices this morning! Yup... and... hopping into their accounts... Transferring all of their money to... Who should it be, sis?"

"No one related to us. It can't be obvious that we're behind this to the outside world."

"Why not?" Ellie asked. "I'd scare the rest of the cheeky bastards away."

"But it will create a frenzy in the news. We don't need that kind of publicity. We're already under the gun for not healing more people, and if we're obviously hurting them, our moral superiority argument won't fly," Supriya countered.

"Even if we're hurting murderous bastards? Grace almost died. Next time it could be Charlie," Ellie shot back.

"Trust me, Ellie. I feel the divine rage as much as you do, but this is bigger than just a few murderous bastards. We have to lead the entire world now on the path of virtue. If we do anything that seems petty or violent, someone will use it as an excuse to do the same. We just don't have that luxury anymore."

Listen to her, Ellie-bean. She is very wise.

Supriya noticed the flash of Eleanor's presence and reached across Neha's lap to squeeze Ellie's hand. "I'm pretty sure that if we do this right, the message will get to the right people in the right way."

"Right... then I'll split it across a set of charities..." Neha returned them to the point. "Medicine for the Disadvantaged, Citizens for the Prevention of Random Acts of Violence... Hold on, look at this... Supriya, do you recognize these names? There's twelve of them who have been transferring money on and off for months... holy shit..."

"Do you think they're the paparazzi who have been hounding us? I recognize those three. They got the pictures last month when that private plane crashed in Devonshire and Edmund and I saved the two children..."

"Holy shit, Supriya... Those two... I recognize those two. They got the photo credit after I pulled those transients out of the burning building in San Francisco..."

"And that one... He was there in Bali when the bus of tourists plunged into the ravine!" Supriya exclaimed.

"Bloody hell," Ellie murmured. "That one there... I know him. He's come by the gallery for months now. He bought a few of my pieces, and I just thought he was an alien groupy, but this photo credit is his! It's from when the homeless man was murdered in the alley just next door! I was away in France, visiting Dad's exhibit at the Louvre with Angus and Duncan. I was so grateful that it hadn't happened while I was home, or the press might have said I was the murderer!"

Neha's hands flew across the keyboard. "Comparing photo credits, these guys have been at the sites of at least seventeen of our rescues on five continents! Do you recognize the pictures?"

Supriya leaned in and watched as Neha scrolled through an endless list of images of their harrowing, bloody, painful rescues. "I recognize all of them. Some of the bloodiest accidents we've stumbled across." Supriya jumped off the couch. "Shiva's wrath! They've been causing disasters for months to lure us into saving the day just for the pictures! How many people do you think have died when we didn't show up where they thought we would?!"

"This is some seriously Lex Luther shit," Neha whispered. "Do you think they tried to *frame* Ellie for that murder just for the photos?"

"Blimey," Ellie murmured.

Supriya began pacing. "This is way worse than some comic book villainy, Neha. This is real. It is organized. They've been maiming and killing people for god knows how long, and now they've targeted us directly."

"You know what we aren't?" Ellie asked as she stood up to join Supriya.

"We aren't goody-two-shoes superheroes," Neha declared.

"We're the gods." Supriya rolled her shoulders and cracked her knuckles. "We don't sit around letting murderous sociopaths get away with their evil shit. It's time to throw some lightning bolts. Sis, have you transferred all the money yet?"

Neha's fingers flew across the keyboard again. "Done! None of them have a cent left to their names."

"Good. Now for step two."

Neha dissolved her laptop and jumped up ready for action, but then Supriya glanced down the hallway and readied herself for the first of many unpleasant tasks.

"There's one more thing I have to do before we go. Wait here, all of you. No invisible lurking, got it?" Supriya threw her sister a commanding look, but as she blurred to the door of Grace's room, Ellie followed.

Ellie's eyes flashed the eerie green of her mother's divine power, and she took Supriya's hand. As she communicated her message silently, Ellie's features subtly sharpened until Eleanor was standing in her place.

Supriya, please indulge me. I have a few things I've wanted to say to Grace for a long time. I will say what Ellie and Edmund couldn't.

Supriya nodded her agreement and pushed open the door without knocking. Grace was sobbing into her pillow, and Supriya sat right down on the bed next to her while Eleanor took the rocking chair on the other side. Neither of them were prepared for Grace to be in such an emotional state.

When she felt Supriya's weight on the old, creaky bed, Grace looked up from her mucus-laden, tear-soaked pillow.

"Are you alright, Grace?" Supriya asked as she felt a hint of sympathy for her misery.

Grace looked over to Eleanor and squinted. "Ellie? Did you come to see me? You look... different."

"Ellie did come to check in on you. And on Edmund and Charlie. But at the moment I am in control of her body. I am Eleanor, Ellie's mother."

"I don't understand," Grace whispered. "Ellie's mother is dead."

"And yet, here I am. Edmund and Ellie cared quite a bit about what you thought, but I know better than that, Grace. I will not apologize for the useful divine talents of the loving family into which you have undeservedly carved a place."

"So I'm surrounded by Edmund's wives?" Grace asked with bewilderment.

"It's your lucky day," Eleanor quipped.

"Are you here to punish me?" Grace asked with a subtle puff of fear.

"Do you deserve to be punished?" Eleanor asked.

Grace paused for a long moment, sniffling as she contemplated her answer.

"I never meant to hurt him."

Eleanor sighed. "And yet you did."

"I know." Grace trailed off into quieter tears.

"Tell me this, Grace. It is something I have always wanted to know: Why did you marry him in the first place? You didn't even really love him on your wedding day."

"I did!"

"You didn't."

"How do you know?"

"I reside in Ellie. I know everything she knows, and she knows what love looks like. She learned it by watching her father. You never loved Edmund."

"And he never loved me," Grace murmured.

"You're right, and it was foolish all around, but I understand his motivations. I have never understood yours."

"Don't you have my memories now?" She looked to Supriya with a more acute burst of fear.

Supriya straightened her posture. "We do not exchange memories like gossip, Grace. They are sacred and private. We don't even delve into the details unless we need them for a specific purpose."

Eleanor reached forward and took her hand. *Tell us, my lost child. Tell us what you need to say. What is in those memories that you are so afraid to share?*

Grace pulled her hand away, startled. "What are you?"

Eleanor's eyes glowed as she invited Uma to join her consciousness. "I am a goddess, my lost child. A goddess so powerful that I can transcend the great barrier between life and death. Shakti has decided that instead of berating you for the years of pain I watched you inflict on my beloveds, I will free you instead. Do not deny this divine gift. You will not get another."

Grace stared into the distance for a while, contemplating her answer. "I thought God sent Edmund to me because he needed to be saved."

Eleanor chuckled. "I suppose we can all agree on how foolish that idea was."

Grace sighed. "It was. It was foolish from the moment we met, not just because Edmund was... who he is. I should have known that it wasn't going to work. Edmund made some offhand comment at a party hosted by my sister about gluttony being his favorite deadly sin, and I assumed that he was Catholic. It took almost six months before I realized what an atheist he was, but by then the prospect of adopting a child had already worked its way into the conversation." She grimaced. "That's how desperate we both were. Can you imagine? Adopting a child with someone you hardly know? I already knew he was a liar, and still I clung so dearly to the idea."

"His lies were always excruciating for him," Supriya informed her. "They were a profound act of love to protect those around him from truths they were not ready to know."

Grace smiled sadly. "He wasn't even lying yet. Not in the way I thought he was. I came by his house for our fourth date, and I noticed his paintings on the wall. I commented on them, and he claimed he'd painted them himself. But I knew the style. There were several in the library where I worked. I knew they were painted by some long-forgotten Victorian artist. I thought he was trying to impress me... that it was childish but cute... We were such desperate fools." Grace trailed off into tears. "Such desperate fools..."

Eleanor reached forward and brushed Grace's hair out of her eyes like a doting mother. "Our beloved Edmund really was quite desperate. I should have realized it was the same for you... In fact, I see something now that Ellie couldn't see. I see tragedy in your eyes, my lost child. A tragedy so great it has imprisoned you in a hell of your own making. But even the most lost souls can find their way to redemption. I've seen it. Perhaps we can save you, if you let us."

Grace closed her eyes and cried for almost a minute, until Eleanor took her hand.

"Tell us, my child. Release yourself from the secret you have been keeping locked deep inside."

"It was so long ago," Grace sobbed. "I repented for decades! I thought God had finally offered me a chance for redemption in Edmund!"

"Repented for what, Grace?" Eleanor coaxed calmly.

Grace sobbed silently until she could bring herself to say the words. "For the child... the child I killed."

Eleanor reached forward and stroked her forehead. "Keep talking. We're listening. You are safe here. We will not judge you like the earthly male priests do."

Grace looked into Eleanor's otherworldly eyes, and a soothing green glow emanated off of her entire body, infusing the meagre creature with a peaceful sense of well-being unlike anything she'd ever known.

"Are you really a goddess?" Grace asked meekly.

"I am the Holy Mother, my child," Eleanor explained. "Not in a Christian sense, but in a much vaster sense than most Christians can imagine."

"I can imagine it," Grace murmured.

Eleanor smiled and began massaging Grace's hands with her therapeutic fingers. "That is a great gift, my lost child. Now tell us. Tell us everything that has been eating away at you for so long."

Grace stared into the distance, avoiding Eleanor's gaze. "I was fifteen. I should have listened to my mother and done what the Good Book said and waited for marriage, but I didn't. I did what Sean wanted, what I wanted... I loved the thrill of it... At first, I was so bloody terrified the nuns at school would notice that something had changed—they'd said so many times that they could tell if we were living in sin—but it lasted for months... seven bloody months. For seven months, I thought I was getting away with something, until the symptoms began..."

Grace trailed off in deep thought, and the goddesses waited patiently for her to continue.

"I prayed that God would end it for me. I begged Him and begged Him, but when I started showing, my mother took me to a doctor in Durham, far away where no one would recognize us. She didn't even tell my father, but I was so bloody terrified he'd find out... The doctor took us in after hours, into a secret dark room in the back. My mother paid him in cash and said no one would ever know, that there would be no record at all that it had ever happened..."

She gave into wailing sobs, and Eleanor stroked her forehead until she could get herself under control.

"But God punished me for it! *He* knew! A week later I was so sick, I had to go to the hospital. I was infected! They did a hysterectomy to save my life, and I wish to God they hadn't. They should have just let me die and burn in Hell where I belong."

Eleanor ran her fingers through Grace's hair. "You are in Hell, my lost child. You have been there for a very long time."

Grace took in a deep breath as she forced herself to continue. "I never told anyone. I never touched another man. How could I explain why I was barren? That it was God's punishment for my mortal sin? I prayed and repented for years and years, longing for a child to make up for the one I'd lost. I knew it was my punishment to never have one, but then I met Edmund..."

She choked on her sobs, and Eleanor rubbed her chest until she calmed down.

"Shhh... shhh, my child. Calm yourself. He is a good man, and he always has been."

"I know!" Grace wailed. "How could you think I don't know that?!"

600

Eleanor threw Supriya a subtle glance of surprise.

"You haven't made it obvious that you feel that way, to him or us," Supriya explained in her most supportive tone. "In fact, you have communicated the opposite quite readily for years."

Grace sobbed for another minute. "He was the only man I'd ever met who wanted a child that wasn't his own. I never even had to explain that I was barren, he just assumed I was too old... and maybe I would have been, who knows... And then... and then he was willing to wait to be with me until marriage... and then... he was so patient and gentle and kind. I hadn't been with a man since... since the sin that damned me." She looked self-consciously back and forth between them. "But he was *too* good. It felt too sinful, too pleasurable for what a mortal sinner deserved."

"You pushed him away because he was *too* good in bed?" Supriya worked hard to keep her supportive tone.

"It wasn't just that!" Grace wailed. "He denied my attempts to save his soul more and more, and with every snide blasphemous comment, I convinced myself that he was a project sent by God, a project to test my faith and my worthiness to inherit the child God was giving me. If I could save *him*, I could save myself."

She dissolved into sobs once more.

"Every day that I didn't save him, I was more and more terrified that God would punish me and Charlie for not holding up my end of the bargain. I spent so much time in church praying for their souls, that I hardly even saw them. I didn't even notice that Edmund was speaking Hindi with our son! That's how often I was gone! Charlie speaks it *fluently*!!!" Grace choked on her tears.

Eleanor gently massaged her forehead chakra until she calmed down. "Grace, the most vengeful god is the one in your head. You built up quite a world in there to punish yourself."

"He did punish me. Just not in the way I expected," Grace murmured. "He showed me that my quest for salvation was futile from the beginning."

"Grace, my poor, lost child, Edmund did not need to be saved."

"He did." Grace looked up at her and then Supriya and gave into another round of tears. "He needed to be saved from me. It was my salvation that was futile."

They let her cry for several more minutes, until Supriya reluctantly brought them back to the original intent of their visit.

"I need to borrow a few of your memories, Grace."

"Why don't you take them from Edmund?" she sniffled.

"He's not involved in this. He's busy comforting Charlie. How much do you remember after they pushed you?"

"You know?"

"We do."

Grace swallowed hard. "I remember just a few minutes before I lost consciousness. I was so bloody terrified. The pain was so horrible, but all I could think about was Charlie. I was so afraid that he would watch me die..." She gave into tears again. "Edmund is the only reason he didn't, isn't he?"

"Yes. You were going to die in the ambulance."

"And I couldn't even bloody thank him... I couldn't find the words."

"You will have plenty of time for that. You still have the chance to use the gift that he gave you to make your life and Charlie's better... and maybe even Edmund's. It was God's will for you to be saved, Grace. If it weren't, you'd be dead right now."

Grace nodded as she wiped away her tears.

"But that's not why we're here. We're going to stop the bastards who pushed you. You were only the last in a string of attacks. They've caused at least seventeen accidents. They've killed and maimed countless innocent people, all for the bloody pictures."

"Are you going to kill them?"

"Do you think we should?"

"I don't know…" Grace murmured. "I honestly don't know right from wrong anymore. It would not be very Christian."

"Plenty of Christians have killed people, over far less of an infraction than this."

"Still… Jesus preached non-violence, and he was one of you, wasn't he? I was not willing to accept it, but now I have nothing left."

"You're right. He was." Supriya took a moment to consider her next move. "You have met him."

"I knew that was what Reverend Rutherford meant…" She crossed herself and whispered a quiet prayer. "I'm not ready to think about it. I thought… I just thought that you were better than killing your enemies."

Supriya smiled. "You're right. We are. Their punishments will be much more poetic than a swift death. I will make their actions matter to them in this life as well as the next, like only a goddess can. Which brings me to borrowing your memories. Focus, Grace. Focus on the agony that you felt after the car hit you. Focus on your pain, your fear, and everything else that you suffered."

Supriya rubbed her hands together until the divine silver light of the Guardian of Memories emerged. She gently placed her hand on Grace's forehead, and after only a few seconds, she pulled away.

Grace took in a deep breath. "The pain… the fear… they are not as sharp as they were before."

Supriya squeezed her hand and smiled. "Take with you Shakti's blessings, my child."

Eleanor squeezed her other hand. "It is not every day that a human receives the blessings of two of Shakti's avatars at once. Accept the peace that we've given you, Grace. It is the only way to free yourself."

Grace gave into a final round of tears and nodded. "Thank you."

Supriya stood up and made her way to the door, and Eleanor followed, but Grace jumped up out of bed, and Supriya blurred to catch her as she collapsed in her arms. "Wait!"

"Rest, Grace. You were moments from death. I have never seen Edmund take so long to recover." Supriya guided her back to the bed.

"Please do not tell Charlie I was pushed. We do not need him looking over his shoulder for the rest of his life."

"We won't say a word about it. And Grace, we will not say a word about our conversation to anyone, including Edmund. You can consider us your mother confessors, if you'd like."

"What a concept," Grace murmured. As Eleanor moved to leave, Grace grabbed her hand. "Holy Mother, put the fear of God in them."

Eleanor smiled and nodded her agreement. She joined Supriya in the hallway and closed the door.

"That was not the conversation I thought we were going to have in there," Supriya whispered as she gathered her wits.

"Shakti works in mysterious ways," Eleanor smiled. "Now come, my sister in arms, we have work to do."

Eleanor took Supriya's hand, and in a blur, they returned to Neha and Kuveni in the library.

"Holy shit, Supriya, it took you long enough!" Neha whined. "I had half a mind to go on a killing spree without you!"

"Let's go. We will start with the ringleader," Supriya declared.

"Do you know where he is right now?" Neha asked.

"Kuveni does."

"Thank god you left a trace!" Neha exclaimed.

"You knew about that?" Supriya asked with surprise.

"Oh please, I'd been trying to figure out how Kuveni did it for years. As soon as I became a Rakshini I began experimenting. It only took me a few hours to figure it out. Boy, would the others be unhappy if they knew... It's really a gross thing to do."

604

"Well, we will all benefit from it now, won't we?" Kuveni countered.

"Let's do this," Neha agreed, but as she joined hands with Kuveni to create a Yakshini vortex around Supriya and Ellie, she stopped and looked at Eleanor with puzzlement.

"I am Eleanor. Ellie has decided to let me take care of our little problem on her behalf. She has never had a taste for vengeance."

"Wicked," Neha whispered as a wide grin spread across her face. "Nice to meet you, Eleanor."

Eleanor pulled Neha into a hug. "We will talk later, *mon amie*. I would like very much to know Mélusine's other half. Ellie finds you a bit overwhelming, but I am certain that we will be great friends."

"Wicked," Neha reiterated. "Let's do this!"

In a flash of light, Kuveni and Neha dissolved, sucking Supriya and Eleanor into their Yakshini vortex.

They materialized in the gaudy marble bathroom of an expensive hotel suite. Horns blared from outside as rain splattered against the windows.

Neha took in a deep whiff. "We're definitely in London. The Thames always reeks of pollution and disease."

"He's just inside the bedroom," Kuveni's disembodied voice whispered. "Celebrating his victory in the heat of passion with a woman he picked up at the bar downstairs."

Supriya shivered once as she brought forth her demonic form, and Neha followed, glancing at Eleanor, who refrained from bringing forth the form that she knew Ellie detested.

Supriya pushed open the door and crept up beside the bed, hiding her disgust at his moans and sighs of pleasure.

"Hello, Sam," she cooed.

Neha snapped her fingers, and all the lights switched on.

The naked woman screamed as she saw them, and Sam scrambled out of her arms, off of the bed, and across the room, up against the far wall.

"Oh, you recognize us?" Supriya asked innocently. "I don't know why I'm surprised. We've seen each other so many times already, it's almost like we're friends."

Neha blurred across the room and gathered the girl's dress up off the floor. She tossed it to her.

Supriya grabbed the girl's hands and stared into her eyes. "You will dress, and leave here now. You will go home. You will sleep. You will not remember meeting Sam." She glanced over at Sam and then sighed with annoyance. "And you will have an uncontrollable urge to go to the doctor and get tested for STDs after you take the morning after pill. Now go."

"I knew I would love you, Supriya," Eleanor winked.

As soon as the girl dazedly put on her dress and stumbled out of the room, Neha slammed the door behind her.

Supriya and Neha walked slowly towards their adversary, while Eleanor held back, considering her options.

"I... I... I don't know why you're here!" he lied as Supriya approached him and ran her clawed fingernail along his cheek until he shivered uncontrollably. "It's my right to take pictures! It's how I make a living! You can't blame a man for making a living!"

"Then why are you so scared?" Supriya asked.

"Is that guilt I see in your expression, Sam?" Neha added.

Supriya slammed her hands on his forehead and ripped the memories from his mind. As soon as she had what she needed, she stumbled backwards and closed her eyes, parsing through the flood of images. As she sat down on the bed to complete her task, the unwise fool glanced at the other two goddesses and made his move.

As he made a leap towards the sliding door to the terrace, Neha grabbed his wrist, and Eleanor blurred forward, calling upon her glowing divine trident as she went. She caught it in her hand

and slammed it up against his chest, pinning him to the wall. Neha let go and stepped back, taking in the sight with astonishment.

"Wicked," she whispered. "I didn't know you were an avatar."

Eleanor's eyes glowed. "I told you we'd be great friends, Neha. I am the vessel of Uma, Avatar of Shakti. And right now, our friend Sam has unleashed the wrath of Durga."

"Wicked," Neha repeated more vehemently.

"Surprise!" Eleanor returned her attention to their victim. "Sam, you have enticed the entire Tridevi here for your punishment. You should be proud. It is an exceptionally rare occasion."

"Twenty-three... twenty-three attacks in all," Supriya interrupted as she stood up and took her place beside Eleanor. "Thirty-one people killed and fourteen maimed, all for some bloody pictures to sell. Is it your right to murder people too, Sam?"

"I... I... I didn't murder anyone! Joe set them all up. He's the one who murdered people!"

"We are the gods, Sam. Do you think you can lie to us?" Eleanor boomed as her trident exploded into glowing green flames.

"All I did was come up with the idea! Joe's the one who made it happen!"

"Who pulled the trigger is irrelevant. You are responsible for all your victims' agony, and now you will face the consequences," Supriya hissed.

"But... but... but, I'll repent! I'll go to confession or something! You're always preaching about being nice to your neighbors!"

"You have made the benevolent gods very angry, Sam," Supriya informed him. "And do you know what that means?"

He wet himself as Eleanor pushed her trident into his chest. "It means that now we are vengeful gods."

Supriya called forth the silver light of the Guardian of Memories and slammed her hands onto his forehead, forcing all of

Grace's pain and fear into his mind. As he squirmed to get away from her, Neha grabbed his arms and held them up against the wall above him while Eleanor kept him pinned with her trident.

Supriya dove in for a second round, transferring all of the agony that she'd absorbed when healing the few lucky survivors of the attacks. He gagged and wailed and screamed like a wounded animal, and when she finally let go, he collapsed into a fetal position on the floor.

Neha kicked him in the stomach.

"That's just the beginning, Sam," Supriya spat. "Every night when you dream, they will be there waiting for you. All of the painful memories of the people you hurt will be there for you to relive again and again."

He looked up at her as tears streamed down his face. "I didn't mean for it to get out of hand."

He shivered as another burst of power wafted off of Eleanor as she spoke. "And yet, here we are, Sam. You had no hint of regret until we arrived to impart your punishment. You are a killer, and the gods know your crimes."

Supriya kneeled down and ran her clawed finger along his cheek until he looked away. "Tell the others that we're coming for them. *This* is our godly lightning bolt. Got it? You tell everyone you know that if they hurt someone, we will know. We will punish them. Got it?"

Eleanor poked his stomach with her trident. "We will know everything you do before you bloody do it. Got it?"

"I… I… I didn't mean to kill anyone… I thought you'd be there every time. You'd save them! And then you weren't! But the money… there was so much money…" His excuses dissolved into sobs. "I wanted the bloody money…"

"And now there's none," Neha spat. "Every cent to your name is gone."

"Was the money worth it? Was it worth the pain that is tormenting you now?" Supriya asked. "That will torment you for the rest of your life on Earth?"

"I didn't think... I didn't realize... They were people... Their pain was so much worse than I thought..."

As he gave into violent shivers, Supriya stood up and sighed with resignation. "We've got a long night ahead of us. Let's go deliver Joe's reckoning."

Eleanor pulled Supriya into a hug and whispered into her ear. "I did not imagine that you and I would deliver divine justice together, Supriya, but you are a worthy ally. The worthiest. I know exactly why Edmund loves you so much."

Supriya hugged her back. "*Jai mata di*," she winked.

Neha and Kuveni encircled them, and with a flash of light, they dissolved, leaving the selfish, sociopathic fool in his fetal position on the floor of the room he would not be able to pay for in the morning.

For hours, they transported around the globe, imparting karmic justice on every member of the gang, leaving a pile of shivering, repentant bastards in their wake.

When the final culprit was wailing with the pain of his victims and begging for forgiveness, they returned to Shambhala just as the grey light of predawn was making its way into the horizon.

"What a privilege it has been to hover by your side, my ladies," Kuveni said as she pulled them all into a motherly hug. "You have done the world a great service with your difficult deeds tonight. Many innocent people will live now that these evil men have been stopped."

Supriya sighed with stress. "I hope it was enough."

"Sometimes we just have to do what we can and let destiny settle the rest," Neha reminded her.

"It was enough. They will not dare repeat their mistakes with the Tridevi looking over their shoulders," Eleanor said confidently. "And now, I'd best give Ellie back her body." She hugged Supriya again, and then pulled Neha into her arms. "It was a pleasure smiting by your side."

"You feel so familiar," Neha whispered as she pulled away.

"That is because your mother and I have some unfinished business," Eleanor replied with ambivalence as she threw Kuveni a knowing glance. "I am the Transformer just as she is, and when the time comes, she and I will become one as we were always meant to be. It is long overdue."

"I'm not sure what my father will have to say about that," Neha replied, only half joking.

Eleanor laughed heartily. "That isn't what I meant, *mon amie*. But I'm sure he'd be thrilled by the development either way."

As Neha blushed, Eleanor winked mischievously, and then dissolved herself into Ellie's softer features. Ellie took in a deep Rakshasa breath.

"Holy shit, Ellie..." Neha murmured. "I haven't been blindsided like that in a long time... maybe... ever!" Neha pulled her into a hug. "Thank you! I didn't know my life could still be this interesting!"

Ellie hugged her back, throwing Supriya a knowing glance. "I knew that if anyone could handle you, it would be her."

"Handle me?" Neha exclaimed with melodramatic offense. "Only one person can handle me, and that is my lovely Mélusine."

Supriya laughed as she pulled her into a hug. "Thanks for everything, sis."

Neha finally let her adrenaline die down. "I'll be in Avalon in Melly's arms if you need me. She's been cheering us on for hours from afar. I can't wait to tell her who joined us."

"She will be floored for sure," Supriya smiled.

Ellie grabbed Neha's hand as her eyes flashed their divine green. "Take with you Shakti's blessings, my child, and share them with your wife." She winked.

"Byyyee." Neha's voice trailed off as she dissolved.

Kuveni put her arms around Supriya's and Ellie's shoulders as she walked them slowly down the hall. "My beautiful boys are asleep in Charlie's room. Do my dearest girls want something to eat before they sleep?"

"My demon has had all that it could feast on and more tonight," Supriya admitted. "I don't think I'll be hungry for days."

"I'm never hungry after Mum's been in control," Ellie admitted. "It takes me a while to get my bearings back."

Supriya hugged Kuveni. "Thank you."

"It is my pleasure to serve, Mistress Supriya."

Ellie followed Supriya as they tiptoed down the hallway, and as they snuck into Charlie's room, he and Edmund both stirred.

"Ellie?" Charlie whispered. "Where'd you go?"

"We just had a few things to take care of. Everything is perfectly fine." She took a seat beside him on the oversized bed.

Supriya took a seat beside Edmund on the other side, and he took her hand into his.

Did you kill him? The one who pushed her?

Supriya closed her eyes and pushed the memories of their long night of divine justice into his mind.

Good lord...

Supriya squeezed his hand.

They will not dare to do it again, Edmund. We put the fear of God in them.

I have no doubt.

He reached over and took Ellie's hand.

Thank you, Ellie-bean... and you, Eleanor.

Darling, we love you. Now let go of your troubles and revel in the joys of this miraculous triumph of light.

We love you, Dad.

"Are you talking about me?" Charlie asked, noticing their silent conversation.

"It is a bad habit," Edmund admitted. "We weren't talking about you, Charlie, but we shouldn't have done it nonetheless."

611

Charlie shrugged. "I'd do it if I could."

Ellie took his hand. *You can practice on me any time.*

His eyes widened, and he smiled for the first time in too many hours as her voice resonated in his head.

Wicked! Can you hear me?

I can.

Wicked! Does it work with Dad?

He took Edmund's hand and tried to communicate a message, but as he heard no response from his father in his head, he sighed with disappointment.

My talent is unique, Charlie. I inherited it from Mum. Only she could communicate like this with humans.

It's cool anyway.

I think so too.

As he caught his father watching them, he politely returned to speech. "Please stay. There's room for everyone." He moved in closer to Edmund, and then glanced at Supriya and Ellie. "We've never really been together like this... as a family."

Edmund kissed Charlie's forehead and then maneuvered to make room for both of them.

Ellie nestled in beside Charlie, and Supriya lay down beside Edmund. They all sighed with relief.

And so, as twelve repentant murderers shivered with their karmic punishments, and one tormented ex-wife contemplated the blessings of her mother confessors, together, in each other's loving arms, with the weight of the world a bit lighter and a child's tears finally quelled, the family of the Preservers of the Universe slept.

~TO BE CONTINUED~

GLOSSARY OF HINDU REFERENCES

Hinduism, the world's oldest continuously practiced religion, is an exceptionally diverse collection of philosophies and rituals practiced by over one billion people globally. There is no single institution and no single written text that defines the 'rules' of Hinduism, and thus it varies widely in practice and belief across the world.

While there is a pantheon featuring a plethora of gods and goddesses with various regional names and stories, there are also numerous sects who worship Vishnu (Vaishnavism), Shiva (Shaivism), Shakti (Shaktism), and combinations/permutations of these major gods and goddesses, and their manifestations (including avatars), as representations of the one supreme being.

The vast and fascinating complexity of Hinduism cannot be captured in a short glossary, and it is not the author's intent to do so. This glossary is meant to give the uninitiated reader some basic context for references throughout the Ashley Mayers universe. Further research is recommended for those interested in digging deeper.

Agni (uh-**gnee**) – 'Fire' in Sanskrit, Agni is also the god of fire and the conveyor of sacrifices to the gods. It is Agni's role in the Hindu pantheon that is invariably linked with the many rituals, both daily and for special occasions, that require a *yajna*, or sacred fire.

Artha (**ahr**-tah) – One of the four aims of human life in Hindu philosophy, sometimes 'meaning, sense, or purpose,' *artha* generally focuses on the 'means to live the life you want,' including but not limited to wealth, career, and financial security. It can perhaps be thought of as 'why you do work.'

Asura/Asuri (ah-soo-ruh/ah-soo-ree) – Originally a term used to describe divine, powerful beings, good or bad, the term later came to represent primarily darker powered beings in Hinduism and is sometimes (but not always) synonymous with demons. Rakshasas are sometimes described as one type of *Asura*. *Asuri* is the feminine form of *Asura*.

Avatar (ah-vuh-tuhr) – In Hinduism, an avatar is a deliberate descent of a deity to Earth. The term is most commonly used to describe incarnations or manifestations of Vishnu, but has been used with other deities, including Shiva, Ganesh, and Shakti. The lists of avatars and consensus around them is dubious. Some sects believe that Shiva, as a formless entity, will never have an avatar, while others believe that Hanuman is an avatar of Shiva. The lists of Vishnu avatars range from ten to twenty-five avatars, and some characters in epics are referred to as 'partial' avatars, such as Rama's brother, Lakshmana, sometimes being considered 'one-quarter Vishnu.' One major thematic element throughout the Ashley Mayers universe explores what exactly it means (and doesn't mean) to be an avatar.

Ayodhya (ah-**yoh**-dyuh) – An ancient city located in Uttar Pradesh in Northern India that remains inhabited today, Ayodhya is considered to be the birthplace and ancient kingdom of Rama. In modern times, tragedy and controversy, fuelled by Hindu/Muslim animosity, have plagued the city after a violent uprising in 1992 that led to the destruction of the 16th c. Babri Mosque, which many people believed was built upon the site of Rama's original temple.

Bhoomi (**boo**-mee) – The embodiment/personification of 'Mother Earth.' Bhoomi is referred to as the mother of Sita, and at the end of *the Ramayana*, when Sita's suffering becomes unbearable, she returns to her 'mother,' being swallowed by the earth.

Ceylon (say-lon) – The historical, British colonial name of modern-day Sri Lanka, Ceylon is a key setting in *the Ramayana*, as the home of the Rakshasa king, Ravana, who kidnaps Sita and takes her back to Lanka to woo her (while she is imprisoned).

Chiranjivi (chee-ruhn-**jee**-vee) – Seven immortals in Hinduism who remain on Earth to lead humans in various paths of righteousness. In this series, we have two: Vibhishana, Hanuman.

Dasara (**Duh**-suh-ruh) – Otherwise known as *Dussera*, *Dushera*, or *Vijayadashami*, depending on the region and language, Dasara is a holiday at the end/culmination of Navaratri, the nine-night autumn festival devoted to the Goddess. Dasara traditions vary across India, ranging from sacred dances of Garba and Dandiya in the north, to a candlelight vigil and elephant parade in Mysore in the south, a city that considers itself the namesake of the Goddess in her defeat of the demon Mahishasura (sometimes referred to as *Mahishasura-Mardini* from the Sanskrit holy mantras). It coincides with the culmination of Durga Puja in Bengal, and always involves great cheer, festivities, and often fireworks and light shows.

Devi/Deva (deh-**vee**/deh-**vah**) – 'Heavenly' or 'divine' beings in Hinduism, *Devi* can be synonymous with 'god' or 'deity' but primarily refers to powerful beings who are 'good,' and can sometimes be contrasted with the 'evil' *Asura*. However, the designations of 'good' versus 'evil' are far less clearly defined in Hinduism compared to Judeo-Christian religions, and so, for example, Kartikeya, the god of war, is still considered a *Deva*. In Hinduism, an *Asura* can ascend and become a *Deva*, with Vibhishana being a prime example, demonstrating that birthright is less important than actions on Earth to define one's character and virtue.

Devi Mahatmya (deh-**vee** muh-**hat**-myuh) – The *Devi Mahatmya* is a religious text (from the *Markandeya Purana*, one of eighteen primary religious texts in Hinduism) devoted to the Great Goddess (Shakti). It recounts her manifestation on Earth in the warrior form of Durga to protect the innocent by defeating the shapeshifting buffalo demon Mahishasura, and her subsequent return of balance and virtue to the world. A text revered by Hindus across many sects, the *Devi Mahatmya* serves as a primary text for Shaktist Hindus, who believe that the Goddess is the Supreme Being. It serves as the inspiration for the festivals of Navaratri, Durga Puja, and Dasara/Vijayadashmi.

Dharma (**dahr**-muh) – One of the four aims of human life in Hindu philosophy, with many meanings, *dharma* is roughly translated as virtue, morality, righteousness, obligations, and correct conduct. The Hindu epics, *the Ramayana* and *the Mahabharata,* both demonstrate that there is often no single clear path to *dharma*, as various 'right' paths often conflict and need to be prioritized, with each difficult choice producing complicated consequences and satisfying drama.

Diwali (Dih-**vah**-lee) – Also known as Deepavali in many South Indian languages, Diwali is one of the most important festivals across Hindu tradition, and celebrates the triumph of light over darkness, knowledge over ignorance, and hope over despair. Based on the Hindu calendar, the festival of lights typically falls between mid-October and mid-November each year, and its observance dates back to ancient times. The rituals vary across the many cultures who celebrate the holiday, but it is generally consistent that people light candles and offer prayers to Lakshmi.

Durga (door-**gah**) – A principle form of the Goddess (Shakti), who manifests physically in many different forms depending on the task at hand, Durga is also called Maa Durga or the Holy Mother (not to be confused with the Christian/Catholic Holy Mother Mary). The primary hero of her own epic, the *Devi Mahatmya*, Durga is most famous as a warrior for justice who wields the power of the entire pantheon, coming to Earth with many arms and weapons to defeat the shapeshifting buffalo demon, Mahishasura. Her triumph in defeating an insidious, ever-changing manifestation of evil can be viewed as a model of perseverance that can be applied in everyday life. Every year her triumph is celebrated during the festivals of Navaratri ("Nine Nights," each celebrating a manifestation of the Goddess), Durga Puja (five nights celebrating her defeat of Mahishasura, primarily celebrated in Bengal), Dasara (the culmination of Navaratri celebrated across India), and Diwali (the Festival of Lights, celebrated across the Hindu world and by other related religions). As the Great Goddess, she is sometimes referred to interchangeably with Parvati, wife of Shiva, and she is sometimes said to manifest as Lakshmi and Saraswati in their roles as the primordial energy that animates the universe. Across most sects,

616

Durga is worshipped as the underlying creative, preservative, and destructive energy of the universe (Shakti), who exists as a formless entity always, and sometimes takes form within the gods or goddesses, to fulfill tasks on behalf of the universe.

Durga Puja (door-**gah poo**-ja) – A five-night festival primarily celebrated in Bengal, Durga Puja coincides with the festival of Navaratri in other parts of India, all in celebration of the Great Goddess (Shakti), manifested as Durga for her defeat of the shapeshifting demon Mahishasura. Known for its *pandals* (elaborate temporary altars to the Goddess), Durga Puja is celebrated with costume, dance, food, special rituals, and bright firecrackers, making the streets of Calcutta one of the liveliest (and most crowded) places in the world to experience the frenetic energy of the Devi in one of her most beloved forms.

Garuda (**guh**-roo-duh) – The 'mount' of Lord Vishnu, Garuda is a large bird, sometimes a humanoid bird, who flies Lord Vishnu around. Sometimes represented as a large phoenix, eagle, or kite, Garuda also exists in Buddhist mythology.

Hanuman (**hahn**-oo-mahn) – Rama's right-hand man and a beloved star of *the Ramayana*, Hanuman is a Vanara, a monkey-like humanoid race who fought by Rama's side in his attack against Ravana in Lanka. In *the Ramayana*, Hanuman uses his flying ability to track and eventually make contact with Sita while she is incarcerated by Ravana, but she refuses to go with him back to Rama. Various interpretations of this interaction range from it exemplifying Sita's purity through her refusal to be in another man's arms, even to be rescued, to a valid observation that had Sita agreed to go back to Rama with Hanuman, the entire war between Rama and Ravana might have been avoided. Hanuman is consistently referred to as one of the *Chiranjivi*, representing loyalty, courage and devotion.

Harihara (**hah**-ree-**hah**-ruh) – A combined form of Shiva and Vishnu (Transformation and Preservation), Harihara is sometimes used to explain/describe the complementary nature of the two gods as aspects of one supreme being. The symbolism evokes the necessary balance (and tug-of-war) between the two primary aspects of existence, each keeping the other in check.

Hiranyakashipu – (**hee**-ran-**yaak**-shih-poo) – A demon evil enough to warrant the Preserver of the Universe coming to Earth (as Narasimha, the fourth avatar of Vishnu), Hiranyakashipu gained a boon from Lord Brahma so that he couldn't be defeated by man or beast, thus requiring Lord Vishnu to take a more clever form, in his case, as a half-man, half-lion, to defeat him.

Lakshmi (**luhk**-shmee) – The female aspect of the Preserver of the Universe, often referred to as the goddess of prosperity (material and spiritual), and the wife of Lord Vishnu, Lakshmi (or Laxmi), is one of the principal goddesses of the *Tridevi*, or 'Trinity of Goddesses.' She is said to be the life-force of Lord Vishnu and is worshipped during the major festival of Diwali every autumn. As the wife of Rama, seventh avatar of Vishnu, Sita is an avatar of Lakshmi.

Kali (kuh-lee) – Hinduism's primary apocalyptic demon—not to be confused with Kali, a fierce incarnation of Shakti (spelled the same in English but not in Sanskrit)—this demon is often depicted with a dog's head. He is said to fan the flames of human greed, violence, and iniquity during *Kali Yuga* ('The Age of Vice'), an era that many Hindus believe describes the modern world. It is sometimes said that Ravana is an incarnation and/or devotee of the demon, Kali, and that Lord Vishnu will incarnate in his ultimate avatar form, Lord Kalki, to defeat Kali and bring the worlds into *Satya Yuga* ("The Age of Truth").

Kali/Kaali (Kah-lee) – A fierce incarnation of the female life-force of the Transformer of the Universe, Kaali (often spelled Kali in English, but too easily confused with the demon Kali), is one of the most misunderstood incarnations of the Goddess. Often referred to as the goddess of time, and represented with blue or black skin, her tongue out, standing on the dead body of her husband, Shiva, wearing a skull necklace and holding a severed, bloody head, she is often thought of as a ghoulish character by those who don't know any better. However, the symbolism of the imagery of her standing on Shiva's body is meant to represent that she is his life-force, and without her, he is lifeless. The life-force of change is fierce, and the ravages of time often frightening, which are two reasons why she is depicted in such a monstrous style. She is, however, a natural manifestation of the destruction required for our ever-changing universe to exist.

Kalki (kuhl-kee) – Lord Kalki, 'Destroyer of Filth,' the tenth and final avatar of Vishnu (the Preserver of the Universe), is believed to be the only avatar who has not already been on Earth. Legends tell of him being born in Shambhala, a mythical place of great spiritual power north of Tibet, a place of great interest to the sages when the stories were written, due to its association and proximity to the homeland of the invading Khans. While references to Lord Kalki can be conflicting, it is consistent in texts that Lord Kalki will come to Earth to defeat the demon, Kali, and restore balance and order, bringing humans back to the path of virtue, and ushering in the Age of Truth.

Mahagauri (Maa-huh-gau-ree) – A manifestation of Maa Durga (considered her eighth of nine manifestations by some sects), Mahagauri is worshipped on the eighth night of the festival of Navaratri in some parts of India. She is said to be "the fair one," with a fair complexion, who offers forgiveness and protection to all of her followers.

Mantra (mahn-truh) – Words or sounds, often repetitive, that are used in prayer.

Moksha (mohk-shuh) – One of the four aims of human life in Hindu philosophy, meaning 'release' or 'liberation,' *moksha* primarily refers to release from the reincarnation cycle of birth and death on Earth.

Naraka (nah-**rah-**kuh) – In Hinduism, Naraka, or the underworld (somewhat similar to Christian purgatory), is a temporary place for expiation of sins to be endured between a soul's mortal death and its return to Earth. There are many different forms of Naraka, each featuring colorful punishments that are related to a person's sins, such as murderers being eaten alive by Rakshasas. As positive and negative actions do not 'cancel each other out' in Hinduism, a soul can repent through their punishment in Naraka and enjoy the peace of *Svarga* (a heavenly place), both before their return to Earth.

Narasimha (Nur-sim-**haa)** – Regarded as the fourth avatar of Vishnu, Narasimha is a manifestation of the Preserver of the Universe who comes to Earth as a half-man, half-lion to defeat the demon Hiranyakashipu, who has immortality against "all men and beasts." He is considered a protector of the innocent and warrior for justice, as well as an example of one of Lord Vishnu's many clever responses to the inconvenient ancient boons held by his enemies.

Navaratri (Nuv-**rah-**tree) – Otherwise known as "Nine Nights," Navaratri is the primary festival of the Goddess and takes place at the beginning of autumn, typically three weeks before the festival of Diwali. Traditions and details of each night's symbolism differ across regions and sects, with fasting and the wearing of special colors to honor various manifestations of the Goddess being common across regions. In Gujarat, sacred dances known as Garba and Dandiya, enact Durga's battle and defeat of the demon Mahishasura.

Parvati (pahr-vuh-**tee)** – The wife of Shiva and one of the three chief goddesses of the *Tridevi* or 'Trinity of Goddesses,' Parvati is the benevolent female aspect of the Transformer of the Universe, and is often referred to as the goddess of power, love, fertility, and devotion. She is also sometimes referred to as an aspect or alternative name of Durga (the root form of creation, preservation, and annihilation), Shakti (the cosmic energy that underlies all life in the universe), and 'one thousand' other names/personas. In the Shaivism sects, Parvati is considered an inextricable force, without which, Shiva (and therefore God) would cease to exist, for it is her life-force that gives them both power and energy. Parvati is the benevolent form of Shiva's wife (a complementary aspect to the fierce form of Kali), and the mother of their two sons, Ganesh and Kartikeya.

Puja (poo-ja) – A prayer or offering, puja describes the manifestation of worship and reverence in Hinduism. Often involving offerings of light (candles or diyas), flowers, water, or food, along with prayers (often in the form of mantras), puja rituals are an important aspect of religious life for most practicing

Hindus, and are particularly common and elaborate on holy days, during festivals, and to celebrate major life events such as weddings, funerals, and baby-namings.

Rakshasa (raahk-shuh-suh) – Shapeshifting demons in Hindu mythology, Rakshasas have been referred to with various characteristics throughout Hindu and Buddhist literature. Ravana, Vibhishana, Surpanakha, and Kumbhakarna are Rakshasas in *the Ramayana*. Due to the varying (and often conflicting) representations of Rakshasas throughout the literature, this series has expanded on the mythological depictions with far greater detail than has been generally used in the past. While there has been a parallel drawn between some vampire representations and Rakshasas, they are not considered to be the same, in the mythology or in this series. The origin of Rakshasas on Venus was entirely invented by the author, upon the suggestion of Neha, as she was writing her own story.

Rama (raah-muh) – The main protagonist of *the Ramayana*, Rama is generally considered to be the seventh avatar of Vishnu. Often referred to as 'the ideal king' and 'the ideal husband,' despite the miserable ending of his wife, Rama is still a beloved figure in modern Hinduism. While there is significant debate about whether Rama should be considered infallible, this series explores the dichotomy between the divine and human aspects of his character, in line with major historical representations across the Hindu world, including the iconic version by the ancient Sanskrit poet Valmiki, that demonstrate his crooked path to virtue in great detail. The festival of Diwali, one of the most popular Hindu festivals celebrated by hundreds of millions of people every autumn, celebrates the triumph of light over darkness, as embodied by Durga's triumph over Mahishasura, and Rama's triumph over Ravana.

Ramayana, the (raah-mah-yuh-nuh) – One of the most well-known and beloved of the ancient Hindu Sanskrit epics, *the Ramayana* follows the many triumphs and tribulations of Rama, the seventh avatar of Vishnu, and Sita, his wife and the avatar of Lakshmi. While the epic covers a range of stories and characters, the primary conflict centers around Rama's battle with Ravana, the Rakshasa King of Lanka, after his capture and incarceration of Sita. While there are many versions of *the Ramayana* referenced across Southeast Asia including in India, Nepal, Thailand, Cambodia, and more, the most famous version is credited to the storyteller Valmiki. *The Ramayana* of Valmiki contains seven *kandas* or 'books.' The seven-book structure of *The Sita Chronicles* is meant to be a nod to the original epic.

Ravana (raah-vuh-nuh) – The main antagonist of *the Ramayana*, Ravana is the Rakshasa King of Lanka. He is said to be a devotee of Shiva, and to have received the 'nectar of immortality' as a boon from Lord Brahma that allows him to withstand any injury from any creature, other than a human. Lord Vishnu comes to Earth as the human, Rama, to take advantage of this epic loophole.

Sanskrit (**sahn**-skrit) – The primary sacred language of Hinduism, it has many forms and served as the foundation for many modern languages in Southeast Asia. Its role in spreading Indic culture throughout the region can generally be compared to Latin's role in disseminating and communicating literature, religion, and secular education throughout Europe for the two millennia spanning the Roman Empire to the end of the 18th century AD.

Saraswati (sah-ruh-svuh-**tee**) – The female aspect of the Creator of the Universe, Saraswati is also considered the goddess of knowledge, music, arts, learning, and wisdom. Saraswati is the wife of Brahma, and one of the principal goddesses of the *Tridevi*, or 'Trinity of Goddesses.'

Satya Yuga (**saht**-yuh yoo-guh) – 'The Age of Truth,' *Satya Yuga* is said to be the peaceful era that will return to Earth after the Preserver of the Universe vanquishes Kali, ending Kali Yuga (the 'Age of Vice').

Shakti (**shuhk**-tee) – The Great Goddess, the primordial cosmic energy of the universe, and the personification of the 'divine mother,' Shakti has many manifestations, including the *Tridevi*, Durga, Lakshmi, Saraswati, and Parvati. She is said to manifest on Earth as the embodiment of creative power and fertility, and of life itself. Some sects believe that Shakti is responsible for all creation and is the agent of all change, as it is her energy that animates everything in the universe, including the gods. In Shaktism and Shaivism, Shakti is worshipped as the animating energy of the Supreme Being.

Shiva (**shih**-vuh) – One of the primary deities of Hinduism, and one of the *Trimurti*, or 'Trinity of Gods,' Lord Shiva is considered to be 'the Destroyer,' 'the Transformer,' and 'the Regenerator.' He is represented by hundreds, possibly thousands, of different epithets. He is often represented as conflicting personas: He can be 'fierce' or 'benevolent,' and he is portrayed as a 'householder' with his wife, Parvati, and their sons, Ganesh and Kartikeya, but he is also portrayed as an ascetic yogi (chaste and focused on solitary prayer)— two lifestyles that are mutually exclusive in traditional Hindu society. Shiva's wife, Parvati (also referred to as Durga, Shakti, Kali, and many other names), is considered to be his life-force. In Valmiki's *Ramayana*, Ravana is a follower of Shiva, and Shiva is said to have given him a divine sword with the stipulation that if he uses his sword for unjust purposes, it will be returned to 'the three-eyed one' (Shiva himself). Shiva is often considered to be 'formless,' and it is common to worship him through the formless idol of a 'lingam' (internet image search recommended).

Sita (**see**-tuh) – The main female protagonist of *the Ramayana*, Sita is Rama's wife and an avatar of Lakshmi. Often referred to as 'the ideal wife' for her desire and ability to make the deepest personal sacrifices on behalf of her husband, Sita's tragic suicidal ending is controversial in modern academic discussions of the ancient epics.

Sugriva (soo-**gree**-vuh) – The king of the Vanaras (non-human intelligent primates who can fly), Sugriva's support is crucial to Rama's defeat of Ravana in *the Ramayana*. It is with Sugriva's army that Rama attacks Lanka. Many discussions around historical validity of *the Ramayana* have centered around the assertion that Rama led Sugriva's army over a formerly existing land bridge from mainland India to the island of Sri Lanka, as NASA images show that a series of lightly submerged sandbar islands do appear to have, at some point in the past, connected the two land masses.

Surpanakha (**soor**-puh-nuh-khuh) – The sister of Ravana, Vibhishana, and Kumbhakarna, Surpanakha is a primary female antagonist in *the Ramayana*. She is often considered the catalyst of the main events of *the Ramayana* (often taking the blame for Ravana's despicable actions). Surpanakha's story is also complex, as one of her primary scenes in the epic is when she falls in love with Rama. When she is rejected and humiliated by Rama, Rama's brother, Lakshmana, permanently maims her by cutting off her nose with a divine weapon. Surpanakha's hatred of Sita and her anger at Rama's rejection is a driving force of her character's antagonistic actions later in the story and in this series.

Tridevi (tree-**deh**-vee) – The 'Trinity of Goddesses': Saraswati ('the Creator'), Lakshmi ('the Preserver'), and Parvati, ('the Transformer'), serve as the female aspects and underlying energy of their male, godly counterpart husbands. Together they create balance between the three main aspects of existence. Each one individually, and the group as a whole, manifest Shakti's energy as is necessary to participate in worldly endeavors on behalf of the gods and goddesses, usually to support the cause of righteousness and restore balance.

Trimurti (tree-**moor**-tee) – The 'trinity' of Hindu gods: Brahma ('the Creator'), Vishnu ('the Preserver'), and Shiva ('the Destroyer' and 'the Transformer'). Together, the trinity complements each other, representing a descriptive model of various aspects of life on Earth.

Valmiki (**vahl**-mih-kee) – The most widely attributed author of *the Ramayana*, he is credited with inventing the poetic structure of epic Sanskrit literature, somewhat akin to Homer's role in codifying ancient Greek verse. In Valmiki's *Ramayana*, he participates as a character in his own work, being said to have taken Sita in after her trial by fire when Rama banished her to the jungle to raise their twin sons alone. Valmiki's own voiced admonishment of Rama's behaviour in the final chapters serves as a valuable, if controversial, reminder of the story's main point of demonstrating the complex and imperfect paths to *dharma* (virtue), along with its tragic consequences.

Vanara (**vaah**-nuh-ruh) – An ancient race of nonhuman, intelligent primates, the Vanaras are supporters of Rama and serve as his primary troops in his battle against Ravana. Sometimes referred to just as 'monkeys,' other times referred to as 'half-man, half-monkeys,' the literature is not consistent in its depiction of Vanaras. Hanuman and Sugriva are the most famous Vanaras, from their important roles in *the Ramayana*.

Varuna (vuh-**roo**-nuh) – The god of water and the celestial ocean, Varuna was the original chief god of the Vedic pantheon and later appeared throughout Sanskrit literature, primarily as the ruler of the sea. He plays a secondary role in *the Ramayana*, and is often referred to as a symbol of *rta*, an ancient vedic concept believed to encompass cosmic order and divine balance or justice.

Vibhishana (vee-**bhee**-shuh-nuh) – The youngest brother of the villain demon king, Ravana, Vibhishana is an important ally of Rama in *the Ramayana*. In *the Ramayana*, Vibhishana attempts to convince Ravana to return Sita to Rama, but his efforts are not successful. He then joins Rama and provides important intel that leads to Ravana's eventual defeat. Rama crowns Vibhishana the King of Lanka after Ravana is dead. Vibhishana's role in *the Ramayana* is a complex one, as he betrays his family and his race in order to follow a path he considers to be more dharmic. Still, there is no perfect path towards *dharma* (righteousness), and so, he is also considered a traitor. Vibhishana is one of the *Chiranjivi*, one of the seven immortals of Hinduism, who are said to remain on Earth to this day to guide humans on the path of righteousness.

Vishnu (**vih**sh-noo) – One of the primary deities of Hinduism, Lord Vishnu is considered to be 'the Preserver of the Universe.' Lord Vishnu is one of the *Trimurti*, or 'trinity' of Hindu gods, along with Brahma and Shiva. Together with his wife, Lakshmi (or Laxmi), who is considered his life-force, Lord Vishnu is mentioned throughout numerous Sanskrit texts and is worshipped as the supreme being by the Vaishnavist sects of Hindus. Rama is generally considered the seventh avatar of Vishnu among the *Dashavatara* ('ten avatars of Vishnu'). Some Hindu texts/sects refer to more avatars of Vishnu, including Mohini, a female avatar.

Vishrava (vihsh-**rah**-vuh) – The father of Ravana, Vibhishana, Kumbhakarna, and Surpanakha, he is described as a powerful rishi or 'seer.' He is said to have left his wife, Kaikesi, the mother of his four Rakshasa children, to return to his first wife after he became unhappy with Ravana's conduct.

Ya Devi Sarva Bhuteshu (**yah** deh-**vee** sar-vuh **bhoo**-teh-**shoo**) – The beginning of the *Devi Suktam,* one of the primary prayers/mantras to the Goddess (often sung in worship), these Sanskrit words celebrate the Goddess's embodiment of power, peace, knowledge, and many other necessary and beautiful aspects of existence in the universe, allowing the worshippers to feel the Shakti, or energy, of the Goddess within themselves, while bowing (figuratively or literally) to the greatness of all that is.

Yajna (**yahg**-nyuh) – 'Sacrifice, devotion, worship, or offering,' it refers to any ritual done in front of a sacred fire, often with mantras.

Yaksha/Yakshini (**yahk**-shuh / yahk-**shee**-nee) – A powerful nature spirit with shapeshifting abilities, generally considered to be the caretakers of Earth. The feminine form of a Yaksha is a Yakshini.

Yama (**yah**-muh) – The god of death, lord of justice, and the gatekeeper of the underworld, Yama is one of several deities who participates in the management of the afterlife. The gatekeeper of Naraka (roughly Hindu 'purgatory'), Yama is said to be one of the judges of human life/morality and 'the first mortal to have died.'

Pronunciation Key:

Rather than using the international phonetic alphabet that is not commonly used by the average reader, these pronunciation notes use references to common sounds in American English, more similar to a foreign language guide for casual travelers. Note that an "h" does not represent an aspiration in this transliteration; it is used to demonstrate various vowel sounds in English. Also note that the consonants have been simplified for an English speaker and do not fully represent the nuanced differences in the Sanskrit alphabet, such as aspirated v. non-aspirated consonants, that a native Hindi speaker would recognize.

Ah – as in "car" and "hard"

Aah – hold "ah" as in "car" and "hard" longer

Uh – as in "under" and "bus"

Ih – as in "in" and "interest"

Eh – as in "extra" and "**e**xcellent"

Oh – as in "over" and "ornate"

Ee – as in "cheese" and "beast," note that this does not indicate an elongation

Oo – as in "choose" and "I do," note that this does not indicate an elongation

This series is dedicated to the Goddess who resides in all of us.
May she give us the energy, inspiration, and perseverance to triumph over all that holds us back, no matter what forms our enemies take.
"We are told too often what we can't do."
May we do it anyway.
Jai Mata Di.
~Ashley Mayers